Pierce Egan

Clifton Grey

Or, Love and War

Pierce Egan

Clifton Grey
Or, Love and War

ISBN/EAN: 9783337082116

Printed in Europe, USA, Canada, Australia, Japan

Cover: Foto ©Andreas Hilbeck / pixelio.de

More available books at **www.hansebooks.com**

RETURN OF THE GUARDS FROM THE CRIMEA.

CLIFTON GREY;

OR,

LOVE AND WAR:

A TALE OF THE PRESENT DAY.

BY

PIERCE EGAN,

AUTHOR OF "ROBIN HOOD," "WAT TYLER," "QUINTIN MATSYS," "LONDON APPRENTICE,"
"THE BLACK PRINCE," ETC., ETC.,

" —————— The god of soldiers,
With the consent of the supreme Jove, inform
Thy thoughts with nobleness, that thou may'st prove
To shame invulnerable, and stick i' th' wars
Like a great sea-mark, standing every flaw,
And saving those that eye thee!"

SHAKSPERE.

LONDON:
E. HARRISON, MERTON HOUSE, SALISBURY SQUARE, FLEET STREET,
AND OF ALL BOOKSELLERS.

TO THE

Soldiers of the Army of England,

IN ADMIRATION OF

THEIR UNFLINCHING BRAVERY IN THE BATTLE-FIELD,

AND

THEIR NOBLE FORTITUDE AND ENDURANCE

in Sickness and Privation,

THIS WORK IS HUMBLY INSCRIBED

BY

THE AUTHOR.

LIST OF ILLUSTRATIONS.

CLIFTON GREY
OR
LOVE AND WAR
A
TALE OF THE
PRESENT DAY

BY
PIERCE EGAN,
AUTHOR OF "ROBIN HOOD," "WAT TYLER," "QUINTIN MATSYS," "LONDON APPRENTICE," &c.

CLIFTON GREY:

OR,

Love and War.

CHAPTER I.

"It is life to move from the heart's first throes,
Through youth and manhood to Age's snows,
In a ceaseless circle of joys and woes."

ANON.

"O what a face was hers to brighten light,
And give back sunshine with an added glow,
To wile each moment with a fresh delight,
And part of memory's best contentment grow!
O, how her voice, as with an inmate's right,
Into the strangest heart would welcome go,
And make it sweet, and ready to become
Of white and gracious thoughts the chosen home!"

LOWELL.

THE TRAVELLER. THE ROADSIDE INN. THE MAIDEN.

THE prettiest town in the south of England is Arundel. Situated on the declivity of a hill, its quaint old-fashioned houses, from the rudest rusticity to the more polished modern mansion, overlooked by the proud castle of "all the Howards," embosomed in rich foliage of all hues, strike the visitor with a feeling of peculiar satisfaction as his eye wanders over the many claims to the picturesque presented to him. It is, however, not in Arundel alone that all the charms of scenery are centred; but turn the gaze in any direction, the landscape is found to be both diversified and beautiful. Here may be observed the grandeur of vast and extensively-wooded uplands; there the calm beauty of undulating valleys, over whose bosoms, murmuring a music that hath no touch of art, glides the clear sparkling Arun, wandering in its course over pebbly stones and through green places, with many a gurgling gushing tone, right pleasant to the ear, and grateful to the eye. From the summit of the swelling downs may be traced the panoramic beauties of highly cultivated counties, enamelled with woods and plantations of every variety of tint, dotted here and there with towns and villages, from which uprise the pointed spires of many a rustic church, and glistening with numberless fields of golden and ripening grain. To the southward, stretches out to its junction with the sky, the ever-varying restless sea; now placid as a sheet of molten silver, anon tempest-tost and surging, under the heavy pressure of a south-west wind, so severely felt upon this coast, in long foam-crested hurrying waves, impatient to expend its fury upon the complaining beach. Along the shore, extending east and west, may be observed scattered small villages or more pretentious towns, yclept watering-places, while upon the sea, shallow and treacherous as it nears the coast, the fisherman's lugger floats lazily and idly, but too just a type of those who man it, stout and trim in the hour of toil and trial, but quite equal to all the sunshine and rest opportunity can bestow. Here and there dart the smartly rigged pleasure-yachts or the row-boat, with one small sail set to woo the favouring breeze. Far out to sea, where the sky seems to arch down to meet the world of waters, may be traced, though dim and hazy, the ship-rigged merchantmen or the leviathan steamers, pursuing their course to far lands or homeward bound, giving in their progress up and down Channel a wide berth to the coast, beautiful and fair though it be to gaze upon. Yea, Arundel is charmingly situated, romantic in its associations, agreeable for its pleasant places and pretty faces, and not the less delightful because, of all the sweet spots the broad lands of merry England can boast, there are few, if any, afford a more bracing, purer, healthier air than this same Arundel.

A few miles eastward of Arundel the road from Worthing winds in close contiguity with the sea-shore; indeed, in rough weather, a south-west wind and spring-tide bring the surf in unpleasant and sometimes terrifying proximity to the traveller, particularly if the time be night and the sky dark when this part of the route be traversed. It is just at the locality described that the road takes a direct turn inland; and, set back a little way from it, a cottage reared its head, palpable enough, if you were in search of it, and bent on finding it, but sufficiently unobtrusive to be passed without notice, unless the attention were specially directed to it. Immediately behind it the ground was cultivated for the production of vegetables, of which there appeared to be an ample supply of those in season, while only a small portion was devoted to the culture of flowers, albeit it was unquestionably rich in dahlias, which, without any design or arrangement, upreared their flaunting heads in all parts of this medley of kitchen and flower garden. The varieties were many, and, notwithstanding the vicinity of the sea, the plants were hardy, and the flowers handsome and perfect. It was evident they were carefully tended, although it was equally apparent they had not been planted with any consideration for effect, or even for successful rearing; nevertheless, they throve well, and surpassed many nurtured under more advantageous auspices. Beyond this garden was an orchard of no very vast extent, neither was it remarkable for the quality or quantity of apples and pears it produced, but it is certain that when the fruit had ripened, the palate might acknowledge that it had been subjected to meaner gratifications than the flavor of apple or pear from trees in this small orchard. Around, beyond, were fields of wheat, until the land ascended swelling gradually into wooded heights, forming the boundary between earth and sky.

At the cottage you could obtain—as a board of small dimensions, and much smaller claim to merit as a specimen of painter's craft, informed you—"Good accomodation for man and beste," the "m" being scandalously left out in the second word, and the designed generic appellation of the quadruped intended shamefully misspelt. You were also informed that it was by W. Waters that the opportunity of accepting accommodation was afforded, and the conclusion to be drawn from the board and the sign exhibited by that portion of the establishment from whence the public entertainment was to be obtained was, that bread and cheese, ale, hay, and water, would be the limit of refreshment 'to be had here.'

With such an impression conveyed by the aspect of the hostelry, no wonder that many a traveller, hungry or thirsty, on horse and foot, pursued his way without testing the hospitality proffered in such homely terms, or without observing that something to wash down the dust on a hot summer's day, or to warm the system on a nipping winter's morn, might be had by fee'ing Mr. W. Waters, because of the modesty both in dimensions and colour of the board that gave the intimation.

Yet there were those who knew such an impression to be ridiculously erroneous, and when purse permitted and inclination prompted, availed themselves very readily of the good cheer to be obtained at the "Bonny Bark;" for such was the sign of the "public," although there did not appear upon the face of the cottage, attached or pendent, any indication that such was the name W. Waters had sponsorially applied to it.

It was towards the close of a hot sunny day in August that a youthful traveller suspended his progress along the dusty road he had been traversing, on his way from Worthing to Arundel, to take advantage of an opportunity suddenly presented to him by a gap in the hedge to cast his eyes seaward and satisfy himself respecting certain prognostics he had been forming during the last quarter of an hour as to the probable continuance of the fine weather he had been making the most of that day. The sun was sinking in gorgeous splendour behind the western hills, casting a crimson glow over the sky above it, tinging the tree tops and crests of hills with hues of golden richness, and throwing into purple shadow the umbrageous woods, the hollow places, and sloping valleys with which this part of the country is adorned. Above, the sky, bare of clouds, was gradually assuming that exquisite tint of the violet, unapproachable by art, from which pale stars began to peep out, and it seemed as though the glory of the day would be transcended by the beauty of the night. Yet not in this direction did the young pedestrian turn his eyes, but, as we have said, his gaze was bent seaward, and he uttered an exclamation which indicated rather vexation than surprise at the signs which met the earnest regard he directed to them.

Immediately above the sea line, stretching from the eastward to the south-west, where the land runs out to a point, a huge bank of dark cloud was rising slowly up, from its volume and density somewhat awful in its character. From the uppermost edge of this mass a thin murky grey vapour sprang rapidly upward in all directions, expanding its filmy serrated edges as it drew perpendicular to the traveller, and in its progress shutting out the clear heavens and twinkling stars, as though to hide from them the ravages the fierce wind and the raging sea had determined on committing.

The youth watched for a few minutes these tokens of an interruption in the serenity which had reigned, until he was startled by a vivid flash of lightning, illuminating all that part of the sea over which the clouds had already cast their shadow.

"I was not deceived," he muttered, "the sea suffers not its calm to be disturbed without a complaining moan. The dull boom of the waves upon the shore, and the mournful roll of the loose beach as it follow the retiring waters, led me to expect a change, but I did not bargain for one so sudden as this. I have yet some miles to cover before I reach Arundel, and unless I am lucky enough to obtain shelter on my way, the storm will burst in its wildest fury over me, and I shall be soaked to the skin without possessing the luxury of a change."

A second flash of lightning more vivid than the first, followed by a low rumbling, admonished him to proceed; and he observed that the pleasure boats, and even such fishing vessels as were in the offing, were running for the shore in evident haste to escape the storm that was brewing, and which was sweeping up with a rapidity almost staggering the belief of even those who observed it.

Springing from the gap, in which he had stood to examine the weather, he proceeded along the road, determining to apply to the first cottage on the wayside for hospitality. He was thinly clad in summer dress, and was fully conscious that the storm would overtake him long before he could gain the destination to which he was bound, and he had no desire to brave the driving rain, when the only result of such daring would be that he must lie in bed while his clothes were being dried. It is true that at his back he carried a knapsack, which appeared somewhat bulky; but, whatever changes of linen and other articles it might contain, a suit of clothes was not among them: so he increased his speed, and, as his attention was on the qui vive, he quickly espied "The Bonny Bark." He at once directed his step thither. As he drew near, his eye caught sight of the board already mentioned; he was too glad of the promise it held out to even smile at the deficient scholarship it displayed, and, on reaching the door, lifted the latch to enter, but further progress was checked, for the door was fastened within. At this moment a blast of wind came howling from the sea—a dense cloud of dust from the road was whirled in the air in fantastic wreaths and carried over the cornfields; big, heavy drops of rain came pattering down, beating against the small panes of the lattice window of the "Bonny Bark," and, with this inducement, the young traveller struck with his walking-cane smartly on the door. The summons did not obtain an immediate reply; he therefore repeated it more violently, using his voice lustily, for the rain was beginning to fall sharply. While impatiently continuing his blows, the door suddenly opened, and a stout burly-looking fellow occupying the door-way, and without offering the slightest opportunity for admittance, enquired roughly what the stranger wanted. The young traveller scanned his questioner from head to foot, and observed that he was young but stalwart; his dress was a compound of the sailor and agricultural labourer. He had a handsome face, but it did not possess the expression which impresses one with the strongest belief in the honesty of the owner.

There was an almost settled frown on the brow, the eye was bright, quick in its movements, and a brilliant black; but while it expressed much determination, unquestionable courage, with the capability of betokening ferocity, it was certainly the great ornament of the face. It was not with such considerations, however, that the young pedestrian regarded him; he looked upon him as an uncourteous boor, improperly impeding his path.

"What do I want?" he exclaimed pettishly. "Pray does not your board state that you afford 'good accommodation for man and beast?' I want accommodation."

"Glass o' ale," suggested the cottager, eying his customer closely, and yet blocking up the doorway.

"Glass of ale," echoed the traveller, with an impatient gesture—"I want to come in and rest myself, perhaps to sleep."

"You can ha' a glass o' ale at t' door," said the Cerberus, still keeping possession of the entry.

"At the door!" cried the youth in indignant amaze, "What do you mean? Don't you admit travellers?"

"Sometimes."

"Why not now?—don't you see a heavy storm is coming up?"

"Ah, that it be—'t'ull be a dirty night."

"Exactly, and I am on my way to Arundel."

"To Ar'ndel?"

"Yes. I have no chance of getting there before the storm comes on, and as time is not altogether an object to me I prefer resting here, and, if need be, having a bed, if you have one to let."

At this moment, a violent gust of wind swept fiercely past them, the heavens each moment grew darker, the rain continued to increase, and a smart flash of lightning again lit up the sea. The cottager threw his eyes seaward.

"T'ull be a dirty night," he ejaculated once more.

"Of course; therefore let me enter, exclaimed the youth," and added, with a curl of the lip, "it is not usual for innkeepers to keep a closed door against a customer."

"Where did'st thou come from?" asked the countryman, fixing an enquiring eye upon him.

"Where did I come from?" repeated the traveller, his face becoming of a scarlet hue, "What's that to you?" Then checking his ire, and seeing the question in another light, he added, "I have come from Brighton; I have walked from thence since the morning, and am tired. But look you my man, answer me yea or nay, am I to come in or not? If yes, let me pass; if nay, I'll e'en hurry on to some shelter, where my money will be more acceptable, and the hospitality more readily accorded."

The countryman, casting a rapid glance over the person of the traveller, as though to form an estimate of his means, called out suddenly to some one within, "Feyther, here's one as wants summut to eat, and a bed—can you do it?"

Immediately obeying the summons, a tall gaunt man appeared from an inner room, and advanced direct to the door; he cast a shrewd penetrating glance at the young traveller, and said instantly—

"Aye, to be sure—that is if he be'nt too dainty with his food, or afear'd of a humble but clean bed."

"Neither" cried the young traveller, making at once almost a forcible entry, "I am ready for a fowl and a few slices of ham, or will be content with bread and cheese; I can enjoy a down bed or a chair, and can pay for either. Do the best you can for me and I shall not grumble, I promise you."

The next moment he had passed father and son, and walking into an inner room, he at once proceeded to divest himself of his knapsack, which he placed upon the table, and removing his cap which he threw by its side, he flung himself into a chair, and drawing a silk handkerchief from the breast pocket of his coat, he proceeded to dust his shoes; while father and son, who had followed him into the room, regarded him with an attention, somewhat beyond that which his dress or even his appearance at their house, or his free and prompt mode of making himself comfortable, really warranted.

The silence which for a minute ensued, was broken by the elder of the cottage inmates proffering to dress a fowl for the supper of his guest, if he desired it, or he would place upon the table at a short notice some nicely cooked rashers of ham, with some new laid eggs, which could not be surpassed in Christendom, notwithstanding what was said and done in respect to Cochin China. The guest preferred the latter dish, and producing a case of cigars from his pocket, he proceeded to light one, and requested to be furnished with a glass of warm brandy and water, while his supper was preparing.

A twinkle was observable in the old man's eyes, and he slightly raised his eyebrows as he said.

"Be you very particklar whether the brandy ha' paid duty or not."

The youth smiled.

"Not at all" he answered readily; "on the contrary, if it has not paid duty, the better my chance to get it "neat as imported" you know."

The old man grinned appreciatingly, and with his son left the room.

When left to himself, the youth sunk into a reverie of a deep and melancholy kind, so profound was it, that he did not hear the approach of a footstep, or observe that the room held yet another tenant beside himself. Twice or thrice, he sighed with such agony, that it was evident he was under the influence of memories inflicting acute sorrow; but as he gave utterance to the last audible respiration, he became conscious that a pair of eyes were intently regarding his features, and he raised his to meet the gaze of as resplendent a pair of orbs as ever were set in the head of the most peerless beauty the world ever saw.

A young girl of seventeen stood before him, holding a tray, upon which was placed the diluted spirit, presumed to have entered the water free of duty, which he had ordered. Their eyes met, the young girl instantly, with a rosy blush mantling her cheeks, turned her gaze upon the ground, and in a low musical voice, said.

"Is this for you, sir?"

The youth sprung to his feet; with ready politeness, he took the tray from her hands, and placing it on the table, answered assentingly.

Simple and common place enough such an act, and there it might have ended, had the young girl presented the ordinary aspect of even good looks, but this was not the case. She was beautiful, and her beauty was of a rare character.

The entrance of a pretty girl, in the capacity of a waitress especially, if with her prettiness there is mixed up cheerfulness and good temper, never fails to excite an interest in the mind, or to influence the temperament of, at least, the male guest. We say at least the male guest, for, strangely enough, women generally are not just to their sex so placed. In their estimation the beauty will admit largely of modification, the cheerfulness is forwardness, and the good nature artfulness. Men do not prove it so—too often the charge is due on the other side, as many a lost creature has experienced—and certainly to them, one of the charms of a country inn is a pretty and good tempered waitress. It will be clearly understood that this bears no covert meaning, nor admits of an improper sense, but those who are compelled to find in the temporary accommodation of an inn, the comforts they command at home well understand how much enhanced are the conveniences afforded when accompanied by a pleasant smiling face, and a willing readiness to oblige.

Our young traveller, although suddenly moved from a deep and painful reverie, formed no exception to the rule. Well educated, possessing taste and refinement, he was fully capable of detecting beauty and awarding it its fair appreciation; it would have been wholly impossible for him to have passed with indifference the face now presented to him, or mete out to it the mere amount of approbation which what is understood by the term pretty face might have claimed. A quick glance developed to him the large and lustrous blue eyes so frequently shrouded by the full deeply-fringed eyelid, the clear snowy transparent skin, the small pulpy mouth, the regular and even features, and the graceful outline of a figure delicately moulded.

It is difficult to define what was his first impression; it was a compound of wonder, respect, and pleasure. It was as though the sunshine, which the hills were just shutting out from the land, had reappeared and filled the apartment, no less to his surprise than his gratification.

It was not altogether easy to talk to her, yet he did find some observations come up to his tongue, to which, at first, she replied readily, and afterwards with hesitation and embarrassment. Why, she certainly knew not; and further, without clearly comprehending her own motives, she suddenly felt impelled to quit the apartment, although the impulse was actually opposed to her inclination.

And so she left him alone once more, and the sunshine no longer gladdened the apartment. This time, the sun had sunk behind the hills for the night; the sky, too, had become a vast murky pall; more distinctly still, was heard the heavy beat of the surf upon the shore, and the long rolling roar of the shingle as it followed the angry waves, which seemed to recede only to hurl themselves with greater violence upon the quivering beach, that trembled under every shock. The wind swept fiercely, yet with mournful wail round the humble building, the rain beat sharply against the casements, and all the indications of a fierce tempest, which had induced the young traveller to seek shelter, were now being realised. As he little noted, in his former reverie, the signs of the brewing storm, so he nothing heeded now the more apparent tokens of a gale. Every faculty was absorbed in reflection upon the vision which he had just witnessed, for such it appeared to him to be. Who was this girl, so fair, so lovely, so delicate in motion and manner, so soft in voice, so well-expressed in language, so neat in attire? A daughter of the landlord, a sister of the churl who had all but denied him admittance from a howling gale? Impossible! if not, what did she there? In service? Preposterous! Certainly it was remarkable. Probably he thought it incumbent upon him to make further observations and some inquiries, and he remembered—oh, contrast to his romance!—that he was to have eggs and bacon for his supper. Would she be the cook—would she wait upon him? At once he was ready, nay, seemed to be absolutely waiting for his supper.

And then he discovered his cigar was out, and he had not tasted his brandy and water. He stretched out his hand to take the glass, but the room being dark, he could not see that it was much closer to him than he imagined, and so he tipped it over, and the glass fell to the ground with a crash.

He chuckled, for he believed that it would bring in some one of the household to make enquiries, perhaps *her*; but no, he stood motionless and listened, silence seemed to reign within the house, albeit there was noise enough made by the warring elements without. This was strange; he remembered he required a light for his cigar, a lighted candle for the room which he occupied, another glass of brandy and water—anything, in short, which would afford him either another opportunity of again seeing the Hebe who had brought him the nectar thus accidentally wasted, or of proposing some enquiries he had the strongest inclination to pursue.

He knew not where the bell was situated, he hesitated to call, and therefore, with a light step, resolved to seek mine host. The dimensions of the cottage were not so extensive that he was likely to lose himself in the search, or to go far before he met with him of whom he was in quest, or some one else.

His first discovery was the bar of the hostel from whence the liquors and ales were dispensed. He, however, perceived by a dim light, that there was no one to perform that operation. He next discovered a room for the rougher guests, and then a passage led to the rear of the premises, where the accommodations of the house had been increased by some out-buildings. Along this he proceeded, and reached a door which was ajar; he pushed it gently open and perceived, standing in front of a cheerful fire, with her hands before her clasped together, and in an attitude no less pensive than that from which she had aroused him, the young girl who had occupied so many of his recent thoughts

CHAPTER II.

"Blue were her eyes as the fairy flax,
Her cheeks like the dawn of day,
And her bosom white as the hawthorn-buds,
That ope in the mouth of May."
LONGFELLOW.

"But other speculations were in sooth,
Added to his connection with the sea,
Perhaps not so respectable, in truth;
A little smuggling.'
BYRON.

THE BREWING TEMPEST. THE SMUGGLERS.

HE approached her on tip-toe, and stood by her side. He heard her breath a low sigh, and then he gently touched her shoulder; she started, and, slightly screaming, retreated a few steps, but on perceiving who had startled her, she smiled, and returned to the spot where she had previously been standing.

"I did not intend to alarm you," he observed, with rather a serious and apologetic expression on his features.

"I am easily terrified," she responded—"that is," she added, correcting herself, "I mean startled—I am nervous."

"You had scarcely need to be weak-nerved to reside here."

"Why? It is very quiet."

"Certainly—just now; but you must often witness some riotous proceedings which can hardly be to your taste."

"There are few such scenes here, I assure you; the house is but little known and less frequented."

"Hem! That is hardly a flattering account of the success of the establishment. I am surprised that your — that is, I mean your—no, I should say the landlord, should carry it on."

"He has lived here many years."

"You are—I presume—a near relative."

"No!"

"No—I thought not."

"Why? You contradict yourself."

"True, I do not believe that you are related to him in even a sixtieth degree."

The young girl caught his look of admiration as he uttered those words in rather an impetuous tone, and the colour rose to her cheeks. Still it was not altogether without an expression of surprise that she said:

"He is my foster father."

"Pooh! a relationship that might exist between a princess and a churl; I knew no drop of his blood coursed through your veins; such a belief would be too absurd to be entertained for a moment."

Again the young girl eyed him with surprise, while her cheeks were suffused with blushes, for it was easy to perceive the tendency of his remarks to be complimentary, although quite unpremeditated. She remained silent, and her eyes sought the earth. The young guest perused the lineaments of the maiden, and each moment with increased pleasure; he longed to touch her hand, not that he had any precise reason for such a desire, or that he felt conscious of possessing it; he was, beside, naturally and by education too well bred to display any act of freedom towards one who excited his respect no less than his admiration, and though, by a power of attraction he did not attempt to define, he was impelled to draw close to her side, it was not with the view of enforcing attentions which would admit of this construction, and so prove offensive. The truth was, that she was the most beautiful girl he had hitherto met, and her beauty was of a rare order—it strangely contrasted with the objects by which she was surrounded, and the people with whom she companioned; the upper lip of the young traveller curled with fierce contempt as he imagined the fellow who had held him in parley at the door of the inn, addressing her with coarse tongue, and pawing her with rude hands. In a moment he hated the idea of her being there at all, and exclaimed, as the repugnance flashed through his mind,

"You do not reside here constantly?"

She could scarcely refrain from a smile, even though surprised by his manner and tone, and answered:

"No, I reside with my mother at Arundel; I am here because my foster sister has been called suddenly away, and she was so serviceable to her father that he is lost without her. I am but a poor substitute for her, but then Master Waters will not let me do half what I would to supply her place."

"I commend his good sense. By the by, where is he?"

"Gone with his son along the shore. A heavy gale is coming up from the south-west, the tide is out, and there is a schooner in the Bay which he fears will be unable to get an offing. If his suspicion prove correct she will drive ashore and—

A vivid flash of lightning, blue to ghastliness, suddenly filled the room for an unusually long duration. The girl gave a faint shriek, and clutched the arm of the youth. A long peal of thunder followed, bursting with a fearful crash, and dying away like the reverberating echoes from a park of artillery. The wind howled and whistled past the building as though it would level it with the earth, and the heavy and incessant roar of the sea was yet more audible than before, even though the tide was running out.

The young girl, with a terrified air, still clung to the arm of the guest, and regarded with blanched features the diamonded panes through which the flash of lightning had penetrated with such startling and lurid brilliancy.

"Do not be alarmed," he said, soothingly: "it is seldom that lightning proves dangerous."

"It is not the lightning I fear, but did you not see that horrid face?"

"No, where?"

"Staring in at the window."

The young man gazed in the direction she intimated, but perceived nothing to justify her assertion; the next moment the latch of the outer door was heard to move rapidly, as though some one was trying it for the purpose of gaining admission. The young girl shuddered with dread, and the youth felt his heart beat quickly.

"It may be some one caught in the storm and needs shelter; it is a wild night to be abroad in."

"Master Waters bade me on no account let any stranger in while he was away. He will himself be back very soon."

The youth laughed.

"A strange inn this," he said, "where the landlord's main object seems to be to prevent people claiming the entertainment he professes to give!"

The movement of the latch having ceased, and the speech of the guest appearing to be uttered with a meaning, the young girl seemed suddenly to awaken to a sense of the fact that the presence of the youth in this outer chamber must have originated in some unsupplied wants, and a few questions elicited that he was without light or refreshment in the room he had quitted, but he turned at first a deaf ear to her offer to supply both, if he would return thither. When, however, he perceived that she repeated her request somewhat earnestly, he complied with a promptness intended to convey a ready attention to any wish she might form.

He said as much, indeed, as with an undisguised look of admiration he prepared to quit her, and as if to escape from the effects of his observation, he hurried in the semi-darkness to the apartment into which he had first been ushered. As he entered, a tremendous flash of lightning not only lit up his apartment, but enabled him to see from the window the sea raging furiously; then all was dark as pitch, and a crash of thunder seemed to shake the house to its foundation. It had barely ceased when he heard voices without, but close to the window. The incident of the man's face appearing at the window, and the attempt to enter, recurred at once to him, and he approached the casement, keeping by the wall in order that he might not be observed by those without, if it were possible to see aught in the room from thence. As he reached the window he heard the voice of the landlord say,

"I tell'ee 't'wull be done; they have shown a blue light twice in the offing."

"They'll never get a line a-shore with such a sea on," returned a gruff voice, and added, "Besides, no boat would live in such a surf."

"It's no concern of yours, I suppose," observed Waters, testily; "you get your people together, and the cart with Galloping Jack, I'll warrant we run the tubs clean enough."

" Why its blowing a heavy gale, and—"

"So much the better," interrupted Waters. "I tell'ee," he continued, "I laid down a line in a snug place, and buoyed it in six fathom water, before dawn this morning. The lugger has made it, she has dropped her tubs by this time, and if you look alive we'll soon have 'em ashore. I promise you it will be a haul worth having—besides there's no fear of Philistines, it's Ben Hartley's spell to night, and he is gone up westward. I met him and gave him a pull at some brandy out of my pistol. He told me he should get under the lee of a cliff, and make himself snug, for he was sure there could be no business done to night. Ha! ha! he said he was sure of that."

"Um! I don't like that Ben Hartley, he always sleeps with one eye open; he carries too many guns for most on 'us. I owe him a pill; he's sp'ilt me a good many times, and got me a year in Dover jail."

"Ha, well you needn't be afeared o' him, he's all right to night; now, away with you, there's no time for jaw."

"How about that schooner?"

"That's just it; she can't claw off this lee shore, and she'll go to pieces in the Bay. I want to run the tubs before she begins to throw up her blue lights, and brings all the people we don't want to see straggling about here."

"Ay! ay!—That's not your Nell I saw in the back there."

"No."

"Who is it?"

"What's that to you? no concern of yours, is it?"

"I like to know my friends. Who's that young luff that was with her."

"With her—with her?"

"Aye, he seemed very smiling like. Looked as if he was laying out an anchor to windward of her."

"Wheugh! Hem! I know, I know; you just spring your luff, and take a severe turn round your jaw. You're getting worse than a woman who has found a hole in her neighbour's character. Just heave a head, and be back by half past ten to a minute."

The two men separated, and almost immediately a light was brought by the young girl into the room. She approached the window in order to place up the rude wooden shutters that fitted in, and were fastened with a bar. Our young traveller hastened to relieve her of the task; as he did so, a bright flash of lightning illumined the place without, and he fancied he caught sight of a man in a rough pea coat, a round hat on his head, and a cutlass by his side, glide from the immediate vicinity of the house eastward. He fixed up the shutter, and on turning beheld standing in the door-way the grim visaged landlord of the house, who was regarding him with a look which could hardly be accused of being violently friendly.

"I am in a smuggler's den," he thought, and with it came the reflection that he was quite unarmed, and totally in the power of his host. It flashed through his mind also that to quit his present location on any plea, would wear the air of pretence, and might precipitate a catastrophe rather than arrest it. The storm still raged, and nothing was left but to wear as composed a counte-nance as he could, and prepare for the worst. What shape that worst was likely to take, he could form at that moment no conception, but he possessed an organi-zation which not only rendered him incapable of fear, but fitted him to meet any sudden danger with energy, with activity, and a readiness to avail himself of such recources as circumstances might place in his power.

His host regarded him, as we have said, with a grim countenance, and somewhat abruptly requested his foster daughter to quit the room, as her services were then unnecessary. He proceeded somewhat roughly, as with a look of surprise on her beautiful face the young girl obeyed him, to ask if his guest was ready for his supper, intimating that in his dwelling folks, unlike Londoners, went to bed early.

His guest expressed his readiness to receive the frugal meal as soon as it was ready, and further said that he would depart to the room prepared for him, when he had concluded his supper, but added haughtily, that as to retiring to bed, he should suit his con-venience or his inclination. The old man bent his brows over his eyes, which glittered like diamonds, but made no reply. He lingered in the room for a minute and then disappeared, and the youth was left to contemplate his position, listen to the howling of the wind, the reverberating echoes of the thunder, and the ceaseless roar of the disturbed sea. He quickly sunk into a reverie, from which he was roused by the preparations made to place his supper before him. The old man alone attended him; the young traveller could perceive that from beneath his shaggy brows his host bent furtive glances upon him, ever and anon; a surveillance under which the youth began to grow restive. He paced up and down the room restlessly, and suddenly turning upon the old man, said sharply:

"You do not make so pleasant an attendant as the damsel who was here just now."

The old man started and grinned at him like a hyena

THE TRAVELLER AND THE MAIDEN.

"Haply not," he replied, through his teeth. "Harkee, young spark, she's here to do me service, and she's not to be made eyes at by any fellow as fancies to do it, unless he would try how hard my knuckles are."

"Nor I either."

"Anan!"

"Why, look you, Mr. Landlord, I have not taken your spoons, and I don't mean to do so. It is my intention to pay honestly for what I have when I leave, or as I have it, or even beforehand if you desire it; therefore, I am not to be "made eyes at" any more than the young lady; that is why I preferred her attendance to yours; she, at least, would not watch my every movement, as if she was in a mortal fear I should take the first opportunity to pocket the salt-cellar."

The old man looked earnestly at him for a moment as though he scarcely comprehended him, then he burst into a laugh, and exclaimed, "Well, you be a stranger, though I don't fear you want to rob me; no, no, it beant that; but, you see, I've known the girl since she's been a baby, mayhap I know more about her than she does herself, but that's neither here nor there, but while I am by I would not see her troubled by word or look. If right be right this be no place for her; let that be how 'twull, while she is here she sha'nt be shamed by a lewd wink or wanton speech."

The knitted brows of the youth relaxed, and with a glittering eye, he said:

"Old man, I honour your feelings. For myself, I would rather lose my right hand than intentionally pain my foster-child by an improper glance, or by the fragment of a sentence which could convey a loose thought"—

He was stayed further remark by a sudden exclamation from the old man. The youth turned his eyes in the same direction in which he perceived him to be gazing, and observed, standing in the doorway, the subject of their discourse. It was evident she had heard what had passed by the expression of her features and the crimson hue suffusing her fair face, as well as by her readiness to retire at the first hint from old Waters, without attempting to explain the reason of her appearance, after having previously been requested, in a somewhat unceremonious manner, to leave the chamber. Old Waters followed her from the chamber, but returned in a moment and said, with a knowing nod, "You'll excuse me, but safe bind safe find, you know," and once more disappeared. Old Waters brought his guest his supper, and waited upon him until it was finished. Then, without giving much time for digestion, he made his appearance with a light, and informed him he was ready to show him to his apartment. The young traveller would fain have exchanged a good night with the young girl who had so much interested him, but Old Waters gave him no opportunity, and he was ushered into a small but clean room, humbly but fully furnished. A glance told him he might sleep well there, very comfortably and soundly,

unless disturbed in a manner he hardly liked to permit himself to suggest. The unfavourable impression created by the conversation he had overheard at the window in the apartment beneath, was, however, fast wearing away, in consequence of the proper feeling the old man had displayed towards the young girl, and by the courtesy, somewhat rough and free, it must be confessed, which he had exhibited to himself. He remembered the sudden apparition of one of the coast guard as he was fixing the shutter to the window below, and it struck him that it would be important to Waters to be made acquainted with it; but even as it flashed through his mind, he heard his chamber door close and a bolt outside drawn with some force, immediately followed by the rapidly retreating footsteps of Old Waters.

At first he was disposed to make a violent dash against the door, with the view of bursting it open, for he did not like to be trapped in this fashion; but he immediately checked himself and went to the window, against which the wind and rain were heavily beating, and from which he could see nothing, all without being of pitchy blackness. He opened the casement, but the wind and rain rushed into the room with such violence, that he was glad to fasten it again.

He was trapped; he sat himself down to reflect, and the result was, that he determined quietly to resign himself to fate. It occurred to him that he should only get into mischief by making an uproar, but that by being quiet he should be enabled to take advantage of circumstances as they might shape themselves. There could be no doubt there was some smuggling going on; that the authorities were on the scent, and no doubt they would do all that was needful, and interference by him was simply out of the question. He did not fear molestation while he remained still; he had no suspicion that robbery of his person was contemplated, for if he had, he might reasonably, also, expect that his life as well as his property would be in danger; but there was nothing to lead to such a supposition. He therefore resolved to put out his light, and merely divesting himself of his coat and shoes, throw himself on the bed, and wait the issue. He determined not to go to sleep, in order to note everything that took place, and so be prepared for any emergency that might arise.

But then he had been walking best part of the day; more than twenty miles had he covered, and that in no manner to save himself fatigue; so that very shortly after he had stretched himself upon the bed and listened to the gushing of the whistling wind, the patter of the heavy rain against the window panes, and the ceaseless roar of the surf and shingle on the beach, he unconsciously became sensible of a change and found himself reclining upon a mossy bank in a paradise of a garden all sunshine and flowers, his head leaning gently upon the shoulder of a fair girl, whose deep blue eyes, beaming with tenderness, looked down into his very soul, while her musical voice, in a low tone, poured a strain of divine melody in his ears; his own hard breathing at the same time being not altogether of so romantic a character as his dream.

CHAPTER III.

"The blue lightning flashes,
The rapid hail clashes,
The white waves are tumbling,
And in one baffled roar,
Like the toothless sea mumbling
A rock-bristled shore;
The thunder is rumbling,
And crashing and crumbling—
Will silence return never more?"

LOWELL.

"Boating to sea again,
Through the wild hurricane,
Bore I the maiden."

LONGFELLOW.

THE WRECK OF THE SCHOONER—THE RESCUE.

ARK! what is that! A loud sharp report rising above the howl of the blast and the roar of the tumbling waters. A ringing sound, that tells a tale of horror, when it comes booming over the sea, startling the ear of those who, on shore, are listening shudderingly to the raging of the tempest. It is a gun—a signal of distress. Hark, it is repeated; see, there goes a blue light; what a ghastly hue it casts around. Behold how it exhibits the sea, foaming and tossing, and boiling—and now how dark it is; how fiercely the blast sweeps over sea and land; how it forces up the huge masses of turbid water; how it bends down and crushes the tall trees and sturdy shrubs, and how it moans and wails, and shrieks and whistles. What an awful night it is.

It is just half-past ten. The schooner is ashore, the sea is making a breach over her, and if the gale continues she must quickly go to pieces.

Another gun is fired, another—the report is brought by the wind with alarming distinctness. The youth springs suddenly from the heavy sleep into which he had fallen, and sits upright upon the bed, unable at first to comprehend his position. A sheet of blue flame lights up the room, a burst of thunder shakes the house; and the young traveller leaps from his bed. He gazes through the window into the murky air, endeavouring to pierce its gloom with his eyes, but is unable to detect anything by his sight, while his ears are almost deafened by the howl of the wind and the never-ceasing roar of the angry waters.

A blue light, solemn and spectre-like, a ghastly claim from the despairing for succour, displayed to his eager eyes the struggling ship and its desperate condition. He impulsively put on his coat, shoes, and cap, and made his way to the room door; it was fast: he shook it vigorously, hurled his body violently against it, dashed his heel fiercely at it, but it did not give way. He shouted lustily; there was no response to his cries. He went to the window and opened it; he waited for a flash of lightning to tell him the height from the ground; it came quickly; he heeded not the tremendous crash of thunder that succeeded, but forced his body through the open space, lowered himself until he hung by his hands from the window sill, then he dropped to the ground; a slight shock to his limbs followed, but he shook it off, and hurried in face of the driving surf towards the point of land nearest to the vessel being wrecked. It was with a very faint hope of being of service that he pressed on to the place where he knew the fisher people would be assembled, but he felt disposed to lend his aid where and when required, and in a moment of emergency it might prove valuable—who should say it would not?

He was not long reaching a part of the beach, where a number of fishermen and their wives had congregated, and where the former were discussing the feasibility of getting out a boat to save the crew, whom the last flash of lightning had shown to be already clinging to the rigging of their ill-fated ship.

The gallant fellows, with true-hearted courage, were trying to argue down their experience; they well knew the difficulty and danger of getting a boat out with such a tremendous surf running, but they were, they said, certain they could save the men belonging to the schooner if they could launch their boat without her being seized by the curling waves as she advanced to face them, and hurled back bottom upwards on the beach. Two gentlemen, both elderly, were among the fishermen, and while they desired them not to throw their lives away, they yet urged them, if there was a chance of rescuing the mariners from drowning, to at least make the attempt. Our young traveller soon joined his voice to theirs, and the result was a determination to make an essay; volunteers were called for. Our young friend eagerly tendered himself; he could pull an oar; was strong and willing; his self-recommendation was accepted. The number required to man the boat was soon made up, and young and old, strong and weak, lent their aid to launch it. It was fortunate that the tide was out, for this enabled the fishermen to actually get their boat afloat in the water forced up by the wind on the flat sands, before it reached the spot where the waves broke furiously upon the land. They got up a sail, and prepared to unfurl it to the gale at the moment they reached the surf, so that it would force their little bark through it, and carry them beyond it; the great danger to their safety being involved in the execution of this manœuvre. With intense anxiety was the moment watched both by those in the boat and those on the land, and it was the will of Providence that this bold attempt to snatch from a dreadful death a number of their fellow creatures should prove successful. No sooner did the vessel meet the boiling surf, than the sail, close-reefed, was sheeted home, a turn only being taken in the sheet, that should the strain prove too much for the boat it might be let go on the instant. Directly the wind caught it, the boat leaped like a courser beneath a lash; it was a fortunate moment, a huge wave had just broken, and the boat flew over the retiring water; rose upon the coming wave, fell in the trough of that, and the following waves still urged onward, the mast almost at a right angle with the sea, and the keel all but lifting out of the water. A murmur of satisfaction burst from the lips of the boatmen; a cheer from those who watched with painful earnestness the movements of the frail vessel in the raging tempest. The first danger had been surmounted; and so long as the gear held, there was every prospect of reaching the wrecked vessel. In this they succeeded too; but it was long before they could contrive safely to remove from the schooner the poor fellows clinging to the rigging; at length the last was with difficulty hauled into the boat. When one of the rescued men who declared himself to be the captain of the schooner, said, in a faint voice:

"Is the young lady alive?"

"What young lady?" asked one of the fishermen.

"There's no young lady here," said our young traveller, whose courage and activity had enabled him to prove of great service.

"My God!" exclaimed the captain; "I had forgotten, she's in the cabin. You've not cast off the line? I'll go on board again and fetch her alive or dead; she's in the manifest, and I must produce her; I swore to put her ashore in England, living or dead. Let me go aboard again?"

He rose, but fell back exhausted, on the thwart on which he had been seated.

"Avast!" cried a brawny fisherman; "You bide there, I'll be aboard and back again with her in the turning of a sheave."

"Stay!" cried our young traveller; "I have been on board twice; see to the line, and be cautious how you haul us into the boat."

In another minute he was over the side along the line, and not without great danger to life and limb, he got on board the vessel. A well-sustained courage and stern determination enabled him to get into the cabin, which was yet singularly free from the water he expected to find washing about in her. A swinging light still burned brightly, and he was enabled to see by its unsteady beams the body of a young female, prostrate in a corner on the upper side, but clutching with death-like tenacity to a fixed portion of the cabin furniture. He could not see her face, which was turned downwards, and her long fair hair was spread dishevelled over her shoulders. He reached her, and spoke to her, but he received no answer; he tried to move her, but it

seemed as though she maintained her hold with a death-grip. He was almost stunned by the beating of the waves, as with thundering shocks they struck the trembling ship; but still above it he heard the shrill cries of the fishermen, who were hailing him, and urging his return, for continued stay was imperilling the lives of all.

It would not be possible to describe the arduous nature of the task this youth had undertaken, or the desperate efforts he made to get his lifeless companion on deck into the blinding hurricane of sea and wind and rain; how he struggled almost against hope, to work his way to where the line was yet fast under the lee of the ship, and by the uncertain aid of which he was to convey her to the boat. But the stout hearts in the boat perceived him as soon as he got on deck; they saw that he had in his care a precious human life; that he had found what he had sought, and was bravely struggling to save it from the remorseless maw of the voracious sea. They hailed him with a cheer, and the young fellow who had first volunteered to seek this young female, at once made the best of his way to the ship, and gave material aid to our young friend in getting the body of the young girl safely on board the boat, in which they succeeded; the line was cast loose, and away they swept with frightful rapidity towards the shore, to gain which in safety was still a task fraught with the greatest danger. But by the time they neared the land, considerable numbers of people from the cottages round, all more or less acquainted with the safest manner of beaching a boat in such weather, were gathered on the sands. They hailed the return of the boat, which repeated flashes of lightning showed to be freighted with the shipwrecked mariners; with loud cheers, they by means of lighted torches showed where an indentation in the land formed a small creek, and into this the boat, half full of water and quite full of living souls, ran. It was no sooner clear of the surf than it was hauled up high and dry; the fishermen jumped out, and the crew of the shipwrecked vessel were led away to cottages, to be cheered by a warm fire, and restored by grog which had not received an introduction to the custom house.

The captain of the schooner proved an exception; he seemed overwhelmed with the misfortune which had overtaken him, and sat down in a state of stupor on the sands, replying nothing to questions which were put to him, unheeding requests to accompany some hospitable persons to shelter, refreshment, and repose; appearing altogether stupified. He took no notice of the girl saved by the young traveller, who tenderly lifted her from the boat, and raising her up in his arms staggered on with her, still lifeless, towards the "Bonny Bark, by W. Waters." Even though he had been obliged to quit, and in so peculiar a manner, it immediately recurred to him to return there. He knew that a female was there, that there would be a good fire and restoratives, and that it was the best step for the restoration of the young girl which could be adopted. So on he went, leaving the captain, who was not roused from his stupefaction until he heard that the wind was rapidly going down, and there was a chance after all that the schooner would not go to pieces, or at least her cargo would be saved; a prospect which kept him on the beach, ready to pay a visit to her as soon as the sea abated. As our young traveller with his lifeless burden drew near to the "Bonny Bark," pretty nigh exhausted with his labors, he perceived that the door of the inn was open, that a strong light issued from within, and that rude and rough voices came thence, presenting a remarkable contrast to its silent condition when he escaped from it.

He did not hesitate to enter, although he perceived it was nearly filled with men whom he judged, by the sounds of coarse laughter and gruff language, to be ill calculated to display those sympathies or afford that assistance the condition of the helpless being, under whose weight, slight as it was, he was now tottering, demanded. His arrival was, for the moment, unnoticed, but his astonishment was infinitely great to find that the larger proportion of the guests were coast-guardsmen, and that W. Waters, his son, and several other men in the garb of agricultural labourers, had their arms pinioned. He a second time cast his eyes eagerly around in search of the young girl whose presence there that evening had so much interested him, and upon whose aid he now so earnestly calculated. She was not there, and a strange pang of disappointment ran through his frame. At this moment an officer of the coast-guard who was present exclaimed, as he cast his eye upon the lifeless companion of the youth:

"Good God, what have you there?—a woman—is she drowned?"

All eyes were at once turned upon the new comer, and room was made for him to bring the girl into the centre of the apartment. He was assisted to lay her gently upon the floor. Her wet garments clung to her slight form—her dishevelled hair straggled wildly over her pallid features—her eyes were closed, and her lips were compressed firmly together; there was an expression, settled on her face, of terror or agony perhaps both.

The officer who had before spoken said, as looking at her features and kneeling down he raised her cold hand, which he commenced chafing between his rough palms,—

"She's not dead yet—Waters, have you a fire?—Speak man, don't let your small trouble swallow up the life of a poor girl, when a word will save her."

"There was a fire in a chamber at the end of the passage, an hour or two back. There may be one now," exclaimed the youth who had saved the maiden from the wreck of the schooner.

Without waiting for any response from Waters, the youth and coast-guard officer raised the still senseless creature and bore her where the young traveller had discovered and conversed with the foster-child of Waters. A fire still blazed brightly upon the hearth, and by its side, crouched down in an attitude of grief and terror, was the young girl just mentioned.

"Hey, my lass," cried the coast-guard officer, as he bent a quick gaze upon her, "hold up your head and lend a hand here—dry your eyes, Waters wont come to any harm; and see here is a poor girl half-drowned; she'll die without help."

The young girl raised her head timidly and with a frightened aspect, but a hurried glance shewed her the young guest and the senseless girl. She rose from her position, and came forward with an exclamation of wonder and sympathy.

"What can I do," she asked eagerly.

"Much," exclaimed the officer, "get some blankets—is there any other woman beside yourself in the house?" he inquired, abruptly interrupting the directions he was about to give.

"No," returned the girl.

"But there are some in the neighbouring cottages," he exclaimed impatiently, "they must be fetched; first, however, get some blankets. Here, young sir, while she is gone chafe her hands well—stay, lay her closer to the fire, so—that's it. Poor young thing—poor girl! she is very pretty."

The youth, regardless of his own cold and soaked condition, endeavoured to restore life by chafing her hands briskly, while the officer drew from his pocket a brandy-flask, and, endeavouring to separate the clenched teeth, moistened her lips and gums with the spirit.

"How long had she been in the water when you picked her up?" he asked of her rescuer.

"I do not know that she has been under water at all," the youth replied, and briefly narrated under what circumstances he had rescued her.

"'Twas bravely done, my lad," exclaimed the officer, approvingly.

"Oh, it was a noble deed!" exclaimed a soft voice near them. They both looked up; there stood the foster-daughter of Waters, and she was bending on the youth a look of admiration with her lustrous eyes, which might well give him cause to be gratified. She hastily tendered the blankets brought, and they were placed close to the fire so as to be made hot.

"I know something of these cases," observed the officer, "for I was destined to be a gallipot, but it did not suit my inclination. This is what my old governor called a case of syncope, and with care and attention she will soon be resuscitated."

The efforts made to restore the swooned female were crowned with success. The warmth of the fire, the application of the spirits, and the chafing of her limbs, renewed animation; a fluttering of the eyelids was observed, and a quivering of the muscles of the mouth gave tokens of returning life. Then the head moved uneasily from side to side, a sigh burst from the lips, followed by a low moan; an effort to open the eyes;

and the by-standers knew that once more she was restored from a death-sleep to life.

At this moment footsteps were heard along the passage, and immediately several persons entered the room. The youth perceived instantly that the two elderly gentlemen who were so active on the beach were of the party, and, what was highly satisfactory, that they were accompanied by several females; a gratified exclamation escaped the lips of both gentlemen, on observing the efforts made to restore the prostrate female, and one of them said:

"The report is true; there is a female saved from the wreck, and the gallant youth of whom Tom Barnes spoke so highly as her rescuer, is here with his charge in safety." He added some complimentary words, and stating that his carriage was in the immediate vicinity, declared his intention of conveying the young female, as soon as she had in a slight degree recovered her strength, to his residence at Arundel, where she would meet with such proper attention as her case required.

The females present now clustered round and took charge of her; the males all quitting the room for that in which the coast-guardsmen and their prisoners were seated.

The men made a gesture of respect as soon as they saw the elderly gentlemen, and the one who had addressed the young traveller, said:

"How is this, Waters, that I see you in the condition of a prisoner?—you have borne the character of a steady and respectable man for years. What charge is this?"

"The coast guard here suspex me o' smuggling," he said, with a sort of gulp. "Ha! ha! but it's only suspex they does. There's nothing can be brought home agin me, I knows."

"I hope not," replied the gentleman; and then turning to the officer, a young man about four and twenty, with an open handsome face, he said: "I trust my good friend, on mere grounds of suspicion you will not make a prisoner of my old friend Waters here; I have known him some years, and really he appears to me to be a very steady sort of man."

The officer touched his cap respectfully, and with a slight bow, said:

"Mr. Gibbon, it is not on light ground he is made prisoner. One of my men overheard him concoct the running of a large quantity of tubs; we have acted on the information, and we have the men and tubs too."

"That is strong presumptive evidence, I must confess. Eh! Waters, this sounds badly. Why, instead of smuggling, I should have thought you would been out trying to save life on such a night as this."

"Sir," exclaimed Waters, "I went out in the gale because I heard there was a schooner aground in the bay, and I thought I might be of service, as I have afore."

"You have," exclaimed Mr. Gibbon; "most gallant service you have rendered, I can testify."

"Well, sir, as I've said, I roused out to see what could be done, when a couple of the phillis—the guardsmen, seize me, and declares m a prisoner: that's all I knows about it."

"Mr. Gibbon," said the officer, with politeness of manner, but much firmness of tone. "This man has been for years a smuggler. We have not before been able to bring it home to him, but I think we have got him this time. However, that will be for the justices to decide. I owe no ill-will to Waters, but I must do my duty."

"Far be it from me to induce you to swerve from it," said Mr. Gibbon. "Justice will be done, no doubt; but I must say, Waters, I am sorry to see you in this position."

"Thank ye, sir," exclaimed Waters. "I aint afeard of the upshot; but if sir, you'd kindly see Mr. Knipe for me, tell him my trouble, and say I'll be glad to see him, I'll thank you, sir. He'll know where to find me."

"Mr. Knipe! Had you not better see Mr. Herbert! Knipe is not a scrupulous man, he is sharp, and has not the credit of being"—

"He has done all my little affairs to please me, sir," interrupted Waters; "for some years past."

"Very well—but your son too, I see, is in custody."

"Ah yes, sir, Saul is as much in the mud as I am in the mire. He's done no more harm than me, yet you see they've taken him."

The officer smiled.

"I have the strongest proofs to connect him with the intended run," he said quietly. Saul Waters raised his head and darted a look of rage and malignity at the officer, which spoke plainly of a fierce revenge when he had the chance of gratifying it. The officer noticed it, but treated it with indifference. Waters, with a quick glance, also observed it, and as if to turn attention from it, said hastily:

"I have another favour to ask you, Mr. Gibbon, if you will be so good as to attend to the wishes of a poor fellow like me."

"What is it, Waters?"

"You see, sir, my daughter Nell is away, and I have only my foster-daughter, Myra Aston, here to look after the place while I am away, if you would please put somebody here"—

"Mr. Gibbon need not be put to the trouble," exclaimed the officer; "I have taken possession of this house and all it contains, in the name of the Crown, until the investigation into the charges against you are over. A proper inventory will be made, and everything taken care of until you are liberated, or it is forfeited to the Crown."

"Very good, Oliver Lawrence, it is your turn now," muttered old Waters between his teeth; and then turning to Mr. Gibbon, he said: "I can't help myself, sir, but perhaps you will be good enough to take Myra with you to her mother at Arundel; she beant included in the inventory at least; I am giving you a mortal sight of trouble, sir, but you see I can't leave her here alone, with any ruffian that Oliver Lawrance may keep here"—

"Waters!" cried the young officer, hotly.

Waters waved his hand, and continued.

"She's young, sir, and delicate, and fit for a better place and better company than I shall leave behind"—

"Say no more," exclaimed Mr. Gibbon; "when the poor girl rescued from the schooner is sufficiently recovered, Myra Aston shall have a seat in the carriage, and I will convey her to her mother's."

"By the way," said the youthful traveller; "it will be as well to come to a settlement with you, Waters. I am in your debt, and there is in the room above, where I retired to rest, a knapsack belonging to me which I claim; the contents are not of much value, still they form my travelling wardrobe, and it would inconvenience me to be without them."

"You had better run up and fetch it," said Waters, with peculiar quickness; for he remembered the bolted door, and he instinctively surmised that it was in the power of his guest, if he at this moment remembered it, to bring it forward in the presumptive evidence to be produced against him. It was certainly a cause for suspicion that a landlord should bolt his guest in his chamber and be shortly afterwards captured as a smuggler's accomplice.

"Nay," said the officer with promptness, "one of my men shall do that;" and added, "You will excuse me, but it is necessary to overhaul everthing here; I have no suspicions that you have anything contraband in your knapsack, but—"

"You might have a score of tubs in it, you know," exclaimed old Waters with a grin.

The officer made no remark. The young traveller guessed instantly why Waters wished him to fetch it. He thought of Myra Aston, and resolved not to add to any evidence which might tend to bring home a charge against Waters, of the truth of which he had not the slightest doubt. He turned to the officer, and said, with some little haughtiness of tone:

"I am of good family, sir; I am travelling only for my pleasure; I have nothing here but a knapsack, which I claim, and therefore I do not see the necessity for the surveillance of your assistant, unless you suspect me of being connected with those you charge with smuggling."

"I do not suspect you, although, were I to be governed by experience, I might be justified in doing so. Many agents for dealers in silks wear as gentlemanly an air as your own, and yet know more about the importation of French goods which never see the Custom House than they would like to acknowledge to a Crown lawyer. However, sir, I will trust you; you can fetch your knapsack yourself, if it please you better, and take it with you unexamined. I have no unworthy mistrust of one who has behaved as you have done this night."

The young traveller bowed, and ascended the stairs; he removed the fastenings, and found the room as he had left it. The window was open; the rain had been driven in by the wind, and the place looked disordered and cheerless; but his knapsack was there untouched, and he took it below at once, being rather quick in his movements, under the impression that delay might give rise to unfounded imaginings. He offered it for inspection, but the officer declined. He said, however, to him:

"As you have been an inmate of this house for some few hours previous to the capture of the landlord and his son, there may be occasion for your appearance before the authorities. Will you oblige me with your name and address?"

"There can be no possible utility in putting me to the trouble of giving evidence; I have none to offer of the least value to your case," exclaimed the youth.

"You must leave that for the authorities to judge," interposed Mr. Gibbon. "If you do not forward the case of the Crown, your evidence may serve to exculpate Waters."

The blood rushed into the face of the youth; he bowed slightly; he remembered the conversation at the window, and he felt that his evidence was more calculated to convict than to acquit the individual mentioned; but he thought of Myra Aston, and strove to wear an air of indifference.

"My name is Clifton Grey," he said; "my address is Gresham Street, London. My guardian, Mr. Jayne, is a merchant; he is well known, and can easily be found."

The officer entered it into a book, while Clifton Grey walked up to Waters and tendered the amount due to him for the accommodation he had received. At first Waters felt disposed not to accept it, but upon reflection he treated it in an off-hand business-like manner, and accepted the money.

This transaction was barely completed, when the females, conducting the young girl rescued by Clifton Grey, made their appearance. She was still extremely weak, barely conscious of her condition, and scarcely able to walk; but the vehicle belonging to Mr. Gibbon was drawn close to the door, and she was lifted in. A few words explained the state of affairs to Myra Aston, who appeared to feel the peculiar situation in which she was placed keenly. She parted with evident sorrow from Waters, who vowed and swore that all was right, and that he should soon settle it when he came before the magistrates; he bade her cheer up, and he would come in a day or so to "Ar'n'del" and see her and her mother; he consigned her to Mr. Gibbon's charge with a profusion of thanks and a fulness in his voice which betrayed that he bore much affection to this young girl.

Clifton Grey noticed that during the time old Waters was seeking to soothe, cheer, and explain his condition to her, Saul Waters bent a steadfast gaze upon her, which it was difficult to comprehend; his brows were knitted, his teeth closed, and his lips pouted. There was great sullenness, almost ferocity in the expression, yet with it all there was a gleam, not of mere affection or love, but of adoration, which contrasted strangely with the gloomy aspect his features wore. Clifton felt his heart throb with sudden violence as he observed it, and a fierce antagonism rose up within him against this man. He did not ask himself wherefore; he could have probably answered the question readily. It seemed to him that there was danger hanging over Myra, and that it was his duty to avert it; he saw the cause before him, and not more steadfast and unwavering than the gaze bent by Saul on Myra was his stern fixed look upon the landlord's son. He was roused from this strange moody musing by the pressure of a hand upon his shoulder.

"What are your movements, Mr. Grey?" exclaimed Mr. Gibbon; "you cannot stay here; your garments are saturated with wet; you look pale and fagged; you need repose. How say you, shall I give you a lift to Arundel? you can get a good bed at an inn I will introduce you to."

"Willingly," replied Clifton. "I confess to being weary."

The matter was quickly arranged; Myra and the shipwrecked female, Clifton and Mr. Gibbon entered the carriage of the latter, and were driven rapidly to Arundel, to which same place the coast-guardsmen prepared to conduct their captives.

CHAPTER IV.

" Behold of what delusive worth
The bubbles we pursue on earth,
The shapes we chase,
Amid a world of treachery!
They vanish ere death shuts the eye,
And leave no trace.

Time steals them from us,—chances strange,
Disastrous accidents and change,
That come to all;
Even in the most exalted state,
Relentless sweeps the stroke of fate;
The strongest fall."

                 MANRIQUE.

NEW FEELINGS—THE GUARDIAN—A CHANGE IN LIFE.

Mr. GIBBON directed his servant to stop the vehicle at the house of Myra's mother. As soon as the sound of the carriage wheels halting at the door reached her ears, that good lady made her appearance there also. She was genteel in manner, kindly in her nature, and having at the time a spare bed, readily placed it at the service of the young shipwrecked girl, upon hearing a brief narration of the events which had brought her to her door. Mr. Gibbon gladly availed himself of her offer, and transferred the young girl to her keeping, with a promise to send medical assistance, and to call upon her on the succeeding day.

He then proceeded with Clifton to the inn he had recommended, and as he parted with him he tendered to him warm commendations for the gallantry he had that night displayed, assuring him that he should make it a point cordially to cultivate his acquaintance, and so quitted him.

It was late on the following day that Clifton arose from a heavy and continued sleep. He was languid, and little disposed for any display of pedestrian powers, but, nevertheless, on reverting to the events of the past evening, he satisfied himself that he had at least strength sufficient to pay a visit to make an inquiry after the health of the young lady he had rescued from impending death, and—quite as a secondary consideration, he was convinced of that—to ascertain whether the girl he had met at the "Bonny Bark" had likewise recovered from the effects of fright and fatigue.

Myra—it was a pretty name—had much interested him; her large, eloquent, thoughtful gazelle-like eyes were present now; he could see them as plainly as he had the night before, when their lustrous beauty was unconsciously admired by him. It was strange that he thought but little of the female he had saved from a watery grave, scarcely at all of the efforts he had made for that purpose; certainly Mrs. Aston had no place in his memory. It was strange that he should be completely absorbed in contemplating the personal qualifications of Myra Aston; that he should have been thus occupied before his eyes had been buried in slumber the previous night, that her face should be present to him while mounted on the crest of a foaming wave in a moment of fearful danger; when he had first awaked that morn; and that he should still be engaged in the same occupation. All this was very strange, but not to him; such a condition of things did not present itself to him; he proceeded in the pursuit of his meditations without arresting them, for they were pleasing, and he checked them only because he reached the abode of their object.

Mrs. Aston opened the door to him; he looked over her shoulder, but there was no Myra; he was invited into a neatly furnished parlour, ornamented with some choice plants, and looking out upon a charming view, but although the apartment was cheerful, the day sunny, the air ringing with the songs of birds, yet the room seemed to him dark, cold and desolate.

His inquiries were common-place enough, his thoughts of a vastly different complexion. The lady he had saved, so he learnt, was much exhausted, but in no danger;

ROBIN HOOD, the Companion Work to WAT TYLER. By PIERCE EGAN.

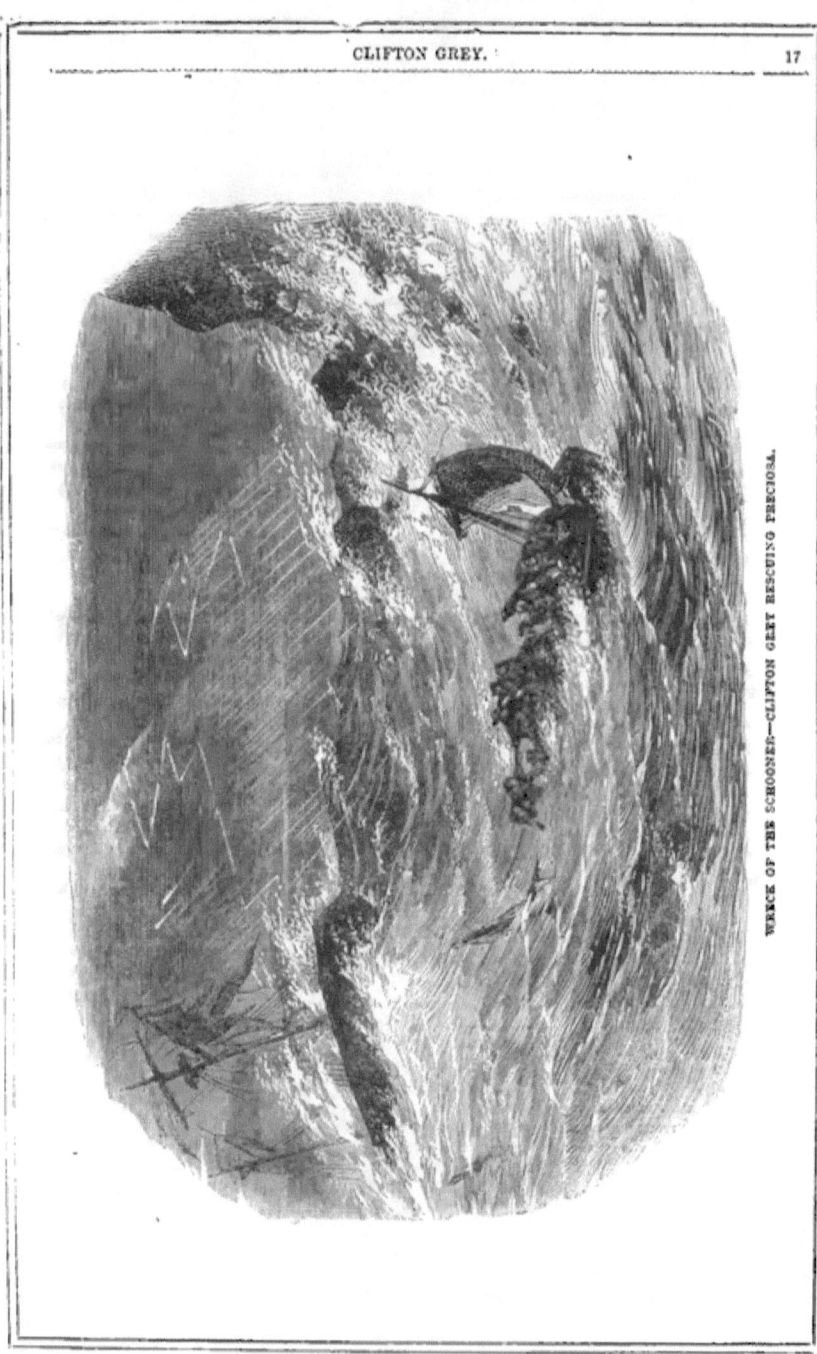

WRECK OF THE SCHOONER—CLIFTON GREY RESCUING PRECIOSA.

The Splendid Coloured Picture—"Clifton is Promoted"—Presented Gratis with

CLIFTON GREY.

Myra was well, and sitting with her. Nothing could be made of the name or condition of the stranger, for she was a foreigner, and spoke a language which neither the doctor nor Mrs. Aston understood. This description of conversation went on for a short time, and, finding the presence of Myra not likely to be forthcoming, he bade Mrs. Aston good day, and sallied into the street, having been warmly pressed to repeat his visits whenever he thought fit to avail himself of the invitation.

He was disappointed, without asking himself why; he was discontented, without attempting to furnish a reason for being so. He resolved to have a walk, yet he would not go into the magnificent park belonging to the castle, although the views were to be obtained there were extremely beautiful; he didn't care about views just then. He would not make a trip to the sea-side; at this moment, it had no charm for him; it was too far, and he was sure to meet only with bathing women and invalids; besides, he had last night had enough sea to last him some time. What should he do to amuse himself?

This question was answered for him.

The exciting and inspiriting strains of a full military band suddenly burst upon his ear, awaking into life the dozy inhabitants, who at once thronged to doors and windows, upon the pathway, and on the balconies, to welcome a marching regiment, which was now entering the town on its way to Portsmouth, to embark there for foreign service. "Cheer, boys, cheer!" rang out from the brazen instruments, the great drum beating sonorous time and the smaller drums rolling out a spirit-stirring accompaniment. The whole town was filled with the martial music. The men cheered, the boys shrieked, the women smiled and waved their handkerchiefs; the dogs barked; the heavy tramp of the men added to the medley of sounds; the gay scarlet of the soldiers' uniforms, the crimson silk flags flaunting in the breeze, bearing names familiar in the annals of English wars, the slim and gentlemanly officers on foot, and the equally slim and gentlemanly officer—a little fiercer and a little older—on horseback, presented a tout ensemble at once attractive and exhilarating to the spectators, the juvenile portion of which, indeed, could set no bounds to its delight.

A latent enthusiasm, dwelling in the soul of Clifton Grey, was roused into action at the sight and the sounds thus suddenly and unexpectedly presented to him. A keen sense of military glory seemed to leap out of the hidden recesses of a nature possessing all the elements of romance, and to take shape and substance. An ambition to emulate the deeds of individual daring done in the Peninsular war, or the campaign in Flanders, every syllable of which he had eagerly devoured, seemed to kindle into a flame within his breast, as though it would consume his vitality. The ringing cheers of the inhabitants of Arundel as they resounded in the air were enthusiastically echoed by himself; the

earnest God-speed uttered by all who had a touch of patriotism—or perhaps relatives among those about to depart, was repeated by him with a misty sense that he might need it himself; the glittering tears sprung into his eyes, as the men, fatigued by their march, but animated by their reception, gave back cheer for cheer; all the lassitude of the morning disappeared, and he waved his hand and shouted until he was hoarse, until, indeed, the last of the men filed off before him, and the roll of the drum mingled with the heartiest cheers, was heard far down the street. Then swept past the tag-rag and bob-tail, and then he turned up the town to wander among the old trees in the capacious and beautifully situated park belonging to the castle.

He found three or four days pass away without any distaste to Arundel arising within him; it was dull and quiet, to be sure, and, excepting the many beautiful prospects, the interest attaching to the castle, and to the sea, did not present those sources of attraction likely to amuse and please a young fellow of his age and education. Yet he neither experienced a sense of weariness nor a desire to leave the place. Every day he visited Mrs. Aston, and his subsequent visits had been more pleasing than the first, for at them he saw and conversed with Myra. If she did not happen to be present at the early part of each visit, the sound of his voice—as it seemed—soon produced her; at least some such frenzy he entertained; and it was remarkable how he raised his voice, and how loudly he laughed when in conversation with Mrs. Aston, until Myra came with smiling cheerfulness into the room to greet him; then all impression of Mrs. Aston's deafness vanished; indeed, a reaction immediately ensued, and he became convinced the hearing of the good lady was a little too acute—not that she betrayed any remarkable faculty of this kind, but it seemed to him that not one of his remarks to Myra was lost upon her mother.

But then, it was strikingly evident that Mrs. Aston was devotedly attached to her daughter, and that this love was reciprocated, so that when either spoke or were addressed, it produced a special attention in both; and therefore Clifton, who began to find that when he talked with Myra his voice took a tone different to that he ordinarily used, and his manner changed into a respectful homage, which, considering the circumstances under which they were introduced, were not the least surprising of the incidents that had yet occurred, he was nervously apprehensive, he knew not why, that Mrs. Aston would observe it, and, as we have said, gave her credit for an auscultatory ability beyond her merits.

All this is very easy of explanation, but Clifton cared not to ask himself too inquisitively concerning the new phase of existence upon which he was entering, or even why he remained in Arundel beyond the ordinary requirements of pleasure-seeking; he knew that the place did yield him gratification; the wherefore was of such a secondary nature, he would not trouble it.

Besides, he had an excuse for delaying his departure; he not yet seen the young lady whom he had saved, since the night of her rescue. She was still too feeble to leave her chamber, a weakness the doctor promised a few days should surmount; he naturally felt a desire to have some conversation with her, especially from what he could gather from Myra. The words she had uttered were Spanish, a language with which he was acquainted. There was yet another inducement to remain; a lawyer had, on the behalf of Waters, applied to him to give evidence upon his case when it was brought before the magistrate, who was at the moment in London, but whose return was to take place in a few days. Clifton had spent some hours in the house, and was required to state that he had seen during his sojourn, nothing tending to show that contraband practices were carried on by Waters and his son. So, without attempting to connect Myra Aston with the motives which kept him in Arundel, he fancied that he had sufficient cause to remain there another week, and wrote a letter to Gresham Street announcing his purpose.

He was fated to leave Arundel more quickly and under circumstances of a totally opposite character to any of which he might have entertained a notion.

On the evening of the second day, after he had despatched his note to London, returning from his accustomed visit to Mrs. Aston, and his usual pleasant talk with Myra, he was plunged into his usual reverie, and for the hundredth time was wondering how Mrs. Aston could have been guilty of the inexcusable indiscretion of permitting her daughter to supply the place of the smuggler's daughter, even though he had obtained through it the gratification of her acquaintance; and he had come for the hundredth time, also, to the determination of remonstrating earnestly with Mrs. Aston against any repetition of what he considered reprehensible folly, in trusting so much beauty in such a dangerous locality, when he was aroused from his abstraction by the waiter, who informed him that a gentleman awaited him in a private room upstairs.

With an exclamation of wonder he leaped lightly up the stairs, tapped gently at the door of the room to which he had been directed, entered the room, and started back on perceiving a tall, stern-looking man dressed in black, standing near the window. He knew him well, it was his guardian.

"Mr. Jayne!" he ejaculated, in a tone of surprise; "to what circumstance am I indebted for the pleasure of seeing you here?" as the gentleman he addressed quietly bowed his head over a very white and very stiff cravat.

"To a circumstance of some importance, I apprehend, to you," he replied.

"To me!"

"To you, Mr. Grey."

There was a pause; then Mr. Jayne said, with a formal and cold politeness:

"You had better take a seat, Mr. Grey, until our conference ends, although I do not foresee an occasion for detaining you any length of time. Still you know that I am a man of business, and like people to thoroughly understand all I have to communicate at one interview; explanations are troublesome, and waste time. You know my mode of doing business, I should imagine, Mr. Grey, by this time, pretty well; I need say no more about that."

Clifton Grey bowed his head. Mr. Jayne at once proceeded to the point.

"You have been under my care upwards of seventeen years, Mr. Grey, and to night our connection terminates."

"To night—terminates—Sir, Mr. Jayne, I—I do not understand you!" exclaimed Clifton, springing to his feet. Mr. Jayne waved his hand calmly, and said:

"Be seated, Mr. Grey; there surely is no occasion for a scene between you and I. We have certainly been connected together for years, but remember it has been a matter of business, not relationship. I am not your father, Mr. Grey, nor indeed am I any kin to you whatever; I have been allied to you in the way of business, and no other."

Clifton Grey felt a rising in the throat; he tried to suppress it, and, as soon as he could clear his voice, he said:

"True, Sir, I believe you are not my father; still I have known no other. My earliest remembrances are coupled with you. My return from school was to your dwelling. You received me in the vacation, and though I confess there was not that communion between us that must exist between relatives—and for which I have so often yearned—still your house was my home, you were its head, and I find it impossible to receive the communication that I am to-night to be parted from you without experiencing some emotion."

Clifton's lip quivered, and he passed the tips of his fingers swiftly over his eyes. Mr. Jayne gave a slight cough, and said, in the same cold tone as before:

"It is not perhaps unnatural, although I do not altogether comprehend it. However, this is mere digression from our business."

"Business!" muttered Clifton, between his teeth.

"I received you," said Mr. Jayne, "with a consignment of goods and money; I was offered a liberal per centage to take the trouble of rearing and educating you, and it paid me well. I sent you to boarding school, and saw nothing of you throughout the year, but for three weeks at Midsummer and four at Christmas. I paid your schooling with the money I received regularly; indeed, I have no remembrance of the failure of a single remittance. You have since gone through the routine of a first-class education, and have matriculated for college; but here we seem to have committed an error."

"Sir!"

"Well, we have gone wrong, that is certain; but I am only the agent in the matter, and I have fulfilled the instructions I received with you; they have not been changed; and I have not only acted up to the letter, but, as I conceive, to the spirit of them. I was desired to cause you to receive an excellent education, and the amount allowed for that purpose and continued was so liberal, so ample, in fact, that as I had not been directed to provide you with a business, I educated you for the position I considered it probable you would be called upon to occupy. It is an unfortunate mistake, but I am not to blame."

"Mr. Jayne—be good enough at once to come to the point," cried Clifton, almost fiercely. "This suspense is to me a torture unendurable."

"It is unadvisable to be at all excited in the matter, Mr. Grey," responded Mr. Jayne, with his usual matter-of-fact tone. "We have to address ourselves to the discussion of one or two very grave affairs, and flurry or excitement will interfere with dispassionate reasoning."

"For God's sake, sir, tell me at once why I am this night to be separated from you, and whither I am directed to bend my steps?"

"Your first question I can answer; your second I cannot."

"You bewilder me."

"The person from whom I received you"—

"My father? I presume."

"No."

"My—my—mother, perhaps?"

Clifton groaned as he uttered these words.

"No—no," returned Mr. Jayne quickly. "It was a merchant, who, like myself, is but an agent in the matter."

"A merchant—an agent," repeated Clifton, with a heaving breast. "Tell me," he asked, with abrupt sternness, "do you know who were my parents; were you acquainted with either or both."

"With neither; I have told you you were consigned to me upon certain terms, which I accepted, and have carried out as I should any other transaction with our house; but I may shorten this relation much, for we ought to have nothing to do with speculation, and the matter of this conversation seems to pain you."

"Seems to pain me?" echoed Clifton, bitterly.

"Yes, and therefore the sooner we get through it the better. Seventeen years ago I received a note from the corresponding partner of a house at a seaport with which we do largely, which was to this effect. 'Can you receive a child of three years old, see to his education, etc., on all expenses being paid, and a liberal commission allowed you for your trouble?' After considering and consulting with my partner, I replied affirmatively. Two days afterwards I received another communication, containing a handsome remittance; the letter said 'The child will reach you on Sunday evening, at nine o'clock. You must answer the summons to the door in person. The child is a boy, his name, Clifton Grey. The amount enclosed will be paid half-yearly, and receive an increase every five years until you receive notice that it will cease altogether. You must on no account mention our name in connection with this matter. In the event of the death of the child, please write us.' Mr. Jayne paused.

"Was—this—this all?" asked Clifton.

"That was all. On the Sunday night named, at the hour appointed, a violent ringing at the door bell took me to the door. You were there alone, crying, affrighted as though just awakened from a sleep. From that hour to the present, you have been under my charge. The remittances have been punctually paid, but no communication has, during this long interval reached me until a few days since, when, with the sum due, came a notice that on this day I was to communicate to you that our further connection terminated, and that as I had doubtless fitted you for some mode of life by which you could earn a respectable livelihood, you were henceforward to maintain yourself, and to seek your way in the world uncontrolled by nought but the laws of the realm and you own promptings. A sum of £25 was allotted to you on the presumption that you might require something as a start in life, and I have now only to give it you"—

"Not a penny—not a fraction!" shouted Clifton, starting to his feet. "I would starve rather."

"Tush!" exclaimed Mr. Jayne, "that is not business, Clifton; you should not interrupt me, for I am just on the finish. I have, during our intercourse, found you obedient and respectful, and I part with you under the impression that you have given me far less trouble than you might have done; therefore, as I have received a liberal per centage with you for so many years, I think, under the circumstance of having overlooked giving you a business, I ought, also, to add to the twenty-five pounds a like amount; here, therefore, are five ten pound notes, for which just give mean acknowledgment."

"Sir—Mr. Jayne—I know you do not mean it—but you insult me. I would perish rather than take one farthing of that money; but tell me, sir, have you no clue of any kind to my unnatural parents?"

"Not the slightest," said Mr. Jayne, shrugging his shoulders, and returning the money to his purse.

"And the name of the member of the firm by whom I was—was consigned to you—will you not tell me his name?"

"I have passed my word not to do so."

"But at some future time circumstances may enable you to do so. Should you be absolved—or feel that you are so, from the promise, will you tell me?"

"Assuredly—why not?"

Clifton thanked him warmly. Mr. Jayne received

his thanks coldly, and looked at his watch; he rang the bell.

"I return to London to-night," he said; "and the train is nearly due. You had better take this money."

"I entreat you not to ask me."

"What will you do?"

"I know not—care not. I will not touch that horrible dole."

"Well, it is not business, Mr. Grey. All your clothes and such other property as belong to you in Gresham Street, I have ordered to be packed and delivered to whoever you may send for it."

The waiter at this moment entered.

"My bill?" he exclaimed, with perfect calmness, and added:

"I bid you adieu, Mr. Grey. You will have a hard struggle to do battle with the world, but look the enemy fair in the face, and never swerve for any man; pay and be paid, take a thorough business view of life, and indulge in sympathy—when you can afford it. Farewell!"

He extended his forefinger to Clifton, who, however, merely bowed.

The waiter brought in the bill; Mr. Jayne paid him, drew on his gloves carefully, and balanced his hat to his satisfaction.

"Not too much time for the train, sir," observed the obsequious waiter. So Mr. Jayne dropped some of his dignity, and, being a punctual man, hurried off to be in time for the train, and left Clifton alone.

Clifton Grey was unable to realise his situation for a moment or two, but at length it burst upon him with its full force. He was alone in the world, without a home, without relatives, without friends, without means or the resources to procure them. He was a pariah, indeed.

He clasped his hands over his forehead, rushed to his room, and fell upon his bed in a frantic paroxysm of grief.

CHAPTER V.

———"The fair,
With flowing sorrow and dishevelled hair,
Sad her complaint, and humble is her tale,
Her sighs explaining where her accents fail,
More generous softness warms the honest breast."
PRIOR.

"It shall be so—it shall be so!
Go bravely trusting, trusting on;
Bear up a few short years, and lo!
HERVEY.

ALTERED CIRCUMSTANCES.—THE RECRUIT.—THE SUBSTITUTE.

WHEN Clifton retired to rest, it was to think with crushing agony upon his position, and the circumstances connected with it. He was however, too much stunned by the suddenness of the shock, too overwhelmed by the vastness of the change, to think calmly, to reason clearly, or to fashion out a future. He lay in a state of feverish excitement, tossed to and fro, moaning, complaining, raging, oppressed with an intensity of mental depression he had never hitherto known; his mind was in a state of hopeless confusion, until at length, utterly exhausted,

"Tired nature's sweet restorer, balmy sleep,"

supervened, and he fell into a deep slumber, disturbed and convulsive, it is true, at first, but becoming sufficiently profound and placid, to substitute for the wildest dreams, visions of the fairest and most fairy-like description. It was not until the morning sun poured a flood of golden beams upon his burning eyes, that he awoke to the consciousness that he was not wandering with Myra Aston in some fair garden-like place, a paradise of sunshine and fragrance-laden flowers.

He saw that it was late, and hurried with his toilet; it was not until he was half-dressed, that the interview of the previous evening with Mr. Jayne recurred to him; and then, like an electric flash, the whole of the remarkable incidents of that conversation presented themselves to him. He staggered, and seated himself disconsolately on the bed, and tried distinctly, and, if possible, calmly to review the past, and look the future in the face.

Who was he? Who and what were his parents, were they living, what their station, what their condition in life—was he—was he a child of shame? How his heart throbbed and beat, the veins in his throat and temple swelled, the big drops of perspiration stood upon his forehead, as this fearful suggestion rose up before him. How he groaned in anguish as he reflected on what he had esteemed himself, and what he really had been; how his pride was crushed out with an iron heel. He had been educated, and he looked upon himself to be a gentleman. He had been reared and instructed in first-class schools, his attire and his allowance had been on an equal footing with that of the sons of gentlemen; he had been admitted among them, treated as one of their own class, had been received and accepted by them as of a condition in no respect inferior to their own. What had been the fact; he had been consigned to Mr. Jayne as if he had been a colt, and which been sent to a trainer to earn his paces; his keep and education had been duly paid for; at length the owner, not caring longer to bear the expense, cast him adrift. There was no parental affection, no maternal solicitude, none of those charms attendant upon close ties of consanguinity, to lighten the hours of his childhood, or smooth away the rugged briars in his progress from youth to manhood; not that he had any troubles to vex him in his career, beyond those trials incidental to schoolboy life; but then, he had none to cheer him, no voice to stimulate, no father's kind word, or mother's fond look, no brother's firm friendship or sister's loving smile. This loneliness of position had caused him many an earnest, sad reverie, but it had not led to the contemplation of a possible contingency like the present. Mr. Jayne had always been cold and distant, never harsh; and he had taken him as he found him, expecting no more, and receiving no less; but even he had never alluded to the possibility that he would be thus thrown helpless on the world, at a moment's notice, had never acted as if such an event could occur, and in no way prepared him how to meet it if it actually came to pass; nor had he pointed out to him a path by which he could henceforward provide for himself; he had told him his struggle with the world would be severe, but in what manner he might hope to conquer the issue, he had not condescended even to give him a hint; he had offered him money, and Clifton's forehead glowed like a burning coal as he remembered it, that was all.

What was to be done? it was a serious question, but it was necessary both to ask and to solve it, and that speedily. What money had he? he referred to his purse; he had one five pound note, two sovereigns and a half in gold, four half-crowns, five shillings, and three fourpenny pieces in silver, and twopence-halfpenny in copper, being, in the grand total, a sum of eight pounds, six shillings and twopence halfpenny to begin the world with; out of this he owed a tavern bill, which, seeing the charge made to Jayne, made him perspire, at the reflection that it would absorb a large proportion of his little all. He at once rang rang the bell; the brisk waiter was quickly responsive, and stared at the announcement that the bill was required, instead of the breakfast, but bowing, he retired, and Clifton finished dressing himself.

Before he quitted his sleeping-room the waiter returned, saying:

"Your breakfast is ready, sir."

"But my bill?"

"My master will wait upon you at breakfast."

Clifton assented; he must have the breakfast, but to continue his meals at tavern prices was wholly out of the question. He therefore looked for the advent of the landlord with some anxiety, as until they had transacted the settlement of the claim against him, he really had no notion of the sum upon which he was to begin life. He had small appetite for breakfast, and had nearly finished it, when the landlord entered with a cheerful, smiling countenance, wished him good morning, and made a few hearty and jovial remarks. At length Clifton asked for his bill, when, to his surprise, the landlord, affecting a grave look, exclaimed:

"Bill—I have no bill against you; stay as long as you will—I am to charge you nothing."

"What do you mean?" exclaimed Clifton. "I do not understand you."

"What, don't I speak plain. Well then, young sir, understand that I take no pay from you for whatever you may eat or drink in my house, not one farthing for bed or board. I have given my word, and I break it to no man—there!"

"Given your word—to whom?"

"Mr. Gibbon."

"Mr. Gibbon?"

"Yes, sir. Mr. Chesney, says he to me, on the night on which he brought you in his carriage, charge me with this young gentleman's expenses incurred by him at your house; no one else, as you would maintain my good opinion. I said I would, and Lord bless you, it would be the worst day's work for me I ever did if I were to take your money after that."

"Where is Mr. Gibbon—is he down here?"

"No sir, he is in London; he will be home in two or three days though."

"Enough," said Clifton; "I will see him on this matter."

"Ay, to be sure; but recollect sir, that the best the house affords is at your service, without charge to you, until he gives me notice to stop the supplies, after that I shall look to you to be paid."

"Exactly so," responded Clifton, and the landlord quitted the apartment.

This unexpected phase of his position, he reflected, would at least give him time to act; he determined, therefore, to await the return of Mr. Gibbon; it would add but little to an obligation he trusted to be able hereafter to repay in some manner, and he hoped to be able to obtain from him some valuable counsel as to the course it would be advisable to pursue to undergo the stern ordeal to which Mr. Jayne had so coolly and callously submitted him.

He found himself too excited, too unsettled, too much under the influence of a succession of distracting thoughts, to be equal to an interview with Mrs. Aston and her daughter; he felt himself wholly incapable of sustaining a conversation on indifferent topics while his brain was in such a turmoil, and therefore he took his way to Arundel Park, and there, under the umbrageous trees, he wandered to and fro, and at length flung himself at the foot of one, to endeavour, by an intense application of his mind to his position and to his acquirements, to select and determine an occupation, which, while it was congenial to his tastes would square with his abilities.

As the event which had thrown him a waif upon the sea of life had been wholly independent of any act of his own, so was the adoption of the career equally the result of a combination of events, over which it cannot justly be said he had no control, but which were possessed of influences too powerful, and in some respects too fascinating for him to even attempt to oppose.

He had passed some hours in contemplation, without arriving at any definite conclusion, when he rose to quit the spot where he had so long reposed his limbs, and took his way towards the town. He felt greatly depressed in spirits, the result of his cogitation was in no respect cheering; nevertheless, although the future before him was vast, undefined, and filled with incertitude, he resolved to face it boldly, and at least not to succumb without a sturdy struggle.

As he sauntered slowly through the park, threading his way beneath the stately trees, now invading the purple shadows, anon emerging into the golden sunshine, there suddenly struck upon his ear a low wail of human woe; he paused to listen, it was repeated, he turned his eyes in the direction from whence the sounds appeared to come, and a short distance from him beheld seated, at the foot of a tree, a young girl, with her hands pressed to her temples and her face buried in her knees, rocking herself to and fro in an agony of grief. Clifton approached her, and addressing her kindly, inquired the cause of her sorrow, but she heeded not his words, and it was not until he placed his hand upon her shoulder that she became conscious of his presence; then she sprung to her feet, and gazed wildly through streaming eyes upon his face, her lips parted as if to speak, but in a moment, with a gesture of disappointment, she turned without uttering a word, and slowly quitted the spot; Clifton followed her.

"Pardon me," he said, you appear very unhappy; believe me I do not wish to distress you by attentions, nor obtrude upon your grief, but if I can render you any service, so as to relieve your mind of some portion of its burden, I will do so with pleasure."

The young girl shook her head mournfully, and continued to sob bitterly; Clifton regarded her attentively; she had, so far as he could catch a glimpse of it, a pretty face, and a well-formed figure, her attire was neat, and its style such as would be worn by a respectable tradesman's daughter; he was, therefore, surprised to find her in such a spot, giving way to a paroxysm of poignant sorrow, as though some calamity had immediately befallen her. He took one of her hands gently within his own, and said:

"Treat me as a friend; I fear some misfortune has suddenly overtaken you. I have no desire to pry into your affairs, but if the circumstances which have occasioned your anguish are of a nature to admit of such intervention as I can offer, you may rest assured of my prompt assistance."

"Ah, sir, you cannot help me," exclaimed the girl, with an expression of misery.

"Unless you show me that I cannot, I shall continue to think I can."

"Oh, no, no; I am ashamed of these foolish tears, but indeed I cannot help it when I think of his poor mother; oh, it was thoughtless—cruel of him."

"Well, but what has he done."

"Charley has enlisted, and is going for a soldier," she murmured; and a fresh burst of tears followed.

"Come, come, it is not so bad, after all," said Clifton, "something may yet be done. Is Charles your brother?"

"My brother—oh no—oh no, not my brother."

"He is a relative, then?"

"No—not—not a relative—I—I have known his mother many years—I am very much attached to her, and this act of his will cause her death."

"Charley is a friend, then?"

The girl was silent, and Clifton at once saw how matters stood. It was evident that Charley was her lover, that he had been enlisted, and her anguish was occasioned by the fear of losing him for ever. Then he said:

"When did Charley determine to become a soldier, and why did he do so?"

"Oh sir, it was all owing to my father, and it is that that makes me so unhappy, for if he goes away his mother will break her heart, and say that I have been the cause."

"You?"

"That is, my father."

"But how came your father to induce Charles to enlist?"

"Why—why—oh, it's no use disguising the truth; Charley loves me, sir; he asked father for his consent to our marriage, and he point-blank refused him."

"When was this?"

"This morning. Charley rushed out of our house mad with excitement, and he fell in with the soldiers. The recruiting sergeant told him all sorts of falsehoods, and as—as—as Charley says—he—he felt as if—he—he—couldn't live without me—and—so—so he took the shilling, and has broken his mother's heart, and—and mine too."

Once more the girl wept bitterly.

Clifton felt a strong sympathy for the anguished maiden, and he proposed that he should accompany her to Charley's residence, with a view to ascertain whether the young fellow was willing to forego his intended martial career, if an arrangement could be effected with the recruiting sergeant, for although he had received the shilling, yet he was not yet attested; and Clifton surmised that by dropping a sovereign into the sergeant's hand the thing might be managed. It was few of these he possessed; what he had were as life-drops to him, yet he was ready to part with one, if, by the gift, peace would be restored to three disconsolate hearts. The young girl was only too delighted at any prospect of effecting the release of her lover, not to fall in with the proposition. Sanguine as youth ever is, she foresaw success because she wished it, she dried her tears, and knew not how to express her thanks to the handsome young stranger, and soon became sufficiently communicative for Clifton to understand that her name was Ellen Fairfax, that she was the daughter of a well-to-do tradesman in Arundel, and that Charley Rowe, to whose dwelling they were directing their steps, was the son of a widowed mother, who had seen better days.

On reaching widow Rowe's cottage, Ellen Fairfax raised the latch and glided in, followed by Clifton, who at once saw the effects of the indiscreet act of an over-excited unreflective youth, in the scene that presented itself. Side by side sat mother and son, the former in a half-fainting state, sobbing hysterically, with her arms round her son's neck and her face buried on his shoulder; he, with a countenance pale as ashes and eyes suffused with glittering tears, sat working his hands convulsively together.

Ellen stole up to the window, and taking her hands in hers, gasped out with quivering lips:

"Dear—dear Mrs. Rowe, this is a sad moment for us all."

At the sound of her voice the son started, he bent a rapid glance upon her, and springing to his feet, strode to the window, and with his fist dashed from his eyes the thronging tears which clung there and blinded him. The widow had no words—no voice; she threw herself into the arms of Ellen Fairfax and sobbed hysterically. The poor girl mingled her tears with the widow's, but making a brave effort, she said:

"Do not take on so, dear Mrs. Rowe, there is hope that Charley may yet be spared to you. This gentleman, who has accompanied me hither, has kindly said he thinks he can procure his release."

The widow ran almost frantically up to Clifton, and poured out a torrent of incoherent words, from which he could, at least, gather that her son was the only tie that bound her to life, that he was all, everything to her, that literally he was her support; that she had not only his loss to endure, but starvation or the workhouse must follow if he was taken from her. It would be doing the widow injustice to assert that any such expression fell from her lips, but it was not difficult, inferentially, to arrive at this conclusion.

Before Clifton had time to reply, the cottage-door opened, and an elderly man entered; an exclamation burst from the lips of the young recruit, an ejaculation was uttered by Ellen, and the widow uttered a shriek and then groaned with intense agony.

"Mr. Fairfax," she exclaimed, gasping for breath; "see what you've done! You stood at the bed-side of my dying husband, who had been your true friend in the hour of need. You gave him a solemn promise as the last breath trembled on his lips, that you would be a friend to the widow and protect the fatherless; how—how have you kept your word, sir? you have done that which will drive my son from his own land, an outcast and a wanderer, and thrust me broken-hearted into the grave."

Mr. Fairfax was evidently much perturbed.

"Mrs. Rowe," he exclaimed, "Madam, I have just heard of this distressing affair—but do not blame me, I am not responsible surely for this most thoughtless—this insane act of your son."

"Oh sir, I do not blame you," sobbed the widow, "that you would not give your child to my son for the asking; but, oh! you might have softened your refusal—you might have spared that which crushed hope out of his young heart, and flung him into the arms of the first temptation that offered itself."

"Who could dream that he would be guilty of such madness," exclaimed Mr. Fairfax, excitedly; "a youth who has always been steady and well-disposed, clever and quick at his work, and with a fair prospect before him—I say, who could imagine that he would destroy all at one sweep, because of a disappointment in a boyish love affair?"

Charley Rowe here advanced from the window to the group. Clifton perceived that he was good-looking, with a clear open countenance, slight in person, but well-formed, and evidently both active and strong. He confronted Mr. Fairfax, and said, with tolerable steadiness:

"Mr. Fairfax, I am fully sensible of the error I have committed, and I acquit you of all responsibility for this worse than foolish act of mine, although, God knows how sorely you probed my heart when you denied me a prize which, though you esteem the desire to win it boyish, will never quit me but with life." A convulsive sob from Ellen came in by way of parenthesis. Charley continued: "But the deed is done, and it must be my duty to repair it the best way I can. When I am gone, my poor mother—oh, my God! I ought to have thought of this," there was a struggle with his feelings, but he mastered them, and went on, "My poor mother will be without a friend—will you, sir, supply her wants, until I can send you some money? indeed, it will not be long before I do that."

"Your mother shall not want while I am in Arundel and have the means of supplying her requirements," exclaimed Mr. Fairfax, emphatically.

"God bless you! sir," exclaimed Charley, with strong feeling, "you have relieved a heavy weight from my soul. I can part now with all with a lighter heart than I had hoped for. The sergeant will be here presently, so I will say what I wish now"—

CLIFTON GREY COMMENCES THE BATTLE OF LIFE.

"But my good fellow," said Clifton, "we must try if we can't arrange with the sergeant to let you off."

Charley looked at him, and regarded him earnestly for a minute, as though he wondered who he was and what brought him there, but he said nothing, he only shook his head.

"Who is this gentleman?" asked Mr. Fairfax.

"A friend of Ellen's," exclaimed the widow.

"Of Ellen's?" repeated Mr. Fairfax, with undisguised astonishment.

"Oh, yes," she continued, "with her usual kind heart she has brought him here, because he has promised to try and procure Charley's release."

"But"— said Mr. Fairfax, perplexed. He was interrupted by a rough summons at the door of the cottage, the latch was raised, the door was opened, and the recruiting sergeant entered. His presence seemed to communicate an electric shock to the heart of every one present. He advanced with a smiling face, he had evidently been drinking, but he preserved well both his equilibrium and his courtesy. He appeared to be a frank pleasant fellow, who was not easily offended.

"Aha!" he exclaimed, "here I am, as good as my word. I told you I'd fetch you in good time, and here I am; so, as soon as you're ready, we'll be off."

"But you told me that we should not leave Arundel for a day or two," said Charley, trying to speak firmly.

"That's true, but then I must collect my recruits at night, and billet them; besides, since you 'listed, orders have been sent to send all recruits to the depôt as quickly as possible."

"Stay," exclaimed Clifton, addressing the sergeant, "can I have a word with you alone?"

"Ten, if you like—by George! you are a fine, likely looking young fellow, well-built, and easy with your limbs. What do you say? Her Majesty glories in such fine young fellows as you; she never goes to sleep without praying for them; promotion's rapid and certain"—

"I can save you much time if you will just step outside the cottage with me," interrupted Clifton, with a smile peculiarly winning in its aspect. It did not fail with the sergeant.

"I am at your service," exclaimed the sergeant, and together they quitted the cottage. Mr. Fairfax at once seized the opportunity to elicit from Ellen a history of her acquaintance with Clifton, which, with some little embarrassment, she gave. In the meantime, Clifton employed all his rhetoric and his bribery upon the sergeant in vain. Skilfully, earnestly, pathetically he pleaded, but without effect. He sketched the misery and destitution of the mother, the anguish of the young sweetheart, the despair of the son, but to no purpose; the sergeant rejected the sovereign firmly but respectfully, and Clifton found it was wholly impossible to influence him in the direction he wished.

"I am sorry for the young man's mother," he said frankly, "and I admire the persevering friendship you show for him, but I have my duty to perform, and while I undertake to do it I'll never shrink, nor swerve from it."

As he concluded, he stayed for no further parley, and entered the cottage.

"Come my young fellow soldier," he cried, "we must not stop here any longer. You will have plenty of time to say good bye to-morrow."

"Oh! Heaven support me!" cried the widow, "Has this gentleman not prevailed upon you to release him?"

"That gentleman has done his best—of that I'm sure," replied the sergeant, "but it don't do to let feelings stand in the way of duty; so, though I give him credit for trying all he knew, yet a better man than him could not make me false to my colours. Come, let us go, my friend."

"Is there no way of releasing him?" asked Mr. Fairfax.

"None," returned the sergeant, "he has taken her Majesty's shilling, and he has the honour of now being in her service. Come young fellow I don't wish to make myself disagreeable, but time's up, and we must march."

Charley attempted to say farewell to his mother, and the poor woman flung herself passionately round his neck, clinging to him and vowing she would be torn piecemeal ere separated from him; Ellen, sunk half fainting into her father's arms; the sergeant walked to the window and looked out; while Clifton, felt a sudden pang rend his heart as he thought, had he known and so loved a mother as it was evident Charley did, how great would be his agony at parting with her under such circumstances.

Then he drew up to the soldier and whispered to him, "I will make the sovereign two." The sergeant shook his head. "Three," whispered Clifton. The sergeant little knew the extent of the sacrifice being made; he did not even attempt to consider what it might be. He turned to Clifton and said:

"Harkye, you do not mean it, but you insult me by these offers. Don't you think these weeping women touch my heart as well as yours. Do you think I would put your offer against my feelings? No, I must do my duty, sir, whatever my feelings may be, and if they would not induce me to give him back to his friends, no offer you can make me will."

Of course this ended the matter, and the scene that ensued became of the most painful description: even Mr. Fairfax found, in spite of himself, the tears coursing each other down his cheeks. Suddenly the sergeant, as if struck by a bright idea, tapped Clifton on the shoulder, and said, "I'll tell you how to stop all this misery, and accomplish the release of this young fellow."

"How?" asked Clifton eagerly.

The observation was heard by all, and it had the effect of arresting the progress of the sorrow until the answer should be given.

"Why," said the sergeant, "I don't know who or what you may be whether you have father, mother, home, and all that, but if you have no particular ties of relationship—and so forth—if such should be the fact, and you are a lad of spirit, as I'll dare be sworn you are, see life, see the world, and be provided for as long as you live. Take your friend's place. I'll accept you as a substitute. 'Go where glory waits you.' I'll take your oath you'll win a pair of gold epaulettes. You'll be a general some day, or I'm no soldier.

'Oh! when glory leads the way you'll be madly rushing on,
Only thinking that by valour true happiness is won,
And when you've won the day, you a general will be,
And proudly in that hour, you'll turn your thoughts on me.'

"Ay, that you will. You'll say 'it was a lucky moment when I met Sergeant Haverel, he chose the path for me to win fortune and a bright and honourable name.'"

Clifton started as the last words fell upon his ear. At first as the proposition became clear, it struck him as being simply absurd, but the last words completed a circle with the first. He did not know who or what he was himself, he had neither father, mother, friends, nor home, he had no ties of relationship, nor had he at command the means of a livelihood. He was certainly not deficient in spirit, and then there came a throng of sounds and sights, the piercing fife pealing out a well known and loved old English tune, the rolling drums giving a thrilling accompaniment, waving flags, glancing steel, roaring of cannon, storming heights amid the cheers of officers and soldiers, he himself leaping over every impediment and cutting his way through all obstacles, until he had carved on the pedestal of fame "a bright and honourable name," unaided, unfriended, unsupported by family connections or any other interests but those of true courage and high and chivalrous honour. Why should he not accept the path to distinction thus singularly presented to him. He turned his eyes upon the group; they were regarding him with eager earnestness, and awaiting his response with intense anxiety, the pale haggard face and swollen eyes of the agonised mother, the wan face of the sorrowful young girl, the troubled countenance of her father, and the grief stamped features of the young recruit, struck him with painful force. He had nothing of this kind to leave behind him, none to weep, or to sob, or to sigh for him. He was a feather in the air, it mattered little where he was blown to, or where he settled down. So on the impulse he turned to the sergeant, and said firmly.

'Give me the shilling: I will go in his place.'

"Hurrah!" shouted the sergeant, and waved his hat in the air.

"One moment," said Clifton, as all crowded round him. "Let us all clearly understand each other before you give expression to your feelings. I am to be quite clear, Sergeant Haverel on this point: if I accept the bounty and enlist, this young man is to be wholly and entirely released from his military engagement with you or the queen?"

"Most decidedly, he will be as free as he was before he saw me."

"Enough," replied Clifton. "And now, Mr. Fairfax, as I only desire to leave peace and happiness behind me, the only reward for the step I am about to take must come from you."

"Name it?" said Mr. Fairfax.

"You have said," continued Clifton, "that this young man has always been steady and well-disposed, clever and quick at his work, and had a fair prospect before him."

Mr. Fairfax bowed.

"His mother has also told you—and you have not denied it—that his father was a friend to you in your hour of need."

Mr. Fairfax silently assented to this.

"And that, at the side of his death bed, you promised to see to and protect them."

"I did," exclaimed Mr. Fairfax.

"Well, sir, as it is very plain that this young man and your daughter love each other, promise me that you will let him pay his addresses to her, and if, at the expiration of two years from this period, you find that he continues as steady and well-disposed as he is now, and has improved his prospects so that he can keep his wife in such comfort as their position in life will warrant, you will give your consent to their marriage, if they both at that time wish it, and I will at once become his substitute in the army?"

"I do not hesitate one instant," said Mr. Fairfax, trying to clear his throat. "I give you my word of honour that I will do this."

"Then, Sergeant Haverel, you will enter the name of Clifton Grey in the place of Charles Rowe," exclaimed our hero, in a clear full tone; and added, addressing Charley : "As we will not have two enlistments, give back the shilling you received from the sergeant; he will give it to me, and I will accept it."

"It is unnecessary," said the sergeant, "for he has not yet been attested, but do as you please."

Charley Rowe, almost in a state of stupor, drew a shilling from his pocket, and handed it to the sergeant, who at once gave it to Clifton, in the Queen's name, and he accepted it, declaring his readiness to enlist and go through the necessary formularies to bind him to the service of Her Majesty the Queen.

"Hurrah!" shouted the sergeant once more, and, turning to Charley Rowe, he exclaimed : "You are free again, my fine fellow. There, old woman, take your son to your arms, he is your own again : and you, my pretty miss, you look sharp after him, and take care he does not again so nearly give you the slip."

The widow fell upon her knees at Clifton's feet, ejaculating :

"The Lord, in his infinite mercy, be praised!" and

then, catching the hand of Clifton, which she kissed and covered with scalding-tears.

"Ob, sir," she murmured, almost inaudibly, "God for ever bless you! I have no words—no voice—to—to tell you—that you have rescued from the grave one who, but for you, would have sunk down into it with a broken heart." Her voice became inarticulate with sobs.

And Ellen Fairfax, too, sunk at his feet, and printed a kiss with her burning lips upon his hand, and tried to murmur out her thanks, but her quivering lips refused articulation.

There was a dead silence for a moment. Charley Rowe had dropped upon a chair, and buried his face in his hands; the sergeant hemmed and coughed, and tried a whistle, which would not come; Mr. Fairfax blew his nose, and felt all the symptoms of an incipient sore throat; Clifton, too, was affected—it was a new situation for him to be placed in. The whole of his life had hitherto been passed without any particular demand upon his affections or those human sympathies which dignify and adorn the race of mankind. His time had been divided between school and the cold home in Gresham-street, where anything out of the pale of business was considered mere waste of time. The emotions he now experienced were, therefore, new to him, and somewhat violent; he was not prepared to control them; he was surprised even to find that he was blinded with tears, and compelled abruptly to move from the prostrate females, whom he would have raised the moment they knelt to him, but for the effect their actions had upon him. It was, however, with him but a momentary weakness; he quickly rallied, and, lifting the widow to her feet, and then the pretty Ellen, he begged them to compose themselves, and try in the future to forget that this occurrence had ever taken place.

"That will be impossible," exclaimed Charley Rowe, springing to his feet, "I shall never forget this night—nor you—nor you. I do not know who you are, but I know that you are one of God's noblest handiworks, and if ever I forget you, or hesitate to do any service you may ask of me, now or hereafter, I hope I may be hanged as a common felon at Horsham."

Clifton suffered his hand to be almost wrung off; and having now adopted his future course, and effected what he came to this cottage for, did not desire to prolong an interview where he felt that, from the extent of the obligation he had imposed, his presence would be embarrassing. He, therefore, prepared to take his leave, and as it was understood that he would not leave Arundel until the next day at least, they suffered him to depart with the promise that they would all be at the station to bid him farewell.

As Sergeant Haverel was, by good fortune, billeted at the house at which Clifton had been stopping, they returned thither together, and on their way the recruiting-officer was especially chatty and agreeable, for he

considered he had made a glorious exchange—a smart, young, well-built and well educated fellow like Clifton, who would always do credit to his regiment, was worth ten of the young man he had released, and he knew that he should obtain praise for succeeding in enlisting him. He, in order, therefore, to clinch his bargain, entered into a long and inspiriting description of the life of a soldier, its pleasures and its duties; the former he exaggerated, and the latter he touched lightly upon, suggesting merely that they were not onerous, but that it was necessary to know and to perform them.

By the time they had reached the inn, his frank vivacity, his open-hearted good nature, his well-chosen incidents, and his highly-coloured prophecy of the "blushing honours" which were to attend the deeds of glorious daring Clifton would be called upon to perform, quite reconciled the new recruit to the step he had taken, nay, rather to rejoice at it, and wonder that, in the height of his despondency, it had never struck him to select it; but, again, he was glad it had not, for, if it had, he might have been debarred the pleasure it had given him of being the happy means of restoring Charley Rowe to his widowed mother and to Ellen Fairfax.

CHAPTER VI.

" She turned and saw him, but she felt no dread,
    Her purity, like adamantine mail,
Did so encircle her; and yet her head
    She drooped, and made her golden hair her veil,
Through which a glow of rosiest lustre spread,
    Then faded, and anon she stood all pale
As snow, o'er which a blush of northern light
Suddenly reddens, and as soon grows white."
                                        LOWELL.

—————————" As her heart would burst,
The maiden sobbed awhile, and then replied:
' Why must such desolation betide
As that thou speakest of?' "
                                        KEATS.

THE EXPLANATION.—THE PROMISE.

As on the previous night, Clifton, on returning to bed, found too much food for thought to be able to retire to slumber until long after midnight, when, wearied and exhausted, he sunk into a state of turbulent dreaming, from which he started at dawn to find that he could sleep no more, and as to lay and toss in bed was only to provoke thoughts which somehow or other would wear a sombre aspect, would float through a cloudy atmosphere, without meeting an opening through which sunshine came, he quitted his bed, and determined to take a stroll along the banks of the cool flowing Arun, until the hour arrived at which he had appointed to breakfast with Sergeant Haverel.

It was a lovely morning, bright, fresh and sunny. He congratulated himself on leaving his heated room for the clear air, and his spirits, which were, despite his own efforts, a shade too low, rose as he inhaled the soft breeze and his eye caught the glittering of the dancing sun-beams on the blue water of the winding river. As he continued his progress along the pebbly banks, he observed, under the green shadows of a wide spreading elm, a female reading. She raised her head as he approached; it was Myra Aston.

He hurried forward to greet her, and she rose to meet him. She held out her hand, he took it, and pressed it warmly; the pressure was returned, slightly perhaps, but it was returned; a strange undefined thrill of emotion shot through his whole frame as he felt the compression of her soft fingers—a sensation of extremest pleasure, coupled with a sense that it was an indication that she entertained a liking for himself.

How much this sudden impression gladdened him it would be difficult to describe; less easy to depict the immediate transition to gloom which succeeded it, or give a distinct idea of the weight that oppressed his heart almost instantly after detecting the presence of a new joy.

Myra detected the change, not without surprise. She had observed the sudden flush of gratification illumine his features—surely she knew why—and noted the look of sadness that followed it, as in a moment of laughter she would have heard the solemn tones of the death bell. She was suddenly smote with a shapeless apprehension of ill, and would have sought to know wherefore, but she felt that she must wait for the elucidation of the mystery without enquiring for it.

Clifton retained possession of her hand: she had no desire to remove it; somehow it was natural that it should remain where it was detained. Clifton spoke first.

"I am very glad to meet you," he exclaimed, "it is unusual for you to walk thus early in this charming valley," he added.

"No, indeed," she returned. "It is my accustomed stroll before breakfast."

"Indeed! you never told me this."

"You did not ask."

"I am punished for the omission, for I should have certainly intruded my companionship upon you in some of these lone strolls."

"Nay, Mr. Grey, not intruded; for had you shared my walks, I should have been the gainer by the companionship."

"It would be difficult, Miss Aston, for me not to believe that the good fortune would be mine."

"You compliment me at your own expense. You, Mr. Grey, have a highly cultivated intellect, and it is rare indeed that I do not reap instruction from our conversation. But pray pardon me, why do you call me Miss Aston? I have not offended you, have I?"

"Offended me! good heaven, no."

"Yet hitherto you have called me Myra; why should it be now Miss Aston?"

Clifton looked earnestly at her, and then said thoughtfully, almost as if communing with himself:

"I am at a loss to say; certainly your name trembled on my lips, yet some prompting which I cannot explain, urged me to address you as I have done. Believe me, however, that I would as infinitely prefer calling you Myra to Miss Aston, as that you should call me Clifton instead of Mr. Grey, which ever from your lips falls harshly and cold upon my ear."

"I have no title to such familiarity."

"What have I?"

"Every one calls me Myra, the very humblest person with whom I come in contact does so; surely your claim at least equals theirs."

"Well, we will not argue the subject: but to bring it to an issue, will you call me Clifton, if I call you Myra."

She turned her large clear deep eyes on his, as though to read whether he spoke in earnest, and there she saw expressed an unwritten language that dazzled her, and made her turn her gaze upon the green turf on which they paced.

She remained silent, and in a little while he repeated his question, and she answered thoughtfully.

"I know not why I should hesitate—indeed I am not reluctant, for in truth I feel as though it would be a pride and pleasure, yet still only natural that I should call you—call you Clifton—but—but yet—"

"But what."

"I do not know how to express the feelings that move me, but I seem to think I ought not to do so—I know not why—would it be wrong?"

"Wrong—how should it be wrong?"

"I cannot see. Still an inward voice seems to suggest that my dear mother should be consulted. I have no withholdings from her, and she ever directs me as my inclination impels me, so that experience proves our thoughts and wishes to be the same. What think you, will be her answer, when the first question I put to her will be that which we are discussing?"

Clifton gazed upon her, with passionate earnestness: he placed his clenched hand upon his heart, as though to keep down its violent beatings. His lip quivered, and his voice was hardly so firm as it had been, when he said,

"Your mother, Myra, will probably suggest that it may lead to a region in which I have made a discovery; but of which I will say nothing now. It is too late; indeed, Myra, our discussion may well be spared, for even if my wish in this matter were complied with by you, there would be small opportunity for its exercise, seeing that I leave Arundel to-day perhaps for ever."

"Leave Arundel—leave us to-day! Your determination is very—very sudden," exclaimed Myra, with a look of irrepressible, almost affrighted surprise.

"It is sudden," he replied, "and not altogether of my own choosing. It is my destiny," he concluded, with much bitterness of tone.

They had now arrived at a very sequestered part of the valley. Arundel was hidden from them by the rising land which skirted the river, and which took the shape of a wooded upland, they could not now, therefore, be observed, unless by some one in close proximity. But there was no one near, they were quite alone.

A silence of a minute or two followed his last observation. Myra had grown as pale as death, and for an instant she experienced a sensation as though she should suffocate. Presently, in a low tone, she said:

"Why do you say you may never return to Arundel, Mr. Grey?"

Clifton took both her hands in his.

"Oh, Myra," he exclaimed, in tones of deep feeling. "You know not what cause I have to say so, you can form no idea of the position in which I am placed; how much the future is formed for me, rather than it can be by me; how entirely henceforth I am to be the sport of circumstances, so that howe'er so much I might wish to come here—to join you Myra—the power to do so will be in the hands of others—nay, even the means, for I know not how soon I may be in a far land, with no prospect of return, Myra, until age perhaps has blanched my hair and thine."

Myra turned upon him a startled look, her face and lips grew whiter still.

"Oh! Mr. Grey," she murmured, "do not talk in this strain: something has occurred to dash your spirits, and you regard the future with a gloomier aspect than facts warrant."

"Nay, Myra, hear me, and judge for yourself. I will be open and candid with you. God knows how long a time may elapse before we meet again, if even it ever come to pass."

Myra withdrew her hands almost angrily. "Mr. Grey," she exclaimed, "You wrong the manliness of your character. I will not listen to such forebodings, they are unworthy of you."

Clifton smiled sadly.

"In some men they would be despicable," he said, "In what I have appeared to you to be, they would be simply absurd; in what I am, they are justified by my condition. Listen to me Myra. I have never known my parents, I have from infancy been reared up by strangers, who have performed their allotted task with care and attention, I confess, but, alas! also with the most frigid coldness. From the education bestowed upon me, from the maintenance extended to me, from the style in which I have lived, and the sphere in which I have moved, I had a right to expect that I should occupy a position of some consideration in life; but at the very moment I was looking forward to a brilliant future opening out for me, the ground on which I stood has without warning, without preparation, been cut from under my feet, and I am hurled into the depths of obscurity, a mere beggar."

Myra uttered an exclamation, and grasped his arm.

"Oh, Mr. Grey! you terrify me," she exclaimed, almost gasping for breath, "I scarcely comprehend you."

"How can I be more explicit, Myra? On my arrival here, I had the expectations and the position of a gentleman; since then, brief as the term has been, I have been reduced to the penury of pauperism, to that of the man who cannot or will not work, and receives alms from the benevolent or the parish by means of the union."

"Merciful Heaven! it is impossible. Oh, Mr. Grey! what thoughtless act have you committed to bring you to this condition?"

"Nay, Myra," replied Clifton, with a curl of the lip, "the circumstance which levels me to the condition of the penniless arises from no conduct of mine, no shortcomings, not even the simplest errors common to my age. It is at least a consolation to know this, indeed, I am unconscious of having been guilty of any deed of which I need be ashamed; they alone who furnished the means for my support and education can best explain why at a moment, without even one small hint to prepare for a struggle with life unaided, that income should be withdrawn, and I, thrust into the arena of a selfish world, without family ties or friends, without even the common resources possessed by those able to earn a scanty pittance, be left to battle on alone as best I may."

Myra uttered an exclamation of distress; the curl of contempt faded from the lip of Clifton, and in a subdued but earnest tone he said:

"Myra, I am the plaything of destiny, that is clear. Had a foreshadowing of my present position crossed me previous to my visit to this vicinity I should have scouted it as the chimera of a fevered brain. I see it plain enough now that I am but a feather on the breath of fate, and this reflection will at least serve to uphold me in trial, in danger, and in suffering, for I cannot but believe that there is shaped out for me a mission which I must fill, and which it would be in vain for me to attempt to evade or thwart. Thus a few fleeting hours have elapsed only since I have been impelled to adopt a new career, towards which I never hitherto directed my gaze, but for which now I feel that nature has especially fitted me. It presented itself to me, I accepted it, and, Myra, it is the new character I have undertaken, that compels my departure hence in a few hours from this, and renders my return as uncertain in its promise as that ever-changing world of waters which, from yonder wooded heights, we may see spreading out to meet the heavens."

Myra had not missed a word, nay, with an intense interest it was impossible to disguise, she had caught up every sentence. As he proceeded, her face grew graver and her cheek paler, at length she faltered:

"And this career, Mr. Grey, is"—

"That of a soldier, Myra."

The maiden drooped her head, pressed her hands tightly together, and burst into tears.

Clifton took her hand gently, his lip quivered.

"Nay, do not weep," he said, softly.

But she drew away her hand, and, hiding her face in her handkerchief, sobbed audibly.

Clifton was much moved, and it was with tremulous tones he said, almost as though speaking to himself:

"I thought at least I should leave none behind to weep for me; nay, when I determined to save Rowe from the consequences of his imprudence, I decided, because, had he gone, he would have left behind him a heart-broken mother and a weeping girl, who had given her heart to him; and I said to myself, thou hast no mother to weep for thy departure, no maiden to grieve for thy absence, and, even though in a far land, a small green mound in some lonely spot may mark thy resting-place, thy only dirge will be the low moan of the sad wind sweeping over the trailing grass, there will be no one to weep thy loss, for in this vast world there is no living thing that cares for thee"—

"Oh! Mr. Grey, say not so—do not think so," interrupted Myra, with tearful eyes.

"And yet it is so," he responded with mournful earnestness. "I felt it to be so at the moment I describe, and so I stood forth to fill the opening destiny had prepared for me, more cheerfully to accept its hazards and its hardships because that while it would be easy to find friends to congratulate me upon a successful career, there would be none to mourn the sudden termination of a life already too long for its happiness."

"You wrong yourself and those who know you, Mr. Grey," exclaimed Myra, with emphasis, "If you imagine that any misfortune could happen to you unregretted by them; indeed, you have endeared one being to you who will not only lament your departure and its cause, but view with anguish the fatal suspension of a career fitted to be both useful and honourable."

Clifton turned upon her an ardent gaze; the glitter of his eye, and its burning expression brought back with a sudden flush the colour to her cheek; his heart beat with a rapidity and violence.

"What have I done, that I should thus obtain such good-will from any one?" he asked in a low tone.

"Have you not saved a l'fe?" she asked of him, with an air of surprise. He turned from her with evident disappointment. "Think you," she continued, that she whom you snatched from the deadly embrace of the deep and angry waters, will hear that you have adopted a profession, however honourable in itself, still

fraught with constant personal danger, without emotion? do you believe that she would learn that you had perished in a foreign land, uncheered by the voice of kindred, your pillow unsmoothed by the hand of affection, and your lone grave unvisited by sympathising friends, without the most painful regret. No, Mr. Grey, it is a poor compliment you pay to the impulses of common humanity, to suppose that under any circumstances you would be uncared for or would perish unmourned."

"Myra, until within the last few days, I, too, was full of romance; I have had it somewhat rudely expelled from me, and the actualities of life brought before me in a manner which I admit has not been unproductive of a shock, but the lesson will not be without its value. Be that as it may, your reference to the young lady whom I have had the good fortune to rescue from a watery grave does not come within the scope of those whose pleasure at my success, or whose sorrow at my fall, I lament as absent. For her and of her I have no thought beyond the mere gratification her existence gives one of having saved a fellow-creature's life. She has not seen me to recognise me, and she will not therefore"—

"Nay, Mr. Grey, you must not depart without seeing her—it is her first constant wish—you would, ere now, have been taken into her presence, but that the doctor, fearing the excitement of such an interview, has forbidden it until now; but you will not, surely, leave without receiving the thanks she so very anxiously desires to tender for the very important service you so bravely rendered her."

Clifton half smiled, and shaking his finger, said:

"Out of your good nature you would call upon your imagination for what you wish, or rather what you think ought to be, rather than what is. This young lady speaks only, as I can gather, Spanish; and as you cannot translate the language, you can have but a very imperfect notion of her wishes on that subject."

"Indeed, Mr. Grey, you are mistaken. The young lady has been brought up in Spain, it is true, but she can speak English."

"Indeed!"

"Yes, she spoke it to me last night with fluency and accuracy, and assigned as a reason for not employing it before, that during the first few days succeeding the shipwreck it left her, and though she heard it spoken round her, she could not recover it until returning health enabled her to exercise her mental faculties with greater freedom. You were the first person she inquired for—you the first whom she expressed a hope to see. You will not, therefore, quit Arundel without complying with her request, I am sure, Mr. Grey."

"It is a needless ceremony; one of the brawny and bold fisherman in the boat with us would have saved her if I had not."

"Still would she have wished to see and thank him."

"And he might have been bound to some distant clime immediately after the occurrence of the wreck."

"Still would she have wished to see him, and have felt aggrieved had he departed unrewarded by her gratitude; and when, in your case, the simile so soon ceases, how much more poignant would be her regret that you had quitted Arundel without accepting any acknowledgment from her that to you she was indebted for her life."

"Myra, I yield the point to you; I have neither the time nor heart to argue it. I will do what you suggest, and say a few brief words to the young lady before I leave—but to you—to you—I have a few words to say ere we part—perhaps for ever—and would say them now."

"Now!" she repeated almost inaudibly, while her large dreamy eyes turned upon him with an aspect, as it seemed, almost of fright.

"Now!" he repeated emphatically.

Twice he sought to commence what he had to say, but there was a swelling uprose in his throat, which prevented articulation, and he paced to and fro for a minute in order to recover his self-possession and control of voice.

Myra followed his movements for an instant with her eyes, and then they sought the earth. She grew pale and cold, and trembled strangely from head to foot. She knew not wherefore. The suspense of that silence had something terrible in it.

Presently Clifton paused, and approaching Myra he took her hand, she did not offer to prevent him or endeavour to withdraw it, but she looked up timidly in his face, as though she longed to hear what he was about to say, and yet feared to listen to it.

He noted it, but his features were calm, almost rigid, and his voice, which was singularly clear when he spoke, had something of coldness in its tone.

"Myra," he commenced, "I have briefly communicated to you my position, and the profession I have adopted—the more immediate occasion which has produced both results you may learn some other day; let it suffice, that the position from which I have been hurled I never disgraced by act or deed—the one I have leaped into shall never be tarnished or defaced by me; and to prevent commencing with a false step, it is necessary that I should be very explicit with you, Myra."

"With me, Mr. Grey," murmured Myra, half fainting.

"Even with you, Myra," he replied. "Between me and those with whom I have lived there is a gulf, which time and circumstance can alone bridge over; when, therefore, I quit England, for I shall immediately exchange into a regiment ordered on foreign service, if that in which I have enlisted should remain in this country, I leave absolutely no one in the world that I can think of with pleasure, or with sincerity care for but—you Myra—you alone of all the living world, as God hears me!"

Myra trembled violently, and her lips grew parched, and her breath came and went in short gasps. She would have spoken if she could, but her tongue found no voice for its accents. Clifton drew a hard breath and went on.

"I would not for the world, Myra, that you should mistake me, that you should for one instant believe that I would take advantage of the circumstances by which we are surrounded, to say more than I have said but now, save to tender with it this explanation. The connection between me and those with whom until my arrival here I have been associated, is as this:" he snapped a piece of twig in two as he spoke, and flung the pieces from him. "Now Myra, with you alone have I since formed an acquaintance—a friendship—whatever, indeed, you will, and whatever you wish it to be so shall it remain; nay, let us—me, rather —tear from it all the romance with which a youthful and an ardent nature invests it, Myra, for I would, in being truthful and honest with you, be also considerate —and honourable. To ask of you more than to sometimes think of me with kindness, sometimes to offer a speculation as to my fate, I may not. I am too keenly alive to my condition, not to feel it were unmanly to hope or hint for more—yet there is one boon I would crave, which perhaps were better refused—and perhaps will not be granted—but oh, Myra, I am so alone in the world that I may at least be pardoned asking it —it is that you will permit me sometimes to write to you a few lines—just a few simple words to say that I am living—that my fate is brighter than I had anticipated or somewhat harder than I had expected— nothing more, not one word that your mother or your friends may not read—not a sentence that might not be addressed to your sister if you had one—to your friend whom I have never seen. I ask for no reply save such as might come through the hand of a friend to tell me that you are alive and happy. Grant this one boon, and I shall quit dear Old England with a light heart, a bright smile, and soul braced to meet every change of fortune."

He ceased, and Myra sank fainting to the ground. With an exclamation of passionate agony he sought to lift her from the earth, but she waved him off, and burying her face in the long grass, sobbed with a convulsive violence that caused every fibre of her frame to quiver.

After his first effort to raise her from her recumbent position had been checked by her, he saw that she would have free vent to her tears, and he had the good sense to see that it would be better to let her ruth have its full play, for she would suffer far less than if he, in his endeavours to soothe, stemmed the torrent. But as he leaned his back against a tree watching her violent ebullition of grief, it is impossible to describe or convey the acute agony he, too, endured at that moment.

At length the paroxysm passed over, Myra dried her

CLIFTON GREY DRIES THE WIDOW'S TEARS, AND ENTERS UPON A NEW CAREER.

The Splendid Coloured Picture—"The Roadside Inn"—Presented Gratis with

eyes and rose to her feet; she approached him, and he advanced hastily to meet her; she tendered him both her hands, and he took them with a gesture of happiness, which gave her infinite pleasure to observe. Making an effort to efface the traces of her tears, and to assume an air of cheerfulness, the estimable nature of which it is impossible to overrate, she said:

"The term of our acquaintance has been short, Mr. Grey, and heaven wills that for the present at least our personal intercourse should end here. I have been taught never to question the dispensations of Providence, which are framed to some wise end, even though while subjected to their influence I suffer deeply. I will not do so now, though I admit the pain they occasion. The commencement of our intimacy has been singular, but sufficiently impressive and agreeable to me to render its continuance a pleasurable anticipation, its sudden rupture—a—cause—for sorrow."

Her voice trembled as she pronounced the word, and he pressed gracefully the small soft hands, which he yet held clasped in his; with an exertion she again compelled her voice to be steady, and continued speaking.

"We are about to part, Mr. Grey—nay, pardon me, if under the present circumstances I feel that I cannot use so cold a term, let me call you Clifton, as you call me Myra, even though my dear mother hereafter may look grave, and tell me that Mr. Grey would be more becoming in me."

Again Clifton pressed her hand, but he could not articulate a word; in its place, however, a tear disengaged itself from his eyelid and rolled slowly down his cheek.

Myra observed it, and modulating her voice even yet more to a tone of gentle tenderness, she said:

"Clifton, we are about to part; events as unusual as those which led to our introduction compel it; let us not repine at what we cannot avert, but endeavour to look with calm fortitude on the trials which may be awaiting us. Not the least singular event connected with our meeting, Clifton, is that a few days back I was a child, I am a woman now; I seek not to inquire by what process this change has been affected, this revolution in my thoughts and perceptions, it is sufficient that it is so, and that I view human actions, with their many springs, through a widely different medium to what I have hitherto done. This enables me to offer to myself some explanation why you should wish to take your real farewell of me here, and why you have shaped it in a form vague in its aspect, but noble in its intention. I recognise it—I most deeply appreciate it, but I will not"—and here again her voice trembled—"further recur to it." Then brightening up, she added: "You have asked me to receive communications from you. Oh, Clifton, I not only shall gladly receive them, but gratefully thank you for the promise. I shall look forward with anxiety to receive them, and shall

peruse them with delight, for I am mistaken in my estimate of your character, if commencing the race on equal terms you do not outstrip your competitors. Write as often, and at length, Clifton, as circumstances will permit, and though there may be little to tell you of what is transpiring in England, still it will be to me a gratification to acquaint you with it, and, if I have health and strength, I will."

"May God bless you, Myra, for your promise," cried Clifton, with a fervent pressure of her hands, and then added with earnestness, "I will not add to what I have already said, for if I did I should lose sight of the course which alone it becomes me to pursue; but I will now bid you a long farewell, pressing on you only to accept this little token of remembrance of me." He disengaged, as he spoke, from his broquet chain a small gold seal, upon which was engraved the device of a dove flying, bearing in its beak an olive branch, while upon a waving riband was the motto "Dum spiro spero," sufficiently commonplace in conception, but beautifully executed, and not altogether inapplicable to the situation. He perceived that Myra hesitated as she cast her eye upon it, and he said solicitously, "Do you refuse me. You know you have promised to communicate with me, and it may not be difficult for you to imagine how welcome the sight of an impression of this little bauble will be in my eye. Besides, it is less in consideration for you than for myself that I ask it, and while you pardon my selfishness I somehow feel that you will not object to minister to it. There, Myra, I have no more to say—at least I will say no more, and will not longer detain you here, the first letter I write to England will be to you, and I hope that it will contain intelligence not unsatisfactory to you."

"I hope so," murmured Myra.

"It shall be my constant aim to regain, by my individual exertion, the position which, by no misconduct of my own, has been rudely torn from me; the steps I take to effect this I shall communicate to you, and I trust that you will comment upon them freely; your remarks will, of course, be received by me with respect, and can scarcely fail to be valuable; and if it should come to pass that I may differ from your conclusion, I shall not question the kind spirit that dictated them. So, now, good bye, Myra, may God bless and keep you until we meet again. I shall cherish your memory sacredly, as the only living tie to this earth, and you will, I trust, remember me as one not undeserving of your sympathy, and who, under brighter circumstances, might have been esteemed as something dearer even than a friend."

Raising her hands to his lips and imprinting on them a passionate kiss, he loosed them abruptly and dashed from the spot, ere the low sobs of Myra smote upon his ear.

CHAPTER VII

"No one is so accursed by fate,
No one so utterly desolate,
But some heart, though unknown,
Responds unto her own.

Responds,—as if, with unseen wings,
An Angel touched its quivering strings."
LONGFELLOW.

THE INTERVIEW. A MYSTERY. THE DEPARTURE.

SERGEANT HAVEREL waited for his young companion that morning until his appetite partook of a savage character, and his patience, like Bob Acre's courage, oozed rapidly from his fingers' ends. He had learned that his young substitute for the rash recruit of the day before had risen with the dawn and quitted the house, but he did not for a moment entertain a suspicion that he would attempt to give him the slip. He was too good a judge of human nature to fear this; indeed, his knowledge, imperfect though it was, of the causes which led Clifton to become the substitute for Rowe, assured him that there was no occasion to doubt the return of the stray-bird, even though he had kept the breakfast waiting beyond all reasonable bounds.

At last, worked up to a pitch of ferocity by the cravings of hunger, he ordered in the breakfast, which consisted of coffee, hot bread, butter, eggs, and rashers of ham, the very smell of which, as it was brought in, nearly took his breath away. Eager for the fray, he was soon engaged in a hand-to-hand encounter with the victuals, an engagement which he kept up with considerable vigour, until at length he grew fatigued, his exertions abated, and ultimately he sank back exhausted, acknowledging himself incapable of continuing the attack any longer, so he shut his eyes, picked his teeth, and with an equanimity of mind which, considering the desperate character of his contest, was worthy of observation, he calmly awaited the advent of Clifton Grey.

At length he appeared, and apologised for having kept the sergeant so long beyond the appointment, but the soldier laughed, and pointed to the havoc he had made in the eatables.

"I waited for you to commence the attack," he exclaimed, "but you did not come up, and, therefore, I stormed the fortress, knife in hand, alone. The enemy poured in upon me a heavy fire of eggs and ham, bread and butter, and tea, and though he succeeded in beating me off, it was not until I had committed great damage to his stores."

Clifton smiled, and seated himself. The sergeant eyed him askance; he noted his pale face, and heavy, swollen eyelids.

"He has been to say good-bye to a girl," he thought, but he said nothing; he only wondered how it was possible to reconcile such an occurrence with the circumstances of the previous evening. He looked at him again, and scanned him from head to foot. "Smart young fellow," he reflected, "well-built, clean-limbed, straight as a rifle-barrel, and plenty of pluck, I'll be sworn! gentlemanly, too, as a soldier should be. He ought to have been an officer, small chance of that, though, unless he has friends to buy him a commission."

Sergeant Haverel had barely arrived at this stage in his self-communings when he perceived that the object of his speculation had dropped into an abstraction yet deeper than his own. He sat with his head leaning upon his hand, and his eyes fixed upon the ground, until he was roused by an exclamation of the sergeant, who, in a voice meant to be cheering and encouraging, said:

"Nay, man, never be down-hearted, pluck up a spirit; come, I know you do not repent the step you have taken to serve the old woman's son up yonder. Eh! I am right, ain't I?"

Clifton started, and shaking off the air of sadness, exclaimed, with some vivacity:

"You judge me correctly, sergeant. Were the same circumstances to transpire at this moment, and I free to act, I would do as I have done. No, I was but casting back over some matters which, henceforth, will be but memories, and perhaps their consideration might have made my face wear an air of despondency I do not really feel. One cannot, sergeant, part from all the old places, the old routine, even the once cherished purposes of life, to enter upon an entirely new phase of existence, without some subjugation of the spirits; it may not be of fear, of apprehension, of sorrow, even though it may wear their garb, but it is scarcely possible for one who possesses the proper sympathies which ennoble human nature to effect this change without displaying a mood subdued even to the character of sadness. Such is the feeling which now impresses me, but let me once enter upon my new duties, you will find me active, sprightly, and as full of animation and aspiration for the future as he who has entered upon a military career out of an enthusiasm for the profession of arms."

"Bravely said," cried the sergeant, striking the table with his fist, "you'll be a general yet. Oh, for a sharp war and promotion by merit! then hurra for active service, a pair of gold epaulettes, or the green turf beneath your head, the blue sky smiling down on your closed eyes, and a grateful country speaking proudly of the son who nobly fell fighting in her cause! Aha! a soldier's life for me, plenty of glory, lots of pay, and no work.

Clifton smiled, for though touched with the seeming enthusiasm displayed by the sergeant, he was still sufficiently alive to the realities of the soldier's life, not to see that the language used by Sergeant Haverel was in a considerable degree the mere jargon of the recruiting officer. However, he had hopes and aspirations half formed, shadowy, indistinct, but yet leading up to a brilliant future, and therefore he was content to receive such impulse and withal such comfort from the expressions of the sergeant as he intended to confer. Clifton made a hastier breakfast than he thought it possible under the circumstances he could have done, premising that he had one or two farewell visits to make, he promised to meet the sergeant at the railway station, at twelve o'clock, in order to proceed from Arundel to the depôt at Canterbury, to enter upon the duties, trials, and enjoyments of a soldier's life.

Sergeant Haverel was both kind and considerate to him; he saw how different he was in education, and principle, to the men he was in the habit of enlisting, and without seeking to inquire deeply into his history, could at once comprehend that having entered the service of Her Majesty, even in so humble a grade, he was not likely to attempt to retreat from the consequences of the step, or the obligations it imposed. He therefore very readily took his promise to meet him at an appointed time and place, and in the interim to go whither he pleased. Clifton directed his steps on quitting the inn to the residence of Mr. Gibbon, to leave his thanks for the courteous kindness he had received at his hands, and if he had returned from London to acquaint him with the career he had adopted, and to profit by such advice as the position and experience of this estimable gentleman, would enable him to give him. But on reaching his residence he found his wish ungratified, and his purpose in some degree rendered null; he, however, was admitted to an interview with Mrs. Gibbon, who he found to be a lady of gentle though dignified bearing, and who listened to him attentively as he briefly mentioned those points of his position with which he wished Mr. Gibbon to become acquainted. The eldest daughter of this lady was present, an elegant girl with an intellectual countenance, full dark eyes and hair, a graceful figure, and manners at once kind and agreeable. It was evident that she regarded with interest the gallant young hero of whom her father spoke favourably for his bravery in rescuing the young lady from the wreck of the schooner, and it was certain that he found no less favour in her eyes, because he was a gentlemanly, and handsome young fellow. The interview was, however, soon over, and though Mr. Gibbon was not present, it was not altogether unsatisfactory to Clifton, for Mrs. Gibbon had strongly urged him to write to her husband whenever he felt a disposition to do so, and assured him that it would be responded to always in a manner that at least should have the intention of being beneficial to him. While Miss Gibbon acquainted him that she had a brother in the army, with whom he might possibly come in contact, and she would so interest him in his favour that if he had the opportunity of advancing his interests,

he would be sure to seize it; and so he quitted the house in better spirits than when he entered it, and made the best of his way to the residence of Mrs. Aston.

Here he was to have an interview for the first time with the young lady whom he had snatched from the arms of death, and respecting whom he had manifested far less curiosity than might have been expected; but this could be explained by the overwhelming nature of the disclosure made to him by his guardian, coupled with the growing interest he entertained for Myra, which indeed had absorbed all other subjects for consideration, and now, that he had adopted a soldier's life, and was about to mix in other scenes in society to which he had been wholly unaccustomed, to dare a future about which he might entertain some shadowy hopes, but of which he could form no real or just conception, he certainly thought an interview between him and the young lady in question but of little moment. He asked no gratitude, and he was in no position to render her further service; but from what had fallen from Myra, he conceived that a special visit to her took something the shape of a duty, and therefore he proceeded to pay it, and not perhaps the less readily actuated to the performance of the act, from the certainty that he should once more see Myra, and once more, although in the presence of others, bid her farewell.

It was with a beating heart he knocked at the dwelling of Mrs. Aston, and not without a depression of spirits, affording a contrast to the elation of the preceding minutes, but before he could note this himself, Mrs. Aston was there to receive him.

At once he perceived by the expression of her features, and the mode in which she addressed him, that she knew all; and if he felt sorry to see that she appeared troubled he could not but be gratified that he had so won upon her esteem that she should exhibit such feelings in his favour. A few words assured him that his surmises were correct—that Myra had put her mother in possession of the principal topics discussed at their morning interview, and he listened in silence to the expressions of regret which she poured forth respecting the step he had taken, when there were so many other paths in life, less hazardous, and more directly leading to wealth, which he should have adopted, forgetting, poor lady, in her earnestness, that the roads to wealth and fame are rarely open to young unfriended men, unless they are possessed of an indomitable energy, and an entire absence of scrupulous sensitiveness. The paths to wealth are many, it cannot be denied, nor that they are favourable to the footsteps of ability; but oh, the briars which unfriended poverty meets at the outset!

Clifton heard her out, and merely replied that the step he had taken was now irrevocable, and that regrets were useless, it was left only for him to extract from his situation, such prosperity as it might possess, however deeply embedded, and he assured her that, if success were ultimately denied him, it should not be for want of a long, steady, and maintained effort to obtain it.

"I am sure you will deserve it," exclaimed Mrs. Aston warmly; "and therefore as Myra tells me you are anxious to write, in order to acquaint us with your progress, understand from me that one of the greatest pleasures I shall now anticipate will be a letter from you."

Before Clifton had time to thank her, Myra entered the room, and, after the usual greeting, acquainted him that the young lady he had saved was in the room above, ready to receive him. He signified his acquiescence to be presented to her, and Myra led him to her presence.

On entering the room he perceived, reclining upon a sofa, a young female, who immediately rose to receive him, and in English, rendered soft by the accent of the sunny South, proceeded to thank him in warm terms for the gallantry which had led him to rescue her from a terrible death, the actual horrors of which, however, she confessed to having been spared by a swoon into which she had fallen when the frightful danger to which she was exposed first presented itself.

After the first complimentary sentences and acknowledgements had passed over, Clifton had an opportunity of observing and inwardly commenting upon the personal appearance of the young maiden to whom he was now for the first time introduced. She was tall and well-formed, pale and delicate in her complexion, but this was evidently the result of her late danger. She had large, clear, deep brown eyes, soft in their general aspect, like those of the gazelle, but very expressive, not a glance emanated from them but what was indicative of some mental operation. Her hair was darker in hue than her eyes, as also were the long silken lashes which bordered them, but it was glossy and smooth, and its arrangement was an auxiliary of no small value to her good looks. Her features were regular, but with Castilian characteristics, and the pure oval form of her face rendered it no less handsome than strikingly interesting.

Before Clifton had time for more than a few brief remarks, a very loud summons at the outer door startled the whole of the party. Mrs. Aston hastened to attend to it, and had barely replied to a few hasty questions put to her by two gentlemen, when they rushed past her, and ascending the stairs, entered the room containing the young stranger, Myra, and Clifton.

It was with no little astonishment that the latter observed the first of the new comers who made his appearance was Mr. Jayne, his late guardian; immediately behind him was a respectably-attired man, whose ruddy embrowned face at once proclaimed the sea to be his profession, and closely following him, a small dapper man, dressed in a suit of black, with a white neckcloth daintily arranged, completed the new arrivals.

The seafaring man pressed forward and stared for an instant steadfastly at the invalid, and then slapping his thigh, exclaimed:

"It's all right, that's she. There you have her, Mr. Jayne; take notice that I deliver according to my contract, alive into your hands, Miss"—

"Yes, yes, yes," rapidly interposed Mr. Jayne, "I see—quite right, no doubt. Permit me to ask the young lady a question; we shall transact the business promptly and with satisfaction to all parties, I am convinced."

Then advancing to the young lady, who regarded with much surprise these preliminaries, he said:

"I hope our sudden appearance will not embarrass you, nor a few questions which I shall put to you perplex you; the fact is of some importance to yourself that you should answer what I ask of you, truthfully and correctly, as you will discover if the worthy captain has not deceived himself and misled me."

"Deceived myself," cried the captain, almost wrathfully, "can't I see! Do you suppose that I was every day in the company of Miss"—

"True, true, no doubt you are right," interrupted Mr. Jayne, "but pray be good enough to let me conduct my interrogations without any further observations."

Once more addressing himself to the young lady whose life had been saved by Clifton, he said, pointing to his companion:

"Will you oblige me, my dear young lady, by telling me whether you know my friend here?"

"I do," she replied. "He is the captain of the vessel that brought me to this country, and which was wrecked upon this coast; an event which would have cost me my life, but for the bravery and perseverance of this gallant gentleman," she added, pointing to Clifton.

A most remarkable expression passed over the features of Mr. Jayne, and something very like a low whistle escaped him, then he said quickly:

"Of course you anticipated being conveyed to London, and when you reached that port to find some one waiting to receive you."

"Yes, I was given to understand that immediately upon reaching my destination, that a gentleman would make his appearance, who, mentioning to me the name of Huerta would convey me to the residence allotted to me until rejoined by"—

"I am perfectly satisfied that you are the young lady whom I have been expecting and with the custody of whom I have at present to charge myself. I am the gentleman who would have met you at the London Docks, and greeted you by repeating the name of Huerta, but that Providence willed it otherwise. Captain Spencer," continued Mr. Jayne, turning to the sunburnt individual at his elbow, "I am willing to certify that you have performed your contract"—

"With a narrow squeak," suggested the captain, with a chuckle.

Mr. Jayne bowed without smiling, and proceeded: "You are entitled to the charges made and agreed upon, and which, by application at my counting-house in Gresham Street, in the city of London, you can obtain, after having complied with the proper forms."

Then turning to Clifton, he said:

"Mr. Grey, I wish to speak a word or two with you."

There was something in his manner which Clifton did not like. He knew him well, and fancied that there was an insolent air of superiority, a sense of the towering eminence of his own position over that of Clifton's, entirely different to what he had heretofore displayed towards him. Clifton felt his cheek burn, and a proud antagonism rise up within him, which would induce him to meet with opposition any proposition that might be made by his late guardian. He instantly formed a suspicion of the purpose with which Mr. Jayne desired him to retire with him, and he said haughtily:

"If, sir, your communication has any reference to the subjects discussed between us at the close of our last interview, you may spare yourself the trouble. My impressions remain unchanged."

"Oh dear, no," returned Mr. Jayne, "you need be under no apprehension of that kind. That question can only be reopened by a proposition on your part, no further offer will emanate from me: such a presumption is unbusinesslike and ridiculous."

"Sir!" ejaculated Clifton, with a sudden fierceness that not only startled Mr. Jayne, but every one else in the room, and the captain at once exclaimed:

"Cheerly—cheerly, let's have no quarrelling, least of all with you, young gentleman. Why you forget, Mr. Jayne, that this brave young fellow perilled his life in a sea in which few boats could live to save the young lady—and for that matter, myself and crew, from Davy Jones', or you would not talk with him in that fashion."

"With what Mr. Grey has done since I last parted with him, I am in no degree connected, it concerns me in no way."

"What," cried the captain, "not if the young lady there had been drowned."

"No, that would have affected you. I should have been sorry, of course," he added, as a growl of disgust escaped the captain's lips, "but, commercially, it would not have affected me; I was addressing myself to a commercial consideration in reference to the question between me and Mr. Grey. I thought that young gentleman had known me long enough to have deemed me incapable of the weakness he seemed to fear. But this is waste of time. Pray, Mr. Grey, spare me a

moment. I have a communication of some importance to you, and my presence being required in London, I am anxious to make my sojourn here as short as possible."

Clifton bowed stiffly, and signified his readiness to grant him the interview he required, and they descended to the room in which Clifton had always hitherto seen Myra. He cast his eyes around it. Was it to be the scene of some further humiliation for him. He bit his nether lip, and folding his arms, fixed his clear intelligent eyes upon the commercial man, and awaited in silence the communication which was to be made to him.

Mr. Jayne hemmed twice or thrice, looked about him as if to detect whether there were any eaves-droppers, and then said:

"Mr. Grey, you know me to be a man of few words, and you are aware that I like, in any communication, to come at my subject at once. I don't wish to hurt anybody's feelings, but it's my way, and it's business. I say what I mean, and there's an end of it."

Clifton bowed, but made no reply. Mr. Jayne went on:

"There is something singular in your history, no doubt; there is something strange in that of the young lady above stairs—with that I have nothing to do. You were entrusted to my care on certain conditions, I fulfilled them up to the termination of our relations with each other. The young lady upstairs is consigned to my care until further notice, accompanied by conditions which I accept and shall carry out; one of them is that on no account am I to permit an interview between you and her."

Clifton started at this announcement.

"Between her and I," he exclaimed, in astonishment.

"Exactly so, such is the nature of my instructions; it is very peremptory in character, and I am commanded at any sacrifice and peril to secure this provision."

Clifton's upper lip curled with the contempt he did not attempt to conceal. Mr. Jayne either did not nor would not see it, he said:

"You will therefore perceive, Mr. Grey, that you cannot return into the presence again of that young lady."

"What but the wish of that young lady, expressed to my satisfaction that it is one of her own forming, shall prevent me?"

"Mr. Grey, I have no desire to approach by assumption any position antagonistic to the state of things which I have explained to you must henceforth exist. The previous interviews you may have had with the young lady in question were simply, so far as I am concerned, impossible of prevention, but I permit no more."

"You!" exclaimed Clifton, sternly, and then said rapidly and emphatically: "Look you, Mr. Jayne, all connection between you and I is sundered as completely as though we had never met. Do you understand this?"

"Assuredly."

"Then I presume you will comprehend that when you tell me I shall not return to the presence of that young lady again, you assume a control over my actions, to which you have not the shadow of a title, and as you favoured me with some gratuitous recommendations, permit me to recommend you, as a business man, to confine your transactions within their proper scope, or your person may have to pay a claim your pocket cannot represent."

"Do you threaten me, Mr. Grey?"

"No, I warn you. I say, and I bid you mark me well, that unless of her own free will that young lady denies me her presence, nor you nor any one else shall prevent me seeking it when I please."

"You may seek it any time you please, Mr. Grey, but whether you gain admission to her it will be my province to control. And I now inform you that I have been appointed her guardian, that I am legally qualified and possess the proper documents to establish me in that position, that she is not of age, and in such matters as I have stated to you is under my control. If, therefore, you persist in attempting to obtain an interview with her after having been solemnly forbidden by me, I shall appeal to the law, and you, who I believe to be wholly unacquainted with its operations, will have occasion seriously to repent having violated it, should you persist in defying the notice I have given you."

"Mr. Jayne, I have listened to you. I know, but too well, what constituted your guardianship and authority over me, not most profoundly to despise it. The man who is an able and practical business man in his transactions in trade, but who has a kind and liberal heart in his dealings with humanity, I esteem and honour; but the fleshly lump of debits and credits, the animated ledger, such as thou, I loathe; and I know at what value to place your fostering guardianship of that most unfortunate young maiden I rescued from a doom which, perhaps, would have been a happier alternative, than living to be placed under your care; I scoff at it. Sir, our interview has ceased: I am about to proceed to the room which you, with your insulting proposition, induced me to quit. Do not seek to intercept me," he added, with a knitted brow and a clenched hand, "for I have no desire to offer you personal violence, nor to make this quiet abode the scene of a riot, but he who seeks to stay me must take the consequence."

Mr. Jayne cast a rapid glance round the room, there was no weapon of which to avail himself. The sea captain was far more likely, if called upon for aid, to side with Clifton than against him, and the little man in black had declared himself a friend of Mrs. Aston; indeed she had recognised him, and in all probability he would side with Clifton. Mr. Jayne resolved to get his new ward out of this house as soon as possible; he had no taste for personal conflicts, especially where everything promised that he should get the worst of it, and he promised himself that once securely under his care, Clifton should have no other chance of obtaining interviews which it was as yet impossible to prevent; so with one more quick glance about him, he said:

"You are prepared to take the consequences of your act?"

"Quite."

"Has it not struck you, Mr. Grey, that there may be very important reasons why you should not meet the young lady in question?"

"No. On the contrary, it has struck me that there may be very important reasons why I should become known to and see her."

"And you persist in forcing upon her another interview?"

"You may invest my intention with such colour as you please. It is my intention again to see that young lady."

"Then I warn you I shall at once proceed to enlist the law in my service to prevent you."

"Do what you please. I care not for your threats, and can afford to despise them."

As he concluded he quitted the room, sprang lightly up the stairs, and entered the apartment, where the sea captain was informing the company of his wonderful luck in floating off, with the aid of the fishermen, his schooner, the succeeding tide to that on which she had grounded, and the wonderful interposition of Providence, which had stilled the wind and calmed down the sea at the very moment when its continuance would have involved the utter destruction of the vessel and the loss of his cargo. As Clifton reached the door of the room he heard the street door slam, and he felt convinced that Mr. Jayne had gone to obtain the assistance of which he had spoken, upon which, however, he would not waste a second thought.

Advancing to the young lady, the subject of his angry interview with Mr. Jayne, he begged to be permitted to say a few words to her alone. She looked surprised at the request, but as he repeated it with some earnestness, she at once assented, and Mrs. Aston, with ready tact, bidding the gentlemen and her daughter Myra to follow her, at once descended the stairs in order to leave together alone the young lady and Clifton. As Myra turned to quit, Clifton laid his hand gently upon her arm and detained her.

"I would have you present, Myra," he said.

"Nay," she said, looking at him with a frank, clear-souled expression beaming in her eyes, "I have no urgings to share your confidence, and our sweet guest, although a stranger to you, has no fear to listen to aught you may have to say to her, alone."

"Nevertheless, I am anxious, for many reasons, you should remain," he said earnestly, and, looking at his watch, continued: "my time for parting with you has nearly arrived, and I hope this last request you will not deny me."

Myra instantly obeyed, and seated herself on the sofa by the side of her guest. Clifton then drawing a chair in front of them, said to the latter:

"In what I have to say I must be brief, as I know not any moment that our interview may not be abruptly terminated. With my name you are doubtless acquainted."

"Oh yes," exclaimed the young girl, eagerly clasping her hands together, "I shall never forget that I am indebted for my life to Senor Clifton Grey."

"As yet I know not by name whom I have had the gratification of saving from shipwreck."

"Ah, it is my name you would remember. Well, it is Preciosa."

"Is that all?"

"All with which I am acquainted. I was reared in a convent, and 'twas ever there Sister Preciosa; since I have left it, it has been Senorita Preciosa, nothing more."

"It is enough; but, Senorita, listen to me; with you and I some strange mystery is connected."

"Can that be possible? You and I! why we were strangers but till now."

"True, but what I say is nevertheless true. Let me explain. The gentleman who is here to claim you and be your guardian for the future brought me up from childhood."

"You!" exclaimed Preciosa and Myra, in a breath.

"He was my guardian. I was consigned to him in infancy, as you have now been in maidenhood, and at an instant's notice I have been cast by him into the struggling waters of the world, to battle with its waves as I best may. Now he has informed me, just ere I regained your presence, that he has received imperative instructions not to permit me to have an interview with you."

"With me!" ejaculated Preciosa, in surprise.

"With you," repeated Clifton. "I am, therefore, fully convinced that we are connected together in our histories and our fortunes by some link which just now it will be impossible to trace and idle to speculate upon—what may be the tie is for discovery hereafter—but I have to implore of you, for your own sake as much as mine, to afford me the means of communicating with you."

"With all my soul!"

"Then, gentle Senorita, be this our arrangement: I have entered the army, and in a few minutes I shall leave here on my way to the depôt; what may be my future destination I cannot guess, but it is, at all events, my intention to join a regiment which may be about to leave England, and whatever part of the world I may be stationed in, I shall communicate with Myra. If you will promise to do so likewise, Myra will, I am sure, kindly receive your correspondence, and thus we may obviate the necessity of attempting to violate the prohibition of an interview, imposed upon us by an unseen authority, assuming a power over our actions by some title as yet a mystery to us. Through the kindness of Myra Aston we shall thus be afforded free communion, and you will be absolved from arbitrary restrictions which Mr. Jayne may be induced to enforce in fear that I may endeavour to obtain speech with you. As I have said before, I believe that in some way our destinies are united, and if they are it will at least be a satisfaction to feel that we possess a channel through which we can address each other, not liable to interception or prohibition, from the fact that its very existence is known only to ourselves."

Preciosa readily acquiesced in this arrangement, and Myra also raised no difficulty in consenting to be a party to it. Then Clifton bade Preciosa farewell. She expressed her regret that she had no token to present to him in testimony of her appreciation of his services in saving her life, and he wanted none, but as she made this acknowledgment she pressed his hand, and with an impulse which seemed perfectly natural, by a simple action, offered him her red and transparent lips to press with his own. It seemed as natural to him to take advantage of this proffer, as it had to her to make it, and he twined his arm round her fair neck and kissed her with sufficient *empressement* to cause Myra's cheek and forehead to become of the hue of scarlet. She knew not wherefore, for Clifton and Preciosa parted very much in the fashion of brother and sister, and yet, somehow or other, Myra seemed to feel as though Preciosa had no right to the prerogative she had exercised; indeed, a hasty reflection failed to suggest to her any female who had; indeed it appeared quite clear to her that Clifton's lips were solely his own property, and no one of her own sex had a right to claim any share in them; she certainly should not think of doing so herself, and—but she had no time to further follow the train of reasoning, for with warm wishes for his future prosperity, and reiterated promise to write to each other, Clifton and Preciosa had parted, and the former sprang lightly down the stairs to complete his leave-taking, having her hand fast locked in his own,

On entering the parlour in which Mrs. Aston was sitting with her two male guests, both addressing conversation to her which was wholly lost upon her, as her thoughts were turned quite in another direction, the little man arose, and at once accosted Clifton. He stated that he legally represented Mr. William Waters, of the "Bonny Bark," who, at that particular moment, was in an unfortunate dilemma, owing to an obstinate preventive officer, who would pertinaciously insist that Mr. Waters had not only connected himself with a gang of smugglers, part of whom were in custody, but that he had, on the night of the shipwreck, been absolutely engaged in running some tubs of spirit to the injury of the revenue and the personal damage of our sovereign lady, the Queen. Now the attorney for

CLIFTON GREY PARTS WITH MYRA ASTON.

The Splendid Coloured Picture—" The Capture of the Sea-Bird "—Presented Gratis

Mr. Waters had strong and legal reasons for believing that he should be enabled to upset the charge against him, but he was, nevertheless, anxious to strengthen the evidence in his favour as much as possible, and therefore, from what had dropped from the lips of Mr. Waters, he thought that Clifton might be able and ready to prove that Mr. Waters did, on the night in question, perform the functions of landlord and waiter in his own house, which he made no attempt to quit, until, accompanied by Clifton, he had sought the bench to endeavour to afford assistance if it were needed; and while engaged on this errand, he was seized by the preventive men and charged with aiding and abetting the smugglers at that time engaged in pursuing their unlawful practices, a charge for which there was actually no foundation.

Clifton, after hearing all the lawyer had to say, quickly and briefly related what had taken place, and suggested that his evidence was not likely to prove of the service to Mr. Waters that the lawyer seemed to anticipate, and therefore he surmised he should be doing Mr. Waters a good turn by being absent on the occasion of his trial, as the counsel for the crown would, if he were present during an examination, probably elicit much that might damage the interests of Mr. Waters in the eyes of an intelligent and impartial jury. The little gentleman in black, before so anxious to secure Clifton's services in the cause, became altogether of his opinion, and at once took his departure without asking further questions, saying, as he left:

"I hear, Mr. Grey, the other side are anxious to get hold of you, and as I am given to understand you are about to leave, the sooner you quit the better, as they have learned somehow or other that you were locked in your room that night by Waters, and they would therefore be glad to produce you if they could, as they would not fail to make use of this incident to the injury of my client. By the way, Waters explained to me his reasons for that act, with which, on consideration, he was certain you would not feel angry. He said he knew you to be a young London spark, and having a young girl in his cottage of whose safety he was tender, he thought it would be simply prudent to prevent any danger arising from any tendency you might have to ramble in your sleep. He! he! he!"

Clifton felt his forehead burn at this coarse allusion, and with knitted brows, he exclaimed, sternly:

"You may tell Waters it is fortunate for him he tendered no such explanation"—

He had not time to add more, for Mr. Jayne at the moment made his appearance, and the little lawyer at once departed.

"You are still here, sir," exclaimed Mr. Jayne, addressing him with the air of a haughty and severe superior.

Clifton drew himself up to his full height, and replied:

"And am fully prepared to remain until my con-

venience suggests a change of place. Before anything more, however, passes between us, Mr. Jayne, let us understand each other. Sir, our relations have been these: You have been a hired and paid servant to connections of mine, who entrusted me to your care; that service has ceased, and with it any control direct or indirect which it may have given you over my actions. I therefore request you to bear in mind that any attempt to assert authority over me I shall treat with scorn, and all assumption of insolent purse-pride addressed to me, I shall punish"—

"Sir!"

"As it merits, Mr. Jayne, by treating it with the supreme contempt such dunghill breeding properly exacts."

"Mr. Grey, you may attribute to the very grossest local mismanagement of police functions your present immunity from a charge before the nearest magistrate. I can, however, very well afford to wait, as I have no doubt another opportunity will be afforded me; at the same time I warn you not to adopt language to me both unbecoming and impertinent, as it will only tend to remove from my breast any disposition to treat you with leniency at a time when you may much need it."

"Mr. Jayne, the future is in the hands of a Higher Power than yours, and it would be well if, before you shape out such a condition, you took that reflection into account. It is not absolutely improbable—and of that you must at least be aware—that a turn in fortune may reverse our present positions; you may need consideration at my hands, and your present conduct towards me may then occasion you some uneasiness. Be it as it may, I am content to take my chance, and promise that if you expect courtesy of language and demeanour at my hands, you must be prepared to extend to me a behaviour which displays no such marked contrast as that which you have exhibited towards me to-day, in contradistinction to what it was when I was under your charge."

Mr. Jayne waved his hand with an air of grandeur, and as if disdaining further speech with Clifton, expressed to Mrs. Aston his intention of speaking a few words in private to Senorita Preciosa, previous to her immediate removal to his residence in London. At the same time, in language and with a tone which brought a flush of heat into the good lady's cheeks, he bade her make out her bill of charges for the accommodation she had afforded to his new ward during the time she had been in her care, and he would liquidate it.

Mrs. Aston, with a quiet dignity of manner, informed him that he was at liberty to see his ward when he pleased; and for the degree of indebtedness for the shelter and attention she had extended to Senorita Preciosa, she referred him to Mr. Gibbon.

Mr. Jayne looked at her with some surprise, but merely said he should have been glad if she had spared him that trouble. Mrs. Aston did not make any reply, and he departed from the room to seek his ward, feeling somehow that he was shorn of his importance, smaller in all respects than he had, on entering the house, felt himself to be.

He had no sooner left them, than Clifton turned to Mrs. Aston, and with much feeling betrayed by the tone of his voice, said:

"Mrs. Aston, my stay with you is brought for the present to a close, I have barely time left to keep my appointment, and must say good bye. I am an acquaintance of very brief standing, and have not, that I am aware of, any claims on your kindness, yet you have freely bestowed it upon me, having received me and treated me with a friendliness rarely won but by years of intimacy, and due to services of no ordinary kind. I can only hope to repay you by striving to deserve the good opinion of me you seem to have formed. It may be years before we meet again, but whatever the extent of the interval, I may at least assure you that if I cannot renew the intimacy ennobled by honours and revelling in the sunshine of prosperity, I never will in disgrace."

"Mr. Grey," exclaimed Mrs. Aston, the tears springing into her eyes," as you have said, the term of our intimacy is brief, but I have faith in its endurance. I am so far acquainted with your singular history as to form the conviction that after the manner in which you have been educated, and taught to look forward to occupy a particular station in life, there is a degree of atrocity in the act which has cast you into the struggling eddies of life, without affording you the common means of deliverance from its many perils by which you are surrounded, for which there is no condemnatory epithet sufficiently strong. It is this consideration for your position which makes me overlook the formularies that govern society, and take you, although so recently a total stranger, to my heart. You will not, I am sure, abuse the confidence reposed in you, for I shall henceforward look upon you, take the same interest in you, be anxious to hear from you, and to help you, should it please God that you need it, and I am granted the power of affording it, as though you were my own son. Apply to me in all your trials and difficulties, remember that a woman's counsel in the matters of life frequently avail where that of man fails; be only unreserved with me, and I will repay your truth and sincerity to the best of my poor ability. Good bye, my dear boy, may God bless and preserve you!"

As Mrs. Aston spoke, she extended her arms, and received into them him who had never enjoyed the tender affection, the gentle soothings, or the fond and loving attentions of a mother, and pressed him to her heart. How at that moment he felt his isolation from such affection! how keenly did he appreciate the womanly tenderness, the more than womanly goodness, which endeavoured to supply to him a loss he never understood so much as now. What a gush of emotion pressed upon him! he could have sobbed bitterly, and it cost him a strong effort to subdue an expression of feeling which, however natural, he shrank from exhibiting. In a faltering voice he thanked Mrs. Aston for the position in which she had placed him with respect to herself, and promised to obey her behest, and he turned to say farewell to Myra. One glance at her told him what she was suffering in trying to look calm, so that his equanimity should not, in her leave-taking, be disturbed on her account. She was deathly pale at this moment; she almost, in truth, looked terrified at feeling so cold, so wan, so like as though she should faint away. He took her hand, it was like marble, he pressed it fervently, and murmured:

"God bless you, Myra! may you be happy. You will think of me sometimes when I am gone." The last word trembled on his lip, and was scarcely audible. Myra, up to this moment, had controlled her feelings with a resolution which had given to her manner somewhat of a cold apathy, which being observed by her mother, had somewhat surprised and rather pained her. She was not less astonished now when Myra sank forward, burying her face on his breast, and cried:

"Oh, Clifton, I will never forget you."

She clung almost convulsively to him, and unable to restrain his impulse, he pressed a passionate kiss upon her cold lips and upon her burning hands, placed her almost senseless in her mother's arms, and with a blessing on his lips, uttered with fervent enthusiasm, he rushed from the apartment into the street.

The sea captain, who had been a spectator of this scene, and had just blown his nose violently, being sure that a coming cold or something else had brought water into his eyes, now sprang to his feet, and cried:

"No—no! Avast there, you are not going to slip your cable in that way, youngster. I owe you a life, and as you havn't got a mother, mayhap you may want a father, and if you do, damme, if you don't enter my name on the books first."

But Clifton was gone, and the captain seized his hat and "made sail" after him. By dint of vociferations he contrived to attract Clifton's attention, and to induce him to halt until he overtook him, when he announced his intention of accompanying him to the railway station, and during their progress he made him a variety of offers of service, pecuniary and otherwise, all of which, while thanking him, Clifton steadily refused. The station gained, he found Sergeant Haveral awaiting him, with about a dozen young fellows, all from the plough's tail, with bundles under their arms and the many-coloured ribbons flying from their hats, denoting that they had taken the shilling, and were going to fight the battles of old England, did she need their aid.

Clifton gave a quick glance at them, and at the people awaiting the coming train, who, with a wonderful sense of their own superiority, were gazing on the recruits, scarcely thinking that here was the material in the rough that aided to establish the proud name England holds among nations; and then he looked at his own dress, which was that of one whose station was far above that of those with whom he was about to mix. The old serpent, pride, rose up in his heart, and he felt a flush of heat in his face and forehead, and an impulse to walk to the end of the platform, rather than join those who henceforth were to be his companions and his equals.

He obeyed his impulse, and in that short walk he questioned this sensation, traced it to its source, and asking himself who and what he was, what his clothes made him, he held it up to his own contempt. He set his heel upon this miserable homage to station, which had nothing to support it, and crushed it out of his heart.

He turned and joined Sergeant Haverel, and with as much frankness as he could put into his manner and voice, he said, pointing to the recruits, who were silently awaiting the arrival of the train:

"Are these to be my comrades?"

"As far as the depôt," replied the sergeant, "and while they and you are there—but you will enter different regiments, according to your physical capacities and inclinations. They are a little rough, but they are well-meaning. You'll manage to get along with them if you'll give and take a little."

"Sergeant Haverel, I am one of themselves, our rank in life at this present moment is the same, and I shall look upon them as comrades and brothers, and pride myself on nothing but the position I may win by good conduct, and my own endeavours to rise in the ranks."

"Well said! bravo!" cried Sergeant Haverel. "You'll certainly be a general some day—if you always think the same—and act up to it. There's the rub, act up to it. Many a smart young fellow has joined a corps with the ball of promotion at his toe, at first he has kicked it before him, but when temptation has come in his way he has forgotten all his good resolutions, and kicked the ball out of his path, putting himself too often in the society of the provost marshal ever after to be worth even being shot at. Don't aim at too much at first, but if you form a determination, keep it. That's how I became a sergeant."

"Your advice is sensible; I will do my best to follow it."

"Aye," said the captain, "but always look aloft. You know when you want to climb to the highest point in a ship—that's the main to'ga'nt-mast truck, you must look upward, ever up—if you look down, the chances are a seventy-four to a bumboat that you come down with a run. But as our friend, the marine, says, don't try to get up to the truck before you have learned how to reach the masthead. I, of course, was mate before I was master, but though I was anxious enough, the Lord knows, I wouldn't take the mate's birth until I could do well a seaman's duty alow and aloft."

Further conversation was here cut short by the arrival of the young man Charles Rowe, for whom Clifton had, under such strange circumstances, offered himself substitute, accompanied by his sweetheart, the pretty Ellen Fairfax, his mother, and Mr. Fairfax. They had come to keep their word and bid him farewell. There was, too, a goodly body of the kindhearted Arundel people, who, having heard the story, thought it a Christian duty to come and see the young fellow who was the author of so kind an act depart on his way, and give him a hearty "God-speed."

The captain took advantage of this sudden arrival to seize hold of the sergeant and drag him into a corner; when there, a busy whispering ensued, accompanied by some rapid pantomimic gestures, with which Clifton was concerned, as the captain frequently pointed to him, and the sergeant nodded his head approvingly, receiving at the same time a packet, which he proceeded to stow away with considerable care.

In the meanwhile, Mrs. Rowe, with tearful eyes, proceeded to take farewell of Clifton, and it was not until he had assured her that he was, to all intents and purposes, an orphan and without friends to leave behind to grieve for him, that she became reconciled to the fact of his having, out of the spontaneous desire to perform a good action, taken upon himself all the troubles, trials, risks, and hardships of a soldier's life.

"I hope," she said, as she held his right hand in both of hers, "that the Almighty will give me the power to make some return to you for the misery you have saved me from undergoing. I am poor, I know, and without influence, but it was a frail, weak little creature that set the lion free from the toils of the hunter, and the day may come—although I pray the Lord to upraise you so that aid of mine will be un-needed—that I may be of service to you, and sir, I would try my very utmost to do it, and if I succeed, then I can well lay down and die, for I shall have nothing more to live for."

Clifton, not without emotion, thanked her; he received, also, the good wishes from the others with gratification, and the offer of service made by Mr. Fairfax, with a feeling that it might hereafter stand him in stead. Neither Charley Rowe or Ellen Fairfax said more than a few almost inaudible words. It was plain, from the expression of the young man's face, that he was struggling with feelings of shame and self-censure, as having been the occasion of the position in which Clifton was now placed; so gentlemanly, so gently nurtured, so much above his present station, did he appear; and Ellen looked wan and gazed at Clifton wistfully, to see how he bore the sacrifice he had made, as much upon her account as upon that of the mother of her thoughtless lover. She had not forgotten a token of remembrance, and she pressed, with tearful eyes, upon his acceptance, a little golden trinket, bidding him not to think of its intrinsic value, but as an earnest of the deep gratefulness she bore to him who had laid her under so deep an obligation, and whose safety and prosperity she should never cease to pray for.

"I have brought nothing with me," exclaimed Charley Rowe, in quivering tones," to remind you of me. You are not likely soon to forget me or my folly, and if I outlive your execration, I shall be happy. Yet stay, I have brought something with me; there is my right hand, and it shall work to do you service when perhaps you are far away, enduring cold and hardships I ought to have undergone instead. It shall work for both of us; when I put away for myself I shall for you too; so, please God, when you come back again from distant lands, there shall be something to show you that Charley Rowe never forgets or despised a true service.

Clifton drew them both aside. He took their hands and they both pressed his fervently.

"When I come back again," he said, "and I fully believe I shall, you will then be, I trust, happy husband and wife; perhaps, with smiling rosy-cheeked children at your knees, who knows. I hope to see it, and to congratulate you; if not, why never mind; and let me beg of you earnestly, if you should at times recal me to your memory, and perhaps you will"—

Ellen burst into tears.

"Do not speak or allude to the circumstances which led to my departure; it can avail nothing, and will only bring back unpleasant reminiscences, therefore promise me that you will forget it, and believe me you will both be the happier for it."

"Oh, do not say so," sobbed Ellen.

"Forget it, cried Charley Rowe, excitedly. "Forget it, never, so help me God!"

"Hush! hush! cried Clifton, placing his hands before his mouth. "However, if you will not grant me that favour, there is one my kind-hearted little Ellen can."

But Ellen, who was easily moved to tears, found it practicable only to assent by a look instead of words.

"Ask it!" exclaimed Charley, with almost fierce earnestness. "I promise it, if we have to go through fire and water to do it."

"It is not so exacting," said Clifton, "and you may not be called upon at all, but this is a changing world, and we cannot depend upon any of its relations for stability. My boon therefore is, that as I know but one family in Arundel, if I could secure them an advantage I would. The name of Myra Aston is not unknown to you?"

"I know her well," murmured Ellen.

"I am aware of that; and I ask you, should any change occur, any unexpected calamity fall upon her and her mother, you will extend to them the same service which you have proffered to me."

"Say no more," cried Charley, "it shall be done, be sure of it, as you are a living man."

"I am only suggesting that they should have a friend near them in their need, and at hand when they require it. They are lonely, and such friendship is most valuable to females thus situated. I think you understand me."

"Quite, and I think I know how you would like the service done, leastwise I think I do, and my name's not Charley Rowe, if they want help, and they don't get it from me when they least expect it."

"I see you understand me, and by doing this you will more than repay any service I may have rendered you."

Further conversation was cut short by a distant whistle, and the porter announced the approach of the train. The loud-voiced bell was heard, and the people, who had been scattered about, some walking, some sitting, now drew together into a little crowd; the porters, who had seemed, like Othello, not easily moved, now darted and ran, and leaped about the railway, as though to show only that they alone were permitted to cross the rails in the face of danger. The long, hollow whistle from the engine, the panting of which was now almost painfully distinct, was followed by the gradual diminution of the speed at which it was advancing, the screeching of the wheels, to which the breaks had been applied, as they clung to the rails, ensued, succeeded by a low rumbling sound as of distant thunder, and the train became motionless in front of the station.

In an instant all was bustle, noise, and confusion. The guards leaped from their boxes and proceeded to open the carriage doors, and the porters to hurry along the side of the train to the whole extent, shouting out, "Arn'del! Arn'del! Arn'del!" Eager passengers looked anxiously for seats in the carriages of the class for which they had booked themselves; travellers who had arrived at their destination vacated their seats, and looked excitedly after their luggage, impressed with a semi-latent horror that the train would suddenly dart at frantic speed from the Arundel station on its way to Brighton with all their luggage under heaps of offensive-looking huge trunks, boxes, and portmanteaus, in the break van employed for the purpose, leaving them in a state of crude speculation as to the possibility of ever recovering it, even after a world of trouble had been undergone in the attempt. In the midst of all this confusion, Sergeant Haverel, with admirable tact, collected his recruits, leaving to the last Clifton Grey, saying to him:

"Now Grey, bid your friends good bye; we are off."

At this moment the sea captain pressed something into Clifton's hand, as he seized it to bid him farewell, and cried:

"God Almighty bless you, my boy. Keep that for my sake. You'd ha' made a good seaman—but never mind, make a good soldier. God bless you!"

He hurried off, as the Rowe family and connexions pressed round Clifton, and fifty hands sought his to squeeze it, and as many voices bade him good bye, and ejaculated wishes for his prosperity.

"Now Grey," cried Sergeant Haverel, dragging

Clifton into the carriage in which his companions were. Bang went the door, closed by the porter as if he had long borne a spite against it, and was now indulging it. "All right here," shouted the porter. "All right," is repeated. Pr-r-r-r-r-r-ew! blew the guard's shrill whistle. The breaks are released from the wheels by the grimy engine-driver, the engine is set in motion. Kaugh! kaugh! kaugh! it pants; with increasing aspirations the train obtains motion, and the faces on the platform and the station itself seem to glide slowly away; then arose a wild, loud, ringing cheer from those left behind; the pace is increased until full speed is achieved, and Clifton sits in a state of bewilderment, contemplating a neat gold watch and appendages, the gift of the captain, and the pretty present from Ellen Fairfax, without for some time coming to a full sense of the mighty transition he had thus commenced and had yet to undergo.

CHAPTER VIII.

"The Russians now were ready to attack."
BYRON.

"A frame of adamant, a soul of fire,
No dangers fright him and no labours tire,
O'er love or fear extends his wide domain,
Unconquer'd lord of pleasure and of pain;
No joys to him pacific sceptres yield;
War sounds the trump, he rushes to the field;
Behold surrounding kings their pow'rs combine,
And one capitulate, and one resign;
Peace courts his hand, but spreads her charms in vain;
"Think nothing gain'd," he cries, "till nought remain,
In Moscow's walls."

JOHNSON.

THE ARRIVAL AT THE DEPÔT—THE CHOICE—
THE DEPARTURE.

IT is quite needless to enter into the particulars of the circumstances which attended Clifton's arrival at the depôt; they were much the same as those which are experienced by recruits generally. At first the change was great, painful, and humiliating, and the struggle to adapt himself to it neither slight nor easily surmounted. The leap from polished circles and refined manners into the very coarsest society could not fail to be productive of much discomfort, but he schooled himself to accept it and take it as he found it, to accommodate himself to it, and to perform his duties to the best of his abilities; to be thankful for advice, and studiously obedient, while he studied carefully the regulations of the service, and conformed to them.

He was surrounded by the ordinary temptations which beset recruits on first joining the depôt of their regiment, and it required no common self-command to avoid many to which he was subjected, for as he quickly obtained the soubriquet of "Gentleman Grey," so any indisposition to mix in the pursuits or practices of his comrades was at once set down to pride, and sneered at accordingly. But matters soon settled to their level, and when it was found that he was high-couraged, firm, and while there was no absurd or false pride about him, he was not to be jeered or taunted into actions of which he did not approve, he was left to follow his own path pretty much as he liked.

Upon his arrival at the depôt he underwent the necessary examinations, and was attested before the magistrate, and then received the bounty-money, and also a sum which Sergeant Haverel presented to him as a gift from the captain of the stranded schooner, who had given it to him at the railway station, to take charge of it until he could place it in the hands of Clifton when no opportunity presented itself for him to return it. He took the money, as he had done the watch, almost as a gift from Providence, which he held in trust in the full belief that there was a superior power watching over his welfare, and that he had a mission to fulfil, of which even such simple accessories to success were indications. He found the non-commissioned officers civil, attentive, and obliging to him. Haverel told him it was because he had possession of money, which Clifton parted with to be put forward in his drill, but never, as it was intimated to him that he might do, for the sake of obtaining a relaxation of discipline, and he had occasion to congratulate himself afterwards upon avoiding such favour, for he found that those who had purchased the indulgence had, in most instances, to pay dearly for it afterwards.

His anxiety to obtain a proper knowledge of his duty, and a desire to go forward with it, soon attracted general attention among the officers at the depôt, who were securing men for detachments for the various corps which go to make up the sum of the army. At this period there were some vacancies in the second battalion of Fusilier Guards, and the colonel of that regiment happening to be at the depôt one morning, observed Clifton under drill; he made some enquiries respecting him, took down his name, and when the drill was over sent for him into a private room in the barrack.

When Clifton entered the room, the practised eye of the experienced military man detected the qualifications he presented for the career he had chosen, and as all officers who know their duty are anxious to secure good men for their regiments, he at once determined to have Clifton in his, if possible. He therefore spoke with less of the military abruptness in his tone than is customary with the officer in addressing the private.

"Your name, I learn, is Grey," he commenced.

Clifton touched his forehead in the most approved military fashion.

"Into what regiment have you enlisted?"

"Momentarily into the 63rd, but I am waiting a vacancy to volunteer into the Grenadier Guards."

"A fine body of men," exclaimed the colonel, emphatically. "A very fine body of men, but so are my Fusiliers; there are two or three vacancies in the second battalion. What do you say, will you join us?"

"Your pardon, Colonel, but I have come to the determination to join the Grenadiers."

"Are you acquainted with any of the officers?"

"Only by reputation, Colonel."

"Then you have no other inducement to join them but the *prestige* attached to their name?"

"None whatever."

"Well, join the Fusiliers; you will still be in a regiment of the Guards, and I can promise you that you will meet with brave, clean, smart, and good companions, considerate officers, and if you are attentive and active in your duties, I can promise you promotion."

Clifton smiled.

"This character," said he, "I hear of all the regiments of the line respectively. I have on such grounds been urged to continue in the 63rd, and as I am desirous of going abroad, and that regiment is now in India, I have, I confess, felt prompted to comply with the solicitation."

"But there is a prospect of active service nearer home; the complication of affairs in the East renders war with Russia almost a certainty, and in such case an army will be despatched to Turkey. The Fusilier Guards will, without doubt, be selected as one of the regiments for such a service, and an opportunity for distinction, therefore, will soon be offered you; prizes will be plentiful, promotion ensured, and in fact everything desirable in the life of a soldier within your grasp. Come, I need say no more, you will join us?"

"Give me until to-morrow, Colonel, and I will decide. There are considerations which necessarily influence my choice of a path in my first start on the great journey of life, and if they should not, on examination, run counter to your proposition, I will join the Fusilier Guards."

"Very well, it shall be so. You have been educated above your present position, and have moved in a very different sphere to that you are now in, it is very clear. I will not, however, now seek your confidence. When you have joined my regiment, opportunities will not be wanting, for I have a habit of closely inspecting my men, of attending to their condition, and seeing that their wants and comforts are properly cared for. It may happen that I shall have the opportunity of befriending your advancement; that will, of course, depend mainly upon your own acts, for while I never countenance irregularities, I am always ready, as far as I can, to reward good conduct."

"I thank you heartily, Colonel," returned Clifton, with an expression and bearing which seemed to strike the colonel, "but as I desire no undeserved favour, I hope fairly to be entitled to all I may receive. I shall strive to get forward to the best of my ability, and if I cannot secure advancement by the honourable discharge of my duty, and a zealous endeavour to win promotion, I will never consent to receive favour at the hands of my officers at the price of conduct for which any man commonly honest should blush."

The colonel expressed the gratification he felt in listening to such sentiments, and after further enlarging upon the advantages to be met with in his regiment, which existed in a less degree in all others, the interview terminated.

The following day Clifton, after duly weighing all the matters connected with the probable consequences of his decision, was entered as a volunteer for the second battalion of Fusilier Guards, and applied himself so heartily to drill, that he soon became distinguished for the correctness and precision with which he went through the military evolutions forming part of the education of a soldier. The sergeant-major soon picked him out, and confidentially informed him that if he continued as he went on, he would very soon obtain his first promotion.

Thus encouraged, he persevered with ardour; the money that others spent in drink he laid out in books; everything pertaining to his duties or the art of war he sought zealously after and studied with intense application; and he profited by his proficiency in drawing to copy some valuable works on military engineering, and the art of fortification. While he devoted every spare hour to the acquisition of theoretical knowledge, he lost not a moment in the effort to master the practical part of a soldier's duty; and in this he succeeded so well, that he became a kind of model recruit; not a little to his annoyance, for he was frequently held up as an example to his comrades, and those who had little of his ambition and less of the education which caused him to take for his motto, "Excelsior!" believed, and hardly scrupled to say, that he became this pattern only to curry favour with the officers.

Such remarks were, however, not made in his presence. He had, at starting, taken his course; he had made a point of not permitting his conduct to be questioned by any of his comrades; he acted freely, openly, and straightforward to them; he was liberal, considerate, and unaffected in his manner; he neither by inference or implication attempted to set himself up as superior to them, except for the possession of the military knowledge open to them all to acquire. He desired not to be considered one jot better than themselves, save by what he had self-obtained since he had joined them. Free, kind, generous, ready to serve, and friendly to all, he at the same time let it clearly be understood that he would resent with his life any unmerited insult or vulgar attack upon his principles. While he sought to be liked, he determined to be respected, and he quite succeeded, for such men as were envious of the praise accorded to him, if they did give utterance to a murmur or two, were careful not to do it in his hearing, less out of fear of standing up before him in a personal contest than from a disinclination to wound the feelings of one who had often done them little, though keenly appreciated kindnesses. His position, therefore, by the direction he had given it in the first instance, and by the firmness with which he had pursued it, was certainly as good as he could, by any possibility, have expected.

Matters progressed much in this manner for some time, when the peaceful horizon of Europe became clouded. The first black spot had been the upstart and overbearing mission of Count Leiuengen, from the imperial court of Austria to the Porte, to arrest the victorious progress of the Turks under Omar Pacha in the chastisement they were inflicting upon those cut-throat thieves and mountain robbers, the Montenegrins. The almost abject compliance of these haughty demands by Turkey, the ease with which, subsequently, the French minister obtained the firman, conferring certain powers upon the Latins at the Holy Sepulchre, to which the followers of the Greek schism were violently opposed, induced the Czar Nicholas to believe the hour had arrived when he could carry out the traditional policy of his nation, and plant the Greek cross on the dome of St. Sophia, extend the Russian shores to the Mediterranean on the East, to subsequently push up the Baltic to the North Sea, and in short, acquire, eventually, sole empire in Europe. The English ambassador at the Court of Russia was sounded by the Czar at this important juncture, as to whether English cupidity would, for the sake of a share in the effects of the "sick man," as Turkey was graphically described by him, consent to the administration of physic, which was but another name for poison, being administered to him by Russia; but though Egypt and Candia were the sugar-plums offered to what was deemed the liquorish tooth of shopkeeping England, the bribe was indignantly spurned. To the honour of England and France, the security of Europe from the rapacious designs of the Northern Power was considered, in preference to these private interests, and though the act was calculated to involve them—and has done so—in enormous expenditure of treasure and of human life, they, with high chivalry and loyalty, interposed their arms between the prostrate Turk and the uplifted lance of the Cossack. As they parried the intended blow, they reasoned with the barbarian against his intended brigandage, but in vain. Having no faith in the possibility of an alliance between the ancient and long-continued foes, England and France—being sure that he had Prussia under his heel and Austria under his thumb—the Emperor Nicholas believed the hour had come when the purposes of Peter and the dreams of Catherine could be realised, and he despatched Prince Menschikoff upon a mission to the Porte, with the undisguised intention of insulting and degrading the Porte in the eyes of the civilised world, and then crushing it upon any effort or attempt it might make at resistance.

To Prince Menschikoff the task was entrusted, and he executed it with a blackguardism which, while it commended itself to the Czar, was alike opposed to what was due to the courtesies of well-bred society, to the respect due to the position of the Porte as a sovereign power, to the dignity of his own station, either as a diplomatist, a prince, or even as a simple gentleman.

The behaviour of Menschikoff rendered a calm consideration of the demands of Russia next to impossible, and though they were of a nature which were not to be complied with by Turkey, without self-immolation, yet they were not examined with the deliberation to which they might have been entitled if presented under different auspices. Be this, however, as it may, the rejection of the Russian propositions—fully and evidently anticipated by that power—was followed by the seizure of the Danubian Principalities, upon the flimsiest pretences imaginable, and Turkey, although advised to submit quietly to this indignity, and display a *politique expectante, à la Austria*, spurned the advice, and with a spirit that did honour to it, declared war with Russia.

It is not within the province of this tale to follow on with the successive events, nor to record the various successes which attended the Turks in the struggles with the Russians on the Danube from Oltenitza and Citate to the raising of the siege of Silistria; it must suffice for our purpose that after repeated and long spun-out efforts at negociation at Vienna, the laying down by the four Governments of England, France, Prussia and Austria, of four points as the bases of negociation by which the future peace of Europe was to be secured, which Russia imperiously scouted, although afterwards glad to assent to them—after, in short, exhausting all the discussions possible in considering the objects of all the Powers mixed up in the complications, the sword was unsheathed, the scabbard was flung away, and a large fleet having been, in anticipation, sent by the Western Powers to the mouth of the Dardanelles, England and France entering into an alliance, offensive and defensive, with Turkey, declared war with Russia.

Now all was bustle, expectation, and excitement in the army of England. A large English contingent was to be sent out to join a yet larger French army, to do battle with the Russ. The most extravagant expectations were raised. The possibility of Russia standing single-handed against England and France was ridiculed; the annihilation of Russia after a brief struggle was confidently predicted; the war was to be sharp and short, and a lesson was to be given to a barbarian Power which had committed several grievous errors, in order to bring about a result which must prove so disastrous to itself, and though probably at some cost, of such advantage to the rest of Europe. But these were all vain miscalculations; the fact was, that but few of the people of England were acquainted with the long-continued persevering preparations

INTERVIEW BETWEEN CLIFTON GREY AND THE MAIDEN SAVED BY HIM FROM SHIPWRECK.

No. 7.

which Russia had been silently making for this grand *coup*. The gradual extension of the frontiers of this great nation, at its extremity, by way of the Crimea, extending along the Circassian coast into Asia Minor, and from Cronstadt up the Gulf of Finland, on its way to the Sound, so that at last, by successive encroachments, it should obtain a seaboard in the Mediterranean, and one in the Baltic, in its efforts to accomplish universal empire, were passed over, save by a few thoughtful men, without remark; and when travellers did narrate the wonders of Sevastopol in the Crimea, and the fortifications at Cronstadt, it was without reference to their real object, and generally coupled with a sneer at their impregnability. Events have shewn how much easier it is to despise an antagonist than to defeat him.

Christmas had succeeded the enlistment of Clifton, and he was yet at the depôt of his regiment, when the peace of Europe was thus violently disturbed, and he was not a little excited at the prospect of active service, which presented itself to him. He had but little doubt, nay, it was the general talk, that his regiment would be one of those chosen to make up the sum of the first contingent sent out, and in the February following this was confirmed; the second battalion of Fusilier Guards received its orders to leave its country station and march to London on its way to its first destination, Malta. Clifton was ordered to join it at the Wellington barracks in St. James's Park, upon a certain day, and right cheerfully did he set about the task of making such preparations as were necessary. He had received, through the kindness of the Colonel, who had taken a liking to him, a timely notice that he might communicate with his friends; and his first act was to write to Myra Aston, to tell her his destination and the chances it offered of that advancement that he so coveted, or of an early termination to his career. It was the first letter he had written to her, and it cost him no little trouble to produce a communication to his satisfaction. He gave her a brief but entertaining history of what had occurred to him since he had parted from her, touched but lightly on the few unpleasantnesses he had endured, and enlarged upon the kindness he had received and the prospect the war would give him of promotion; he promised to write again to her at the first place at which he arrived, where an opportunity permitted him. He spoke of Senorita Preciosa, and of the certainty he entertained that in some manner his destiny was connected with hers. "I should be sorry," he said, "to lose the opportunity which your considerate kindness gives me of occasionally communicating with her, as by this medium I hope some day to realise what I am convinced, and my heart tells me, is only too probable, and therefore I earnestly remind you of your promise, though I am sure it is unnecessary, because, comprehending the importance I attach to the advantage you will, I know, preserve it for me." A few other remarks and the letter was closed and despatched.

On the eve of his departure from the depôt, Sergeant Haverel made his appearance there, and evidently in extravagant spirits. He came up to Clifton, and seizing his hand, shook it warmly.

"Congratulate me, my boy!" he cried, with a chuckling laugh.

"Upon what?" asked Clifton, smiling also.

"Upon my appointment. Look ye here,"—he cried, showing his left sleeve handsomely embroidered, "I am sergeant-major of the second battalion of the Fusilier Guards, and join the brave fellows to-morrow."

"It is my regiment; I also join it to-morrow."

"I know it. But hang it, man, you have not congratulated me."

"I do, with all my heart, for I believe you deserving of it. I have cut some of my eye teeth since I have been here, and I know the value of a good-hearted and honest sergeant, who does not, in sharing, count three for himself and a promise for the recruit."

"Ha! ha! ha!" laughed the sergeant. "Many thanks, Grey. I believe you understand me, and so have the officers under whom I have served, and for that matter, my comrades. I have no reason to complain if they have not."

"What besides general good conduct brought you the promotion—the war?"

"It is too long a story just now. Some other time, Grey, you shall have chapter and verse. Let it serve you now that I got the vacancy in ours, and have exchanged into yours. But I'm thirsty, and we must have a glass together, for

To-morrow, comrade, we,
On the battle plain must be,
There to conquer or both lie low—lie low.
The morning star is up,
There is wine still in the cup,
So we'll take another quaff ere we go, boy, go.

"Ay! Grey, I know you are not much of a hand at the bottle, and I do not recommend sucking the monkey too much, but we'll have a glass to-night together. You have some new comrades to say good bye to. I have some old ones; we'll take it together. Come along, and forget for to-night that you are 'Gentleman Grey.'"

Clifton laughed, and consented to accompany him to the canteen; and there a carouse ensued, of an exciting kind, for there were many there who, if not actually ordered out, were in early expectation of being so, being told to hold themselves in readiness for foreign service; and there were others, not expecting to be sent abroad, who wished to have what was termed a jolly parting with their comrades. It was with difficulty Clifton was able to preserve resolution to prevent taking more than he could bear; while the jolly Sergeant Haverel, who sang an excellent song, was a famous teller of anecdotes and stories into the bargain; and, therefore, as a first-rate boon companion, had liquor forced upon him from all sides, seemed to drink with all, and as frequently as all there, and yet without any visible effect beyond a red and shining face, and an eye that glittered like a diamond.

A strict disciplinarian, with all his jovial habits, the sergeant was ready to quit the festivity the moment the time arrived to return to barracks, and though many there sought to detain him with entreaties and proffers of drink, he was proof against all, and with Clifton reported himself at the proper time, even though he knew that under the circumstances a latitude would have cheerfully been allowed without any comments being made. As they journeyed together to London on the following day, Sergeant Haverel himself referred to it, by complimenting Clifton on the readiness with which he could quit the enticements of joyous company when duty called him.

"You understand, I see, Grey," said he, "the advantages attending discipline. I am very particular in this matter, because I say to myself, if I do not set an example I cannot expect that others will be more attentive than myself; I therefore never knowingly commit a breach of discipline, and I never permit it. I tell you this, Grey, not that I believe you will ever require me to relax my rules on the score of friendship, for I wouldn't for my own brother, but because I would impress upon you the necessity of a very decided observance in it; it will bring you out for promotion, and if you get the lift it will enable you to be strict with those who were of the same rank as yourself before it, because they know that having done your duty yourself you will insist upon others doing it, and they cannot produce instances of your own lax observance of duty as an excuse for shirking it."

"You are quite right, sergeant," exclaimed Clifton, "those very considerations have weighed with me, and have done more to aid me in adapting myself to my change in life than aught else. I have had some rebellious struggles, some bitter pills to swallow, and some hard gulps to get down language from men who so short a time back I held as in a position immeasurably inferior to my own; but reflection taught me that our relative positions had changed, and that I could not expect subordination or respect hereafter from men if I refused to show it when in their position."

"That's just it. I have seen plenty of service, Grey, and I hope to see plenty more," rejoined Sergeant Haverel; "and we shall, unless we get our billet with a bullet at the first brush. You are new to it all; I am an old hand; let me give you, therefore, a few hints, and if you treasure them up, I'll bet a month's pay to a glass of mild ale that you'll prove the benefit of them."

"It is just what I want. I have been reading, with much attention and application, books on tactics; but a few practical hints will be of no little value to me, I am sure, and I shall indeed be thankful to you."

"Well, Grey, in commencing with the first and most important consideration, I need say but little about it

to you, because education has already done it for you."

"What is that?"

"Cleanliness: a dirty man, without a jest, Grey, never makes a smart soldier; he is looked upon with contempt by the officers, and shunned by his mess. He is the first to catch disease and to hold it, and the last to rise from the ranks. That will never be your case; nor need I say anything to you about looking always well and constantly at your arms. You tell me you have been a sportsman: and, you know how necessary it is to keep your gun in good order, for at the moment you want to bring down your bird your weapon may miss fire from want of common attention to it, and you suffer disappointment from it; but that is nothing compared with aiming at your enemy, because a failure here may cost you your life, and perhaps help to destroy the advantages anticipated from an important manœuvre, and thus involve hundreds of other lives."

"The fault seems but a simple one; but, sergeant, I thank you for showing me the great importance of avoiding it."

"Ah! Mr. Grey," cried the sergeant, warming into his subject, "Trust in Providence, and keep your powder dry, said old Noll, and he knew what a soldier's duties were. You are a sportsman, as I said before, and you know that you can't place any faith in a bullet if your powder's damp. When you are blazing at men armed like yourself it is something different to letting fly at a frightened bird, because, if you don't hit him, the chances are that he'll wing you. So always keep your powder dry, Grey, whether you trust in Providence or not."

"I shall not forget."

"No! nor be afraid of the trouble of making yourself a crack shot: as much depends upon that as upon the state of your rifle—for, Grey, we are to be armed with the Minié rifle, and there is some sense in that —you see it is not much consequence if you can't hit a haystack at a reasonable distance, whether you discharge your piece or not. You must trust, then, to sound pluck and cold steel, but if you are a good shot, as a soldier you befriend yourself, and you do your country good service, and I'll show you how. Are you acquainted at all with outpost duty?"

"Only by reading, and what the sergeant has communicated to me, as well as a little drill in picquet and fatigue duties."

"Not much use when you come to the real duties. I do not suppose you, as one of the Guards, will have such duties often, because it is the Rides who are generally selected, but you may; and on a dark night, when out on outpost duty, you will know the advantage then of being a good shot. I don't mean, by a good shot, the merely firing point blank at a given object in fine weather, and in broad daylight, but at an obscure object in a dim light, a stiff wind blowing, the enemy on a different level with yourself, and, like you, perhaps dodging about for cover: then's the time a man's shooting is of value to him."

"So I can believe."

"Ay! and yet you would hardly believe how little most of our men care to become good shots, even though their own lives pay forfeit. But, Grey, if a man feels like a soldier, if he is a soldier at heart, he'll become a soldier every inch of him. Why, if a man is clever at outpost duty, I'd trust him with the execution of any thing else."

"Why," asked Clifton, anxious to elicit as much practical information as he could, from one whom he was well assured was "a soldier every inch of him."

"Why! because all that he knows of manœuvring he has to practice in that duty, and he has to think too, because he cannot always be governed by the word of command, as in obtaining cover he may be quite out of hearing. He must reflect, and judge, and consider what is best to be done; he must feel that he is the sentry for the army, and be able to catch the true character of all the sounds that may greet his ear, whether they are indicative of the approach of a small or large body of men. He may be sure that the enemy knows he and others are thereabouts, and will use all their cunning to deceive and capture him, while he must not be in a hurry to get away, until he knows something of the advancing force, so that he may retire slowly, and by continued discharges draw sufficient aid to the front to keep in check the advancing skirmishers until the general is on the spot, and the army is prepared for action with the main body of the enemy, which is probably rapidly following up the advance of the light troops thrown out by them."

"He may then leave the responsibility to the general in command," said Clifton, with a smile.

"Yes," replied sergeant Haverel, "because he has done his duty; and if he has done it well, he deserves the good opinion of his comrades; for every good soldier knows how much the safety of an army in active service depends upon the outpost duties being well performed."

"I can understand not only that," said Clifton, "but also that there are many things which a soldier, if he has any regard for his comfort—nay! his life, while on active service, ought to make himself acquainted with."

"Now let's hear you! What are they?" asked the sergeant.

"Why in all the narratives of campaigns which I have read, I have found in all cases that the soldiers have suffered immensely from two causes."

"And they?"

"Are the weather, and want of provisions."

"Very true; but while on the march through perhaps an enemy's country, and just at such time as circumstances make the opportunity, you can neither ensure fine weather nor a supply of provisions. You must therefore do the best you can."

"Exactly, it is the best you can, to which I allude.

You are all aware of the possibility of bad weather, and a failure in supply is a contingency that may occur at any time; it is as well, therefore, to endeavour to foresee and provide for them by creating resources where none would otherwise exist. Economy of rations for the one, and the careful study of resources and contrivances to meet the want of them for the other, I consider as an important part of a soldier's education. His comforts depend so much upon his knowing how to avail himself of any resources within his reach, and substituting others for those which may not be, that he ought to be able to recognise and employ them whenever they exist; and if he did, I am convinced that many of the sufferings of which I have read would never have existed."

"Very true, Grey; but we have had a long peace, and the bulk of the English army does not know anything about active service, but what they picked up at Chobham, and that wasn't worth much to them. No! they ought to know how to do everything for themselves, and then the bad weather and short rations would lose half their power and fatality. Well, we must see what we can do with our comrades after we have joined them. Here's London at last."

The drafts of the detachments on their way to join their respective regiments were now gathered together, and marched to their destination. As they proceeded, Clifton perceived, from the expression of the faces of the civilians, who stopped to gaze upon them as they passed, or thronged to accompany them on their way, and from the remarks he overheard freely uttered on all sides about thrashing the Russians, that the war would be hailed with popular enthusiasm, and if the Government willed it would be prosecuted and promoted with vigorous energy and ready sacrifice on the part of the people. On reaching his destination, and in making himself as comfortable as he could among new faces in a strange place, he found considerable assistance and no little mental support in the presence of sergeant Haverel, who, after he had done his utmost to keep Clifton in high spirits, as he parted for the night from him, handed him a letter.

"This arrived," said he, "just as we were leaving Chatham barracks, and I took it of the post-man to give it to you. It is a returned letter; and as I knew you had no time at the moment to take notice of it, and as it might be from some friend to whom you were anxious to write respecting you going abroad, I thought I would'nt damp your spirits at the moment of setting off; but now I think it my duty to give it to you, as we are in London, and there may be some little opportunity left for you to make other arrangements respecting it if a chance offers. Good night, Grey; we shall meet in the morning."

The sergeant departed, and Clifton, as soon as his back was turned, tore open the packet. Within there was a printed communication addressed to him, to the effect that the enclosed letter, for reasons stated thereon, had been returned to the dead letter office, where it had been opened, and was now returned to the writer. Clifton looked at the letter, and a glance told him it was that which he had despatched from the depôt to Myra Aston. Upon the upper edge of the letter, just over the superscription was written, in a very rude style of penmanship, "Gon aWay not none ware."

Clifton crushed the letter in his hand with a sensation of acute agony; he then opened and carefully examined it, and his cheek burned with a fierce flame as he imagined the sardonic smile upon the cheek of the official who had perused it ere he returned it to him; although in this he gave himself needless pain, as the overworked functionary has but little time to peruse the epistles he opens; it must be indeed under unusual circumstances, if, after having ascertained name and address, adopting it as the means by which he can return the communication, he does not pass on to the next without further inspection. Clifton at another time would have been the first to suggest this explanation, in reply to a surmise such as brought the burning blood to his brow; but he was too overwhelmed by this most unexpected occurrence to reason upon it. He slowly tore the letter up in small pieces and flung them into the fireplace, and threw himself upon his humble pallet; but not to sleep.

Once more he was isolated in the world, without friends or home, and so what mattered it whither he went, or what became of him?

CHAPTER IX.

"The little ones cling round her knee,
    And lisp their father's name;
They cannot tell their country has
    For him a greater claim :
Yes, wife and children, house and land,
    Must be by him resign'd—
But honour calls——."

"Cease, cease those sighs, I cannot bear;
    Hark! hark! the drums are calling;
Oh I must chide that onward tear,"
    Or kiss it at its falling."

"We still may hope that happier days
    In store for us remain,
And though we part in anguish now,
    We yet may meet again."

THE NIGHT BEFORE THE DEPARTURE. THE CAPTAIN'S BROTHER, AND THE SERGEANT'S SWEETHEART. THE PARTING.

HAD Clifton Grey been plunged less suddenly into his position of isolation, it is probable that the acuteness with which he felt every successive trial would have been less severe, and that he would have met them individually or collectively with more firmness;

but, although it cannot be said that he had been at a moment violently expelled from the bosom of a loving family, and all his connections with them abruptly sundered, yet the even tenor of his past life, the character of his education, and the expectations it had given rise to, led him to look forward to a position the very opposite of that in which, without the slightest warning, he was now placed. The first blow delivered by Mr. Jayne hurled him from his estate, without leaving him a single friend with whom he could take counsel, or to whom he could look up to for advice; and the frail ties of sympathy he had since formed were successively torn from him just at moments when he could least afford to part with them. No wonder, then, that he felt these visitations of Providence keenly. But there was an alloy in the very bustle and confusion which surrounded him in his new career; constant society, the light-hearted reckless mirth ever ringing in his ears, the calls upon his mind and body in the performance of his regimental duties, prevented him brooding over his misfortunes, and all tended to rouse him from a depression which, if suffered to have sway in a mind constituted like his, might have had a fatal result.

His friend, too, Sergeant Haverel, having a shrewd notion of the friendless condition of the young recruit, and believing that the forlorn situation in which he stood had received some painful addition by the returned letter he had presented to him, exerted himself to cheer and encourage him in the task of banishing sad thoughts, and in creating visions of glory and wealth as the destiny of the future, enlarging at the same time with all the ardour and romance of his sanguine temperament upon the honours to be achieved, the glory to be won, and the fortunes which were to be made with such ease in the ensuing war with Russia, now set down as a certainty, although it had not yet been declared. At first he made but little impression on our hero, but at last his persevering efforts were rewarded by the returning smile, the brightening eye, and the elastic step which denote a healthful tone of mind, and he felt that whatever were the secret griefs Clifton had to endure, he had passed out of despondency, and had attained a frame of mind which enabled him to look his troubles fairly in the face, and hopefully gaze into the vast field of the future stretched before him, in trustfulness that the sorrow would pass away and happiness yet be realised by him.

Clifton soon had the opportunity of witnessing some of those peculiar features of a soldier's life, seen only when he is about to enter on active service, and many of the scenes he beheld were painful enough to give him the heart-ache. That a soldier's pay was small he had found out long since, and but for the kindness of the sea captain he would have more unpleasantly experienced it, and therefore it was with wonder he observed how many soldiers, with their scanty pittance, were married.

One shilling and one penny per day is his pay;

with this he has partly to clothe himself, wholly to feed himself, to pay for his washing, hair-cutting, and what is called barrack damages. What can possibly be left on which to keep a wife—not alone a wife, but usually a number of children—the poorest persons generally have the largest family? It is not to be expected that as soon as a man volunteers to fight the battles of his country he is to be dead to the natural affections, or to be debarred from exercising them with others who in the nation fill posts less onerous and honourable. Nor should it be presumed that if he is to indulge those softer feelings to which the sternest and harshest are at times susceptible he is only to do so at the expense of morality. But what is the fact. Some soldiers marry with leave, the proportion being about five in one hundred. Marrying with leave means that the wives are so far recognised that they live in barracks, claim medical attendance, can send their children to a regimental school, and do washing for the officers as well as needlework, if required: the money obtained from this source helping to eke out the miserable balance left of the soldier's pay, when he has liquidated the regimental charges upon it. But where there are five in one hundred marry with leave, there are fifty married without, and unless the wife, who has none of the above advantages, be hard-working, industrious, and thrifty, her fate may be imagined. Her husband can help her but little, and if he is not in some degree steady, not at all. The privation and wretchedness which follow these imprudent alliances it is almost impossible to exaggerate, and how they are contracted to the extent to which they exist is little short of a marvel; it is the men who share the pleasures of matrimony, the women who bear the burden of it, and example, remonstrance, persuasion, and counsel are all in vain. If the girl loves the soldier, there is no picture, however vividly painted, of miserable destitution ensured, unless she devotes herself to a life of slavery, will deter her from joining her fate to the man who has won her heart; many leave the service of good families, some the good homes of their immediate relatives, to unite themselves to a life of penury and pain. There are exceptions to this view of the subject, but they only serve to prove its truth; for a woman once infatuated with a man will not look into the future, will not reason at all. What cares she for self-sacrifice? she thinks not of herself for a moment. To be with him, to be to him what he can most desire, to afford him happiness, and to save him pain, she will encounter and dare anything, and she does. Fearfully in some cases does she pay the penalty of her devotion.

Bad as at all times such marriages must prove, how much is their wretchedness enhanced by the departure of a regiment for active service. The little advantages possessed by the wife of the soldier married with leave are taken from her, and those which the married without leave possessed in the presence of their husbands, are lost to her entirely by his absence. Both classes are now on a par; they are not only left desolate, but they are left destitute.

The night before the departure of Clifton's regiment, ordered to Malta, he had some unhappy realizations of the results of such marriages. He had made all the arrangements required by his departure, and took advantage of an hour or two left to his own disposal to take a stroll in the vicinity of the barracks. As he quitted by the small wicket, he came suddenly upon a small crowd, chiefly composed of women; some were young and smartly dressed, others were plainly, and many wretchedly clad: no inconsiderable number were accompanied by children. He was at once accosted by several, asking after some of his comrades, a few that he did know and some that he did not. Different as were their respective attires, their countenances had but one expression—one of hopeless grief. He answered the queries put to him as satisfactorily as he was able, and they all wound up with one enquiry, "When do you march?" "Our orders are to be ready at four o'clock in the morning," was his response; in most cases it was received with a low sob. With an aching heart, at the sight of so much misery, he was not sorry to get clear of his questioners; and was, as soon as he got beyond, accosted by several civilians, who, putting the same question respecting the hour of departure to him, offered him their good wishes: some asked him to come and drink, while others thrust cigars upon him, and one offered him money. All had something kind to express, and none failed in uttering a wish that he might escape the dangers of the battle field. It was impossible to receive all this attention from persons of whom he knew nothing without emotion, and his heart swelled within him as his busy imagination sketched out desperate engagements, and successes only obtained by the most valorous deeds, entitling his name to be uttered praisefully by those who now spoke to him hopefully.

He was a fine young fellow, and his dress as a private of the Fusilier Guards set off his well formed figure to great advantage, the saucy rake of his cap, with its small chequered band of red and white, detracted nothing from his handsome manly face, and many were the bright glances and smiling countenances of pretty girls turned towards him as he passed; but he remembered his position, and the condition of those who were waiting to take their farewell—only too probably their last for ever on earth—of his companions in arms, at the barrack yard gate and he almost shuddered.

As he strolled up St. James' Park, he perceived before him a young girl hurrying towards him: she was closely attended by a gentleman dressed in the height of fashion, who sought to keep pace with her. As her course appeared to be somewhat serpentine, and her pace increased when she saw him to a run, he very naturally concluded that her companion was keeping her society with the purpose of insulting her. No sooner did he entertain this impression than he slackened his not very fast walk, and put himself more decidedly in her way. He had no intention of getting into a disturbance at such a moment, it would be only of too serious moment to him, but he determined if he found the girl—for she looked young—was annoyed by her unwelcome companion, to give her the opportunity of getting rid of him; nothing more. He was in no disposition to quarrel, he was about to leave England, perhaps for ever, and he had no wish to part in anger with one of her meanest or basest sons.

As soon as the advancing maiden perceived his movement, she appeared to guess its purport, and she ran up to him. Her face was scarlet with exertion in walking at a rapid pace, but no loss at the act upon which she had suddenly determined. She placed her hand upon his arm and said eagerly :

"Are you one of the Fusilier Guards."

"I am," he replied.

"Do you know Sergeant Haverel?" she asked earnestly.

"I do," he replied. "We are the best of friends."

"Thank God!" she replied vehemently, "You will protect me from the man who is following me—will you not?"

"I will. Take my arm."

The girl seized it, and clung to him as though she was about to be torn from him, while Clifton turned his gaze upon the man advancing towards him, with a cool effrontery and a steadiness of purpose which rather surprised him. He had just caught a sufficient glimpse of the young girl who had claimed his protection to see that she had a very pretty face, and was very neatly dressed. By this time the pursuer confronted them.

He was a stylish looking man, as we have before said. Well dressed,—that is fashionably, which does not always mean "well" dressed. He had long fair hair, and full fair moustaches; he wore an eye glass which he held with the most perfect command before his left eye, detaining it there only with his eye brow and cheek bone. When he reached the couple he stopped, and eyed Clifton from head to foot with a slow and supercilious gaze.

"You aw a soldyaw," he exclaimed, with an affected accent upon the last syllable.

"You are not," responded Clifton, looking full at the fair moustache, and feeling the colour mount to his cheek and his lip curl.

"I mean a pwivate soldyaw."

"Well?" responded Clifton.

"What wegiment?"

"If you will not see for yourself, why do you ask?"

"Why, as I stwongly suspect, you intend to intawfewaw with my little pawsuits. I shall wepoort you unless you leave that young girl, and go about you' business at once."

"Suppose I care nothing for your 'weport,' will not leave this young lady who has claimed my protection, and do not go about my business—what then?"

"Oh, she has claimed your pwotection, has she?"

"She has."

"Vewy well. Then I shall see if I cannot compel you to do what I wequire."

"Proceed."

"Mind I'm not to be bullied with impunity, and if you'll civilly wetire, leaving me to have a few words with the little wench, I'll say no more about it."

"Oh, pray do not leave me!" exclaimed the girl, earnestly clinging to Clifton's arm as she spoke.

"What are you afraid of, you little spooney?" exclaimed her annoyer. "You know I don't want to hurt you. Wefleet upon what I have promised you, and come and have a few words in pwivate, and settle the matter."

The girl made no reply, but drew yet closer to Clifton, as if she would be shielded from his very words. Clifton felt a tingling about his knuckles, and an almost inexpressible desire to knock the fellow down; but he remembered his position and refrained. Regarding the insolent intruder with a stern look, he said :

"Do you know this young lady?"

"Of course I do," responded the hero of the eye-glass, again subjecting Clifton to a very close inspection from boots to cap, "but cuss me if I think you do."

"Whether I do or not," replied Clifton, "is not to the purpose; but even supposing you do know the lady, it is very evident that she has no desire to improve the acquaintance; and to prevent you forcing attentions upon her which disgust and offend her, she has requested me to interfere: and I shall do as she requests."

"Disgust and offend her!" cried the fellow, in a rage. "Why many a lady of wank and wiches would wejoice to weceive those attentions."

"Take them to them, then; they are as undesirable here as your presence. Do you wish to see Sergeant Haverel?" asked Clifton of the girl, who yet clung tremblingly to his arm.

"Oh yes, I—I must see him. The regiment leaves to-morrow, does it not?" exclaimed she, in tremulous tones.

"Yes; we leave here at four in the morning," responded Clifton, turning to retrace his steps towards the barracks, where he had left the sergeant.

"But you are going to leave that young woman here, you know?" exclaimed the tormentor once more, impudently confronting Clifton.

"I am not, you know," replied our hero, losing gradually the command of his temper, "but I am you; and if you would not desire that it should be on the broad of your back on the gravel path, you will stand out of my way, nor molest me and my companion further."

"I would not advise you to twy any wuffianly attack upon me, soldyaw. I know your wegiment now, it is the second battalion of Fusilier Guards. My bwother holds a commission in it, and your back shall smart for it, if you endeavour to cross me in my playshaw."

Clifton placed his hand upon the man's shoulder and compressing it with a firm grip, he, with a passion-impelled effort of strength, sent him flying far away in the darkness. They heard him fall heavily upon the ground. The young girl screamed slightly, and Clifton stood for a moment, expecting to see his prostrate enemy leap up and advance to attack him, but he did not make his appearance, and as Clifton was desirous to avoid any squabble upon the eve of his departure, he said to his trembling companion:

"He will not trouble us again. Come, if you want to see the sergeant we must away at once, or the opportunity will escape you."

So saying, they proceeded towards the barracks. Clifton was not long in discovering that there was a love match between this young girl and Sergeant Haveril; that she was heart-broken at the thought of his departure, the more especially as within nine or ten months from that time she would come into possession of a legacy which would enable him to leave the army, marry her, and go into business together. However, there was no help for it, and she was in despair at his departure and the prospect of his death; which, not actually improbable, was conjured into a certainty by her fears. Her name too, he learned, was Lizzie Hastings, and that she was an orphan, with an aunt living; that she was a milliner; and that she could earn enough money now for both, if the sergeant would leave the army.

"But he wont," she said, mournfully.

"Why not? I am sure he must love you?"

"Oh yes, I believe he loves me very dearly and truly; but he says he has no notion of my working and slaving on his account, and until he can be sure of keeping the wolf from the door by his own exertions, I shall not sacrifice my health and strength upon him."

"But you don't like him any the worse for that, do you?"

"Oh no; but then he is so foolish on these points, and so obstinate. Ah! I had much rather he would stop here and let me work for him, even if it was night and day, than he should go away and be killed."

She took out her handkerchief and sobbed.

I see now, thought Clifton, how these marriages between soldiers and their wives are contracted; if the man lets his love get the better of his judgment, if he does not resolutely stick out, and refuse to enter into the contract by which so much misery is entailed and the woman immolated, she will never hang back from the sacrifice.

They had now reached the barrack-yard, and Clifton found the crowd had much increased, there were more civilians, more weeping women, and more children.

They worked a passage among the sad groups, and Clifton, leaving Lizzie Hastings close to the barrack door, entered, and quickly found Sergeant Haverel, who squeezed his hand hard when he learned the visitor he had brought to him: he lost not a moment in proceeding to the spot where she had been left. She was yet there, and Sergeant Haverel, taking both her hands, struck up

"Although I leave thee now in sorrow,
Smile my light, my love, to-morrow."

He paused, for her streaming eyes were raised to his, and even though they were surrounded by crowds of people, she could not prevent her head falling on his breast, while she sobbed audibly. He pressed her to his heart and whispered:

"Don't be soft-hearted, Lizzie darling. Come, my lass, I must have a word of a sort with you, and teach you how to act bravely, or you'll never be fit for a soldier's wife. Did you not offer always to obey the word of command, eh!—eyes bright, then—ah! at it again, Why, my little bird, how you shiver and shake! There, there, catch tight hold of my wing, let us get out of this bustle, for I want to talk you out of your trembling, darling. Come and listen to me, and I'll wager my first medal against your silver thimble, that when we say good bye you'll do it without a tear in your eye, a wrinkle on your face, or a sigh quivering on your lips."

As he uttered these words, he drew her away from the clustering people, whose numbers were increasing, and whose curiosity betrayed momentarily less and less reserve, and together at a slow pace they wandered among the shadows of the fine old trees in the park, where they could say what they listed unnoticed and unheard.

Clifton Grey in the meanwhile sauntered back into the barrack-yard, where much bustle and confusion was manifest, and all the indications of a regiment about to depart on active service were everywhere apparent. Having accomplished all that was necessary in his own case, he had nothing left but to watch the preparations of others, and tender his services, where he thought they might prove acceptable. He had been but a short time thus employed, and was in the act of assisting a comrade who required his aid, when he felt himself suddenly and rudely seized by the shoulder, and a voice which he at once recognised exclaimed hastily and excitedly:

"I have him, Chawles. This is the wuffian, Chawles, who wegaled me with his wascally impertinence, and on my wefusal to wender a weply to his insolent wequests, felled me like an ox."

Clifton turned quickly and found himself in the grasp of the individual from whose insults he had released Lizzie Hastings. He recognized, also, in the person of "Chawles," a captain of his regiment, for whom, even after a very brief observation, he found himself

THE SEPARATION.

"It must be for years, and it may be for ever."

already entertain a strong dislike, because of his haughty bearing and the almost brutal manner he displayed towards the men under his command. Shaking off the hand of his detainer, and drawing himself up, he made the usual military salute to his officer, who at once said, harshly:

"Now, fellow, answer—are you the man who assaulted this gentleman?"

Clifton could not help feeling that the captain had delivered himself of a contradiction of terms. He, however, made no allusion to it in his reply, but said:

"If, sir, he has aught to complain of in my conduct, he has only to thank himself for it."

"I am to understand, then, you were the fellow who dared to knock down my brother?"

"Your brother, sir, forgot his position as a gentleman; he ought not to have been surprised at the consequences."

"No blackguard insolence, if you please. Did you or did you not strike him?"

"I did, but"—

"Enough; I shall order you under arrest, and see if I can't teach you to comprehend the difference between a gentleman and one of your scoundrelly associates."

"But, sir," exclaimed Clifton, indignantly, "you have not heard the circumstances which led to my act."

"Weally," exclaimed the captain's brother, who was applying a white handkerchief to his discoloured eye, "weally, this is too good a joke. I have wecounted to him the particulars of our wecontre, my fine fellow, and you shall smart for it. Wecollect I pwomised you a wubber for your bowl, and you'll weceive it."

"Sir, you will not surely condemn me unheard," cried Clifton, appealing to the captain, who, however, with a frowning visage said, angrily:

"You scoundrel, what do you want me to hear—that you had the audacity to step in between my brother and a young person whom he honoured by speaking to, and then because he naturally felt indignant at your presumption, you crowned your insolence by felling him to the earth like a ruffianly prize-fighter—"

"Yes, exactly," echoed his brother, "like a wuffianly pwize-fighter."

"I therefore shall immediately order you under arrest. Hey! corporal!" he cried to one at that moment hurrying past; but, before the man could obey the command, an officer attired in military undress, who had been leaning against a pillar close to them, but unobserved by all, stepped forward and said, in a mild but firm voice:

"For what would you place this man under arrest, Captain Winslow?"

All turned: it was the colonel who had induced Clifton to join the regiment. The latter breathed freely again: he knew that at least he should have an im-

partial hearing. Captain Winslow coloured and bit his lip, but he touched his cap, and said:

"He has committed a most scandalous outrage upon a gentleman, a civilian."

"Yes, a wevolting attack upon 'me," cried Beverly Winslow—for that was his name—thrusting himself before the colonel, who simultaneously stepped back a pace; with a stern brow, which the captain knew well how to interpret, he said:

"I will attend to you presently."

Then, addressing himself again to the captain, he said:

"Was the soldier—Grey—I think it is"—

Clifton touched his cap: the colonel continued:

"Was Grey upon duty or upon leave?"

"Upon leave, I imagine, colonel," was the reply.

"Were you present at the altercation?"

"No, colonel, but I have heard the whole of the circumstances."

"From whom, permit me to ask?"

"From—from—my—this gentleman," exclaimed the captain, reddening and pointing to his brother, and added quickly, "he addressed his complaint to me, and as the man was about to quit England, begged me to afford him such immediate redress as laid in my power."

"Which you were about to comply with?"

The captain bowed.

"What defence has Grey offered?" enquired the colonel.

"None," returned the captain, with a scowl at Clifton which said pretty plainly: 'Contradict me if you dare.' Clifton affected not to notice it, and the captain added, "Indeed, he admits the commission of the assault."

"And what led to it?" asked the colonel, sternly regarding the captain. The latter was not prepared to utter a palpable lie, and he therefore remained silent. The colonel paused a moment, and then turning to Clifton, he said:

"Grey, have you explained to Captain Winslow the causes which led you to knock down this—this gentleman." The word, as he pointed to Beverley Winslow, seemed to stick in his throat.

"I have not, colonel," replied Clifton, without adding that he had not been permitted, for he believed that the colonel might guess as much.

"There, Grey," said the latter, "I think you were wrong." And then addressing himself to Captain Winslow, he said, speaking with marked emphasis, "Will you do me the favour to walk a few steps with me. I was present during the whole affair, and as you have listened to an exparte statement from that person, who it is probable is somewhat interested in the matter, you will not refuse to hear a narration from me, who at least cannot be accused of having an undue leaning on one side or the other."

The captain bowed, and the colonel taking his arm,

they moved down the barrack yard together, leaving Clifton Grey and Beverley Winslow confronting each other. Beverley drew near to him, and Clifton, folding his arms, prepared to receive his taunts, for he expected no less from him, without trusting himself to reply. He was not deceived. Beverley Winslow approached him closely, and exclaimed,

"Well, my man, ain't you wather distwessed at the pwedicament you've wun you'self into. I told you not to int'fere, but you would wesist all pe'swasion and a pwetty mess you've made of it. Don't you wish you could wetire fwom you' position."

'No," returned Clifton, who could with difficulty refrain from smiling.

"Meah bwag. But come, I don't think it was so much your fault, as it was that widiculous little dwessmake's, so if you will beg my pawdon before the captain, my bwother, and expwess you' wegwet in vewy wespectful terms, say how sowwy you feel, pewhaps I'll get you out of the scwape—mind, I only say pewhaps."

"I cannot accept your offer," replied Clifton laconically.

At this juncture, Sergeant Haverel joined the party. He had caught sight of Clifton, and came running towards him; he seized him by the hand and wrung it heartily, saying in a loud voice:

"Grey, you have done me another good turn, and I shall put one more notch on the stick. Lizzie has told me all. You have acted like a true comrade, and I only wish I had been near that short tongued Mary-Jane, if I had'nt spread his features out with my ten knuckles in a manner so that his own mother would'nt have known him, may I never obtain my dear little Lizzie for a wife. I would have "wequested him to wetire," over the "wailings," with the toe of my boot."

At this moment, Beverley Winslow, who had not lost a word of Haverel's, saw an imaginary friend in the distance, and hastened towards him. He was stopped in his hasty retreat by his brother, who had quitted the company of the colonel; saying a few words to him, he pointed to the wicket at the barrack yard. Beverley nodded, and made his way hastily towards it, without turning his head to snatch a glance at Sergeant Haverel, whom he at once understood was the sweetheart of Lizzie Hastings, the pretty little milliner, whose place of business was opposite to his lodgings at the West End. Her pretty face had won his regard, and he resolved that his tribute of affection should if possible be to effect her ruin: he had found out that she had a soldier for a sweetheart, and at first, thought Clifton was the man. He now discovered that it was the sergeant-major of his brother's regiment, and taking all things into consideration, he did not make any demur to his brother's request to him to quit the barrack yard, and meet him at dawn in the morning,

at the terminus of the South Western Railway. On the contrary, he shook his hand hurriedly, and a little to the captain's surprise, hurried away.

Captain Winslow now turned towards Clifton Grey, advanced to him, and addressed him in a tone which bore a meaning very different to that his mere words would seem to convey. "Grey," he commenced, "the colonel desires me to inform you, that he has related to me all that has transpired between you and my brother. He says that he witnessed the whole transaction. Were you aware of that?"

"I was not," returned Clifton.

"Oh !" ejaculated the captain drily, as much as to say, I don't believe it, and then went on. "Having heard both sides of the question, I am bound to believe my colonel's version in preference to that given by the gentleman, whom I ridiculously enough imagined, having been the sufferer, would be likely to be well informed about the matter. However, under all the circumstances, and taking into consideration the fact that it was you who interfered in the first instance with the actions of the gentleman, and not he with you, of whom but for your conduct he would not have taken the slightest notice, I am bound to say that you acted with commendable spirit in this affair, and have not incurred the punishment I had designed for you. You will therefore not consider yourself under arrest, but at the same time, I think it prudent you should remain in barracks until we march in the morning. Permit me to thank you for preventing me committing an injustice, and let me beg of you to believe that I will reward it at the very earliest opportunity." He bowed as he concluded, with mock politeness, but neither the malignancy with which he uttered the last words, nor the look with which they were accompanied were lost upon Clifton. He understood their meaning instantly, and knew that he had an enemy placed just where he was capable of doing him the greatest injury. The captain turned on his heel, and his departure was attended by a prolonged whistle from Sergeant Haverel, who as soon as he was out of hearing, said :

"So ho! Then it was Captain Winslow's brother who insulted my Lizzie, and was therefore knocked down by you, eh !"

"So it seems."

"And our good colonel luckily happened to be by and saw it all, eh !"

"He has said so, but I did not see him at the time."

"Ah, Grey, you were fortunate in having him for a witness; it might have turned out badly for you if you hadn't, and you must look precious sharp that it doesn't now. I know the gentleman who has just left us, by report; he don't forgive being crossed, and he has got the power of making your life as miserable as the very devil. You must therefore be constantly on the watch not to give him a chance of exercising his

power over you, to your discomfort, or else down goes
your house. Thank God! I shall be able to help you
and circumvent him a little, and if I don't, d—n me!
that's all. You shan't suffer, Grey, for having stood
the friend of those I love, if I can help it; but don't
you drop a hint likely to reach the captain's ears that
it was my little Lizzie you saved from his poodle
brother, or you may lessen my chance of serving you at
the needful moment."

"Be under no care for that. I shall think no more of
it," exclaimed Clifton.

"But you must. Captain W. will not so easily
forget it nor you. He has had a drilling from the
colonel about it, I can see, and he'll be revenged on
you; but he must look infernally sharp to do it, for
I'll stick to his heels like a leech to a cow's hoof in a
pond on a hot summer's day, and if he does contrive you
harm, d—n him! he must keep wide of me, or—"

"Tush, tush!" interposed Clifton, "think of this when
it comes."

"All right, my boy. Nevertheless, take my advice,
don't give him a chance; he's like a wasp, if you give
him one he'll sting you. So look out; I shall look out,
I can tell you, and so must he—so must he."

Sergeant Haverel ground his teeth and clenched his
hand as he said this with much excitement, but Clifton
drew him away from the spot, and by directing some
enquiries respecting Lizzie Hastings succeeded subsequently in turning the conversation into quite
another channel. He retired to rest early, for the
regiment was ordered to parade at four o'clock, in
heavy marching order; and at that hour, long before
the day began to dawn, the rolling drum and shrill fife
awakened the sleeping, spurred the sluggish, and summoned the alert to the rendezvous.

It was a cold, grey, damp morning in February,
when the men were paraded preparatory to marching
for the terminus of the South Western Railway to proceed
to Southampton, and there embark for Malta. Without
the barrack gates groups of persons had remained
all night; they were mostly composed of the wives,
relatives, or sweethearts of the soldiers, and were in a
state of almost frantic grief at the coming separation.
They had already had what was presumed to be a
parting interview with their husbands and lovers; but
they yet remained to bid the last farewell; to utter
the last good bye, and to take their last long and
lingering gaze of those who were now in all the pride
of manly health, but who might soon be laid beneath
the green turf, either by the bullet of the enemy or the
fell disease that rarely spares those on whom it firmly
fixes its scorching claws.

As the dawn approached, the throng increased
rapidly; the streets in the immediate line of march
displayed numbers of people moving to and fro, waiting
for the appearance of the troops, and as the first
streaks of light touched the house-tops, the faces of
those who seldom rose with the sun began to make their

appearance at the windows. Fast men, whose return
home is the advent of the milkman, arrived in cabs to
witness the 'fellows' of the Fusiliers take their departure for the East. Citizens and tradesmen, who contribute largely to the taxes, tumbled out of bed to see
the gallant men whose allotted task and profession it is
to fight the battles of England, for which the men of
business pay the piper, go off; women and girls who
had not husbands, brothers, or lovers among the
departing troops, mingled with those who had, and
were also to be seen clustering in the highways or
crowding the windows of the houses along the route.

At length, when the assembled groups had grown
weary of waiting, and the hour at which the men were
expected to march had long passed by, the exciting
sounds of a splendid military band suddenly woke up
the still chilly air. A buzz ran through the crowd
that surrounded the barracks; it pressed closer up;
presently the barrack-gates were thrown open, and
the well-skilled martial musicians, playing with
unwonted emphasis the popular air of "Cheer, boys,
cheer!" made their appearance, followed by the whole
battalion in heavy marching order. The tune was
well selected; it had an immense effect upon the
populace, who at once greeted the appearance of the
magnificent body of troops with a stentorian cheer,
which was taken up and carried through the whole
line of spectators as far as the eye could reach, and
maintained with vigorous energy from the barrack-
doors to the railway station. Along the crowded
thoroughfares, every doorway, window, and housetop
was crowded with anxious gazers; in the streets
arrested omnibuses, carriages, cabs, carts, all bore their
animated burdens, who enthusiastically waved their
hats and shouted themselves hoarse. White handkerchiefs were fluttered by fair owners, whose bright eyes
glistened with the unrepressed tear, and whose lips
murmured a prayer for the safety of the brave men
passing them with tramp so even and such solidity of
movement, who, with their drums beating and their
colours flying, were on their way to meet and fight the
barbarous Russ.

On all sides, around, above, beneath, wherever
Clifton's eyes turned, he saw the expression of earnest
enthusiasm, a popular tribute of affectionate admiration
for those gallant heroes who perilled so readily and so
boldly life and limb, existence and strength, to maintain
the honour of their country; and his heart glowed
responsively to this warm ebullition of popular feeling.
No doubt he, in common with many of his comrades,
made a secret promise that the reliance on their
courageous exertions to maintain the glory of dear old
England, thus openly expressed, should not, so far
as his best ability went, be abused.

But while thousands of faces were glowing with
enthusiastic patriotism, he could not but observe that
immediately accompanying the men were vast numbers of females, some the very minions of poverty,

others neatly, and not a few gaily dressed; many dragged children with them, keeping the poor little things at a trot in order to keep pace with the quick march of the soldiers. They presented a painful contrast to those above described; their faces were pallid, wan, and sorrowful to despair; in the midst of the cheering they were weeping; while hats were twirled in the air and handkerchiefs waved to and fro, they were wringing their hands. Clifton's heart chilled as he gazed on their woe-stricken countenances, and he could not but feel a thrill of consolation rise up against his sense of loneliness when he reflected that among the anguished sufferers there was not one suffering the acute misery he witnessed on all sides on his account. It seemed as if the band-master had noted the unhappy faces in the immediate vicinity of the troops, for he changed the air to "Oh! Susannah, don't you cry for me." It was strange to see what an effect this simple and beautiful air had upon the multitude; it was responded to by the women with a low sobbing wail, by the men with a glistening eye, which told that the injunction had the contrary effect to what was intended. Not one who heard it but instantly felt the force of the allusion, and how much real cause there might be for tears, when the bloody hand of War began to deal its fatal blows; for though from their very heart of hearts they freely put up wishes for the success and safety of their brave countrymen, it was impossible not to feel that out of the many gallant fellows with such handsome faces and such fine forms, the incarnation of young, vigorous, manly health, now passing before them, but few would return to their native land, and of those few the larger proportion would be maimed in body and wrecked in health for life. That the whole battalion, in fact, was a holocaust to the god—nay, the demon, of war.

At length the terminus of the South Western Railway was gained; thousands of curious and excited spectators surrounded it, and the rush to obtain a place on the platform was tremendous. Frantic women rushed into the midst of the troops and were surrounded and carried to the platform to give and receive the final good-bye, in spite of the officials, who had orders to admit only the soldiers about to be forwarded to Southampton. The scene became here heart-rending, for numbers who hoped to have taken their last farewell on the platform were debarred admission, and their screams and cries were agonizing; many of the men thus prevented from pressing their last kiss on their wives and sweetheart's lips, dragged their shakos over their moistened eyes, bit their quivering lips, and hastened to take a seat in the carriage awaiting them, praying inwardly that no delay might take place in their departure.

At the moment of entering the gate, Clifton Grey felt his arm pulled with a sudden and almost vigorous jerk; he turned, to see Lizzie Hastings at his elbow. With an ashy and agitated countenance she looked up in his face: she said in beseeching tones:

"Where is he? where is he? I have run all the way here; they tried to prevent me, but I should have died if I had not said good-bye to him. Oh! take me to him—you can—you will not refuse me. Oh, for God's sake! do not, if you would not see me fall dead at your feet."

"Now then, stand back there!" cried an excited railway official to Lizzie Hastings; "you must go back—you can't go in—go back, I say."

Lizzie shrieked and shuddered, and clung to Clifton's arm. He turned his eye to see what comrades were near him. Three or four were close to him, with whom he was on very good terms; with rapidity, and in a low tone he begged them to make an opening for her to slip through into the station, at the same time he pressed heavily against the railway official, who was but doing his painful duty, and forced him back against the archway a few steps only, when he released him, and passed on. A momentary movement—Lizzie was no longer visible, and the policeman was quickly engaged in squabbling with the next person who attempted to infringe the regulations.

When Clifton reached the spot where the long string of carriages were stationed, waiting to convey him and his comrades to the first stage of their destination, his heart smote him, as he observed the passionate and agonized leave-taking going on between those soldiers and their female connections who had succeeded in gaining admission. It was impossible to witness the writhing agony, the wild grief of those who, in parting with their husbands, were left not only in desolation, but in destitution, without sharing some of the pain; it was not possible to note the despairing sorrow, or hear the convulsive sob of those who parting with their lover weighed down by the fearful foreboding—alas, too frequently realized!—that grim, and bloody death would step in, and forbid a reunion, without an aching heart; it was not possible to listen to the despairing exclamations of the women, or the hopeful aspirations in their efforts to cheer the crushed spirit of their betrothed uttered by the men, unmoved. Turn which way he would, Clifton saw nothing but sadness, desolation, and despair, in the countenances of those about to be left behind, and mentally thanked heaven that he was at least spared such a trial. The thought had barely passed through his mind, when he felt a tap upon his shoulder, and he was accosted by a railway porter, who said:

"Is your name Grey—Clifton Grey?"

"It is. Why do you ask?" replied Clifton, with considerable surprise, looking hard at the man, to see whether he could recognise him; but he knew him not. The man handed him a card.

"A lady," he said, "told me to give you this."

Clifton took it, and perceived that it bore some words

written in pencil; when he had perused them, he raised his head; but the man had disappeared. On the card was written hastily, in the Spanish language, "I have this moment recognised you; I cannot get to you, for I am not permitted. You are about to start on your career of glory—or death. My heart aches and my eyes are blinded with tears, farewell—but we shall meet again. Heaven will preserve you and bring you to me. God bless you, and have you in his custody; farewell, my heart is bleeding, dear—dear Clifton."

It was signed "Preciosa." Clifton looked in all directions, and at length across the wide station; he perceived a train waiting the departure of the special train which would convey the troops. From the window of one of the first class carriages he perceived a waving handkerchief; with a throbbing heart, he removed his shako from his head, and placing it upon the muzzle of his rifle, he elevated it, and moved it to and fro as a token, not only that he had received the note, but that his heart responded to the contents: and thus he bade her once more farewell.

As he did this he thought of Myra. What had become of her! what would he not have given of all he possessed, small as the stock might be—but therefore, the more valuable to him—to learn why she had so abruptly left Arundel. It was not possible to cross the line, neither would he have been permitted at that moment to have made the circuit of the extensive shed even had he attempted it: he was therefore compelled to content himself with this demonstration, and to trust to providence not only for an elucidation of the mystery, but to grant him the opportunity of corresponding with her.

It was no consolation, however, to remember that Preciosa did not know what regiment he had joined. He therefore sought, in waving his shako, to draw particular attention to such distinguishing marks in his accoutrements as would enable the young creature now gazing towards him to make herself acquainted with it, and thus know how to address a communication to him.

From the window of the carriage a white handkerchief fluttered agitatedly; he perceived presently the small hands which held it, clasped prayerfully together; then above them, leaning forward, and turned towards him, he saw a face from which a veil had hastily been withdrawn, and though so far from him, he at once recognized it as that of the young girl whom he had rescued from a watery grave off the coast of Sussex, and further that she evidently acknowledged him to be that Clifton Grey to whom her hurried pencil lines were addressed. An emotion of gratification passed through his breast, and, on returning his shako to his head, he laid his hand impressively upon his heart. One of those small hands wafted a kiss to him in return, and then the face was suddenly withdrawn, as though its fair owner

had fallen back to give way to a violent passion of grief.

And so, notwithstanding his self-comfortings on this head, ungracious as they were, there was one present at his departure from England to bid him farewell, with tearful eyes, with mournful forebodings, but earnest wishes for his immunity from danger.

He walked slowly up the platform to find the place that was allotted to him in the carriages fast being filled by his comrades, when he encountered Sergeant Haverel, and Lizzie Hastings in the act of leave taking. She had dried her tears at the bidding of her lover, but her efforts to look cheerful under the same influence were anything but successful. He had tried his utmost to raise within her soul trustfulness and hopefulness, he had brought into full play his own sanguine temperament to effect his object, and if he had not altogether succeeded, he had at least lifted up her spirit beyond the gloom of despair: it might not have been into sunshine, it is true, but it was to a more genial region than many there, with better reason to be satisfied, could boast of. The sergeant, as he caught sight of Clifton, beckoned him to him with an assumption of cheerfulness, which his swelling heart made difficult to simulate. When he drew near, he said:

"Come, Grey, my boy, you have been boasting that you leave none behind to weep for you. Here at least, is a little girl who will pray for you. You know that every bullet has its billet, but it don't at all follow that there is one made out for either you or I. God is good; and if he sees fit to strike us down we must not grumble; but with all respect, and no wickedness, he may just fancy to let a couple of fine young fellows, like you and I, off easily. However, let that be as it will, you have done Lizzie a service, and very near got yourself into a scrape for doing it; and she has told me that when, like a good little girl as she is, she says her prayers before she goes to bed every night, she will offer up one for your safety."

Clifton took her hand, and pressed it; he said emphatically, as he looked with an earnest gaze into her pretty face, and thought to what strong temptations a young girl so good looking and so placed might be subjected to:

"The prayers of the virtuous will ever prevail. If you have made the promise and will keep it, Lizzie, I shall fancy I bear a charmed life."

The tears sprung into the girl's eyes:

"Oh! Mr. Grey," she exclaimed, as she warmly pressed his hand, "You deserve my prayers for the kindness you have shown me, and indeed—indeed, I will pray for you to be spared."

Her voice faltered at the last word, and she covered her eyes with her handkerchief.

"Nay, nay, Lizzie," cried the sergeant, "no tears, if you would have me start with a light heart. Come, give Grey a kiss, poor fellow, he has no lass to see him off, although I'll be sworn he'll find one—" 'Where he is going to,' he intended to have said, but that it struck him such a remark would not tend to tranquillize the mind of Lizzie, as she might adopt an impression that he, Sergeant Haverel, might possibly make a similar discovery, therefore he gently let his sentence down with the words "some day."

Lizzie, however, did not supply the sentence as he had surmised, but she complied with his request, and gave Clifton such a really warm hearty kiss that it was not possible for him to respond to it coldly, and he fairly hugged her in his arms and felt the hot tears gush to his eyes. As he released her, squeezing her hands with vigour, he said:

"God bless you, Lizzie; keep your heart like polished steel, as true in temper and as unsullied in brightness; remember the breath of shame will encrust it with a rust nothing will ever remove. Good bye, God bless you!"

Lizzie wrung his hands, but could only murmur "God bless you!"

The colonel advanced up the platform at this moment, and as he passed he said, with a smile on his kind face, "Now, sergeant, take your farewell kiss, and tell off your men into the carriages."

Haverel touched his forehead, and then caught Lizzie in his arms and strained her to his breast, imprinted a long and passionate kiss upon her lips, muttered a few inaudible words, once more kissed her lips, her hands — gave her one more convulsive embrace, one hoarsely uttered good bye, and he tore himself away, coughing to clear his throat; the next instant he was busy in obeying the command he had just received, while Lizzie fell back fainting against a pillar. It was only by such an exertion of the will over physical weakness as, in some remarkable instances, will control it, that she preserved herself from falling lifeless flat upon the platform. The struggle was severe, but she so far mastered the deadly tendency to swoon as to keep herself conscious of what was taking place, and to follow the movements of Haverel with burning eyes, feeling as if spell bound in some horrible dream.

At length the men were all placed in the carriages, the doors were all fastened, the flags floated idly but proudly in the cool and gentle breeze, which penetrated the space of the extensive shed slightly though gratefully to the sense of the inurned; the band, which had on entering the terminus played the national anthem amid the applauding voices of the loyal thousands assembled, now struck up the beautiful Irish air of the "Girl I left behind me," lively and spirit-stirring enough it seemed, but as

"The sincerest laughter with some pain is fraught."

so the mournful associations to which the tune gave rise seemed to make the sprightliness of the air a mockery. The station-master waved the signal for departure, the attentive engine-driver turned the scalding vapour into the steam whistle, which blew loud and shrill, and smote the hearts of many of those left

behind with the chill horror of a death note; the train commenced its slow gliding movement, a wild, long, tremendous cheer burst from the lips of those moving away and those remaining. Again and again was that stentorian cheer repeated and re-echoed, drowning the shrieks, the sobs, the wailing of those unhappy females who were left a legacy to their countrymen, and who felt they had spoken the last words and taken their final farewell of the beings dearest to their hearts. The train soon obtained accelerated motion, and was quickly lost to sight, but as it slowly emerged from beneath the shed there might have been seen from the pillar on the platform and the window of the railway-carriage handkerchiefs wafted to and fro by the hands of two sobbing women, whose eyes were so blinded by scalding tears as to prevent their perceiving that both were gazed upon to the last by those for whom they waved their tribute of farewell in the air.

Clifton Grey, the friendless, homeless outcast, thus, in spite of human probabilities, in opposition to his most certain calculations, found that his departure from the scenes of his youth was attended by a farewell kiss imprinted on his burning lips, and by the bitter tears of one who, in regretting his absence, shudderingly hesitated to look into the future. This consideration was, indeed, a balm to his desolate heart, and a proof how vain and profitless it is to shape out coming events, which results shew to be but falsifications, and the inscrutable decrees of the Almighty Disposer of events.

CHAPTER X.

"Existence may be borne, and the deep root
Of life and sufferance make its firm abode
In bare and desolated bosoms."

BYRON.

"Who loves raves—'tis youth's frenzy—but the cure
Is bitterer still."

IBID.

"He stood: some dread was on his face;
Soon Hatred settled in its place:
It rose not with the reddening flush
Of transient Anger's hasty blush,
But pale as marble o'er the tomb,
Whose ghastly whiteness aids its gloom.
His brow was bent, his eye was glazed;
He raised his arm, and fiercely raised,
And sternly shook his hand on high."

IBID.

THE PAST. THE ENCOUNTER IN THE WOOD. THE LAWYER AND THE FUTURE.

THE charges of smuggling and otherwise defrauding the Queen's revenue, brought against W. Waters and Son, although favoured by many strongly suspicious circumstances, failed of proof upon the trial. A sharp lawyer and a keen quick-witted counsel, unscrupulous in the use of his prerogative, upset the case for the Crown, and the pair were acquitted; not without being informed by the judge that they had had a very lucky escape, and he warned them to be more careful in future, as a similar piece of fortune might not attend an attempt to cheat the excise laws. Old Waters grinned as he listened to the exhortation, and with flushed cheeks quitted the bar, bowing humbly to the judge and the jury as he retired, on its being announced to him that he was no longer in custody, and might go. His son displayed no such humility; but giving a stern glance of defiance at the ministers of the law, and one of malevolence at the principal witness for the crown, whom he saw in the body of the court, he strode out with the air of one who had been wronged and was bent upon having his revenge.

Shortly after this the "Bonny Bark" once more displayed its quiet allurements to the public, and presented an aspect so precisely like what it had formerly exhibited, that any one who knew the place and had been absent for a short term would never have imagined events so important to the landlord and to the fate of the establishment had taken place in the interval.

There was one exception—and not a trivial one either, if the opinions of two persons were to be consulted—Myra Aston was not there. Old Waters, upon his release from the fangs of the law, had waited upon Mrs. Aston, and having acquainted her with his "honourable" acquittal, requested her to permit Myra to return to his house, as his "Nell" had not been able to get away from the friends with whom she was staying, and he did not expect her back for a week or two at least. Mrs. Aston at once firmly declined.

In former years, at the time of her marriage, Waters and his wife had proved of important service to her. She had married far above her station, but her husband was a younger son, and in all such cases to wed beneath the dignity or position of the family in violation of the wishes of its head, was tantamount to being discarded a beggar. The condition of Franklyn Aston was not different to others of his class, his immunity from human affection no greater. Myra's mother, when a girl, was exceedingly beautiful, at least in the eyes of Franklyn Aston, and as his mind was of an order far too high to permit him to sacrifice the woman of his affection to his love, he married her. Information of this attachment reached his family too late to prevent the union, with which, however, they were unacquainted; but having a full comprehension of the honourable sentiments which influenced the actions of Franklyn Aston, they feared such a catastrophe. His father, possessed of influence with the government of the day, obtained an appointment for him at Sierra Leone, "the grave of the Englishman," which admitted of no delay in departure if accepted. And this was communicated to him at a moment when resistance

was hopeless, for he was in delicate health and entirely dependent upon his father. At first the intelligence of his appointment fell upon him like a crash of thunder, and for a time he was utterly prostrated; he was not only married but he had an infant female child, the little Myra, and what step to take he was utterly at a loss to conceive. To leave his young and pretty wife alone with his tender infant to fight the hard world's battle, he would not; to declare his marriage and defy the anger of his family was a step which would ensure destruction. In this dilemma he took counsel of a college friend, who had embraced the profession of the law. He advised that the child should be left in England with foster-parents; that Mrs. Aston should go out to Sierra Leone in the same ship with her husband as a passenger, and under an assumed name. Franklyn would, on his arrival, be enabled to provide for the emergencies of the situation as he best could, and probably without difficulty, as he was removed from the control of his family, would be placed in a situation of comparative independence, and they could send for the child as soon as it had age and strength enough to bear the voyage. It was a dreadful alternative, but it was the only scheme that presented a favourable prospect of realisation, so as to secure the society of this young couple to each other, and it was determined on and put into execution.

Acquainted with Waters and his wife from living in the same vicinity, a proposition was made by Mrs. Aston to Mrs. Waters to take charge of the little Myra, and as she had recently presented her husband with a girl, named Ellen, afterwards exclusively known as "Our Nell," she offered no objection to the proposition, and an arrangement was effected, under which Mrs. Waters promised to act as a mother to the child for certain considerations, pecuniary and otherwise. Franklyn Aston and his wife sailed to their destination, and remained there for some years in comparative happiness, remitting with the utmost regularity the sums agreed upon to Waters, and learning with gratification of the healthy progress of their darling. At length news reached Franklyn Aston of the death of his father, who had never been made acquainted with his marriage, and he was summoned home after an absence of ten years, to hear of something greatly to his advantage.

His father had, in reward for what he termed his obedience in quitting England at his wish, secured to him an annuity, over which he gave him the entire control to leave to whom he pleased at his death; it was not large in amount, but it was sufficient to keep the wolf from the door. This he settled at once on his wife; and fortunate it was for her that he did so, for on their passage home he died, and was buried in a deep sea grave.

On reaching England Mrs. Aston, for the sake of her child more than herself, through a friend all unskilled in such an undertaking, made a represen-

SERJEANT HAVEREL OBTAINS HIS FULL RANK.—CLIFTON GREY COUNTS ONE FRIEND IN THE SERVICE.

tation of her connection with her husband's family, to them, but her claim was scouted with scorn and insult. Secured from want or penury by the sum her husband had settled upon her, she retired to Arundel; she did not persist in her demand to be recognised, but having gained possession of her daughter, a beautiful but decidedly rustic girl of ten years old, she determined to mix no more in the world beyond the secluded circle into which she had settled down, but devote herself to the cultivation of her daughter's intellect, for which office her husband had fitted her in sharing with her during their long sojourn at Sierra Leone his scholarly acquirements, so that she might at least have an education in some degree worthy of the position her father's family occupied.

In the course of time Mrs. Waters died. Myra had been reared by her in a homely manner, but with the most affectionate kindness; she therefore loved her fondly, and although the arrival and the unwearying tenderness of a maternal parent had awakened in her all those filial affections which had lain dormant during their separation, they did not weaken her attachment to her foster mother. Nor did she forget or desert the playmate of her childhood, Nelly Waters, who had all the good qualities of her mother, and none of the bad ones of her father or brother; they were much together, and such advantages of education as Myra could convey, or the other desired to attain, she communicated to her. Each visited the other, Mrs. Aston having too warm a recollection of the faithfulness with which Mrs. Waters had executed the trust reposed in her to desire to curb or contract the intimacy between the two girls, especially as Nelly had neither vices of manner nor morals. When Mrs. Waters died, the frequency of their interviews abated, not because aught had arisen on such an event to occasion a coolness, but that Nelly's duties in the household had increased twenty-fold; indeed she had taken her poor mother's place, while Myra's increasing studies left her much less time to devote to friendship.

When some family affairs called Nelly to the residence of a branch of the family in another part of the country to transact some business to which her father was unequal, she had with much earnestness begged of Mrs. Aston to permit Myra to take her place during her absence; she complied with the request, and hence the meeting between Myra and Clifton. The circumstances which had attended that transaction had resulted in a manner by no means agreeable either as regarded the charge brought against Waters, of which Mrs. Aston did not for a moment entertain a doubt he was guilty, or in the impression she entertained, that Myra had not met Clifton without danger to the future serenity of her mind. When, therefore, Old Waters asked her to permit Myra to again return to his house during the continued absence of his daughter, she gently but firmly declined; declined also to give reasons for her resolve.

The old man spoke bitterly. He challenged her with permitting her scruples to be affected by the base and lying charges made against him by Ben Hartley; he taunted her with being 'afear'd' of people's opinions against her own convictions; he reproached her with forgetting the years of care and attention paid by him and his wife to her child, when for such conduct no amount of gold could equal its value; he twitted her with being a friend in fine weather, but a lee-shore in foul. All in vain; she listened to him, replied to his reproaches, and persevered in her resolve; and so he flung himself off to obtain the services of one Sal Chinnick, "who'd sarve his turn well enough, although his Nell had a mortal dislike to her, but he couldn't help that, and he didn't care one d——n what became of him an' the hull lot; for what was the odds if liars was to be believed and rewarded, and folks were to forget services and grow so mighty grand, they didn't know themselves even if they stared in the looking glass? What did it signify?—let it all go to Davy Jones for what he keered."

Mrs. Aston acquiesced, and, worked up to a culminating point of savage and reckless resolution, Waters flung himself from her presence to execute that mission to Miss Sarah Chinnick, which was to elevate her into the position of mistress of his public mansion, until the return home of his daughter Nell. Now, Miss Chinnick was certainly no favourite with Nelly Waters; indeed, she held a very low place in her estimation, and there was a strong probability, that, upon her return home, as soon as she found who had been installed queen of the feast, she would neither feel overpowered with gratitude for the services that might have been rendered by her, nor loud in her congratulations to her father for the selection he had made in the substitute for Myra. It was by no means an impossible contingency that the advent of Ellen Waters would be followed by a prompt disappearance of Sal Chinnick, and an estimate of character presented to Waters pater, which would afford him more food for reflection than self-gratulation. He felt this; he knew it; he had a sense of the impropriety of which he was about to be guilty. But what then? Mrs. Aston, by her refusal to again permit her daughter to become the locum tenens of Ellen Waters, roused his ire. He knew she would feel vexed and angry by his choice of Sal Chinnick, the reputation of that damsel being more extensively known than respected; but for the immediate consequences of his rash step, he nothing "keered;" it was enough for him that Sal Chinnock would succeed Myra Aston, to the infinite chagrin of Mrs. Aston, because comparisons might be raised which would make Myra's occupation of the same post a town talk. He calculated on avenging himself for the refusal of his request, by inflicting a wound on Mrs. Aston's pride; so, leaving the house, he hastened to perform his purpose, with a speed which seemed to fear some sudden interference from some quarter in which it might be least expected. His anticipations were not altogether remote from realization. Miss Chinnick was, however, duly installed into the Bonny Bark as the *pro tem.* mistress; but if, on her elevation, she increased the trade of the establishment, it was very certain that she did not improve its character, and therefore a comparison between her and Myra began to be discussed in Arundel, and people wondered how Mrs. Aston could ever have permitted her pretty, lady-like daughter to have filled the same office. Thus far W. Waters had his revenge, for he succeeded, as he calculated, in making, in some degree, Myra a town talk.

It was not this event which had been the occasion of the sudden departure of Mrs. Aston and her daughter from Arundel, without leaving even with a neighbour an address to which communications intended for them could reach them.

Neither was it because the gentle Myra was subjected to annoyance from the younger Waters, yet more vexatious than that which her mother had experienced at the hands of the old smuggler, even though that annoyance came at a moment when she was least prepared for it, when it was most unexpected, and could not have been less desired.

It was not unnatural, after the departure of Clifton, having discovered that he was dearer to her than she even liked to acknowledge to herself, that Myra should find a pleasure in wandering among the old trees, in the spot where he had disclosed to her his position, and announced to her his future intentions; where, indeed, she first awakened to a sense that her peace of mind was as much dependent upon the predilections, the welfare, and the happiness of another, as upon her own. Frequent as had been her visits to that now, to her, memorable locality, previous to the event above mentioned, they were constant now. It was only when a flooding rain rendered walking, at least for the purposes of healthful recreation, impossible, that she did not retrace the steps they had together taken previous to his leaving her. It was seldom that she had a companion in these walks; the presence of one was irksome to her, for it interfered with thoughts devoted to him alone. Of those who had attempted to share her lonely walks, Ellen Fairfax was almost the only one who succeeded; and she had obtained the ascendancy because she found an inexhaustible theme in Clifton Grey's conduct in saving Charley—her Charley—from the consequences of his rash act, and Myra a never-tiring pleasure in listening to the praises of one of whom she thought so highly. Sometimes Charley Rowe joined them—the subject was still the same—and he commended himself to the favour of both girls by the warm and grateful terms in which he spoke of the benefit he had received at Clifton's hands, and his hope that an opportunity would yet arise, which would enable him to show his appreciation of it.

When Charley sought the society of Ellen, and he learned that she had gone for a stroll with Myra, he knew where to look for them both, and find them.

One morning Myra took her accustomed walk, but alone. She was somewhat depressed in spirits, for she had expected ere this to have received a letter from Clifton. Two months had elapsed, but there had been no communication from him, and silence was unfavourable to her wishes in his favour. She felt convinced that he was not one who would promise earnestly, and yet lightly forfeit his pledged word; she could only, therefore, surmise that his advancement had not been what he expected, and so, in deep disappointment, he had abstained from writing to her. Two months was not much, it was true, but yet, in her estimation, it was quite—quite long enough for any one to entertain a favourable opinion of Clifton, if they were not quite captivated with him; and, as she imagined that promotion would follow liking as a natural consequence, she could hardly bring herself to believe that he was not on the high road to become at least a captain. She forgot that the authorities did not see with her eyes, or that, under the old system, interest wholly superseded merit; she thought only of his handsome exterior, and, better far, his fine manly heart, and his true perception of the noble and the good. She was sure that his pain at not having pleasing news to communicate equalled her disappointment at not hearing from him, but she thought that it was a pity that any circumstances should chain him to a silence as unpleasant to him as it was certainly distressing to her.

Occupied with such thoughts, and conning over the best means of finding out the depôt at which Clifton was stationed, and of inducing her mother to write him a few lines of inquiry respecting his progress, which must provoke a reply, she became suddenly conscious of the presence of some one in the lone place through which she was strolling beside herself; nay, that whoever it was, deliberately stood in her path, as if to stay her further progress. She looked up—it was Saul Waters.

She did not like Saul Waters; she never had, even though she had been brought up with him from childhood until she was in her eleventh year; he had always been a brutal boy, rough in his manners and cruel in his disposition. Mostly sullen, he yet had been kind to her, but sometimes ferocious. To his sister Nelly he had been the same, save that in his kindness there was a difference: to the latter it was circumscribed without exception; to Myra, when displayed, it was sometimes profuse and extravagant. To Nelly his conduct bore a species of uniformity; to Myra he was impulsive. She had grown to fear him when she was living beneath his father's roof as his foster-sister; she had subsequently added an unconquerable aversion to this fear; and upon the occasion of her last visit to the Bonny Bark, when she first met Clifton Grey, that dislike, although she saw but little of him, was confirmed. His conduct to her then had been unpleasing, because it was mixed up with that familiarity which, to a modest female, is insult, and he would have been absolutely rude but for the intervention of his father, who emphatically assured him "he would cut him in half if he tried that game on again." Then he became as obsequious as he had been insolent, and pestered her with attentions and allusions to her pretty features, no less offensive than his former roughness. Her visit had been brought to an abrupt termination, and one of its most pleasing features was that which had liberated her from her daily proximity to this young man. Just now, and in this place, she could not help a shudder as she perceived who intercepted her: with a start of surprise, she exclaimed:

"Saul!"

"That's me," he exclaimed, with a short laugh, while there was a "frowning devil" in his eye. He held out his hand, but she did not take it. He bit his lip, and bent a fierce look upon her.

"What!" he exclaimed, "won't you shake hands with me, Myra? Why should you be ill friends with me because the old man's quarrelled with your mother?"

"I am ill friends with you for no such reason," she replied, coldly.

"It ain't about Sal Chinnick, sure-ly?"

She made him no reply; the supposition was too absurd.

"You know," said he, deprecatingly, induced by her silence to speak, "that I had no hand in her coming to our house. It was all the old man's doing; besides, as you know, Myra, she's not the girl that will do for me, so you needn't take on about her."

Take on about her!

Myra replied not; she scarcely heard him, and as little heeded. She only thought how she could get back quickest to a frequented place, and so home. He regarded her almost fiercely—for in her silence, and her averted head, he could decipher no flattering evidence of her good opinion of him.

"What, sulky still!" he exclaimed. "Come, Myra, I have given you no cause to be sulky with me, and I won't leave you or let you go till you tell me we are friends."

He attempted to lay his hand upon her shoulder as he spoke, but she shrank from him. However, she did not attempt to retire, but, looking him firmly in the face, she said:

"You cannot, nor ought you to forget, Saul, that if I entertain an unfriendly feeling towards you, you have yourself been the occasion of it, nor have you acted in any way calculated to remove it; any difference that may exist between our parents has had no influence upon me, but if you wish to regain my good opinion, it must be by conduct very different to the annoyance to which you subjected me while beneath your father's

roof, at a time, too, when I was there to do him service."

"Bah!" he cried, gloomily, "don't bring that up again;" and then added, with some earnestness of manner, "You know, Myra, I am fond of you; I like you better than any girl in the county;—I've told you so afore; and if, when we were brought up together, boy and girl, I didn't treat you so kindly as I ought to ha' done, it was because I was a fool, and didn't know the truth of the matter; for, by the Lord, if I hadn't a' cared for you, I'd never taken the trouble to quarrel with you—"

"I've no desire to listen to, nor share in, this kind of conversation," interrupted Myra; "I am desirous of returning home, and—"

"Not yet—no! You don't go until I've spoken out what I have been wanting to say for a long time; this is a good chance, and I won't lose it."

"You will not attempt to detain me by force, Saul!" she exclaimed, with alarm.

"Not if you'll stand quietly still and listen; but you know me, Myra, and when I say you shall listen to me, you will think it, perhaps, the wisest plan not to thwart me."

Myra did know him, and, dreading some violent outbreak of his terrible temper, felt that, under all circumstances, it would be the most advisable course to follow his counsel. She, therefore, remained still, with her eyes bent upon the grass, and her lips compressed, as though she feared trusting herself with the utterance of a single word. He saw quick enough that his acknowledgment of the tenderness he entertained for her had awakened no corresponding feeling in her heart; but his was not a nature to be deterred by such a discovery, and he would persevere in the prosecution of his suit, even if he had to recommend its reception by round oaths, and enforce its adoption by hard blows. He was thoroughly a ruffian, and even the supremacy of the tender passion made him neither gentler in his manner nor kinder in disposition. He was bent now on making a revelation of his love for Myra to her, without troubling himself to think or care much whether she would actually respond to it or not; he reflected only that, if he knew himself with any degree of correctness, it would be her most prudent course to accept his attention, and act as if she was passionately attached to him.

As we have said, she remained still, dreading to listen, but unable to see any escape from a position in many respects both painful and distressing to her, and he prepared himself to make a plain confession, leaving to her what course she would pursue, and—to take the consequences.

"Look here, Myra," he commenced, having cleared his voice, "I've told you I'm fond of you,—I repeat it : there is no girl in this county—nay, nor in the wide world beyond the seas—whose love and license I'd care half so much for as one of your pretty smiles. I didn't know this when I was a boy, when I had a real fine chance to make you fond of me, but I know it now, and if you'll let me, I'll make up for lost time. My heart's yours; I'll share with you all I have, and I'll make you my wife. Not such a bad offer, Myra, all things considered; the old man has plenty of money, and all he has 'll be mine—you may be sure o' that, you may be right sure o' that. I'm going to France for a trip in a night or two, and I'll bring you home some mortal pretty things, and I'll do for you or get for you anything you want. You're the girl of my heart, and woe to him as says a word to you, or looks at you, or talks of you in a way I don't like; if he does, he may say his prayers, for I'll have no mercy upon him. Come, Myra, what do you say, will you walk with me?"

Myra returned him no answer. His countenance fell, his frowning eyebrows nearly rested upon his cheekbones, but his gleaming eyeballs glaring upon the delicate girl were plainly visible; he bit his nether lip as though he would sunder the soft flesh, and then, after waiting silently for a minute or so, he exclaimed, harshly:

"Why don't you speak?—ain't I worth talking to? I've asked you a civil question, don't you mean to give me a civil answer?"

Myra turned her full clear eyes upon him.

"I am not free to speak what I feel here," she said, in subdued tones.

He laughed.

"Why not?" he asked.

"There needs no explanation," she returned, reproachfully; "you cannot fail to know. Ask your questions in the presence of my mother; I will then answer them unreservedly."

He uttered a bitter laugh.

"What!" he cried, "ask you to walk with me before your mother, after her row with my old man about Sal Chinnick! No, I ain't such a fool, I hope. Besides, what has she got to do with it? I ask you if you'll have me, not her. If you said yes, who'd care, do you think, if she said no? and if you said no, where would be the good of her saying yes? Hang your mother! I want nowt to do with her; I want you to say yes or no to my offer. It ain't every girl as can get such a chance, I can tell you; there's three or four farmer's daughters, not many miles from this, would jump at it, and don't you make a fool of yourself and throw it away."

Saul exhibited here, by such talk, a miserable knowledge of the way to win a lady's assent to his suit, unless, indeed, she was on the verge of desperate old-maidism. Upon Myra the effect was to increase the antipathy she already felt for him, and to add to it the most profound contempt; it seemed, also, to restore her courage, for, with a clearness of tone, and with an emphasis which seemed rather to surprise him, she said:

"You would have the answer to your proffer, from my own heart now, without hesitation or equivocation?"

"Aye, lass, as you really mean it."

"Then to your request I say, at once and for all, no; I will not accept your offer, and neither promises nor persecution can ever induce me to alter this intention; therefore abandon any impression that I am not in earnest, or that I may be induced to change my mind. Select of those you have mentioned, the maiden you most prefer, and be happy with her; to me, or with me, you can never be other than you have been. You are answered, Saul, and now let me pass."

"Not yet. You won't have me, eh?"

"I have given you my answer. Do not seek to detain me further. I will not remain here longer."

"But you must—ay, girl, must; if I knock you senseless to the earth, you shall stop till you've heard. So you hate me?"

Myra's upper lip curled contemptuously. Hate him! he was not worthy such a feeling, at least in her estimation. His face grew livid, as he noted the scornful expression of her pretty mouth.

"Well," he added, "You despise me. Its all the same to me; and for that matter, it will be to you. I know why you scorn me, and look down upon me now. Its because of that young fellow that came to our house and then made himself so mighty agreeable at yours. You know who I mean—the *gentleman* who's gone for a common soldier. Ah! you need'nt turn so red; I know all about it, though you fancy you kept it so snug. And to be so upstart and proud about him too—Ha! ha! a common soldier! he must ha' been a mighty rogue. Gentlemen don't turn common soldiers unless it's to escape Botany Bay."

"Let me pass."

"You must stay here until I've done. I'm not good enough for you, eh? I'm to be scouted for a common soldier, a shilling a day, and dear at that. A fine gentleman truly! but then he was pretty and genteel, and I dare say he hugged you tenderly, and kissed you nicely."

"You are an unmanly ruffian, to dare thus to speak to me," cried Myra, the tears springing into her flashing eyes. "I will not be stayed to hear such cruel insults."

She made a spring, and attempted to dart past him, but he was too quick for her, and caught her in his arms; she struggled with her utmost strength to get free, but his power far surpassed hers, and the attempt to escape was hopeless.

"You shall not go," he cried, with a fierce oath, "until I choose to let you. You'd best be quiet, you'll only hurt yourself in trying to get away."

She again made a desperate exertion to liberate herself, but in vain; breathless and exhausted, she ceased her efforts, and bursting into tears, exclaimed:

"You will have occasion to repent this treatment to me."

"Not I," he replied with a chuckle, holding her as if she were in a smith's vice: "I told you I've a good deal to say to you, and I won't let you go till you've heard it all. I want to speak about your gentleman sweetheart, and—who knows—perhaps to have a kiss or two, as well as him—only his were given and mine will be taken; but then, stolen fruit is always the sweetest. Myra," he added, addressing the half-fainting girl with deliberate emphasis, "you know my temper; you know I won't be thwarted; and if you persist in flouting and scorning me, it will be the worst whim you ever took into your head in your life—you know it—a dark deed won't stop me. I love you; my blood leaps and boils in my veins when I think of you; and mine you shall be, cost what it may—ah, its no use cowering and shrinking. I've sworn it, and I am a likely fellow to keep my oath when it is taken to gratify my own pleasure. D'ye heed me; you'd best be wise in time; you'll be happier, I can promise you, by having me, than spurning me. Come, forget what you've said, and promise me to think better of it. Your soldier has gone away, and he'll think no more of you; I'll make you as happy as the day's long. Look up, Myra, gives us a kiss, and make a bargain of it."

He tried to press his lips to hers as he spoke, but she dashed her hand in his face, and struggled wildly; she uttered a succession of wild and terrified screams; but the ruffian, growing excited, heeded them not, and persisted in his efforts to pollute her lips with his hot sensual kisses. For some time she successfully resisted him, but his blood growing heated, the devil became paramount within him, and there was every prospect that he would recklessly and villanously proceed to the very worst lengths, under the insane idea that such atrocity would compel her to become his in despite of her predilections for another person. In the frenzy of despair she exerted a strength which for a time kept him at bay; but she was fast losing power to continue the struggle, and it was with a species of maddened horror she grew conscious of her increasing inability to prevent herself becoming a prey to the lawless brutality of the abhorred scoundrel, who held her with a giant's grip. In the intensity of her terror she shrieked frantically, and called for help in piercing accents. A dreadful faintness seemed creeping over her, numbing and paralysing her limbs; desperately she strove against it, for she knew if it obtained the mastery over her faculties, that she would be utterly in the power of the merciless wretch from whose fatal embrace she was employing her utmost strength to liberate herself. He all this time endeavoured to force his hand over her mouth to stifle her cries, and fling her to the earth.

It was at the very moment when the power to accomplish this, so far as the struggling maiden was concerned, was his own, that Heaven interposed.

There arose in the immediate vicinity a sudden and violent crashing of boughs, and the hissing rattle of roughly displaced leaves. Through the impeding underwood, just behind where Myra and Saul were contending in a worse than death-struggle, a figure forced its way with impetuous speed; it was that of a young man, whose indignant features at once betrayed, as he leaped into the copse, his determination to attempt the succour of the oppressed. With a firm grip he seized the young smuggler by the neckcloth at the back of his throat, fastened with his other hand upon his right wrist, drew the arm suddenly straight out and gave it a wrench, which made the ruffian release his hold of Myra and give a howl of pain. They struggled tremendously for a minute, but it was in vain; Saul was pinned as if in a vice; his efforts to get free seemed to promise no result but a dislocated arm; he therefore became at once quiescent. With a cry of joy Myra darted from the spot, and would, upon the impulse, have fled without even expressing the intense gratitude she felt towards her preserver, for her horror at her situation had been so overwhelming, and her joy at her deliverance so great, that save a hearty thanksgiving to heaven, she had no other thought than to be far away from the dreadful scene, nestling in her mother's arms. But her flying footsteps were arrested by the sound of the voice of him who had saved her calling her by name. She turned to look upon his face, it was Charley Rowe.

She uttered an exclamation of gratified surprise and thankfulness for his timely interposition, while he, in terms of no measured astonishment, referred to the struggle which he had so fortunately interrupted.

"Why, Myra Aston," he exclaimed, "how came you to be thus subjected to the unmanly roughness of Saul Waters? I thought he was your foster brother, and if so, you, at least, should be safe from his ruffianly behaviour."

Another sharp struggle ensued this speech. Saul Waters uttered some desperate threats against the personal safety of Charley Rowe, but he was compelled once more to succumb, after discovering that the only effect of his struggling was to inflict torture upon himself. He could not shake off the firm grip Charley Rowe had obtained of his wrist, nor could he prevent the twisting which the latter slowly applied to his arm, and which promised, if continued, to wrench his limb from the socket at the shoulder. Once more he became quiet, and enabled Myra Aston to say, as she supported herself with one hand resting upon the trunk of a tall beech.

"Saul Waters can best explain the reason of his wicked conduct. He has wronged me deeply, and insulted me grossly. I never gave him cause. I am too exhausted, too ill to say more now, but there will come a time for reparation; he may look forward to it

—and fear it. I would return home, I have strength enough, I hope, to reach there; but I entreat you to detain him until you think I have gained a spot sufficiently near the town that he will not dare attempt a repetition of his horrible brutality to me."

"Never fear," cried Charley Rowe, renewing the firmness of his grip of his prisoner. "If he gets away from me until I am sure you are safe and sound at home, put me down for a paltry numbskull, whose acquaintance it is better to cut than to keep. Hie away with you, Myra. I have no doubt you will meet with Ellen on your way home. She is on the look out for you, and I, being on the look out for her, arrived here at a lucky moment."

Myra shuddered, and responded.

"Fortunate indeed! for you saved me from degradation, and from—death."

Saul Waters scowled at her beneath his black and bushy eyebrows, as she emphatically enunciated the last word, but she did not look towards him. Essaying a faint and grateful smile, with pallid face and tottering steps she quitted the copse, and Saul Waters and Charley Rowe were left alone. As her form was lost to sight, the former burst into a coarse laugh, and said:

"Let go, Charley, the game's over. I shan't go after her."

"No," said Charley coolly, "I'll take damned good care you don't have a chance."

"Come, don't be a fool—let go I say."

"Not if I know it."

"You won't?"

"No?"

"What d'ye mean? Do you suppose, just because I had a spree with Myra, I meant her any harm. Bah! aint she my foster sister. I was only having a talk with her, and she's such a namby pamby fool, she squirled out directly I touched, her—that's all."

"And enough too. You ought to have known better: you are big enough, and for that matter, ugly enough."

"Take your hands off me."

"I shan't."

"Charley Rowe, you know me. I've licked you many times."

"When we were boys, and you were twice my size. We are a little better match now, Saul: it won't be quite so easy to lick me now."

"Won't it? Off with your hands, and I'll show you."

"No! I promised not to let you go for some little time yet, and I'll keep my word."

"If I get loose, I'll beat your brains out." Saul coupled with this speech a tremendous oath. Charley Rowe uttered a contemptuous laugh.

"You won't frighten me by bounce," he exclaimed. Saul gave a sudden and infuriated bound, as though to jerk himself from the strong grasp of Charley Rowe, but although he employed his best strength and sub-

mitted to the agony of having his arm twisted round, until the torture of the rack could not possibly exceed it, he found it impossible to get free. He gnashed his teeth, and the veins of his forehead swelled like cords; he foamed at the mouth with a paroxysm of passion frightful to witness; he hurled the most terrific imprecations at the head of Charley, threatening him at the same time with a sanguinary and terrible retaliation. Charley Rowe was not, however, to be induced to relax his hold, and although it was not a little trying to his muscular powers to maintain it, he held on as a bull dog to the lip of a bull when it has once made its true grip.

At this moment there appeared upon the scene another character. No sooner was the heavy tread of a man heard close to the spot and advancing towards them, than the eyes of both were bent upon the new comer. Saul suddenly uttered a howl of triumph; the stranger was no less a person than the host of the "Bonny Bark," W. Waters, his father.

The grisly old man stared at both with an aspect of undisguised astonishment. He could see that they were engaged in an act of hostility to each other, and though both were young, their struggles wore nothing of the air of boy's play. He saw, too, that his 'boy,' usually in the ascendant in affairs of this kind, had in the present instance caught a Tartar; that Charley Rowe held him securely, and did not exhibit the slightest design of parting with him in a hurry. Somehow he was apprehensive that this condition of things had arisen from no mere brawl. The late arrest upon a charge of smuggling had made him suspicious, and he could not help, on the first glance at the relative positions of the two young men, fearing that Charley Rowe was in some inexplicable manner invested with the powers of a special constable, and had seized his son upon a charge of defrauding the revenue of Her Majesty, a crime of which the old man knew him to have been very recently guilty. As he was rather thickly tarred with the same brush, and as he had not the slightest desire to again test the conveniences of Horsham Jail, he came to the immediate conclusion that under any circumstances, it would be advisable to rescue his son from the clutches of Charley Rowe, and temporize afterwards, if occasion required it.

"What are ye quarreling about, lads?" he exclaimed drawing very close; "Aint ye a couple of fools to be striving and wrastling, instead of being friendly o'er a cup o' ale?"

"I don't know about a couple of fools—I know there's one rogue," exclaimed Charley Rowe, emphatically.

"Beat his brains out, feyther," cried Saul, between his teeth.

"Don't you interfere, old man," cried Charley, sternly; "the best thing you can do is to be quiet."

"Make him let go his hold," ejaculated Saul, grinding his teeth as he uttered the words, so that they were scarcely intelligible. The old man drew nearer to the contending pair.

"Keep off," shouted Charley, excitedly, as he perceived the evident intention of Old Waters to effect, if he could, the liberation of his son. "Keep off, old man! if you attempt to interfere I'll hang on to Saul like a leech, and give him two years in Horsham gaol for what he has done to-day."

This unfortunate threat for his conduct to Myra, so ambiguously expressed, decided Old Waters at once to liberate his son and get him away beyond the reach of the officers; to permit him quietly to be made prisoner for what he had done "to-day" was only to ensure the result he so much dreaded. So he said to Charley, with a forced, but vindictive grin:

"Let un' go—let un' go, I say."

"I will not, until the proper time, if I drag him into Arundel," cried Charley, forcing Saul back as though he would compel him to retire thither.

Old Waters held in his hand an ash stick, surmounted by a formidable knob; he advanced upon Charley, and cried:

"But you must let un' go now. You must let un' go now. I say you must let un' go, and you shall. We'll talk about making matters square bimeby."

While speaking he struck Charley Rowe upon the forearm of the hand which so firmly gripped the wrist of Saul; his blows were delivered with such rapidity and sharp violence, that the hold which Charley had maintained hitherto with success was rendered powerless. Saul, quite alive to the effect of his father's blows, seeing where they were delivered, made a desperate dash to set himself free, and succeeded, for Old Waters had paralysed Charley's strength by his assault with the stick. No sooner did Saul find himself at liberty, than he snatched the ash stick from his father's grasp, before the old man was aware of his intention, and delivered a terrific blow with its knob on the forehead of Charley Rowe, felling him instantaneously to the earth insensible. He would have repeated his murderous blows upon the skull of his prostrate foe, and beaten it to atoms, but that his father sprung upon him, closed with him, and obtained possession of the stick. At the same time, he fastened upon the collar of his son, and dragged him from the spot.

"Art mad, Saul," he cried; "thee's done enough to 'un. Come away, or ye'll make it hanging matter; its bad enough as 'tis; ye'll have to hide away now—"

"Aye, and for something, too; gi' me the stick, old man. I swore I'd beat his brains out, and I will; gi' me the stick, or I'll throttle you."

His father was, however, capable of coping with him, and succeeded in dragging him some distance; and then, partly by threats, and partly by such expostulation as was likely to have most weight with him, he succeeded in inducing him to accompany him on his return to the "Bonny Bark." He had left this esta-blishment in charge of Miss Sarah Chinnick, who had not failed to make the most of her opportunity while the elder Waters had been absent on business, in which his son had materially aided, and for which both had rendered themselves amenable to the Excise laws. W. Waters had not unshakeable faith in the unswerving integrity of Miss Chinnick; and though it had been much to his interest to pay the visit he was now returning from, he felt nevertheless that it was also greatly to his interest to be at home, at least while Sarah Chinnick was in charge of his establishment.

He was much distressed at the incident which had just taken place; he considered it very unfortunate, inasmuch as being unacquainted with the real cause of the struggle between Charley Rowe and his son, he attributed it to some discovery of the transaction in which his son had that morning been engaged; and as he remembered the judge's warning to him, that he would not always be so lucky as he had been upon the occasion of his trial, he was in a sweat of apprehension at the bare thought of falling again into the grip of an officer. He viewed, therefore, the presumed discovery of Saul's smuggling and his capture as unfortunate, and his own share in rescuing him as no less unpleasant; but to have added murder to it would have been a piece of sheer madness; with cunning and caution the present difficulty might be got over—but murder, that was not a thing easily to get away from. He hoped by rapidity of action to escape observation, and, if needful, to establish an *alibi*; he hurried Saul by a retired and slightly circuitous route to Arundel, which he entered by a path whose direction really led to a different locality to that which they had so recently quitted. Having up to this point avoided notice, they entered Arundel boldly, and rather courted observation than shunned it; they yet walked at a quick pace, although they endeavoured to prevent this being apparent. On nearing the house of Mrs. Aston, the quick eye of Saul detected the form of Myra slowly drawing towards it. He smiled bitterly as he noted her tottering gait, and overtaking her as she reached the door of her dwelling, he muttered hissingly in her ear:

"Turn and turn's fair play. I had mine, you've had yours; mine has come again. If you don't see your bully-bo' before the week's out, you can find him where you left him."

He passed on rapidly; Myra's frame was thrilled by a horrified shudder, as she heard these words and recognised the voice; she uttered a faint scream, and fell swooning on the doorstep.

CLIFTON GREY RESCUES LIZZIE HASTINGS FROM INSULT.

CHAPTER XI.

"His was a brow where gold were out of place,
And yet it seemed right worthy of a crown,
(Though he despised such) were it only made
Of iron, or some serviceable stuff
That would have matched his sinewy brown face.
The elder, although such he hardly seemed
(Care makes so little of some five short years)
Had a clear, honest face, whose rough-hewn strength
Was mildened by the scholar's wiser heart
To sober courage, such as best befits
The unruffled temper of a well-taught mind,
Yet so remained that one could plainly guess
The bushed volcano smouldering underneath;
He spoke"——

                  LOWELL.

THE fall of Myra upon the threshold of her home, although it attracted no attention from those within the dwelling, was not unobserved. A gentleman sauntering along the pathway with an enquiring look at the houses on either side had observed the slowly advancing Myra. Unconscious of the semi-swooning state in which she happened to be, he drew towards her with the view of addressing some questions to her. He likewise noted the rapid approach of the two Waters', perceived that the younger bent his head on reaching Myra, as though he whispered an observation in her ear. Some piece of rustic insolence, he thought, intended for low wit. Both men quickly passed him with hasty step, and he turned to gaze after them. When next he directed his eyes towards Myra, whom he expected to be at his elbow, he saw her lying evidently in a fainting fit upon the door step.

With one quick glance to note the route they took, he ran forward and raised the senseless girl in his arms. He knocked loudly at the door, at the foot of which she had sunk, and, when it was opened, he uttered an exclamation of surprise no less emphatic than that which had burst from him on discovering Myra in her swoon, having the moment before seen her walking in apparent health.

Mrs. Aston opened the door to the rapid and violent knocking of the stranger, and uttered a cry of horror on beholding her daughter lifeless in the arms of a stranger. Another minute, and they were within the house, with the outer door closed and Myra lying upon a sofa, her mother applying such remedies as were immediately at hand and experience dictated to restore her to life. In her terror, she had scarcely addressed a word to the gentleman in whose custody she found her senseless daughter, and she certainly had not looked in his face. She was overwhelmed at the condition of her child, and, much as she marvelled as to the cause, she dreaded to ask it of him whom she considered best able to acquaint her with it. Wherefore she dreaded to obtain the knowledge she knew not, nor sought to know; she was almost frantic, for she remembered no occasion upon which Myra had been in a similar state.

Nor was she reassured when returning animation brought with it to the only yet half-conscious girl a violent attack of hysteria.

At first, Myra had, on recovering from her swoon, raised herself up and gazed wildly and shudderingly round her; then she burst into a violent passion of tears that soon became hysterics of a convulsive character, and ceased only when she relapsed into a swoon. The gentleman counselled medical assistance, and proffered his aid to procure it. Mrs. Aston thankfully gave him the name and address of the family medical attendant, and he departed to find and bring him back with him. She had some sense that this gentleman was no stranger to her, that his person and his voice were known to her, but she gave the passing thought no consideration, she was too much absorbed with a sickening horror at the state of her beloved child, and a dim dreadful fear to what it was owing. She had quitted home in her usual health, and if slightly depressed in spirits, still of the same calm equable temperament as she was wont to be, and how had she returned! With a face the hue of death, her hair disturbed, rough, and straggling, so opposite to its usual exquisite smoothness, and her dress disarranged and disordered, and to crown all, in a death-like swoon. What could it all mean! She fell upon her knees by the side of her lifeless daughter, and called upon God not to afflict her with a heavier trial than she had yet known. She could bear contumely and want, she could prepare herself to endure a life of continuous poverty and labour without repining, but she could not prepare herself to hear a recital she feared was waiting to be communicated to her, and which she had an agonized apprehension would scatter to the winds all her anticipations for the future, and crush her heart to powder. She prayed with earnest agony, and the scalding tears which coursed each other down her blanched cheeks seemed by their violence to herald a convulsive fit similar to that which had prostrated Myra, but a rapid knocking at the outer door awoke her to the necessity of controlling her feelings; she arose, and drying her eyes, gave admission to the strange gentleman who previously had arrived with Myra, and was now accompanied by Mrs. Aston's medical attendant, who on a former occasion will be remembered as having restored Senorita Preciosa to health.

He approached Myra, and applied some restoratives to her, which speedily brought her back to life, and directed that she should immediately be placed in bed.

"She has undergone some extraordinary and unwonted excitement," he observed, "both mental and bodily, and she should be kept perfectly quiet for some days. You must not be surprised, Mrs. Aston, if she is attacked slightly with delirium, but be under no alarm, for although the present affair is somewhat violent, there are no dangerous symptoms. Are you acquainted with the causes which have thrown her into this condition?"

"No—no. I have not the faintest conception, and, God help me! I fear to enquire."

"Take my advice, Mrs. Aston; do not seek to ascertain it just yet; let her communicate it of her own accord. By seeking too soon to know the occasion of her excitement you will only throw her back."

Mrs. Aston assured him of her compliance with his directions, and the doctor departed, promising to send something to allay the mental excitement Myra suffered under. When he had disappeared, the stranger whose assistance in this emergency had been so valuable, said to Mrs. Aston.

"It is somewhat strange, madam, that I was in search of you, when fate led me to the spot where I discovered your daughter senseless. This is no moment for explanations, but it is important that I should have an interview with you, to talk over matters of the greatest moment to you and to your daughter. I will defer this for a day or two; but in the meantime I trust you will permit me to make enquiries to-morrow after the young lady's health."

Mrs. Aston's heart was too full to make him any reply; she only bowed her head acquiescently, and he quitted the house; a vague sense that she had seen him somewhere again passed through her brain, but she dismissed it, and proceeded to fulfil the directions of the doctor. With aid she placed Myra in her bed, and watched with weeping eyes through the long night the successive paroxysms of delirium, not of a violent but rather of a wailing character, which Myra suffered, but failed to extract from her incoherencies any clue to the event which had brought her to this pass. Now and then Myra cast her eyes shudderingly round the apartment, as if in fear to behold some dreaded being; and twice or thrice she struggled with an expression of loathing horror to remove some imaginary hands from her waist and shoulders, but all that was really intelligible referred to Clifton Grey and his unfulfilled promise to write to her; this, she murmured, made her spirit very weary and her heart heavy and sad; the burden of her complainings during the slowly-moving, dreary night was, "Why do you not write to me, Clifton; only one little line to say I am not forgotten. I ask of you but one little line, and you will not write it." And she moaned so sorrowfully and so sadly her mother's heart ached as she listened—ached not alone at the mournful wailings, but at what they disclosed. She gathered but too surely that her darling child had given her first and passionate love to him with whom they had had but such short acquaintance, and whose prospects were in no respect such as promised happiness to the attachment it was plain Myra had conceived for him; for what was he but a common soldier, by his own account without an acknowledged or known relative. Of what would his future be formed? The probabilities, under the most favourable prognostications, were hard service for some years, if he escaped death by bullet, weapon, or disease,

and possibly a sergeant's stripes; according to the ordinary expectations he might toil on upon his scanty pay without rising, or fall in the first field, or worse, be fearfully mutilated and return to England unable to earn a livelihood and drag out a miserable existence upon his meagre pension. Such was the picture of Clifton's future, which Mrs. Aston sketched out; and was this a fate for Myra to ally herself to and share? She could not endure to even believe it could be realized. Clifton Grey was in appearance gentlemanly, nay, an elegant young man; he was handsome even to a fault—just the clear open manly face a woman could love with her whole soul. All that was true; but coupled with it was a position, in which griping want must be a constant presence; nay, he could have no home to offer his wife if he married while in service; less than a home, if discharged from wounds or incapacity longer to serve: therefore, Mrs. Aston found it impossible to contemplate an alliance between them without a shudder. There was a prospect of avoiding it, she could see that; Clifton had joined a regiment ordered for active service, of that she had no doubt, for she remembered well what he had said on parting and she had no difficulty in imagining that he would be engaged in the war on the eve of taking place between this country and Russia. She was sufficiently well acquainted with the ordinary chances of such a position not to comprehend that they were decidedly against his return. He was ardent, new to the battle-field, hopeful of promotion, and would court danger to obtain distinction. Such men, but too frequently, were the first to fall in the deadly strife, and she might spare herself, she believed, the pain of contemplating an union between Myra and him, for it was an event which the ordinary course of circumstances rendered improbable; but Myra had given her heart to him, and her mother could but too well foresee that, her peace of mind was so inwoven with that gift, she would know no happiness unshared with him. This, as we have said, was her first and passionate love; her mother, acquainted with the recesses of her truthful, faithful nature, knew but too well, that to her applied the lines of the poet:

"Man's love is of man's life a thing apart,
'Tis woman's whole existence."

She believed that Myra was unconscious of the extent of her liking for Clifton, and it was not her intention, in any degree, to assist to enlighten her; but she had not the faintest hope that it would remain undeveloped, more than it had been, or, that the first time occasion called upon her to make a preference, she would fail to elect Clifton at once to the empire of her heart, or glory in investing him with the treasure.

It was a sad, and night to Mrs. Aston, and when she saw, as morning dawned, that her daughter had fallen into a calm slumber—the sign that the danger had subsided; she knew not whether she ought to have rejoiced or grieved.

Then, with an agony of grief at the wickedness of

such a thought—for she doted on her child and her death would make life unsupportable to her—she fell by the bed side upon her knees, and wept, and prayed.

In the morning there was a report through Arundel, that Charley Rowe had been discovered on the previous afternoon in a copse near one of the curves of the river Arun, with a deep wound in his skull, lying senseless upon the ground. That with great difficulty he had been restored to life, but that he had not recovered his senses, and was in a state of raving delirium. It was added that the police had taken it up and were engaged on investigating the circumstances. Mrs. Aston, when she heard this report from a neighbour, could not help associating it with the strange condition in which Myra had reached home. She had learned from Myra, when she left her the day before, that it was her intention to walk in the neighbourhood where Charley Rowe had been found nearly murdered, and on hearing this report, she was yet more perplexed to trace a solution to the mystery which enveloped the present state of both.

It was nearly mid day when Myra awoke from her slumber, much refreshed, and free from a wandering brain; but the doctor was present, and himself administered another potion, advising her to keep herself as calm as possible, and urged her mother not as yet to advert to the circumstances which had occasioned her prostration of body and mind. Mrs. Aston complied, not without reluctance, for she was in a state of the deepest anxiety to know the worst, that she might shape her course accordingly.

Towards evening, the gentleman who had discovered Myra in the condition described, made his appearance at Mrs. Aston's, and was admitted. Myra was in a deep slumber, and her mother, therefore, was at liberty to receive her guest, and reply to his questions, as well as to receive his congratulations upon the prospect of her speedy restoration to health. When the usual common-places on such a subject were exhausted, a silence of a minute ensued, then the gentleman, clearing his throat, said:

"It appears to me, Mrs. Aston, that you do not remember me!"

Mrs. Aston started as he made this observation. She regarded him attentively, and once more a floating perception that she had seen him before and under different circumstances passed through her mind, but without affording her any assurance of the fact; she slowly shook her head.

"I have once or twice since I have seen you fancied that we had met before," she exclaimed, "but I cannot call to my memory when."

"I will enlighten you," he said. "It is many years since we have met, and though under ordinary circumstances the probabilities are that you would have forgotten me, yet as we did not meet under ordinary circumstances I am disappointed to find that you do not recollect me. I knew you again the instant I beheld you."

Mrs. Aston scrutinised his features once more, but without further recognition than the undefined sense she at first received of having somewhere met him in years long gone by.

"You forget," she observed, "the change that Time impresses on our features, where incessant duties and great mental activity prevails. The change, too, is greater in man than in woman; few would recognise in the bearded and whiskered countenances now so frequently seen, the pale smooth faces of pleasing boyhood of a few years back; and unless privation and misery of a severe kind imprint their rugged furrows with an iron harrow, women do not exhibit in their countenances those marks of the battle of life which men, who have to encounter, dare, and endure these ever-succeeding struggles, betray. My life, for many years, with one terrible exception, has been even and placid, and would leave but few marks upon my features. Yours probably, though not actually one of unhappiness, has suffered from the attrition of a constant intercourse with the world, and your face would present therefore a different aspect now, to that it wore when I first beheld it, even under circumstances which you say ought to have rivetted it on my memory. Notwithstanding all this, however, it is many years since we met, and I, whose every thought and whose whole life was devoted to my husband, may be excused if the face of another of his sex, failed to impress itself indelibly upon my memory.

"I attach greater force to your last reasons than to your first," observed the stranger; "but there can be no doubt there is much truth in your observations. I have had to do battle with the world in that arena where its struggles are the most severe, the law. Mrs. Aston, your husband and I were schoolfellows, and I was present at your marriage."

"Good Heaven, Mr. Frederick Maule!" exclaimed Mrs. Aston, with excited astonishment.

"The same," he replied, with a smile; "but known to the world now and for some years as Randolph. I inherited property left to me by a relative, on condition I took with it his name, which, but for such an arrangement, would have terminated with him. And as this was more than his self-love could quietly permit, he obtained from me a very readily given promise that in consideration of receiving the whole of his landed and personal property, I should henceforth consent to bear the cognomen of Mr. Frederick Maule Randolph, and to hand that name down to posterity, should Providence bless me with family, which it has."

"This accounts then for my inability to find you upon my arrival in London from Sierra Leone, after the death of my husband. I discovered one or two of the name, but not you."

"You did search for me, then?"

"I did. I was anxious to prove my legal title to the

name I bear," she replied, a crimson flush mantling her cheeks and forehead. "And by your able aid I knew I could compel my husband's proud family to admit my claim to be recognised and acknowledged by them as his wife. But alas! I was unable to meet with you, and I perceived that my affairs were much mismanaged by those to whom they were entrusted. To prevent further loss and shame, for the sake of my beloved child, who was now all to me on earth, I gave up my purpose, and came down here to live, in order to devote my life to her education and improvement, so that one day, should the chance ever occur, she might prove herself worthy of the family—at least on his side—from which she has sprung. But now heaven alone knows what is in store for me; the sad accident of yesterday, the details of which I have not yet learned, nor of which I can form any conception, may be of a nature to crush all my long and fondly cherished hopes to dust."

She burst into a paroxysm of tears as she spoke, and Mr. Randolph was able to form a shrewd guess at the mental agony she was enduring, through the suspense to which she had referred, by the convulsive character of her emotion. He suffered it for a short time to have its sway, and then he strove to arrest it: he referred to the fact of her ignorance of what had occurred, and argued that although she had been terrified and alarmed to a most serious extent, such a condition gave no just foundation to the horrible apprehensions which were crowding in her mind.

While yet, with professional subtlety and skill, urging his view of the subject, and, as he did so, relieving in some degree the weight of fears which oppressed the mind of Mrs. Aston, they were greatly startled by a soft low voice ejaculating:

"Mother!"

Both sprang to their feet in alarm, and before them beheld Myra, pale and wan as any ghost, but dressed in her usual attire, and regarding Mr. Randolph with an air of surprise. He at once controlled his astonishment; advancing, he took her hand, and in soft tones congratulated her upon being sufficiently restored to make her appearance in the sitting-room. Not so Mrs. Aston, who, affrighted at her sudden appearance, feared a return of her delirium; she caught her by her hand, and passed her arm round her waist, saying:

"My darling child! why have you quitted your bed; you are not strong enough. Come, darling, return to it, I implore you?"

"Nay, mother," she replied, "I am much better; far too well, in truth, to let you suffer any painful forebodings. You must have been so shocked and terrified on my account, that on awaking a short time since, and remembering that I could not have given you any relation of what had happened to me yesterday, I resolved at once to rise—for I felt quite strong enough—and relieve your curiosity. Do not banish me, therefore, until at least I have done that."

"Well and wisely said," ejaculated Mr. Randolph, rubbing his hands, for at once, with professional sagacity, he foresaw that the disclosure would not involve any serious cause for grief or such destruction of hopes as Mrs. Aston had hinted at. Mrs. Aston was only too eager to receive some explanation to persist in her request to Myra to return again to her couch: and then, all three seated themselves, and two with no small curiosity listened to the recital which Myra gave them, with alternate emotions of indignation and surprise. Mr. Randolph took notes of the heads of the outrage, together with the name of the young ruffian who had subjected her to his infamous insults, and promised to obtain redress from Saul Waters, and to reward Charley Rowe for his manly defence of her.

Her mother had not intended at present to have informed her of the state in which he had been discovered, until she had more strength to bear it; but just at this moment there came a summons to the door, and in a few minutes Mrs. Aston, who had left the room to reply to it, returned with Ellen Fairfax and a police officer. It seems that in his frenzy, while engaged wrestling with an imaginary object, Charley had frequently uttered the name of Myra Aston. As the same medical man attended both, these incoherent utterings of her name led him to mention the circumstance of his having been called to attend her, and finding her in a state very similar to that of Charley's, save that she had received no such murderous blows. As the police officer was engaged in making minute inquiries, the remarks of the doctor respecting Myra came to his ears, and he announced his determination of at once proceeding to her residence, with a view of ascertaining whether, as he suspected, one event was connected with the other. Ellen Fairfax, who was present when he declared his intention, resolved to accompany him, for she was devoured by an absorbing curiosity to ascertain what extraordinary circumstances could have occasioned both Myra and Charley to be thrown into such a dreadful condition, and for which it appeared impossible to assign a cause.

Myra's narrative at once gave the key to the mystery, and the police officer immediately quitted the house with the purpose of taking young Waters into custody. He knew him to be desperate and cunning; he must be prepared to combat him with his own weapons, and he hastened to make the necessary preparations. Ellen, desirous of asking a thousand questions of Myra, induced her to return to her bedroom, and once more Mrs. Aston and Mr. Randolph were left alone, he to narrate and she to listen to the cause which had brought him in search of her to Arundel.

"I have mentioned," he commenced, "that I was your husband's schoolfellow. We formed a boyish intimacy when first thrown together, and afterwards, saving my life by rescuing me from drowning, and subsequently espousing my cause when oppressed by bigger boys belonging to our school, our acquaintance-ship ripened into a friendship on his part, and an attachment on mine, that nothing ought nor shall obliterate. From school we passed to the same college, and there I still found him the same steadfast, self-denying, disinterested, tender friend I had proved him in our earlier associations; and when we quitted college I entered upon a life of unceasing application,—the practice of the law; he, with large expectations, although a younger son, from his wealthy family, was removed from the sphere of my action. But we corresponded, and when his attachment to you was first created, I became his confidant, and was made acquainted with all its successive stages as they occurred until your marriage, of which I was not only a witness, but I acted as your father, as you will remember, upon the occasion, and gave you to him,—a prize I am sure he estimated at its true value, and never ceased to acknowledge as such while he lived."

Mrs. Aston, albeit she tried to preserve her equa-nimity, could not repress the tears this eulogium upon herself and kind tribute to her husband's memory called forth.

"Nay, never weep, Mrs. Aston," exclaimed Mr. Randolph, as he observed her apply her handkerchief to her eyes. "His virtues here won for him an immortal crown, and it is difficult to conceive that had he been spared longer to us, he would have been happier than he is now. But let us pass over all such reflec-tions, and proceed to the matter in hand before us. After I had changed, with the aid of an act of Parliament, my name to Randolph, I wrote to my dear friend Aston, acquainting him with the whole of the circumstances pertaining to it, to which I received no reply; I wrote a second time—a third time with a similar result. I never heard again from him; made enquiries respecting him at his father's house, but his family either could not or would not afford me any information concerning him."

"They could, but would not," observed Mrs. Aston.

"I have no doubt of it," he replied, but at that period, and for some few years, I was engaged in a very heavy case, which caused me almost intolerable labour, incessant application, and the very greatest anxiety. At length it was brought to a successful close, and a brief opportunity enabled me once more to think of myself—of my friends again. I made enquiries respecting my friend Aston, to learn that he died on his return voyage from Sierra Leone to England. Questions respecting you, my dear madame were treated as arising from some ridiculous hallucina-tion on my part; your very existence was ignored; and being once more called to conduct a case of great magnitude and vast responsibility, I was reluctantly compelled to suspend the prosecution of my endeavour to learn some tidings of you until a more favourable opportunity. At last that time arrived, and with it a series of circumstances so remarkable, that it would be

rank blasphemy to deny the visible interposition of a Supreme Hand in the ordering of them. I need hardly add that both you and your daughter are intimately connected with them, and that I trust to be the humble instrument of restoring the wife and child of my beloved and much-lamented friend to their undoubted rights, and to the position to which they properly belong."

"In heaven's name, what do you mean?" asked Mrs. Aston, with marked agitation.

"Pray calm yourself," he returned, "I speak advisedly; but at present you must be content with this instalment. Your claim to be recognised as the wife of Franklyn Aston is in the right hands to be enforced, and in a fair way of success. 'It shall go hard,' as the playwright has it, 'but you shall ride the Barbary courser yet.'"

Mr. Aston raised her eyes to heaven, and ejaculated "For his sake and for hers, oh, may this be true!"

"Never doubt it, my dear madam," exclaimed Mr. Randolph. "It is not my intention to raise hopes which, like some frail glittering bubble, will be blown into air by the first adverse puff against it. Neither is it my desire to mislead you by any statements until I am pretty well assured that I am justified by facts beyond the power of fate to change. I have only to add that with difficulty I was enabled to trace your departure from Sierra Leone to England in company with your husband, your arrival in this country, and your ultimate departure for the south coast; the precise spot I eventually ascertained to be Arundel—also by a communication not less remarkable than the other, to which I have alluded, and which I may accidentally mention. Acquainted with a merchant named Jayne, I, at a recent interview, enquired after a fine young fellow, a ward of his, named Grey; he appeared rather averse to respond to my inquiries; and, as I had no title to penetrate into what he seemed not to care to disclose, I contented myself by hearing that the last he had seen of him was at the house of a lady named Aston, at Arundel. At the moment, strange to say, your name did not strike me as being that of the lady whose residence I desired to discover, and I parted with him; I was unable wholly to get out of my head his strange reserve respecting his ward, a young man whose general appearance and intelligence of manner had much interested me. Wondering in mere idleness of thought what he could be doing at Arundel, and why that should be their last place of meeting, the name of Aston suddenly appeared before me as if written in letters of fire. 'Aston, Aston,' I repeated, it must be the same. I hastened to Mr. Jayne, and from him, with evident reluctance, indeed a marked repugnance, for which I am at a loss to account, and which I did not seek to decipher, he gave me general directions by which I hoped to find your abode. I at once set out on my journey, and arrived at the moment that your daughter, terrified by the scoundrel she has named, sunk in a swoon upon your doorstep."

He paused for a moment to take breath, and Mrs. Aston said:

"I know not how to be sufficiently grateful for the kind interest you have evinced in behalf of myself and daughter. I believe that I am now fully aware of your object in seeking us; but may I, without offence, request to know what course you advise us to pursue, and what means will be required to support it. It will be most important for me to know this, as I should be opposed to entering upon an undertaking to which my means would prove inadequate. Better not commence it at all, than fail while on the road to success, for want of the resources to proceed to the end."

"You will have no occasion to waste a thought upon that. You must leave all that to me; the case is in my hands, and there will be no falling short for want of resources. My immediate object in coming down to have a personal interview with you, is to prove my title to have a sincere interest in your affairs, and to make plain to you wherefore you should place implicit reliance in me. I hope I have succeeded in this, and I shall likewise do so in persuading you to quit this town, and with your daughter accompany me back to London. My dear sister will be proud and pleased to receive you at my house, which I hope to induce you to make your home until you have gained the cause which in duty and justice to your daughter you are bound to prosecute. I will not, however, at this moment, dwell upon these minor points, but will return in the morning to discuss them if occasion should demand such an alternative, by which I mean, that you, as ladies will do—may raise some objections to the latter part of my plan. If you should, I trust you will at least patiently listen to the arguments with which I shall advocate the step, and I shall not despair of securing your consent to adopt it, as well as your acknowledgment that my counsels are both wise and prudent, and that you and your daughter will be guided by them. I will leave you now. You have had much in the last four-and-twenty hours to disturb and excite you; and you are much in need of repose. I will not intrude upon you until mid-day to-morrow, and hope then to see your agitation allayed, and your system perfectly refreshed. In the interval of our separation I shall pass the time at my disposal by following up the search after that ruffian—Waters, I think that's the fellow's name?"

Mrs. Aston replied in the affirmative.

Leaving the further consideration of this point for the present, he took his departure, reiterating his assurance to Mrs. Aston, that she might disarm her mind of all suspicion, and place the firmest faith in his sincere and disinterested friendship. The memory of the opinion entertained by her departed husband of this gentleman, and her own recollection, slight though it might have been, of the part he had taken in an important epoch of her life, induced her to believe that she might, without danger, do so, and she retired to rest in a state of mind which, if bordering on bewilderment, was, at least, of far a happier frame than it had been on the night previous.

Mr. Randolph, a thorough man of business, did not let the grass grow under his feet in his endeavour to secure the person of Saul Waters; but that young gentleman—it is true, stimulated by the almost frantic urgings of his father—was far from Arundel by the time that the policeman looked in upon old Waters to taste his ale, ostensibly, but really to take his son into custody.

Upon the entry of the official, the old man uttered a common-place exclamation of recognition and welcome, but his face wore that peculiar hyena-like grin with which he met Clifton's observation respecting the difference he found in the attractiveness respectively possessed by Myra and him, and he appeared quite prepared for the casual remarks respecting his son which dropped from the policeman. He replied to them with well assumed indifference, and to one who knew the circumstances, and listened to the conversation, considerable amusement would have been afforded by the keen encounter of wits that took place between the pair: the one making enquiries so framed as not to excite suspicion; the other replying as if he had not the least idea that the questions were put with a covert motive. The old man professed not to know where his son was, believing he had gone by train to Portsmouth, with some pal, upon a spree, but his son, he said, did pretty much as he liked, and it was seldom he knew much of his whereabouts until Saul told him afterwards. The policeman elicited nothing to give him a hint of the direction in which Saul had fled, but he contrived to make the old man confess that he and his son were together on the day on which Myra and Charley Rowe had been assaulted, and to cause him to prevaricate much respecting what had transpired while they were together; and when he had got out of him enough to satisfy him that the old man, if not actually engaged in the assault, was cognisant of more than he chose to reveal, the policeman requested him to accompany him to the inspector of police, and abide the result of an interview.

Old Waters assented with painful misgivings—not alone for himself or son, for of his own share in the transaction for which Saul had rendered himself amenable to the law, he felt sure that he had incurred no danger, and Saul had gone on board a fishing-yawl, which would put him ashore at Hastings or Dover, and from thence he would make his way to London, where the old man believed, from what he knew of the Modern Babylon, it would be impossible for the Arundel police to find him out, so that his misgivings for Waters and son were not very serious, but for the safety of his property they were. Miss Sarah Chinnick was yet in the ascendant, albeit her empire was on the wane and pregnant with an ignominious fall, inasmuch as the return of Nelly Waters was expected to occur at the expiration of the following day, and Waters, senior, had detected the rapid disappearance of the stock, for which there was no corresponding increase in the till in lawful coin of the realm. Sarah Chinnick had many relatives, and however much they might have hitherto neglected her, they made up for former absence by the court they paid to her while the domestic department of the "Bonny Bark" was under her control. They came often, but never without being attended by large appetites and much thirst; of course Sarah did not ask payment of them for what they so copiously partook of, and, to be sure, they indignantly scouted the notion of offering to pay, if any such mean notion had obtruded itself. The expectations of W. Waters, himself, upon this head, were never taken into contemplation, but he had become seriously alive to the manifest discrepancy between the disbursements and the "takings," and, at the very moment of the arrival of the policeman, had brought himself to the conviction that the only remedy to be provided for the very unsatisfactory position which he discovered his business to have assumed during the advent of Sal Chinnick, was by unceremoniously kicking her out. This was the conclusion at which he had just arrived on the arrival of the policeman. His motive for selecting Miss Chinnick had been an absurd attempt to revenge himself upon Mrs. Aston for not permitting her daughter to reoccupy the post she had taken upon the first departure of her foster sister Nelly Waters, and he discovered that the result of this act proved to be, not only that his selection of the damsel in question was a matter of indifference to Mrs. Aston, but that it had involved a very serious loss to himself; that indeed, he was the person punished by the act, and not Mrs. Aston. It may therefore be well understood that to leave Sarah Chinnick once more in undisputed possession of his goods and chattels created in him considerable uneasiness, for he felt morally certain that his departure would be the signal for the gathering of a large family party of the Chinnicks under his roof, during which there would be much feasting and great revelling at his expense. But he was unable to help himself, for the policeman was deaf to any arrangement which would leave Waters at home, and so the housekeeper *pro tem.* was summoned and she made her appearance. She was a smart and decidedly handsome girl, but there was a very apparent indication, both in the character of her features, as an index to her temperament, and her manners, that her sense of morality was not at all likely to interfere with her inclinations. She laughed nodded at the policeman in an impudent manner n as she entered the bar, and in a very familiar nquired of Old Waters what he wanted with ith a frowning growl the old man told her he

was just going a little way, and would be back in about half-an-hour, and that while he was gone she was not to admit any one.

"What, nobody!" she cried, with affected surprise.

"No one," repeated Old Waters, fiercely.

"What! not my cousin Bob?" she asked, with a saucy laugh, as if she knew it would enrage the old man.

"No!" he roared, and added, with an oath, "let cousin Bob wait outside till I come back."

"Won't you be gone more than half-an-hour?" she asked, in the same saucy, familiar strain.

The old man ejaculated a negative with the voice of a Stentor, but the policeman caught her eye, and winking at her, held up his ten fingers, which intimation was readily understood to be the number of half hours that Waters would probably be away—it might be days for what she actually knew, but presuming it to be half hours only, there was ample time for a little enjoyment, and so she, as soon as Waters and the policeman turned their backs, set about preparing for a gala.

Waters sought the aid of Knipe, his lawyer, on reaching Arundel, and upon going before the inspector, the evidence tendered, it was submitted by Mr. Knipe, was insufficient to connect Old Waters with the murderous attack upon Rowe; the objection was considered good, as there was no proof of his being present when the deed was committed; and therefore he was liberated on bail, until such time as Rowe himself was in a condition to explain the circumstances necessary to implicate him with Saul Waters in the deed which had placed Charley in the state in which he was discovered. Waters therefore arrived home, by the help of a borrowed horse, in a few hours after he had quitted, and found, as he had surmised, the friends and relations of Sarah Chinnock gathered in strength from various distances, with a remarkable celerity, in a high state of festivity; and although they had been kept well supplied with refreshment, they were uproariously, at the moment of his arrival, calling for more.

Waters, on making his appearance, quite perceived his return was unexpected, and sternly resisted all the proffered tokens of love and amity with which he was greeted by the relations of Miss Chinnock. He proceeded to turn all of them out of his dwelling, there and then, not excepting even Miss C., an undertaking accomplished only by the greatest amount of perseverance, a black eye, and a large quantity of earthenware and some glass destroyed. He would, indeed, not have been ultimately successful in obtaining more than a severe thrashing from the guests, who strongly objected to their summary removal, if it had not been for the opportune arrival of the officer of the coast-guard Oliver Lawrance, with a couple of his men. Upon understanding the wishes of the host, he assisted him, and, as he said, "cleared the decks in the turning of a capstan bar;" a favour Waters repaid the young

DEPARTURE FOR THE CRIMEA.

officer and his men by treating them to spirits which had never been introduced to revenue officers before.

While they were thus occupied, Nelly Waters returned home, a day before she was expected, and the wild confusion of the whole household at once presenting itself to her organ of order, extracted questions from her which produced a rambling story from her father, that determined her, at the earliest opportunity, to pay a visit to Mrs. Aston and Myra, and learn more. As she quietly formed this resolve, Oliver Lawrence formed one also. He had seen Nelly before, it is true, but as she stood before him now, she presented an aspect vastly different to that under which he had previously seen her, and therefore, as the present aspect was one which mightily pleased him; his resolve was that he should visit Waters more frequently, and be on more friendly terms with him than he had been. He addressed Nelly with much respect, but at the same time with an impressiveness of manner she could scarcely fail to observe, or, as it came from a good looking young fellow in the attractive garb of a sea officer, to be pleased with. She felt the colour come unbidden into her cheeks, and her eyes brightened as he pressed her hand in bidding her farewell; and when he announced that he should come again soon to see her and her father, if Old Waters did not express himself delighted at the anticipation of the promised visit, at least Nelly told him as if she meant it, that he would find a ready welcome, and that her father and herself would strive to prove it.

Oliver Lawrence had written to the authorities the day before to request the favour of a change in his locality, as he did not feel comfortable in it; he proceeded direct from Waters's house to the station to write another letter retracting it.

At the expiration of a few days, Nelly Waters went to Arundel to see Mrs. Aston, quite resolved that her father's dissension with that lady should not interfere with the attachment she bore Myra; for she loved her, if possible, more dearly than if she had been her own sister She was not a little staggered on reaching the house, to find it shut up and to let, while upon the door was fastened and painted a plate, informing those whom it might concern, that all letters, parcels, or communications for Mrs. Aston were to be forwarded to F. M. Randolph, Esq., Solicitor, Paper Buildings, Temple, London.

Disappointed and sad, Nelly returned home and made her father acquainted with the ill success of her visit. He listened with attention, and chuckled with pleasure, for he believed that the chief evidence against his son Saul was removed, and in the dead of that night the plate giving the information as to where Mrs. Aston might be communicated with was abstracted; so that when the postman, a week or two subsequently, came with Clifton Grey's letter, nobody to whom he applied remembered the address, and he therefore was com-

pelled to communicate to the authorities of the General Post Office that the lady to whom the letter was addressed, had "Gon a Way," a fact which they subsequently put Clifton in possession of, much to his anguish.

CHAPTER XII.

"NEVER did a set of finer fellows leave Old England for the good and glory of their country than the brigade of Guards.

"The long swell from the westward began to tell on the troops, the figure-heads began to plunge deeply into the waters, and the heads of the poor soldiers hung despondingly over the gunwale, portsill, stay, and mess tin, as their bodies tumbled to and fro in the creaking tumbling tabernacle in which they were encamped.

*   *   *   *   *   *   *   *

"The happy arrival of the Simoon, after a voyage of sixteen days from Portsmouth, while it eased the anxiety of the timid, deprived many of an interesting subject of censure and speculation.   *   She came into harbour with the Scotch Fusilier Guards on Saturday night (18th inst.), and the troops were disembarked the following day, and landed at their quarters in the Lazaretto."

W. H. RUSSELL.

"Here's a coil."

SHAKSPERE.

HE journey to Portsmouth, the first step in the progress to the East, was quickly performed. The train flew swiftly along the rails, the panting engine every now and then shrieking, as if with delight at being the medium by which an opposing barrier was to be presented to arrest the aggressive progress of the Great Barbarian of the North. The ride through the cool fresh breeze that swept over the extensive commons and waste lands, both in Surrey and Hampshire, through which the South Western Railway runs on its way to the coast, served to restore many of the men who, through the questionable kindness of parting friends, had indulged a little too freely, and to exhilarate those who, in despairing grief, had separated from the connections they loved most dearly on earth. Others who had left none to mourn, if they had some to hope, and who, without a sad thought at quitting friends and country, looked forward to the chances of war for promotion and prize-money, received additional exhilaration as the cold clear wind blew freshly in their faces. There was plenty of excitement—vociferations, songs, wild hurrahs, repeated as every successive station was arrived at, and but little abated until Portsmouth itself was reached. And here a repetition of the public enthusiasm awaited the arrival of the men. Upon quitting the train, and forming into marching order, the band heading, the regiment struck up a popular air, and the lusty throats of thousands who lined the route, on the roads, on the pathways, at windows, and on house-tops, gave utterance to a succession of hearty cheers, until the men had reached the

dockyard, and indeed until they absolutely were embarked on board the Simoon screw steam-ship of war,
and became busily occupied in ascertaining the whereabouts of and securing the berths appointed for them.

At dawn on the following morning, after a night
three parts of which was passed in bustling activity
and preparation, the Simoon tripped her anchor, and,
running down the Solent, cleared the Needles, and stood
away to sea, direct for Malta, a destination to which
the Ripon, Orinoco, Manilla, and Niagara, all large
merchant steam-ships, freighted with the Guards, had
been despatched. The Simoon vessel of war, with her
full complement of guns and seamen, was not expected
to make the passage with the same rapidity as the fast
ocean-going mercantile steamers, but she was known
to be a sound sea-boat, with an agreeable captain and
a first-rate crew: the voyage was therefore looked forward to with no dissatisfaction, even though it promised
to be longer by a day or so than those performed by the
vessels belonging to the Peninsular and Oriental Steam-
ship Company. This expectation was not falsified.

The incidents of the voyage were few, and confined
to the ordinary circumstances attending the transport
of troops. At first there was great jollity, much card-
playing, an infinity of smoking, and unbridled hilarity,
which subsided, ere the Bay of Biscay was reached.
As there happened to be a stiff breeze, a resolute head
wind with a long swell, the noisy became silent, the
uproarious speechless, and the active motionless, close
under the gunwale on the lee side, to which they
clung with tenacity, albeit every other part of their
frames were helplessly immovable. The ruddy were
ghastly pale, the reckless drinker loathed the smell of
spirits, the inveterate smoker hated the sight of his
pipe, his heart heaved at the thoughts of it. The
glutton abhorred his victuals, the singer could not
pipe a note, unless it was a groan extorted from him
by a cold sweating faintness, and the ready joker
looked dismally lachrymose. If the hardy tars
smiled at the very unwarlike aspect of the stalwart
guards, they took pity on their prostration, and lent
them assistance with a hearty good will. However,
the demon sea-sickness took his flight with returning
fine weather, and the whole battalion brightened up
again. The ruddy once more sported highly tinted
visages; the drinker returned to his rum with renewed
affection, the smoker wondered how he could have
suffered even the deadly sea-sickness to put his pipe
out. The ever-hungry satisfied with increased goût
the cravings of his appetite; the singer, of whom
Sergeant Haverel was a very conspicuous type, trolled
forth verses of every known or popular ditty more
joyously than ever; and the joker returned to his
"chaff" with a force which seemed to have gained
strength from its temporary lull.

Clifton Grey happily spared from being a victim to
this distressing malady, was enabled to render much
assistance to his comrades, and made himself very

popular with them, by the untiring and cheerful
efforts he employed to relieve them from the nauseat-
ing influence under which they laboured, or to supply
them with such comforts as their position required,
and which were at the time doubly acceptable. Never
seeking to affect a condition above their own, but,
accepting that accorded to him by a natural deference
to his superior education, he was, in a degree, more
looked up to by them than either their corporals or
sergeants; there was less familiarity, and more real
respect. Their feeling was excited by a just appreciation of his actual worth, which was sufficiently palpable
in all his acts, and under every phase of circumstances
in which he had been thrown in common with the
men; they knew the metal of which he was composed
was genuine; there was no false or meretricious glitter
about him; he affected nothing, but he possessed much,
and was ready at all times, without profession or
parade, to share it with his comrades; he could afford
information as readily as he could give counsel; and as
he submitted at no time to even the implication of an
insult, so he commanded alike the respect and good
will of all those among whom his present lot was
cast. If they had liked him before, he was endeared
to them now; for their tenderest connection, or the
dearest and most attached friend, could not have been
more constant in attendance upon them, while they
were struck down by the miserable sea malady, than
was he, and the kindness was, as he afterwards proved,
golden grain sown upon no barren soil.

As the Simoon ran up the straits, every available
spot from whence a good view of Gibraltar could be
obtained was occupied; the seamen manned the
yards; Tarifa was passed; and then, lining the walls
of the stern sea-girt fort were to be seen the soldiers
of the garrison, who cheered their brethren in arms
bound to the East, and the Fusileers echoed back their
shouts with hearty good will. Not a vessel was passed,
but the like expression of good will passed on both
sides; and at last, on the 18th of March, on Saturday
night, sixteen days after Portsmouth had been left in
the hazy distance, the Simoon let go her anchor in the
harbour at Malta; a contrast to the two months' trip
of olden time, but on the other hand, altogether as unfavourable when compared with the seven days and
three hours' run of the Himalaya.

"The Fusileers disembarked in excellent order,"
wrote the correspondent of the Times, and he spoke
not unadvisedly. Quarters on the Lazaretto, a range
of stone buildings of no height, but running to some
considerable length along the edge of the Quarantine
Harbour, were assigned to them, and they had no reason to complain of the selection. Originally built for
hospital purposes, it possesses all the conveniences
necessary for such an object, and was both well venti-
lated, and shaded from the heat. The men, once
installed, quickly commenced making its advantages
available for the promotion of their personal comfort.

Clifton, through his friend and comrade Sergeant Haverel, was well posted, and had a place assigned him near to a casement which overlooked the blue waters of the harbour, and from which an agreeable view could be obtained of the life and bustle attendant upon a military and naval port, the services of which were in full requisition. Clifton did not obtain this considerate kindness in opposition to the rules of the service, but there are in all institutions opportunities of evading the regulations without violating the strict letter of them, or trenching upon the spirit; such was the fact of Clifton's case; he would have been no party to a disobedience of rules, but he had the common sense to accept an advantage when it benefitted him without injury or wrong to his comrades.

Clifton availed himself also of the earliest opportunity of paying a visit of inspection to all those parts of Malta worth seeing. He was struck with the mass of fortifications it presented; wherever the eye traversed there were long extended lines of smooth white stone walls, pierced at equal distances, with huge embrasures from which looked down frowningly massive cannon, with tapering mouth, and bulky breech, gazing eagerly down, as if on the *qui vive* to belch forth fire, flame, and shot upon the devoted heads of those who might provoke it. The straight lines were broken and diversified by many-tiered bastions, and not a point from whence destruction might be hurled or invader repelled seemed to be overlooked.

Clifton found much to interest him in the beetling defences, and the buildings public and private; he derived also no little amusement from mixing with the Maltese, and as he spoke Spanish well, he was enabled to obtain many articles, and to save himself from extortion, denied to his less accomplished comrades. In this way he was serviceable to some of his officers, and received their warm thanks for his assistance. To this however, there was an exception.

Some few days after their arrival, while strolling with Serjeant Haverel through a street in Valetta, he observed Captain Winslow bartering with a Maltese for some fruit. Overhearing the demand of the man for the stock selected, he, knowing it to be preposterously extortionate, touched his cap, and informed the captain that he was being swindled, and mentioned both to the latter and the Maltese the proper price —less than one third of that demanded. Captain Winslow turned round and looked him hard in the face, and then with a haughty and contemptuous air, said:

"You are officious sir, impertinently officious. When I require the assistance of your cleverness, I may ask it; until then, don't obtrude yourself or your information upon me."

Clifton Grey never winced while this insulting speech was being meted out to him, but there was a slight cast upon his lip; he only touched his hat. While Serjeant Haverel, biting his nether lip hard, said, in a tone not very deferential to the presence of his officer,

"Come along, Grey, don't throw away your time, you've none too much of it."

And then as they moved hastily on, he sang loudly:

"Let us speak of a man as we find him." "I tell you what Grey," he observed, after they had proceeded a short distance, "if it would not be altogether wise to speak of Captain Winslow as you find him, it is very necessary to think thus of him. He's a bitter pill—one of the men who does more mischief in an army than a whole regiment of careless drunken rascals. He is the man who sets in motion the spirit of insubordination, by doing his best to excite the hatred and contempt of those placed under him. He treats all the men of his company worse than dogs. He is running up an account which he'll have to pay some day; but I don't think he'll admire the settling."

"By education and position he should be a gentleman," said Clifton; "but those advantages have failed to place him in that category. His ungracious rudeness to me in return for a service—for, though slight, it was one—I can only attribute to ignorance of what is due to his station, and regard it accordingly."

"Very true, Grey," returned Haverel, "but you cannot afford to despise it. You are a marked man on his list, and he has made up his mind to let you have the full benefit of it. He asked many questions concerning you of me the other day. I gave him all he wanted, and a little more, perhaps. Then he indulged me with some insinuations in regard to my treatment of you. I know what he meant pretty well. I could have spat in his face; but that would have been against the regulations; so I told him never to fear for me— I knew my duty pretty well, and I would keep you to your tether. Let me warn you once more to beware of him; he means you mischief, and he has the chance of working it, too. You may hate him as much as you please, but it will not do to despise him."

Clifton, with a smile almost of derision, promised to comply with his suggestion.

At this moment a thundering salute was fired from the fortifications of the harbour, attended by a succession of loud cheers, and vast bodies of soldiers and civilians hurried to the harbour to ascertain the cause. It proved to be the arrival of the "Christophe Colomb," from Marseilles, having on board Lieut.-General Canrobert, Lieut.-General Bosquet, Lieut.-General Martini Pray, forty-five officers, and 800 troops. The soldiers of both countries cheered each other lustily; and when the Frenchmen landed, the troops of the nation that had always hitherto met them with deadly weapons in their hands, now lined the landing-place—those hands outstretched, instead of deadly conflict, in cordial welcome. It was strange to witness the enthusiasm on both sides, and how the soldiers of both countries scanned the persons and appointments of each other;

how unequivocally expressed was the astonishment and admiration of the French soldiers at the massive proportions of the Guards; and how equally a similar feeling was displayed by the latter, who, while they marvelled at the somewhat diminutive build of the French soldiers, could not fail to admire the compactness of their accoutrements. The French troops were no sooner marched to the temporary quarters assigned them, and released, than they spread themselves all over Valetta, making themselves as free and at home with whatever they came across, whether new or strange, as if they had been previously long and well acquainted. The soldiers of both armies quickly fraternised, although few could speak the other's language, yet the language of drinking to and with each other was soon understood and practised. Clifton, from his ability to speak the language of the others fluently, found his services in incessant request, both by his comrades and the French soldiery, not only to translate their mutual friendly feelings, but to express the readiness with which each professed to employ their good offices to consolidate the alliance, and render each other such favour and assistance as might be desirable or they might require; and thus he not only grew further in favour with his own comrades, but he made friends among his companions in arms in the French service, as we shall see.

For several days subsequently vessels successively arrived, containing English and French troops, until Valetta became like a thronged fair, and Clifton found every moment not occupied by his regimental duties engaged in interpreting. One of the lieutenants belonging to the battalion not unfrequently employed him in this service. One morning after practice with the Minié rifle, this officer addressed him, requesting him to hold himself disengaged that evening from all other employment to attend him at Sliema, where a wealthy merchant had given up the best portions of his mansions to the officers of the Scotch Fusilier Guards. An invitation had been given to some French officers, and the ease and rapidity with which Clifton could translate French into English, or vice versâ, induced Lieutenant Linder to believe that he could pass a pleasant evening with the French visitors, even though he could not speak a word of their tongue; and he was not far wrong.

Upon the approach of the hour appointed for him to be at Sliema, he quitted the barracks at the Lazaretto, and made his way towards Sliema. On his road he overtook a young black-eyed damsel, who looked archly at him, though her head and face were nearly shrouded in a mantilla, and let drop a few words in Spanish, which implied that if he were to slacken his pace, she might have a word to say to him. He thanked her, but informed her that he had a prior engagement, which would prevent him availing himself of an opportunity, which at another and happier time, could not fail to delight him.

"A lady, of course," suggested the black-eyed damsel, with an ill disguised curl of the lip.

"Nay!" he replied, "I am not so fortunate."

"That must be your own fault, senor."

"No—I am a soldier, and my duty has the first claim upon my time."

"Ah! you are on duty, that is unfortunate, senor. Let me be plain with you, and assure myself as well that I am right. You were at practice with your rifle upon the sea-shore this morning, at targets, with your comrades."

"You are right."

"And you had the good fortune—I beg your pardon—the skill to hit the centre more frequently than any other soldier."

Clifton looked at her with some surprise.

"Well," he exclaimed, as she paused for his answer, "was it not so?"

"It was, but then I have practised rifle shooting with a stadium before, and there was small merit in what I did. But why do you mention it."

"Because I can now tell you that there is a person who much desires to have an interview with you."

"An interview with me! that's strange. Why did not the person seek me himself?"

"Himself," exclaimed the girl, with a scornful toss of the head. "Senor, are all your countrymen so dull of comprehension when addressed as you have been by me."

"I do not care to answer the question, beyond hazarding a supposition that your ways are not our ways, and to tell you also that experience has taught me that an honest confession of ignorance, in many matters not to be acquired by intuition, has saved both time and error. As my time is short, suppose we be, as you said but now, very plain with each other. Who is it wishes to see me?"

"A Senorita—her position high—her fair name is unsullied, and must not run a chance of taint. I dare not therefore mention it, nor where she dwells, nor can I say when or where she will consent to receive you."

"This is mere absurdity. If such is your position in the affair, why make a mystery of what was possibly a passing remark, forgotten, perhaps, as soon as uttered, and which can have but little interest for me, who have not seen the lady, and probably shall not, for our regiment will shortly leave this for Turkey."

"Listen, thou gallant in form, but cold and ungallant in heart. This lady was this morn on the sea-shore and saw the firing; she observed you, and started when she did so. After her first glance she never took her eyes off, and before the firing had ceased she drew my attention to you. 'Note that Englishman well!' she said, 'learn his name and where his troop is lodged; I would have speech with him.' That was all that took place, but unfortunately I suddenly lost sight of you, and I have walked my feet nearly off in trying to find you in Valetta. At last I found one of your soldiers of the same dress, who could not understand a word I said, nor I a sentence he uttered, and I was returning in despair when you overtook me. Now, Senor, I wish to know your name, and where and when a communication will reach you."

"I am afraid I must confirm your opinion of my want of gallantry," said Clifton, with a smile. "I am, as you must or should be aware, here but for a brief term, and cannot place any expectations on ever returning here. I confess, therefore, in consenting to an interview with the lady, who you say desires to see me, an affair which on both sides it will be only prudent to avoid."

"Bah! You are flattering yourself, you iceberg. The lady of whom I speak is young and lovely, and can command a train of noble cavaliers, without being reduced to seek a lover among the English troopers. It is with no such object she wishes to speak with you upon, but on some matter of grave importance, or she would not have betrayed so much earnestness to obtain an interview with you. Come, your answer to my question, you glacier!"

Clifton laughed at her pettish observations. "I do not always wear a frosty surface," he said; "there is a volcano here," he continued, placing his hand upon his heart, "it upheaves its burning lava at times."

"It is needful that it should."

"Ah!" he responded, with a sigh, "there has been warm summer time there."

"Any one can see," she exclaimed, quickly, "it is winter now."

"You would have a change in the seasons, would you not?"

"Not to cold weather—especially cold weather in men, I hate it. Ah! your comrades are not all natives of the North Pole. It was very hot weather with the one I met a little while back. He had a raging volcano, the fire burst out at the top of his head, his hair was of the hue of flame. We spoke not the same language, but, Mother of Mercy! he soon addressed himself to me in a language comprehended all over the world; he nearly squeezed the breath out of my body with his arms, and almost suffocated me by stopping my breath with his lips."

"You should have screamed for help," said Clifton, with a laugh, "and then he would, if caught in the fact, have been punished for the outrage."

"I could not have screamed, if I had tried; besides he was a nice fellow, and no iceberg; I should not have liked to have got him into trouble."

"Well, but I shall get into trouble if I remain here talking with you. I ought to have been at Sliema by this time."

"Sliema!" cried the girl, "where is Sliema?"

Clifton mentioned the name of the loyal proprietor of the mansion where the officers of his regiment were quartered.

"Madre de Dios!" she exclaimed, "the senorita will be there to-night. There is to be a grand party; her

father will be with her. Are you to be a guest?" she added, with further surprise.

Clifton felt the blood rush to his forehead; the old leaven had not been worked out yet.

"No," he replied, "I am only to act as interpreter, and therefore at the disposal of the officer who has engaged my services; as I have reason to believe that I shall immediately attend on his movements, it is not altogether improbable that, although not received as a guest, I shall mingle with them."

"Enough, you will see the senorita."

"How shall I know her?"

"It will not be necessary for you to have any such information. If she desires to confer with you, she will very soon make it known to you; if she does not, her incognito will thus be strictly preserved."

"And so farewell. When next we meet I hope you will entertain a more favourable opinion of me; now, you are angry with me."

"Angry with you; oh no, I pity you."

"Pity me, wherefore?"

"Because you are insensible to your own advantages."

"Farewell Senor mio, and when next you meet and have converse with another of my sex, whose face nature has fashioned with no unskilled hand, and whose heart is filled with the most generous sentiments towards good-looking fellows of your race, don't stand and talk to her as if you had been originally made out of the spray from a fountain, and afterward changed into solid ice, or however kindly she may at first feel disposed toward you, she will assuredly end your interview as I do, by running away from you, for fear you should turn all the love flowing in her heart into a frozen stream."

As she uttered the last words, she waved her hands contemptuously towards him, and drawing her mantilla over her roguish countenance, she turned from him and exhibited a very pretty pair of ankles in rapid motion.

Clifton watched her disappearing form for an instant, and shrugging his shoulders, hastened on to his destination. Ought he to have followed the example of his freehanded comrade, and put her freedom of breathing into danger; it seemed as though such was her opinion upon the matter; it was one with which he did not happen to coincide, and what was more, on conning over in his mind the strange circumstance of an interview with him being desired by her mistress, to him an utter stranger, he could hardly help connecting with it motives not flattering to her purity. Somewhat nettled, he scarcely knew why, by the taunts of the girl, he resolved that the mistress should not, any more than the maid, induce him to a rapid thaw, notwithstanding the recommendation he had just received; and when he came further to reflect, he dismissed it, either as being mysterious or ridiculous.

On reaching the villa at Sliema, he found the greatest activity and bustle prevailing; not a window but exhibited a blazing light; and domestics were hurrying to and fro, busily preparing for the feast that was on the eve of consummation. Lieutenant Linder was informed of the arrival of our hero, and immediately sent for him. As the latter entered his dressing-room, "I am glad you have come, Grey," he said, "for I expect to meet to-night a French officer, whose father and mine made an acquaintance in the Peninsula. My father, I believe, saved his life, although he took him prisoner in one of the many engagements fought in that war. During the peace they have frequently corresponded, and some services have passed on both sides; but the son and I have never met. My governor happened to learn that his regiment was ordered for active service, and that therefore a probability existed of our meeting; he furnished me with credentials, and I have no doubt my expected guest will possess them likewise; but, unfortunately, scarcely a word of French do I know. Serious efforts were made to drive it into me at school, but without effect; and, though I have since made attempts, I cannot advance beyond a common salutation. How did you pick it up, Grey?"

"With other languages, at school, sir," replied Grey.

"With other languages!" echoed Lieutenant Linder. "What other languages?"

"Latin, Greek, German, and Spanish."

The lieutenant whistled.

"Why, Grey, you have had the education of a gentleman."

Clifton bowed.

"You have not always been in your present humble condition?"

"I was brought up to expect to fulfil a position not second to your own, sir."

"Indeed. Adverse circumstances, I suppose, have wrought a change?"

Clifton bowed.

"Well, well," said the lieutenant, kindly," never repine; brighter times will come. Let us hope you may become rich yet, and purchase your promotion."

"I hope to win it," exclaimed Clifton.

"What—a serjeant's stripes. I spoke of a commission."

Lieutenant Linder then explained to Clifton Grey those army regulations—which have since been altered —by which he could not rise beyond the rank of full serjeant. Unlike the admirable principle of promotion that obtains in the French army, where, as Napoleon forcibly remarked, every soldier carried in his knapsack a marshal's *bâton*, no act of superhuman bravery— no display of military skill, under trying and difficult circumstances—could earn or entitle the non-commissioned officer to the promotion of a commission. It is true the Field Marshal Commanding-in-Chief could recommend to her Majesty to grant a commission to the common soldier—even to a civilian; but at the moment Lieutenant Linder was speaking, although the

date is so recent, instances of such an exercise of prerogative were almost if not absolutely entirely unknown.

Clifton Grey's knowledge of the regulations which governed the military service—that precious routine, an insane adherence to which has been so productive of disasters—was, on enlisting, of the most limited kind. The romance of his nature had induced him to lend a ready ear to the exaggerations of Sergeant Haverel, to believe that if his career was not suspended by an envious bullet, while engaged in desperate assaults on well fortified cities, or amid a storm of iron hail winning fame in the open field, he might rise to be a general, or some post no less high or honourable. When he began to study his new profession, to learn his regimental duties, to examine the prospects his new career were likely to open up to him, he found that, as it appeared, an insuperable bar was placed to his farther advancement when he had reached his highest rank as a non-commissioned officer. He had, in frequent conversations, mentioned to Sergeant Haverel his discovery, and the check it gave to his ardent determination to distinguish himself in the first conflict in which he happened to be engaged, but that light-hearted individual had always got rid of the subject by pooh-poohing the regulations, and assuring Clifton that if he dared and did so well as to be honourably mentioned in the General's despatches home, he might make sure of obtaining a suitable reward—so he might, but he might, nevertheless, be doomed to a miserable and sickening disappointment, as to many a brave, skilful, and able soldier in the commission has proved.

Clifton explained to Lieutenant Linder that he was not ignorant of the position in which he stood, but he hoped, if opportunities presented to win the highest rank as a non-commissioned officer, and then he had a vague notion he might, by means which did not now develope themselves, receive the presentation of an ensigncy, and from thence he should date his real start upwards, until he had achieved a position of which he might well be proud.

Lieutenant Linder shook his head and smiled.

"You forget, Grey," said he, "that little word that comprehends so much—'interest;' by its side merit stands no chance. However, I will not dispirit you, for as we were taught at school, 'it is the exception that proves the truth of the rule.' You will have, at least, one advantage over many of your comrades, aspirants for an upward progress like yourself, that, as an educated man and the son of a gentleman, you will, if you obtain an ensigncy, be received on equal terms in the officers' mess, notwithstanding fortune had originally placed you in the ranks; but with men whose fathers were, perhaps, of the lowest class, or nobody knows who, they would find the change from the rank of sergeant to ensign but to be most painful instead of gratifying."

The usual indication of strong feeling—a scarlet

flush, mounted the forehead of Clifton, his lip curled, and he said, with some emotion—

"The poet has said—

"Honour and shame from no condition rise,
Act well your part,"——

"Aye!" exclaimed the Lieutenant, with a laugh. "The poet has said so: but in a question of associates, the officers of a regiment have a weakness in respect to birth. You need hardly distress yourself about the matter, Grey; it will be some time ere you have the chance of testing the truth of my observation; but if it should come to pass after some of our hand-to-hand meetings with the barbarous Russ, that fortune metes out to you such reward, you, as I have said, are likely to escape the cold shadow, because one can see by your language, manners, and general address, that you are a born gentleman, and it requires a gentleman to detect this. I repeat, adversity is no bar to intercourse, for too many of our class are as poor as Job; but to claim it, there must be birth and blood. You, Grey, have both—is it not so?"

Clifton felt an inward conviction that he had; but, alas! the proof was wanting: his eyes sought the floor, and he remained silent. Lieutenant Linder placed his hand kindly upon his shoulder, and added—

"I have no doubt of it; but I should ill support my claim to be a gentleman, if I sought indirectly to obtain a confidence you did not think fit to repose in me directly; and therefore let us change the subject. Come, you must polish up your knowledge of French, for I shall tax it to-night to the utmost."

"I have read French from my boyhood," returned Clifton, "and, admiring the literature of the nation, I made myself, if not master of it, extensively acquainted with it, and my knowledge of the language nearly equals my acquaintance with my own tongue."

Lieutenant Linder, now bidding Clifton follow him, descended to the drawing-room, in which were assembled a number of officers and gentlemen, all chatting and laughing together in a somewhat boisterous manner. Several French officers were present, two or three of them being officers of Zouave regiments. Clifton felt keenly the new position he filled in entering this society in the capacity of a servant, to speak only when addressed, and then confine himself to a simple reply. An observation from him, he was well aware, would be met by a stare of surprise, or an insulting rebuke, but the hope that there was yet his day to come made him thrust down the uprisings of pride, and determine him, not only to remain as quiet and unassuming as possible, but not to hear remarks which were calculated to wound his *amour propre*, even if they were intended for his ear.

His appearance at the heels of Lieutenant Linder attracted immediate attention, and many who were speaking became immediately silent, as though expecting an explanation of such an apparition.

Lieutenant Linder did not apparently observe it, and spoke cheerfully and chattingly to one and another, while Clifton quietly retreated to a corner of the room which was unoccupied. He was not permitted to remain there long before one of the officers of his regiment present walked up to him and said abruptly, but in a tone loud enough to be heard by all the room:

"Pray, my man, for what are you here?"

Clifton saluted him in the usual military fashion, and said.

"Lieutenant Linder will explain."

"What have I to do with Lieutenant Linder, I ask you the question?"

Before Clifton could answer, an officer engaged in conversation turned quickly round and came up; he had overheard what had passed and Clifton's second reply.

"I gave you that answer, sir, because I presumed that information would be more satisfactorily and perfectly given by Lieutenant Linder."

The new comer was Captain Winslow, he turned his grey eyes and pallid face upon Clifton, and with an excitement of manner, quite uncalled for, he exclaimed, "Aha! I know the fellow, he is the most insolent, and presuming scoundrel in the regiment. How dare you enter a room where gentlemen meet; you impertinent rascal! Did you think you had a chance of purloining something. Get out of the room this instant, you vagabond, and proceed to barracks. In the morning I'll arrange an interview between you and the Provost Marshal."

O the marvellous effect of discipline! In any other relation but that of captain and private soldier, Clifton would have struck him to the earth; by a violent exertion of self-control, however, he kept down his wrath, but he stood his ground, fixed his clear eye firmly and unwaveringly upon the shifting cat-like orb of the captain, and disdained to make a response.

The loud tones of Captain Winslow drew the attention of all present—among them Lieutenant Linder. He had heard the insulting observations, and advancing hastily, he confronted the captain, saying;

"Winslow, you are not addressing those remarks to private Grey."

"Indeed, but I am, Linder. Pray what should hinder me?"

"A respect for truth."

"Lieutenant Linder!"

"Captain Winslow, the application of the epithets scoundrel and rascal, accompanied by the imputation of dishonesty to private Grey, has not the shadow of a foundation in facts, and you know it."

"I! sir."

"You Captain Winslow. A smarter, more obedient, sober, cleaner, honester soldier, there is not in the ranks than private Grey, and notwithstanding your promise respecting the Provost Marshal, you will permit me, if you don't know it already, to acquaint

CLIFTON GREY EXAMINING THE PORTRAIT IN THE SIGNORA'S VILLA AT SLIEMA.

you that he is one of the few who has not only not been presented to the notice of the provost marshal, but is not likely to need the introduction."

"Possibly, Lieutenant Linder," said Captain Winslow, with an assumption of authority which made the young officer wince again. "As you seem to know so much about your amiable protégée, you will be able to explain the exertion of modesty which forced him into the presence of the present company, no member of which I opine, even you will admit, is accustomed, however much he may respect the common soldier in his place, to share the hours off duty with the men he commands when he is on."

There was a laugh, which made Lieutenant Linder chafe, and Clifton as cold as marble.

"To those who have a right to demand that question, I am ready to reply," remarked the young lieutenant, haughtily.

"I shall certainly assume that responsibility, Lieutenant Linder," returned Captain Winslow, in the same offensive tone. "As I am seeking information respecting one of the men of my company, I, as your superior officer, require of you the particulars which you acknowledge you are in a position to give."

"As you take that ground, Captain Winslow, it will be enough for me to say that Private Grey is here at my request, by permission of Colonel Hay."

"And the object of his being here with you, by permission of the Colonel?" asked Captain Winslow.

"I decline to reply to a question which, at least, you have no right to demand," responded the Lieutenant.

"Not, perhaps, as your officer, sir, I admit, but as a gentleman, who objects to be 'hail fellow' with the lowest scum, I am entitled to ask the necessity for such contact."

"And as I, Captain Winslow, am infinitely above the imputation of introducing the lowest scum into the society of gentlemen, I consider an explanation, such as you ask, wholly uncalled for and unnecessary."

"Then, Lieutenant Linder," exclaimed Captain Winslow, with an insolent sneer, "permit me to inform you that, on this point, we join issue. You are welcome to the congenial society of your friend, if it pleases you to indulge in it; but you really have no right to expect that others should do less than decline to share its multifarious advantages, or to protest against its being forced upon them at times and in places when they cannot escape from it, unless by a forcible expulsion."

Lieutenant Linder threw back his shoulders and drew himself up to his full height, while with a very palpable movement he rested his left-hand upon the hilt of his sword, and in a very clear voice said, "I do not presume, Captain Winslow, that you are likely to attempt such a feat."

"Certainly not. The servants of the house would take the trouble off my hands, if a picquet were not handy."

"I cannot admire your respect for the uniform of your regiment, Captain Winslow, any more than I do your proceeding in this matter."

"Lieutenant Linder!"

"Captain Winslow, I have a right to defend my position, and I will. If men are alone to be associated with according to their gradations of rank, pray, upon what terms ought I to accept the society of Captain Winslow, seeing that my grandfather is an earl, and his immediate ancestor a rag-merchant."

A suppressed titter ensued. The sallow face of Winslow became livid.

"S'death!" he exclaimed, in guttural tones—"Linder, this is an insult."

"Lieutenant the Honourable Cuthbert Linder, if you please, Captain Winslow," cried the young officer, proudly. "We are standing now upon our positions, although I must strongly dissent from the assumption that rank or birth will make men gentlemen, as much as I shall henceforth disbelieve that holding a commission in Her Majesty's service necessarily makes an officer a gentleman."

"You have proved it, Lieutenant Linder," hissed Captain Winslow through his teeth.

"I trust so," returned the Lieutenant; "and permit me to add, Captain Winslow, that I am equally prepared to prove myself an officer and a gentleman, when he who dares to express a contrary opinion exhibits the courage to maintain such a false impression."

"Tut, tut, gentlemen, you are both gentlemen and men of honour," observed a major of the regiment who was present, and who advanced for the purpose of interposing. "You are both becoming hot in your desire to prove that you should, as well-bred men, be cool. There is some misunderstanding here, it is evident, and I have no doubt it is quite capable of being easily explained—in fact, my knowledge of Linder assures me of this, and so much as may be necessary he will be willing to offer—more no gentleman can expect."

"Be this the proof," returned Lieutenant Linder, quickly: "I will in private submit the whole position to you, Major Thorpe, leave in your hands an explanation, and act precisely as you may counsel."

"Enough, enough," cried several voices—"more cannot be expected nor desired."

Captain Winslow shrugged his shoulders, bowed with affected deference, and said—

"With all my heart! I have never questioned more than the right of Lieutenant the Honourable Cuthbert Linder to introduce into the company of gentlemen a man whose condition widely separates him from them."

"Bah! Winslow," cried the major. "Have you been spending a month with your evangelical friends, that you have grown so precise of late? You will have your explanation, and will give as well an admirable instance of that social wisdom at whose fount you have drunk so deeply, if you find another subject of conversation until my return."

So saying, he took the arm of Lieutenant Linder, and quitted the room, while the remainder of the party returned to the centre of the apartment, leaving Clifton standing like a pariah rather than one of those brave fellows of whom the nation has so much reason to be proud. An exception to this occurred in the instance of a French officer present, who, unable to comprehend more than that some division of opinion had occurred between Captain Winslow and Lieutenant Linder, understood not its connection with Clifton, and somewhat to the surprise of those who had comprehended what had transpired, he walked deliberately up to our hero, and saluting him, proceeded to examine his accoutrements, and to put one or two questions in very broken English, to which Clifton replied, and, with a gentlemanly tact, which the French officer readily detected and appreciated, he, without informing him that he spoke his language, gave him an opportunity of discovering it, and of eliciting by a direct question the fact. Immediately the French officer commenced an animated conversation with him, in which Clifton took his part so ably as not a little to surprise those who were gradually drawn to listen, and to fill with rage and vexation the heart of Captain Winslow, who burned to revenge the knock-down blow received by his brother, and the severe lecture he had received from Colonel Hay, of both of which injuries, as he esteemed them, Clifton was the author.

The conversation between Clifton Grey with the French officer was exclusively on military matters, and the replies the former gave to questions put by the latter, proved not only that he had acquired a very considerable amount of information upon the *mechanique* and tactics of his profession, but that he was equally master of the language in which he was speaking. As will occur in such matters, an observation caught by one of those who were attentive, drew from him a remark, and he was soon borne upon the stream; others were drawn in and carried away, until Captain Winslow found himself standing alone with an officer of his mess, who suffered himself to be very much of his opinion in everything.

It was with the most bitter annoyance that he observed several of those who had smiled at his sneers at Clifton, now addressing him in terms which displayed unmistakeably a respect for his communications, or listening to his explanations with marked attention. It was just as this altered condition of things had reached its maximum, that Major Thorpe returned with Lieutenant Linder. Both looked surprised, and, as it was easy to see the real state of things, no less pleased. Major Thorpe at once cleared his voice, and said:

"Captain Winslow and brother officers. Lieutenant Linder has explained to me that, requiring the offices of Private Grey, he obtained permission to employ them, and to perform these offices it is necessary Grey should be within earshot. As men of the very highest rank have availed themselves of persons far beneath themselves and those with whom they associated in station, for a similar purpose, there can be no possible objection to Lieutenant Linder doing the same thing in the present instance; and I certify that he may. Indeed, the whole thing is so ridiculous, that it needs no such explanation even as this, and I must confess my surprise that Captain Winslow should have extorted it in the manner he has done."

"And why, Major Thorpe?" cried Captain Winslow, with fierce hauteur.

"Oh, pray, Winslow, drop that tone and manner with me. You know it does *not* do with me," exclaimed the major, with marked emphasis. "I will answer your question to your ample satisfaction, without being pricked to do so. I repeat, I am surprised, because you do not know Private Grey."

Captain Winslow waved his hand impatiently.

"I repeat, sir, you are mistaken in the man. Grey bears not only the best character in the regiment, but I have reason to believe that, but for adverse circumstances, he might have held a rank certainly not second to yours, Captain Winslow, to which he is entitled by his birth. In no way, therefore, will the dignity of any gentleman be lowered by his presence, to which, at the same time, Lieutenant Linder is fairly entitled; and here ends, I trust, all further feeling on the matter."

And so it did in the breasts of all but Captain Winslow, who now more than ever resolved to accomplish the disgrace of Clifton Grey. He was vexed, annoyed, insulted: Clifton was the occasion. He estimated himself as immeasurably his superior, and was further troubled that his equanimity should be disturbed by such a thing. Grey was "a spider crawling offensive in his sight," and if he could not get some friendly hand to brush it from his path, he was determined to do it himself. He would stick at nothing to accomplish his end; and with a rapid comparison of their respective positions, he could see no difficulty in it, if he exercised ordinary cunning.

He bowed in reply to the speech of Major Thorpe; and as several fresh arrivals were at that moment announced—among them ladies—the whole subject met with an immediate and entire change. Dinner was announced; and many of the officers, favoured with introductions, secured, with no small pleasure, a fair companion each at the magnificently-spread table.

Clifton Grey took up his post at the shoulder of Lieutenant Linder, who, strangely enough, in the French officer already mentioned as having addressed Clifton, he found the friend whom he expected to meet. Their intercourse was of the most friendly kind. Lieutenant Linder found the services of Clifton Grey inestimable. The rapidity and precision with which he conveyed to each the other's sentiments, expressions of good will, observation, and information, while it afforded a striking proof of his proficiency, was also an example of a superior order of intelligence. While thus engaged, he several times observed the large dark eyes of a young and beautiful girl fixed upon him. Ever as he noticed this he turned his own away; fully alive of his present subordinate position, he feared that even to be aware that in some way he attracted her attention might be misconstrued into an act of monstrous presumption on his part. And what made the affair more embarrassing was, that at her side sat Captain Winslow, exerting himself to the utmost of his powers, neither limited nor wanting in attractiveness. Twice or thrice he had observed the fixed expression of her eyes, and following their direction, found, to his chagrin, that they were fastened upon Grey. At first he attributed her fixed gaze to abstraction, and rallied her upon it. She smiled, without denying it, but suddenly she completely upset the charge, and confirmed Captain Winslow's first impression, by observing, in Italian, which he spoke well:

"I believe you are an officer of the Scotch Fusilier Guards?"

"Captain Winslow; devotedly at your service," he said with a bow.

"Pray—is not yonder soldier, who appears to be interpreting between the English and French officer, attached to your regiment?"

"He is, Signora."

"He is a fine, handsome young man."

Captain Winslow's cheek burned with a sudden rage. He twirled his moustache, and fixing his eye insolently upon her, said:

"You are entitled to judge, where I can form no opinion. I would rather be asked what impression your charms had made on me."

"You know his name, of course," persisted the young lady.

"Pshaw!" he returned, with an affected laugh, "we take no heed of our common men. It is by such beauty as thine we are attracted."

"You can ascertain his name for me, Captain Winslow, if I request it, I presume," she asked, as though she did not hear his observation. Somewhat astonished at her pertinacity, he bowed, and remained silent. She did not attempt to disturb the pause, but her eye was upon Clifton, as though the fascination was too strong to permit its gaze in any other direction. It was evident that she entertained no desire to converse with Captain Winslow, beyond obtaining from him information which it galled him to be asked. It was apparent that he was indifferent to her, and equally plain that there was some strange interest raised in her in respect of Clifton Grey. He above all others! Had it been Linder, or Major Thorpe, or Lieutenant Thistlethwayte, who was a smart fellow, he should not have cared; but for this man, who had already given him such ground for dislike, to be preferred to him, by the most beautiful girl present, was too much for his equanimity.

As he watched her soft, though earnest gaze, always in one direction, he felt slighted, and, once more insulted. He resolved to retaliate. Turning to her he said, as he gently touched her arm:

"Pardon my waking you from a blissful dream, and suggesting that you must, indeed, have made an entire surrender of your heart, for this gay scene to have no claim upon your attention."

"Nay, I was but forming a wish."

"May I ask what it is?"

"You can gratify it."

"Put me to the test."

"Comply with the request to obtain the information I mentioned but now I desired to possess."

He shrugged his shoulders with impertinent discourtesy, and, leaning across the table, cried in a loud tone—

"Lieutenant the Honourable Cuthbert Linder, may I claim your attention for one moment?"

Lieutenant Linder bowed haughtily, but made no further reply. Captain Winslow, having obtained the attention of several others as well as the Lieutenant, abandoned his Italian, and adopting the English, in a tone modulated to convey an impression that he was indulging in very severe sarcasm, exclaimed—

"Your *protégé* increases in attraction. A lady, beautiful exceeding imagination, and romantic beyond conception, struck by his personal merits, is anxious to learn his name. Will you favour her by indulging her in so *harmless* a wish?"

These observations were rewarded with a laugh, an evidence rather of the unexpected character of the communication, presumed to have been made in joke, than of any real want of good breeding. The faces of three persons, however, became of the hue of scarlet—the lady's, the lieutenant's, and the soldier's; but although the maiden's cheek burned, and her eye lighted up with an almost unnatural brightness, she preserved the most perfect calmness of demeanour. The instant silence was restored, and before Lieutenant Linder could speak, she exclaimed, in very pure English, and with clear, vibrating tones—

"Had Captain Winslow been desirous of yet further displaying his polished gallantry, and of exhibiting his acute sensibility of that exquisite delicacy pertaining to the true gentleman, which would submit to any sacrifice rather than call a blush into the cheek of a woman, be her position elevated or humble, he might have gained the information for the lady whom he so figuratively described, at the expense of such trouble as would have prevented those less interested being fatigued by having to listen to it. As his gallantry, *sans peur et sans reproche*, it may be, has abruptly taken fright, I may take upon myself to add, Lieutenant Linder, that I should be obliged by your permitting your protégé to make the communication to me personally."

Captain Winslow, as she ceased, smiled, and drank up his wine. But why did he shrink from turning his eye to the right or the left, anywhere but upon the glittering lace upon his embroidered cuff?—why did he feel like the hound who has incurred a thrashing, and is not anxious to make his whereabouts too prominent? Why did he suddenly resolve to bully through the affair, which was assuming uncomfortable proportions? It was easy to answer the question.

Lieutenant Linder drained his glass to the dregs. While Captain Winslow was speaking, he had filled it and emptied it again. As the lady ceased he leaned forward, and in a subdued voice—a marvellous contrast to the bubbling and boiling volcano raging within his breast—said—

"Madam, it is as easy as it is gratifying to comply with your request—not so easy, possibly, to make you comprehend that Captain Winslow's gallantry, as recently displayed, is not national, but peculiar to his family—ancestral, I may say, and, therefore, to be estimated by you as such."

"I dispute your being a judge, although your grandfather is an earl," responded Captain Winslow, with affected nonchalance, notwithstanding the wring the taunt gave his pride. Lieutenant Linder scarcely attempted to subdue his contemptuous explanation, but turned to Grey, who had, with ill-concealed pain, heard all, and requested him at once to pass round the table to where the young lady sat, who desired to have speech with him.

Clifton bowed and obeyed. He had no difficulty in guessing that the Senorita spoken of by the girl in the faldetta and this lady were identical. One glance at the expression of her face was sufficient to assure him that he had wronged her in his thoughts, and that if the maid detested icebergs, the mistress was as pure as one. It was strange that she should desire to speak with him—strange that to him her face seemed familiar, but it was no less painful and humiliating to him to be placed in his present position. At first, a battle with the world to earn the common necessaries of life had startled and shocked him; but he had soon recovered it. Young, strong, ardent, he was fitted for the struggle, prepared to meet it, ready to maintain it, and sternly determined to come out from it the victor. He had expected hardships, scarcity, labour, privations—all those trials the needy have to stand to win bread; but for such an ordeal as he was now undergoing he was quite unprepared, because it was not possible for him to foresee it. It is beyond description to convey the acute agony he was suffering, and had suffered since he had entered that house. He believed, with such a gratified confidence, that he had trodden out all his pride—that he had passed through the fire and was annealed; but, alas! he had never been submitted to such an intensely heating process as this. And this torture he had to endure, with his hands—his whole body in chains; he was a soldier—a mere machine in the hands of his officers: he had only to hear and be silent—to hear and obey—to submit to

the most subtle torments, and yet not lift an eyelash in retaliation. Clifton groaned almost audibly, but he had mastered the fearful temptation to risk all, so that he might have a fair hand-to-hand struggle with Captain Winslow. Fortunately, his better sense displayed to him the insanity of such an act, which would involve his own destruction, without insuring in the least the gratification of a satisfactory retaliation. He almost prayed now, as he advanced to where the Captain sat, that the insults which he felt were in store for him—unmanly and dastardly they were sure to be, would not so exasperate him beyond the possibility of endurance as to impel him to dash his fist in the Captain's face, and thus insure for himself an ignominious death—a death he earnestly hoped would, if it were to overtake him, early be allotted to him in the face of the enemy upon the battle-field.

He determined, at least, to give Captain Winslow no idea that his treatment of him so deeply wounded his spirit; but while he exhibited towards him the respectful manner imposed upon him by the military rules regulating the conduct of a subordinate to a superior, he should at the same time see that duty alone forced him to observe it, while he entertained for him, apart from his military rank, the most profound contempt.

As he made his way to where the lady who had summoned him to her presence sat, he attracted the notice of many a fair maiden, who, had he been decorated with golden epaulettes instead of cotton, would have received his attentions with a delight fully equalling their admiration of his person. He walked with an erect bearing; his well-formed figure thoroughly developed by his military drill, and his person set off by the regimental attire; his handsome face, his clear bright eyes, his open, white ample forehead, his shining, neatly arranged, and parted curling hair, all rendering the laconic but expressive description of him given by the signora to Captain Winslow perfectly just. Well might he have excited the envy of his sallow-faced officer. Well might this man hate him in his heart, when he perceived the cold indifference of the signora directed to himself change into the gentlest courtesy, accompanied by an air of undisguised and undissembled interest, when addressed to Clifton. Fixing his pale grey eye upon our hero, Captain Winslow said, in tones of brutal authority—

"Come here, sir—closer, sir—attention! This lady, sir, smitten by your pretty face, would indulge in a little chat with you; but because she has had the remarkable fancy to descend to your level, be careful to subdue your usual vulgar insolence, and, for the sake of your country, try and remember some of the early lessons in good behaviour received from your gentleman father or lady mamma, for I am assured you had one or the other, or both, I don't know which, and don't much care. Mark me, sir, as the provost marshal has already got his eye upon you, see that your conduct to this lady does not provoke him to add to the amount of reproof he will have to administer."

Clifton Grey's eye fastened itself upon that of Captain Winslow, and the latter could neither release it nor fail to read the language printed there in letters of fire.

"This fellow," he thought, "if he gets a chance, will make a shuttlecock of me. He must be got out of the regiment."

"Captain Winslow," exclaimed Clifton Grey, with a slow clear emphatic enunciation, "I do not deserve to receive from anyone, certainly not from you, such an exhortation as you have just delivered. I have learned to respect myself, and in the achievement have, I trust, acquired the power of doing that which is the truest sign of an English gentleman—abstinence from disrespect to others, especially if their condition be beneath my own. In reference to the provost marshal, I deny that I am under his penal notice. Your assertion has not been made of your own knowledge, and as I presume you are not desirous of repeating that which is not true, I tell you the individual who gave you such information will not dare to reiterate his lie to you in my hearing."

"Oh! you add the bully to the category, I see!" observed the captain, curling his lip as he uttered the sneer, and then added roughly, "No replies to your officer, fellow! Do what you are bid!" and then turning to the signora, whose knowledge of English was not so imperfect as to prevent her understanding the speech the captain had made, and its reply, he said in Italian, "Here is the pretty fellow at your service; shall I put him through his paces?—I know some which will display the elegance of his form to much advantage. Say, signora, in what shall I oblige you?"

"By ceasing to address your unmanly and most contemptible insolence to me; by not even inflicting upon me word or look; and I counsel you to obey me, for I have many friends here, one word to whom will call for the production of all the courage you may possess—a virtue rarely allied to ungentlemanly discourtesy—to face their anger."

Captain Winslow bowed with affected submissiveness.

"I have no wish to offend you," he said, "I am afraid you have misconceived me; if I have, however, undesignedly offended you, pray pardon me. I wished you only to understand that I had no desire to enter the lists, in competition for your fair favour, with one of my men."

The signora arose from her gilded chair with a crimson flush upon her forehead, and an eye glittering like a diamond. The captain quailed beneath her proud, contemptuous, and indignant glance, like a lashed whelp, and rose to permit her to retire. He bowed low, with the endeavour, by an exaggerated air of politeness, to prevent those around perceiving that he had openly insulted her: he had gone too far; and he was alarmed for the consequence, although his was not the nature to show it. He attempted to assist her departure, but

she disdainfully shrank from his offer; she even most scornfully plucked part of her dress from his grasp which he was releasing from an ornament of the chair, to which it had entangled itself, preferring to rend it piecemeal rather than it should be in contact with his hand. She turned to Clifton, who could perceive the tears in her eyes, which she strove hard to keep back in their fountain, and, in tolerable English, she said to him in tones, which, but for an effort, would have been agitated, "You are, I believe, one whom my guardian is desirous to have an interview with. Will you kindly follow me to where we shall meet with him? If we are mistaken in our surmise you shall not be one moment detained."

Clifton bowed, and, with much respect, signified acquiescence. Captain Winslow would have interfered out of mere malice, but he fancied he had gone far enough, and it would be wiser to halt where he had reached. The short colloquy had, however, given Lieutenant Linder, who had been watching Winslow and the lady with a very shrewd surmise as to the real state of the case, an opportunity of reaching the spot and tendering his arm to the signora, to escort her to the door of the room. She looked at him with surprise for a moment, but there could be no mistake as to either his intention or manner, and she accepted with a feeling of gratefulness his prompt attention.

As he bent to her on parting at the door, he said, hastily:

"Pray judge not hastily of British officers by the sample submitted to your inspection during dinner; and be charitable enough to believe, that although there may be some spurious imitations, there are many gentlemen among us."

"I thank you for affording me an evidence of the truth of your observation," replied the Signora, with a gentle inclination of the head, as he passed out of the room. Clifton followed; as he did so, Lieutenant Linder grasped his arm.

"Return as quickly as you can, Grey," he said, "for your services between I and my French friend are invaluable."

Clifton touched his forehead with his extended fingers, and hastened after the lady, not without feeling the peculiarity of his position, or the complexion it might in the minds of the depraved assume. He was not in a clearer atmosphere, when, instead of entering a large saloon where already a number of ladies and gentlemen were assembled, she turned from it down a passage, beckoning him to follow; he obeyed, and after ascending a narrow flight of stairs, which were intercepted by a small corridor, and, pursuing it, she turned out into a wider passage, and pausing before a small door, unlocked it, and bade him enter. He complied, and found himself in a small library, but furnished from floor to ceiling with books. She took up a lamp and elevating it so that the light fell full upon his features, she regarded them with earnestness for a minute, and then proceeding to a part of the room where hung a picture hidden by a curtain, she withdrew it, and disclosed a beautifully painted portrait of a young man in the full dress of an English diplomatist. She gazed upon it, and murmured with some agitation: "This cannot be mere coincidence. Oh no, my heart tells me so. It would not have throbbed so painfully, when suddenly from his fellow soldiers he stood forward upon the sea shore, and turned that face upon me which drove all others from my sight. No, no; it is impossible that I can be mistaken!"

Then recovering herself, and laying her hand gently on his arm, she looked in his face with an expression of soft tenderness, which made every nerve in his body thrill with emotion, and said, "Wait thou here until I return with my guardian—the interval will be but short; but I trust the result will be of grave importance and much happiness to us both."

She quitted the room, and left him alone completely mystified. As he heard her retreating footsteps, he seized the lamp and hastened to inspect the picture, which by her act seemed to have some connection with him; and it was with much astonishment he saw that it presented a most remarkable resemblance to himself, nay, were he similarly attired, it would have served as a faithful likeness of him. Absorbed in the many reflections which this singular discovery created, he did not hear approaching footsteps along the corridor; nor did he even notice the entry of an elderly gentleman attired in deep black, and attended by the Signora who had introduced him to the apartment, until an exclamation from the former roused him from his reverie. He turned at the sound, and hastily apologized for his seeming inattention, and then silently waited what was to follow—the unravelling of a mystery to which he possessed no clue.

The old gentleman, upon catching sight of Clifton's face, now turned full towards him, uttered a hasty ejaculation, and betrayed a motion of surprise; but quickly recovering himself, he turned to the young lady and said in Italian:

"The resemblance is marked indeed. Still the probabilities are so remote, and the evidences so vague, that I am afraid I am but giving way to your romantic infirmity in proceeding thus far."

"Nay, you admit the extraordinary coincidence of feature, dear guardian," she replied, almost entreatingly. "It will be well not to omit accepting any chance lending to discovery which fortune may throw in our way."

The elderly gentleman shrugged his shoulders and exclaimed, "*E meglio cader dalle finestre che dal tetto.* If I do not assent to your present caprice, I shall have to submit to a never-ending complaint of having apathetically parted with a brilliant opportunity of making a grand discovery; in self-defence I assent."

"*Mia cara amici!*" she ejaculated with earnestness, and the old gentleman turned to Clifton and addressed him in very good English, although with a strong foreign accent.

"You are surprised at being called upon to take part in this interview, and without an explanation. This is only natural. I am sorry at present that I am not at liberty to indulge in interpretations, but must confine myself to questioning you. Should your answers prove confirmatory of the expectations aroused in the mind of my sanguine ward, further meetings will be necessary, at which it is more than probable matters now strange and complicated may be elucidated. If your replies shut out the hope entertained, nothing will remain but to thank you for your courtesy, and to part as though we had never met."

"I have no objection to accept your questions," resumed Clifton; "but I may, I hope, be permitted to suggest that I have my reserves, and if I decline to answer some questions you may put to me, it will be looked upon rather as the result of a necessity than as an act of discourtesy."

"Most assuredly. We can demand nothing; we simply ask—it rests with you to reply or refuse, as you are impelled. Will you favour me with your name?"

"It is Grey—Clifton Grey."

"The Signora repeated it with an air of disappointment. "Are you sure?" she asked.

He smiled. "I have known no other" he replied.

"Are you a native of England?"

"I do not know—I fancy not."

"No! Did you never hear your birth-place mentioned?"

"Never. My earliest recollections are connected with London, the capital of England."

"But your father and mother—they were natives of England?"

"I know them not."

"An orphan?"

"I cannot say."

"Pardon me: your replies confuse me. Have you any objection to be more explicit?"

"My birth is enshrouded in mystery."

"In mystery!" ejaculated both the maiden and her guardian, with some eagerness.

"So far, that in infancy I was placed, by whom I know not, in the hands of a London merchant, who reared and educated me. With him I lived until recently. Events unexpected but imperative occasioned our separation. He remains as before a merchant prince. I commenced actual life as you see me, a private soldier in the ranks of the army of England."

"May I ask the name of the merchant who reared and educated you?"

"Oh, certainly. His name is Jayne; his residence is in the city of London, near to the Bank of England."

"Hem!" coughed the old gentleman. "Perplexing—very. There is wonderful likeness of feature, similarity of age, mystery of birth, but total discrepancy in names and places. Pray tell me, as I presume you mingled among merchants, did you ever know one of the name of Huerta?"

"No—stay!"

He put his hand to his forehead to remember. Surely he had heard the name—it was familiar to him; but where or when he had heard it, after some reflection, he found it impossible to recollect. Certainly he did not know any one of that name, and he reiterated his negative.

"Then here ends our inquisitive examination, and your further trouble," observed the old gentleman; while the young lady uttered a sigh of disappointment, stopping before her guardian, and repelled with her hand an evident intention on his part to apply to his money-case, and perform an act which would have been felt by Clifton, if not exactly an insult, yet as one of the painful penalties of his position, although it might have gratified many of his class. She addressed our hero with some earnestness of manner—

"I am less easily satisfied than my guardian," she exclaimed, "with inquiries which, notwithstanding his good will, are more important to me than to him; but I am not without the sense to perceive that although your resemblance is great to one whom we are most desirous to discover, the circumstances of our meeting would render the probability of your being so yet more remarkable. Still the possibility did exist; and as I feel with the proverb, '*L'ultima che si perde è la speranza*,' so I deemed myself justified in making, through my guardian, the inquiries which I wish had met with a more favourable result. Accept this, I pray you, in memory of me, and as some slight acknowledgment of the trouble I have occasioned you."

She handed him, as she concluded, a very handsome and massive gold ring. He accepted it with a grateful inclination—

"I have no claim to this," he said; "but I take it because I would bear with me some token that if the friends I have known in brighter days have fallen from me, there are some who, in more adverse times, have treated me with gentle courtesy. In my tent, by the watchfire, nay, in the hour of battle, when it presses my finger as I grasp my musket, it shall serve to remind me of one who, overlooking the humble position I occupy in contrast to her own elevated condition, did not permit me, during our brief interview, to detect the disparity which others have sought to make me remember with bitterness. Farewell, signora; and, believe me, I too regret the inquiries made have not resulted as you wished. You, it is evident, are on the search for a lost relative—I should only be too glad to penetrate the mystery that veils my origin. Should I survive the war and return to England, my energies will be directed to the accomplishment of this my first, at least my chief object; and as—as I feel some strange, undefined impression since I have gazed at yon portrait, I may be pardoned by you if I acknowledge an impression that future researches may lead me in this direction,

even though the examination which has taken place seems opposed to such a presumption. Will you consider me improperly forgetful of my condition if I ask you for the opportunity of reopening this subject, should circumstances, at a future day, seem to require it?"

"There can be no possible objection," observed the guardian. "We are too anxious to discover the missing heir to throw difficulties in the way of any researches, come from what quarter they may." He produced a small pocket-book, and drawing from it a card, gave it to Clifton, adding:

"When you think there are grounds for addressing to me a communication, it will reach me there."

Clifton took it and consigned it to a place of safety, and then, receiving the necessary directions to enable him to regain the room he had quitted with the Signora, departed, feeling, as he did so, that the lustrous eyes of the beautiful Signora were bent earnestly upon him, and that they followed him so long as he was in their sight.

While he gazed upon her face, as they stood together in the library, as he listened to the soft tones of her voice, he could not help remarking to himself, how much her eyes, her voice, her manner, were like to those of Preciosa. It was strange he should have made no mention of it. Had he done so, how changed might have been the events now awaiting him, but he did not. It was not intended that he should; he had a mission to fulfil—let us see how he fulfilled it.

When he returned to the dining-room, all the ladies had disappeared, and the gentlemen were over their wine. He gained the side of Lieutenant Linder without attracting the notice of Captain Winslow, and thus escaped taunts that might have got the better of his sense of discipline. The lieutenant had been engaged in hopeless efforts to make his friend, Captain St. Victor le Marchant, comprehend him, as the gallant Frenchman had the most imperfect knowledge of English, and Linder none whatever of French. The evening passed over without further incident, and on some of the following days the regiment was exercised, again, in the use of the Minié rifle: Clifton, as before, proving the best shot, and eliciting from the Colonel some favourable remarks, much to the annoyance of Captain Winslow, who was not only unable to fire with anything approaching the accuracy of aim displayed by Clifton Grey, but was equally incompetent to fulfil his promise of drawing our hero under the notice of the provost marshal, as he had boasted. In fact, so completely did matters take the opposite direction that, in the presence of Captain Winslow, the Colonel who had from the first been struck by the gentlemanly bearing, the well-developed form, the clear, open, manly face of the young soldier, assured him that it was with much gratification he had learned that he had filled the office of interpreter with such knowledge of the language, and with so much intelligence. He recommended him to prize and maintain the good character

CLIFTON GREY AND THE MALTESE GIRL IN THE FALDETTA.

to which he was already entitled, and not to fear, if he did so, that he would be passed over when promotion was a-foot.

Especially gratifying was this praiseful notice, for it was said in the hearing of many who had been present, on the previous night, when Captain Winslow had so defamed him; and they turned their gaze upon the Captain, and shrugged their shoulders, very much as if they thought he had a weakness for lying. Two or three days afterwards, Serjeant Haverel called him on one side, and said with an affected gravity:

"I want to speak with you, to give you a little friendly caution. There has been some one here, enquiring for you."

"Caution—enquiring for me, Serjeant?"

"Hush! there's no need to blow it all over the Lazaretto. This is a devil of a place, this Malta, Grey. The number of girls here is awful, and then they have such black eyes, and such pretty little ankles, and they really are so very friendly that—that ——"

He paused and scratched his head.

"That what?" said Clifton.

"Why daumie, if I was not to think of the girl I left behind me, and whistle it, too, pretty often, I should get fancying half-a-dozen of them to be my darling little Liz,—but no, God bless her pretty little face! I gave her my promise that I would never, while I was away from her, kiss another woman—unless it was impossible to help it—I popped in that clause, you know, Grey, because there are occasions—that is there are ——"

"Well, but you have not taken me aside in this secret manner merely to warn me against the blandishments of the pretty girls of Malta, have you?"

"Why no, not entirely, although it has a great deal to do with it; for you see you are my pupil, as I call you, and I don't mean to let you make a fool of yourself if I can prevent it."

"Thank you."

"I mean it: and why I say it is, there came here to-day a pretty little brunette with her head folded up in that shawl thing the women here wear."

"The faldetta."

"Ay some such fidd-lddle name. Well, with the wickedest black eyes glittering upon me, and the prettiest little foot, which she popped in and out like a mouse at play, dodging my toes—she asked for you."

"For me!"

"For you. I soon found that she couldn't speak much English—she mixed up a lot of French—and Dutch I think—with it. Strange it is, Grey, that the people about here can't speak our language, and it is so easy too. She should hear Lizzie, when the fit's on; she'd have talked in one half-hour as much as would have taken the other a twelve month to get through. But I see you are impatient. She was disappointed that you were not here, and at last, when I told her you was my friend, and if she'd a message to leave I'd give it

to you, then she said something about you being cold and reserved, and there was no embracemong* about you. I told her she laboured under a trifling mistake, and just to save your character—with no other motive in life—I embraced her a little."

"A little?"

"Only a little; and I told her that if she would come amongst us Scots Fusiliers, and give us a fair chance, she would find there was a good deal of embracemong about us, and then —"

The Serjeant paused.

"Then what?" asked Clifton.

"Well, I'm afraid I gave her a kiss—that is to say, if I was put on my oath, mind you, Grey, I should assert positively I gave her a kiss."

"Really, serjeant, I think the caution must come from my side."

"Not at all. I am an older soldier than you, and can take a pretty girl in my arms and give her a kiss just in a friendly way."

"Platonically."

"Platon-ically—no, one buss only, and have done with it. Present arms, fire, and fall back. You, you young villain, would be for keeping up the fire. As for me, though I confess that a pair of sparkling black eyes, and two ruddy, soft, pouting, impudent lips, just close enough to mine to make me smell primroses, does not make me feel pious, yet somehow it does make me think of my own darling Liz:

'Her brow's like the dawn, Her step's like the fawn,
With her beauty there's none can compare;
For the work that she makes, and the hearts that she breaks—
Oh, there's none like sweet Lizzie the Fair!'

Oh, Fortune and Fate, and every other spirit or destiny, if that little black-eyed wench that I taught to have a good opinion of the bold Fusiliers had only been my Lizzie—wheugh! do you think I should'nt have reloaded after one fire? Lord! how I should have hugged her; but I didnt. No—instead, I let her go directly I had disturbed the bloom on her tulips.

'Oh, ducks and peas,
And Stilton cheese!'

It is dangerous work moving the bloom. I thought so, and let go at once, and therefore think it proper to give you a friendly caution; for

'There's danger in that dark blue eye,
And mischief on that curling lip;
There's peril in that low, soft sigh—
The honey of her breath to sip.'"

"Admitting all this," exclaimed Clifton, as the serjeant ceased singing, "and promising to be both cautious and wise, did the lady of the faldetta leave any message for me?"

"No, sir. If she had, I should have been able then

---

* The serjeant probably had heard the French word *empressement* used.

to judge whether she or you required advice. I might
have hinted to her—

    ' Were it not for the men girls would ne'er do amiss,
    Nor papas nor mammas disobey.'

" While to you I should have sung—

      'I know a maiden fair to see—
        Take care !
      She can both false and friendly be—
        Beware ! Beware !
        Trust her not;
      She is fooling thee !' "

"Serjeant Haverel," cried Clifton, laughing, and
turning away, "you are musical to-day, and merry.
I leave you; for I am hardly in your mood. Neither
sermons nor songs suit me at this moment."

"Will a letter answer the purpose ?" cried the serjeant, with a loud laugh.

"A letter ?" echoed Clifton; and his heart beat
violently. A letter for him. Had a mail from England
arrived ? Had Myra discovered his destination, and
despatched a letter after him ? Oh ! that it might be
so. He turned to the serjeant, and held out his hand.
"Give it me," he said, briefly.

The serjeant shook his head gravely as he produced
from his pocket a small, neatly-folded note, and, holding it between his forefinger and thumb, passed it
backwards and forwards about a foot beneath his nose,
"It smells," he said, "like Atkinson's shop in Bond
Street; and if it does not say inside, 'Young soldier—
you are just my style—Pray give me a call,' I'll
eat it."

    ' Will you walk into my parlour ?
    Said a spider to a fly;
    'Tis the prettiest little parlour
    That ever you did spy.' "

Clifton snatched the note from his hand with an
impatient exclamation, and abruptly quitted him, in
order to inspect its contents alone. As soon as he
found himself unobserved, he tore open the missive.
The characters were evidently traced by a female hand
—small, and beautifully formed. They ran thus:

"My DEAR FRIEND,—Since our brief interview, and
its unsatisfactory revelations, I have had my first imperfect convictions strengthened by my remembrance
of your features, your form, voice, and manner. This,
in defiance of statements all in opposition to that impression, which induces me to believe you are he whom
they say you are not. This is a mystery the future
can alone decide; but as you have resolved, at a coming
time, to make search for those from whom you have
been separated, and as a clue may be furnished from
sources the least expected, and existing in directions
not likely to be examined by you, I have determined
to draw up a brief history of him we would discover,
accompanied by much minutiæ of detail. Should circumstances, therefore, direct you, during your own
search, to the path wherein our lost one may be found,
you, out of the generosity of heart which distinguishes
your nation—and you, especially, as I have already

proved, will be able, not alone to inform myself and
guardian of your so much desired success, but him
whom we are waiting with such weary expectancy,
where he may find those whose existence will prove to
him of priceless value. This favour will add one more
weighty obligation to those already incurred. It will
not be refused, that I feel. As yet I have no return
to make, but to pray constantly to the Queen of
Heaven to intercede for your safety in performing
your part in the vast and dangerous enterprise undertaken by your gallant nation and the brave French in
defence of the oppressed Turk; but the time may
come—I pray it may—when I shall be permitted to
record more appreciably the sense I entertain of
the service you have rendered me. I will forward to
you the packet herein mentioned to-night by the same
trusty messenger, who will bring me any response you
may think necessary to send me. May God preserve
you.   "SYLVA."

Clifton perused the billet twice or thrice; the whole
affair was sufficiently remarkable to cause him to
attach to it an importance which no ordinary circumstance could have occasioned, and he at once retired to
a small inn in the city, and there wrote briefly the
particulars of his own history, so far as he was
acquainted with them. He was struck by the resemblance between himself and the portrait; it haunted
him. Why should it not have some connection with
his origin ? Upon reflection, the improbability was not
so great as it had first appeared. At all events, no
harm could arise by placing in the possession of the
sweet-faced and gentle Sylva those links in his history
which might hereafter afford a clue to the discovery of
his family; and he now longed to receive those papers
mentioned by the lady in her note, for from them he
quite expected to glean information respecting himself.
Wild and visionary such speculations might have appeared to calmer reasoners, but he seemed to feel there
were wanting only some minor links in the chain of
evidence to confirm him in the impression which he in
common with Sylva had formed, that he was identically
the being of whom they were in search, although
absolute identity was wanting, and was not just at
present likely to be forthcoming. Now he bethought
himself of Preciosa, of what Mr. Jayne had said
respecting the instructions he had received to keep her
and himself apart; and now he had some confused
notion that it was in her presence that he had heard
the name of Huerta mentioned. He would have
alluded to this in his communication to Sylva, but he
had finished and closed it before it crossed him, and
the hour for his return to the Lazaretto had arrived;
he had not a minute to lose, so he determined to leave
it to another opportunity, and made the best of his way
to quarters.

He had been back but a few minutes, when he was
summoned to meet the lady in the falditta, Sylva's
messenger. He at once recognised her as the same

lively dark-eyed girl he had met on his memorable visit to Sliema, and expected to be bantered with by her. But no; her eyes flashed, it is true, with unusual brightness; he fancied even a tear glistened in them; her face was flushed and heated, and her smooth shining hair somewhat disturbed. There were several rents in her faldetta too, which she exposed in her endeavours to hide them, by arranging it to prevent their being seen. She was haughty and distant in her manner, and scarcely spoke. When she saw Clifton, she drew close to him, and handed a packet to him tied with blue ribbon. He thanked her as he received it, but impatiently she interrupted him, and, with a frowning brow, enquired if he had any reply to make. He gazed earnestly upon her; he could not understand her manner, so different to what it had been. He did not, however, seek to induce her to change it; he addressed her in kind terms, gave her the packet he had written, and begged her somewhat anxiously to be careful in her return to avoid the rambling soldiery who might be on their way to barracks, as those who had been drinking were not likely to pause at a common insult. Her lip curled and her eye flashed; she threw her head back haughtily, and shewing him a small poignard she held in her hand, she said disdainfully,

"This will answer for men. O Dios mio! Your officers are more dangerous than your comrades. Say," so added abruptly, dropping again the hand which held the poignard, upon which, at a second glance, Clifton fancied there were stains of blood yet moist. "Say, Senor, is there one here who will escort me unmolested five minutes' walk from this. I ask no more, but I wish no less?"

Before Clifton could reply, Sergeant Haverel came, and was about to speak to the girl in familiar terms, when she impetuously repeated her request to Clifton, who translated it to the sergeant.

"I have a whole half hour under my control," he exclaimed, rubbing his hands; "and I am more fit to be trusted with this young woman than you, for you know, Grey,—

'I left my love in England,
    In sadness and in pain,
The tears hung heavy in my eyes,
    But her's fell down like rain.'

I have remembrances to check my exuberance—you none; so, I'll see her safely down Valetta, and if any one offers her a word of offence, he will have to put himself on his defence. Damme! I'll wring his neck as a hungry gipsey does a barn-door fowl's."

"You are brave man and true," said the girl, suddenly, in broken English—"I will go with you."

She took the sergeant's hand, and would on the instant have hurried away; but Clifton stopped the sergeant, and whispered to him—

"There is something in the manner of the girl, Haverel, that assures me she has been ill-treated. Do

not trifle with her, for God's sake, but try and elicit the truth from her."

Sergeant Haverel gave a quick glance at her, nodded hastily to Clifton, and led her away. Clifton retired to consult the contents of her packet, and the moment the opportunity presented itself, he tore it open with trembling hands. What was his astonishment and dismay at discovering, written in large characters, the following words—

"Popinjay! are you advanced enough in charity-school lore to remember the fable of the jack-daw in peacock's feathers, or the ass in the lion's hide? Apply either or both to your own case; they fit you more closely than ever your tailor, Moses, did in the days of your pseudo-gentility. Remember your shilling a-day, and do not mistake yourself for a general. Profit, if you can, by this exposé of your contemptible swagger!"

There was no signature; the hand was disguised; but he did not for a moment entertain a doubt of the quarter from whence this scandalous and insulting epistle had emanated. He was sick with rage and wonder—wonder that for the simple circumstance of having prevented Captain Winslow's brother insulting a modest and respectable girl—he should thus vindictively pursue him. He could not help believing that there was some deeper motive in the captain's hostility than the cause to which, hitherto, he had ascribed it. It was impossible not to feel the greatest contempt for him, as well as rage most difficult to keep in subjection, and at the same time a very justifiable apprehension that he would leave nothing unsought or untried to ruin him. Clifton was therefore compelled to stifle the anger and disgust the conduct he had so unjustly received had given birth to, and inflexibly determine to discharge his duty with correctness and precision, to persevere in that observance of discipline which had already won for him the good opinion of the most influential and observant officers; and he was sure that, as gentlemen and men of honour, they would come forward in the moment of trial, and do justice to his character. He knew how much self-protection from the machinations of Captain Winslow rested with himself. His own clear intelligence taught him that he was placed in a condition which prevented him adopting the course which first and naturally presented itself; and, bitter as was the task, rendered it necessary for him to swallow the bitter potion the captain had prepared for him; but, nerving himself to the prosecution of his purpose, he determined to BIDE HIS TIME. It would come; of that he felt sure. He would not, therefore, hazard its success by a premature exhibition of the many emotions the behaviour of Captain Winslow had excited. Nay, he further schooled himself to show no sign of the wrong he had been compelled to endure, until the proper time. To exhibit to Captain Winslow any other manner than one of freezing coldness he would not do. Sooner might all his prospects perish; but he determined that he should not be gratified by witnessing the pain which the evident abstraction of the papers from the nymph of the faldetta had occasioned him. He resolved to enter upon a careful investigation of the circumstances under which they had been purloined, and when he had secured evidence, which should bring the infamous act home to Captain Winslow, he would then appeal to the Colonel, from whose hands he was sure of justice, whatever the rank of the culprit, superior to his, Clifton's, might be. With some anxiety, he awaited the return of Serjeant Haverel, expecting that he would be able to throw some light on the subject, and when that individual made his appearance, Clifton eagerly questioned him as to the cause of the girl's disturbed manner. He shook his head.

"There's been some rascally behaviour attempted with that girl," he replied, "and we must find it out; but we must proceed with caution. When she came here, she enquired of one of our officers—I suspect who —for you, and he told her to follow him and he would take her where she would see you. I can hardly make out what ensued, because she mixed up such a many languages with a very little English, but I could make out that she was in a room with two or three officers, who, under the pretence of joking with her, were very rude, and stole a parcel with which she was entrusted. She was detained some time, and subjected to much insult, until at last, outraged beyond endurance, she used her knife, and wounded one of the jokers. After that they restored her parcel and let her go. Her enquiries of some of the men enabled her to find you, and that's all the story I have to tell; but, look out, Clifton, we shall soon see who is on the sick-list, and if your parcel has been tampered with, we shall know on what horse to put the right saddle."

"It has been tampered with!"

"The devil! How do you know?"

"The whole contents have been abstracted, and others substituted. I guess at the author of the outrage, and he shall not go unpunished, trust me, Haverel."

"Do nothing rashly, Grey. Get the proofs together, and then appeal to the Colonel; he is the soul of honour and truth: he'll see justice done to you."

"That is the course I intend to pursue, and, unless fate is more than cruel to me, my turn shall come."

"That is certain. Your spoke in the wheel is down now; it will come up as the wheel goes round, never fear."

And so it did.

CHAPTER XIII.

"Pass we the long, unvarying course, the track
Oft trod, that never leaves a trace behind;
Pass we the calm, the gale, the change, the tack,
And each well-known caprice of wave and wind."
BYRON.

"We are 'an army of occupation' at last. The English and French armies have laid hold of a material guarantee, in the shape of some score of square miles of the soil of the Crimea, and they are preparing to extend the area of their rule in their progress towards Sebastopol."
W. H. RUSSELL.

"They have half way conquered Fate
Who go half way to meet her,—as will I.
Freedom hath yet a work for me to do.
So speaks that inward voice, which never yet
Spake falsely, when it urged the spirit on
To noble deeds for country and mankind."
LOWELL.

THE DEPARTURE FROM MALTA—THE ZOUAVE—THE LANDING IN THE CRIMEA—THE FIRST SKIRMISH.

THE declaration of war against Russia was followed by immediate orders for embarkation of the British troops for the new destination, Gallipoli, and all was bustle and preparation. Clifton had no opportunity of communicating to his fair and kind correspondent the loss he had suffered by the robbery of the MSS. forwarded to him by her, but he was enabled to ascertain that Captain Winslow, in consequence of some sudden disorder, was on the sick list, and there was a doubt whether it would not be necessary to leave him behind at Malta; but, although Serjeant Haverel expressed a devout wish that this might occur, yet he was sufficiently patched up to follow in another vessel less crowded and inconvenient than the one in which the Fusiliers embarked and were conveyed to Gallipoli.

It is not the purpose of this history to enter into detail respecting the movements of the British army subsequent to its departure from Malta, and previous to its arrival in the Crimea. Few accidents worth mention occurred to Clifton Grey to interest the reader of this narrative, either at Gallipoli or Varna. In both places Clifton Grey had a sharp taste of what constituted a soldier's life on active service, not only in the hard labour imposed upon him in the regular military duties, the privations which the men had to undergo from the miserably-defective arrangements made for the comfort and the protection of the health of the army by the authorities at home, but as well from the influence of the climate, which, however beautiful its aspect, struck down with mortal blow some of the strongest and healthiest. Clifton had always been very regular in his habits—by no means a free-liver; careful in his diet, and very moderate in the gratification of such appetite as he might possess for strong drinks; he, therefore, escaped the violent attacks of the disease which prostrated numbers of his comrades, and proved fatal to many, and when at last the order for embarkation arrived—to the general satisfaction of the whole army—Clifton had recovered from his slight sickness, and never was in better or robust health. Indeed, his handsome face, and clear but somewhat embrowned skin, looked the personification of sound health, and formed a remarkable contrast to the sallow countenance of his arch enemy, Captain Winslow, who was slowly recovering from the threshold of death, to which he had been hurried by excesses following close upon a partial recovery from a wound received under circumstances with which but few were acquainted. He was but the shadow of himself, and scowled like a demon at our hero on accidentally encountering him, and perceiving how well he looked. How heartily he wished him fast in the grip of the cholera—how futile was such wish! Clifton Grey, however, in the interval between his departure from Malta, and his disembarkation in the Crimea, picked up another staunch friend—a Zouave, whose life he saved one night at a café in Varna. He had entered the place, and partaken of some coffee. A party of French soldiers were in one corner of the room, actively engaged in refreshing themselves, and conversing with each other with no small amount of volubility. The Zouave in question was one of the party. In another part of the coffee-room were seated several Greeks, engaged also in conversation, but there was this difference: that their tone was not so joyous, nor their manner so free and jovial as that of the Frenchmen; indeed, they regarded the latter with fierce and scowling looks, and delivered themselves of remarks varied enough, but comprising only the most insulting observations upon the French nation in general, and the French soldiers before them in particular. Clifton, who had been well be-Greeked at school, had, on his arrival in the East, set himself to work to master the Romaic spoken by the Greeks, by whom they were surrounded, and who were at once servants and dealers in all things. Perseverance and natural aptitude soon enabled him to get sufficiently well acquainted with the language to keep up a common conversation, and though he was hardly so well conversant with it as to properly translate all that was said by the Greeks on the present occasion, he gathered enough, and took an opportunity of remonstrating with them for thus publicly insulting those who were members of a brave nation, undeserving of such remarks as they had made, and who, personally, could have given them no cause for offence. One of the Greeks turned upon him a fierce scowl, and, with a sneer, exclaimed—

"Πολλά περάζεσθε"—("You take too much trouble.")

Clifton assured him he entertained a different opinion. That were the French soldiers to know the tenor of their discourse, they would feel hurt and enraged.

"Τόσον τὸ χαλίτερον"—("So much the better,") responded the Greek, contemptuously.

"I do not intend to listen to language insulting to

men who are friends and allies of my nation; therefore if you desire to speak derogatively of France and Frenchmen, remember you are in a public room, and I should advise you to utter your comments in an under tone, or you may compel me to interpret your remarks; you then will have occasion to repent it," exclaimed Clifton with some warmth.

The Greek waved his hand with contempt, and pointed to a group of Cavasses, Zaptics, and Bashi-Bazouks, informing Clifton that if he knew as much of Turkish as he did of the Romaic, he would hear them indulging in the most scornful remarks concerning the " Giaour Pesevenk " allies of the sultan. He further informed Clifton that if it would afford him comfort and satisfaction, he might interpret what he said, as neither he nor those around him cared the value of a base coin for one or all the Frenchmen assembled there. It happened that the person of Clifton Grey had been the subject of admiring observation to this party of French soldiers; they had observed him address the Greeks, and as in the course of the few remarks uttered, they noted that the looks of the Greeks and Englishman were several times directed to them, they suspected that they were in some way the cause of the conversation, and when Clifton returned to his seat, determined, in a very marked manner, to interfere if observations of a similar character were indulged in by the Greeks, his eye caught that of one of the French soldiers, who politely motioned to him that he wished to have speech with him. Clifton approached him, and a few questions and replies explained the position of affairs. Upon which, one of the party, a Zouave, making profuse acknowledgments to our hero for supporting the honour of France, arose and advanced to the Greek, and addressed him in French, which the other both understood and spoke.

"You have amused yourself and comrades by some very contemptuous remarks about France?" he commenced.

"Well," replied the Greek, "if I have, what then?"

"And of Frenchmen?"

"True. I speak as I find them."

"Are you an Armenian?"

"Yes."

"Mark me, one Jew is equal to three thieves, but it takes nine Jews to make one Armenian. Do you understand me? one Armenian is a greater rascal than twenty-seven thieves. I speak as I find them," added the little Zouave, and turned away with a dignified wave of the hand; having, at the same time, recommended the Greek to introduce his observation into the bowl of his pipe along with his Turkey weed, and smoke it. The Greek had no notion of treating it in such a reflective manner, but whipped a long-bladed knife out of his belt, and sprung from his seat, following, with an exclamation of rage, the short individual who had thus vituperated his whole race; and here would have terminated the career of him who had been one of the *gamins de Paris*, and was now an admirable soldier of the empire, but that Clifton Grey leaped to his feet, and arrested the hand of the Greek; as vigorously grasping the hilt of the knife it was descending on its way to the back of Monsieur le Zouave. With a sharp jerk of the wrist and elbow, he wrested the weapon out of the hand of the infuriated Greek, and flung him on his back; in an instant the whole place was in confusion; the Greeks rushed to the aid of their fallen companion, and the Zaptics, Cavasses, and Bashi-Bazouks advanced to assist the Greeks, but the French-men turned to Clifton, assisting with right good will; and without doing any mischief or injury, they cleared the place of the disagreeable individuals, and sat down to finish their wine, discuss the events which had occurred, and the little Zouave vowed eternal friend-ship to Clifton for having saved his life, which, was however, destined to run another very narrow escape. When the wine was drunk, and the party left the *café*, a volley of musketry from the upper windows was poured on them, immediately after they quitted the threshold of the door: two of them were mortally wounded, a bullet passed through Clifton's cap, and one passed near enough to the Zouave's cheek to make a small gutter there, and give him a ringing in the ears which lasted for some time to come. The assassins were discovered and were afterwards punished, but the additional incident only seemed to add to the fervor of the affection which the Zouave had conceived for our hero. He was a strange little fellow, jauntily dressed; upon his head, with a saucy inclination over his right eye and ear, he wore a kind of red fez that possessed a roll of cloth at the edge, which, set on the head, was intended as a protection. His head was small and bullet shaped, the hair being cropped so close as to make pulling it fabulous; his face was a series of decided developments, nose prominent, cheek bones prominent, forehead prominent, eye-brows prominent, moustache prominent, little piercing black rat-like eyes, and a skin not unlike that which adorns a goose's legs, only a little more coppery. There was not much of it when all were put together, but yet, there was a prominence about the *tout ensemble*, that more than compensated for the want of size. His body was covered with a vest of bright red, which reached to the hips; over it was a bright blue jacket with red facings, entwined by ornaments, neither numerous nor elaborate. A broad silk sash, wound several times round the loins, served the double purpose of keeping up the flowing pantaloons, and acting as a support to the back. The pantaloons, a brilliant scarlet, and copious in dimensions, were caught at the knee, over which they bellied in loose folds; upon his legs were greaves of yellow leather embroidered, which were laced down the back, and set over the shoe. His throat was open and untrammelled by the detestable stock; his beard and moustaches, of the hue of real Spanish leather, were as black and shining as that estimable article

for shoes or travelling bags, and of luxurious propor-tions. He was clean, smart, sharp, but not dapper; he had nothing of that offensive quality so often seen making the principal feature in neat little men. He had served some years in Algeria, and was a perfect type of the class French soldier, genus Zouave.

He admired Clifton's appearance, possibly, because it formed so great a contrast to his own; he liked the chivalry which had induced him to take the initiative in the quarrel with the Greeks; he especially appreciated the ready nimbleness with which he intercepted the descending blow that would have introduced him into purgatory, before he considered that his mission had been fulfilled. He was in ecstacies with the fluency which Clifton displayed in speaking his language, and fraternized with him in a spirit of enthusiasm, which, if it made Clifton smile, at least disposed him, as he had faith in its sincerity to himself, to carry out the *entente cordiale* with a warmth quite up to the antici-pations of M. le Zouave.

Having thus introduced one who proved of no slight service to his English friend, let us proceed with the course of events. A council of war, held at Varna on the 26th of August, and attended by all the English and French generals of full rank, came to the decision of moving at once on Sebastopol. Marshal St. Arnaud issued an eloquent and spirit-stirring order of the day, addressed to the French army; Lord Raglan rose the spirits of the British forces to a pitch of enthusiasm by issuing a memorandum instructing "Mr. Commissary-General Filder to take steps to insure that the troops shall all be provided with a ration of porter for the next few days." A recommendation which, if unromantic and of the earth earthy, was yet received by the men with acclamations, and a kind of presentiment that after their beer they would be able to fight the Russians like devils.

After many anxious hours and false alarms, the order was given for embarkation, and the Scotch Fusilier Guards were stowed away on board the steam transport No. 14, the *Kangaroo*, and as soon as they were on board, sharp work began to be speculated on, and the landing was expected to cause many a brave fellow his life. Still all was animation and spirit on board all the vessels; it is impossible to describe the cheerful eagerness displayed to embark—anything to get away from the valley of death in which they had been encamped, and the life of monotony they had endured while there, a condition which had led to the reckless and thoughtless wooing death by every act calculated to ensure it. Lord Raglan issued very copious instructions, and which were characterised as being remarkable for simplicity, clearness, and pre-cision of language; and when at length all the troops were embarked, and the order was given for sailing, such a sight as presented itself can scarcely be imagined, cannot be described, could only be really comprehended by being seen.

There departed from Varna bay a gigantic squadron of transports, numbering six hundred vessels "covered and protected on every side by a fleet with a battery of 3000 pieces of artillery, and manned by the bravest seamen in the world." What a sight it presented! The vessels extended in long lines NINE MILES ; indeed, it would not be an exaggeration if a yet longer distance were named ; for many a straggling vessel, whose presence was the result of private enterprise, accompanied this enormous fleet—an armada surpassing anything the world had ever heard of, and dwarfing into insignificance the long-famed Invincible Armada of Spain and its 130 war vessels. The orders for sailing were concise and plain ; the Light Division of the British army were ordered to get under weigh on Thursday, September 14th, 1854 ; the Fourth Division to sail at two ; the First at three ; the Third and Fifth to sail at four. The ships were ordered to sail S.S.E. for eight miles, to rendezvous in lat. 45 degrees, and were not to go nearer to the shore than eighty fathoms. And so they sailed.

Clifton was, during the whole time, in a state of restless, feverish excitement it is impossible to describe. He could not rest in one spot for a moment, but elbowed his way here and there among his comrades ; now looking at the amazing extent of the vast fleet, now at the grey sky, anon at the blue water ; then he would think of the future in store for him, whether he should be struck down by an envious bullet, blasting every hope, ere he put foot on shore, or whether he should win distinction in his first fight. How heavy was his sigh, when he reflected how desperate must be the soldier's exertions, how palpable and repeated his deeds of valour, ere he would win his way to preferment ; how crooked the path, how filled with barriers, uprising as each one was surmounted, until success seemed impossible ; how many temptations there were to overcome, to avoid flinging down by one act the task of years ; how determined and incessant the adherence to strict discipline ; how, in fact, almost insuperable were the obstacles to the advancement to which he looked forward. His spirits were dashed as the magnitude of the labour before him presented itself with its full force to his consideration, and for a time he felt downhearted indeed ; but, presently, with the fresh sea breeze, the animated conversation of his comrades, the motion of the vessel, the wondrous sight that presented itself as he gazed over the vessel's side, before, beyond, behind, and around him, the sadness gave way, and with an enthusiastic determination to signalize himself in the coming battle on the shore of the Crimea, he broke into as extravagant spirits as he had been before silent and dejected. He looked around him for some heart sympathising with his own to confer with upon the prospects of the future, upon the sanguine hopes he entertained of carving for himself a bright name. He saw Sergeant Haverel, who, advancing, shook his hand warmly on encountering him, saying :

"You will soon show how you have benefitted by my teaching :

'For now, my boy, we go
To face the Russian foe,
And we'll never leave the field
Till we've made the Russians yield,
And cry quarter from the British blow, hey ! ho!
And cry quarter as our bullets lay them low,'

Ha! ha! and we will lay them low, too, we mean that. See, Grey, we are not going to land at that place there," he continued, pointing to a large town on the shores of the Crimea, which the vessels were slowly passing.

"It is Eupatoria," returned Clifton Grey ; "there runs in the Caradoc with a flag of truce at her bow ; what is that for I wonder ; do the commanders expect the place to surrender without a blow ?"

"That we shall know in good time. I should say now, that would make a good base for operations for an army. A town well fortified on the land side, and with the sea open to the fleet, nothing could be better to enable an advancement upon the interior by easy stages, so as to bring up all the material in good order. Sebastopol, the impregnable, as some of the Frenchmen call it, might then be invested."

"It will take a larger force than we have with us to invest it, if the description I have received of it is correct," replied Clifton.

"Let me whisper in your ear," returned Sergeant Haverel, with a laugh, "We English could take it alone—what, therefore, shall we do with the help of the French, who fight like wild cats. I tell you what, Grey, we shan't need to invest it, we shall carry it by the bold stroke, you'll see."

"We shall," returned Clifton, with a smile,

They did see.

Eupatoria was passed, and at length a place was selected for the landing of the troops—a task of great difficulty and hazard, and involving a large amount of time. The spot chosen was a long low strip of land, which was the result of incessant washing of the waves upon the spot where may be said, at this part, to commence a plateau, rising, by a regular ascent, to what is called the Tent Mountains. A salt lake, a mile in length, and half a one in breadth, runs inland just beyond the sandy beach ; and this low flat coast ran along the borders of the Euxine, until it reaches the mountain ranges immediately in front of Sebastopol.

As early as seven in the morning of Thursday, September 14th, the vessels were off this spot, and drew up in parallel to the beach. The French ships drew closer into the shore than the English, and they had the honour of first landing and planting the French colours on the shores of the Crimea. A small galley, belonging to one of the French men-of-war, freighted with only some sixteen individuals, cut their swift way through the limpid waters, and within a few minutes after the keel of the little craft touched

THE LANDING OF THE BRITISH FORCES IN THE CRIMEA.

"Grey, you are new to it; you will see how we shall go forward; let them blaze away as they will, for every man who falls others will close up. We will show the greasy bears that fighting to us is like parade duty, and do what they may, they can't stop us from taking those heights. What if some of us bite the dust?

> 'The soldier knows that every ba'l,
> A certain billet bears,
> And whether doomed to rise or fall,
> Dishonour's all he fears.'

And not to take the position before us will be dishonour, such as I hope not to see. No, if the retreat is sounded by our bugles, let my hearing be stopped by a Russian bullet."

"Amen!" said Grey, "that is not, however, probable, for though many of us must fall, yet there are others to supply their place, to avenge their deaths, and to maintain the honour and glory of that flag we are all so proud to fight under. No, it may and will be a deadly struggle, but I feel somehow not the least presentiment of death; I only have a dim vision that I shall find myself in yonder frowning redoubt, with the colours of our regiment proudly waving above. By the way, Haverel, Lieutenant Linder is brave to recklessness; you will be near him with the colours—if you can, protect him should he need it; you will, for my sake, do it."

"And my own—and his; he is a gentleman in spirit and in heart, and he shall have my best support, if he requires it—it will not be for the promotion of the health of the foe I encounter for his sake. But see, Grey, the aid-de-camps are galloping to and fro; I want a word with you before we fall in; we may not have another opportunity. We can't tell what the Almighty may have in store for us; but we can make such preparations as in the event of receiving the bullet as a billet, may soften the sorrow of those we leave behind."

"I am glad to hear this from you, Haverel, for it has opened the ground for a communication I would have with you."

"I understand. Well, see here!" he produced from his breast as he spoke a paper packet, sealed and directed, he placed it in Clifton's hand. "I leave behind me if I fall," said he, "the only two persons in the world who may drop a tear to my memory, and for whom I am anxious to provide. One is my dear, good, simple-hearted old mother,. God bless her soul! for she has ever been good and tender to me, rascal and scapegrace that I have been; and the other is—is—you know," he said, hastily coughing, as though some dust had suddenly got in his throat; "it is my Lizzie. My pretty, soft-hearted, fond, darling little Liz, Heaven preserve and keep her. I have heard from her thrice; so fondly she expressed herself, so loving, that dam'me I—I—hem, never mind me, Grey, if I do appear a little weak and foolish—but you see—this girl—this Liz of mine, found out my poor old mother, and told

her she would act as a daughter to her, while I was away from her, and I know she visits her often, and treats her tenderly, and takes her little comforts—in short, more than supplies my place. Now, Grey, though we have not been married, for our courting wasn't over when I was ordered away, yet, don't you think I ought to look upon and consider her as my wife?"

Grey wrung his hand, and said, warmly:

"She deserves no less from you, Haverel."

"And no less shall she have, by God!" he replied, excitedly. Well, in this paper I have put down what I wish done, should the Russians give me my last pill, and if you escape, you will promise to open it and see to my wishes."

"But if I fall too?" suggested Clifton.

The sergeant scratched his head for an instant; it was a poser, because it was so probable; then suddenly his eye brightened, and he said:

"Well, I'll mention it to the surgeon, and he's a good fellow. If you are hurt, you will be brought to him; if you fall dead on the field, he will know where you are when the muster-roll is called, and search you, and then he will open it."

"But why not entrust it to him now?" asked Clifton, "that appears to me to be the wisest plan."

"Because he will be too busy to remember anything about it when perhaps I may ask it of him. If he wants any paper during his operations, he'll tear up my packet to a certainty, and so let it be as it is."

"As you wish," replied Clifton, "I will take the utmost care of it, and if you fall, and I am spared, I will, to the best of my ability, carry out your intentions as you desire them."

"God bless you, my boy! and whatever be my fate, I hope you will come out of the fight without a scratch."

"That is more improbable than your being knocked over, and in anticipation that my career may be cut short, I too have written a few lines for the eyes of one who may heave a sigh when she hears I am of the past. I think it quite possible that you will attend the muster roll, and that I may not; therefore I wish you to take charge, until I request its return, of this small packet. Iit is addressed to Miss Myra Aston, to the care of Mr. Jayne, Gresham-street, London; although I know not her present address, it is highly probable that he may, and knowing that, before that paper reaches his hands, I have been killed, he will not hesitate to give it to her."

"I will take charge of it, but I hope, Grey, to-night we shall shake hands together over supper, and tell each other what he did to day for dear old England and her Queen, God bless her!"

No more was said after this. They both returned to their places with their comrades, and soon the rolling drums announced the hour had come for the capture of the Russian position, or for a terrible reverse of the arms of the allies.

The whole of the allies, after receiving the word of command, were soon under arms, and an advance was made upon the river and within three miles of the village. Here the British halted, and at half-past twelve the French commenced shelling the heights. The smaller war steamers, French and English, now edged in near the shore, and commenced throwing up shells, which went crashing among the Russian troops in their position on the extreme right. The *Vesuvius*, Captain Powell, was eminently conspicuous; the practice it exhibited was splendid for its accuracy, and great in its advantages, for it occasioned such havoc in the enemy's squares that they were compelled to retreat until they were at least three thousand yards—nearly two miles—from the sea. The Russians fired at the ships furiously, but without the least avail. The French artillery on land was also well served, the shells poured in among the enemy with admirable precision, committing great execution. But 40,000 Russians were on the heights, and though for one hour and a half the French kept plying their artillery, no displacement of the Russians from their position was the consequence.

Suddenly a cloud of French skirmishers appeared struggling up the heights, covering the French columns which pressed forward in their rear compactly, resolutely, and rapidly; the Russians poured into the advancing troops terrific volleys, which the French skirmishers returned with deadly accuracy. A mass of Russian infantry now unmasked themselves in a most commanding position above the approaching French, and poured in rapid and murderous discharges of musketry among them. The skirmishers were at once drawn in, and then the whole force made the *pas de charge*, and scattered the Russians like a flock of frightened sheep, and the French troops continued their rapid progress successfully up the heights. Lord Raglan, at ten minutes to two, after anxiously watching the movements of his allies, threw out a line of skirmishers. The Russians now set the village on fire, and dense volumes of smoke rolled over their position so as to obscure them from sight. This was a military manœuvre—designed with forethought, and executed with skill. Still the rifles advanced, firing their miniés with clever precision they were followed by columns of infantry of the various divisions until the village was closely approached, and then a halt was commanded. The skirmishers were now within 1,200 yards of the Russian batteries, which immediately commenced belching forth shot and flame, the balls sweeping between the open spaces, between the nimble riflemen, and bounding over the uneven ground until they reached the columns standing motionless, or ploughed up the earth in front, and buried themselves.

Clifton's eager eyes strained themselves in noting all that was going on. With beating heart he watched the brilliant movements of the French, who, in spite of the devastating fire to which they were subjected, pressed still forward, scrambling like cats where no human being could be expected to maintain a footing; and now his pulse throbbed, as he saw a blaze of fire shoot out from the Russian batteries, and direct itself —a storm of red hot iron hail—along the whole British line. Clifton grasped his musket convulsively, and set his teeth; but the shower was short, it did not reach their column, though he saw a number of the rifles swept away before it. An aid-de-camp now came galloping up; the French had crossed the Alma, but as they had not yet succeeded in occupying the position agreed on, Lord Raglan ordered the troops within range of the Russian fire to lie down, rather than to fall back, and the British artillery was ordered to direct its fire at the masses of Russian infantry, gathering, extending, and thickening under the protection of the batteries. The British guns did severe execution, and it could be perceived that hundreds fell after each discharge, but the troops were impatient, and longed to be engaged; they murmured as they lay there, for several of the poor fellows had limbs taken off before they had obtained a chance of striking a blow in the service of their country.

A comrade who lay next to Clifton, a light hearted Irishman, named Mickey Dunigan, whispered to him:

"Musha bad luck to the taste that likes this better than fighting. Sure, it's time enough to bite the dirty ground av a blagguard of a Rooshan kilt me intirely. Ah, now! I've kem into possession of my 'dirty acres' any way. By my sowl its give up my share of the estates I will to them as hungers for the likes of 'em."

A round shot fell within two feet of their heads at this moment, threw up a cloud of mould, passed over them, and by a groan of pain which rose up behind them, they knew some poor fellow was horribly mutilated by this anything but agreeable visitor.

"There's a dirty spalpeen for you," said the Irishman, in a louder tone. "Blur an ouns. Them Rooshins are throwin' dirt in our eyes. O'thin, wait till a while ago, an' I'll give some of 'em mud enough to kiver 'em, an' the Lord steps atune me an' harm."

"You may not have the chance," returned Clifton, who felt restive at laying on his face, for some unlucky ball, that might deprive him of all his future hopes. "If we stop here long enough, there's a strong likelihood that a good number will answer the muster roll short of an arm or leg."

"Ah now! be asy, God's good. Sure, I'd like to have a prod at the Rooshans, if its only for the honour of dear ould Ireland, but, if its God's will that my billet's made out for this spot, sure I'll die asy. Haven't I done my duty with the priest, Mr. Wheble, blessings on him! and sure, hasn't his riverence tould me I'll stand a chance for—"

"Silence, there, my men!" cried an officer, in a cheerful tone, "look to your arms; we shall have the word of command to be up and at them directly."

A deep, hoarse, though suppressed murmur of approbation, ran among the men at this observation. Meanwhile, the hail of shot—round and case, and shell—grow thicker and heavier. Lord Raglan was getting fidgety, for he knew he had an army of untried men, but he knew their character too. He knew they had, as a body, superior intelligence to the troops, in those days of yore, when he fought under the Great Duke, who bravely as they conducted themselves, were still men experienced in many a hard fought field, and he therefore, felt, that as the men now under his command were conscious that the honour of England was entrusted to their keeping, he might safely rely upon them, whatever their lack of experience, to do and dare all that he could expect from them. With an excited and a throbbing heart he gave the order for the whole line to advance.

The word ran like an ignited train of gunpowder, through every division.

The men, with a wild stentorian cheer, uprose as if by magic, and in the face of a hurricane of flame, shot, and shell, sprung forward, led on and cheered by their gallant officers. Into the river Alma they plunged with a yell of delight, and in another instant the foremost were on the opposite banks. Of these was Clifton Grey.

His hour had come. His dream, his aspiration, the problem of his future life, was now to be solved. His breath came short and quick; he who would not have trod on a worm, in hours of peace, was now about to smite down and slay his fellow man; this thought did not intrude itself upon him, he compressed his lips, and gripped his musket. He breathed the name of Myra twice or thrice, and murmured.

"For you! for you, dearest, you shall, hear my name spoken of in honour, or of my death."

Up went the brave soldiers, pressing up the steep heights in the face of a blistering blaze of shot and shell, which knocked down hundreds of the men, never to rise again. The progress of the First Division, bravely led by the Duke of Cambridge, who did honour to his connexion with the royal house of England, directed their attention to a most formidable battery on the left, from which issued a tremendous shower of round and grape shot. Above this advanced an immense mass of Russian infantry, prepared to attack the Guards and Highlanders if they carried the battery. The quick eye of the commander-in-chief perceived this, and directing two guns to be brought up, their fire was brought to bear upon the menacing foe. The execution of these guns was tremendous; they cut channels through and through the mass of Russian infantry, and created such a panic that, after wavering and staggering, they turned and fled.

On pressed the brave Fusiliers, supported on either side by the Coldstreams and the Highlanders under Sir Colin Campbell. As they passed through the small vine yards, the Irishman next to Clifton coolly pulled down a handful of the grapes, saying to Clifton, as he crammed them into his mouth:

"Taste some; sure they're swater than thim grapes the Russians are shying at us, any way."

Clifton's eyes were, however, only on the bold officers who led them, or on the colors, borne with a proud and noble air by Lieutenants Linder and Thistlethwaite. At last they were face to face with the battery.

"Reserve your fire, lads, and take them at close quarters," cried the firm and manly voice of the major. The men responded with a cheer; their line was as even and firm as at a review. Suddenly a blasting blaze of flame came from the battery, a roar of thunder and a terrific storm of shot poured into the ranks of the advancing men, who answered with a wild cheer which rose up ringing loud above the tremendous din of cannon and musketry.

"A sergeant's stripes for the first man in the battery!" roared the Duke of Cambridge at the top of his voice.

"Clifton Grey claims it!" almost screamed a youthful voice, and one of the Fusilier Guards bounded from the line right into the belching flame incessantly flashing from the battery. In another instant a single human form was seen to leap bodily into the side of the formidable redoubt, a smart crack of a piece, scarcely heard, followed, and the gunners in charge of the deadly instrument where this bold adventurer sprung upon them found themselves attacked by one who fought with the desperation of frenzy.

"Whroop for ould Ireland!" yelled a voice, in the rear of the brave youth, who it will be easily recognised was Clifton Grey, and who was striving to maintain his ground. "Good luck to the likes iv you, my bould Fusilier; sure here I am to help you. Kim out o' that, you dirty, grasy blayguards. Whroop! Here's Paddy from Cork among you." And the Irishman used his bayonet right and left with desperate skill.

"Bravely done, Sergeant Grey," roared Lieutenant Linder, leaping into the redoubt, and elevating the colours of the regiment. "Hurrah for England! God save the Queen! Give it 'em lads."

The Lieutenant, attacked by a score of Russian bayonets, was supported with brilliant courage by Clifton Grey, whose strength seemed to be, under his excitement, superhuman; while Lieutenant Linder, now joined, though at a short distance, by Lieutenant Thistlethwaite, both nobly carrying the proud colours of England, fought bravely. He was followed up and supported by Sergeant Haverel, who shouted and fought with the most determined valour, his sentences being composed of words which had no connection with each other, but were something like:

"England for ever.—Hurrah.—Cold iron, boys, let 'em taste it.—Lizzie for ever.—Down with them.—Hurrah England.—Cold iron to 'em, boys.—Down goes your house."

'If enemies oppose us
When England is at war
With any foreign nation—

"Ha! would you, you thief—that's the lieutenant and the colors; that's one for my Liz. Hurrah!—

"We f..r no wound or scar,
Our roaring guns shall t.ach 'em
Our valor for to know.

"Give 'em cold iron, boys—that's it—fall back, you——."

All this was the work of a moment. A cloud of glittering bayonets in the hands of powerful and determined men flashed over the redoubt. The Scots Fusileers, honour to the brave fellows, were into this death-dealing battery at a bound.

Almost at the same moment, the Grenadier Guards and the Coldstream Guards reached the earthen walls and poured over; and, on the left, a loud, wild, ringing cheer announced the advent of the Highlanders, who, at the express wish of their gallant leader, Sir Colin Campbell, had not returned the Russian fire until they were in close contact, when they poured in a fearful volley upon their opponents, and came clattering over the left of the battery with wild yells, and sweeping away all opposition as a March wind does dry dust.

The battery was won.

The Second and Light Divisions having performed prodigies of valour, and having suffered severe loss, which had not deterred them from their arduous purpose nobly achieved, now crowned the heights. The French at this moment turned the guns they had taken upon the Russian masses; the troops in the redoubts, and the infantry which had again advanced to support them, were now flying, panic stricken and in confusion. The Guards were preparing to follow; the different divisions, indeed, as well as the French, were forcing back the Russian army, and then a body of cavalry, some thousands strong, was noted; the Russian army was in full retreat,—the cavalry was here to cover it. The guns from the French poured, with frightful effect, round and case shot in the masses of retreating Russian infantry, which the Cossacks and lancers vainly sought to shield,—the retreat became an apparent flight.

THE BATTLE OF THE ALMA WAS WON!

CHAPTER XV.

"Hang round the bowers, and fondly looked their last,
And took a long farewell."
GOLDSMITH.

"Can I forget—canst thou forget?"
BYRON.

"Long in its dim recesses pines the spirit,
Wildered and dark, desponding y alone;
Though many a shape of beauty wander near it,
And many a wild and half-remembered tone
Trouble from the divine abyss to cheer it,
Yet still it knows that there is only one
B fore whom it can kneel and tribute bring,
Yet be far less a vassal than a king.

"To feel a want, yet scarce know what it is,
To seek one nature that is always new,
Whose glance is warmer than another's kiss,
Whom we can bear our inmost beauty to,
Nor feel deserted afterward—for this
But with our destined co-mate we can do—
Such longing instinct fills the mighty scope
Of the young soul with one mysterious hope.
So Marguret's heart grew brimming"—
LOWELL.

THE DEPARTURE FROM ARUNDEL.—THE TWO FRIENDS.—THE MUTUAL PROMISE.

WE must now return to Myra Aston, whose first visit to London, which was to become her future residence, was made shortly after her restoration to convalescence, in consequence of the plans adopted hastily, but with sound judgment, by Mr. Randolph.

At an interview, after it had been discovered that nothing could be done at present in bringing Saul Waters to punishment for his outrage on Myra, Mr. Randolph impressed upon Mrs. Aston the necessity of leaving Arundel. In the first place, in the prosecution of her affairs, which accident had placed in his hands and which had brought him to Arundel to find her, as he had already fully explained to her, he would have frequently to consult her, and, from the nature of his professional avocations, repeated journeys to Arundel would be most embarrassing to him. Then, on Myra's account, it would be advisable to change the scene, to save her from being the subject of further attacks from the young ruffian who had so scandalously assailed her, and might return, as well as from being the subject of constant remarks extended throughout the town by all the gossips, who, with a very small quantity of bread, doled out a very large quantity of smck. Mrs. Aston saw the force of the reasoning, and, further, felt it would be very advisable to withdraw Myra from scenes which would all tend to bring Clifton Grey back to her memory—nay, to keep his form ever present in her sight, while the very loneliness of the place would help to make her imagination feed upon his personal and mental qualifications —charms which, by absence and the very romance of her nature, would be much heightened, and therefore induce an indelible impression, which no after proceedings would be able to erase. It was not without a feeling of sympathy—not without a pang for Clifton Grey, in whose situation she was truly interested—that Mrs. Aston felt this last consideration a very strong inducement to quit Arundel; but then her daughter was so very dear to her, that to permit her to form an attachment to one whose means could scarcely fail of being inadequate to keep her even in moderate comfort, were they united, she could not but feel would be acting in a manner unnaturally inattentive to her interests. It is true she remembered her own love match, but she also recollected that if she had been happy in the devoted love of her departed husband, her peace of mind had still in no small degree been embittered by the hostility of his friends to their marriage, and to the want of the resources to procure those comforts and luxuries to which her husband had been accustomed throughout his previous life. To quit Arundel, and withdraw Myra from whatever would tend to remind her of Clifton, and to put her in a position of meeting others who, with advantages of affluence, might possess no less personal attractions, would be the best way of weaning her from the feeling of attachment it was evident she entertained for Clifton, but which might after all be but a first impression on a young heart disposed to love, and, if not fed by intercourse with the object, be effaced by the first really passionate admirer who preferred his suit to her, and pressed it with ardour.

No arguments brought forward, and supported by Mr. Randolph with weighty reasons, had so strong an influence as this; which was, on her part, a quiet, mental operation, in which Mr. Randolph took no part, and with which, to say the truth, he was unacquainted.

Mrs. Aston decided to quit Arundel—that was enough for her professional friend. His presence was required in London, and he was anxious to take Mrs. Aston and her daughter with him. He at once requested Mrs. Aston to take an immediate inventory of her goods—select those things only which she had a strong desire to retain—pack up all her wearing apparel, and leave the rest to him. The good lady did as he desired, and, within a few hours, her part was done. Mr. Randolph was equally prompt. A broker residing in the town was called in, and offered a price for all the furniture it had been determined to dispose of; his offer was accepted, and the money paid down. The dealer followed the transaction by appearing with a cart, which at once conveyed the articles to his own premises. A vehicle from the railway station next appeared, and the packages for London were quickly conveyed thither. The board declaring the house to be let made its appearance, and was affixed to the place from whence Old Waters had carefully removed it the night afterwards; and then the inmates, each female hanging on an arm of Mr. Randolph, quitted the house

for the railway station to leave Arundel—for ever? We shall see.

Myra had taken no part in these movements. Mr. Randolph had begged her to remain still, informing her, with an attempt at pleasantry, that she would assist more by looking on. Her mother begged her not to interfere, because she would make herself ill if she did. Listless, spiritless, indisposed to exert herself, she scarcely knew why; dull, jaded, sad, unconsciously hopeless in the future, she acquiesced, and sat in a sort of dreamy consciousness that something very disagreeable was going on, and something painful was about to happen.

When her mother brought her her walking attire, she put on her bonnet and mantle quite mechanically, only saying:

"Where are we going, mother?"

Her mother stared at her with a frightened look, and replied:

"Have you forgotten we are about to go to London, to stay at Mr. Randolph's."

"For long?"

"I do not know, my dear, perhaps—really, it is impossible to say."

"Pray, mother, shall we be long away from Arundel?"

"God knows! Myra—I cannot tell you. We may never return to it."

"Never! Oh, mother!"

The tears sprung into Myra's eyes, and it was plain that she was now arrived to a consciousness of what was going on, and she gazed with such a beseeching curiosity into her mother's eyes, that the latter could not refrain from saying:

"It is Mr. Randolph's doing, Myra dear—it is for our future welfare. I thought you had understood it so."

"Oh no. Why are we to go away, never to come back here?"

"I do not say we shall never return. I have no reason to say so. That we shall return here to live, as we have done for so many years, is highly improbable; it is for our benefit that this change occurs; surely you, Myra, will not repine at an alteration which can hardly help to much increase your happiness and mine."

"And yours, dear mother?"

"Have I not said so, Myra."

"Go where you will then, mother. I will accompany you without one reluctant word, for your happiness is ever my constant prayer."

Her mother kissed her tenderly on the forehead, and then attired for their journey; they descended to the room in which Mr. Randolph awaited them, prepared to conduct them to the railway. He complimented them on the speed with which they had put on their travelling gear, which, for ladies, was marvellous.

"It is true, you had no glass," he said, with a laugh, "either of you, and that aids a woman's operations singularly. Come, let us say good bye to Arundel for

THE BATTLE OF THE ALMA.

good, it cannot fail to be for wealth and happiness. I hope—and intend it shall be for both."

They moved to the door. Myra gazed round the room; it was here she had first come to a sense that by no man had her heart been so moved as by Clifton; that no being in the human form had raised the emotions in her breast which he had kindled there. It was here she had received him in her real character; it was here she had parted from him, perhaps for ever; and now she was about to quit it, probably never more to return to it; was she, therefore, to give up the memories attached to it—and him with whom they were associated, never! Ah, he was away from her, still lonely and friendless, enduring all the hardships of a soldier's life; danger, illness, death, were around him; a speck of glory only in the long vista before him. She was yet in comfort and competence, before her a world of affluence and position was opening; was she to forget him to whom her heart clung, because fate had made him a private soldier instead of a general officer, as in her estimation he was entitled to be? No; ten thousand times no; she looked at the blank walls; the desolate aspect of the unfurnitured, once comfortable room; her eyes swam in tears, her lips quivered, but she uttered no word. She, too, had her mental operation, as well as her mother: Clifton was likewise the hero of it. Ah! but what different conclusions mother and daughter came to.

As we have said, each female, mother and daughter, taking an arm of Mr. Randolph, quitted the house and made for the railway station. As they, under the influence of that gentleman's movements, hurried on, they were not long in sighting the station. It was at this moment that Ellen Fairfax, advancing towards them, uttered an exclamation of surprise, and stopped Myra. The latter, quitting Mr. Randolph's arm, requested him to proceed, informing him that she, with her friend, would follow.

"Heavens, Myra! what does this mean?" asked Ellen.

"I must tell you some other time, Ellen," returned Myra. "I hardly know myself; but as we have no time for prolonged conversation, let me first ask you after Charley Rowe, whose brave interference on my behalf I can never forget or repay."

"Thank God, Myra, he is out of all danger, but very low, and he is ordered to be kept very quiet. He is very weak and low, but the doctor says there is no fear. How he'll make Saul Waters smart for this when he gets well enough!"

"Mr. Randolph says that terrible being has disappeared, and is not likely to return here soon again; but let us not speak of him. I shudder with horror when I hear him spoken of, or his form crosses my memory. I am about, Ellen, to go to London."

"When?"

"Now, this moment. We are on our way to the station."

"Going to London! Oh, Myra, how I should like to go too. You must write to me."

"It is my intention."

"And I will write to you, and tell everything that has taken place since you left. What part of London are you going to stay in?"

Myra paused for a moment. She did not know if she had heard it mentioned—she could not recollect. She told Ellen suddenly as if struck by a thought—

"You will find it on a painted board at our door; but I shall write to you. Ellen, I want to ask a favour of you, will you grant it?"

"Will I—why, Myra dear, you know I will, not only because I love you, but because somebody else loves you too."

Myra grew paler, but said nothing, and Ellen ran on with her light talk.

"I am bound to do so for his sake. Did he not restore my Charley to me, and did he not say to me, when, poor dear fellow, he stood at this very railway station going off to fight the beastly Russians, all on account of the folly of Charley, did he not say to me, 'You know Myra Aston?' and I said Yes. Well, and then he said, 'I ask you, should any change occur—any unexpected calamity fall upon her and her mother, you will extend to them the same service which you have proffered to me?'"

"Clifton said this, did he, Ellen?" murmured Myra.

"He did, his whole thoughts full of you to the last moment; and I said I would, and so did Charley promise too, as he was a living man, and so he will too, or I'd run away from him if ever married to him, should he decline to do it when he ought and was wanted."

"Thank you truly and sincerely, dear Ellen," said Myra, in low but earnest tones.

"Oh, no thanks to me; see what we owe to him. Yes, Myra, the last words he said to me—and I remember them as well as if they rung in my ears now—some sailor told father when Lord Nelson died he had 'frigates' engraven on his heart,—I believe Mr. Grey's words are carved on mine. I often hear them so loud they startle me, and I turn to see if he is there——"

"What were his last words?" exclaimed Myra, with some earnestness, "have you not told me?"

"Never, because I thought you might fancy things which you ought not, and which would not be true; for as certain as that I am here, I and Charley mean to keep our promise from the very bottom of our hearts—that we do."

"I am sure of it; but the last words he said, dear Ellen?" interrupted Myra, with such a look of appeal, that Ellen's heart was full in a moment; a loving woman herself, she could tell how dear the anxiety Myra felt to hear what had last fallen from his lips, when he was borne away—perhaps because she felt that she was in some way identified with them, and she replied:

"He squeezed my hand hard, as Charley promised to befriend you if ever you stood in need; he said, 'I see you understand me, and by doing this you will more than re—re—repay any—any—any service I—I I—I—I ha—aave ren-ren-rendered you.'" Ellen sobbed out the last words, and Myra, with a mental blessing upon him, felt that she could not have uttered a word, had her life depended on it.

There was a silence of a moment, and Ellen, still wiping the tears from her eyes, continued:

"Then instantly before we could any of us say a word, the disgusting train came up, and there was a ringing in my ears and a flashing in my eyes, and then Clifton—I mean Mr. Clifton Grey, squeezed my hand and kissed my cheek—"

"Your cheek?" faltered Myra.

"Well—no—no—I—oh yes, I remember; he pressed my cheek with both hands, and kissed my forehead, and I felt so cold and sick, and ill, so dizzy, breathless, and blind, that I—could'nt say anything—in fact, when I got a little better, the train had gone, and father was frowning and blowing me up, and telling me, with such a fierce face, that I ought to have known better than to faint before so many people, as they would think I had done it because I was parting with my sweetheart. How absurd of him to fancy such rubbish, and Charley standing by my side, too."

Perhaps Myra for an instant—only for an instant—thought that the father had not delivered himself of such rubbish as his daughter chose to imagine; however, brushing away at once any such impression, she said to her companion:

"I have told you, Ellen, I want to ask a favour of you?"

"And I have just shown you, Myra darling, that you have a right to command it. What can I do; for only tell me, and you shall see whether I am not anxious to serve you.'

"Well, Ellen, I expect—while I am away—a—a—a letter from—a friend—"

"From him—," Ellen pointed her thumb over her shoulder.

Myra gave a slight cough, and turned her long, dark eyelashes towards the ground.

"From—from him—" she repeated, interrogatively, "from him?"

"From him, Myra, who has gone away from us—from whom should I mean? from Mr. Grey, to be sure. Oh, Myra, how, if he loved me—as I am sure he loves you, oh—" she clasped her hands with fervor, "how proud and happy I should be to own it." She paused for a moment, and as though reflection had come to her aid, added, "I mean—if I had not already loved Charley, of course."

Myra, really in her heart, thought so too; why should she hesitate to acknowledge it: she could not say—somehow it was a topic she would have had

no one comment on, speak on, think upon, but herself and Clifton. She scarcely saw that it was not out of any feeling of false pride, of any ridiculous perception of difference of condition between them, that she shrunk from hearing others allude to an attachment between her and Clifton, but that it arose from an emotion which invested with a sacred halo everything connected with him and her affection for him. To fling upon, around him, every spare thought; to build up fairy schemes of fabulous happiness, of exquisite impossibilities; to hear him, in imagination, address her with words of tenderest composition; to see him, in her mental vision, regard her with looks of fondest devotion, was all—all delicious; but to hear any one speak, suggest, allude to it in any way, was altogether distasteful. And yet, anomalous as it may appear, she listened with a degree of pleasure to the rambling chattering of her friend; she could have listened to her for aye, provided the theme were the same, and her own emotions imperceptible. She cast her eyes upon Ellen Fairfax; there was the stamp of truthfulness and sincerity upon her youthful, pretty healthy face; flushed as it was, too, by the feelings and emotions thronging her innocent bosom, raised by the remembrance of Clifton, and all those grave associations with which he was connected; and Myra felt that there was something golden in her honesty of speech; her integrity of spirit; and that to her, of all maidens, to affect an indifference she did not feel, would not be to deceive her, but to call forth perhaps a worse feeling than pity. This train of thought was but the action of a moment, and pressing her arm, Myra said:

"I do expect a letter from him, Ellen, and if not sent to me from this, wherever I may be, will you recover it from the post-office, and address it me the moment you get it."

"That I will, Myra, without even pulling open the edges to peep inside, if it should not happen to be in an envelope, which I dare say it will, for he is a gentleman, every bit of him, that I am sure, let anybody say what they like."

"Nobody does say anything else, do they?" asked Myra, quietly.

"Not that I ever heard of, and they had better not, in my hearing. 'Handsome is as handsome does,' I say; but then, many folks don't think so. There are plenty, Myra, not fit to hold a candle to him, will look upon him as dirt, because he is only a common soldier now."

Myra sighed.

"But never you do so—but there, you never will, I'll be sworn; and who knows, he may come back a general, and a duke, like the great grand old duke that's dead and gone, and then let us see what folks would say—"

"Here we are at the station," cried Mr. Randolph, suddenly pausing at the entrance of the railway building.

"Now Myra dear, bid your friend farewell, for we shall be off in a moment."

"Oh! but I shall come on the platform with you," said Ellen, with a sort of defiant look at Mrs. Aston, as much as to say, 'prevent me if you can'. "For I haven't half said to Myra what I want to."

Mr. Randolph shrugged his shoulders.

"Woman's privilege," he muttered, "which they claim with a pertinacity and perseverance quite equal to the volubility with which they exercise its marvellous, never flagging possession."

Mrs. Aston smiled, and Ellen looked at him, a little mystified. She thought him a frump, and would have said so, but he was Myra's friend, and perhaps it was better to do nothing of the kind.

When they were on the platform, Mr. Randolph and Mrs. Aston made some enquiries respecting the luggage, and Myra and Ellen pursued their tête-a-tête.

"Tell me, Myra darling," whispered Ellen, and at the same time pressing both her hands with earnestness. "Is it any change such as Mr. Grey prophesied, that takes you away from Arundel?"

"No indeed, Ellen."

"Because, dear, do not disguise it—at least, tell me the truth. You have known Nelly Fairfax too long and too well to doubt her truth or her affection. Withhold no such secret from me, out of mere pride, for if it is so, and you will only make a real friend of me, come back to our house, darling, and make it your own. I'll work for, wait on you hand and foot, and if ever I say a wry word, or show a pout on my lip—why—beat me. I'll never complain, so that you are happy."

Ellen, full hearted Ellen, was watery-eyed too; she burst into tears; Myra caught her to her heart, and strained her there, the tears were in her eyes too, as she said: "I have one true friend in the world, Ellen dearest; you have never proved it to me more forcibly, more dearly than now. Heaven bless and reward you for your tender consideration, for your generous purpose! Be at rest, Ellen, my own dear friend; I leave here, as I understand, only to make a change of my position, for one wealthier, higher—but not happier—no! oh, not happier."

"Myra, ought I to be glad that you will be higher in station, and richer in purse, than you have been; no doubt I ought, but some how, I am not. I seem to hear it with a feeling of fear."

"Fear, Ellen?"

"Well—apprehension, and that's all the same, isn't."

"What have you to fear or to apprehend?"

"Me! oh nothing. I did not think of myself, I—I thought of him who is far away."

"What—again Ellen?"

"Why not, Myra."

"You would not make me jealous, you wicked little Nelly, would you."

"I make you jealous? O Lord, not for the world! How could I?"

"You are so very anxious and interested for him."

"Oh Myra, ought I not to be? What has he not done for me, as well as Charley? How should I be, if he had gone away—why, as you are, Myra—and that—that does make me at all times—so miserable, so wretched."

She hid her face in her handkerchief. Myra pressed her arm—and said, with affectionate warmth:

"Have no such thoughts in future: rest assured Clifton was happy in doing what he has done; and whatever he may suffer, he will have no other thought of you and Charley, but those of kindness and friendship."

"God bless him! I know he will not, because he is so noble; and that is why I think of him, and why I ask you—entreat you, would go on my knees to implore you, if I thought there was the least tendency on your part to require it—when you are rich and great, not to forget him—him, Myra, who would die for a kind look from you; who would, if he were a monarch, and you—as he first thought you, a waiting maid at a little public, lift you up to his heart, proud to have you there."

Myra squeezed her hands.

"Forget him, Ellen," she said with a tone and clearness that made the girl start. "Forget him, because I were somewhat richer, no! I shall forget him, only when I am capable of no other remembrance."

Ellen pressed both her hands with enthusiastic fervour.

"Now then, the train? whose for Lun-dun, now—Lun-dun," suddenly shouted a brisk porter, darting suddenly from the down side of the platform, and performing a series of evolutions over the rails, chiefly composed of running backwards and forwards, with no perceptible object but that of throwing nervous people into a sweat of apprehension at the insane indifference the man displayed to being changed into a pancake by the advancing engine;—a feat it was quite capable of performing with more celerity and certainty than the bat of any harlequin the world had a notion of. The worst part of the whole affair being, that the porter, who at least has won from those who observe his antics the title of a reckless fool, is fully aware of the danger he runs, and you know he is.

The Portsmouth and Brighton train now made its appearance in very close proximity.

"Now then, ladies," complacently ejaculated Mr. Randolph, looking with a sharp keen gaze at the advancing train, and dropping a glance to where the luggage was piled for depositing in the luggage van.

"God bless you, Ellen—God bless you!" cried Myra hurriedly, embracing her warmly, at the same moment whispering as she did so. "You will not forget my request, will you, Ellen."

"Oh no, that I won't. I'll go to the post office every morning," responded Ellen, kissing her affectionately, and in her turn whispering. "And when you are a lady, you will not forget what I have asked of you ?"

" You make me laugh, Ellen. My visions of grandeur and rank are not so defined as you would make them appear; but be assured of this, I will not suffer any change to make me forget, where I wish to remember; least of all, shall your truthful sincerity be forgotten or silenced."

"But you will not forget, or look coldly on him, because you may be lifted into a station much higher than his."

"No! as I hope after death to go there," said Myra with solemn earnestness, pointing Heavenward.

"Thank God," ejaculated Ellen heartily. "I am satisfied now."

"I really must, young ladies," exclaimed Mr. Randolph suddenly interposing, speaking although a little excited, quite blandly. He had seated Mrs. Aston in a first class carriage, had secured seats for himself and Myra, and now, to prevent the latter being left behind, abruptly terminated their interesting last words.

"Now, Worthen', Lancin', Shoreham, Brighton, and Lun-dun," bawled the brisk porter, running along the side of the railway carriages, delivering the above names of the places with a pronunciation which defied any one but himself to decipher it.

Ellen followed her friend to the carriage, to which she was conducted with urbane politeness by Mr. Randolph, saw her seated opposite her mother and next to the door, which had been closed as soon as she was seated, and then followed, as usual, the last shake of the hand through the open window.

"Good-bye, Ellen dear," murmured Myra.

"Good-bye, Miss Fairfax, make my remembrances to your father," said Mrs. Aston, with a kind smile and nod.

"Um—a—Good-day, miss," ejaculated Mr. Randolph, with a polite bow.

Poor Ellen Fairfax! she stood and looked at them as though gazing through a heavy falling rain; her lips quivered and trembled, her throat swelled, but though she tried to respond she could not articulate a word.

There was now a cessation of the bawling, but a noise of running feet; and slow and stupid people, who appeared to be woefully ignorant of the only things they were required to know, and the brisk porter, pushed and trundled them into carriages with a bustling movement, as though a frightful accident would occur to the train if it remained in front of the station for another instant. There was the banging of the doors by an excited guard, the brass-bound peak of whose cap was flattened fiercely over his eyes, and the mottled hue of whose face gave him the appearance of having been in angry hostility with a north-easter, and that he had had the worst of it. With a frowning look down the line, as

though a number of persons who had no business to do so were about to get into the train, he shouted :

" All right behind there ?"

"Re—yight here," yelled the brisk porter, giving the handle of the last door he had closed a twist, and himself subsiding into a slow walk. The guard blew his small trilling whistle, the engine moved on, dragging the train after it, and Ellen was left standing alone.

She watched the snake-like line of carriages as it receded, rapidly growing smaller until it whisked round a gradient and was no longer visible to her. Then with a sigh, heavy-hearted and sad, she returned to her home, whither, after a visit to Charley, she was directing her steps when she encountered Myra.

CHAPTER XVI.

" Making their common atmosphere
An interchange of thought and soul ;—
Yet chaining down eye, voice, and ear,
To custom's stern control;

"The encourag'd strife, the cherish'd thought
Still combatting, and still denying ;
The flying fervour to be caught ;
The lingering hope in flying ;

"Until with each poor hunted hart,
To its last covert fairly run,
Life stak'd on that convulsive start."
KINSTON.

" She's mine !

You may settle
Your claims—I'll make mine good."
BYRON.

THE DWELLING IN LONDON.—LIZZIE HASTINGS.—
LETTERS FROM ABROAD.—THE CAPTURE.

MR. Randolph's place of business was in Paper Buildings, in the Temple; his private residence in Baker Street, Portman Square. It was to the latter place he conducted his female companions, on their arrival in London. With his usual business habits he had telegraphed the announcement of his return, and his brougham was in waiting at the station to receive him upon reaching his house. Mrs. Aston and Myra were met and welcomed by his wife and two eldest daughters, two handsome girls, elegantly accomplished, and the manner of their reception was such as could not fail to place them at their ease at once. Mrs. Randolph took charge of Mrs. Aston, and the two Miss Randolphs of Myra, and they led her off to her sleeping chamber at once. Myra, on entering it, gazed somewhat timidly around her; she thought of her own dear little bed-room in Arundel, and of the many happy hours she had spent in it; she wondered what was to be in store for her here. What cheering hopes!

what fond surmises! what forebodings! what tears! She sighed; she could not help it; she would not have had it noticed, but it was not possible to prevent it. The two sisters looked at each other, and then the eldest, who had observed the direction which Myra's eyes had taken, said:

"The room is small, Miss Aston, but we have endeavoured to make it as comfortable for you as we can, and if you should find out any deficiencies you wish supplied, only let me or my sister know, and mamma will directly see that you are furnished with them."

This was said in a tone in which disappointment was slightly visible. Myra turned to her, and with evident surprise said:

"Indeed, Miss Randolph, a hasty glance assures me that nothing which considerate thoughtfulness would place at my command is absent. It is impossible not to be struck with the aspect of the room; if one could be happy any where, surely it could not fail to be here."

Miss Randolph's eyes brightened.

"And yet you sighed?" she exclaimed.

"Did I?" said Myra. "It is very probable; I thought of the many happy hours I have passed in my own little room at Arundel, though bare in its lack of comforts to this, and the uncertain future presenting itself to me at the same moment—I no doubt did sigh."

"We hope to make the future as happy as the past; that is, as long as we are permitted by fate to be together," exclaimed the eldest girl.

"You are very kind," responded Myra.

"Give us a character when you know us better, Miss Aston," exclaimed the youngest, with a laugh. "I am afraid if you say anything good-natured now, you will find out you have been premature in your remarks."

"Indeed, Miss Randolph, that is scarcely possible," returned Myra, with a smile.

"My name is Isadore, when you speak to me, and not Miss Randolph," cried the young girl laughing. "My sister, there is Miss Randolph, if you please."

"Not to you, at all events, Miss Aston. My name is Sophie," exclaimed the elder, joining in her sister's merry laugh. Myra felt a rush of blood to her face, neck and ears; she remembered her conversation with Clifton upon the same subject, and it almost seemed as though these young ladies had obtained possession of it, and were joking her. She felt, however, it was too absurd for a moment to entertain such a thought, and she joined in the laugh too, saying:

"My name then is Myra, and not Miss Aston: you will understand young ladies, that you will call me by no other."

"Myra, what a pretty name!" both exclaimed in a breath.

"Not prettier than Isadore, or Sophie," returned Myra.

"Well, I think Isadore is a pretty name," exclaimed its fair owner, and giving a sly look at Myra, she said: "It is fortunate, that if one does part with one's surname at some period of one's life, that the christian name remains one's own property."

"Not always," replied her sister with more gravity. "Supposing you are successful in catching Everett's friend, nobody will call you Mrs. Isadore Winslow, they will style you Mrs. Beverley Winslow. So you will, you see, lose the name of Isadore."

"Never. Why, Sophie, you must be mad to think that I am other than disgusted with that senseless puppy, who thinks himself and all belonging to him, 'fust wate.' Have him? I would sooner marry a common soldier, and it is not likely that I should degrade myself so low as that, do you think it is, Sophie?"

"Marry a common soldier! why what are you thinking of," cried Sophie, with a recoil. "For mercy's sake don't let mamma hear you even express such a sentiment as that; she would faint at it."

"Better, nevertheless, than Mr. Beverley Winslow," cried Isadore, with a toss of the head.

Poor Myra, how acutely she felt these unfortunate remarks. The first observation by Isadore of the alternative she would adopt rather than accept the hand of Beverley Winslow was to her like a stab from a dagger in her heart. She became crimson, the eloquent blood displayed itself in her cheeks and forehead, and as Sophie took up the subject and pursued it, she turned from scarlet to a ghastly paleness. What would Clifton have suffered if he had overheard these remarks? Yet was it possible that he could have felt them more acutely than she did at this moment? She thought of Ellen Fairfax's homely proverb, "Handsome is that handsome does," but she had the discretion to see that to enter upon a discussion of the principle just now would be out of place. The sisters, unconscious of having uttered a word to wound her feelings, had only sought to raise a smile by their observations; they found they had not succeeded, and were at a loss to understand why.

"You look pale, Miss Aston," exclaimed Isadore, in a tone of interest.

"Myra, if you please, Isadore," said our heroine, with a soft smile and gentle tone.

"Myra dear I meant to say, of course," cried Isadore, laughing again.

"She is tired, and we are fatiguing her dreadfully," exclaimed Sophie, adding, "We will leave you to yourself for a little time, and then we will come and fetch you into the drawing-room."

Myra thanked her, for she did, indeed, wish to be alone, even for a short time; and both kissing her, skipped out of the room.

After a general survey of the room which was to be her own for some time, and perceiving that many imaginary wants had been supplied in addition to the actual, that, in short, it was impossible for careful considerateness to exceed what had been done to ensure her comfort, she changed her dress, and sat waiting until the return of Isadore and Sophie, feeling that she was about to enter upon an entirely new life. She had only a dim and dreamy notion of what Mr. Randolph's intentions were, and of what his exertions promised; in fact, he had not been very explicit even to her mother, but he seemed to entertain no doubt that Mrs. Aston was entitled to a considerable fortune, a far more elevated position than she now held, and that he could secure it for her. She soon began to have a sense that the supplication of Ellen Fairfax on behalf of Clifton Grey was not unwarrantable; that she should indeed probably be placed in a position in which to forget him entirely would be what the world—such as it is that claims that title—would deem proper and prudent; but would she? No, not to be elevated to a throne: she felt that. Strange that in so short a time their relative positions should be so reversed. When he first met with her at Arundel she had presented herself to him in the capacity of waiting maid to a gentleman of first class education, looking forward to a rank in society the first of its kind. How had he treated her then? As a gentleman who has any claim to the real title always treats a virtuous woman—with the most respectful attention, with the tenderest consideration; neither by look, by gesture, by word, had he acted to her other than if he had considered her of a station far higher than it was even now. And was she to repay this with ungracious and ungrateful pride? She had not a second thought about it. Conduct so contemptible was out of her pale, and she dismissed at once remembrances of what his standing in society was for what he was himself. She loved to dwell on that; she thought him first so noble and so clever, so well read, so fluent in speech, so able in criticism, and sohandsome—so very handsome, for that unquestionably had its weight with her, and she loved to sit and imagine his clear musical voice conversing with her, his deep expressive eye bent on her own, and to believe that though actually apart they were absolutely present in spirit—a communion which would, even to dream of, have thrown Clifton into raptures, had he known what she imagined him to say, and in what terms she fashioned her reply.

She was thus employed when she became conscious that a young girl was in the room coughing, and trying to draw her attention to her presence. She started, and rose up.

"Oh! if you please, Miss," said the girl, "I came to do your hair, and dress you; but I see you've did it."

"Oh, yes, thank you," returned Myra, smiling. "I have been used to do it myself."

"Yes, Miss; but if you please for the future I'm to do it for you."

"Who sent you?"

"Mrs. Randolph, Miss; and if you please, Miss, Miss Sophie bid me tell you she'd be here in a minnit; and if you please if you have any commands for me, Miss, because I'm your maid, Miss."

Myra looked at her. She was young, about, sixteen, good looking, smart in her attire, and strikingly clean; while the arrangement of hair, collar, cap—if these circular pieces of net trimmed with lace, and garnished with such brilliant narrow ribbon and popped so saucily at the back of the head feminine can be called caps—dress, and other parts of her attire, was in such apple-pie order that it would have been impossible to have found an article awry or out of its place.

Myra elicited from her that her name was Lucy, and that she was one of a large family brought up in the country; that her cousin had sent for her to London, and had taught her how to wait, and had paid for her to learn dress making and hair dressing, and in fact had been at all the expense of the education which fitted her for the position she now held, and although her first essay, for which she was more capable than many who had been in such situations several years.

"How old is your cousin;" asked Myra, somewhat interested in her story.

"Just nineteen, Miss," replied the girl.

"Oh!" thought Myra "I see how it is;" and then aloud "He is young to have acted with such thoughtful goodness."

The girl opened her eyes until they appeared of the circumference of tea cups; she turned a violent scarlet and said:

"He'm! its a she'm! my cousin Lizzie Hastings, fust hand with Mrs. Stewart, up in the corner of this street, Miss."

"Oh!" said Myra, quietly, and felt to be growing red too. To her relief, Sophie and Isadore Randolph made their appearance, and they descended to the drawing room, leaving the girl in the room, and promising to be rather a pet of Myra.

She soon felt at home. Mr. and Mrs. Randolph were capable of doing to perfection the social honors of their table, so as to place at ease in a few minutes the greatest possible stranger.

"I have invited no one, and declared the family out to every one to-day," said Mrs. Randolph,

"So that you might, my dear Miss Aston—"

"Myra!" exclaimed Sophie, in a mock heroic tone.

"Myra!" ejaculated Isadore, much in the same strain.

"Myra," said the young lady herself faintly, but with a pleased smile.

"Oh! ah! I see," remarked Mr. Randolph, rubbing his hands. "That is just what I wish—a compact which will be observed on both sides."

"Signed, sealed, and delivered," cried Sophie, in her semi-tragic tones.

"What is signed, sealed, and delivered?" cried a young man sauntering into the room, screwing his eyes up, looking—evidently very near sighted—as if desirous of picking out of the mist before him the various individuals composing the party, being for the moment in a state of the greatest indecision as to whether those present were members of his own family, or strangers as much unknown to him as a tribe of Chippewa Indians. After deciding that an object of only gradually developing feminine proportions and attire was Isidore Randolph, and an individual in dark was her father and his, he halted before Myra, and said:

'Soph—Hallo! Soph—ha ha! why you've been dressing your hair in another style. What a vain puss you are!"

A shout of laughter followed this discovery, and he knew a *fiasco*, of which he was the hero, had been performed. Immediately he popped a pair of handsome gold mounted glasses to his eyes, and saw, looking with some curiosity up into his own, a pair of the loveliest eyes he had ever seen in his life or could ever hope to see, and with these a countenance not a jot less beautiful. He felt hot; he made a bow, and said hastily:

"I beg you ten thousands pardons for making such a mistake. I have no excuse to offer; I ought to have known better. Governor, pray introduce me."

Mr. Randolph at once explained, and Everett Randolph—for the new arrival was Mr. Randolph's son—being aware of the circumstances connected with her case, being with his father in the profession, ejaculated, "By Jove!" and at once proceeded to engage Myra in conversation, but not until his father had explained what he had been about to observe when interrupted, that, for that night, it would be exclusively a family party, so that they might get well acquainted. They did so, and on retiring to rest, none appeared to be dissatisfied with the prospect of having to spend some time in the company of each other.

And some little time passed away, Mr. Randolph had placed it in Mrs. Aston's power to draw upon his bank for a certain sum, much larger than she was likely to require, and set her mind quite at ease, by assuring her, that he had in his possession documents which made her the legal possessor of a much larger amount than he had placed to her credit, but that it would take some little time to realise, and in the interim he was prepared to supply whatever cash she might have occasion for, and this, with the exhortation that she was not to look upon it in the light of an obligation.

Myra, thus surrounded, thus circumstanced, soon lost the rusticity she had possesed. She was still quiet and reserved, but now it wore a different aspect. No one for an instant would construe her retiring manner for bashfulness. Perhaps the pure, simple, child-like diffidence, might have charmed the lover of unsophisticated nature more, but it would be ridiculous to deny that the polish of society of a first class character had not added to the elegance of her bearing,

the ease of her movements, the general impression that her beautiful face and figure conveyed to every one who turned eyes upon them.

One of the most moved was Everett Randolph's friend and school companion, Beverley Winslow, who, one quiet evening, had been brought home by Everett, "just to please the girls," who, when nothing else was on the *tapis*, were glad to have Beverley Winslow to jibe at. Like Everett, he was near sighted, but not so much; nevertheless he trusted to nothing but his glass, and the manner in which he held it to his eye, by the attraction of eye brow and cheek bone, was in its way a clever feat. At first sight, he declared that he succumbed, and that same night requested Everett to put him in the way of a proposal, which, however, his friend declined. He had fallen in love himself at first sight; but almost immediately awoke to the certainty that his suit would be rejected, and therefore had the good sense to set to work and master it. He had no notion, consequently, of assisting a proposition he felt would be infinitely more ridiculous than his own; for though he kept the society of Beverley Winslow, he was not a moment in doubt in respect to the estimate to be formed of his character, and really in a friendly spirit advised him to relinquish his advances in that quarter.

'Wheffo' ?" he asked. "It weally seems to me no wale, because you wevewing and adowing her, a' afwaid to weveal you' passion, that I should be debawed doing so. You must admit, my dea' Evewett, that the lady will have to decide fo' herself, and might not wejoice that you took that pwovince on yourself. You know too, that women are stwuck—unaccountably stwuck by a man's appeawance; now yon'll acknowledge Evewett, my boy, that the' is a dwiffewence between us."

"I do," laconically responded Everett.

"Well, it would weally be pwesumptuous of you, to shut one up by the monstwously widiculous conception, that it would be impossible for her, to sufficiently like me to wewawd my adowation with her hand. You'll excuse me, Evewett, but it is weally too absw'd. It won't beah weflection."

Nevertheless, Everett extorted from him a promise, that he would, for the present, take no steps to prosecute a suit, that without the smallest necessity for shrewdness, or foresight, Everett was certain would be rejected imperatively, and which, therefore, could not fail to be troublesome and annoying if pursued, but which he was very decidedly determined it should not prove.

Beverley Winslow, however, was a more frequent visitor than ever, and as often as consistent with the rules of good breeding, would make a morning call, hoping to see Myra, in which he was not always successful; for when she heard his voice, before entering the room, she retired to her chamber, and regaled herself with a book. She could not extract the fun

THE ABDUCTION OF MYRA ASTON AND LIZZIE HASTINGS.

No. 16.

out of his folly that both Sophie and Isadore Randolph did with much cleverness. He was distasteful to her, she cared not to analyze the feeling, it was enough for her, that there was a sense that he was unpleasant, and though his absence or presence really did not make much difference to her, still, if there was a choice, it would have been, that he should have kept away.

Yet his visits eventually were productive of no little importance to Myra.

Let us in a few words here explain, that soon after Myra's arrival in London, she wrote a long letter to Ellen Fairfax, particularly acquainting her with her present address, and begging her to communicate with her, especially if she had received a letter. This letter was given to the footman to post, who, while on his way to perform the operation, met with an old friend, and immediately the pair adjourned to a neighbouring public-house, where many were the drams—and the 'just one more!' which they swallowed. At length by the time the footman got into the streets he was three parts tipsy, and wholly oblivious of what errand he had been sent on. A few days subsequently he found the letter very dirty, and horribly crumpled, in his coat-tail pocket. He remembered in an instant the circumstances connected with it, and fearful of his neglect being found out, he burnt the missive, purposing stoutly to swear that he had posted it on the day he had been commissioned to do so. In ten days after he received from Myra another letter directed to the same address: he remembered it in a moment. He went out, as though for the purpose of doing as ordered, but really to destroy that also. He went into a tap room of a public house, opened the letter, and commenced perusing the contents which began as follows:

"Dearest Ellen, why have you not answered my letter of the 6th. Pray, dearest, explain your silence."—

He read no more, it went into the flames; he rammed it into the burning coals with the poker, until consumed, and then he returned as before, ready to swear that he had posted it in Old Cavendish Street, and that a little man with spectacles, and a green cotton umbrella, had put a quantity of letters into the box at the same time. Thus Ellen receiving no communication from Myra, could not communicate with her, for Waters destroyed the board which had borne Mr. Randolph's address in the Temple, and the clue for a correspondence between Myra and Clifton by this channel was thus lost. She had written too to Preciosa, but had received no reply, for that young lady had not been permitted to have her letter. Mr. Jayne intercepted it. He smelt communications between Clifton and Preciosa; it was part of the duty he had undertaken to prevent them, either by personal interviews, or by letter; so he skilfully opened the lady's epistles, whether forwarded by her, or addressed to her. Those of no moment to the general instructions he received, he permitted to pass; those which trenched upon them he unhesitatingly and unscrupulously

destroyed. Thus a letter from Senorita Preciosa to Myra, communicating the brief circumstances attendant upon the incident, with which she was connected, in the departure of Clifton from London, was taken possession of by Mr Jayne, read, and with a grin consigned to the fire. This source, as a means of information, was therefore closed against her.

But there was another, and thus she became possessed of it.

Her maid Lucy had become a pet, the girl was anxious, willing, respectful, prompt, and active. She went about her duties with a cheerful spirit, and strove her utmost to give satisfaction. With Myra this was quite enough to ensure it, even had she been less expert, but then she was handy and clever, could really dress hair with taste, make or retrim a dress with skill, and under the tuition of her cousin really do wonders with a bonnet or cap. Her Cousin Lizzie Hastings was not a girl who did her work by halves; though but Lucy's senior only three years, she was much her elder in practical sense, worldly knowledge, and self reliance; and she made it her duty to see after her protegée, and keep her up to the proper standard. Myra had rather encouraged her visits, for she could not but see they were of advantage to the girl, and she could not help liking the cheerful manner and pretty face of Lizzie, or to be struck by the proper and womanly view she always took of the general affairs of life.

One night Myra had declined to go to the Opera, not feeling well. The rest of the family were gone, Mr. and Mrs. Randolph her mother, Everett, and the two girls. She sat for some time in the drawing room reading until she fell into a reverie, and then, though her attitude was the same, her eyes failed to trace the words before them, her memory went back with her to the night at the inn when she first met Clifton. The frightful storm—the subsequent visit—that eventful morning by the Arun; all passed in review before her. Where was he now? had he forgotten her—was he yet alive? The British Army was known to be encamped at Varna, and many had died from disease there; she knew not his regiment—nay she knew not how to set about making any enquiry respecting him. She waited in dreary suspense a letter from him—it came not. Ellen wrote not; it was strange, mysterious, and made her despond. In the midst of the luxury by which she was surrounded, there was an aching void. Oh! had Clifton Grey but been in the position of Everett Randolph, that he might have visited there, or even Beverley Winslow! How hard was fate, that would deny so small a favor to one so worthy, and yet grant it to another in all respects his opposite!— At this moment her eye caught the figure of Mr. Beverley Winslow, sauntering, with affected step and slow, towards the house—now adjusting his eye-glass, anon twiddling the end of his mustache, and all the while twirling and swinging his cane, to the manifest disadvantage of passers by. He was yet some distance off, and a curl of scorn turned the beautiful lip of Myra, as she thought of the disparity in position between him and Clifton.

Her attention thus drawn to him, she perceived that by his carelessness he had contrived to strike with his cane a young female, who, proceeding the same way as himself at a quicker pace, had attempted to pass between him and the railings in front of the houses. The young female evidently stopped, and made an exclamation, and Beverley Winslow paused also; in an instant he gave a kind of tragic start, and seized the young female by the wrist. She struggled for a moment, and then, breaking away, darted down a street, at the corner of which the incident took place, closely followed by Mr. Beverley Winslow. Both disappeared, and Myra felt a little mystified, and, perhaps, a little curious to know what it could all mean. She remained at the window for a minute or two to watch for the *denouement;* but as nothing more was visible of the pair she turned away. As she did so, and before she could leave the window, she saw appear lower down the street from another turning—Mr. Randolph's mansion standing between the two—the same young who seemed to be very neatly and well attired, Beverley Winslow had so suddenly seized. She was hurrying forward almost at a run, and crossed to the same side of the way as that on which Myra was standing; when she reached the house, Myra lost sight of her. Beverley Winslow evidently kept up the pursuit, and as she cared not to watch his movements, she quitted the window. Almost at the same moment there was a loud knocking at the door, and a ring at the bell, and in less than a minute the footman appeared with the announcement that Mr. Beverley Winslow begged to be permitted the honour of paying his respects to Miss Myra Aston; she looked at the man with some astonishment as though she scarcely heard aright, but immediately recovering herself, sent back a request to be excused, being ill, and at the moment retiring to her own room.

The man departed with her message, and she at once went to her chamber, not caring, after the excuse she had sent, either to be seen or to be placed in the way of importunities, which she knew Beverley Winslow, when he ascertained she was at home alone, would be capable of. On reaching her apartment she found there Lucy and her cousin, the latter in her street attire. A glance was sufficient to inform her that this was the young female who had broken away from Beverley Winslow, and whom he had pursued. The girl's face was flushed and heated, and she looked ready to cry. Myra greeted her kindly, but made no allusion to the event she had witnessed. Lizzie Hastings, however, apologised for being in her room in her mantle and bonnet.

"I did it only, I assure you, for the best, miss, for I felt it was the safest—"

"The safest?" repeated Myra.

"Yes, miss," repeated Lizzie, "it is a strange story; I should like to tell it you, if you will not mind letting Lucy go to her own room for a few minutes."

Myra felt awkwardly situated. She was somewhat curious to hear the story—not very much so—but hardly desirous of being made a confidant on such a subject as this promised to be; but still her natural good nature got the better of pride promptings, for she could see the girl was eager to communicate all to her, and she acquiesced. Lucy thereupon went to her room, seemingly as cheerfully as she went about everything, really dying to know what her cousin could have to tell to her young mistress.

Lizzie sat for a moment, hesitating and speculating where to begin her history, and at length, clearing her voice, she said:

"I saw you standing at the window, miss, as I entered the house, and I suppose that you saw me followed by a troublesome and annoying ruffian."

"Ruffian!" echoed Myra, almost with a smile, "why it was Mr. Beverley Winslow, was it not?"

"That is the name which was written on a card which he once sent to her," returned Lizzie, a little excited, "and perhaps I ought to call him a gentleman; but I cannot think him one from his conduct to me, and it goes against my very heart to call him a gentleman—gentleman indeed! Ah, miss, you should have seen a young comrade of—of—of a sergeant in the Guards that I know; ah! he was a gentleman, although he was but a common soldier."

Myra, though she smiled at her earnestness, was struck by the observation.

"You laugh, miss; but you should have seen the young soldier I mean, you would have been more likely to fall in love with him than have laughed at him."

"Indeed!"

"Yes, miss; he was handsome in person, gentle in manner, noble in spirit, and brave as a lion. He knocked down like a pepper-castor that mean wretch Mr. Winslow for annoying me; and he helped me to see my—my husband that will be, if God in his infinite mercy spares him—at the last moment when he left England. He might have been in the ranks, but, oh, he was the true gentleman! I never say my prayers at night without imploring the Almighty to hear me, and send back to England, safe and well, Clifton Grey."

Myra turned pale as death; she clutched Lizzie by the wrist so as to startle her, and gasped out:

"Who?"

Lizzie looked frightened, and replied:

"I hope you'll pardon me, miss, but indeed I trust I have said nothing to offend you."

Myra shook her head impatiently.

"No, no, oh no!" she said, hurriedly, "repeat that name you uttered just now again."

"The soldier's, miss?"

"Yes—yes."

"Clifton Grey."

"It *is* the name!—you saw him—tell me what you know of him—all—all?"

"I do not know much, but all I do I'll willingly tell. I have a sweetheart, miss—it would be affectation to conceal it, and I will first tell you the plain truth."

"Who—him, Mr. Grey?"

"Oh, mercy! no—he's a gentleman"—

"You said but now he was a private soldier."

"That's true, and so the sergeant told me, though he said he believed he was a thorough gentleman who had left his friends out of some quarrel. He entered the army in the ranks."

"Where did the sergeant first meet him—did he enlist him?"

"He did, miss; it was at Arundel, in Sussex. The sergeant told me the whole story; he became a soldier to save a widow named Rowe breaking her heart on account of a son who had enlisted."

"It is the same," mentally ejaculated Myra, and again urged Lizzie to proceed with her narration.

Lizzie Hastings then told her all that the readers already know, something they do not know, and something, too, that Myra had long wanted to know—the name of the regiment which Clifton Grey had joined.

"Have you heard from your friend since he has been gone?" asked Myra, in a quiet voice.

"Oh, yes," replied Lizzie, "I have had three letters from him; two from Malta and one from—from—what is the name of the young prince who had a wonderful lamp?"

"From Aladyn?"

"Yes, that is the place; and there's in each a good long piece written to me by Mr. Grey."

Myra uttered an audible sigh. Clifton had written to this young girl, but not one word to her; still there might be some sound reason for his silence; she had no wish to misjudge him. She felt an intense desire to read the letters—at least, what Clifton had written; the outpourings of Sergeant Haverel's heart to the young girl before her could hardly possess much interest for her; acting on the impulse, she turned to Lizzie, and said:

"If you would not object, I should much like to see those letters?"

"You, Miss?" exclaimed Lizzie, with astonishment, and a rose blush mantling her face and neck. "You would hardly like to read the foolish nonsense Walter Haverel writes."

There was a tremulous motion in Myra's eyes.

"I—I—have some reason to believe—nay, I think I must have known the Mr. Grey you have referred to, I could be better assured of this if I were to see his handwriting."

It flashed through Lizzie's mind that Myra was one of the rich relations of "Gentleman Grey," as Sergeant Haverel was fond of calling him.

"I have not got them with me. They are at my aunt's," she said.

Myra exhibited a motion of pained disappointment. Lizzie Hastings grew hotter in her speculations. "Lor!" she muttered to herself, "perhaps this beautiful young lady is his sweetheart, and her ill-natured friends won't let her have him. I'll be no party to their wickedness, I promise them." Then she said aloud:

"I will try and bring them to you next Sunday, miss, if that will do?"

Next Sunday! This was Tuesday. Myra felt sick at the idea of waiting such a dreary length of time, and then hit upon a simple and very foolish idea. All the family, including her mother, were at the opera; perhaps this aunt did not live a long way off, and she might accompany Lizzie there, peruse the letters, and no one be any the wiser of the mode she had adopted to secure the means of communicating with Clifton, if only to know why he had never written to her.

She glanced at the timepiece upon the mantel-shelf; it wanted a quarter to nine. Looking very earnestly at Lizzie, she said:

"Does your aunt reside very far from this?"

Lizzie felt sure now that she was right in her surmise. She, too, looked at the clock, and exclaimed:

"Dear, dear, I didn't think it was so late. Let me see, my aunt lives in the city; a 'bus from Orchard-street will set us down at the corner of Bread-street, in a little less than half-an-hour, that will be a quarter past nine, and then a quarter-of-an-hour and that'll be half-past nine, then if we run to a 'bus—and don't get one—oh, dear, I'm afraid there's no time to-night."

"Not if we stop here cogitating," replied Myra, and added, with firmness, as though she had quite decided upon the step she would take, "Will you take me there?"

"With all my heart, miss," replied Lizzie; "but I must be back at Mrs. Stewart's by ten or a quarter past at the very latest."

"A cab will not be long taking us, will it?"

"Oh no, much quicker than the 'bus, and much safer, because you can't be annoyed by any impertinent puppy, as you too often are in a 'bus; but then the fare—"

"I'll pay all expenses," exclaimed Myra, putting on her bonnet and a large shawl, which folded entirely round her. She rung the bell, and her maid Lucy appeared.

"I am going out for a short distance," said Myra. "Your cousin will attend me. I shall return in about an hour."

"Yes, miss."

Another minute and the two females were without the house. A cab happened to be passing was hailed, and in they got. Said Lizzie—

"Drive to Little St. Thomas' Apostle, No. 12, next door to a green grocer's, opposite a carpenter and pack-ing-case maker's. There's five bells with brass handles at the side of the door, and a—"

"All right, mum!" cried cabby, who would have been satisfied and proceeded correctly to the destination required if he had received only one-fifth of the above direction.

He drove there at a swift pace along the nearest route, and pulled up in the narrow Bread-street, at the corner of the turning to which he had been directed, in a quarter-of-an-hour from the time they started. Here he was told to wait until they returned, and as the man expressed a very unequivocal desire to possess some security that they would keep their word, Myra readily agreed to pay him his fare, the amount of which he quickly perceived they had no notion of. In answer to the usual question, he said—

"Why my fare's five shillin'."

"Five shillings!" almost screamed Lizzie. "Nonsense, that's impossible. Why it aint five miles."

"You walk it an' try it," said the cab driver; "but that's neither here nor there: I say my fare's five shillin', and I should think I ought to know best. But seeing you two young wimmin are alone, and, generally speaking, you females don't have much money about yer, why say four bob an' its a bargain."

Myra, who understood his offer simply by the amount mentioned, said—

"But I want to return to Baker-street, and that I suppose will be eight shillings."

"How long are you going to stop, mum, because it depends on that?" enquired cabby, affecting caution.

Myra looked at Lizzie.

"A quarter-of-an-hour—not longer," exclaimed the young milliner, quite shocked at the price the driver demanded.

The man scratched his head as if communing with himself; at length he arrived at a decision. Apparently he let his generosity get the better of his mercenary promptings—actually he had made up his mind to be guilty of a scandalous piece of roguery.

"Tip us the dibs," he said, "and I'll take you, though I can tell you I didn't want to go westward agin to-night."

Myra paid him the money, and Lizzie convoyed her to No. 12, St. Thomas' Apostle. She pulled the fourth bell four times, and then took the hand of Myra to guide her up a long winding staircase, dark as Erebus, and which felt damp and shaky to the feet, until the door of the room, occupied by a relative, was reached.

At the same time, cabby, satisfied that neither of the "young wimmin" had taken the number of his cab, drew his horse at a gentle pace into Cheapside, and let it remain near the curb for a few minutes, occasionally raising his little finger to foot passengers as they went by, in hopes, by a new fare, to go away with a pretext. His expectations were answered by a gentleman suddenly pulling open his door, and exclaiming, as he entered and seated himself in the cab, "Regent Street."

Cabby answered "all right," jumped on his box, and drove off at a tremendous pace; immediately afterwards a city policeman appeared from the entry of a neighbouring shop, and, taking out his note book, entered the number of the cab, intending to summons the driver, for plying for hire in a place not appointed by Act of Parliament. In the meanwhile, the girls, thus unconsciously deprived of their means of return, had reached the door of Lizzie's aunt, and knocked for admission, but there was no response; they knocked again, and then Lizzie tried the door, but found it locked. She uttered an exclamation of vexation.

"I'm afraid she is out," she said to Myra, giving, at the same time, a series of hard raps with her knuckles. No response. She shook the door by the handle; no answer. She repeated her efforts still more violently as her expectations grew hopeless, and then suddenly a door on the flight above the one at which she knocked, opened. A head made its appearance over the banisters, and a female voice exclaimed:

"Who did you want?"

"Mrs. Watney," replied Lizzie, quickly.

"Mrs. Watney?" repeated the woman.

"Yes, is she at home?" asked Lizzie.

"Is she at home?" repeated the woman, "no, she is not."

"Do you know where she's gone?"

"Do I know where she's gone? No, I don't."

"Did you see her before she went out?"

"Did I see her before she went out? Yes, I did."

"Did she say how long she would be gone?"

"Did she say how long she would be gone? She said she'd be back in about half an hour."

"How long is that ago?"

"How long is that ago? She went out at eight o'clock."

"It's now past nine."

"Oh yes, it's gone nine."

"Can we wait a few minutes for her?"

"Can you wait a few minutes for her? Well, yes."

"Where?" asked Lizzie, sharply, almost out of patience at the incessant repetition of her questions.

"Where?" echoed the woman, true to her habit, "why in my room if you like. Come up."

Lizzie led the way with a brisk step, ascended the stairs, followed by Myra, and entered an apartment in which there burned a large fire and there stood a large bed. Round the fire were a variety of cooking utensils, and upon the walls were cooking utensils; against it, on shelves, there were plates and dishes of various dimensions; a few pictures were hung up, they had all black-ribbed frames, with a circular brass ornament at each corner, and the pictures were very highly coloured, as in days gone by charity boys' Christmas pieces were, the reds and yellows being very predominant. In the bed were ranged five small heads in night caps, the wearers in deep slumber. The woman, part owner of the apartment, clean and tidy in her attire, had a baby in her arms, making the number then present six, Lizzie looked at the woman, who invited them in kindly terms to be seated, and then at her baby, then at the five in the bed, and then at Myra; she touched the latter on the fingers, and whispered:

"If this is what comes of being married, really I shall begin to fancy we are better off by being single."

"A thousand times!" exclaimed the woman with the baby, who overheard her, "you take my advice, young ladies, if you don't want to sup sorrow by spoonsful, never get married. I've had enough of it, I can tell you; my hands are always full; I'm never still a minnit. What with one and the other on 'em I'm worried out of my life. Don't get married, that's my advice."

"But," cried Lizzie, with eyelids rather extended, "every person who marries has not so many—troubles," she changed her word, though she looked at the babies.

The woman comprehended her meaning instantly, and said:

"Ah, you may well call 'em troubles: plagues they are, and no mistake. I've heard talk of the pleasures of matrimony: I've never experienced it, I can tell you."

This was rather hard upon the young girls, who were not only disappointed in perusing the letters from beings to whom they were warmly attached, but they were doomed to listen to a mournful homily upon married life, in which it was depicted in the harshest terms, and the strongest advice given never to enter its bonds, and that too by one, albeit she had had little in connection with it but toil and struggling poverty, would, if left a widow the following day, terminate her widowhood at the very earliest opportunity.

After sitting a little time, Lizzie grew uneasy and restless; time was going on, and she was anxious not to be out later than the appointed hour for her return. At length, in the midst of a recital of the woman's sorrows and trials, St. Paul's chimed a quarter to ten, and addressing Myra, Lizzie exclaimed:

"Good heavens! we shan't get back by ten, miss. We had better not wait any longer, had we, miss? I am afraid it will not be any use, and my aunt may be much later. If I stop to see her I shall be very late, and as Mrs. Stewart is very particular with her young ladies, I may lose my situation."

"Not for worlds on my account," said Myra, rising, ready to depart.

"Will you leave a message for her?" asked the owner of the apartment.

"Yes," cried Lizzie; "and what a pity I did not think of this before. Will you tell her that her niece Lizzie Hastings has been here, and wants to see her particularly in Baker-street to-morrow; mind, very particularly, and tell her to bring those three letters sent to me from abroad; be sure you tell her that. She must not forget them on any account, for there's life and death connected with them; tell her that, will you, if you please?"

"I will," responded the woman."

"Thank you; that's all. She is to come to see me at Baker-street to-morrow, and bring three letters with her."

"I shall remember."

"And will you let your little things there buy some sweets to-morrow?" exclaimed Myra, placing two half-crowns on the table.

"God bless you, miss!" exclaimed the woman of the apartment, "I don't want that, indeed I don't, for the little attention I have shewn you."

"Never mind, keep it," said Myra, gently; and added, "you'll not forget the message?"

"That, indeed, I will not."

After exchanging farewells, the passage of the stairs was commenced, and, saving a few slips, was successfully accomplished, and the street was gained.

Lizzie ran forward to awaken the cabman, for she was sure he must be asleep by that time; but when she got into Bread-street, there was no cab; she looked right and left, but there was no cab to be seen. She ran back to Myra, and out of breath, she exclaimed:

"There is no cab, it is gone!"

"Gone!" repeated Myra.

"I can't see it anywhere."

"Are you sure you looked in the right place for it?"

"Quite. We came into this street from that end, did we not?"

"I don't know. This place is quite strange to me, and bewilders me."

"We might have come in at the other end, let us go and see, miss."

Myra complied, and the two girls hurried down the street, and after a hasty look down Bow-lane, they saw a cab standing; Lizzie uttered a cry of delight:

"There is the stupid fellow. What made him go mooneying down there?"

They hurried to the cab, and Lizzie opening the door, Myra was about to enter, when the cabman pulled the door rudely out of her hand:

"Now then," he cried, "what are you arter—where are you goin'?"

"Why to Baker Street, where you brought us from, and where we've paid you to take us back to!" exclaimed Lizzie, indignantly.

"Not me—aint been West'ard to-day," replied the cab driver, with the accustomed nonchalance of the genus. "That game won't suit me."

"Not you!" cried Lizzie, indignantly, and at the same time became conscious that it was not the driver to whom Myra had paid eight shillings; and when she became alive to this fact, she told the man the story, and her conviction that they had been infamously cheated. He whistled and laughed:

"He was in a good thing, he war," he observed, with a somewhat envious tone.

Myra ended the remarks by requesting him to take them back to Baker Street.

"I can't," said he, "My fare's Alderman Carden. I'm waiting for him, and he'd be safe to pull me; but look here, take the first turning to the right, and the second to the left, and the first to the right agen, and that'll take you into St. Paul's Churchyard, and there you'll find lots of cabs."

And away they started to follow his advice; but somehow they became mystified, and got into an old fashioned churchyard, and that was not St. Paul's, and then some one directed them again; but they only became further perplexed, and went down some steps through a short alley, and arrived in a long, narrow street, with tall, frowning warehouses, clustering in every direction. Having been told to keep straight on, they crossed over and went down a narrow passage, and soon found themselves in an open space, but where there were high stacks of material piled up in every direction, and in the greatest profusion and confusion.

"We are surely quite wrong," said Myra.

"Oh!" cried Lizzie, wringing her hands, "we have lost our way. I, too, that never did such a stupid thing before. Let us go back again, and find somebody to put us right. Where can the policeman be? there is never one when you want him. We are close to the River Thames, can't you see it flowing through that opening there?"

Myra saw it plain enough; a dark murky sky over head, a swiftly moving, black looking, solemn mass beneath, hurrying silently, heedless of impediment, ever onward. She instinctively shuddered. "Let us go back at once," she said.

At this moment, two men came from the water side; two dark, bulky looking objects, swaggering on, and approaching the spot; one said:

"When do you drop down—with this tide."

"Yes," replied the other, "in half an hour from this, so don't be playing Tom Coxe's traverse, or we shall go away without you."

"Never fear," said the other, "I'll keep within hail of you."

Both Myra and Lizzie were this time retracing their steps towards the streets, when the men overtook them. Lizzie, who had a terrific sense that her fate was in the morning to be brought into the stately presence of Mrs. Stewart, to be treated to a severe lecture, which would be accompanied by a prompt dismissal, although she was a first-rate first hand, and they were busy, and first hands were not to be had at a moment's notice, was distracted at her position, and thankful to catch sight of any one likely to advise her in her strait, and direct her how to get out of her dilemma. Suddenly she turned round, and accosted the men following:

"Can you be kind enough to tell us the way to Baker-street?"

"Baker-street, my lass," said the man, passing in front so as to stand between her and the street to which she was directing her steps, "Baker-street?"

"Yes," and she repeated the word clearly.

"Why, I should say," he returned with a coarse laugh, "through the miller's yard. Come, what are you two girls doing down the wharf here at this late hour?"

"We have lost our way; we want Baker-street—Oxford-street, Cheapside—any where out of this horrible place," exclaimed Lizzie, wringing her hands.

"Give me a kiss, my dear, and I'll show you Cheapside," retorted the fellow, with a boisterous laugh.

"Stand away, man!" almost shrieked Lizzie, as she clutched hold of Myra's wrist: "Stand away, man, or I'll scream for the police, and have you put in the station house, if you dare to lay hand upon either of us."

"Whoo! here's a row of teeth from a small cutter," exclaimed the fellow with a chuckle. "I like your pluck, girl, but I must have a kiss. You had better take it quietly, and then I'll let you go."

"Stand away, man!" cried Lizzie, with flashing eyes, the courage of a lion, and with an assumption of strength far beyond what she actually possessed: "Let us pass—do not insult us for mercy's sake! Do not—dare not touch us! I'll scream for help if you attempt to lay one finger upon us!"

As she uttered these words, she attempted, still firmly clutching Myra's wrist, to glide past the pair; but the fellow dodged them, laughing almost good humouredly, as though he sought only to terrify them. He did not touch Lizzie, but danced before her, with out spread arms, completely intercepting her path. His companion, who had scarcely interfered, now said impatiently:

"Don't be all night over this d—d folly. Have your kiss, and heave a-head. Here, I'll show you how we do it down on our coast."

In an instant he seized Myra—who had shared in this scene with a species of stupified horror—round the waist, and threw her head back. At that moment, the gas light threw a strong glare on her face, and on his:

"Saul—Saul Waters!" she cried, gasping with horror.

"Myra—Myra Aston!" he yelled, "Mine, by God!"

In a moment, he flung the heavy cloth jacket he carried on his arm over her head, and shouted:

"A prize, Bill—a prize such as I never hoped to have. Stop the piping of that screeching cat, and bring her on board with this 'un."

"What the hell are you up to, Saul?" cried his companion, having all but stifled Lizzie with his huge pea jacket.

"Ask no questions now," replied Saul, lifting up Myra, struggling in his arms, and darting down the dark wharf.

"A lark's a lark, and a spree's a spree," said his companion Bill, "but d——n me if I understand this game; however, here goes, in for the pitch in for the pot."

He lifted up Lizzie in his arms; it was in vain she wrenched and twisted herself about with the most desperate exertion of all the strength she possessed. She was but as an infant in his arms. He shot off with his burden into the darkness, making his way to the sombre, sad, soundless, yet swiftly-moving river.

Then all was silent where they had stood.

A moment after, a policeman, yawning and stretching his arms, although he had not been an hour on duty, passed the end of the turning leading to the wharf. He stood at its entrance a minute, with his back towards it, looked up and down Thames-street, and then, with one hand on his lantern, perhaps to warm his fingers, he moved slowly on towards London-bridge.

Upon the wharf itself there was not a sound, and no traces visible of Myra Aston, Lizzie Hastings, or the men who had borne them away.

St. Paul's clock struck the hour of ten, and Mrs. Aston was laughing heartily at the acting of Lablache.

CHAPTER XVII.

"The Guards had stormed the right of the battery ere the Highlanders got into the left; and it is said the Scots Fusilier Guards were the first to enter."

THE TIMES CORRESPONDENT.

"So inspir'd,
The Scipios battled and the Gracchi spoke:
So rose the Roman state. Me, now of these
Deep musing, high ambitious thoughts inflame,
Greatly to serve my country, distant land,
And build me virtuous fame; nor shall the dust
Of these fallen piles, with shew of sad decay,
Avert the good resolve, mean argument,
The fate alone of matter."

DYER.

"On he proudly strode,
As who should say, 'Back fortune, know thy distance!'
Thus steadily he pass'd, and mock'd his fate.
When lo!"

BROOKE.

THE MOVE FROM THE ALMA.—THE FLANK MOVE-MENT.—THE ROYAL DUKE AND THE CAPTAIN.—CLIFTON'S STAR STRUGGLING THROUGH THE CLOUDS.

S we have said at the close of Chapter XIV., the battle of the Alma was won; Clifton Grey had made his first essay, fought his first battle, and won his first distinction. He was the first in the battery; there were, he believed, many living to prove it, but to make assurance doubly sure he had, the first moment he had the opportunity, whipped out a piece of pipe-clay from where he kept it, and marked in large letters "C. G." on the gun he had faced, stormed, surmounted, and by which, in spite of all opposition,

he had kept his position till followed up by his comrades.

In the heat of the fight he had done this, when a very hail of bullets was pinging and whistling through the air on every side of him, and he determined, if possible, not to lose the benefit of his daring. He had had the good fortune twice to save the life of Lieutenant Linder, and once that of Lieutenant Thistlethwaite, by beating down a Russian gunner with the butt end of the musket, as the man was about to pierce him with his bayonet.

Among his own comrades, even before the fighting was over in the battery, he heard his name mentioned with glowing praise, and his blood being up, he was ready to dare anything it was possible for the General to have commanded, however impracticable and fatal in its result.

The flying and panic stricken Russian infantry were pursued by the excited soldiers, but the Russians threw out their large masses of Cossack cavalry, which, ineffectual to protect the retreating columns from the French artillery, yet prevented the pursuit by the British and French infantry. The Allies had no adequate force of cavalry to employ in the pursuit, and the departure of the defeated army, under Prince Menschikoff, was molested only by the guns turned on them on the hills, by the French. When they were out of range, the firing ceased. The battle was over; the first meeting between the Russians and the Allies had ended in a victory for the latter. A glorious victory, which history will not fail to do justice to.

And now the men spread themselves over the field, to search for wounded comrades—too many, by the way, for the sake only of plunder, but still a large proportion engaged in the noble duty of assisting the bandsmen, and giving as much assistance and relief as they could to the brave fellows, whose chances had not been so favourable as their own.

Clifton Grey set himself lustily to work; many of his comrades whom he liked well were not within ken, when the regiment to which he belonged had made a hasty muster up the hill, and he was anxious to see who were living, and needed help. He departed to try and render it.

He had not far to go. He took the line facing the redoubt, up to which he had rushed in the face of a sheet of hot red flame, and there, by fifties, his gallant comrades and the men of his division were lying—nay, over that vast expanse of hill, where, were they not lying, acres of them.

It was a frightful, sickening sight, that field of death—and glory!

Clifton's heart sunk within him as he saw the fearful effects of the case and round shot upon the dreadfully mutilated corses of many whom, in the pride of health and strength, he had seen that morning laughing, joking, animated, eager for the event which had annihilated them; and his feelings were painfully ex-

CLIFTON GREY AFTER THE BATTLE OF THE ALMA.

cited as every now and then he came upon men he
knew well, who were pale and ghastly, gasping for
breath, calling hoarsely for water, bleeding horribly
from desperate wounds, and yet bearing their agonies
with a brave dignity which was yet more noble than
their conduct had been that day.

To many he rendered assistance, which they acknowledged with blessings; and night came on and
there were yet hundreds of men lying wounded on the
hills to bring in, but he had not paused nor flagged
while any of his comrades had needed his aid, and now
darkness had set in. Faint and exhausted, he proceeded
to where the Scots Fusilier Guards were to bivouac for
the night.

During his attentions to his wounded comrades, he
was struck by the face of a young Russian officer lying
dead; his brow was bent and his teeth were clenched;
the aspect of the face was not that of rage, anger, or
despair—even pain, it was rather that of one bent on
deeds of daring, of an ambition to excel, to accomplish
some achievement of great daring. Clifton recognized
in the expression the same character as he believed his
own features wore when he captured the first gun of the
redoubt.

The Russian was dead, had been for some time; a
Minié bullet had passed through his heart; by his side
in his clenched hand was his sword, bright and un-
fleshed. He had been shot down before one hope or
aim had been accomplished.

"Such might have been my fate!" muttered Clifton,
as he knelt down by the soldier's side, and breathed a
brief prayer of thankfulness to the Almighty for his
escape from injury. It was with no thought of plunder
that he opened the grey coat at the breast of this
young officer, for he could plainly see he was of that
rank, but he looked for what he felt he should find,
and he did not look in vain. He brought forth, from
the yet warm breast, near the heart, where the life
blood had oozed out and lay in a coagulated puddle, a
packet sealed, tied with ribbon, and directed.

"I knew it," he said; "it may give me a clue to his
friends, I will preserve it for them; enemies we may
have been in life, I will act a friend's part in death."
He took also his watch, his purse, and a diamond ring
from his finger, and put them carefully away. Then,
hastily drawing off the long Russian coat, he threw a
British one over him, and upon his head he fastened
the shako of a grenadier, which lay upon the ground
near him, having fallen from the head of one of the
men who had been wounded. He knew by this he
would ensure him burial.

On reaching the place where his comrades were regaling themselves upon their evening meal, he heard a
warm discussion going on, and Mickey Dunigan taking
an active part in it.

"Why thin, bad luck to the likes iv him that sez it,
and the back of my hand and the soul of my fut to
him that thinks it," he cried, angrily. "Wirra! is it

my own name I know? To the divil with 'em! we
was the fust in—and it's the gun we won, and we'll
have the stripes, too."

"What, over the back, Mickey?" asked one of the
men, with a laugh.

"No, you villain; sure I'd not wear the stripes
where you've had 'em, bad cess to you! many's the
time, an' the Lord knows it. Why, the Provost Marshal's ashamed to look you in the face, you omadhaun,
he's seen yer dirty back so often," roared Mickey. There
was a shout of laughter at his comrade's expense; and
then another quietly enquired:

"What do you mean by we? How many of you
claim the sergeant's stripes, Mickey?"

"What is't I mane, you dirty spalpeen!" cried
Mickey; "shure you pushed up in the rare, or you
wouldn't ax me that; it's not in the front you were,
any way."

"Ah, well! I saw who was first on to the redoubt,"
cried another of the men.

"Did you?" said Mickey. "You were to the front,
av coorse?"

"I was."

"Well, it wasn't you, you blayguard; so don't try
to be getting the dark side av us wid any of your
blarney."

"I didn't say it was."

"No; it's well for you you didn't. Perhaps you'll
oblige your friends by telling 'em who it was?"

"It wasn't you, Mickey."

"Faith! I know that; but I wasn't the last there,
av Gintleman Grey else," cried Mickey, with a knowing
wink.

"That's the man who was first in the battery," cried
the soldier.

"An' I know it, for I was second," cried Mickey.
"I saw Gentleman Grey leap out of the ranks, as
we rushed up to the battery, and with a cheer that
rung on my heart as the sound of a trumpet, he leaped
like a roebuck on to the earth walls; and there he was
when we came tumbling in after him," exclaimed the
private.

"Well said," cried the round tones of Sergeant
Haverel's voice, "spoken like a poet; he did go in like
a reindeer, and fight like a devil:

> 'Fast he stealeth on, but he wears no wings,
> And a staunch old head hath he!'"——

"Thank you, sergeant," said Clifton Grey, drawing
up and shewing himself. He had been a listener to
the foregoing without being able to help himself, for he
had been detained in his approach by a knot of men
arranging their rations, and at last was able to pass up
to the camp fire, around which the men were squatting
like Indians, nearly all smoking short pipes.

Sergeant Haverel held out his two hands to Clifton,
and shook both his warmly; the tears stood in the
honest fellow's eyes, as he said:—

"Safe and sound, Grey—wind, and limb—touched no where? tell me that, and I'll sing:

"Hurrah for brave old England,
And the dear ones left behind!
Who would not be a soldier,
If Dame Fortune proves thus kind?"

"I believe I am untouched in person," replied Clifton, "but my chin-strap was shot away, my coat has got several rents, and my belt has been ripped by bullets; but thank God, I have not got a single hurt—and you Sergeant?"

"Free as a duck in its fatting time; some near touches, just a rip and a scrap as you say, but all right this time.

'My name's dy'e see TomTough,
And I've seen a little service.'

"Ha! ha Grey, if my face is as black as yours, we should do for a couple of ramoneurs, instead of Fusiliers."

"Black!" he echoed with surprise.

"Ay," said the sergeant, "honourable soot—the real charcoal grime. Talk about the battle's smoke, who say's you've not been in the chimney."

And he had, for his face was blackened by the powder, his teeth and lips sullied by his cartridges, his hair and eye-lashes singed, and altogether, save for his regimentals, he might have been taken for one in the occupation of a tinker, instead of the usually smart Clifton Grey. He laughed at the allusion to the hues of his face, especially as it came from the sergeant, whose face had not lost the fierce brick hue it had won in the battle's heat, though, like Clifton's, it was somewhat dulled by the powder-smoke.

"Well," said our hero, "I have been in the smoke and fire too; but I've won my stripes by it—it was worth the risk, one leap brought me another."

"Hurra!" shouted Mickey, "stick to that, Grey. I'll back you wid that as long as I'm by your side. Sure did'nt the Duke, long life to him! promise the sergeant's stripes to the first man in the redoubt; and wasn't Grey the first, and a blackguard named Mickey Dunigan forerinst him—at laste in his rare, I'd like to know to that?"

"Who disputes it?" asked Clifton, quietly.

"I do," said an authoritative voice.

The soldiers looked up, and there stood Captain Winslow, with his pale face and glaring eyes bent malignantly on our hero. A movement of respect to his position made the men stand up. He ran his eyes uneasily around.

"It is time enough to settle that question, my men," he added, "when His Royal Highness summonses before him those who make the claim. As for this fellow, with his boasting braggardism, if you listen to him he'll make you believe the fortune of the day was won by his single arm; we know the brave man never boasts. You all fought well, and Lord

Raglan is proud of you; but, take counsel from me do not be too eager to put forth claims which may cause you to reap, instead of honour, contempt."

"Pardon me, Captain Winslow," said Sergeant Haverel, glowing like a turkey-cock, but still touching his hat respectfully, "the Scots Fusiliers were first in the battery."

"The Grenadiers claim it, Sergeant," said Captain Winslow: "and I must say that I've seen the gun upon which 'G. G.' is chalked."

"Musha bad luck to the Grannydeer that did it, Sure an' it stands for Clifton Grey, an' its meself saw him do't after he'd prodded a Rooshan into purgatory, av the likes of 'em over go there," cried Mickey.

"Silence there!" said the Captain, sternly. "His Royal Highness will give the promotion to the man who is honorably entitled to it."

"That's Grey!" cried Sergeant Haverel.

"Grey, Grey, Grey!" exclaimed several of his comrades, who thought too well of him to be jealous of what he had so bravely done, and who disliked the captain just as much as they were attached to a true-hearted comrade.

"Where is private Grey?" cried a voice at this moment, and Lieutenant Linder bustled into the group, closely followed by Lieutenant Thistlethwayte.

"Here," answered Clifton, almost sorry the kind-hearted officers appeared, for he knew it would only be a prelude to a contention between them and the captain on his account.

Lieutenant Linder caught his hand in his, and, as the tears sprung in his eyes, he said:

"Twice, Grey, you saved my life. Believe me, I know how to be grateful, and will not forget the obligation while I breathe."

"Nor I, Grey," said Lieutenant Thistlethwayte," with much earnestness. "Had it not been for you, I should have been lying where many a brave fellow now takes his last sleep."

"I did no more, indeed, than any other of my comrades," replied Clifton, drawing back. "They fought with courage and desperation, and supported you nobly; I do not deserve your kind praise."

"I should think not, indeed!" exclaimed Captain Winslow with a sneer.

Lieutenant Linder turned round as if he had been struck.

"Captain Winslow, permit me to suggest that you are quite unable to judge what are the deserts of private Grey," he said, sharply.

"I think not. I believe you have already had my opinion on that subject," responded the captain, drily.

"We were speaking of his conduct in yon redoubt," said the Lieutenant, angrily.

"Oh, to be sure; he has been piping his self praise to all his friends, I find. Ha, ha! Your protégé, Linder, was first in the redoubt, and claims the promotion promised by His Royal Highness. Ha, ha!

—has the cool audacity, in the teeth of his comrades, all better men than him, to make the claim of being first man in the battery! Ha, ha!"

"Sure I know who was the *last* there, any way," muttered Micky Dunigan.

There was a suppressed titter among the men.

"Do you dispute it, Winslow?" asked Lieutenant Thistlethwayte, with a steadfast gaze into the face of the captain, which the latter found it difficult to support.

"Faith, it is worth no such trouble—the fustian is too palpable," returned the captain.

Lieutenant Linder uttered an angry exclamation. Lieutenant Thistlethwayte grasped his wrist to keep him subordinate, and remarked:

"I only say, Captain Winslow, that you cannot dispute it."

"Cannot, Thistlethwayte, why not?"

"Because you know you were not present."

"Not present! S'death! what do you mean, sir?"

"Only this. That when we crossed the Alma, and the bullets were rattling like hail in front of us, you fancied you were hit and retired to the rear; in fact, I am told there was a race between you and Annesley, who *was* hit, and that *you* won it; therefore, you are in no position, you see, to dispute or testify to it."

"Lieutenant Thistlethwayte, you are impertinent; I shall order you under arrest if you presume to attempt to bring me into contempt before the men——"

"Tut, tut, tut!" interposed a pleasant voice; it was that of the colonel, who had been actively employed in seeing to the wants of the wounded; "no angry words now. We have been all too near our Maker this day to think of or to speak harshly to one another. You no doubt grieve, Winslow, at having been unable to distinguish yourself to-day; and I am sure a moment's reflection will teach you to think with kindness and speak with gratefulness to heaven of those who have escaped the bloody penalty of daring. Linder and Thistlethwayte, I am proud to see you both unhurt. You carried yourselves nobly—you bore your country's colours with bravery, and have reaped the admiration of your comrades, the esteem of your superior officers. Right proud, too, am I of my brave Fusiliers, and though I understand the Grenadier Guards claim being first in the battery, I know my Fusiliers were not far behind."

"With the greatest respect to the bravery of the Grenadiers, Colonel, we Fusiliers were first into the battery—and there's the first man that shot out from the advancing columns, and with a wild cheer, which I can hear now, sprung into the blazing flame," earnestly exclaimed Lieutenant Linder. "I followed close with my colours, and I know I assert what is truth."

"Of whom do you speak?" asked the colonel.

"Of Private Grey," replied Lieutenant Linder. "Stand forth, Grey."

The colonel smiled, and returned Clifton's salute, as he obeyed the command.

"I am truly glad to hear this," he said, "although I might have guessed that Grey would do credit to himself and to his regiment. I must tell this to His Royal Highness the Duke of Cambridge. As a colonel of the regiment, he will be proud of the deed. Of course, I shall be understood to speak in no spirit of detraction, if I say this admits of proof."

"There is plenty of proof, colonel," exclaimed Lieutenant Linder. "I saw him go into the redoubt like a stag over a thickset hedge."

"And I!" cried Thistlethwayte.

"I saw him there when I got there, may it please your honour," exclaimed Sergeant Haverel; "and I was not long after the first over the sides of the redoubt."

"Sure an' av your hanner ud let me spake, I can give ye the best proof in the world that Gentleman Grey was first in among the Rooshians who held the batthery," exclaimed Mickey Dunigan, making an obeisance to the colonel.

"Speak out my brave fellow," said the latter. "You Irishmen have fought to-day as bravely as ever."

"An' the Lord bless you for that good word," said Mickey, heartily; adding, "but then your banner knows that fighting's mate and dhrink to an Irishman, and where there's plenty av it av coorse he'll be there."

"And the last to leave it while there is any left," remarked the colonel, with a laugh; and added: "but the proof you proffered just now?"

"Sure, yer hanner, its that same thing I'm keming to, an' its none can give it you the likes of meself, seeing that when the Royal Duke schramed out 'A sergeant's stripes for the first man in the bhattery!' sure that's Mickey Dunigan sez I to myself, sez I; an' sure you blagguard, sez I, maning meself, your honner, you'll do this same for poor ould Ireland, blessings on her.—'First flower of the earth, first gem of the say,' sez I to myself; an' I meant to kaap my word; but wheugh! just as we kem up to the battery—it was hailing lead, your honner—I boults out av the lines, but the divil a chance I had, for Grey, with a yell and a lape that ud bate the best hunter in Galway, wint slap into the redoubt. Bad luck to my stiff legs! he was in first, but I was second, your honour, and that's truth, plase God."

"I believe you, it sounds like truth," said the colonel.

"It is the truth, your honour, for I followed poor Will Stevens, who lost his number, and lies in the battery, and he was third in," exclaimed a private belonging to the regiment.

"I am sure it is correct," observed the colonel, "and shall not fail to represent it in the proper quarter. England had need be proud of her sons, when thus they conduct themselves in their first action. Grey, I shall name you to His Royal Highness; and you, my brave

Irishman, shall not lose promotion, though you did not, by your own showing, win the rank you aspired to."

"Hurroo! Long life to your honner," shouted the Irishman. "Sure its them at home will be proud of this day."

Clifton thanked the colonel for his promised interest, and could hardly refrain a glance at Captain Winslow, to see what feelings he betrayed at the turn matters had taken, but he was no longer there. The colloquy had grown hot and painful to him, and he retired more incensed and more determined than ever to ruin Clifton Grey; while Lieutenants Linder and Thistlewayte were as equally resolved to push forward his fortunes. They both seemed to feel that he was of gentle birth, and would grace a higher station; the obligation he had placed them under in saving their life only gave fresh impetus to their good intentions. They knew what harm Captain Winslow could do him if he chose, and they agreed together to watch him narrowly, and shield their young *protégé* as far as laid in their power. A fortunate thing, this, for Clifton it proved, for they not only had the power, but the good sense to know how to wield it with advantage when its exercise was required.

After some close enquiries and inspection, listening to some details, and giving counsel to the men, the colonel passed on to the next group, followed by the two lieutenants, who did not, however, quit without intimating to our hero that his interests should not be lost sight of while in their keeping. Some trifling conversation, interlarded with the congratulations of Sergeant Haverel and a few of his comrades, ensued, and then, worn out with fatigue, he was glad to roll himself in his grey coat, sink upon the damp ground, and woo sleep on the bloody field of the Alma.

As his upturned eye caught the dark deep blue of the sky, studded with diamond-like stars, his thoughts turned to Myra Aston. A sanguinary battle had been fought and won by the allies. What would they say in England? What would be her emotions when she heard of it? She must know that he would be engaged in it; that he would take no idle part in it. Would she wonder what had been his fate? Would she offer up a prayer for his escape—shed a bitter tear if he had fallen? Would she think of him at all? Whither had she gone? why had she been silent, even though he had asked her only to reply to a communication she should receive, and which she had not received. And dim and misty forms seemed slowly to whirl around him, and amid the din, confusion, choking obscurity, there stole over him an impression that the spirit of his dead mother, holding the hand of Myra, hovered over him, watchfully and protectingly, and so he sunk into a deep, deep sleep, lying on the wet grass, on that dread plain of slaughter and death.

At daybreak the army was once more astir. The cold volumes of mists rolled down the valley, or wreathed curlingly upwards from the hill sides, exhibiting here and there a patch of verdure, or a mass of troops. As the dawn merged into day there pealed down from the heights, occupied by the French, the shrill blasts of their trumpets, and the long incessant rolls of their drums, waking into active motion, not only the troops of their own nation, but those of the British. The men leaped from their dewy bed and shook off the moisture that clung to their garments, prepared to swallow a hasty breakfast, to fall in, and proceed to the interior of the Crimea, and yet further struggle for advanced position, until they were fairly set down before Sebastopol, for well they knew, or believed, that the first scene in the bloody drama to be enacted had now only been played.

As the white fogs wreathed upwards, Clifton, who had at the first shrill peal of the clarion leaped from his heavy slumber, and shaken off his drowsiness, saw, slowly developed, masses of French infantry in battalions, on the eve of marching. Along his own lines all was bustle and activity, but no confusion. The men were occupying their respective places in the ranks, and now more palpably finding by the gaps they had to fill up how many a poor fellow had the night before been billeted with a bullet. Along the plain lay in patches, horrible for the extent it embraced, the dead and wounded Russians, the latter tossing and writhing in dreadful agonies, hoarsely begging for water, and gasping for aid, which could not be afforded. Save the solitary help given by Dr. Thompson of the 44th regiment, who remained behind with the wounded and dying, to render them such service as lay in his professional capacity, and he had power to afford. All honour to that noble surgeon, who perished shortly afterwards, mainly in consequence of the arduous exertions imposed upon him! It was a sickening and wretched sight. Clifton felt that he should be glad when he had left it behind.

Now the General Commanding-in-Chief was in motion with his staff; aid-de-camps were galloping to the various divisions with orders. The sun was fast clearing off the mist; it was eight o'clock. On the heights to the south the French infantry was already advancing; along the sea coast was a line of war-steamers at low speed proceeding in the line of coast parallel with the advance. Now the whole British army was in line, and the order was conveyed to all the divisions to march, and it was obeyed with alacrity. The colors of the Scots Fusilier Guards being proudly borne by the lieutenants in charge of them; as they fluttered in the breeze, sixteen bullet holes might have been counted through them, and their staff was split. Well might the two young officers congratulate themselves in passing through their first action in such a bullet storm unwounded. With honour to themselves and country they were sure to do; with safety, under such circumstances, was little short of a miracle. The line of march was upon the Katcha, and soon tokens of the retreat of defeated troops, and the advance of a victorious army became palpable. Buildings, as they appeared, had been rendered desolate and uninhabitable by the flying Cossacks; the affrighted inhabitants had fled, most of the furniture had been carried off, and such as had been left behind was smashed or rendered useless. China and glass lay in shattered fragments, pictures smashed, boxes, desks, and drawers rifled, and their contents mercilessly destroyed, or ruthlessly scattered about. In some of the villas on the banks of the Katcha the traces of elegant refinement were left; but, alas, the traces only, for although the evidences of female presence were, by many articles of attire or accomplishments, to be met with, they had been ruthlessly damaged or destroyed. As it was, every building as soon as reached was overrun and ravaged by the advancing conquerors; and pillage, wherever an article worth taking was to be got, was adopted by the soldiers as a right prescriptive, and pursued with a perseverance admirable if devoted to a worthy purpose. It was almost laughable to see how many a man fatigued himself to exhaustion by carrying plunder absolutely of no use to him whatever.

With the exception of three or four articles, which he purchased to give as remembrances to—in truth, he knew not—Clifton contented himself with rifling a few pears, and grapes, and apples, which were growing in vineyards and orchards in the greatest profusion; it was a delicious change from the rations on which he had been living for some time. Moderate, however, in this, as he was in all matters of personal indulgence, he benefitted by what he ate; not so many of his comrades, who, eating inordinately, laid the foundation for cholera, which afterwards swept them off with terrible rapidity.

That night the army bivouacked in the valley of the Katcha. On the following night in the village of the Belbek. No brush with the enemy, even with the outposts took place, save a few shots fired by the French at some Cossacks who showed in front of their outposts; and though the firing aroused some out of their slumbers in anticipation of having to take part in very arduous and dangerous duty, it proved a false alarm.

On the following day, no little to the surprise and counter to the expectations of those who believed that the positions of the Russians between them and the famed City of Sebastopol were to be carried, as at the Alma, at the point of the bayonet, a sudden order was given—having been concerted between Marshal St. Arnaud and Lord Raglan—for both armies to make a flank movement on Balaklava; the object being to avoid the batteries raised by the Russians to prevent the advance of the Allies, to save life, to effect a bloodless turning of the military works, and obtain a new basis of operations, while their concentrated fire would be directed upon Sebastopol from a side where an attack had not been expected, and where the preparations necessarily were weaker for them than at the north side, which at first it had been contemplated to attack.

The masses of infantry turned as if by magic, and,

without guides or other direction than such as could be imperfectly furnished by the officers, they plunged into a thickly-wooded region, forcing their way through or over every obstacle, but almost necessarily falling into a desultory mob, so far as preserving any form of order was concerned, but yet sufficiently attentive to discipline not to take advantage of the unavoidable straggling confusion into which they were thrown. On they pressed, and rounded the head of the harbour without molestation from the Russians, who were being shelled in Forts Constantine and the Star Fort by the man-of-war steamers. As they proceeded—now passing over the tops of hills from which they could catch glimpses of the white houses of Sebastopol and the sea beyond—now deep in the difficulties of thick underwood in the valleys, and again scrambling over heights which revealed to them the city before which they were doomed to lay so long or give up their life either under the death-dealing ball or the no less murderous ravages of want and disease. Their progress, though irregular, was continuous. Among those who pressed on in front, eager to be foremost in the fray, or to discover aught important to be known, was Clifton Grey. He, in company with several of his comrades, brave and active, pushed on in advance, in skirmishing order, ready with loaded rifle, to give a good account of themselves to the foe, or prepare the troops following them for an enemy if they came upon one. Over heaths and half-cleared plantations, across narrow lines, and through heavy ground on went Clifton full of hope to meet with an adventure, and seemingly unconscious of fatigue. He was now in a wooded plantation, from which he caught sight of a winding road, promising better and easier progress than the route he was pursuing, and he soon leaped into it. Hark! surely he heard the roll of heavy wheels before him, the tramp of many horses, the heavy and regular tread of infantry. He was far in advance of his own battalion—some distance in advance of the nimblest of his comrades. Those in front of him could not, therefore, belong to the Allies, but must be Russian troops; he ran on at once rapidly; he cautiously cocked his rifle, and under the shadow of the spreading trees he advanced until an abrupt turn of the road brought him upon a couple of Russian soldiers, seemingly tired, dragging on with weary steps and slow, with their pieces over their shoulders in an easy and careless way. Clifton followed them for a minute, and then, creeping closely after the laggard nearest to him, he seized his musket by the barrel, twisted it out of his grasp, flung it behind him, and dashing in front of the other, he presented his piece and bade him halt. So perfectly surprised were both soldiers, that the armed one, throwing down his musket, which proved to be empty, they yielded themselves prisoners without a struggle. One of them, a Pole, addressed him in French, and he replied and ordered both to sit down by the road side and await his return;

If they did so he would promise to save their lives; if they attempted to escape they would only meet with certain death. Both men, who seemed worn out with fatigue and want of food, readily complied, and squatted down beneath a tree. Clifton, with no less caution than before, pushed on; and just as the road emerged from its wooded vicinity to an open space, he saw before him an extensive Russian convoy, accompanied by a large body of infantry and Cossack cavalry. He retreated instantly to give the alarm and bring up troops. On coming up with his prisoners, he ordered them to accompany him. At this moment there was the rattle of horses' feet advancing briskly along the road, and before he had time to make a disposition for defence if it should be a party of the enemy, Lord Raglan, closely followed by his staff, swept round the winding way. With an exclamation of surprise as he caught sight of Clifton and his prisoners he reined in his steed, and a few rapid questions put him into possession of the facts. He made inquiries of the Russian soldiers as to the force discovered by Clifton Grey and was informed that it was the baggage guard of a large detachment of the Russian army. His lordship's resolve was taken very quickly. Turning to Grey, he said:

"Your name, my friend?"

"Clifton Grey, my lord."

"Your number?"

Clifton Grey gave it to him, and he made a memorandum of it.

"Take charge of your prisoners until your comrades come up; I shall not forget you."

Clifton put his hand to his forehead, the commander-in-chief returned the salute, turned his horse's head, and returned, followed by his staff, leaving Clifton alone with his prisoners. It was not for long. Almost instantly he saw some of his comrades breaking through the wooded plantation, and they uttered a shout as soon as they saw him. He was soon surrounded, and he got one of them to retire with the prisoners to the main body, yet some distance behind, while he informed his comrades that there was a large baggage convoy a-head, a splendid prize, and bade them get ready to share in its capture, but to await the disposition Lord Raglan, who was aware of its proximity, would make to secure it. Not they.

"Come on, Grey," they cried, "lead us on, and let's begin the fun; we can throw ourselves out in skirmishing order, and get half the booty before the others come up."

Yielding to their solicitations, joined as they were by many others, he and they pressed on, and as they emerged into the open roadway they perceived the convoy, some hundred yards in front of them, and extending a considerable distance. At once, with a loud shout, they commenced a dropping fire upon the Russian infantry, who, thus unexpectedly attacked, betrayed the greatest astonishment, and, very soon, disorder. Still their numbers were numerous, and they poured in a volley in reply, which, however, did no harm. At this juncture, a portion of the first division of artillery made its appearance. The guns were unlimbered, and several rounds poured into the petrified enemy. The second battalion of Rifles now appeared on the scene, and, joining the small detachment of guards who had first appeared on the scene, they spread out, making good use of their Minié rifles, and threw the Russians into disorder. Detachments of the 8th and 11th Hussars now galloped up and charged; the Russians took to instant flight, and never exerted their speed so heartily, and to such advantage, as upon this occasion. They left behind them the whole of the baggage, and the booty was enormous. On Lord Raglan's arrival, he gave orders for it to be fairly divided, and every man got a share of the spoil.

Clifton Grey's attention had been directed to a carriage which he perceived among the carts and vehicles comprising the baggage train, and suspecting it to belong to some Russian officer, he at once proceeded to search it, while others were occupied in hunting for the military chest and for wines and spirits. He found in it some papers, apparently of an official character, and also some rich and valuable orders, gorgeously decorated with diamonds, evidently belonging to one of very elevated rank; he seized them. There was, also, in one of the pockets beneath the carriage window, a handsome purse well filled with gold pieces. He made a parcel of them all and bore them to his colonel to convey to the Commander-in-Chief.

"The papers will no doubt prove of much service," exclaimed the colonel. "The orders are of a high description, and his lordship may desire to possess them, but he will give you an equivalent. The purse of money I will take upon myself the responsibility to say you may keep."

"If it so please you, colonel, I would prefer that the whole parcel be placed in his lordship's hands intact."

"As you please. Do you know, or have you heard to whom the carriage belonged."

"I have reason to suppose that it was Prince Menschikoff's."

"Ha! was he in it when the Russian guard were attacked?"

"I think not. From what the prisoners let fall he is in Sebastopol."

"Where I hope we shall soon be!"

"I hope so, colonel. If we were to go on now, animated as the men are, we would be in before sundown."

"The commanders-in-chief know best; we must be governed by their judgment. Let us get before Sebastopol, we shall soon learn what is next to be done."

"The battle of the Alma, Colonel, has roused the lion in the men's hearts; they are ready to dare anything the general may entrust to them; that I know. They would not let the honour of England be stained by any faltering or faint-hearted conduct, however desperate the task set them. If only the word was given now to close up, advance on the vast fortifications in front of us, storm and carry them, the men would answer with a cheer, and never fall back, but as the shot of the enemy laid them low."

"I know the brave-hearted fellows," exclaimed the colonel, his eye lighting up with enthusiasm. "The safety of the world may be entrusted to their keeping."

"You will, I hope, colonel, pardon the freedom I have used in thus speaking to you, but your own kindness leads me perhaps beyond a barrier I ought not to cross, and which I never pass intentionally."

"Your own good conduct, your sense of what is due to yourself, gives you a discretion, which you well preserve. I have not to be told that your present is not your proper position. I am sure it will not continue so."

Clifton bowed, and thanked him, and being dismissed, returned to where the soldiers were, still actively engaged in appropriating the booty, which was fairly their own. Soon, there was not a thing but empty and broken carts and arabas to be seen, and then the order to march was once more given, and the troops went on in high spirits to Traktir, and halting near Mackenzie's farm, bivouacked for the night there.

On the succeeding day, Balaklava was reached, taken and occupied, and, subsequently, the different divisions were placed on the heights above, which were thus taken possession of by the allies; and, Lord Raglan moving his head-quarters from Balaklava to a spot near the farm of Dzeudo-otar, the British Army was fairly settled down before SEBASTOPOL.

The succeeding days passed away rapidly. Some skirmishes with outposts—some shot and shell from Sebastopol forts—some work between the French and Russians—but nothing of a general character in the shape of assault or sorties took place. Then that mysterious but deadly disease—the cholera—began to tell upon the constitutions of the delicate, the thoughtless, or the reckless. Clifton subjected himself to a strict training for the life he knew he should have to endure, and omitted nothing which tended to harden his frame and keep him in health. Many of his comrades succumbed; and he failed not to do his best to procure them medicines, or such comforts as he could obtain by soliciting from the officers, who never hesitated to grant them when asked for for the sick.

On the night of the 11th of October the terrible trench work commenced, and eight hundred troops, under Captain Chapman, R.E., turned up the first earth in front of Sebastopol. They worked rapidly and silently in the dark, occasionally visited by shot and shell from the Russians, but without much damage being done. The labour was very severe, the ground

being rocky; and those who wanted strength, and had not been inured to such labour, soon found it tell fearfully upon them. The sick hospitals every day—nay, every hour—received fresh accessions; and it was only such men who had been inured to the hardships of active service, or who, like Clifton Grey, absolutely trained themselves for it, that were able to stand it. He was sorely tried. Captain Winslow at last thought he had got a turn, and he put him upon a working party, and so contrived the relief that his pet hate was left forty-eight hours in the trenches. Upon being relieved, and returning to his tent, cold, faint, weary, and hardly able to stand, he was ordered out again for outpost duty. As he appeared without strength, hardly able to shoulder his rifle, Captain Winslow said to him:

"I think, Grey, I once overheard you give a lecture to some of your pot companions upon outpost duty; you can give them twelve hours' example now how that duty should be done."

"I beg your pardon, Captain Winslow, but Grey has been already forty-eight hours in the trenches," said Sergeant Haverel, brusquely.

"Is that all?"

"All, sir?"

"I had intended him to have sixty. No matter, he can make it up in the valley."

"I am going out with this picquet, sir, and I prefer having men who have strength to do their duty," said Haverel, sturdily.

"Naturally, sergeant; and you can take Grey, who can teach you yours. You can prick him with the point of your bayonet if he grows lazy and shams sleep."

"Shams sleep, Captain Winslow!" cried Sergeant Haverel, indignantly; "What would you be likely to do, Captain Winslow, if you had a spell with a spade of two days and two nights on trench work? Human nature can't stand it: it is no better than murder."

"Sergeant, you grow insolent and insubordinate; another word and I order you under arrest. To your duty, sir, and take that fellow with you, unless he desires the provost-marshal to quicken him to a sense of obedience to orders."

"I have made no complaint, Captain Winslow," exclaimed Clifton Grey, hoarsely, whose white face and black lips told a tale of fatigue, almost beyond human endurance.

"No!" said the captain. "You are cunning enough for that. Forward!—March! Keep your eye on that fellow, men, and, if he attempts to desert, shoot him—March!"

"Halt!" cried a loud voice, almost at the same moment; and there, on horseback, attended only by a single officer, was the Duke of Cambridge, a colonel of the Scots Fusilier Guards, and a general of division.

"What is the meaning of this, Captain?" exclaimed the duke. "You are, surely, not about to entrust outpost duty to men of whose fidelity you have a

MYRA ASTON AND LIZZIE HASTINGS ON BOARD THE SLOOP.

suspicion. Who is the man? We want no man in the Guards whom we are unable to trust."

Sergeant Haverel, with his face almost purple, his lips quivering, advanced, and, saluting the duke, said, in a very perceptibly agitated manner:

"We have no such man in our battalion, your royal highness; I would shoot him myself if I knew where to single him out."

"Of whom was Captain Winslow speaking?" asked the duke, sternly: "He would not have given any such injunction as that I overheard unless there were some foundation for it."

"No man in this picket deserved to be outraged by such an observation," said Sergeant Haverel, emphatically.

His royal highness looked at Captain Winslow, who shrugged his shoulders in a manner that by no means commended itself to the duke.

The Captain pointed to Clifton Grey, and said:

"Your Royal Highness, there stands a fellow—"

"A soldier!" exclaimed Sergeant Haverel, with spluttering emphasis.

"Avery inch av him," ejaculated Mickey Dunigan, loudly, "an' he wor as high as the Ture of Babal."

All the men gave a loud murmur of approbation.

"Silence there!" cried Captain Winslow, fiercely.

"Macdonald, be good enough to alight with me," said his royal highness to his companion, and, looking at Mickey, said: "Here, you Irishman that spoke, hold the bridle of my steed while I dismount."

Captain Winslow, white even as Grey, ordered him at once from his position to obey the duke's command. Mickey, only too delighted, for he foresaw justice to the oppressed looming large, held the noble steed with firm grip, while the royal duke placed himself upon terra firma. As Major Macdonald joined him, he said to him:

"This smacks a little of insubordination—we will enquire into it; there is too much paraphernalia about court-martials for trifles, eh, Macdonald? A kind word will do more than a harsh sentence."

The major bowed.

"Now, Captain—I beg your pardon, I forget"—

"Captain Winslow."

"What is this I have overheard? You have a refractory man, and a bad soldier—for it is only the meanest wretch on earth who will desert his country's colours—a troublesome man. Why, instead of sending him upon important duty, do you not employ him upon menial, irresponsible duties?"

A gleam flashed in the eyes of the captain:

"In truth, your royal highness, I confess I did not think of a very palpable and proper way to deal with him."

"I thought not; let me have a word with him. Which is he?"

"Step to the front, private Grey," exclaimed Captain

Winslow, relying upon the stern, military discipline which on active service makes a word, a look insubordination.

"Grey—private Grey," muttered the duke, thoughtfully; "where have I heard that name?"

He gazed upon Clifton, who stepped forward, and drew himself up with a determination to stand up like a soldier, without one shudder or falter, even if he fell dead with the effort, and said:

"A fine-looking young man—I am really very sorry, I assure you."—

Major Macdonald whispered in his ear. The duke looked at Clifton closely, and said:

"Truly—yes; it must be so. Are you ill, my man? speak."

Clifton's tongue was dry and swollen, his mouth was parched, so that the roof and sides were like tight leather, but he contrived to gasp out:

"I am greatly fatigued, your royal highness."

"You look sinking with exhaustion; upon what duty have you been employed?"

"Trenches."

"How long were you at your post?"

"Forty-eight hours."

"When were you relieved?"

"A quarter of an hour back."

"Good God! Captain Winslow was about to send you on twelve hours outpost duty."

Captain Winslow interposed.

"Pardon me, your royal highness," he said.

"Silence, sir!" cried the duke sternly, "I'll conduct this interrogation without your aid, if you please." He repeated his question to Clifton, who answered him in the affirmative. Then, turning to Sergeant Haverel, he said:

"Sergeant, you ought to know the man well, what his faults or failings are, and what his good qualities. Speak out, without fear or favour, I want to know the truth."

Captain Winslow interposed.

"Perhaps your royal highness," he exclaimed, "will kindly permit me to be absent while the praises of the man in question are chanted, and permit me to suggest that I fail to see how the service is to be benefitted by stubborn and evil-disposed men being supported against their officer."

The duke screwed up his eyes until they nearly closed, while regarding Captain Winslow as he spoke, and then he said—

"Well, no, Captain Winslow, I cannot spare you just yet, and with respect to your suggestion I may discuss the matter with you hereafter; at least, I may say, however, I confess my inability to discover the benefit the service can receive by working men to death. Now, sergeant," added the duke, "we will hear you."

"I haven't much to say, your royal highness," said the sergeant, "but I hope what I do say will be found to the purpose. Private Grey, your royal highness, is a gentleman born—he enlisted to save a widow going to the workhouse with a broken heart—he knows and practises his duty, as a soldier, as well, I say, better, than any man in the army: he is the best hearted, truest, the most high-souled, generous, and faithful comrade, soldier ever had; the kindliest and friendliest in health; the tenderest and untiring in services in sickness; the noblest, bravest, best friend, I, or any other man ever had in the wide world, and I defy any living man to gainsay me, without being, saving your royal highness's presence, the damnedest liar that ever lived in this world from its commencement."

"He never failed in his duty!" cried one of the men.

"Never was up for punishment!" cried another.

"Never in the black hole!" said a third.

"An' the first in the redoubt, as God's my judge!" roared Mickey Dunigan, unable longer to restrain his anxiety to say something in addition to the general commendation.

The Duke turned sharply at the last remark.

"What redoubt?" he asked of Mickey.

"O wirrastru! does your royal highness forget that as we charged up the Alma heights, yer hanner's hanner bawled out a promise of a sargint's stripes to the first man in the Russian battery."

"Now, I remember it well," replied the Duke, "and would willingly keep it, if the opportunity is given me to do so."

"Sure an' Grey was the first in this, an' me, Mickey Dunigan, at the back iv 'im. Oh, the blessed God! the Rooshans at the guns could tell your highness, av we'd let 'em live to do it, who first leaped among 'em, like an Irish fox into a flock o' geese. An' I die this minnit Grey was that man."

At this moment Major Macdonald, kind hearted as he was brave, started forward and caught Clifton, who would have fallen flat upon his face as if dead; his musket fell upon the ground and discharged, fortunately the bullet hit no one. Excessive exhaustion, coupled with the ordeal to which he had been thus subjected was too much for him, and he sank under it into a deadly swoon. The major, interested by what he saw of his features and manner, as well as by what he had heard, kept his eye pretty much upon him, and perceiving him suddenly lose all perception caught him ere he fell heavily. Several of the men went to his aid, and the duke said:

"Nature is overdone; bear him to his tent, and fetch the surgeon to him. Captain Winslow, private Grey, will be released from all military duty for three days. In the interim, you will probably hear from me."

Captain Winslow, with ill concealed chagrin, made a deferential motion of acquiescence. Clifton Grey was taken up carefully by four men, and borne to his tent, while the duke remounted his steed, saluted Captain Winslow with distant hauteur, and, attended by Major Macdonald, rode slowly away, saying thoughtfully.

"Private Grey, the name recurs to me, as being one mentioned to me for promotion. I must refer to my notes."

Then turning to Major Macdonald, he said:

"This is not the only instance of disaffection which has come to my knowledge, and which I am convinced has arisen from an absurd and improper mode of treating soldiers as slaves, not men. There must be an alteration, Macdonald. We must try the effect of private expostulation."

The major assented, and further discoursing upon this point, they proceeded on to head quarters.

The men, who had borne Clifton Grey to his tent, and had communicated with the surgeon, now fell in to proceed to their duty; Clifton's place was supplied by the man whose turn it was properly to take part in the duty; the order to march was given, and they proceeded on to their responsible and dangerous duty. Sergeant Haverel, who accompanied them, humming almost loud enough for Captain Winslow to hear:

"'Let us speak of a man as we find him,
And censure alone what we see;
And should a man blame let's remind him
That from vice there are none of us free.'"

"Thrue for you, sergeant," said Mickey Dunigan, "but av we are not all free from vice, sure there's some wid a purty much larger share than they've any business wid."

"Ay!" said one of the men, "and are cunning enough to hide it, too, from those they don't want to see it, but they can show the devil's hoof plain enough, to those they fancy they may tyrannize over."

"Just my sentiments," said Haverel, and sung lustily

"'If the heart from the veil could be torn,
An' the soul could be read on the brow;
There is one I would pass by with scorn
I must duck to as captain just now.'"

There was a general laugh, and as general an acquiescence in the sergeant's impression. The men, having thus vented their feelings, went to their dreary and hazardous post, as cheerfully as though they had been going to guard the entrances of one of the royal theatres in London.

CHAPTER XVIII.

"Gone, gone from us! and shall we see
  Those sybil-leaves of destiny,
  Those calm eyes, never more?
  Those deep dark eyes, so warm and bright!"
                                    THRENODIA.

"The morning watch was come; the vessel lay
  Her course, and gently made her liquid way;
  The cloven billow flashed from off her prow
  In furrows formed by that majestic plough;
  The waters with their world were all before.
      *   *   *   *   *
  The gallant chief within his cabin slept,
  Secure in those by whom his watch was kept.
      *   *   *   *   *
  Alas! this deck was trod by unwilling feet,
  And wilder hands would hold the vessel's sheet;
  Young hearts which languished   *   *   *
      *   *   *   *   *
  They skim the blue tops of the billows; fast
  They flew, and fast their fierce pursuers chased.
  They gain upon them—now they lose again—
  Again make way, and menace o'er the main."
                                    THE ISLAND.

THE SEARCH FOR THE MISSING.—THE CABIN OF
THE SEA-BIRD.—THE OPEN SEA.—THE CHASE.

MRS. ASTON was agreeably entertained at
the opera. "L'Elisor d'Amore" was played,
and the music was sung to perfection.
The acting of Lablache had never been better, his
impersonation of the Quack Doctor never more
ludicrous. The queen was present, the house crowded
with all the beauty, fashion, and nobility of the empire.
Mrs. Aston largely enjoyed the entertainment, laughed
heartily, and on her return, was quite in high spirits.
They had been joined in their box rather late by
Beverley Winslow, who paid great attention to the
Misses Randolph, and their brother, in order to
propitiate opportunities for seeing Myra. The lively
girls, pleased at having a butt at which to level their
shafts, seemed rather to accept his presence, as an
agreeable addition to their circle, than as an object to
jeer at; and Mr. Randolph, who set him down as an
insufferable puppy, and an ass, but withal, very
harmless, made no objection to his intimacy with the
family, upon the principle that he was an individual of
that description, whose absence or presence was a
matter of no moment to those whom he visited. The
compliment was passed to him to accompany them
home, and he caught at it. He rode with Mrs. Aston,
and after some remarks upon the opera, said:

"I much wegwet the absence of Miss Aston from
the opwa this evening, the mowa as I understand at
the house that indisposition compelled her to keep her
woom."

"This evening! Did you call, Mr. Winslow?"

"Merely en passant. I was on my way home to
dwess."

"Did you see her?"

"No—oh no! I sent in my name, but the man
bwought a wequest to excuse her, on the plea of indisposition; of course, I at once expwessed my gwief,
and left for the opwa."

Mrs. Aston thought there was something strange in
this; she had not left Myra so indisposed as to induce
her to keep her chamber, why she should therefore
have denied herself to Mr. Winslow, unless she really
had become ill, she could not comprehend. She regretted now, that she had not persevered in persuading
Myra to accompany her, for she believed, that though
nothing ailed her physically a secret grief was undoubtedly preying upon her, and change of scene, life,
and gaiety, were the best antidotes; silence, and
loneliness the food on which it increased. She became
silent and thoughtful the remainder of the ride;
although Beverley Winslow enlarged upon the vocal
and histrionic merits of "Gwisi, Mawcyo, Tambuwini,
Cawedowi, Wubini," and others of operatic celebrity,
pointing out with much loquacity, what was "gwate,"
and what "indiffiwent." What in fact, during her
stay in town, she should seek of this kind of entertainment, and what she should avoid. Mrs. Aston replied
in monysyllable, and did not understand anything he
said. She was thinking alone of Myra, with a foreboding of ill for which there seemed to be no occasion;
but which, nevertheless, possessed her. Again and again
she wished she had induced Myra to accompany the
party to the theatre, or that she had remained at home
with her. It seemed an excess of maternal feeling,
degenerating into foolish weakness, to give way to this
impression, but in spite of her sense of this, she continued to wish she had done one or the other. It had
been well if she had.

On reaching home, one of the first persons she saw
in the hall close behind the porter, was Lucy, Myra's
maid. The face of the girl seemed to wear a perplexed,
and anxious air, and she looked eagerly at those who
entered, and then retreated hastily upstairs. Presently
her bell rung, and down stairs she went like a roe.
Mrs. Aston, still in her cloak, as she had left the opera,
was on the landing.

"Miss Aston," she exclaimed, as soon as Lucy
approached her. "How is she?"

The girl looked confused, and with a singular
expression of countenance, said:

If you please 'm, I don't know 'm."

"Has she retired to rest?"

"No 'm."

"She is in her room, is she not?"

"No 'm."

"No! where then?"

The girl looked much frightened, and ready to cry.

"Oh! if you please 'm. I don't know 'm," she
said, and clasped her hands at the same time.

Mrs. Aston grew cold and faint. The girl's manner
rendered her horribly apprehensive.

"You don't know!" she repeated faintly, "explain
yourself."

"Oh! if you please 'm, Miss Aston went out about a quarter to nine to night, and she aint come back yet."

Mrs. Aston uttered a cry of astonishment.

"Went out at a quarter to nine to-night!" she reiterated.

"Yes'm," said the girl; "Miss Aston said she'd be back in an hour, but it's now past twelve. Oh dear! oh dear! I hope nothing has happened to her!" she added, wringing her hands.

Mrs. Aston felt the place swing round with her, but making an effort, she caught the girl by the hand, and said:

"Come with me! Explain to Mr. Randolph what has taken place."

She hurried the terrified and now sobbing maid into the drawing-room, where Mr. Randolph, his family, and Beverley Winslow were engaged in discussing what they had seen that evening, and she gasped out:

"Mr. Randolph! Mr. Randolph! interrogate this girl; there is some horrible mystery. Myra has left the house."

"Left the house!" repeated every one present, not the least astounded and the loudest ejaculator being Beverley Winslow.

"Gone—gone!" cried Mrs. Aston, bursting into tears, and sinking upon a chair. "Oh, what fresh afflictions has heaven in store for me!"

"Gone!" repeated Mr. Randolph, in amaze. "You astonish me. Come hither, girl."

"Oh, sir, if you please, sir, it ain't my fault, sir; I have had nothen' to do with it, sir. I couldn't help it, sir."

"No one said you could," he replied, at once adopting the professional coolness requisite to cross-examine in a manner best calculated to eliminate the facts. "Now, leave off your tears, and answer me clearly and truly. When was the last time you saw Miss Aston?"

"At a quarter to nine."

"Where?"

"In her own room."

"Was any one with her besides you."

"Mr. Randolph—papa—papa!" ejaculated both Mrs. Randolph and her daughters, in a deprecatory tone.

Mr. Randolph waved his hand for silence, and repeated his question.

"Yes, sir," replied Lucy.

"By Jove!" exclaimed Beverley Winslow, and whistled.

"Who was it—no equivocation?"

"Lizzie Hastings, sir."

"A female?"

"Oh, certain'y, sir."

"Who is she?"

"My cousin, sir."

"She came here to see you, then?"

"Yes—no—that is, sir, she came to speak with Miss Aston."

"Upon what subject, do you know—conceal nothing?"

"I don't know exactly, for I was sent out of the room, but I believe it was something about that gentleman?"

"Who?" cried Mr. Randolph, sharply.

The girl pointed to Beverley.

"What, Mr. Winslow?" he cried.

Lucy nodded her head.

Beverley Winslow started as if a galvanic shock had been applied to him. He turned intensely scarlet—he looked in an instant as if he had had just a year in India. He uttered a kind of winneying laugh—half hyena, yet an empty laugh, as he remembered the chase he had given Lizzie Hastings that evening, and also that he had lost her momentarily on that immediate spot from having been violently run against and almost knocked down by a drunken bricklayer.

"Well, upon my word!" he almost shrieked, "this is weally pwepwostewous; about me? Ha! ha! don't know any young woman named Lizzie Hastings."

"Are you sure—recollect?" said Mr. Randolph, eyeing him closely and detecting his confusion.

"What's the use of twying to wecollect what it is not possible to wemember; I wepeat the name's unknown to me, and the person also, of course."

"Well, that is not quite such a matter of course," responded Mr. Randolph; but, although not satisfied with Winslow's denial, he proceeded with his interrogatories of Lucy; and from her he elicited that after Lizzie had conversed with Miss Aston about half an hour, she was summoned, and found her young mistress dressed to go out. Her last words, which she was made several times to repeat, she communicated to them: "I am going out for a short distance, she said," exclaimed Lucy; "your cousin will attend me. I shall return in about an hour."

"Nothing more?" said Mr. Randolph.

"Not a word, sir," replied Lucy.

"Not anything as to the way she was going, or upon what business?"

"Not a single sentence, sir."

"Did they go on foot or in a cab?" asked Everett.

"I don't know, sir, replied Lucy. "I did not follow them to the door."

"Where does your cousin live?" asked Mr. Randolph.

"Mrs. Stewart's, in Baker-street. She's first-hand there."

"Then there will I go first," said Mr. Randolph, "there is something mysterious in the whole affair. Can you supply no clue after what you have heard, Mrs. Aston?"

"Oh, none whatever. I cannot imagine any motive whatever to take her abroad at such an hour, unless her feelings have been artfully worked upon by the girl who has induced her to go out with her, and thus made her the victim of some diabolical scheme."

"I'm sure, 'm, my cousin Lizzie has done nothing artful 'm," burst forth Lucy, "and she—she'd die—be—before she'd do—do—do any—anything dia—dia—bolly—bolly—bolly—cal, that she would!"

"Silence!" said Mr. Randolph, sternly.

" If you please, sir—can't—can't have my cousin spoken against, and she—she—don't deserve it."

"Silence!" I tell you."

" If any harm's come to Miss Aston," persisted Lucy, "it's come to my cousin too, for she'd lay down her life for Miss Aston, and I know it, too.'

" Will you hold your tongue? Answer only questions put to you," exclaimed Mr. Randolph, and then bidding Mrs. Aston keep herself as calm as possible, and assuring her that he had no doubt he should bring her back some good tidings, he prepared to pay Mrs. Stewart a visit. Everett and Beverley Winslow expressed their intention of accompanying him, so that if they obtained no satisfactory information there, they might be able to devise some plan of prosecuting their search in various directions. Mrs. Aston was left in the care of Mrs. Randolph and her daughters, and as soon as the gentlemen disappeared, Lucy was again subjected to a most searching cross-examination, especially so far as the young ladies were concerned, upon the part relative to Mr. Beverley Winslow; but Lucy persisted in saying she did not know what it was. She confessed only that she had overheard his name mentioned—that is through the keyhole, which she did not acknowledge—but that was all.

In the meantime, Mr. Randolph proceeded to Mrs. Stewart's, and, after some little delay, saw that lady. She expressed her surprise at Lizzie's absence, was both angry and vexed at it, for she gave her a very high character: said nothing of the kind had ever before occurred, and she was at a loss now to conjecture what had happened; but she could afford no other clue than that Miss Hastings had an aunt living somewhere down in the city, but where she really did not know—what was more, she did not even know her name, she might have heard it, but could not remember it if she had; and, further, she thought it extremely improbable that she would have gone there at the hour she was said to have left Baker-street, seeing that her time to be in Mrs. Stewart's establishment was a quarter past ten.

Mr. Randolph did not prolong the interview to discuss possibilities; he believed he had hold of a slight clue, however faint, at least it would aid in prosecuting further enquiries. He returned home, sent for Lucy, made enquiries about the aunt, and she produced a strip of paper, upon which was written, "Mrs. Watney, 12, Little St. Thomas Apostle, near Cheapside, City, fourth bell." Lucy had purposed to visit this relative on her first day out, and Lizzie had written it out for her. Mr. Randolph seized it, and away went the three, called a cab, and drove down at a swift pace to the address.

On reaching there, Mr. Randolph jumped out of the cab, and selecting the fourth knob, gave it a hard pull: a bell rang furiously. They waited a short time, and then, just as the bell ceased ringing, Beverley Winslow tried in rapid succession the first three. Almost im-

mediately the first, second, and third windows went up, and three heads were put out; three voices asked what was the matter, and Mr. Randolph called out that Mrs. Watney was wanted; the three windows were instantly indignantly slammed down, and it is certain that the name of the lady was not repeated with expressions conducive to her welfare in the state hereafter.

Beverley Winslow then plied the fourth bell vigorously, but with no success. He tried the fifth; the bell answered promptly enough, but there was some delay; at last, they heard the top window open, and a large quantity of night-cap protruded. A shrill female voice cried out :

"Now then, what's wanted ?"

" Mrs. Watney."

" Mrs. Watney? she ain't come home. Stopped at her friends, I s'pose."

" What time did she go out to-day ?"

" What time? about eight o'clock to-night."

" Ha! were there two young ladies with her ?"

" Two young ladies ?" screamed the woman, "no; they could'nt after she was out."

" About what time ?"

" What time? a little after nine."

Mr. Randolph rubbed his hands.

" We are on the scent now," said he.

" By Jove !" exclaimed Beverley Winslow, and gave a loud whistle.

" Pray step down immediately, ma'am," shouted Mr. Randolph, "I have some important questions to ask you, and every instant is of consequence."

" I ain't dressed," screamed the woman.

" By Jove !" cried Beverley Winslow. " Ha! ha!"

" Of course. Dress yourself as quick as you can, and come down here; I'll reward you well for your information."

The woman soon slipped on her things; her good star was in the ascendant; she had already received a handsome bonus from Myra, she was promised another, which might be more. She came down stairs, and a series of interrogations were put to her, every one of which she faithfully repeated before she deigned to reply. However, Mr. Randolph learned that Myra had been there, and her visit was connected with some letters in possession of Mrs. Watney, which letters he determined, if possible, to obtain. The next thing to ascertain was what route the two girls had taken; the woman had no notion which way they went when they left her. Mr. Randolph gave the woman half-a-sovereign, and telling her he should probably see her again the following day, he departed, attended by his son and Beverley Winslow, and turned into Cheapside. Here he searched for a policeman, and, strange to say, found one immediately. To him he gave a description of Myra and her companion, and asked him if he had observed a couple to correspond with that which he had given. The man, after calling upon his memory, replied in the negative. He was asked if he observed a cab set down in Little St. Thomas Apostle. No; he had not, but he had seen one draw off from there, and the man ply for passengers at the curb, and he had taken his number. Mr. Randolph asked the policeman to give it him; he complied with the request, but there the enquiries in that direction ended, and Mr. Randolph said, as he turned down to St. Thomas Apostle again:

"It is clear to my mind, that they did not come up into Cheapside, or they would have returned in that cab, for in that cab they came here, I feel satisfied."

"By Jove," muttered Beverley.

"Let us pursue our enquiries this way: there is a station-house near here; we may perhaps glean some information, or obtain some assistance."

His companions assented, and he led the way, at a quick pace, following the exact course which Myra and Lizzie in their ignorance had taken. Before a house, lighted up, they saw some four or five cabs. At once Mr. Randolph proceeded to enquire whether any of them had had a fare westward that night. They all replied in the negative.

"I had the offer o' one," said one of the cabmen, "but I could n't take it."

"Who were the parties who wanted to engage you?"

"Two young wimmen."

"At what time?"

"A little afore ten."

Mr. Randolph gave a brief description of them.

"That's 'em," said the cab driver, slapping his thigh, "and a pretty bilk they were dropped into."

"What's that?" cried Mr. Randolph.

"They guv'd a kebby eight bob to bring 'em from Baker-street"—

"The very place," ejaculated Everett Randolph.

"By Jove!" cried Beverley Winslow.

"Yes! down to St. Thomas 'Postle and back," said the cabman.

"Quite right," said Mr. Randolph "proceed, my good fellow."

"And back," repeated the cabman with emphasis, "but," he continued, "when they come out o' the house they'd been to, and wanted to go back, he'd miked off."

"Ha! ha! ha!" laughed all the cabmen, with infinite gusto.

"By Jove!" ejaculated Beverley Winslow, "what a wascally wobbewy."

"Well?" said Mr. Randolph.

"Well, they wanted me to take 'em to Baker-street, but I'd Alderman Carden to take home, an' he's a bitter pill—you can't get the best of him—so I told 'em to go to St. Paul's Church-yard, and they'd get a cab there."

"Did they proceed in that direction?"

"Yes, I told 'em the way, and off they went at a trot."

Mr. Randolph thanked him for the information, and hurried to St. Paul's Church-yard. There he was at fault—quite thrown off the pursuit. All his inquiries ended in nothing, and he was compelled to proceed back to Baker-street, with a faint hope that they had lost their way, and had to walk a long distance, and that he might find when he got back that they had returned.

He had gained, however, something—enough to raise hope, but when he got back to Baker-street, it was with pain he learned that neither of the girls had come back, and nothing more was known than what had transpired before Mr. Randolph and his companions had left the house.

However, what he had gathered satisfied him as to the facts of the case, up to a certain point. It was evident that Myra and her companion had gone to the City to obtain possession of some letters, that they had fully purposed coming home direct, but that some accident had occurred which had prevented and detained them. What it could be it was impossible to surmise, only something fatal, or at least of a desperate character could have occurred, and those most disposed to solace Mrs. Aston could not help coupling with this mysterious incident some dreadful occurrence. Nothing could be done that night, and they were obliged to retire to rest sad and dispirited, to commence the search where it had left off, but without being able to trace what had become of them after they had left the cabman who had directed them to St. Paul's to follow the route he had pointed out. All trace ceased there, and notwithstanding Mr. Randolph throughout the following day, and the next, and the next after that, pursued his inquiries with the most indefatigable and close research, employed the best detectives to be had in that useful and valuable force: it was all in vain; not the least clue could he obtain to their fate, after having, up to a certain point, followed up so closely their track. It was this that made the affair so mysterious and alarming.

On the following day, in a state of trepidation, Mrs. Watney presented herself in Baker-street, and produced the letters. Her first visit was paid to Mrs. Stewart, but no tidings had been obtained of Lizzie Hastings there; the mistress of the establishment expressed herself amazed, shocked, grieved, nay, mystified. She had had so high an opinion of Miss Hastings, she said, but there was no telling anybody; so, as Mrs. Watney was Lizzie's immediate relative, she communicated to her the dismissal of her niece from that moment, unless she could, on her return, give her the most satisfactory reasons for her absence. And all the while this colloquy was being carried on, Mrs. Stewart and Mrs. Watney mingled their tears, for with all the former lady's strong sense of propriety, there was much genuine feeling in her composition, and in her heart she really believed something dreadful had happened to her "first hand" to compel her absence. It was not possible that, unless the girl was the most artful she had ever encountered, she could be wicked enough to have eloped with any individual, or have done anything of a nature to prevent her re-admission to her establishment.

Mrs. Watney then, with a heavy heart, went to Mr. Randolph's. She could not make out what the letters could possibly have to do with the disappearance of her niece and the young lady, but when Mrs. Aston received them and hastily ran her eye over them, she soon came to a conclusion why Myra, at an unseasonable hour, under the guidance of a comparative stranger, and in secrecy, had quitted her new home. She was most pained at the discovery; unacquainted with the true circumstances, she arranged them in her own way, and only so as to give herself shame, mortification, and agony, alas! to no end. The motive for quitting Mr. Randolph's was thus developed, but the continued absence was shrouded in the deepest mystery.

Let us withdraw this veil from the reader's eye. Saul Waters and his companion, each bearing a struggling girl, hurried, after they had effected their capture, to the wharf's side. The former, animated by, as it appeared, almost superhuman strength, moved on, despite the agonized exertions of Myra to escape from such horrible thraldom, as though he bore a mere infant in his arms. His friend, equally strong, but not moved by the same impulse, found more difficulty in conveying his prisoner, for he feared in his attempts to overcome her resisting to hurt her, but still he followed Saul up, and with him passed over the decks of several vessels until the furthermost was reached. Past its sides flowed the deep, dark waters of the Thames.

Peering into the darkness, Saul raised his voice, and cried, lustily:

"Sea-bird, ahoy!"

"Hecoh!" responded a voice in the dark and misty distance.

"Bring a boat. Heave ahead," hallooed Saul.

"Bear a hand, Dick," shouted Saul's companion.

"Ay! Ay!" was heard, and then the plash of approaching oars.

In less than three minutes, a boat with a man and a boy at the oars, made its appearance out of the mist, its nose touched the side of the vessel on whose deck they stood, and the man with the painter in his hand drew it up close alongside.

"Take a turn with that painter round the cleet there," said Saul, to the man who had just arrived, "and then jump into the boat, and hold her steady, while we get on board of it."

The man did as he was bidden. Saul, without for an instant, loosing his grip of his prize, slid into the boat, and sat in the stern sheets; his companion did the same.

"Cast off, and give way," said Saul, laconically.

"Hey, boy!" cried his friend Bill. "Jump aboard and let go the painter, heave a head, and shake some of the dust out of your eyes, or I'll work it out with a rope's end."

The boy, in a blue shirt, and white, coarse canvass trowsers, but without shoes, stockings, or hat, leaped on to the vessel from which the others had embarked, cast loose the line, and, returning to the boat, took his place on a thwart, pulled with his companion, exerting his best strength, until the side of a smart trim sloop was made: he leaped lightly on board, and made the boat fast, and assisted the captives on board. Both girls, exhausted with their struggles, were now powerless to resist, and tacitly obeyed the impulse given to move in certain directions, though as yet they had not been allowed to escape from the heavy jackets thrown over them, and which, in drowning their cries, all but stifled them. They were, as soon as they were on board, hurried to the cabin, the captain of the vessel, who happened to be Saul's companion, saying to the boy:

"Make that boat fast aft, and let me know as soon as ebb begins."

"Ay, ay, sir," replied the boy, and the captain with his fair burden squeezed himself through the small square opening which led down into his sitting, sleeping, only apartment on board the vessel which he commanded.

Immediately he had deposited his burden on a seat, which also served the purposes of a locker, he returned to the ladder he had descended, and ascending a few steps, drew over the hatch, and securely fastened it.

"Now?" said he, "to examine the prizes we've made, Saul."

His intention to remove his pea jacket from Lizzie had already been anticipated by her, and she was endeavouring to use her eyes with an intense anxiety to see what means there were for self defence near around, any where within reach. Saul had taken his thick coat from about Myra, who was in a state of semi-insensibility, and flung it upon the ground. He placed her tenderly upon the seat, watched her head fall against the bulk head of the cabin, and her pantings to recover her breath. The light shone upon her face, pale and almost without sign of life, but yet so beautiful, that his passion for her became more intense than ever.

"Myra, lass, fear not!" he said, "thee'll be better presently. Nay, thou did'nst think o' meeting me, I'll besworn; nay, nor I thee. But ha' gotten thee now, Myra, and sooner then let thee go, girl, I'll be run up to the foreyard arm for 'ee, that I 'ull."

Myra buried her face in her hands, and burst into tears; if she had not, she would have gone mad, so frightful were the workings of her emotions at the position in which she was placed. She saw keenly the consequences of her act, simple in itself, and without intentional harm. In what had it resulted? She dared not trust herself to think of her mother—the Randolph's—aught—save that she was in some dreadful hole, with the being of whom she had as much horror as

BALACLAVA.

hatred. She scarce heard what he said; she made no attempt at reply. He paused for a minute, and then said:

"Come, lass, it's no use crying; thee know'st me before to-day, and thee must do as I've been 'bliged to do many a time an' oft, take matters as they come. You don't like me now, I know, but you will by an' bye. I'll never give you reason to do other. I'll take any oath to't you like to propose, I'll always be kind to you, you shall have your own way in everything, and you shall see how well and how long I'll love you, Myra."

"Ay!" cried his companion, with a laugh, although he was a little mystified by what he heard, "until you range up alongside of another as pretty, eh, Saul?"

Saul turned fiercely to him, and in a tone it was quite easy to understand was the reverse of jesting, bade him hold his tongue, and not interfere in this affair.

"Look'ye Myra," he said, turning again to her, "let us be good friends. We used to be once, you know. Come, give us a kiss, and if it be a bad job, do you make the best of it."

He took a step towards her, but she rose up with a shudder and a shriek; he at the same moment felt himself pulled back, and though the strength employed was not so vast, its suddenness compensated for what it lacked in power. A figure interposed between him and Myra, and a glittering knife flashing before his eyes, he started, drew back yet further apace, to see Lizzie Hastings standing before him, erect, firm, determined, from her flashing eyes almost frenzied, bearing unmistakeable evidence of being equal to any act of daring.

"Touch her at your peril!" she cried, looking with extended eyeballs into those of Saul. "Approach her with any such purpose as you have said, and as God hears me, I'll plunge this knife into your heart."

A large sharp-pointed knife had lain upon the table, she had possessed herself of it, and grasped it with all her strength. She did so quite with the determination to use it. Saul saw that she did. His upper lip trembled as he looked at her; that was a dangerous sign with him. He called her a foul name.

"Put down that knife," he said, "or I'll clutch your windpipe between my fingers till I squeeze the breath out of your body."

"That be d——d!" said the captain of the Sea-bird, who had seated himself on a locker, and rather enjoyed Lizzie's exhibition of spirit, as he admired her features and figure the more he gazed upon them. "No, no, Saul, the girl's a right to take care of her friend, and I admire her pluck. I don't carry the colours of a saint at the peak of my mizen, but d——n me if I stand by while any fellow lays a rough hand on a woman's throat. No, no."

"Oh, sir, have mercy upon us, and let us go!" cried Lizzie, earnestly. "You seem at least to have come of the heart of a man about you—heartily I'll forgive

you the fright you've caused us, if you will now put us on the land without further harm."

What the captain would have replied boded very much in their favour, for to say the truth, as he said, 'a lark was a lark and a spree a spree,' but here were two evidently respectable young girls, with one of whom and Saul there was some former acquaintance, of which he knew nothing, but which was certainly not favourable to his friend, and to have them on board his vessel absolutely kidnapped, and so liable to all the consequences, without any particular inclination for such a position, was going beyond either lark or spree. The girls were both much terrified, and were there to their utter fright and horror; they ought either to be put ashore, or crime would be likely to ensue, and where it would stop he did not like to look forward to. So he felt very like ordering one of his men and the boy to put them both ashore at once, and thus end the matter. If Saul chose to go on shore with them he might, and go through the adventure to the end, but his impression was at once to wash his own hands of the whole affair.

It was not permitted.

A loud knocking was heard at the companion, and on the captain giving a hoarse acknowledgment that he heard it, a voice cried,

"There's a strong ebb, shall we get under weigh?"

"Hold on," said the captain, "I'll be on deck in a minute or two."

"All right, sir," returned the voice, "only a Thames pollis boat hailed us just now, and one of the phillistines said they was going on board a foreign steamer that's just made the bridge, but they wanted to see you as they come back; they wont be long, and you was not to be missing."

The captain gave a whistle.

"Saul, you're wanted," said he.

Saul uttered a fearful oath.

"We must get away at once," he said.

"Had'nt you better go ashore?" exclaimed the captain.

"No—no! If they've tracked me aboard of you, they'll nose me ashore. No, let's clear out at once, we shall be right down the Pool before they miss us. Come on, Bill."

Saul strode to the companion ladder, but the captain, pointing with his thumb to the two young girls, shook his head.

"Can't be done," said he. "We must put they ashore, first."

"Heaven bless you!" cried Lizzie, heartily, "for your kind intention."

Saul again uttered a terrific oath, and seizing the captain by the arm, he said, anxiously,

"Come on deck, I'll make this all right with you."

"Do'nt see it, Saul," said the captain.

"Come on, I'll prove it," cried the other, fiercely almost dragging the captain up with him. They disappeared, and fastened the companion down, so that any attempt at escape by the poor helpless girls was quite hopeless. Still, Lizzie tried her utmost to cheer and sustain Myra, and raise up hopes of liberation which she had no faith in herself. There was at least some consolation in the fact that, however great a ruffian Saul Waters might be, his companion was not by many degrees so bad; and, unless he was induced to change, he would not permit Saul to perpetrate any decided act of villany: thus, if they were determined to perish rather than submit to wrong, they might, even if prisoners for some little time, escape without further violence. At all events, Lizzie secured a knife, and hunted for one for Myra.

"We have one certain friend in it," she exclaimed, "and, frightful as the alternative may be, I'll use it, if I am compelled.

Myra had no power, strength, or disposition to rouse her spirit to the same condition into which Lizzie had worked hers. She was overwhelmed by what had occurred. Not so Lizzie; simply because she was not, as it were, so largely the victim. She was placed in a position of peril and difficulty, Saul being an utter stranger to her. In all ways it was an accident of a painful and trying character; but Myra was differently situated, and the past as well as the new position into which she had recently been thrown made this utterly unexpected adventure of a more agonizing character, for it was not alone that she was placed in such imminent danger, but it was her mother's agony at her loss, the strange wild conjectures which would necessarily attend her disappearance, and the unjust but natural presumptions that would be indulged in by those who judged the actions of one half of the community by the follies, weaknesses, and crimes of the other, all—all which so completely bore her down when she needed her whole courage, strength, spirit, and self-reliance.

Soon they heard with beating hearts and dreadful forebodings the heavy tread above their heads of many feet, the crashing of falling chains, the creaking of ropes being hauled upon, the rattle of blocks, the increased heave and fall of the vessel, accompanied by signs that she was in motion and about to leave her moorings. Sounds, too, as if some persons in anger were flinging down heavy weights; then the noises by degrees subsided, the position of the vessel took a decided incline, there was a gurgling, bubbling, dashing sound at the sides, and Lizzie, clasping her hands, said:

"We are going—we are going! The wretches are bearing us away!"

For hours, the pictures of despair, both sat there. The vessel was proceeding at great speed, that was certain, and by the occasional noise on deck, the groaning and creaking, the rolling of the bark, a stiff breeze, if not a gale, was blowing. After a time it was plain that the Captain and Saul were too much occupied in their duties in working the vessel to attend to their prisoners, who were not sorry for such a respite;

indeed, Lizzie, at a great risk of a fall, made her way to the companion, not with the intention of opening it, but to find if there were any means of keeping out those that were out, but none could she find, and so she returned to Myra, and tried to engage her in a conversation, but, for a time, without success.

When, however, hour passed after hour, and still, beyond the uneasy surging motion of the vessel, no one appeared to disturb them, they both began to grow calmer, to look their evil in the face with a more collected spirit than before, and they began to converse upon it. Lizzie, blamed herself hastily for what had occurred, and the trouble into which she had drawn Miss Aston, and Myra lamented that Saul's mad passion for her should have proved the occasion of bringing Lizzie into a position almost as perilous as her own. Thus, each blamed themselves for what had happened, and feeling that it was their duty to cheer each other up as much as they could, brought both into a more peaceable frame of mind, and more willing to trust their fate into the hands of the Almighty, who would not, in their moment of need, refuse them help, but for some special purpose that would prove wise and good in the end.

Insensibly, from talking of what brought them there, they got to the subject of the letters, and Lizzie repeated all nearly word for word that Clifton Grey had written to her—words of gentle counsel, of tender thoughtfulness, of cheerful hopefulness, all that could tend to make her worthy of the man who loved her—whom she loved very dearly, too—or could give her sanguine expectations of a glad and happy meeting in the time to come, looked for so earnestly by both of them when he should be released from the wars, from its dangers and its trials, the horrors of suspense, and the weariness of long expectancy, they should both sit down hand-in-hand together by their own fireside, never more to part until the hour arrived to render up their living spirit unto the hands of Him from whom they received it.

Myra listened eagerly to every word, and as Lizzie repeated sentence after sentence verbatim, she could detect the happy felicitous turn of expression she had so often admired when Clifton had held converse with her; it lost none of its charms now that she heard it under such different circumstances.

Fortunately, though much inconvenienced by the motion of the vessel, neither suffered from the horrible malady of sea-sickness. That, at least, had not to be added to their other discomforts; but Myra, who had spent the principal part of her life on the sea coast, had not to learn that the lurching and surging forward of the vessel, the straining of the seams, the creaking of the cordage, the tramping on the deck, and the low hoarse roar which seemed incessantly to continue above them, was caused by what seamen call dirty weather, and that this commotion of the elements would command the exclusive attention and employment of every hand that could assist in working the sloop; so, for the present, there was no fear of intrusion from their captors; but although wearied by what they had undergone, and the many hours which had elapsed beyond the time at which they usually retired to rest, neither had the smallest inclination for sleep. They did not have sufficient faith in security from interruption for that; but as daylight began to dawn, Lizzie, who throughout had proved the more resolute and energetic of the two, looked about for something in the shape of a weapon which should prove quite if not more efficacious than the knife she had already obtained, and which she, in some degree, congratulated herself had saved Myra from insult. It was with difficulty she could use her locomotive powers, but she made the attempt, and displayed not the smallest hesitation in opening every drawer or small closet that presented itself to her view, in the recesses of which she thought it probable she might find what she searched for.

She did not search in vain, for in a small drawer, beneath a cupboard of the narrowest dimensions, she discovered a brace of revolvers, with all the appliances, powder, ball, and caps. She shuddered as she looked upon them, and even turned pale, but it was a momentary weakness only.

"'Courage! Lizzie, my lass!' Walter cried to me when he placed the pair in my hands he bought before he went to the war. 'Courage! say I to myself, 'if I am to be a sergeant's wife.' Heaven grant me strength of mind to emulate his bravery!"

Lizzie plunged her hand into the drawer as she spoke, and drew out the pistols singly. She examined them; they were new—one of Colt's last patterns, they were loaded too, and each nipple fitted with a cap. They were on half cock, but would not discharge unless from some remarkable accident. Lizzie knew this, and closing the drawer carefully, returned with her prizes to her companion.

She held them out to her in exultation. Myra, with an apprehensive cry, drew back.

"Nay, do not be afraid, Miss Aston, for here are protectors indeed. With these, and a firm determination, we are as safe as if we were on land. Take one, and secrete it; there may come a moment, when you may be glad to have it to rescue you from a horror worse than death."

Myra, animated by her words, held forth her small white hand, and took the offered pistol; it was heavier, being loaded, than she calculated upon, but she grasped it firmly, and said: "I pray to Heaven that moment may never come; but should it, I know how to die, and would not hesitate for one second."

"You!" cried Lizzie. "You die—kill yourself because a wretch chooses to act like a diabolical ruffian. No! no, Miss Aston, I do not intend to do any such thing, if"—

The companion at this moment gave sounds as of being unfastened. Both Myra and Lizzie secreted instantly their weapons, and clinging close together sat in a dark and furthermost corner, awaiting the coming of their visitor.

Through the companion-way, and upon the ladder, a heavy huge pair of leather boots made their appearance; they slid with an agility, remarkable in their seeming immobility down the worn steps, and, enveloped in a shining waterproof coat of large dimensions, a sou'wester fastened under his chin by a piece of cord, Captain Bill stood before them. He looked hard at both, and then cast a glance round the cabin.

"Been frightened, lasses?" he said in a hoarse voice. "Dos say you have," he added, "for its been blowin' hell's bells, but the saucy Sea-bird can weather worse tempuses than this. The gale has lulled, and the sea's goin' down—we shall have fair weather, and smooth sailing in an hour or two, so I just come to see whether we can't make a good land fall for you, and cheer you up a bit. You're hungry and tired, no doubt—so are we—and I'll send down the boy into the cabin to make a good landfall of grub. Come, now, gals, don't look so shy. Bah! don't lower your peaks as if you were a brace of byster dredges dropping to le'ward of the spanking frigate of a enemy. Cheer up! I'll see no harm comes athwart hawse of you."

The two maidens, still crouching and clinging together, offered him no reply, but looked very dejected. The man eyed them wistfully, and worked his hands in rather a fidgetty manner about his buttons; he seemed more disposed to make friends with them than to take advantage of their forlorn condition. He writhed about a little in his clothes, and ejaculating an oath, added:

"Come, freshen up! carry your peaks higher! for I tell you, I, Bill Poole,—there's a rattling French frigate with my name, I tell you—won't let any harm fall foul of you while I am within hail. Now, you mind me; lay in a good breakfast, and when you've filled up the hold, just run a signal aloft there, so that the boy can clear decks; then I'll fasten down the companion, lay on it myself, so that nobody shall range up alongside you, and you can turn in for a few hours, and sleep off them white faces. When you have had your spell out, you can come for a watch on deck, and I'll show you blue water and sea-birds, and other fine sights, only to be seen without land on either bow or quarter. Then that'll make you happy, I should think."

"Why, if you are disposed to consult our wishes, do you not put us on land?" observed Myra to him, appealingly.

He shook his head.

"That would be dangerous," he said.

"I will promise you, that if you will do so," she urged, "you shall not be placed in danger on our account. Nay, I will ensure you a reward."

The captain of the Sea-bird scratched his whiskers, and became thoughtful; then he sighed, and returned,

"Can't be done now, at all events; we are stretching away with a fair breeze for the French coast—"

"France?" cried both girls, apprehensively.

"Well," said he, deprecatingly, "you'll be no worse off there than aboard here; and, perhaps, you'll stand a good chance for a quick run home. There, its no use palavering more about it. Backing and filling won't give us head-way, and so we must stand on as we are. Now, you fill up your lockers with grub, and go to sleep. It will be all right bimeby. You'll see."

So saying, he went to the closet above the drawer from which Lizzie had obtained the pistols, and from it took a bottle of spirits and a horn, which he hugged up as prizes of inestimable value, and retreated upon deck, saying,

"Rouse up!—the red flag at the fore! Whoop! I've said I'll take care of you, girls, and I will, too, or may my grog be stopped by a run up to the fore-yard-arm without help of hands or feet."

Keeping bottle and cup in tight embrace, he disappeared up the companion way. When he was gone, Myra said,

"Heaven be praised, there is a hope of escape, although it is distant."

Lizzie Hastings shook her head,

"Do you speak the French language, miss?" she asked, hesitatingly. Myra answered in the affirmative. Lizzie clapped her hands and snapped her fingers.

"Then I don't care," she said, exultingly. "I'll scream for help the moment we land—up will come the French soldiers—you will say to them that they are our allies, now, and fight for us—that we have been carried off, and want to go back again; they will say, 'Ah! wee, wee, wee'——"

"You speak French, Lizzie?" interrupted Myra, with the first smile that had illumined her features since her abduction.

"No," replied Lizzie, "not I. Mrs. Stewart does, and I have heard say that's French for 'yes,' though why they don't say yes when they mean it, I never for the life of me could understand; but the French are for ever saying it to everything, whether they mean it or not; however, they will protect and send us back once more to dear old England."

"If we are permitted to leave this vessel when we reach the French port," said Myra.

"I will, I am determined," returned Lizzie. "I did'nt take this pistol for nothing."

"I am afraid you would faint at the first discharge," said Myra, more cheerful than she had been, for she saw hope in the distance.

"Well, I should scream, of course," replied Lizzie, but I should terrify my—"

A pair of cold, white feet suddenly obtruded through the companion way, and they were followed by a pair of wet blue trowsers, and an equally wet blue shirt; above the collar rose a white, haggard face, and curly hair of much the same colour. It was the boy of

whom the captain of the Sea-bird had spoken; he had come to spread the table for breakfast. He looked worn out with fatigue and want of rest; his eyes were hollow and sunken; lines of care were round his mouth, and even his forehead, young as he was, was furrowed. A hard, very hard life had produced this aspect; but he was in the process of inuring—a kind of pickling, in order to preserve for future trials of endurance upon the frame. This boy in time would lose his pale face 'for one of mahogany hue; his skin, now soft and fair, would ultimately rival leather; his delicate frame would expand sideways —it rarely lengthened—until he took somewhat the aspect of a beer cask, built more for strength than size.

Both Myra and Lizzie regarded him with compassion, but he took notice of neither; he proceeded to the little closet, brought out some crockery of a very plain description, and without exception, cracked in more places than one. The table upon which he placed them was provided with a rim, so that unless the sloop fetched rather a heavy lurch, they would not slide off. Having disposed of them by arrangement, he came to the locker on which the two girls were seated, and said bluntly:

"By your leave, ladies?"

They rose, and he produced from the locker, ham, soft bread, a basket full of eggs, some cold salt beef, all of which he placed on the table, and then looking Myra in the face, with a stolid air, he exclaimed:

"Cap'en wants to know which you'll have, tea or coffee, or both?"

At first they would have declined, but nature asserted her rights, and Lizzie took upon herself to order tea; he poured from a canister nearly a quarter of a pound of that invaluable plant into a very black looking can, which boasted a spout and a handle above it, to hang on to a hook over the galley fire; this can had a lid to it, to keep out the soot and keep in the strength, and when it had received its contents, away darted the boy up the ladder, and soon reappeared with the can, the smell from which at least was fragrant. He ran his eyes over the store of eatables, and said:

"Capt'en says you're to stretch along the eating haliards, and keep a good full."

They both said they could'nt eat. The boy's eyes opened wider still, each glared like the bull's-eye of a policeman's lantern, as they once more roamed over the food on the table. He gave a gulp, but said nothing; both Myra and Lizzie understood it, and the active benevolence of both was at once excited. Lizzie cut a thick piece of the soft bread, and Myra a stout piece of ham.

"You are tired and hungry," said Myra to him. "You can eat this, that we have cut for you."

The boy cast a quick glance at the companion way, and stretched out a pair of eager hands to receive the proffered bounty; he stowed away the gift within his shirt next his skin—not the cleanest safe in the world, but the only one he had at hand ; he pulled his forelock with finger and thumb, and then whipping up four eggs, danced up on deck again. He was soon back with these articles cooked, they had given him the opportunity of putting away the food given to him, until he could revel in it.

While he was gone, Myra and Lizzie had conferred together. They needed a friend, and they thought they might secure one in the boy ; a mouse had set a lion free, who could tell but the boy might effect their release. A few remarks respecting his jagged appearance enabled them to learn that he had been on deck all night, that a complete gale had at one time been blowing, but that it had subsided, and the Sea-bird was now bowling along before a fresh and fair breeze ; he expected by night fall, or soon after, if the wind held, they would be off the French coast.

"Is there no way by which we could land first in England?" asked Lizzie eagerly.

"Do you want to go ashore first?" he asked.

"Yes," cried both girls with eagerness.

"Ask the cap'en, he can bear up for Ramsgate as soon as we're off the foreland, and land you there."

"Ah! but he will not do that," said Lizzie. "He has dragged us from our homes, and, in spite of our tears and prayers, is carrying us to France."

"Ah!" said the boy, "he's a regular nigger driver," and added an epithet which was infinitely less elegant than expressive of the antipathy he bore him.

"Can you assist us to get on shore?" enquired Myra, with an anxiety of manner which was not without its effect on the boy.

"Me!" he answered, biting his thumb nail in a thoughtful manner, "me—no—no—that is, I don't see how I could."

His thoughtful hesitation seemed to suggest that he had some notion that it was to be done, and Myra caught at it.

"I will give you a sovereign, if you can contrive it," she said.

Lizzie drew out her purse, and shook forth its contents : there was in it one half crown, a two shilling piece, one shilling, three sixpences (one with a hole in it, never to be parted with but under the last agonies of starvation) a key, a ring, a small knob of orris root, twopence in halfpence, and two farthings, making in all —excepting the sacred sixpence, the gift of Haverel— the sum total of six shillings and eight pence halfpenny. The question was, how much of this could she spare, for after landing, she knew not what she might want ; so after counting it rapidly, and jumping to a conclusion, she added to Myra's offer her own :

"I have not much with me, but I will give you half a crown now, and send you ten shillings, when we get safe to London.

The boy mused a moment, and then said to them :

"If I do this, do you think you can get me out of

this craft into the merchant service—anything, so I am out of this?"

"To be sure," promised Lizzie ; "anything you like—a banker's clerk if that's all."

The boy told them then in a whisper he would do his best ; but they must not expect too much. They must ask no questions, and not even notice what he did if they saw him on deck or anywhere else.

"What is your name?" inquired Myra.

"Jack Melbury," he replied. "My mother lives at Littlehampton—you can always hear of me there."

At this instant a voice shouted hoarsely for the boy, and he flew upon deck ; ere he went up the ladder he placed his finger on his lip. It was strange what a degree of intelligence had lighted up his face when he promised to exert himself in their favour. How plain it was that beneath that dull heavy look much real ability lay concealed, but which, by harsh usage and over labour, was being hourly forced deeper and deeper beneath the surface. He again put on the same dogged look he had previously worn as he quitted them, and received, on reaching Captain Poole to know his will, several cuffs for having been so long performing his task below when he was wanted to go aloft. He expected the task, and obeying it, he went up to the mast-head.

Myra and Lizzie, further cheered by what had elapsed, partook of the breakfast, and when the boy returned to "clear the decks," he hinted they might go on deck, and 'twould be as well if they did. Why, he did not inform them. Myra inquired if Saul Waters was there? and was informed he was in the "fo'kstle," or forecastle, asleep, and was not likely to turn out for some time. He had done a hard night's duty, and had drank a bottle of brandy before turning in, so they need not be apprehensive of the pleasure of his company.

Lizzie, who watched the boy's face attentively, thought she could read there honest intent ; and though he did not explain why they had better show themselves on deck, she counselled that they should comply with his suggestion ; there might be an advantage in it, and it was their duty to take every advantage that came in their way. Myra suffered herself to be convinced by her reasoning, and, to say the truth, was not sorry to get upon the deck of the vessel, in order to change for the close atmosphere of the cabin the pure fresh breeze, which was forcing the Sea-bird swiftly on its way.

The boy led the way, and as soon as he got on deck said, in a loud voice :

"Come on deck!"

A grunt from the vicinity of the steerage responded. There was a sturdy sailor at the helm, and rolled up in a huge sea coat, reclining on some loose stuff under the bulwarks, in a doze, lay the captain of the Sea-bird.

"Ladies on deck," said the boy.

An accustomed sound might not have roused the

captain; but an unaccustomed observation woke him up. He sprung to his feet. The two girls stood shivering, white-faced, and half-bewildered by the light and the breeze; they were holding on by the companion, and looking about them mystified.

"You are cold, lasses," said the captain, "the breeze is too strong for you at first. Ah! you'll soon get used to it. Jump below, Jack, and fetch out of my bunk two pea coats—you'll see them there."

The boy obeyed, and re-appeared with them. Captain Poole fastened these protections from the weather and cold—wonderfully odorous they were of tobacco—round the trembling girls, and bade them pluck up a heart and look about them. They soon felt the effects of the warmth and the fresh air; it invigorated their weak frames, and enabled them to cast their eyes around, observe where they were, and what was their chance of escape by aid of the boy.

In good sooth, that prospect was small enough, the natural prospect altogether as extensive. Quite away on their right, almost behind them, lay a long blue line of coast; before them, on their left, nothing but sea; above them sky—clear, blue, and cloudless.

What aid could the boy possibly render them, here on the wide, wide sea? It seemed simply hopeless.

We shall see.

The captain of the Sea-bird for a short time tried to engage them in conversation, but they were not at all communicative; at length, as he learned they intended to remain on deck for some time, he expressed his intention of 'turning in' for an hour's sleep. He gave his directions to the man at the helm—who seemed too drowsy to be at such a post, if the safety of all on board was a consideration—and descended to his cabin.

Half an hour passed; two men who were in the fore part of the Sea-bird threw themselves down under the lee of the vessel's side to snatch a brief slumber. The boy alone was wakeful; presently he disappeared into the cabin; scarcely a minute elapsed before he appeared again with a roll of bunting; he gave an anxious glance coastwise, and then he affixed this bundle to the pennant halliards. In an another instant it was up at the truck, fluttering in the wind a blood-red flag.

The boy shot forward and dived into the forecastle.

The man at the helm, if he had seen the boy's act, took no notice of it. Myra and Lizzie did not understand its purport; they were made acquainted with it hereafter.

They talked but little; they sat and watched the coast they were leaving behind them, growing sadder as it perceptibly lessened in their sight, when all at once, as if by magic, a large cutter made its appearance on the weather beam. Myra pointed it out to Lizzie, and grasped her hand vigorously.

"Do you see that vessel yonder?" she asked with an anxious and an eager tone.

"What, with white sails—like this?" asked Lizzie.

"Yes," she replied.

"That is a revenue cutter," she said.

"What is that?" asked Lizzie, innocently.

"A queen's ship on the search for smugglers. Oh! could they but have a suspicion of this vessel, we should be saved."

"How?" enquired Lizzie.

"They could compel this vessel to bring to, and come on board to search her."

"Can't we wave our handkerchiefs?" suggested Lizzie—they might see us."

"We are too far off."

"How large it keeps growing, we seem to be going towards it."

"No," said Myra, hardly able to articulate for excitement, "no, it is pursuing the same course as we are, and is nearing us fast."

"It may overtake us?"

"It may."

"And come close up, so as to see us?"

"I hope so."

"Thank God!"

There was a silence for a few minutes. It was evident the cutter was fast increasing her speed, and lessening the distance between them. There was no look-out, and the helmsman mechanically every now and then opened his drowsy eyes and cast them on the sails, and then at the compass, but he edged the vessel only a little closer to the wind as she shewed a tendency to fall off before it.

Both girls bent a gaze of painful interest upon the approaching vessel, which seemed to have been gradually rising out of the sea; her hull was now visible, and her course slightly altered, so as decidedly to follow in their wake. A slight scream suddenly burst from Lizzie's lips, a white puff of smoke broke out from the bow of the revenue cutter; presently it was followed by a low boom; it was the sound of a discharged gun. The helmsman's practised ear caught it; he opened his eyes wide in a moment, and looked in the proper direction. He gave a silent grin.

"The Snapper!" he muttered. "She wants to overhaul us, s'pose. Nothing aboard here."

He cast his eyes around him; the sleepers were in deep slumber at the forepart of the vessel; the captain and the rest were below. Only two girls, who could know nothing of the matter, were huddled together near the companion, and there was no one to thwart any purpose he might form. He growled a horrible oath:

"There's Lootenant Spencer aboard o' her, I know. D—n him, I'll gi' him a dance."

He brought the vessel more before the wind, and she, in obedience, surged forward and greatly increased her speed. Another puff of smoke followed this act; once more the distant boom of a gun was heard, but the helmsman only looked at the two girls, the sleepers, and his sails, and held on to the helm. For a short time there was not a sound but the dashing of the sea, as the Sea-bird plunged over and through it; the mast and cordage strained and groaned, and the foam from the crests of the dancing waves flew high up over the bows of the vessel as she darted on her course under the guidance of a practised hand.

The helmsman bent his keen eye, glittering beneath his shaggy brow, upon his pursuer, and an oath escaped him.

"There goes her gaff taupsail up," he muttered. "If the breeze freshens, whoop! that spar will snap, like a rotten cabbage stump. Ha! ha! he'll have a precious run for nothing, how he'll splutter and swear!" He indulged in a silent grin again, and eased off the head of the vessel a little more before the wind to give her yet greater speed.

It was quite clear, however, that the increase of sail upon the Snapper, and the much larger surface of canvas she could spread to the wind, gave her the advantage over her competitor, though the Sea-bird, built for a dangerous trade, had a very light pair of heels, and could compete with any boat of her tonnage. The Snapper gained rapidly on them every minute, although the man at the helm adopted all such artifices as were calculated to enable him to hold his own; but his attempts were useless, for, in spite of all, the Snapper ran with them two feet for their one. It was with intense anxiety the two girls watched her coming, prayed in utmost earnestness at heart for the success of the pursuers, for their release depended on it.

Boom! another puff of white smoke, a blaze of flame, told of the discharge of another gun from the Snapper. Ha! a black object whirling through the air struck the crest of a wave ahead of them, dashed up the spray in a sheet of mist, rose up, struck the sea again further on, and then expending itself in a series of short bounds, disappeared.

"Ha! ha!" grinned the helmsman, "he's a shotting them guns." Again he gave the Sea-bird more head, and she leaped on in obedience.

The two vessels once more kept on their way in silence, the Snapper increasing in size every minute; at length a sheet of flame rose once more from her bows, Lizzie screamed, it was so near. Bang! the report was loud and sharp. The sleepers sprang from their slumbers. Crash! came the iron messenger, whistling through the air, struck the mast, shivered it into fragments, and the whole fabric of spars, ropes, gear, above where the cannon ball had struck, fell with thundering uproar upon the deck, over the side, and into the sea.

In an instant the Sea-bird was a hopeless, helpless wreck upon the waters.

CHAPTER XIX.

"Can I not serve you! You are young, and of
That mould which throws out nerves; fair in favour;
Brave, I know, by my living now to say so;
　　*　　*　　*　　*　　*
You are made for the service. I have served.
Have rank!"
　　　　　　　　　　　　　　　WERNER.

"And now the bugle's warning note
　Rings out a summons clear,
'Up, up, to horse!' the shout resounds,
　From vanguard to the rear!
Then hurriedly the order flew,
　These dreadful guns to take,
Where dreadful fire, in that dark vale,
　Did fearful havoc make.
　　　　　　　　　　　　　　　SONG.

"The foe's at hand; why, let them come;
Steep are our hills, nor easy of access,
And few the hours we ask for their reception.
　　　　　　　　　　　　　　　GUSTAVAS VASA.

THE FIRST STEP IN PROMOTION. THE CAVALRY CHARGE AT BALAKLAVA. A MURDER ATTEMPTED. THE BATTLE OF INKERMANN. THE FORTUNE OF WAR.

THE considerate thoughtfulness of His Royal Highness the Duke of Cambridge in releasing Clifton Grey from duty for three days enabled him to win back his strength again. As we have said, ever temperate and moderate in his habits, nature had not disease, nor the ravages and inroads made by drink upon the constitution, to contend with; his system was perfectly sound and healthy; the prostration, therefore, from sheer exhaustion, was soon recovered by rest, and by the many little kind attentions paid to him by his comrades, in return for the numberless services he had rendered them. Before the three days had expired, he was fit for any duty again, however arduous.

The Duke of Cambridge, as he promised, enquired into Clifton's claim to being first into the battery upon the heights of Alma, and took some trouble to examine the evidence which from various quarters he obtained; but though it was conflicting, and in some quarters even asserted that the Scots Fusiliers were broken and disordered under the terrific fire from the redoubt, and while they were reforming the Grenadier Guards obtained the coveted first admission, yet his Royal Highness was satisfied by the corroborated testimony afforded him, that Clifton Grey had at least earned the promotion he had promised. Enquiries in all directions served only to assure him that Clifton possessed all the requisites to make a valuable member of the army. Quiet and gentlemanly in his manners, his lips unpolluted by foul language, scrupulously clean and neat in his appearance, abstemious in habits, strict in discipline, well conversant with his military duties, free from the taint of official reprimand, confinement, or other punishment, brave to a fault, he was, as the Duke observed, quite a model soldier. This character

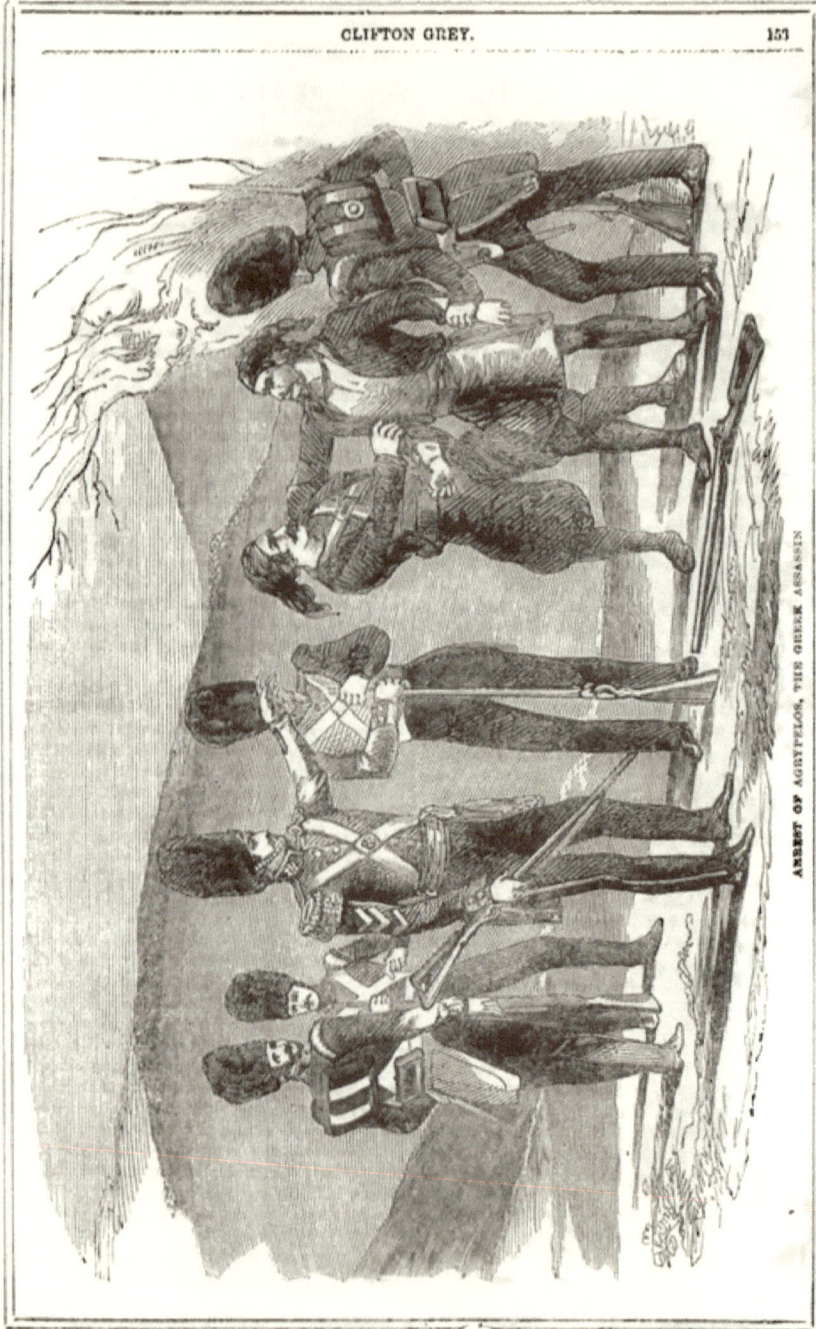

ARREST OF AGRYPLOS, THE GREEK ASSASSIN

had been elicited from a colonel, from lieutenants, from non-commissioned officers and privates, comrades manly enough to speak the truth of one who had been, and did prove a true friend to many of them; and so the Duke rewarded Clifton for his gallant conduct in the field, and his good conduct in the camp, by promoting him to be colour-serjeant, in the place of a brave soldier who had been killed in the battle of the Alma.

The duke spoke kindly and flatteringly to our hero, in informing him of the step to which he had been promoted, and assured him, that though it appeared to have been tardily presented, the delay had arisen rather from the difficulty of deciding upon conflicting claims than indifference in bestowing the prize plucked out of the blazing throat of death. He further assured him that her Gracious Majesty had resolved upon presenting with commissions those non-commissioned officers who highly distinguished themselves by valour and ability in the field, and he confidently hoped, from what he had ascertained from all quarters respecting his merits, as well as his very creditable character, that he should have the yet greater pleasure, hereafter, of presenting him in the name of her majesty with a commission in the army, of which he was already so honourable a member.

The barrier had been broken down, and to the common soldier at length the door was opened, through which he might pass to become a general, if not a field marshal, who knows?—great changes in the whole military system are imminent. May they turn out free from red-tapeism, and be framed solely for the good of the service, and in that, for the nation! Clifton Grey thanked his royal highness in brief but energetic terms—he had been called to the front, to receive his promotion, in the presence of his comrades, who had fought with him; and the officers under whom he had served, including Captain Winslow, whose feelings were not of the most gratifying nature, although he affected to feel the utmost indifference—and he promised his royal highness that the favour he had bestowed in such flattering terms, and with such royal grace, should never be dishonoured by him.

The Duke bowed, and smiled approvingly, and the men cheered lustily. Many promotions were made at the same time, for the losses had been very heavy, and among them Mickey Dunigan became Corporal Dunigan, infinitely to his delight. As the Duke departed, his royal highness informed Captain Winslow that he would be prepared to receive him at an hour on the following morning which he named. The captain bowed obedience, and the Royal General of Division returned to his quarters. We may briefly say, that Captain Winslow kept the appointment on the following day, and on being asked the occasion of his conduct to Clifton Grey, he sought to exculpate himself by declaring him to be an artful, designing hypocrite, who by great skill and cunning had succeeded in deceiving every one.

"But you, Captain Winslow," observed the duke, looking at him fixedly.

Captain Winslow coloured, and bowed. His royal highness then sternly addressed him, and remarked that he must be candid enough to say he did not think his superior sagacity had acted honestly by him. If the young man was artful, he was at least neither a drunkard, a thief, or was he undisciplined; his artifice had at least induced him to be steady, obedient, cleanly, smart in his duties, and brave in the field, and so long as such results sprung out of artifice, his royal highness said he should not object to the whole army—cavalry, artillery, and all, being in the highest degree artful. He further informed Captain Winslow it was easier to lose men than to replace them, especially men whose cunning made them such good soldiers, and he might be assured, that if he repeated the act of ordering a man who had taken his turn at the desperate trench labour, on outpost duty, before he had had his rest, it would be more than probable that the commander-in-chief would mention him in his despatches to the home authorities in terms not likely to advance his interests. Captain Winslow, in conclusion, was informed that his royal highness had determined to keep Sergeant Grey in his eye, and any attempts at petty tyranny would be detected, and treated accordingly.

The captain retired, mortified beyond expression, but unable to reply, beyond that he knew his royal highness was, like many others, deceived in the man; he had no desire to injure or oppress him, and since his royal highness had thought fit to take him into favour, he would treat him with all possible respect. If, however, his royal highness found hereafter that his sympathy and favour had been showered upon an unworthy object, he at least would be free from blame.

"Or from praise either," said the duke, with emphasis; "as you certainly was proceeding in the way—if the man were as bad as you insinuated, of making him much worse. Good day, Captain Winslow."

Captain Winslow came out of the quarters of the royal duke, very much as if he had been in an oven, and was restored to the air in a white heat.

To be sure there was rejoicing that night among those who had been promoted, and those who, looking forward to it, were still not jealous of it being bestowed on those who were fairly entitled to it. If there was favouritism at the Horse Guards, and at head quarters—if nephews, and cousins, and relatives got pitchforked on to the staff irrespective of capacity or fair claim, at least the humble corporal and the modest serjeant had nobly won their reward. Mickey Dunigan bore his blushing honours with a pride and gratification which could not have been surpassed by that felt by him who made the leap which converted a plain major into a general and head of the Staff.

"Mickey, is it?" he cried to a comrade who addressed him thus familiarly, "bad manners to you for the ignorant blaggard yo are. *Corporal* Dunigan—you'll be plazed to mind—*Corporal* Dunigan—you onmannered thafe! when you're spaking av a man that's had a royal duke for a godfather."

And Corporal Dunigan strutted away to quiet places, where he could laugh to himself with glee respecting his new dignity, and commune with himself thereon with the most entire self congratulation.

"Mickey, you'll be getting proud thin, ye villin!" he said to himself, "av your new grandeur, and not know yerself, av you meet in a crooked lane. Sure, Corporal Dunigan is it? the top of the morning to you, Corporal Dunigan—that's me. Hoo! but the ould people in the dear ould Ireland, it's grand they'll be when they get the bit o' money I've saved, and hear the news, blessin's on 'em! Sure its the ould gal will be off to Michael Lynch, and knock him down wid her tongue. 'Sure Misther Lynch,' my son's a corporal in the quann's army,' sez she. 'Whoo! thin,' sez he, 'that rogue 'll bein back a giniral.' Ha! ha! an' av the ould fool should spake truth, who knows. Ha! ha! Thin Bridget will bear the news, and she'll turn as red as the fairest flower in the garden of Paradise, ah *Brighidin bou mo store** ! Pulse of my panting heart, its joyful you'll be when you know your bould soldier boy's a corporal. Its fancy your swate self kissed, you may, just now, atuno the eyes, and on the cheeks, and on the lips—on the lips—on the lips! Oh, murdher! an' I wish, Bridget darling, you was here on this spot at this moment, sure I belave its hug you to me heart I should. Ha—ha! Full Corporal Dunigan, sez the duke. Full Corporal Dunigan—whisht—whisht! sure I'll go an' see Father Wheble, for its proud I'm gettin, an' I may be losing honest Mickey in full Corporal Dunigan."

So Mickey, still laughing ever and anon with satisfaction at the thought of his new dignity, went to find the priest to confer with him, so that his vanity might not get the upperhand of him.

The siege of Sebastopol proceeded slowly, but in due form, according to the stereotyped rule of warfare. Every battalion contributed its quota of men for the trench-work, and the labour was most severe. At the same time there began to be felt the consequences of gross incapacity and infamous jobbery in the various departments; somehow there was a scarcity of food, of clothing, of everything that ought to have been in plenty, with an unexampled transport at hand. The consequence was, that the number of sick began to show an awful increase. The worst, however, was to come—it was only beginning as yet to be felt. Towards the latter end of October it was observed that the Russians had marched several battalions of their infantry across the Tchernaya, and stationed them in large numbers in the gorges and mountain passes on the roads to Inkermann and Sim-

pheropol. They threatened Balaklava, which was however, considered a secure position, and had been also strengthened by entrenchments made by the French, while the Turks had thrown up earthen redoubts on four hills receding from each other to the mountain chain, each armed with two or three guns, and defended by about 250 men. On the morning of the 25th of October, 1854, the first redoubt was attacked by the Russians in considerable force, and the news was instantly conveyed to head quarters. The Duke of Cambridge was ordered to get his division into motion, and Sir George Cathcart the fourth division. General Canrobert received notice, while the blast of the trumpet called the cavalry under the Earl of Lucan into the saddle. All was life, bustle, and activity. The roll of the drum, coupled with the rattling of musketry, and the heavier sound of guns of heavy calibre, told that an action had commenced.

Clifton Grey had now a species of command, and he shewed himself quite equal to the task; he got his men together with an alacrity which it was impossible not to praise; but, much as he wished, he had not the opportunity this day of distinguishing himself. The division had been placed by Lord Raglan under the orders of Sir Colin Campbell, and marched to the front in advance of Balaklava. Already had the Russians obtained possession of the redoubts held by the Turks, who fled at their approach in terror and disorder. Already had the 93rd Highlanders, in one long thin line, only two deep, received the storm of Cossack cavalry 1,500 strong, with a fire, at first discharged at too great distance, to stop the horde; but, on the second discharge, within a hundred-and-fifty yards, of such deadly accuracy, that the whole force of Cossack cavalry wheeled about and fled. Already had an immense body of Russian cavalry advanced down the hill to where the noble Scots Greys and the Enniskilleners were in saddle, impatiently awaiting the word to go at them. That was given and responded to by a wild cheer from the dragoons, who went away, Scot and Enniskilleuer, at a hand-gallop, to meet in deadly conflict thrice their number. Nothing could resist them—they closed with the foe, and absolutely cut their way through them, but only to encounter other formidable squadrons of Russian cavalry. At this moment the trumpet sounded for the 1st Royals, the 4th and 5th Dragoon Guards, to charge, for the Russians first dispersed were closing compactly up to entirely surround the brave Scots and Enniskilleners; but with a ringing cry that went to the hearts of all who heard it, the high-hearted dragoons went at full gallop at the Russians, checked nor paused not, swept them before them, and scattered them as if they had been a flock of sheep. Five minutes sufficed; the whole Russian cavalry turned and fled in terror and disorder. "Well done!" cried Lord Raglan, with a burst of enthusiasm. It was well done!

The First Division and the Fourth were now upon the ground, and the cavalry on the left front, then after such brilliant performances, followed the celebrated but fatal cavalry charge. The First Division, embracing Guards and Highlanders, had filed off to the extreme right; they faced the redoubt, and were fired on by the Russians, but without effect. The Russians made a retiring movement. As the cavalry retreated, their infantry fell back to the heart of the valley. One redoubt was abandoned by them, and the other three were held in possession. Then came an order—either the result of incapacity or misconception, God knows—the responsibility, on whose ever head it may lie, is a fearful one. While gazing on the retiring Russians, and longing for the order to move on in pursuit—though he knew it would not be given—Clifton, to his astonishment, and to that of others, who were as well acquainted with the rules of warfare as himself, under which cavalry never advanced to capture guns unless supported by infantry, saw the light cavalry, led by Lord Cardigan, at a trot, advance upon the redoubt—nay, upon the whole enemy in position. He cast his eyes round, and saw that the only support they had was a reserve of cavalry far away in the rear. The madness of the attempt was apparent to all—it was a mere holocaust to the sanguinary Moloch of battles. On they flew—no trumpet sounded the recal. The redoubts poured upon them a murderous fire from the guns and from rifles. Unheeding, the cavalry dashed onward. Flame belched forth from the guns; a dense mass of white smoke, and the gallant cavalry disappeared in it. The glitter of sabres, like minute flashes of lightning, could be observed in the sullen mist. The roll of guns and musketry on all sides was awful. Clifton's heart beat quick; his breath came and went with difficulty. He could hardly restrain himself from uttering a wild cry to his comrades to follow him and bound off to their aid, but discipline chained him where he stood, and with sickening anticipations he awaited the re-appearance of the cavalry, if any of them returned to tell the dreadful tale. They did come out of that gulf of smoke, but not until they had been into the redoubt and sabred the gunners as they stood. They charged a column of Russian infantry, and dispersed it like a cloud of sparrows; but exposed on all sides to a withering and destructive fire, they fell almost in masses. Troopers without horses, and horses without riders soon told how fearful had been the loss under this fatal mistake. As the light cavalry were getting towards their lines, the Russians threw out a mass of lancers in order to annihilate them, but the 8th Hussars, miserably unequal in point of numbers, but infinitely superior in pluck, charged them, and passed through them, committing great havoc. The retreating cavalry reformed and charged again—noble fellows!—although they had already undergone the devastating consequences of a frantic enterprise. At this instant, while the cavalry were engaged in a fearful hand-to-hand encounter, the Russian gunners, with an infamy which has no parallel in the history of war, discharged their guns at the contending masses, slaying indiscriminately friend and foe, shooting down, like dogs, their own cavalry as well as that of their enemy.

A shout of execration burst from the troops who witnessed this indiscriminate slaughter, and had it been wise to have given the order to advance, although it might have been in the face of certain destruction, a desperate effort would have been made to have taken a full revenge.

As the shot and shell from the redoubts reached the ground where the guards were posted, they were ordered to lie down in two lines, but ultimately were moved on towards the Russians, who commenced slowly retreating, and endeavoured to lure the advancing allies into a gorge, where no doubt they would have been able to have effected serious injury on the pursuing troops, but Lord Raglan and General Canrobert were alive to the stratagem, and though they extended their front, and retook three of the redoubts, they were not to be seduced into an action where the advantages to be gained were most problematical—where the loss to be suffered was large and certain.

Night came on, and the troops returned to camp; as the Guards marched back to quarters, they were replaced by a French division of considerable strength, among whom Clifton recognised his friend, the Zouave, whose life he had saved at Varna. The little soldier uttered a shout of recognition, and rapidly conveyed to him an intention he had formed of seeking him out and enjoying the pleasures of his society, when the cares of duty would not interfere with the delightful communions of friendship.

Two nights subsequently, Clifton marched out with a picket to an outlying position, and posted his men where they could quickly detect the advance of an enemy long before they could approach near enough to effect a surprise. He had Mickey—we beg his pardon, Corporal Dunigan with him; this Irishman had conceived an affection for our hero, for he had been kind to him in sickness, and a friend to him when in need, and he would at any time have hazarded his life in his service, had such a sacrifice been required of him. After placing the men at their post, Mickey said to him:

"Ah now, sergeant! sure it's a deep grievance you must have done captain you know who, with the yaller face, like a hound sickening for the distemper, for he's bitter agin you, an' you may swear that any way."

"Captain Winslow."

"That same gruelly-looking spalpeen—saving the service."

"I have neither done him harm, nor even now wish him harm. I have a loathing contempt for him, nothing more. Why do you introduce the subject? it is not a pleasing one to me."

"Plasing, is it. Ugh! about as agreeable as a morning at the triangles under the provost-marshal. Murther! I wouldn't spake of it, but the blaggard"—

"The captain."

"Sure it's all one—tould me on the quiet, the other day, when he heard me say in joke, which he thought earnest, that you was a murthering villin, that he thought so too, an' he was glad some of his comrades had found the rascal out. He offered me a crown, which I took, for his dirty money would buy claan bacca, an' I ax'd him what it was for. So he sez to me 'for yourself, my bauld fellow, an' you ought to have been the sergeant,' sez I; 'Bow, wow,' sez I. 'His banner's grace knows best,' sez I, 'an' he made me corporal.' 'So,' sez he, an' his face grew like the skin of an ould sow after its kilt and drest, 'I hate him,' sez he, 'I hate him from my sowl.' 'Sure, captain dear,' sez I, 'it's no harm he's done the likes iv you, anyway,' sez I; sez he 'He has done me the deepest, an' he stan's in my way with a large property. 'Does he now?' sez I; sez he 'He does, it's only lately I found it out, an' if he knows it I shall be ruined,' sez he. 'Murther! captain,' sez I, that's bad, anyhow.' Sez he, 'My friend'—he called me his friend, ha! ha! I was a corporal, and his friend. Sure, I'm coming to my honours mighty fast"—

"Go on, Mickey, for heaven sake! you know not how you have excited my interest."

"Sure you'll wake up when you know more, I'm thinking. 'Well,' sez he, 'my friend,' sez he, 'this fellow has crossed my path from his first joining the regiment, 'but it was not—although I had a strange hatred to him from the first time I encountered him—it was not until we was at Maltha,' sez he, 'that I found him out.'"

"Malta—found me out—what did he mean?"

"'At Maltha?' sez I. 'At Maltha,' sez he, 'an accident,' sez he, 'a mere accident placed in my hands a dockyment'"—

"A document! Merciful heaven, can it be"—

"Thrue for you, sargeant darling, that's what he said —'placed in my hands a dockyment,' sez he, 'which told me who and what he was, an' that he stood between me an' a large fortoon.'"

"Is this possible?"

"It's what he said; it may be a lie, I won't swear it isn't; but av it is, he tould me as av it wor truth. 'I hate him,' sez he, 'an' I'd give a thousand pounds,' sez he, 'if any one quietly would put a bullet through his heart.'"

"So murderously vindictive! bad as I deemed him I did not think he would have descended to this."

"'Sure,' sez I, 'a Rooshin 'ud do it for less money,' sez I. 'I will undertake to give it,' sez he, an' he caught me by the wrist with a grip that made me cry out; 'you may win it av you plaze,' sez he. Sure I looked hard into his grey, cat-like eyes, an' I sez, 'Captain,' sez I, 'maybe you know the hearts of men you make the likes o' them offers to.' 'I think I do,' sez he, wid a wink o' the eye. 'I think you don't,' sez I, wid a wink o' the eye too; 'an' before you've such a whisper for me again, reflect, captain darling, that a bould soldier boy who'll charge slap into the face of an inimy won't shoot a comrade in the back,' sez I, 'an' he won't take it kindly av the man as axes him to do do it,' sez I."

"It was well said, Mickey," exclaimed Clifton, thoughtfully.

"So wid that I bid him the top of the morning, an' I turned my back on him, kase, you see, I was afeared the corporal 'ud forget he was talking wid the captain, and the man might have spat in the blaggard's face"—

Mickey's speech was interrupted by a loud 'ping' in the air, instantly followed by the sharp crack of a rifle. A Minnié bullet passed close to the ear of Clifton, and struck a tree by which he was standing, threw up some fragments of bark, and buried itself in the trunk. In an instant Clifton and his comrades were on the alert, but the bullet was from within their own lines, and how it could come from a foe seemed a mystery. Sounds of footsteps were now heard, with voices in contention. Clifton, Mickey, and two or three of his comrades, with rifles ready for action, advanced in the direction whence the sounds emanated and challenged. A voice responded "La France!" and quickly added, "Un ami, mon brave Anglais!"

Clifton rushed up, and found a Zouave, who had fast hold of a man by the back of his neck and his wrist. The prisoner was struggling to escape, but in vain. At a word from Clifton, two of his men took charge of the Zouave's capture, who proved to be a Greek—a chapman from Balaklava; and Clifton sought from the Frenchman an explanation of the circumstances under which the capture was made by him.

"Aha!" cried the Frenchman, suddenly. "Voilà! C'est mon bon ami de Varna."

Clifton instantly recognised the little Zouave, with whom the incident occurred, narrated in a former chapter, previous to the embarkation of the army for the Crimea, and whose life, on that occasion, he, at a critical moment, saved. After mutual acknowledgments had passed, the Zouave related how he had, after an adhesion to labor to which those of the doomed spirits, in the infernal regions, were light amusements, obtained a release from duty, and had taken a stroll to recover his elasticity of mind, and preserve his elasticity of frame. In the course of his perambulations he found that he had lost his way, and as he was pondering—not sure that he was in the vicinity of the English, or whether he was straying direct into the arms of the Russians—suddenly observed the Greek on before him, adopting, alternately, a shuffling, running, crouching, creeping, sneaking, progress, which assured him all was not as it should be, and so he determined to follow him. Together they proceeded onwards, at about equal distances for a short time, and then Monsieur le Zouave gained on his chase, until he saw him fall upon the ground and lay motionless. The Zouave copied his example, except in remaining still; he crawled towards him on his belly, and was almost within reach of him, when the Greek suddenly rose to his knees, and taking an aim with a rifle with which he was armed, discharged it; as he did so he found himself struggling in the arms of the Frenchman. Clifton thanked him heartily, and mentioned how narrow his escape had been, the hand of M. le Zouave had diverted a ball which would have stretched him lifeless to the earth. The Zouave would not acknowledge the merit, but said it was the hand of Heaven which always interposed its protecting hand over those whom it considered worthy such favor. Motive for the deed was now sought, and Clifton questioned the Greek as to the cause of his act; but the man, who wore an air of sullen ferocity, refused to speak. He was kept in safe custody until the picket was relieved; but, before that hour, the Frenchman departed, being put in the right way to find his own lines again, and quitting with a promise from Clifton to pay a return visit to the French camp, to which he assented.

When the picket was relieved it returned to camp, and reported what had occurred—the duty falling upon Clifton Grey, and that of receiving it upon Captain Winslow, who became violently scarlet as soon as he heard what had occurred, and turned towards where the Greek stood, with his arms folded and his head cast down. He bit his lip, but with an effort he recovered his nonchalant manner:

"What stuff is this you tell me?" he said, sternly. "This man belongs to Balaklava—a trader with the allies—and could have no possible motive for firing at any member of the English army. Pray, sir, did you see him discharge his gun?"

"No," replied Clifton, "but his bullet passed within an inch of my head, and proceeded from where he stood. The Zouave, in whose hands we found him struggling, not only saw him fire, but diverted the rifle, so that it missed me."

"Where is the Zouave?"

"He has returned to his regiment."

"What is his name?"

"I do not know; but I can obtain it." He then briefly narrated the scene at the café at Varna, in proof that the French soldier was not unknown to him.

"Bah!" cried Captain Winslow, contemptuously; "do you suppose the man can be detained upon such wretched evidence as this? Do you assume, because you got kicked by this man in some wretched brawl at Varna, you are at liberty to make others the authors of a revenge you have not the courage to take for yourself? I shall order his discharge. Release him, there! Agrypelos, you are at liberty; be off with you, and take my advice, don't get rambling over the hills at night, or you may, as you have done, get into trouble, and not get off so easily."

The Greek did not need further telling; he was off like a shot, not a little to the astonishment of those who had brought him in prisoner, and of Clifton Grey, who, struck by the remark made by Captain Winslow,

perceived that this Agrypelos was the very fellow who had attempted at Varna to stab the Zouave, although previously neither the Frenchman nor himself had recognised him. He turned to the captain, and said:

"Captain Winslow, it is not for me, as a subordinate officer, to comment upon your proceedings, but I beg to suggest, that Greek is a dangerous man, and should have been examined, at least, before he was permitted to depart."

"Because you happen to be afraid of the man, are a number of gentlemen and officers to be inconvenienced by your pusillanimity? Let's have no more of this; dismiss!"

"Captain Winslow, as my superior officer you shelter yourself from reply. You know how much truth there is in your observations, and I know that there is a limit even to your insults. The time must and will come when you will have to account for the unmerited indignities to which you have so long subjected me."

"What, do you threaten me, fellow! I will order you under arrest"—

At this moment a frightful spasm interrupted further speech; he grew a ghastly white, and would have fallen but that Clifton caught him. He writhed and twisted, and became so faint as to be almost powerless; large drops of cold perspiration poured down his forehead, and he gasped out:

"To my tent—to my tent!"

Clifton saw that he was seized with the cholera, and bore him at once to his tent as tenderly as if he had been an infant, or his nearest and dearest relative. Having deposited him there, he rested not until he had obtained a surgeon, and remedies were being administered to arrest an attack of a most severe kind.

He was at no loss to guess, although Sergeant Haverel saved him the trouble, by the suggestion that the Greek Agrypelos had been hired to do the assassin's work by Captain Winslow; and, coupling this with the story told him by Corporal Dunigan, he arrived at a conviction that Captain Winslow, by some means which had been denied hitherto to him, had arrived at the knowledge of his extraction; and, further, that he stood between him and some important interests. This, at present, was all speculation and surmise, it was true, but, nevertheless, having once got hold of the idea, it took firm possession of him, and he determined, as soon as he had an opportunity, to endeavour to obtain some confirmation of it. Fortunately, he knew where to write to Sylva, and he determined to inform her of the loss of the contents of the packet she had addressed to him, and entreat her to forward to him another with similar contents; but, for the present, he had not time to apply himself to penning letters, for the siege was opened, the bombardment of Sebastopol had commenced, and what with trench work, outpost duty, repelling sorties, and snatching the few hours of repose indispensable to maintain his strength, there was no opportunity for writing. Many of the men began to fall ill with dysentery and cholera; the army was imperfectly supplied with food and clothing; the weather began to change for the worse; cold, wet, and foggy nights were succeeded by bitterly-cutting, windy days, while the tent accommodation, the only protection from the inclement weather, became daily worse.

On the night of November 4th, Clifton Grey again had duty with a picket belonging to his division, and marched down the valley of Inkermann, where they were posted in connection with the pickets of the Light and Second Divisions. The night was dark, gloomy, and misty; there was a dripping fog, which could not be called rain, but deposited a moisture equally wet and penetrating with severe rain; just the night for an attack by a cunning and determined enemy, and the greatest vigilance was therefore necessary. At the same time, it was so wretched and trying to the spirits of those that had to endure it, that Clifton exercised more than usual watchfulness in visiting the sentries, seeing that they were wakeful and attentive. While doing this it seemed to him that he could hear the sounds of wheels moving in the valley below where they were posted, and not only that, but the tramp of men. He reported it at once to an officer on duty, and this was again conveyed to the major, who arrived at the conclusion that the sounds distinctly heard by others as well as himself, when he drew their attention to it, were those of ammunition carts and arabas, going into Sebastopol by the Inkermann road. No notice was therefore taken of it. About five o'clock, Brigadier-General Codrington, subsequently Commander-in-Chief, an active and intelligent officer, riding round the brigade of the Light Division, received everywhere the report "all's well." He entered into conversation with a captain on duty, and the same reflection made by Clifton crossed the minds of both, and became the subject of remark. The Russians had shown themselves always ready to assault, if they could do so, by a surprise. This was the very morning to accomplish such a feat. Struck by the force of the suggestion, Brigadier Codrington determined to retrace his steps to the pickets, and warn them to be on their guard, as day was breaking. He turned his horse's head, and had not proceeded far, when his ears were greeted first by a solitary discharge of a rifle, then a sharp volley of musketry, followed by a dropping fire, from the pickets commencing slowly to fall back.

The Russians, in enormous strength, were upon the pickets of the Second Division before it was known they were in the valley. Clifton's ears had not deceived him; he had heard the movements of artillery and infantry on their way to commence an attack which was confidently calculated by the foe to result in driving the allies into the sea. The pickets of the second division fell back, closely followed by the Russians, who soon came up with the pickets of the light division. The practised eye of Brigadier Codrington told him what had occurred,

and he galloped back to the lines to wake up his division, who as were, the other divisions of the army, in their tents sleeping; some few had risen, and a few camp fires were being lighted, but the bulk had not yet turned out. Now the alarm rang through the camp. "The Russians are advancing in force!" In what direction! who will be first to repel them? The pickets were still fighting bravely, and retiring slowly, but the dense masses of Russians rapidly pushing on to them, made resistance out of the question. Brigadier General Adams now had got together the 41st, 47th, and 49th regiments, and hurried with them to the brow of the hill, to arrest the advance of the foe. Brigadier General Pennefather, who was commanding the Second Division in place of General Sir De Lacy Evans, who was ill, next despatched his own brigade, composed of the 30th, 55th, and 95th regiments, to operate on their flank. The shrill blasts of the trumpet were sounding in all directions, the expressive roll of the drum, calling the men to arms, and cracking fire and rolling volleys of muskets, attended shortly afterwards by the heavier discharge of artillery, made the whole camp soon one scene of wild and exciting activity. Sir George Brown got his division under arms, composed of the 7th Fusiliers, 19th, 23rd, 33rd, 77th, and 88th regiments—at least, all that the Battle of the Alma and sickness had spared, under Brigadiers Codrington and Buller.

His royal highness the Duke of Cambridge was quickly in the saddle, and as soon had his troops under arms; the Highlanders were at Balaklava, but the Grenadiers, the Coldstreams, and the bold Fusiliers, with loud cheers marched quick time in up to the front, on the right of the second division, and in front of a dense column of Russian infantry.

Lord Raglan was made acquainted with the approach of the enemy, and with his staff rode to the scene of action, which had already commenced, and was raging with tremendous violence,—in what direction was only indicated by the rattling of musketry and the roar of shot and shell. The morning was dark, gloomy, and foggy, and a drizzling rain was falling; it was impossible to see many yards in advance—impossible to detect the manoeuvres of the enemy, or point out where to out-flank or out-general them. The fight, therefore, became a sheer bull-dog encounter—hand to hand—bayonet to bayonet. One of the bloodiest on record, it is one, at the same time, which must ever redound to the honor of the Englishmen engaged in it, and further evidence that wondrous pluck, that sound bottom, that thoroughbred game, which never knows when it is beaten, and holds on to the foe while life or power to strike remains.

It is not the province of this history to give full details of the battle; we have but to do with the acts of one battalion—or, rather, those of one man in a particular battalion—and though we may not record the deeds of this division or the other, they are patent to the world, they need no praising word, nor the labors of a humble chronicler, to recount what is written in letters of gold in their country's history.

Clifton, with his picket, rejoined his regiment, which, as we have said, with loud shouts and cheers were rushing on to the enemy, and soon were face to face with five times their number. Now was heard the voices of their officers, directing them to fire low and not too fast, cheering them with round-toned voice, and animating them—if they had needed it, which they did not—by brave example.

The word was given to charge, and that tremendous line of steel, as in obedience to the command, and under the influence of a ringing cheer, was something to strike terror as it came sweeping on into the ranks of the enemy. It was irresistible, the Russians gave way before it, driven like a flock of cattle. But now it was discovered that the Guards were deficient in ammunition, and what reserve was in the rear it was not possible to say. At this moment a large body of Russian infantry broke through the fog and appeared on their right, and far in their rear. At this instant, a terrific volley of musketry from the massive columns of the advancing Russians was poured into their ranks. A frightfully murderous storm of bullets, which cut down no less than fourteen officers, and hurled into eternity nearly half the division. To remain where they were was to be overwhelmed and annihilated; they were deficient in ammunition, deprived of their leaders, confused, staggered, and in this desperate position they made for the lower road of the valley to re-form and return to the charge.

Now it was that Clifton Grey shone pre-eminent among his fellows in animating and encouraging them to maintain the fight, even against such enormous odds. He adopted that vigorous though concise language which at once appeals to the *amour propre* and to the heart. Unwounded, though his dress had been ripped in several places with ball and torn by bayonet, and he had been engaged in close and fierce conflict, he thought not of danger, saw only danger in being overwhelmed by the masses of the enemy's infantry; he saw, also, that nothing but right down dogged endurance, accompanied by successive dashing charges on the part of his division, could arrest this evident intention of the enemy. And this conviction he tried to make palpable to his comrades, who listened to him with stern emotion, their fierce eyes and clenched teeth telling that the devil was roused within them, and that they meant to drive the Russians back from whence they came or to perish where they fought.

It may be here stated that the point of attack chosen by the Russians was just that portion of the British position which was alone open to surprise. The sharp and practised eye of the old and able soldier Sir De Lacy Evans had detected this, and he represented it to the proper quarter. The authorities listened, promised to examine, did examine, admitted the truth and the

force of the representations which pointed out the unprotected character of a series of slopes ascending to the summit of the hill unbroken by entrenchment or outwork of any kind. At length, precisely the very species of work for defence which ought not to have been adopted was commenced. On the slope of the hill just over Inkermann, a redoubt or battery, composed of gabions and sand-bags, was thrown up. As soon as General Evans saw it, he suspended the progress of arming it with the "two" guns designed for it, inasmuch as, barren of all support, it was more calculated to invite assault than to repel it, and it was well that his advice was followed, for on this day even two guns, turned from this battery upon the British troops, would have done incalculable mischief.

It was from before this battery the Guards had retreated to the road below. Here they were reinforced by the indefatigable exertions of the Brigadiers and the Duke of Cambridge, and with a small supply of ammunition they prepared to charge the Russian infantry, who were in the battery, and who no doubt deeply lamented at that moment to find that it was without guns.

"Now, lads, remember the eyes of England are upon you," shouted the duke. "It must not be said that even the whole Russian army could make the British Guards give way. Forward!"

"Hurrah!" shouted the men, grasping their rifles—the Minié, with which they fortunately happened to be armed—fortunately, for that weapon did tremendous execution that day.

"Hurrah! boys!" shouted Sergeant Haverel, "we will remember dear old England!

"'My ancestors were Englishmen, an Englishman am I,
And 'tis my boast that I was born beneath a British sky;
I prize my peerless birthplace for its freedom and its fame,
In it my fathers lived and died—I hope to do the same.'

and lick the Russians too, boys. Hurrah!"

"Hurrah!" shouted the men.

"Reserve your fire, lads, until the word is given," cried Brigadier Bentinck, "then fire low, and charge; use your steel freely."

"Hurrah!" shouted the men.

"Sure it's myself will do that, anyhow," exclaimed Mickey Dunigan. "For it's mighty fran the Rooshans are wid their toasting irons, an' by Gorra! av we don't spit 'em like larks, they will be after doing that same for us."

A laugh and cheer responded to his words. Clifton reserved his speech for the moment of encounter. On they went at a rapid pace through the wet, prickly brushwood, and the dark, drizzling rain; a blazing fire of musketry meeting them as they advanced at double quick time. The battery was before them, occupied by a dense mass of Russian infantry, the deadly Minié with which they were armed would reach far beyond where these men clustered:

"Make ready, present, fire!" was suddenly shouted by the commanding officer.

DISCOVERY OF SERGEANT HAVEREL ON THE FIELD OF INKERMANN.

Down went the guns with the precision of parade-firing, crash went a fearful volley into the column of Russians:

"Charge!" shouted the officer.

"Charge!" roared the sergeants.

"Hurrah!" shouted the men, and with a wild yell not to be described—only to be conceived by being heard—they dashed upon the enemy, who held possession of the battery:

"On, boys!" shouted Clifton Grey, springing out in advance. "Clear the battery, the French are coming up; let us show them how we carry a position."

A wild shout followed, as Clifton, ever in advance, closed with a body of Russians, bearing down the guard of the man in front, bayoneted him, recovered his weapon, and leaped over the sandbags and fascines forming the battery with a loud, ringing cheer, to be heard far above the sounds of musketry, and amid a hail of bullets he plunged into the redoubt, crying:

"Fusiliers, you're wanted."

"Here's one av 'em," yelled Mickey Dunigan, leaping in close after him. "Faugh a ballagh! Whoop, for ould Ireland! St. Patrick sends ye that, ye ugly thafe!"

"Give it 'em, Fusiliers," roared Sergeant Haverel. "Forward, tumble 'em over. Up, Guards, and at 'em! Hurrah!"

"Down among the dead men,
Down, down, down!"

"Drive them out, boys," shouted Clifton Grey, "they give way; they are retreating; tumble them out and down the hill after them."

And now the fight became terrific. The Guards, with tremendous impetus, dashed into the battery, and were masters of it in a minute; the Russians were beaten back by the mere force of the shock they had to encounter; and the Guards sent them flying before them, but they were instantly replaced by another mass, heavier and more formidable than the first. With admirable discipline the Guards restrained their impetuosity in pursuing their retiring foes, and prepared to receive others, whom they charged as soon as they came within reach with irresistible fury. The Russian columns were broken and dispersed, and fell back in absolute flight, but another dense mass was brought forward to supply their place, and these men fired as they advanced, and then charged with the bayonet. The struggle was tremendous; column after column of the Russians poured up, and to save themselves from being entirely surrounded, the Guards had to fall back. Once more out of ammunition, opposed to more than four times their number, they had no alternative. The number of dead Russians and of the Guards, who lay stretched on that bloody patch of ground, told with what devotion they had struggled for the honour of their country.

With a stern, determined front, they moved slowly back, and the Russians could tell that to charge them

in this movement would not enable them to rout them, but expose themselves to fearful loss without a corresponding success. The Russians once more occupied the battery, and threw out a body of the infantry to keep the Guards employed, and to prevent them, if possible, from advancing to retain possession of it.

At this moment the Duke of Cambridge was conspicuous in cheering and rallying the men, not that they required it, God knows, for on that dreadful day they all fought like heroes. They needed no spiriting up to return to the fight, they had too much to avenge; they knew there was too much at stake for them to give way. No, noble fellows all, they were ready to dare every danger that could be opposed to them, and to lay their lives down cheerfully if they could secure the victory for the land that gave them birth, beneath whose flag they would scorn to do a dastard's act. The cocked hat of the royal duke, and his glittering epaulettes, attracted the attention of a body of Russians, who advanced to a spot where they could bring their muskets to bear on him. Clifton observed it, and seeing near him Mr. Surgeon Wilson of the 7th Hussars, who was attached to the brigade, he pointed out the imminent danger of his Royal Highness to him.

"I will caution his royal highness," exclaimed Mr. Wilson.

"We can send those fellows flying if a dozen of us charge them with the bayonet," said Clifton.

"Right," cried Mr. Wilson, "gather up a few of your men and I'll lead you."

In less than a minute Clifton had twenty volunteers. Mr. Wilson uttered a cheering cry, and rushed on to the Russians, closely followed by Clifton Grey, Mickey Dunigan, and the rest of the brave fellows; they came on to the Russian detachment at a bound; the bristling British bayonets were too much for the foe, they were scattered like chaff before the wind; routed, they fled at the top of their speed, and the life of the Duke of Cambridge was saved.

Around and in the two-gun battery the Russians were thickening and effecting a lodgement, from which it would soon be impossible to displace them; and as Clifton, with nervous anxiety, detected this, he saw their only chance was once more to be led up to the battery, and clearing it out, maintain the position against all comers. Just at this time the Russians had, from another point, obtained possession of the batteries of Captain Wolehouse and Captain Turner, having obtained the advantage from the gloom of the wet fog, the artillerymen as they advanced hesitating because they were unable to tell whether they were friend or foe. The Russians, in enormous force, rushed on and overbearing all opposition, took possession of the guns. But they were not permitted to retain it long, for the Light Division made a desperate charge, and swept the Russians before them like a herd of deer. This was enough for the Guards, for Clifton Grey, who under the excitement of the moment, uttered a loud thrilling cry, and sprung forward in a second; the whole of the Guards, whose numbers had been sadly thinned, dashed on, turning with fierce ardour to not only recover what they had surrendered, but to drive back the Russians from whence they came. With animating shouts they plunged forward, not waiting for—not heeding the word of command, increasing their quick march to a run, they swept with irresistible force into the battery, driving out every Russian and forcing them partly down the hill. Here the struggle became tremendous and deadly; the Russians here opposed to the guards, were evidently the *élite* of the Russian army; they crossed bayonets, and fought with a courage and perseverance worthy of a better cause; but though fresh masses succeeded each other, the guards kept their sanguinary ground against all odds, fighting with a heroic bravery and endurance unsurpassed by any like feat on record. And now, when the Guards maintained the battle against enormous odds, only yielding up ground with their lives, and the struggle was continued by the most determined valor alone—for column after column of Russians were being added to the force already employed, and were slowly, but surely, making their force so overwhelming as to enable it to bear down all opposition, Clifton, yet without a wound, but almost exhausted in this bloody field of slaughter, as he saw regiment after regiment of Russian infantry charging up the heights, shrieking and hallooing, began to have forebodings of the result. No base thought of yielding crossed him; he seemed to bear a charmed life. He had, with a pang not to be described, seen Sergeant Haverel fall, while pursuing the Russians down the hill; he no longer heard the inspiriting cheers of the brave Mickey Dunigan, who on that day nobly sustained the character for bravery so well earned by his most brave fellow countrymen in the many engagements in which they have fought: he believed him therefore to be struck down. Lieutenant Linder was also not to be seen: in fact, it was plain that an immense number of the division had fallen; in addition to which some confusion existed, for the men belonging to the different battalions were now mixed together, Grenadiers, Coldstreams and Fusiliers, but all engaged with one mind, one soul, in battling with the enemy, without a thought of giving way.

Three hours had passed: long hours were they under such circumstances, but the Guards, almost decimated, were yet on the old spot; now almost surrounded by Russian infantry, then breaking their way through them, retiring to re-form, and again with wild and deafening cheers charging the opposing Russians, scattering the front ranks like a flock of geese, and only checked in their advance by enormous numbers pitted against them. There is a limit beyond even which superhuman bravery cannot pass; and it seemed that this limit had now been reached by the enduring and nobly courageous British Guards. It was a critical moment. It cannot be denied that it was a very critical moment. Hark! the shrill blasts of a trumpet, the rapid rolling of drums, the quick ear of Clifton caught the sound. The tears of joy sprung to his eyes.

"Hurrah, lads!" he shouted, "the French have come up, the day's our own."

The French had come up. Three battalions of Zouaves came spinning on at the *pas de charge*. The screaming blasts of their trumpets, as they reached the hill, rose up above the roar of artillery, the crash of mingling steel, and the roll of unceasing musketry discharges. They took the Russians in flank, and at the same time their artillery opened upon the right wing of the enemy; the effect of which fire, fierce and fast as it was, speedily became visible.

"Now, lads," cried Clifton Grey, at the top of his voice, "ply them with cold steel. Hurrah! shoulder to shoulder; they give ground. On, boys, the Russians are on the retreat!"

"*Faugh a ballagh!*" shouted a husky voice, and a man, with his head tied up with a bandage sopping in blood, pressed close to the side of Clifton; "the Rooshans retreat, bad luck to the likes of me av I'm ont o'that! Hurroo! St. Patrick's still our protector. *Faugh a ballagh!* here's a Fusilier coming."

It was Mickey Dunigan; wounded he had been, but had hastily bandaged his head, and risked all chance of recovery rather than be out of the glorious opportunity of driving back the Russians, and securing the victory of "one of the bloodiest struggles ever witnessed since war cursed the earth."

With a tremendous shout and an impetuosity not to be resisted, the Guards charged the Russian infantry, and broke their ranks in several places. At the same moment, the French charged them on the right with brilliant effect, and the artillery all along the line had now fairly got into play. At this last and turning moment of the battle, never was the hellish din at greater height. The roaring of the artillery of both armies, the rattling of incessant volleys of muskets, the rolling of drums, the shrill blasts of trumpets, the shouts of soldiers charging with passionate impulse, the groans of the dying, the shrieks of the wounded, the clashing of the fatal steel, all combined to make the most unearthly union of sounds it is possible to conceive and impossible to describe.

The Russians made one more desperate effort to establish themselves upon the heights, but it was too late. With the advance of the French, the English divisions pressed forward, and the Russians, repulsed on all sides, gave way, and began to retreat even more rapidly than they had advanced. The fierceness with which the French, under General Bosquet, fresh from camp, charged the enemy in flank, forced them directly into the fire of the British divisions, and then the tremendous effects of the Minié rifle were apparent in an eminent degree. Often one bullet took down three or four men, and the guns, getting into range, mowed them down in files. Sixty thousand Russians had been opposed to eight thousand five hundred English and nine thousand French infantry, and they were now in full retreat. They were, however, so well furnished with artillery, and a thick, dense fog, which had reigned all the first part of the morning, and retired for an hour, now re-appearing, that it would have been madness to have followed them up close; but they were severely peppered as they retired into Sebastopol; the Lancaster gun, under the guidance of Lieutenant Hoare, strewed the road to the city with dead every time a chance presented itself of discharging this terrible war engine upon the retreating ranks of the enemy.

Soon after the advent of the French, the battle of Inkermann was over; it was won; the Russians, who had confidently anticipated driving the allies into the sea, had retreated, beaten, discomfited, shamed, into Sebastopol. And who had defeated them, these sixty thousand Russians, the flower of the Czar's troops? Why the remnant only of the divisions which were left from the battle of the Alma, and the ravages of sickness; they numbered only 8,500; they were roused from their slumbers, and fought that day through, hungry, wet, and famished; they had been on outpost duty four nights out of the seven; had toiled for twenty-four hours at a stretch, or some, even as Clifton Grey had been, compelled to a spell of forty-eight hours at a stretch in the dreadful trenches. For three long hours they withstood the most desperate efforts of the enemy, alone, unsupported, frequently without ammunition, and only cold steel or a clubbed musket to rely upon, they confined the Russians to the crest of the heights; at no time, not-withstanding their tremendous excess of numbers, did they get beyond it. They, in their turn, sought to achieve what the allies accomplished on the heights of Alma, but failed. They retreated when the English gained them, but the English maintained their ground with unshaken tenacity throughout a long and dreadful day, when the Russians sought to copy the example which had been set them.

At half past twelve the Russians were in full retreat; by two o'clock there was not one in the immediate vicinity, save the wounded, the dead, and the dying. Now the trumpets sounded to gather the regiments together, and rations were served out; while fatigue parties were appointed to gather up the wounded as quickly as possible, and bear them to the ambulances to hospital.

There was a rough muster of the Guards; and the Duke of Cambridge, who was yet labouring under great excitement, thanked the men with much emotion for their magnificent gallantry—it had no meaner title; and he assured them that in England the people would be proud to hear recited the feats they had that day performed; while he should take especial care, when

the opportunity was permitted to him, to lay before the Queen a plain, unvarnished tale of how her Guards had fought for her and maintained the honour of her name under circumstances unexampled in history.

The men responded with a cheer, even though they were worn out with their desperate exertions and want of food.

His Royal Highness then called Mr. Wilson in front of the regiment, and publicly tendered to him his grateful acknowledgments for having, as he believed—and of which there is no doubt—saved his life; his royal highness subsequently called forward Sergeant Grey, and complimented him upon his arduous exertions:

"I many times observed you, Sergeant Grey," he exclaimed, "setting an example of valour to the men, cheering them on with words and gestures, and leading them where, if danger was plentiful, yet honour was to be plucked by handfuls. We have passed through a serious and critical occasion; and to the pluck and endurance of the British troops, nobly supported by our allies, England is indebted for one of the most glorious victories to her arms which history can furnish. All those individuals who have largely aided to contribute to the success of the day are deserving of the warmest gratitude of their countrymen, and the best reward which can be bestowed upon them. You, Sergeant Grey, have this day exhibited many signal instances of courage as well as an intimate knowledge of your duty, which has enabled you to operate against the enemy with great advantage to the result. You have nobly done your duty as a soldier, as a man, and as an officer; it will be my care, therefore, to recommend you to the notice of the Commander-in-Chief, that you may be rewarded with one of those commissions which her gracious Majesty has been pleased to command shall be bestowed upon non-commissioned officers whose bravery and ability entitle them to such distinction."

Clifton's heart was too full to speak; he could only place his hand on his breast and bow; and then the troops were dismissed to obtain refreshment and rest after the dreadful labours of the day. Clifton, just gnawing a piece of biscuit, could not rest until he went in search of Sergeant Haverel, whom he had seen fall, and also of Mickey Dunigan, whose spirits were greater than his strength, and who, albeit he had shouted to the Russians to clear the way, was one of the first to fall and encumber it. Clifton esteemed it his duty, if neither were dead, to get them into the hospital as quickly as he could, in order that their hurts might be attended to, and their lives, if possible, spared. He made his way to the sand-bag battery, where he had seen Haverel, bravely fighting, struck down by a bullet. As he advanced on to the position, he saw the ghastly evidences of the tremendous struggle which had taken place in that particular locality, strewed about in all directions. Upon the patchy grass, in the sloppy hollows, beneath the scrubby brushwood, dripping with fog and blood, lay the dead and dying Russians; with them mingled the British Guards and French Zouaves, showing that over the same slip of ground the troops of both nations had struggled with the enemy; had not only successfully opposed their advance, but had driven them back in disorder and defeat.

Around the sand-bag battery, the scene of so many desperate exploits—so many feats of individual bravery and daring, the dead, dying, and wounded lay in heaps. The sight was absolutely horrifying; on this one spot alone lay upwards of twelve hundred dead and wounded, Russians, more than half the effective strength of the Guards. Here lay, too, in sad numbers, the stalwart forms of the Guards, the hardy frames of the French Chasseurs of the Indigènes, and others of the French infantry and line.

Clifton commenced his sad search; terrible, indeed, was the occupation, and shocking the sights which met his gaze. Of the dead, some were lying calm and still enough, with a placid smile on their countenances, as though they had not been engaged in their fierce and murderous duty; others wore the aspect of vengeance in its most ferocious form, the knitted brows and projected jaws, the eyes wide open and staring, sightless, it is true, but seeming to be glaring with the ferocity of madness. Some, stark dead, were on their backs, with knee up and arms raised, in the very act of discharging their musket, when the the terrible Minié ball had cut its way through the man's heart, killing him on the spot and hurling into eternity the soldier behind him, and probably also his rear rank man. There were some of the English who had been wounded by ball, and while on the ground had been ruthlessly bayonetted by the Russians as they had passed them; these men in their death agonies had wrenched up the grass, wet with their own blood, and lay with their clenched hands towards Heaven, as though calling down maledictions upon the barbarous wretches who not content with the havoc of the bullet, had stabbed repeatedly the helpless men who lay upon the ground powerless to resist their damnable barbarity. Nor was this alone the villany of which they were guilty, for while shrieking for water to cool their parched and burning mouths, many of the wounded Russians, receiving that or spirits from the canteen of the soldier, who, having been opposed to them in mortal combat, was now engaged in the duty of humanity, seized their musket and shot down in cold blood the very man who had afforded them the essential succour for which they had been imploring. So generally did this take place, that before affording them the help for which they lay groaning and entreating, it was found necessary to destroy the guns within their reach, and empty the cartridges upon the ground.

Four or five times was Clifton fired at by the scowling and mutilated wretches lying on the threshold of death, among the entangled bloodstained brushwood, as he passed them, the scarlet coat, in the eyes of the Russian, being the type of the Antichrist

Russian fanaticism had been called upon to extirpate. Still did he escape unhurt. An especial providence seemed to put a protective shield over his person, which glanced off bullets, and warded off bayonet thrusts. On reaching the redoubt or battery, he commenced to look for Haverel. There was a fearful pile of dead to turn over, a fearful number of his division were down here. As he was proceeding to the spot where, as well as he could remember, he had seen Haverel fall, he heard a voice, faint and barely audible, exclaim:

"The blessed saints have heard me, an' the blessed Virgin has interceded for me. Sure I'll repeat ten Hail Mary's for that same goodness to a poor fellow av the likes o' me. Oh, thin, there's a Fusilier kem to help me. Hroo! there, sure man, ye'll not pass on an' lave Corporal Dunigan to die here the death of a dog. Sure I've been kilt twice entirely, an' I am bleading to death."

Clifton turned sharply to where the man lay, who had uttered in a low voice, quivering with agony, the words we have given, and he saw his Irish friend and comrade lying on his back, helpless, and bloody from his wounds. In an instant, Clifton knelt by his side, and raised him tenderly to a sitting posture, leaning his head against his breast.

"Cheer up, Mickey," he exclaimed. "It is Sergeant Grey who holds you; he'll not leave you until you are in safe hands."

"Hurroo!" cried Mickey. "Is it safe you are?"

"Quite safe Mickey."

"Is it wounded you are?"

"Not a scratch, Mickey."

"Blessin's on the Lord for that same! an' its fight like a divil ye did too. Ugh! Grey, have you dhrop ov wather—ugh! my throats chokin' with drought, an' me tongues like a rasp."

Clifton, who had filled his canteen with brandy and water, now moistened his mouth and throat with it, and used a little on his temples. Micked rolled his eyes gratefully upon his companion, and murmured:

"God's blessin's on you for that, avich! I'm a made man again, an' if I got to the tent now an' have a slaape, I'll be ready for a sortie in the mornin'."

"You must lay here a little while Mickey," said Clifton. "I'll make you a comfortable bed, and will soon get an ambulance to carry you to hospital, but poor Haverel has, I fear, lost his number, and I want to find him."

"Sure, has the sargeant gone! The saints recave him—he was a strict man, but good comrade."

"I do not know that he is killed, but I saw him fall, and I hope to find him, if wounded, still alive."

"You do! oh musha! look at that now, an' a vagabone like me kaaping you from findin' him. I'll do well now; lave me here sargeant dear, and look for Sargeant Haverel, he may be dying for a taste av the cordial you brought me to life wid."

Clifton would not, however, leave him until he had made him a bed of some of the coats of the dead soldiers strewed everywhere, and when he had placed him on a softer surface and covered him over, he, with a shake of the hand, a few words of comfort, and a promise to soon return to him, hurried to seek for Haverel. Poor Mickey! he felt a gulp in the throat, and the tears sprung into his eyes as he murmured:

"Why thin' its me own mother couldn't do more for me to put me up an' make me lay soft, an' me in a strange land, an' his the hand o' the stranger. Oh, Bridget, darlin'! av you knew how tenderly that bould-hearted Fusilier had minded your own Mickey as he lay on the wet grass bleeding and chill beneath the cold grey sky, sure ye'd offer up a prayer from him to the Blessed Virgin! as I do now."

And with feeble strength but earnest meaning the honest fellow breathed a prayer to the Throne of Grace for the man who had just shewn him the attention of a gentle, sympathising woman, under circumstances in which they were not to be expected, but when they came so peculiarly grateful.

Clifton found his search for Haverel commence very shortly after quitting Mickey Dunigan. The red coats were strewn upon the ground far too numerous. He had need of haste, too, in his search, for the gloom was thickening and daylight fading, and delay in discovering him might be death. As he turned over the bodies of men in his own uniform whom he knew not, he lighted upon others with whom he had been in light converse the night before. Many were quite dead, others so desperately wounded as to render recovery next to impossible. With burning indignation he saw that numbers of his comrades, who had fallen wounded only by a ball, were pierced with five or six bayonet wounds inflicted by the Russian soldiers, and, upon the impulse, he all but made a vow to retaliate in a like manner when the opportunity—not likely to be far off—was afforded to him. Such consequences result from inexcusable and infamous modes of conducting warfare. At length, as he passed a heap of slain Russians, he saw from beneath the bodies of two of them the red-sleeved arm of a British soldier stretched forth. He cast a glance at it—it bore the sergeant's insignia upon it, and it stayed his farther progress at once. It was the work only of a moment to lift the senseless bodies of the foe from that of the prostrate Englishman, and place them on one side while he raised up his countryman in his arms to find that his search had been rewarded—that he held Sergeant Walter Haverel in his arms.

He was quite senseless and cold. His hand yet grasped his rifle, and it was only by force that Clifton withdrew it from his clutch and cast it away. He was not dead—his clenched teeth told that, but he had bled from a bullet-wound in the chest, which had passed obliquely through his body and out under the arm. Clifton laid him gently down, and, as he had

done in Mickey's case, gathered hastily together a few coats, and upon this bed he laid him, and commenced bathing his temples with brandy-and-water—to chafe his hands violently—to try and separate his teeth so as to get some of the liquid down his throat. He breathed up his nostrils—he again bathed his temples, and then rubbed his hands, trying all those suggestions for the restoration of life, under such circumstances, with which he was acquainted.

As he did this, surrounded by the dying and the dead, his hearing racked by the groans of the wounded, his sight shocked by the mutilation swarming round him, he gazed on the white face of Walter Haverel, and he thought of Lizzie Hastings; he remembered well her tearful, anxious countenance, on the day she had parted with himself and Haverel. He had read there how deeply her young heart was devoted to her soldier lover, and as he looked upon the wan yet stern features, still rigid, of him who was flickering between life and death, he thought of the agony of that young girl when, with beating heart, her wild eyes ran down the list of killed and wounded at the battle of Inkermann, and saw the name of Sergeant Walter Haverel, of the second battalion of Scots Fusilier Guards. He had a thought of Myra too, but with a sensation of pain he dismissed it, for it seemed to him that she had cast him from her memory—that she had effaced him from her mind for newer, wealthier, brighter friends, and such thoughts following, or rather accompanying the re-action from the tremendous excitement he had endured throughout the whole of the forepart of that dreadful morning, made him terribly depressed, and he was surrounded by everything to increase the miserable sense of loneliness which suddenly fastened itself upon his heart.

Still a conviction of his own desolation did not interfere with the active duties of his philanthropy and friendship; he persevered with Haverel, hoping yet to find his exertions rewarded by his restoration to life. He noted not a few wounded Russians huddled in some bushes not far from him, who scowled upon him with glances of malignant hate, and who took an opportunity, though wounded, and themselves on the way to signalise their departure from this world by an act of butchery in cold blood; they elevated their guns and discharged a volley at him; but though the bullets whistled past him in startling and dangerous proximity, he was not hit. He rose up and advanced hastily upon them; he could have had a terrible retaliation, for all of them were powerless of self-defence, being more or less desperately mutilated. He stayed the hand which under the first impulses of passion was raised to smite, and contented himself with removing from their reach all the muskets, rifles, and cartridges which would enable them to repeat their dastardly deed.

On returning to Haverel, he, with emotion and pleasure, saw signs of returning animation in the uneasy writhing of his limbs and a slight convulsion of his frame, and he resumed his efforts to recover him; and at length succeeded in getting down his throat a little of the brandy and water. It bubbled and gurgled, but it went down; and then the chest began to heave and fall, with short pants; and low moans, as if of pain, were uttered by him, and then his breathing became more regular; he sighed heavily several times, or rather took deep inspirations, but still panted; gradually however his lungs seemed to have quite recovered the power of action, and he subsided, as it appeared, almost into a gentle slumber.

Clifton gazed upon his every movement with the deepest anxiety, and as he was about to endeavour to rouse him by repeating his name in his ear, the sergeant began to murmur and mutter some words. Clifton bent down his ear to listen, and his words seemed to tell that when first struck down, the sergeant was conscious of the fate which the ball of the enemy appeared to promise:

"Hush—hush, Lizzie!" he whispered, "be a woman, darling! dry up your tears, a soldier looks for death on the battle field. Don't weep for me, my girl; in my dying hour I think of you; pray that the great God before whom I'm about to stand, will support you, sustain you, bear you up, till we meet again in heaven—in heaven!" he paused; then he went on again: "It is hard to die before we have tasted the happiness we promised ourselves in the prospect of living with and for each other; but God's will be done. God bless you, my darling! I have so loved you, that it is hard to part; Liz, my own Liz!" Again he paused, and a gush of scalding tears forced their way through Clifton's eyes, a commentary upon what he was listening to. Nay, now he would have roused him to consciousness, but that he fairly sobbed at the thought that the hopes, anticipations, love, the whole faëry schemes of the future indulged in by the poor girl of whom he was speaking, and in whose welfare he, Clifton, had become warmly interested, would be buried in the far-off grave with this man. Again Haverel spoke in a low tone. "We shall meet again," he said, "yes, we *shall* meet again, Liz, my pet!" and then in a low, plaintive voice, he chanted:

"You'll be coming, coming, coming,
    You'll be coming with the flowers,
You'll be coming with the summer
    To this new land of ours;
And we'll forget all our sadness,
And I'll kiss your lips in gladness,
And bid you joyous welcome
    To this new land of ours."

He ceased, with a sad sigh, and turned his face uneasily on one side.

Clifton, with an effort, recovered the emotion this touching soliloquy had produced, and he called in his ear intentionally, a little smartly.

"Haverel!"

"Here!" repeated the sergeant instantly.

Clifton repeated his name, and bathed his temples again. The sergeant put his hand on one side, and tried to raise himself up to a sitting posture. Clifton assisted him, and then for the first time, and with difficulty, he opened his eyes.

"Where am I?" he ejaculated.

"With Clifton Grey," responded our hero.

He looked wildly around him, listened for an instant attentively to the repetition by Clifton of his exclamation, and then he seemed to comprehend his situation. "Oh God!" he said feebly, "this is the reality then—I have been knocked over. Is—is the fight over?"

"It is," replied Clifton, and pressed his hand in a congratulating manner.

"And the Russians?"

"Are beaten—they have retreated and fled into Sebastopol. The day is ours, Haverel; the victory a glorious one."

"Thank God—Hurrah!" cried Haverel, with a burst of relief, and a feeble shout in honour of the success to which he had bravely—as long as he had power to strike—contributed.

"Where are you hurt?" enquired Clifton.

"I don't know—somewhere about the body. I am very faint, I should like to get to my tent."

"I will see to that without delay, Haverel."

"Thank ye. Have you got off scot free?"

"Heaven has been as kind to me as before, I have not one scratch, and yet, I did not get out of the way of either balls or blows."

"I know it; but you see, Grey, every bullet *has* its billet, and a ball with yours has'nt been yet moulded. I'm very cold and faint. Grey, answer me honestly and truly—Am I on the march for my long home?"

"I hope not."

"Don't hesitate to tell me. I am not afraid of dying, you know, but I *am* afraid of stepping out of the world before certain arrangements are made about which I am anxious."

"We will hear what the surgeon says. Ah! by heaven there goes Mr. Wilson, he's as good a surgeon as he is a brave officer. Lie still for a moment, Haverel, and I will bring him to you."

Without waiting for a remark, Clifton laid the sergeant gently down, and rushed after the officer, who stopped, having heard his name called. He recognised Clifton again, and with a compliment upon the gallantry and skill he had displayed while under him, charging the Russians, he readily complied with his wish to step a little out of his path to examine Haverel.

On reaching the sergeant, though so short a time had elapsed, they found him nearly insensible. The surgeon, however, produced a bottle from which he poured some fluid into the sergeant's mouth, which appeared to have almost a miraculous effect in restoring him to consciousness. Then the surgeon carefully opened his jacket. Ugh! what a ghastly mass of blood presented itself, but the surgeon, with professional know-lodge and practical skill, soon found the wound, and traced the progress of the bullet.

"It has gone clean through you," he said, "but it has missed the vital parts in its vicinity. We must get you into hospital as quick as possible."

"Is there great danger?" asked Clifton in a low tone.

"There is always much danger in this kind of hurt," he replied; "it produces other ills, which may have a fatal effect on the frame; but there is no immediate cause for apprehension. The sergeant was not a hard drinker?"

"By no means; on the contrary, since I have joined he has been quite temperate."

"So much the better—all in his favour. However, yonder comes an ambulance, run and secure it; we will get him into it, and when in the hospital I will pay him the best attention."

"God bless you, sir!" muttered Haverel, who had heard all.

No less fervent was Clifton's expression of gratitude and he hurried off to obtain places in the cart for the wounded, both for Haverel and Mickey Dunigan, and succeeded. The sergeant was raised tenderly from the ground and placed in the ambulance, and then Clifton prevailed on the attendants to help him with the body of Mickey Dunigan, who was lying patiently and uncomplainingly where Clifton had left him.

Our hero did not seek his tent that night until he had seen both his humble friends and comrades as comfortable as they could expect to be under the circumstances, for the accommodations were far below what was required; the number of wounded was so large, the preparation for this terrible contingency so small, that many a brave fellow who would have been now living, able and fit for duty, perished from sheer want of assistance. With a sense of sickening horror, from the terrible sight of the dead and dying everywhere strewed around him, and a painful feeling of loneliness—for he looked to England in vain for friends to rejoice at his escape, and exult at his promotion—he returned to his tent. He thought bitterly of Myra; remembered their meeting alone; the last—the only kiss he had pressed upon her lips, as though it were the seal to an attested deed, by which he had covenanted to love her with a truth and constancy which must never be violated so long as he should exist. How, in his first sanguine aspirations, he had valued that undertaking! how he had hugged it to his heart! and what splendid schemes of future happiness he had raised upon it! What was it now; mere waste paper. Months, which seemed in duration years, thousands of miles, vast seas, divided them. While all around him were receiving communications from their friends and relatives, he had not one little line from a living soul. He was doubtless uncared for by the only one whose good opinion he prized, or why had his letter **not** found her—he was, perhaps, forgotten. He

threw himself upon his humble pallet, in dejection and exhaustion, and sunk into a slumber, compelled by excessive fatigue, only to be aroused by dawn on the following morning to aid in superintending the removal of the wounded and the burial of the dead.

CHAPTER XX.

"The cordage creaks and rattles in the wind,
With freak of sudden lunch; the reeling sea
Now thumps like solid rock beneath the stern,
Now leaps with clumsy wrath, strikes short, and falling
Crumbled to whispery foam."—LOWELL.

"Hark to the boatswain's call, the cheering cry!
While through the seaman's hand the tackle glides.
          *   *   *   *
Blow! swiftly blow, thou keel-compelling gale!
Till the broad sun withdraws his beaming ray."
                                        BYRON.

"There have been tears and breaking hearts for thee,
And mine were nothing had I such to give."—IBID.

THE SEA-BIRD. THE CAPTORS CAPTURED. THE CAPTIVES RELEASED. HOMEWARD BOUND. DISAPPOINTMENT.

WE left the Sea-bird a helpless wreck upon the waters, reduced to that condition by a shot from the bow-gun of the Snapper. The crash with which the whole superincumbent fabric came down and fell over the side was tremendous, while, by its weight and the force of its descent, it promised to capsize the ill-fated vessel. Lizzie and Myra shrieked and clung to the vessel's side as she heeled over, and at the same moment the captain appeared through the companion way, and Saul Waters, followed by two seamen, rushed up from the fore cabin. It is impossible to depict the fury and astonishment displayed in the countenances of the captain and crew at the sight which presented itself to them. The danger was, however, too imminent to pause for questions; axes were instantly obtained, and the wreck of topmast, sails, &c., were cut adrift, and the so recently swift-sailing Sea-bird now rolled heavily in the trough of the sea, the sport of every wave.

Captain Poole was scarcely able to articulate for passion: he cast his eyes over the sea and saw the Snapper bowling down upon them like a race-horse. He turned like a tiger to the man whom he had left in charge of the helm, and uttered a succession of terrific oaths.

"What the hell does it all mean," he yelled, "have you been to sleep and let her broach-to?"

The helmsmen gave a ghastly grin, and shook his head. Captain Poole fastened upon him as a bull terrier upon a rat, and shook him.

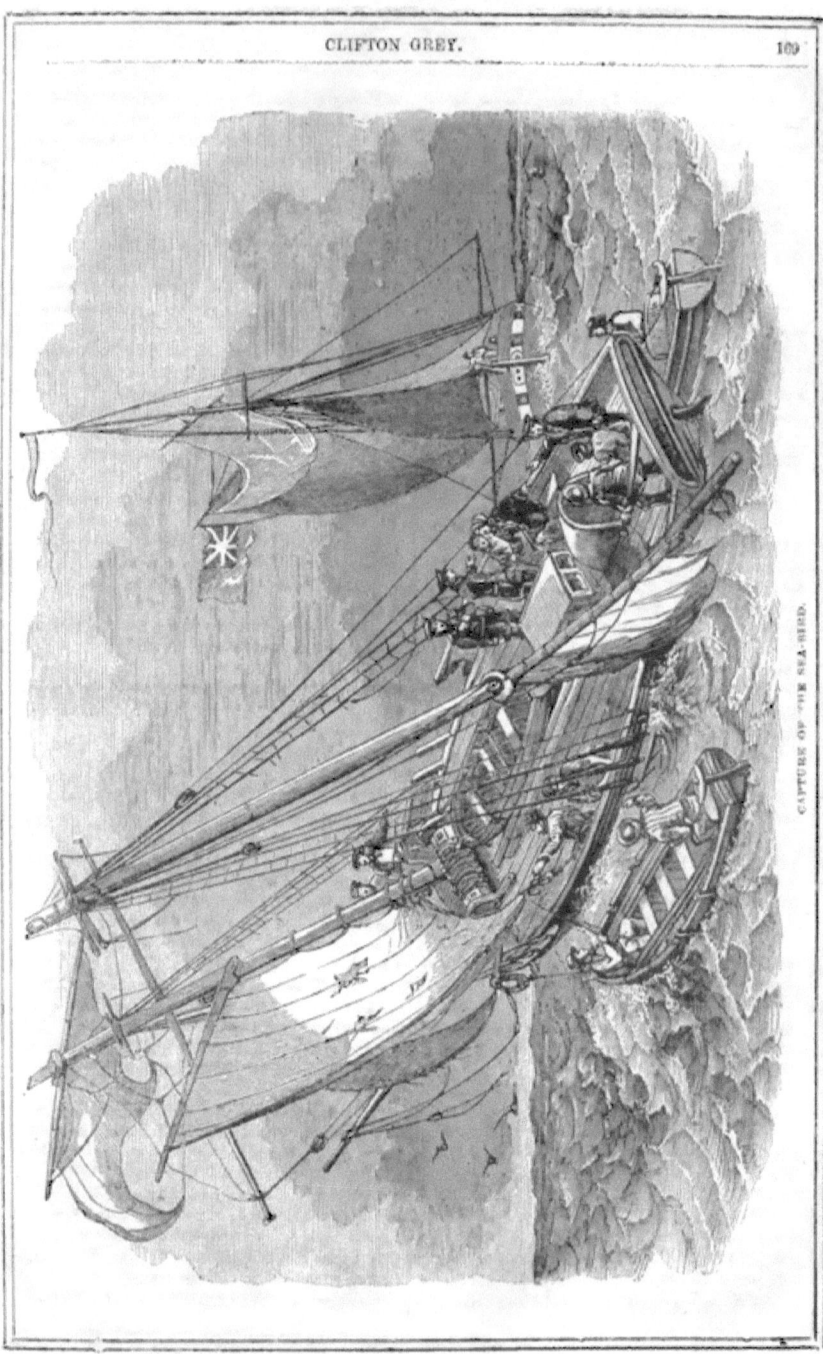

CAPTURE OF THE SEA-BIRD.

"I left you in charge," he spluttered, with frantic passion, "and everything is carried by the board; tell me how it's happened—and tell me how it's happened, or I'll heave you overboard."

"'Taint my fault," said the man, trying to shake himself free.

"You lie, you rascal, it must be; how else could it happen?"

The man pointed with his thumb to the rapidly approaching revenue cutter.

"She did it," he said.

"Why—how?"

"Ax Lootenant Spencer when he comes aboard."

"Lootenant Spencer," echoed Saul Waters, hastily, with a look of alarm at the coming vessel; "is he aboard that cutter?"

"A' course he is."

"D—n him! What's to be done, Bill?" cried Saul Waters, biting his thumb-nail in feverish anxiety, and regarding the Snapper with evident uneasiness.

"Done!" shouted Captain Poole, "why fling this infernal thief into the sea. Done! how should I know, or what should I care now what's to be done? A pretty damned mess you've been and got me in among you. Tell me, you old thief," he added, shaking the helmsman's neck, "didn't the Snapper hoist signals, or fire across the forefoot before she made us a wreck?"

"Didn't see her," said the man, with a ready lie. "I was only holding my own when bang goes a gun and down comes the hull lot."

The captain flung him from him, and folding his arms paced up and down the deck with gloomy forebodings. As for Saul, he dropped down the forecastle hatchway with precipitation after hearing his friend Bill's reply to his query.

Myra and Lizzie sat clinging together, watching the Snapper draw near with throbbing expectancy, but they did not utter a word; and when the revenue cutter was within hail, and shortened her sail to enable her to bring up alongside the Sea-bird, Captain Poole cast his eyes rapidly and anxiously on the two girls, and stopping before them, he said:

"You'll have your turn now, girls. The people aboard this Snapper will take you home to your friends. Come now, I haven't done you much harm; you'll make it as light as you can?"

"I have no desire to injure you," said Myra. "You might have behaved cruelly to us, and you have not done so; you are to blame in having taken us from London, but you have since done nothing of which I have to complain—on the contrary, rather to be thankful for."

"Thank'ye," said he. "It's all along of Saul Waters; I shouldn't have done it but for him. Howsomdever, you won't be much the worse for your trip, and you may have it in your power to save me from unpleasant consequences by a good word; and I say, pretty one,

you'll give your good word too, won't you?" he added, addressing Lizzie.

"I shall tell the whole truth," she said, nodding her head, "and you'll have the benefit of that, if there will be any benefit in it," replied Lizzie, feeling wonderfully disposed to "speak out," now help was at hand.

And now the Snapper was up with them; the Sea-bird was hailed, her captain replied, and then a boat was lowered from the revenue cutter, and two officers with four seamen to row the boat, pulled up alongside and jumped on board. One was the Lieutenant Spencer, before spoken of, and the other Oliver Lawrance, who, by one of those mysterious dispensations of Providence not possible to fathom, had, from being well acquainted with the person of Saul Waters, been set—now that he had fallen in love with his sister, and the duty was especially irksome to him—to discover his whereabouts, and if successful, to capture him, further charges of defrauding the revenue having been made against him.

Lieutenant Spencer was a handsome young officer, but with sharp manners, and a stern aspect; the moment he put his foot on the deck he asked for the captain, and Captain Poole stepped forward.

"Aha!" said he, "it is you, Poole, is it? I told you I'd have you, and my prediction is verified."

"I should like to know what you've made me a wreck for. I've nothing contraband aboard; I'm on a run out in ballast," said Poole, folding his arms, and putting on an injured look.

"Indeed: that remains to be proved."

"Search us."

"I intend. But if you have nothing wrong aboard, why did you run away from us?"

"Run away; nonsense, we only kept on our course; you should have hoisted signals for us to heave to, if you wanted us to do it."

"Hoist signals! why we fired half a dozen guns, and as you refused to take notice, the gunner gave you a proof of his skill. It's your own fault you are a wreck."

Captain Poole sprung upon the man he had left in charge of the helm, and dragged him forward, addressing Lieutenant Spencer, he said:

"This man was left in charge while I turned in; he says you fired but one gun, and that brought us up a wreck."

"He lies!—Ho, ho! What, it is Jack Heywood, eh! I don't wonder that he should lie. Why, Captain Poole, if you had turned in, and this man was in charge, let me tell you I have a proof which I do not think proper at present to mention, that we were seen from the Sea-bird; but when I ordered the bow guns to be fired, the only answer each time I got was putting the Sea-bird more before the wind, so as to show us a clean pair of heels, if possible."

Captain Poole uttered a cry of rage, and the chances

of a long swim would have beeen submitted to the unfortunate wretch the helmsman, had it not been for the presence of the officers; Poole, therefore, contented himself by shaking him violently and hurling him from him.

Captain Spencer laughed.

"Enough to vex you, Captain Poole, if you really would have hove to for us had you seen us. Well, you may not have any contraband articles on board, but there are persons—"

Captain Poole opened his eyes to their widest extent, and with a mystified air, he pointed to Myra and Lizzie, quite at a loss to guess how the lieutenant could possibly have learned they were aboard.

Lieutenant Spencer and Oliver Lawrance turned in the direction in which he pointed, and in their turn were quite astounded to see two females clinging together, just emancipated from the coats of the captain, eager, yet hesitating to approach and claim protection.

"Women—ladies!" cried Lieutenant Spencer in a tone of surprise. "What is the meaning of this—are they passengers?

"Passengers, no sir," replied Lizzie Hastings, promptly. "We have been shamefully seized, and carried off from London."

"Against your free will?" asked the lieutenant.

"Of course: you don't think we should have come for pleasure," she returned almost indignantly.

"Explain," he said.

"I, and this young lady by my side, were last night returning home, when we were suddenly seized upon by a ruffian—who is not here now, but is some where about the ship—and brought here. They were going to take us to France, when your ship luckily stopped them."

"Luckily indeed," said the lieutenant. "This must be enquired into. Your names, if you please, ladies?"

Oliver Lawrance, who had been gazing hard at Myra, now advanced, and said to her:

"I believe we have met before.'

Myra looked at him, and shook her head.

"I do not remember you," she said:

"You recollect the night that a schooner was on shore below Arundel, and a young gentleman saved the life of a young lady: you attended her on that occasion."

Myra gazed upon him, and at once recollected him as the officer who had taken Waters and his son into custody.

"Your name is Aston," he said.

"It is," she returned. "I remember well the occurrence of which you speak."

"You have quitted Arundel?

She bowed.

"I do not desire to appear impertinent, or to prove inquisitive, but I have a purpose in saying, you did

not leave with any one in Arundel an address by which you might be communicated with."

"Surely it was affixed to the house when we quitted it."

"Then it has been removed. You remember Ellen Waters?"

"In truth I do, most affectionately."

"Although you have received ill usage from the hands of her brother, she is not to blame."

"I am very sure of that."

"Would you like to see her again?"

Myra looked at him with surprise. Who was he, and why should he be so interested in her? She answered him affirmatively, wondering why he asked her such a question.

"Then you shall," said he, "and that before you are much older."

Not a little disconcerted was he, that at this moment, two of the Snapper's crew made their appearance aft with drawn cutlasses, and Saul Waters between them; one of them said:

"Lootenant Lawrance, we've made a prize; we have rowsed out from fo'k'stle the man you' been in chase on—here's Saul Waters."

"Aha!" cried Lieutenant Spencer, "the very man. I told you, Lawrance, we should find him aboard this craft. I knew it."

"That is the man who seized us, and carried us off last night," exclaimed Lizzie, pointing to Saul.

"You are in for it pretty deep this time, Mr Waters," observed Lieutenant Spencer. "I don't think you'll get to windward of judge and jury this trip."

"Saul scowled ferociously, but made no reply; his quick glance round told him there was no chance of escape for him—at least at present, and therefore the best thing he could do would be to remain quiet.

"Have you searched the vessel from heel to deck?" asked Lieutenant Spencer of two other men.

"Ay! ay, sir," was the reply.

"Anything contraband?"

"No sir! the sloop's in ballast."

"Your papers, if you please, Mr. Poole," exclaimed the lieutenant to the Captain of the Sea-bird.

"I'll go below and fetch them," returned the captain with a sudden alacrity.

"Very good, and I'll accompany you," exclaimed Lieutenant Spencer.

"You needn't give yourself that trouble," said Poole hastily.

"Ah! but I shall," replied the lieutenant decidedly, and then turning to his boat's crew, he exclaimed:

"Go on board the Snapper with your prisoner; put him in irons where he'll be out of the way; say so to Mr. Paul, he'll pick out a berth for him. Then come back here, and get on a hawser from the bitts to the stern of the Snapper; we must give a tow-rope to the Sea-bird, and save what we can of her. Heave a-head.

Now, Captain Poole, if you'll make sail, I'll bear you company."

Professing an alacrity he did not feel, Captain Poole led the way into his cabin, closely followed by Lieutenant Spencer. In the meantime, Saul Waters was conveyed on board the Snapper. As he left the Sea-bird—there was no help for him, for even his associates used bitter language to him, as they considered him the proximate cause of their disaster, inasmuch as the Snapper was on the look out for him when she fell in with them, and seemed glad to get rid of him, so there was no help—as he quitted the side, he cast his burning eyes on Myra. She did not meet their gaze, although she felt they were fixed upon her; it was hard to tell what was the predominant expression of that parting look, whether it was one of intense and passionate love, or malignant hatred; his eyes glittered like fiery planets, his lips moved, as if he would have spoken to her either words of adoration or of fiercest loathing; before he could force an exclamation through his grating teeth and parched lips the boat shoved off, and was borne by the sweep of the sea in an instant twenty yards off. Saul then felt that he was divided from her for ever: he uttered a despairing cry, and burying his face in his hands, sunk upon a seat in the boat, and bowed his head to his knees.

Oliver Lawrence saw at a glance that there was some wild attachment on the part of Saul Waters for Myra, which was not returned by her; nay, he had heard something of it previously, without attaching much interest to it; now, without intending to appear inquisitive, he put a few questions which satisfied him as to the truth. Lizzie Hastings answered very readily everything relative to the share Saul Waters had in bringing them there, and it was not difficult to gather the rest. He made no remark, but he felt pained at the position in which he was placed—that at the moment he was desirous of winning the affection of Nelly Waters her brother within an operation of the law, which would condemn him for some years to penal servitude.

He, however, imparted much comfort to the two maidens, if he failed in bestowing it upon himself, for he informed them, that they were now in perfectly safe hands, that, by the following morning, they would probably be in Shoreham Harbour, and they would then be able to telegraph their safety to their friends, and follow by the first train, so as to personally relieve the apprehensions their absence must have occasioned.

The men belonging to the Snapper, which had been standing off and on, now made their appearance again with a tow rope; they soon went through the labour of fixing one end to the Sea-bird, and attaching the other to the Snapper; by the time this was effected, Lieutenant Spencer made his appearance on deck, followed by Captain Poole, and without making any allusion to what might have transpired in the cabin between them relative to the sloop's papers, the former made arrangements for all on board the Sea-bird to be transferred to the Snapper, and then the revenue cutter prepared for her run up channel to Shoreham, where it was proposed to land the prisoners and the rescued, and report the events which had taken place.

Myra and Lizzie were ushered into the Snapper's cabin; it was elegantly fitted up, was more roomy than that of the Sea-bird, and it had the charm of safety, as well as being the bearer of both to the arms of their friends. They both readily partook of the refreshments afforded them, and were unquestionably pleased with the respectful attention paid to them. Lizzie was in extravagant spirits, and quite won the heart of Lieutenant Spencer, who believed her to be, without the ghost of an exception, the prettiest lass he had ever clapped his eyes on; in fact, he told her in confidence that her majesty's yacht the Fairy had nothing like so pretty a figure-head as hers, and as he insinuated with an unmistakeable gravity and seriousness, that she was a frigate of which he should most decidedly like to take the command for life, she nipped his hopes in the bud, by telling him, that though she had a high respect and admiration for the brave tars of her country, still she had given her love and heart to a brave fusilier, who was fighting the battles of his country in the Crimea, and rather than do his affection for her, or her love for him, wrong or shame, now he was far away perilling his life for his country, she would surrender the world and all it contained. Lieutenant Spencer applauded her truthfulness, although it carried his wishes by the board, and carefully abstained from alluding to the subject again.

In the fulness of her own gratification at this providential rescue, Myra did not forget her promise to the boy, through whose instrumentality she believed her and Lizzie were mainly indebted for their escape, and she asked Lieutenant Spencer what had drawn his attention to the Sea-bird, so as to cause him so pertinaciously to compel her to heave to. He told her that he was acquainted with a woman, by name Melbury, at Littlehampton, who had a son on board the Sea-bird. The mother was anxious for the well-being of her son, and had put some inquiries to him respecting the probabilities of his advancement in life under the auspices of Captain Poole; he had, in reply, informed her they were of a character likely to end in advancing him to the yard-arm, and advised her, if she possessed any anxiety that he should do well in the world, the sooner she induced him to slip his cable from under the lee of Captain Poole, the more likely would he be to reap the desirable advantages of the world. Indeed, he comforted her by saying, that if the lad was smart and willing he would enter him on board his own craft and in the Queen's service, where he would have light work and good pay, and, if steady and able, he would rise to the top of his profession. As the lady in question looked upon that elevated point as a pinnacle in the clouds to which monarchy itself was alone of equal height, she knew not how to express her gratitude, and promised that her son should cut himself adrift from the captain of the Sea-bird, and follow in the wake of the captain of the Snapper.

To this, however, Lieutenant Spencer had attached a condition. The Court of Exchequer had decided that Mr. Saul Waters was a person whom it was not politic to suffer to remain at large, so long as it was deemed necessary not to suffer the customs revenue of our Sovereign Lady the Queen to be defrauded, and it had instructed Lieutenant Spencer to seize his body when and wherever he found it, and lodge it in one of her Majesty's jails, &c., &c., &c. Now, Lieutenant Spencer, fully alive to his duty, was quite prepared to comply with the command thus given him, providing he should fall, as he declared, "'thwart hawse" of said Saul Waters; but that individual, independent of certain warnings of his conscience, had also been warned by companions in iniquity—for in the eyes of the State defrauding the revenue is iniquitous—of the attachment the Court of Exchequer had developed for his person; and as it was not reciprocated by him, he determined to prove himself a very Joseph, and fly from the embraces of such a Potiphar's wife as the Court promised to be. He had not to learn that being once safely locked in her arms, getting free from them would only take place at that figurative period when the golden argosies of the indulgent maternal parents of longing juveniles return to port, or, in humbler phraseology, when little boys' mothers' ships come home. So he resolved to keep out of reach as long as he could. For some time he was successful. But men—especially if they have done wrong and sinned in company, cannot keep away from their old haunts or their companions in sin; and Lieutenant Spencer, a man of the world, experienced in the characteristics of the men with whom he was in constant antagonism, was well assured, without putting himself much out of the way, that he should fall in with Saul Waters some fine morning in the company of those whose society he was known to affect. Now, the captain of the Sea-bird was one of these companions, and sooner or later with him Lieutenant Spencer felt sure he should overhaul the man he was in search of. Hence the condition he imposed on the boy's mother. It was to the effect, that at any time when Saul Waters was on board the Sea-bird on a voyage between England and France, and the Snapper should heave in sight, the boy was to send up to the truck of the smuggling sloop a flag of red bunting. This would be enough, and if he would do this then he might be sure of escaping the consequence of being caught on board a vessel endeavouring to run contraband goods, and Lieutenant Spencer would take him henceforward under his especial care, and, to a certainty, make his fortune,—such a fortune as would render comparison with the riches of an Eastern monarch a mere absurdity. The fond mother listened with eager ears and

promised with anxious hopes. We do not attempt to defend the morality of the stratagem; we only repeat what Lieutenant Spencer said and did; and add, that the boy being at home soon after for a few days 'spin,' his mother had used her most potent eloquence to convert him to the way of thinking and to the wishes of the commander of the Snapper. The boy took the bunting, but made no promise. He did not see those realms of fairy happiness in the exchange which dazzled his mother's vision, and he had a kind of undefined dread that the scheme suggested to him was only a ruse to get him into the grip of the law, from which there was no escape. Captain Poole had pictured to him the necessity of keeping clear of all officers of revenue and customs, had painted them in the worst colours, and had given him reasons why he should dread coming in contact with them. He therefore had formed a resolution to make no use of the bunting, and to give at any and all times the Snapper and its crew a wide berth, should he sight it while on the ocean. But the kindness of Myra and Lizzie to him, at a moment to him when, half famished, food was more desirable to him than gold, and when he heard their request to him, induced him to think of the Snapper, all his mother had said, and at once to believe the fact of saving two young ladies from being carried away and never heard of more would outbalance the crime of which he had been guilty in the eyes of the law—that of being engaged in contraband traffic. So, as we have said, up went the red bunting to the topmast head.

When Lieutenant Spencer, with his glass, sighted the fast sloop the Sea-bird, he saw his own bunting flying aloft—he knew wherefore; he would not else have overhauled the Sea-bird on her outward passage; hence the gun to bring her to—hence the shot which brought her up with the loss of her upper rigging, when the man at the helm put her before the wind to spite the commander of the Snapper.

This explanation ended, Myra spoke in the boy's behalf, but the Lieutenant assured her it was unnecessary, for he had determined to take care of the boy's interests, and he would keep his intention good. He told her that beyond giving him a private intimation to that effect he could take no further notice of him at the moment, in order to save him from the anger of his late companions, but as soon as they were ashore he would do the best for him.

As soon as they were ashore!

Myra presumed it would be that night; Lizzie set it down for an hour or two. Providence did not so ordain it.

As they were beating down Channel, on their way to Shoreham, the Snapper was hailed by a man of-war brig on the cruise, and informed that a schooner laden with silks and spirits was clearing out from Havre, with the intention of landing her cargo on some secluded port of the English coast, and running it to avoid paying the duty. As the brig would have no chance of coping with her in speed, the Snapper was ordered to proceed in search of her, and keep her in sight until she attempted to run the goods, and then to effect a capture.

Not a moment was to be lost; the brig lent a few hands to put on board the Sea-bird, to rig up a jury mast, and take her ashore. She also took charge of the prisoners, except the boy, Jack Melbury, whom Lieutenant Spencer kept back, as well as the young ladies, because both lieutenants assured them they would from their cruise return to Shoreham sooner than the brig would anchor off Woolwich, so as such was to be the case, and they were both treated with the utmost respect and deference, they consented to what appeared to be the best course to be pursued.

The vessels parted. Up went the gaff-topsail of the Snapper, and she shaped her course for the French coast direct, as the Captain of the brig had stated that the schooner would hug it for some distance after she cleared her port. The wind freshened into a cap-full, and then sail had to be shortened; the Snapper skimmed the water like a sea-gull, and with like speed. The French coast was soon made, and then Lieutenant Spencer gave to his cutter as much the appearance of a private gentleman's yacht as possible. . He hoisted the burgee of a member of the Royal Yacht Squadron and bore up for Havre. The breeze increased to half-a-gale, with the prospect of becoming worse, but Lieutenant Spencer still held his course. The seas increased in height and force; now the Snapper was elevated, trembling from truck to heel, upon the crest of a huge wave; anon she surged with fearful rapidity into the trough of the sea, mounting with equal celerity another wave of yet greater bulk than the last, to be borne on to another. The mainsail was trussed up, a storm jib set, and all made snug, yet the force of the wind was added to and became tempestuous. The bright sky grew hazy and gloomy, the wind cold and sharp, the teeth of the sea to windward to look spiteful and shew incessantly. The motion of the cutter was severe, and, acting upon want of rest and long borne anxiety, prostrated both Myra and Lizzie. To a violent sea-sickness was added a deadly helplessness, almost hopelessness. The thoughtful consideration of Lieutenant Lawrence had procured for them all such comfort and aid as was at his disposal, and advising them to take such advantages as the berths, commodious and well furnished with bedding, afforded, he left the cabin, promising to send Jack Melbury to wait upon them; and the boy soon appeared and waited upon them hand and foot, with all the tact and experience of a stewardess, and without either short temper or unwillingness. A complete tempest sprung up, and the Snapper was glad to run for shelter to Havre. It was not without both difficulty and considerable danger that she made the port, but a good sea-boat and first-rate seamanship will go far to master and surmount the fury of the contending elements. It was nearly dawn before Havre was reached, and then both Myra and Lizzie were in a state of complete exhaustion. The boy who had waited on and watched them unwearyingly through the night, became frightened; as his practised ear told him that the Snapper had let go her anchor, and was on smooth water, he hammered at the companion way, which had been battened down, and after some perseverance he was heard and attended to. Oliver Lawrance followed him into the cabin, and saw that the poor girls were really dangerously ill, and after a brief conference with the commander of the Snapper, he went on shore, summoned a medical man, and then proceeded to the house of the British Consul, whom he roused up, and stating shortly the circumstances connected with Myra and Lizzie, asked for counsel at the same time, suggesting that he should receive the unprotected girls into his house. The consul, a kind but cautious man, declared it to be out of his power to comply with his wish; but suggested that he should apply to the Convent of the Sisters of Charity, who, under such circumstances, would receive the invalids and carefully tend them until they had communicated with their friends.

He offered to accompany him and represent the case to the consideration of the mother superior, of whom he gave the very highest character, and he put it to Oliver Lawrance, whether this would not be by far the best arrangement, both as regarded the preservation of the fair fame of both girls, and for nursing advantages of a nature impossible to be obtained elsewhere. The young lieutenant jumped at the offer, and the consul at once accompanied him to the convent, where they rang at the bell, and had not to wait for admittance.

An interview with the superior was granted at once, and upon hearing the tale of the lieutenant, she at once entered into the views of the consul, and summoned two of the sisters to accompany Oliver Lawrance on board the Snapper.

"We shall have to be away as soon as the wind lulls a bit," said Oliver Lawrance to the consul, "but I trust you will not lack in your attentions to the young ladies, and whatever expenses you may be put to you shall be paid."

The consul bade him think no more of the matter with anxiety, for he should communicate to his wife what had occured, and she would, he was sure, do all that was necessary.

When the Sisters of Mercy, accompanied by the medical man and the lieutenant, reached the Snapper and descended into the cabin, they found both of the girls in a state of semi-insensibility. The doctor pronounced for their instant removal; they were wrapt in the boat-cloaks of the officers, and most carefully and tenderly conveyed to the shore, and thence in a vehicle to the convent.

Oliver Lawrence left them not until he was certain they were in no danger, and would have every attention paid to ensure their entire recovery to health. He promised to communicate with their friends, wholly forgetting that he was unacquainted with their address. But he thought only of pretty Nelly Waters. To her he intended to relate the meeting with her foster-sister, and hoped by his narration of the attention he had paid to her, to compensate in some way for the unavoidable share he had in the capture of her brother.

With daylight the wind fell, and the sea went down. Then a schooner, with raking masts, saucy trim, build and rig of the true clipper character, worked out of the port of Havre, and stole away to sea. She was soon followed by a yacht-like sloop of large size, which it was understood had run into Havre only from stress of weather. No very long time elapsed before neither were to be seen. It was only observed that the schooner, on reaching the sea, had hugged the French coast up Channel, and that the yacht, after some seeming hesitation, had adopted the same course.

A composing draught was administered both to Myra and Lizzie by the medical attendant, and when towards evening they awoke, feeble, dreamy, yet unconscious of what had transpired, they were fed with some weak chicken broth, another dose of the composing draught was administered, and slumber again supervened between them and a return to consciousness.

The sun was streaming in through the windows of the little dormitory, or rather the cell of the dormitory in which Myra had been placed early on the succeeding morning, when she opened her eyes, and after a minute's consideration became sensible that she was not dreaming, and was in a strange place. She was yet very weak and faint, but she raised herself to a reclining or recumbent position, and gazed around her with an astonishment it is impossible to describe.

Her eyes took a rapid survey of the small apartment, almost bare of all kind of furniture, for save the pallet on which she rested, a small table and a little bench, there was nothing else for the ordinary uses of a sleeping apartment. In a niche in the wall was a small figure of the Virgin Mary with the Infant Saviour upon her knee—before it knelt one of the Sisters of Mercy in her grave costume; she was motionless, soundless; her lips moved, but they only told that she was in the abstraction of deep and earnest devotion. Myra looked once more around her, above, below, pressed her hands over her eyes for a moment. Was she in a dream? She opened them; no! there was the pale and silent nun kneeling still; there were undecorated walls of stone, the small table, the little bench, upon which lay a missal, and there was the pallet upon which she had been asleep, and had now awakened to a feeling of the greatest and most complete mystification, and a kind of shuddering terror.

She yet felt a strange, surging motion; the rushing and dashing of waters in her ears, but she was not, could not be on the sea—where was she?

She turned her trembling eyes again on the nun, but she remained as statue-like at her devotion as before. Hark! that voice—surely it was that of Lizzie Hastings. She listened intently, and in the adjoining cell certainly heard her late companion, in a hysterical tone, a compound between a laugh and a cry, propounding a variety of questions, which a soft, mild voice was trying to respond to in French. What could it all mean? At this moment, the kneeling Sister of Mercy, disturbed by the colloquy just mentioned, turned her quiet eyes upon Myra. She uttered a low exclamation, and rising from her knees hurried towards her, and in a soft, musical voice, enquired how she had rested whether she was better, and if she could bring her anything.

She spoke in the French language, with the Norman accent enough to make it sound very pleasing to the ear.

Myra looked at her face; it was colourless, nay, very pale; young, pretty, and wholly devoid of any trace of passion or worldly care. Her eyes, a very dark brown, were almost supernaturally bright, but soft, tender, and affectionate in their expression. It was impossible for Myra not to be drawn towards her with an emotion of fond reverence; hers was just the nature to which such a being would peculiarly address itself. Brought up in a different religious communion, she could yet see that unless the hypocrisy was beyond something it was possible to imagine, there was pure devotion in the religious offerings of this young female; that if the mode was different to her own it was as earnest and—she could not be so gross an impostor for it to be otherwise—as sincere. It was fortunate Myra could speak French, even though but moderately, for a few questions and replies enabled her quite to understand the change in her situation, and to reconcile herself to her lot. She would have dressed herself and risen, but the nun forbade it, and waited upon her with such constancy, such thoughtfulness, such attention to her wants, and such a quick perception of what she would probably need, that Myra quite exhausted her category of thanks—a gratitude at once repressed as often as it desired to express itself—that it was no wonder she was almost entirely restored to health on the following day.

Her interview with Lizzie took place on that morning; she, too, had been no less kindly treated, and had quickly recovered her natural strength. She was so delighted to see Myra again; she embraced her, and seemed not to like to part with her; she even, when they sat down together, caught hold of a portion of her dress and held it.

A singular compound was Lizzie. She was grateful

for the kindness she had received here, quite conscious of its disinterestedness, of its value to her; was fully sensible of the really religious, unselfish, angelic natures of the religious women by whom she had been ministered to and tended so carefully; had not a word derogatory to say of them, a thought unjust to give birth to; but she did not like the place they were in, and every now and then a kind of crawling shudder crept over her frame as she saw about her the emblems of death, mortality, and the world to come everywhere present. She believed all she witnessed to be sincere—nay, it was too real. She felt as if she was absolutely in the valley of the Shadow of Death. She was unaccustomed to it, and did not comprehend it. The only thing she thought unreal in the place was the cheerfulness of the nuns. When she looked upon the desolate-looking chamber where they passed so many of their devotional hours, and slept so few—when she gazed on their garb so staid, so austere, she could not understand that a smile could ever honestly play on their features, or a cheerful word pass the portals of their lips. She expressed as much to Myra, and asked what it really meant? Myra was scarcely in a condition to explain; she had been brought up to view the members of this religion, and its votaries, through a peculiar medium, and was really incapable of replying to the questions which Lizzie put to her; but as Lizzie's was not a nature to be content with wondering only, she suggested to Myra the advantage of asking a few questions to make it plain to her—to both, if that were all—how persons who spent their whole lives in devotional exercises, or the ministrations of charity among the poor, the wretched, the miserable, the sick, the destitute—all who had need of aid, of consolation, of whatever human charity could afford—could, compatibly with the austerities of their religious observances and incessant intercourse, find it in their hearts to smile, speak cheerfully, and, instead of the unhappy, sad, solemn, grave beings their garbs seemed to indicate, be really happy, contented, amiable, and even sociable individuals. Myra, with some embarrassment, put this question to the nun, who told her readily that, as they did everything for the love of God, and they strove to their utmost truly, honestly, and fearlessly to carry out this precept, and hoped for that salvation which had been promised to those who loved, honoured, and feared Him; and as they had given up the world and its cares, so far as their own personal interests were concerned, they really had nothing to be unhappy about. It was true they could sympathise with the sorrowful and the miserable, but when the weight of another's sorrows was not upon them, there was no earthly reason why they should not speak cheerfully, smile happily, or sing like birds.

These remarks led to conversation, and they were presently joined by two sisters, who were going to the Crimea, to wait upon the wounded French soldiers in hospital. The very idea brought a rush of tears into Lizzie's eyes, and she looked upon the two delicate-looking young girls who were about to dare pestilence, fever, epidemic, contagion of all kinds, to minister to the wants of the wounded and helpless, to cool the fevered brow, to moisten the parched tongue, to listen to the last words of the dying, to minister to the last fleeting hopes of the despairing, and afford consolation to those who shudderingly deemed it no longer within their grasp.

Both the sisters, thus newly arrived, could speak a little English, and they were delighted to find two young English girls with whom they could converse, and although the term of intercourse would be brief, by whose aid they could improve their knowledge of a language which they might find valuable, for the purposes of charity in the far distant place to which they were bound; and so, quite in a methodical way, they sat themselves down with pencils and paper, and soon arranged what was likely to prove to them a most serviceable vocabulary.

The organizations of Myra and Lizzie were unlike; their characters, manners, habits, temperament dissimilar; yet the one passion by which they were both influenced, operating in a different manner on both, led to precisely similar results. So soon as Lizzie knew that Sister Marguerite and Sister Geraldine were destined for the Crimea, she at once concluded that either one or both would meet with Serjeant Haverel; and in assisting Sister Marguerite to form her vocabulary, she helped her to a few phrases which, if addressed to the sergeant, would strike his ear with great familiarity; and, gradually, from mere expressions, Lizzie got to narrations, and so on to confession. So that before they retired that night to repose, Sister Marguerite was quite aware that a sergeant in the Scots Fusilier Guards, an Englishman, very good-looking, tall, well-made, good tempered, musical, everything that was agreeable, had got with him in his custody hard and fast, and on no account to be parted with, even to return to its late owner, the heart of a young female, who thought of him all day, prayed for and dreamed of him at nights, who was most anxious that he should know she had been true to him, had never looked, nay, even thought of another—that she would not do so for the world or all it contained, and that she should continue to pray for his health, his success, his promotion, and watch for his return, that if—and here she sobbed heartily—Heaven should please to permit one of the horrible and barbarous Russians to slay him, she would never forget him, never—never—never! Nothing should efface his image from her soul, and for his sake, she would die as she had lived, a maid, and unmarried. She wept a flood of tears at the bare thought of such a thing; but the sister Marguerite soon found the means of consoling her, and promising her that should she ever see this said Sergeant Haverel, she would acquaint him with her interview with the treasure

MYRA ASTON AND THE SISTER OF MERCY IN THE CONVENT.

he had left in England, and make him promise to prize its value, and never abuse the confidence, the love, the happiness placed in his keeping.

Myra reached this very goal by a different road. She helped to form a vocabulary too, but, it led to no allusion to Clifton Grey, from it, if anything. Yet, to sister Geraldine was confided the fact, that there was a member of the English army in the Crimea, without a relative or friend in his own land—save one—who would be glad of a kind word in his loneliness, who would be pleased to learn, that, of all of whom he had left behind him when he shouldered his musket, and left the English shores, to fight the barbarous Russ, there was one, who still wished that the high hopes he entertained, the bright visions he had formed would be realized; that though upon his cold, damp bed in the battle field, he might be saddened by a sense of desolation, he might yet believe the only one he had asked to remember him, when seas divided them, had not forgotten him. Here the different pathways of the two girls joined, for Myra pressed her hands together, as the tears sprung to her eyes, and ejaculated, "Never—never!"

Sister Geraldine understood all, for though Myra had given the admission she made, the air of a feeling of more than common interest in one, who was but as a friend, a relative—even a brother, the nun saw well that those human affections, which woman places upon one of the opposite sex at some period of her life, so long as she is a denizen of the secular world, and which Myra had her full share of, were showered upon him of whom she spoke.

The nun gazed wistfully on the beautiful, earnest young face turned towards her, animated by a recital, which, though not openly, tacitly admitted the vital interest the speaker felt in the youthful Crimean soldier, in whose favour she sought to enlist the sympathy of Sister Geraldine.

She sighed, for she saw that this young girl's entire happiness was settled upon the friendless youth to whom she alluded, and she, young as she was, had seen how often these first attachments were widely and effectually sundered for ever by separation, especially when that separation was occasioned by war. She had, in France, seen too many instances of the parting of a young and simple couple, whose affections were mutually shared, whose faith had been plighted to each other, but, in spite of all their hopes, their prayers, their promise, the result they had anticipated had never been realized. He had been doomed to no early grave in Algeria, and his fate had usually given a complexion to her after career, in most cases the occasion for sorrowful reflection.

Sister Geraldine, as we have said, sighed, as she foreshadowed the result of this passion—a dreamland of faëry regions, flowers, sunshine, paradise, where sorrow and unhappiness never dare show its foot, a reality of sackcloth and ashes.

Her sigh was so heartfelt and audible, that it attracted Myra's attention.

"Why do you sigh?" she asked, "but now you were smiling and cheerful, yet, since I have spoken of the existence of a friend in the far distant country, to which you are destined, you seem to have changed your manner, and become sad. Why is this?"

"I have a failing, *ma chère enfant*, of which I strive to deprive myself, but I have not yet succeeded," replied sister Geraldine. "It is a habit of sketching the future."

"But, why should that make you sad, who, having devoted yourself to heaven, can have no painful forebodings for the future?" observed Myra, with surprise.

"It is not for myself that I am *triste*," returned sister Geraldine. "I left, behind with my worldly attire, the trials and afflictions which could pertain to my own destiny, but, I am permitted to grieve for the sorrows, the happiness, and the sad—sad trials of others."

"I understand that—it is so natural, seems to be so much a part of your heavenly mission; but why sigh just now? For whom—for what do you sigh?"

Sister Geraldine suffered a faint smile to light up her pale, passionless features, fixing her eye steadfastly on Myra, she said:

"You are anxious, because you feel that I might possibly have sighed on your account, is it not so?"

Myra drooped her head.

"It is even so," she faltered.

"You too, from that sigh, might rapidly sketch the future. See, I am not old, yet I accepted the vocation to which I was called some years back. I have mixed much among the young of both sexes, and have had much confided to me. I have seen the fondest hopes, indulged, in the fairest prospects attending them, and yet they have been utterly swept away, leaving nothing behind them but despair."

"Have you foreshadowed such a fate for me?" asked Myra, turning cold and pale.

"*Ma belle*, it is but at least a speculation, a fancy, a contingency."

"Founded on experience."

"True, but that experience has its falsifications; yet, I would guard you against setting up a human idol from adorning it with flowers and gems, from worshipping it, from investing it with all your best and brightest affections and sympathies, in the anticipations that one day it will be united with you—in fact, that the time is coming, when it and you will be one, and walk together through life's pathway, hand in hand, heart in heart, until the term allotted for an earthly sojourn has expired; for if the idol be shattered, the affection, the sympathies, the hopes, the aspirations, will be shattered too, and trail in the dust never to rise again. Some hearts, like the pliant reed, will bend before the storm, and when it has passed away, will rise again; but there are those which are laid prostrate, are utterly crushed and destroyed by the first hurricane, that tumbles to the dust the human deity which has been idolized."

Myra's head drooped yet lower; she uttered not a word, but the most painful despondency seized her, as she essayed to make the sketch of the future, to which sister Geraldine had referred. The nun regarded the expression of her features with an aspect of tender anxiety—perhaps commiseration would be the better word. She laid her hand gently upon Myra's, and said, in a soft, low voice:

"I would not have you, *ma fille*, meet your sorrow before it has started on its journey: I would only have you prepared for it when it arrives. It may not come; Happiness and joy may unseat it, and travel to you in its place. It is not more just to be too sorrowful without hope in a brighter future, than it is to be overjoyous in anticipation of a coming state of bliss which may never approach you. I would have you cheerful without being overbuoyant; but, if you must be sorrowful from the compulsory endurance of affliction, I would equally counsel you not to despair. It is time enough to be sad when the hour of trial reaches us; it is well always to be amiable and lively, so long as we have a right to be so; besides, you know *le chagrin altère la santé*, and we owe a duty to ourselves as well as to others."

"But why then do you raise sorrowful reflections before, as you have suggested, the occasion for grief may have even set out on its way to oppress me."

"I have not purposed to invite sorrowful forebodings to visit you, *ma chère fille*; it is your duty to refuse them admission to your soul, but it is equally your duty to place your affections so much under the control of Him who rules all things, that in the event of His decreeing the annihilation of your hopes. You shall bow beneath the chastening, and not determine because one great source of happiness has been arrested that all others are dried up against you."

Myra crossed her hands over her bosom.

"I comprehend you," she said. "Your counsel shall not be lost upon me."

"I trust it may not—I feel it will not," said Sister Geraldine. "See why I speak. I am going out to the Crimea, to attend to the wants of the sick; the wounded, and mark me—the dying. Already has sickness, contagion, plague, swept off a frightful number of souls, but also accursed war has added its dreadful contingent, for in the last dread battle, how many thousands fell, never to rise again."

"Battle!" exclaimed Myra, clasping her hands, and regarding the nun with breathless eagerness.

"Battle! when?" cried Lizzie Hastings, who was present, growing as white as a sheet, and clutching at the dress of Sister Geraldine in her nervous excitement. "Oh, for mercy's sake, tell us all you know? A dreadful battle to be sure it must have been—

thousands killed. O my God, sustain me! Thousands killed! I have wearied heaven with prayers for Walter's safety. Oh! surely the Almighty has not disdained to hear me."

Myra found speech denied her; she only sat motionless, fearing, yet waiting to hear further, a horrible consciousness upon her that she had but to hear—but to hear a name uttered as being among the killed and wounded, to fall down upon the stone floor senseless.

Sister Geraldine paused for a moment, that the excitement might have its vent in tears. This was the case with Lizzie, but not with Myra, she felt as if she should suffocate, but she had no tears.

"We have received intelligence," said Sister Geraldine slowly, "of *La Bataille d'Alma* fought in the Crimea, on the 20th of September. The Russians were completely defeated, and compelled to retreat."

"Thank God!" gasped Lizzie.

"It was a glorious triumph for France, and *les braves Anglais*, but *O mon Dieu!* at what cost! France had fourteen hundred killed and wounded. England, three thousand!"

Lizzie screamed, and Myra buried her face in her hands.

"It is very sad," exclaimed Sister Geraldine, but you must not despair. Every thing is possible to the good God, and he may have listened to your prayers, and spared those to whom you are attached."

This announcement put a stop to the conversation. Myra felt so oppressed by terrible fancies, that she could not utter a word; while Lizzie Hastings wept and dried her eyes, assuring herself by turns that her Walter was killed, and that he had outlived the strife, winning medals, prizes, and promotion. She alternated between hope and horror, and had not the subject, and even her excitement, been in themselves painful, her conduct would have partaken of the ludicrous.

The consul now made his appearance, and informed the two maidens he had taken a passage for them in a steamer, bound to London, and which would sail in two days' time, if they found themselves well enough for the journey. In the meantime, any courtesy, either he or his lady would show them, in chaperoning them over the scenes and sights to be found at Havre, they would cheerfully render. Myra, however, thanking him for his kindness, declined to quit the convent until she went on board the steamer, and expressed her gratefulness for the attention and genuine hospitality both her and her companion had received at the hands of the inmates of the convent, and from himself. Myra did not forget to question him about the battle of the Alma, and he confirmed it; he further acquainted her that he had just received a copy of the *Times*, which contained a list of the killed and wounded; which paper he would beg her acceptance of, in order, that she might, on her return to London, while on board the steamer, peruse its contents at her leisure.

At her leisure!

Even Lizzie echoed those three words with a gulp. How eagerly Myra accepted his offer! what present could he have made her which would have had half the value in her eyes of that copy of the *Times?* How she thanked him when she got it.

On the morning appointed for their departure from Havre, they were ready for their journey long before the hour named for the steamer to sail, and had time to take an earnest and affectionate farewell of Sisters Marguerite and Geraldine, whom they might never meet again. Sister Geraldine had entered among the English sentences with French translations, "M. Clifton Grey, Soldat Anglais, 2*. Bataillon, Scots Fusilier Guards," beneath it, the name "Mdlle. Myra Aston," and the words "*La Souvenir douce.*" Lizzie Hastings had taken care that Sister Marguerite should write down in her note book the name of Sergeant Walter Haverel, his station and regiment. Also, that his friend Miss Lizzie Hastings, of London, had sent him her affectionate remembrances, hoping that he was well, and would soon come home a general, and begged to inform him that she was as well, and as happy as she ought, or there was any right to be expected to be. And so they parted.

The consul gave unto the special charge of the captain of the steamer the two young ladies who had so strangely been placed under his protection, and requested him to pay them every attention, and afford them the means, on landing, of proceeding at once to their homes in London. The steamer, at the appointed hour, started, and was soon on her way up Channel. The moment Myra and Lizzie had an opportunity of placing themselves where they were not likely to be observed, they opened the *Times* newspaper, and referred at once to the list of killed and wounded.

What a fearful array of names! Their hearts beat, and their fingers trembled as they went slowly down the long, long list. They passed no name over, but, when they had reached the last, and found the terrible collection of names included neither that of Clifton Grey nor Sergeant Walter Haverel, they instinctively clasped each other in their arms, and fervently ejaculated, "Thank God!"

CHAPTER XXI.

"This is, indeed,
A cup of bitterness, the worst to taste—
And this thy heart shall empty to the dregs.
Endless despair shall be thy Caucasus,
And memory thy vulture; thou wilt find
Oblivion far lonelier than this peak.
Behold thy destiny!"
                                    LOWELL.

"Sounds not the clang of conflict on the heath?
Saw ye not whom the reeking sabre smote;
Tyrants and tyrants' slaves!—the fires of death,
The bale fires flash on high—from rock to rock,
Each volley tells that thousands cease to breathe;
Death rides upon the sulphury Siroc,
Red battle stamps his foot."
                                    BYRON.

CAPTAIN WINSLOW SKETCHES THE FUTURE,— STRUGGLES WITH THE FOE.—PROGRESS.—NEWS FROM HOME.

THE morning after the battle of Inkermann, Clifton Grey turned out and assisted and directed the party under his command, either in burying the dead, or in removing such of the wounded as needed help and aid. It was a sad task, and took the whole of the day, so that he was unable to pay a visit to the sergeant or the corporal of his regiment, who were both in hospital.

That night he was ordered to the trenches, and took his twelve hours' spell of work, returning in the morning fearfully fagged, but otherwise without injury, although the Russians did not suffer the men to work at the parallels without striving their best to destroy as many as they could.

The days went on pretty much the same: the siege proceeded slowly, and illness began to make rapid strides. There was an insufficient supply of clothing, and the weather was growing wet and cold; men's boots were worn out, and there was none in store to replace them. Even the officers were dirty and ragged, and began to assume the appearance rather of beggars who had donned—after they had well patched them—the old discarded costume of officers of the guards, rather than guardsmen, at once the pride and admiration of Rotten Row and the most splendid *salons* of the *haute noblesse.* Food, also, was scanty, and without the necessary change to preserve health. The toil, too, became excessive. It turned out that the generals in command had accepted more ground than they could manage with the strength they possessed. Thus was it, that the soldiers had four nights out of the seven engaged either in out-post duty or in the trenches. In the latter arduous and dangerous labour, twenty four hours at a stretch unrelieved was common, and even forty eight hours in them not altogether the exception.

As might have been anticipated, the men fell ill, attacked by dysentery and cholera, and were swept off at a fearful rate. The hospitals were full, and those at Scutari and elsewhere were in a fearful condition. Men not only died by hundreds from incurable wounds, from disease and its attendant horrors, but they died under neglect—or rather from sheer want of attention, or the application of the commonest remedies. There was a fierce struggle between Routine, and plain Common Sense. Routine proved victorious. If medicines were needed they were not in store; if beds on which to lay those stricken down by cholera were wanted, an order had to travel from one, to be taken to another, to be counter-signed by a third, to go up to the General Commander-in-Chief at head quarters, and from him to the head of the Medical Store Department, and again from him, to whoever might have charge of these beds.

" Six men under my charge," said a surgeon with feverish earnestness to a store keeper to whom he applied for beds for them, " are beaten down with the cholera, and I want six beds."

"Have you got an order?" said the official, with the accustomed departmental coolness.

" No!" replied the surgeon, who thought the fact, that British soldiers seized with so dangerous an epidemic would be enough for a member of that very army. Innocent fellow! no such thing.

" Must have an order, signed, and counter-signed by the Commander-in-Chief?" said the official.

"But it is seven miles to head quarters."

"Can't help that."

" Seven miles back will make fourteen miles to journey for this order."

" Must have the order?" said the official.

"But, good God, the men will die!"

" Can't help that: there must be an order before I can part with the beds."

" Let me have them on my responsibility?"

" Your responsibity."

"Yes, and I will afterwards get you the order properly signed."

" Pooh! what are you dreaming about? If I let them go, it will be my responsibility."

" But you will not let the men die, if even it be your responsibility. Curse the responsibility! what should such responsibility weigh against a number of men's lives?"

" Am not expected to answer that question. All I know is, that you must bring me an order, signed by Lord Raglan, before I dare part with any beds. No order—no beds."

" The men will all perish."

" Sorry, but can't help it: must have an order."

The surgeon went away with a sigh—and an oath too, and proceeded for medicines to the authorities at Balaklava. He requested to be provided with some medicines for the diarrhœa, and was met by the reply,

" We haven't any!"

" Nonsense—anything—opium will do."

" We have n't any!"

" Some castor oil?"

" We have n't any."

" Any thing you have I'll take."

" We have n't any."

The surgeon gave up his cholera and dysenteric patients, but he had some ten or twelve in raging fevers. He asked for some fever medicines, and received promptly the reply:

" We have n't any."

" Can you give me some for rheumatic patients?"

" We have n't any."

" What, nothing."

" We have n't any."

And the surgeon had to return without anything to aid any of his patients: so, of course, they died off at once.

Unfortunately, there is no romance in this statement. It is FACT.

The mortality became frightful, the weather assisted it. The approaches to the camp from Balaklava were broad troughs of sloppy mud, or heavy adhesive clay, which for tenacity had no parellel on earth. The commissariat horses were knocked up, and the poor soldiers, in addition to their already overwhelming labours, had to bring up the army supplies, and the ammunition to the siege batteries. Is it surprising that in less than one little month, upwards of 3,500 British troops, sick and dying, were forwarded from the camp to the Hopitals at Scutari?

Clifton Grey suffered with the rest of his companions; but, as in previous trials, his constitution, good and unimpaired by excesses of any kind, sustained him through all. Abstemious in his habits, regular, so far as he could be, ingenious in providing appliances which his situation denied him, clever in contributing substitutes for wants when the actual article required was not forthcoming, apt at cooking, and in all respects all that can be required in a soldier, he got over the fearful difficulties better than he anticipated.

The frightful storm of the 14th of November, which caused so much destruction in the bay and on the land, and which added so much to the discomfort and prostration of the army, as usual caused him but little damage. His tent was swept down, and everything during the hurricane was whirled into the wildest confusion, but in a few hours it was up again, and the interior restored pretty much to its former state. The men under his immediate control were, like himself, spared from the attacks of dysentery or cholera—they stood the climate, fairly performed their duties well and unmurmuringly, and were always ready to turn out and meet the foe the moment they were required. But it was only the unceasing attention, energy, and example of Clifton Grey that kept them in this condition. He made them steady, he enforced cleanliness, he shewed them how to vary the cooking of their food, he roasted himself the green coffee, and bruised it in a substitute for a mill of his own contriving, so that they might not have their stomachs disorganised through the frantic folly of some pump at the head of affairs. One of the men having been bred a shoemaker, they relieved him by turns while he worked and kept them well shod—although the substitutes for boots were not of a pattern which would have gained them admission to a ball-room; but their feet were kept dry and warm, and so their health and strength was preserved, and thus they were always ready for the trenches or other duty; and it was at last noticed by the heads of the regiment that whatever captain, failed to bring up his company, through sickness or any other cause, that of which Clifton Grey was serjeant was never wanting; and now that Captain Winslow was in hospital he received the full benefit of his labors, and was frequently in receipt of a praising comment from the colonel.

Then, too, when he could spare a moment, he attended like a sick nurse upon Sergeant Haverel and Mickey Dunigan; and, as a great favour, he obtained permission for them to be suffered to remain in the hospital, instead of being sent to the hospital at Scutari; and when the room was imperatively required by those in a worse condition than themselves, he had been removed to his own tent, and his comrades, who had come to feel the strongest attachment to him, vied with him in waiting on the wounded men, supplying them with comforts and necessaries, while Clifton, taking his instructions from Mr. Wilson, the surgeon, devoted himself to dressing the wounded and administering medicine, while he was rewarded by hearing from the surgeon they were progressing well and rapidly, and that an assistant surgeon could not have performed the necessary duties better than he did.

At this period, the middle of November, he succeeded in completing a letter to the young lady residing at Malta, who had professed such an interest in him, and who evidently identified him with some missing relative by the resemblance he bore to a certain portrait. He acquainted her with the interception of the packet which she had forwarded to him, and therefore with his ignorance of its contents. He also related to her the story he had heard from Mickey Dunigan, in which Captain Winslow had figured, as informing the corporal that he had obtained possession of a document that put him into possession of certain facts by which he ascertained that Clifton Grey stood between him and a large fortune.

"I am induced by this," wrote Clifton, "to believe that the secret promptings which have impelled you to consider that my resemblance to the portrait of your near relative is not merely accidental, has some real foundation. I was myself, on examining it, struck by the great similarity of features between my own and those there depicted, but at the same time had no positive reason to suppose it other than one of those freaks in which Dame Nature occasionally delights. I have since, by the circumstance just mentioned by me,

and a review of the past, been led to think there may be some truth in the surmise that this likeness is less accidental than hereditary, and am thus induced to entreat you to repeat the contents of the document you sent to me at Malta, but which I did not receive, in order that I may be enabled to trace some clue to the truth, and, if possible, discover how far the possession of that document by Captain Winslow induced him to hire a Greek mercenary to shoot me."

He added a few more lines, briefly alluding to the share he had taken in the various engagements, and his immunity from wounds hitherto. The mail went the next day, early, at least so it was said; for at this period it was not at all regular, and depended upon the will of Lord Raglan, who had, on two or three occasions, named an hour for its departure; and despatched it some three or four hours earlier, the reports of the sailing of the mail were, therefore, not founded upon any data, and were more often wrong than right. However, Clifton took his packet to the post office, along with some letters from some of the officers, and was at least satisfied that he should be in time. But he had only just reached the post office and deposited his letters, when an orderly from the commander-in-chief arrived with the command to close the box and make up the letters, as Lord Raglan would, within the next three hours, start the steamer with despatches for the home government.

On his way to his tent, Clifton encountered one of the hospital orderlies, who halloed to him to stop. Clifton turned.

"Hey, sergeant!" he cried: "Is your name Grey?"

"It is."

"Oh, then, you are wanted down below at the hospital tent yonder."

"Who wants me there?"

"Captain Winslow. I have been looking for you this hour. He embarks almost immediately on board the steamer for England. You must look sharp or you'll be too late; and he is very anxious to say something to you before he goes."

Clifton mused a full minute before he determined to comply with the summons. He asked himself, did the captain wish to inflict upon him a parting insult? Captain Winslow had been fearfully ill, and almost miraculously saved from the jaws of the gaunt slayer, cholera; during his complete prostration Clifton had frequently visited him with such delicacies as his brother officers could spare or he could procure for him. He had waited upon and assisted him when utterly helpless and unconscious, but as soon as the danger was past and Captain Winslow, though very slowly, began to recover and recognise those who were about him, Clifton came to his side no more. He felt convinced that the captain knew nothing of this, and could not, therefore, desire to see him to pay him with ironical gratitude; at the same time he was at a loss to conjecture what he really could want with him; but as this speculation answered no purpose, and promised to bring him no nearer to the truth, he resolved to obey the order, and within a few minutes of the time he reached the tent and presented himself before Captain Winslow.

The captain was reclining upon a substitute for a couch, and was swathed in rough coarse clothing; he was but the shadow of what he had been—a mere wreck of bones and tendons remained of what had been a powerful frame. His face, always sallow, now looked the colour of green gold, his eyes still retained their furtive glance, but were heavy and dim, his breath was very short, and he did not speak without difficulty. As soon as his eye lighted upon Clifton it flashed for a moment, and ran up and down his figure from head to foot. He gave a sickly smile.

"Well, Gentleman Grey," he exclaimed, in a feeble voice, "you don't look the same smart, handsome, clean dandy you did at Malta."

He did not, indeed. His red coat, with incessant exposure to the weather, to the smoke of powder, to the bayonet, to the mud of the trenches, was greatly changed in its aspect. The scarlet hue had disappeared, and was replaced by one of port wine; despite the scrupulous brushing, it had lost all pretensions to brightness, and the facings were no less dingy. In several places it was patched, and where it had been merely rent was mended. His trowsers bore similar signs of wear and tear—that is, as much of them as were visible, for he had extemporised spatterdashes from his ankle to the top of his knee, which were attached to his legs with strips of leather, wound round very much in the fashion of this portion of the costume of an Italian brigand. His smooth, clean face was now ornamented with an ample beard and moustache, and altogether he looked more like the pioneer of the regiment emerging from arduous service than the smart, clean, gentlemanly looking soldier he appeared when, as Captain Winslow said, at Malta.

Clifton intuitively glanced down his person, and he too, smiled; he turned his eye upon Captain Winslow and said:

"It has been no holiday work that has caused a change in my appearance, Captain Winslow. I am not alone in this altered aspect: you are yourself not so bright as you were."

"No impertinence to your officer: remember your station, sir!" cried Captain Winslow.

"I shall not forget it sir, so long as you will condescend to remember yours," returned Clifton haughtily; and then he added, "yousent for me, Captain Winslow—may I beg to know the purpose for which you require my presence."

"I am about to return to England on sick leave," said the captain, with a sneer, "you will carry my luggage down to Balaklava."

Clifton Grey made an impatient gesture.

"Captain Winslow," he said, "cannot you understand how infinitely you yourself raise me above you by these petty exhibitions of personal animosity and malignity. You know that I would not—neither would it be expected of me—respond to any such order. My duty commands me elsewhere, and is of a different complexion. I, at least, Captain Winslow, have seen some hard fighting. I have so borne myself in the several engagements, as to win my promotion. Even your hostility to me cannot find a peg to hang a charge of unsoldierly conduct upon, therefore let me suggest that if you have any pretensions to the character of a gentleman, you will have more regard for the estimation in which you wish to be held than to descend to such paltry proceedings as to summon me to bear your luggage to the ship at a moment when the honour of the country—which pays me—and you, Captain Winslow, to do its work—is at stake, and requires the best energies of the few left fit for duty in the trenches or on outpost duty to protect the camp. I, Captain Winslow, had twenty-four hours in the trenches, terminating at twelve last night, I turned out at six this morning, and have been doing regimental duty since then. I am to take out a picket to-night. Shall I report to Colonel Upton that you, Captain Winslow, who have not yet drawn your sword in one engagement, and are now away to England on sick leave, insisted upon your power, as my superior officer, to command me to be your porter, and so prevent my doing the more important regimental duty required of me by the service and commanded by the colonel?"

Captain Winslow ground his teeth, but remained silent. Clifton Grey saw his advantage, and followed it up.

"You have sent for me, Captain Winslow, only to make me feel, if you can, more bitterly, the position in which fate has placed me, after having permitted me to enjoy a status equal to your own. You have, from almost the day I joined the regiment—at least since the hour when I protected a defenceless girl from the unmanly outrage of your brother—heaped upon me the most trying insults it is possible for man with any sense of the dignity of his own nature to bear, and without the shadow of a motive"—

"There you lie!"

"Captain Winslow, you presume upon being my superior officer, and your present illness, to use those words."

"Bah!"

"If you live, and I am spared through the siege, you may have occasion to alter your tone, and to render an account which it may not be palatable to you to meet."

"Pshaw!"

"Your contemptuous exclamations serve the purpose only of rigidly fixing me in a determination I have formed; and I may as well now intimate to you that it is my intention to exact reparation from the man who hired the Greek scoundrel Agrypelos to assassinate me."

"Pah! what is that to me?"

"Much. At least it may suggest itself to you that it is likely to prove important, when I tell you that I know the man."

Captain Winslow's lip quivered and curled. He hissed some sentence through his teeth, but it was inaudible. Clifton gazed upon his pale face and shifting expression of countenance sternly, as he said:

"Aye; it is even the same man that sounded Corporal Dunigan, and would have enlisted him in the murderous service, but that the honest though humble soldier spurned the guilty action which his superior in station, but infinitely inferior in the nobler qualities of manhood, wanted the hardihood, or some yet less estimable qualification, to do himself."

"You are talking enigmas to me," said Captain Winslow, "which I care not to solve. I am ill and weak, with scarcely strength for this interview; but I am resolved to go through with it, even if it knocks me over altogether, because—because I hate you—do you understand me, hate you as much as it is possible for man to develope that passion! I need not give you any other reason—it is enough."

"Ample—but powerless of ill to me."

"We shall see. Mark me! I know more about you than you think for—I know who and what you are, which you do not—I know that you inherit an enormous fortune, if you knew when, where, and how to claim it. Failing you, it reverts to me, who do know how, when, and where to claim it. With it is the hand of one of the loveliest women God ever formed; young, exquisitely beautiful in feature, no less elegantly formed, accomplished, high born, and already half in love with you—"

"I?"

"With you! Nay, I will not hesitate to say that she is wholly in love with you. Here is fortune, rank, beauty—all that man on earth can desire—within your grasp. You know not where to seek it. If you did, you know not how to claim it. I possess the link of the chain you need. I go to receive all; to enjoy your wealth, and revel in the arms of the beauty who pants to call you her own. It is to tell you this I sent for you, that you may chew the bitter cud which your hours on outpost and your days and nights in the trenches will give you an opportunity of doing. While resting on the deep clay of the unhealthy trench, surrounded by the blood and brains of slaughtered comrades—in the deep snow, the cutting sleet, the flooding rain—while in the dreary hollows on dangerous outpost duty—on the muddy turf upon which you stretch your exhausted limbs after toil beyond the limit of human endurance—sing ever to yourself the burden that you are entitled to great wealth—to high station—to the embraces of rare beauty, but that instead you are a wretched sergeant of the line, exposed to the horrors of an ill-conducted campaign, ragged, shoeless, half famished, doing the duties of two men and performing the labors of three, spared by some strange fatality from sickness and the bullet or bayonet of the enemy, but yet, ever beneath their ghastly shadow hanging over you, as the sword by a thread over the prostrate form of Damocles—this the enjoyment of your vast estates and personal riches, the hugging of your Minié, the only embrace of beauty permitted you. Now go, and think over this. Go and ask yourself whether, hating you as I hate you—it is not possible for hate to be in excess of that—whether I need lack gratification when I reap all that should be yours, all that awaits your taking, if you but knew how to set about it? Ask yourself if my hate should not be gorged to satiety by this? Ask yourself whether I could quit the Crimea, this island to which you are chained, Prometheus-like, with a vulture preying upon your vitals, without sending for you to inflict the torture you must feel—knowing what I have now communicated to you—when I have departed? Go, I have no more to say to you."

"But I have to you. Mark me, Captain Winslow. I believe in the truth of what you have stated, so far as my title to rank and wealth extends; I have no common reason for my faith in this; beyond it I leave the issue in the hands of Heaven. You have proposed certain issues, it is not for you to dispose them according to your wish or your will; however cunningly you may weave your plot, you cannot ensure its success. I take the benefit of that doubt; it supersedes your malignant suggestions; it is the dove with the olive branch winging its way to me over the dark and overwhelming waters. Go your way—I go mine; do your worst, I dare and defy you. Each retires with his conscience—you to luxurious ease, but yet to act the part of the burglar and swindler, by taking possession of that you admit not to be your own. I to the death-exacting trenches, to meet the murderous sorties, to pass the long nights in the black valley of the Tchernaya, exposed to the fatal influences of the wintry elements, or the no less dangerous missile of the active foe, to the damp earth upon which alone such rest as can be snatched is to be obtained, to meet at any time and in all seasons the foe in bloody combat. Yet, withal, I, with turmoil, toil, and danger, the happier, prouder man than you, with your wealth and comfort, obtained through a cheat, and indulged in with an ever present apprehensive horror."

Without another word, or waiting to hear one, Clifton quitted the hospital tent and returned to his own tent, to await the hour when he was to take charge of the picket.

Captain Winslow was borne on board the Medway, and steamed away for Constantinople, to carry out the infernal project he had, with such brazen coolness, acknowledged his intention of doing. How he succeeded we shall see hereafter.

Clifton Grey, at the appointed hour, marched out with his picket. It was under the command of Lieu-

CLIFTON GREY SAVES LIEUTENANT LINDEN FROM BEING TAKEN PRISONER BY THE RUSSIANS.

tenant Linder, and was of greater force, in respect of numbers, than it had hitherto been, on account of its being destined for a ravine where it was known the Russians had accumulated a number of the infantry, who were posted in small natural caves, from which they were able to inflict great mischief upon the working parties of the French right attack, and also upon the English in their left attack. It was determined to dislodge them, and the advance of this comparatively small force was more in the nature of a *reconnaissance* than with a view to attack the foe in their cover; but it was not the less dangerous, nay, if anything, it was more so than if it had been an attack in any force.

The night was miserable indeed—the sky was of a pitchy blackness—the wind howled and moaned, and the ground was ankle-deep in sloppy mud, or a thick tenacious clay. Nevertheless, the men pressed on, heedless of the weather, some passing a joke, and others laughing at it, all bent on doing their duty like brave men, and none raising a word of objection to the miserable state of the ground, or weather, or the dangerous character of the errand upon which they were bound.

As the heavy rain pattered against the cabin window of the Medway, as the vessel surged over the turbulent billows, and the wind shrieked and whistled through the rigging of the vessel, Captain Winslow drew the warm clothing in his comfortable berth over him, thought of Clifton Grey, and smiled.

Our hero, as he pushed on, facing the cold beating rain, and tramping through the miry slough to the spot where he might meet with his death from the bullet of a Russian, thought of Captain Winslow, shrugged his shoulders, and pitied him. He was startled at the moment by Lieutenant Linder observing to him, as if he divined his thoughts:

"Winslow has left this for England."

"I am aware of it, sir. I saw him before he left for Balaklava to go on board the Medway."

"It was nearly all up with him; however, the devil always provides for his own. Did he make friends with you before he went away?"

"He sent for me, sir."

"Ah! to read a recantation, I'll be sworn; and to promise, if he reached England alive, to give a donation to a church, and offer up prayers for your safety. Eh? Was it not so?"

"Something different. He sent for me to say, that he had the right to a reversion of rank and property to a vast amount, on my failing to claim it. As he assured me I knew neither where to make my claim, or even if I did, how to substantiate it, and he did, I might comfort myself under the performance of my duty, with a conviction that he was enjoying all the luxury wealth and station can give, which properly should be mine."

"The devil! And do you believe that there is any truth in what he said?"

"I have not a doubt of it."

"Um! that's not at all agreeable. One thing, by-the-bye, is fortunate, and may prove a solace to you, my friend Mandeville, of the 33rd, who had the misfortune to lose his left hand at the Alma, has gone home in the Medway. He is an idle man, unless he has a pursuit, and once fairly on it, he will follow it out to a result with untiring energy. He asked me to give him an idea to kill *ennui*, going home. 'Jack,' said I to him, 'there's Winslow going in the same ship with you. He is a fellow who cannot exist without a plot, a plan, or contrivance of some sort on his hands, and always for a bad object; of that I would stake my life. Watch him narrowly, and ascertain what new game he is up to. You will then have plenty to amuse yourself with on your voyage home.' 'I will,' he replied, thanking me for the suggestion; 'and if he arrives in England without my being in possession of his scheme he is either a much cleverer fellow than I have yet met with, or I am losing my powers of unweaving a tangled web.' I am glad that you have told me he has a nefarious purpose which he intends carrying out, for I am sure Jack Mandeville will unkennel it, and not rest until he has completely and utterly thwarted it. It may, too, be the means of working you good in the end. Strange what important results spring from unforseen circumstances! I'd wager my existence that Winslow never took Jack Mandeville into his calculation, and that very omission will fling him to a certainty."

Clifton expressed his satisfaction at what he heard, but breathed a devout wish that he might be one of the parties in the action before the *dénouement* took place.

The men had now reached the limit of their march, and they were posted in certain numbers on particular spots, with orders to advance when they saw their comrades engaged, only on a given signal, and in the full character of a support.

Clifton Grey, with a dozen men, now prepared for the commencement of the work, and he said to Lieutenant Linder, before he advanced,

"Can you see those four stone huts down in the left of the ravine—they are hardly visible in the hazy gloom—away there in the gully to the left."

"I see them now."

"They are full of Russian riflemen armed with the Minié. They can bring their rifles to bear on the French right and our left attacks, and—ah! there goes one!" he suddenly interrupted himself by observing, as a flash of light, a puff of white smoke, and the sharp crack of a rifle from one of the places indicated showed it to be tenanted by the men he had named.

"The Russians are lodging there, safe enough," said Lieutenant Linder, "How do you propose to get them out?"

"We shall steal on to that further one to the left first, by crawling along the ground till we have got far away to the left, and then advancing in Indian file, as noiselessly as possible, until we get close upon the hut, then make a dash for it—we are sure to take it. I shall immediately blow a blast on a bugle I have with me. You will then advance upon the hut I have got possession of, and we will dash out upon the next; the other men will advance at full speed upon the two we have captured, and we can then advance, followed by our supports, on the other two, drive out the Russians, and thus take possession of all the huts."

"The plan is a good one. I'll do my best to follow it out."

"There are some caverns, too, with some Russians in them, whom we must dislodge, but we shall know more about them when we get down there."

"All right; sound the bugle the instant you are ready for us, and we will be down with you with the speed of three-year-olds over the flat at Newmarket."

Clifton Grey moved off with his dozen comrades, proceeding slowly and stealthily under cover of the ridgy ground until they reached a particular spot, when they lay down and trailed themselves along the wet grass, preserving, however, their rifles from the damp, for life and death were involved in that precaution. They crawled noiselessly on until the uneven ground enabled them, by stooping low down, to take the hut in flank, without in that dark, gloomy atmosphere, running the risk of discovery, until they were close in the vicinity of the hut.

They reached within a hundred paces of the hut, when Clifton halted and motioned to his men to do the same. They stood still and remained as silent as the grave. They plainly heard the Russians laughing and talking, and apparently unconscious they had an enemy so near. Clifton now whispered to each man his allotted duty, and when they had all declared they were quite ready, he bade them not to utter a sound but to follow him at the very top of their speed. They had fixed bayonets, because he was anxious, if possible, to take the first without a shot being fired, and hoped, if he succeeded, to make easy work of the others.

Grasping his rifle ready to use it either for firing or for the bayonet, he sprung forward like a deer pursued by the hunter's hounds. In an instant he was in the hut, and cried in French:

"Surrender yourselves prisoners, or we will bayonet every man of you."

At the same instant his comrades crowded into the hut. The Russians, completely surprised and panic-stricken, cried for quarter, and threw down their arms; they were all made prisoners and their arms secured. Leaving two men sentry over the prisoners with their rifles cocked and presented, he blew a blast from a small bugle he had with him, and strained his eyes in the direction in which he knew Lieutenant Linder would advance, and soon saw a black mass moving forward with great rapidity towards the hut where he was stationed with his men.

They were evidently seen by the Russians in the nearest hut, for they discharged several rifles at them, but Clifton, leading his men, dashed at them before they had time to reload, and was soon engaged in a hand to hand conflict, as he quickly found, with nearly treble his number. Occupied as he was in the deadly struggle, he had no opportunity of directing Lieutenant Linder where to aid him by a blast of his bugle, and the little party were placed in imminent danger. However, by skill in the use of his rifle and bayonet, he disposed of his antagonist by a death wound, blew the bugle lustily, and cheering on his men to fresh exertions, plunged again into the struggle with an ardent fury that made his opponents give ground before him. Still, the odds being so manifestly unequal, the Russians took heart, maintained their ground, slowly but surely closed around their assailants, and subsequently, in language which the English neither understood nor heeded, called upon them to throw down their arms or be slain. The British replied only by shouts, and fighting more fiercely than ever.

At this moment, Lieutenant Linder and his men came up at the *pas de charge*, a large proportion of the Russians were panic stricken at the sight; they threw away their muskets, and fled at the top of their speed; the others surrendered.

On went Clifton, followed by his chosen comrades, to the third hut, where he arrived as soon as those who had fled thither, but the men in possession of this cover were by this time aroused to a sense of their danger, and they met the advancing guards by a volley, which made several of the poor fellows bite the earth. Without pausing, however, Clifton and his companions rushed on, and again, a desperate hand to hand conflict ensued. Here, as before, the Russians far outnumbered their antagonists, and the struggle therefore was proportionally desperate. Once more Lieutenant Linder arrived with his reinforcement, and made a dashing charge, but the Russians at the same instant were reinforced, the relative numbers were thus perceived, and the Russians still maintained the superiority of force.

They crossed bayonets; but though they fought with bravery, they were no match with this formidable weapon for the Guards, who drove them back by physical force, seconded by a cool and daring courage, not to be exceeded by any troops in the world—by in fact a display of that *solidité* which the French officers spoke of in such high terms of admiration. All this time, men on both sides were loading and firing as fast as they could, or, if too closely pressed, using the cold steel. Clifton ably supported Lieutenant Linder, who took the direction, the moment he arrived, of the affair, and fought with his accustomed reckless daring, cheering on his men to emulate his deeds, which were worthy of the high character he sought to carve for himself.

But as there is many a slip between the cup and the

lip, so Lieutenant Linder, at the moment he made a plunge forward with loud and animating cries to compel the retreat of the Russians to whom they were opposed, stumbled, and fell prostrate on the ground. Before he could arise a Russian sprung on him, and with both hands upraised his musket to bayonet him. Before he could thrust it down, the bayonet of Clifton Grey pierced his chest, and he was hurled to the blood-stained turf. Others, however, rushed to either capture the prostrate officer or to slay him; but Clifton Grey sprung across his body, and, clubbing his musket, swung it round him, and kept the Russians at bay. He shouted to his comrades to close up and support him; while the Russians, believing that, from the exertions made by the sergeant and privates to rescue and save him, that the lieutenant was of more consideration than he appeared to be, redoubled their efforts to capture him. In vain. Clifton Grey maintained his position. Fired at, thrust at, even flung at—for some of the Russians, who cared not particularly for close quarters, took up large stones and threw them—he was yet neither wounded nor injured, nor did he budge an inch; he only animated his companions by lusty exclamations—by appeals to their courage, and to their prowess, and at length had the satisfaction of finding, by a renewed effort by all his party, the Russians were made to fall back, and Lieutenant Linder gained his feet again.

"I am unhurt, Grey!" shouted the lieutenant, when fairly on his legs once more." "Hurrah! England and the Queen! Give it them, lads; here comes our reinforcement. Drive them before you, lads!"

The men responded with a wild shout. The Russians were shaken; they hesitated, gave way, and fled to their last hut in the vicinity. They were not permitted a moment's respite; with loud and vociferous cheers the Guards pursued them, loading as they ran. By the advice of Clifton Grey, and under the command of Lieutenant Linder, as soon as they came up with the Russians, who were at their last post in this spot drawn up to receive them, they fell flat on their faces at a word, and as if by the stroke of an enchanted wand. At the very instant the Russians discharged a deadly volley of bullets, which, like a heavy storm of hail, went whistling and hissing over their heads, the ping ping note telling that the Russians, like themselves, were armed with the fearful Minié.

The sounds of this discharge were yet in their ears when up sprung the bold Fusiliers, let fly a sharp volley, and with shouts sprung upon their foe, to do battle with them with the bayonet. The line of steel glittered brightly and fearfully in the gloom of the night, and the force and speed with which these powerful fellows rushed into close quarters would have compelled a body of equally stalwart men accustomed to such tremendous warfare to have received the sweeping charge unbroken. The Russians opposed to them were not of this character, for they fell back before the bristling bayonets presented at them so compactly and so formidably. Not an instant to recover was allowed them.

"They run! they run!" shouted Clifton, "drive them in boys, hurrah! On with you, lads, the huts are our own!"

And so they were. Utterly broken, disorganised, and beaten, the Russians stood no longer, but went at full speed towards their lines, the Fusiliers pursuing them until the bizz-bom-bish of a shell from the artillery of the Russians advised them to give over the pursuit, and return to those who had established themselves in the huts so lately possessed by the Russian riflemen.

Within they found blankets, great coats, raki, muskets, and ammunition in plenty. Clifton, who much doubted whether they would be suffered to retain their victory without a struggle to regain it, made the men cram their cartouche boxes with the cartridges, which were in profusion stored away in the hut. Loading himself with a quantity, and supplying likewise two or three of the men with a bundle of them, he, leaving Lieutenant Linder in charge of the hut nearest to the Russian main body, hastened to those huts which were garrisoned by small bodies of his parties, and filled up the boxes of every man with ammunition—a wise precaution, as it turned out. On making his way back, he heard the rapid tramp of armed soldiers, and as the sounds advanced from his own lines, he paused until they came up, and then he challenged. An officer replied, and Clifton went up to him; he found three companies of the Rifle Brigade under Captain Tryon, who enquired of him the occasion of the firing. Clifton told him in brief terms.

"It is well done," he replied. "We came out for the very purpose; however, we had better on to the hut held by Lieutenant Linder, for surely the Russians will not let a handful of men retain posts of such importance."

"Such is my impression," said Clifton, "and for that reason I have served the men all well out with ammunition found in the furthermost hut; there is yet a large number of rounds there."

"Of which we will avail ourselves," exclaimed Captain Tryon.

"Hush!" cried Clifton hastily. "By heavens! a body of Russians are advancing upon Lieutenant Linder's post. I hear the rifles of the men at play on them; follow me, Captain Tryon, we have not an instant to lose."

"Rifles!" shouted Captain Tryon, "show the Russians how the Rifle Brigade handle the Minié. Quick march. Forward, lads."

And forward they went, at a trot.

A strong column of Russians was pouring down from the main body of the Russians upon the captured post, and already, as they advanced, the small body of Fusiliers were doing fearful execution with their rifles, and yet the Russians pressed on. And so did the Rifles. It was a race as to who should be at the coveted spot first; and it was decided by both reaching it together; but the Rifle Brigade poured in such an overwhelming, well-directed, and fatal volley, that the column of Russians at once fell back in disorder, with a considerable number of killed and wounded. Once more they fell back on the main body; and now the Fusiliers prepared to give up possession of their huts to the Rifles, who proceeded to establish themselves in them; but before the Guards retired, the huts were again assailed by another strong body of Russians, composed of several columns, and they made desperate exertions to regain the huts and caves out of which they had been driven by so small a force. But, once out, they were not permitted to enter again. The British troops maintained themselves with their accustomed pertinacity, and, after a terrible loss, the Russians were forced to retreat. The Rifles and the Guards having succeeded in demoralizing them by the fearful execution their Miniés had made, rushed out to give them a parting speeding on their way. The grey-coated Muscovites, thoroughly repulsed, finally retreated to their lines, their path marked by their dead and dying.

The last brush was, however, fatal to the brave Captain Tryon, whose gallantry and soldierlike qualifications made him a valuable servant to his country, and whose estimable qualities endeared him to all who had the happiness of his friendship or the pleasure of his acquaintance. While cheering on his men, exhibiting that energy, and at the same time the coolness so essential to military success, a Minié bullet pierced his brain, and he fell, never to rise again. Clifton Grey was close to the spot, and was the first to raise him as he fell. He bore him tenderly to the hut, but saw that any further attention to him was useless. The soul of as gallant a soldier as ever headed a company, had winged its way to its Maker, and he had but to utter a prayer and leave his lifeless form to the care of his own men, who would pay his lifeless remains all the respect to which it was entitled. And there was no fear of this, for the men were much attached to him, and would pay the last tribute to him with emotion, and little less than reverence.

The grey dawn of the morning shewed itself over the heights, when the picket under Lieutenant Linder was relieved and returned to camp. The night's work was reported, and the men were dismissed to sleep, while others went on with the work of destruction and death.

On the following day Clifton, released from another twelve hours' picket duty, was ordered to attend his Colonel, and when he entered his presence Colonel Upton said—

"Stand forward, Grey. I have heard from Lieutenant Linder an encomiastic account of your be-

haviour at the taking of the Ovens the night before last. It was a very smart affair—a very smart one indeed, and reflects the highest credit upon those who conceived and executed it. Lieutenant Linder tells me that it was you who planned the scriatim capture of them, availing yourself successively of the support of your reserves until the whole of them were in your hands."

Clifton bowed.

"It was skilfully designed. He tells me you commenced the work and completed it?"

"Lieutenant Linder's modesty, Colonel," said Clifton, hastily, "has induced him to sacrifice his own large share of credit to advance unduly my interests. To his great bravery, his coolness, his military knowledge—"

"True—true, Linder is a good soldier and a brave one, but he detailed the circumstances to me exactly as they happened; and for myself, uninfluenced by what he said in your favor—and he did praise you, I confess—I can judge pretty nearly what share you took in the affair. It affords me the very greatest pleasure to tender you my approbation, and to inform you that General Canrobert has sent to Lord Raglan to thank him in the name of the French army for the important service rendered by dislodging the Russians from those covers, for the loss and annoyance to the French Artillery of the right attack, as well as our own, was considerable. The Commander-in-Chief has sent for Lieutenant Linder to give him the details, and you have my permission to accompany him. As I have reported to Lord Raglan the share you took in the capture of the huts and caves, his lordship may be desirous of speaking an approving word to you."

"Colonel, believe me I am deeply grateful for your most considerate kindness;" exclaimed Clifton, as the colonel ceased to speak.

"Nonsense, man! To me it is a gratification of a very high nature to award praise where it is deserved —to confer reward where it is merited. You are entitled to all I have said and done—perhaps more. Indeed, I am by no means sure that I have gone so far as I ought; for I have noticed you frequently of late for your admirable discipline—for your soldierlike conduct—and for the able condition of the men immediately under your superintendence; and it is only proper that such conduct should be estimated at its right value, and openly commended and encouraged. Here is Linder; you will accompany him to head quarters. Good day, Grey! I shall speak to you again on this matter. Linder, your papers are ready."

Lieutenant Linder, who at that moment entered, smiled at seeing Clifton Grey with a deeper flush upon his embrowned skin than it usually wore—for he knew that it was the result of no unpleasant communication. He took the dispatch—made his obeiance—he had been previously instructed—and catching Clifton by the arm with his left hand, they quitted the tent and proceeded to head quarters.

Lord Raglan and his staff were located near the farm of Dreuzde-otar, and as Clifton mounted the rising ground in front, he saw the white walls of Lord Raglan's house standing, with the sky for a background, and in front of it a number of horses—some with riders, others without. Officers of various regiments were lounging upon anything which afforded a lean, or were seated on their steeds awaiting communications. Sentries were posted, pacing slowly to and fro, to keep off intruders and strangers; and soldiers, off duty, were in large numbers sauntering to and fro, looking on nothing in particular and everything in general.

The deep booming of the siege guns was proceeding as it had been day after day, and the white smoke wreathing up in the air, tinged with rainbow hues won out of sunshine, told the direction in which the struggle was going on without ceasing. A delay of an hour and a half, expended in conversation, chiefly about the affair of the 20th, by Lieutenant Linder with a number of officers, during which a knot of them gathered round Clifton to ask questions of detail in respect to the engagement, and then admission was obtained to the commander-in-chief. Clifton remained without—but not for long. An orderly, some ten minutes after the lieutenant had been in the presence of Lord Raglan, summoned Clifton to appear before him, and with an increased throbbing of the heart he obeyed.

He was led into a room, meanly furnished, but presenting evidence that the commander-in-chief had plenty of employment for his pen as well as his head and military knowledge in the government of the army. A large table, at which sat two clerks, was covered with papers and forms, at which they scribbled with exemplary perseverance. Lord Raglan's own table was likewise covered with papers of remarkable variety, written and printed, and exhibited chaotic confusion, except to his experienced and practised eye. Upon the walls were large maps, hastily affixed, bearing marks of being frequently consulted.

Lord Raglan was standing with his back to a fire, and facing Lieutenant Linder, who was standing before him in an attitude of respectful attention. By his side stood a French general officer. Some other individuals of position were in the room, but Clifton had no eyes for them. He turned his gaze on Lord Raglan, whom he had hitherto only seen in the field, and scanned his pale, thoughtful, but kind looking face, and somewhat spare figure, with considerable interest, but he was not permitted time for more than a casual survey. The quick eye of Lord Raglan noted him as he entered, and he fixed a close scrutinizing glance upon our hero, and said:

"Oh, this is the sergeant of the Fusiliers of whom Colonel Upton speaks in such flattering, and you in such high, terms. Stand forth, sergeant. What is your name?"

"Grey, my lord; Sergeant Clifton Grey," he replied promptly."

"Your age?"

"In my twenty-second year, my lord."

"Um! You are well developed for your age. How long have you joined?"

"Twelve months in September last."

"And before that?"

"I had just matriculated for college."

"Ha! and enter the army as a private; from what cause?

"Circumstances my lord, over which I had no control whatever, threw me on the world penniless."

"And you enlisted?

"I did, my lord."

"To save a foolish rustic, who, in a love frenzy had taken the Queen's shilling, from being torn from his mother, whose only support he was; briefly, my lord, that is the truth of a very touching story told to me by the serjeant, who accepted Gray as a substitute," exclaimed Lieutenant Linder, with earnestness.

"Enough," said Lord Raglan, "that, coupled with what you have said, Grey, explains the mystery: men of position rarely enlist in the ranks, unless under circumstances not quite favourable to them. However, I have heard a high character of you, Grey. By the bye, I remember you were at the Alma, and received your promotion from His Royal Highness the Duke of Cambridge, for being the first to enter one of the Russian redoubts."

Clifton bowed to him.

"Ah!" he added with a smile, "a moot point, but where all did so bravely, the last has but little depreciatory attached to him. You were at Inkermann too?"

Lieutenant Linder answered this by a glowing eulogy upon his actions that day.

"You have a warm friend in Linder, sergeant," said his lordship, with a smile.

"He has thrice saved my life, my lord," exclaimed Lieutenant Linder, energetically.

"True—true, true!" repeated Lord Raglan expressively, as though he was pleased by the gratitude evinced by the lieutenant.

They now came to the struggle of the huts, and Lord Raglan made Clifton repeat all that took place: he listened attentively, and when he had ended, he said with a sigh:

"Poor Tryon! he met a soldier's fate, he deserves the kind remembrances of his country."

Then he spoke some warm words of praise to Clifton, approved of his military manœuvres displayed in the affair of the huts, and of the gallantry which led to success in the undertaking, declared him a

Sergeant Major, and promised to recommend him to the notice of Her Majesty for a commission. "Yours is an example which I trust, Grey," said his lordship, "your comrades will emulate. You entered the ranks unfriended and unknown; by steady conduct, sobriety, by strict attention to discipline, by uniformly performing your duty, by respectful and proper demeanor, by great bravery, and excellent military acquirements, you have placed yourself in the fair road to obtain all the honours the army affords. At the highest point as a non-commissioned officer you can reach, a door has been graciously opened by her majesty to that rank which, once obtained, leads up to the position I have now the honour to hold. I imagine it will be quite unnecessary for me to impress upon you the prudence of proceeding as you have commenced, but, I may assure you, that if you persevere in your most honourable course, you will reap the reward to which you are most fairly entitled."

Lord Raglan having repeated that General Canrobert had expressed his great admiration of the spirited affair of the huts, and the considerable service he had rendered him, intimated to *Captain* Linder that the interview was at an end.

To be sure, Clifton Grey retired from the room greatly gratified by what had taken place. Praise from so high a quarter and in such terms was enough to make him proud. Oh, that there had but been some one to share his intense pleasure at this recompense for his arduous labors, for his defiance of danger and death, for all he had endured and suffered! It was true Lieutenant—now Captain Linder shook him warmly by the hand upon what had passed. It was true that Sergeant Haverel would grow husky with emotion and pleasure at hearing it; that simple full-corporal Dunigan would express his delight in terms of extravagance; but there beyond the seas, in the home—for withal it was home to him—he had quitted, he needed, yearned for one to whom he could pour out his full heart to. He would have bated one-half of what honor he had now received if that to Myra he could have related the other portion—if he could have said to her, "I promised you that the position into which I have leaped should never be tarnished or defaced by me. I promised you to move ever onward and upward. I whispered 'Excelsior' in your ear; and see, I am keeping my word." He had not, however, the opportunity to say this to the only one he had yet known to whom he cared to say it, and he therefore felt commingling with his gratified pride a sense of loneliness and desolation which quite robbed it of its value.

He knew to a certainty that Sergeant Haverel and Corporal Dunigan, both now fast progressing to convalescence, would be pleased to hear from his lips a recital of what had occurred at his interview with Lord Raglan. It would be, at least, some relief to that terrible want to which we have alluded, and which he so keenly felt, to tell it them, no matter how briefly or with what modesty of colouring. So, having yet some little time to spare before he would be again actively engaged on duty, he repaired direct to the hospital tent, where his brave, though humble comrades, were striving to win back strength again.

When he entered it and advanced to the convalescent ward, limited in its proportions, he found pale-faced Mickey Dunigan seated upon a stool, with a short pipe in his mouth—unlighted by the way—wrapped up in his long grey coat, with the collar standing up above his ears, his head yet bandaged, and his whole appearance that of one still hovering on the threshold of death. He was in an attitude of intense attention, and his eyes were winking and blinking as if to stay a bright tear which disengaged itself now and then, and rolled down his weather-beaten and sunken cheek. Opposite to him, and quite close, was Sergeant Haverel, who was endeavouring, through a paroxysm of gulps and gasps, laughs, and moistened eyelids, to read the contents of a letter to him. As Clifton approached he heard Mickey say—

"Thrue for you, Sergeant dear. Sorra a doubt o' that, any way. She's the jewel av the world. Oh! thin, but its a bould heart she has. My Bridget would shriek and turn her eyes to the back av her poll as soon as any one began to talk to her av fighting, like a bould Fusilier, them murtherin' Rooshans. An' its praying for the blagguard that sits in front av you she is this blessed minnet. Holy Mother! av she'd seen me when Sargeant Grey picked me up all blood an' brains, it holler she would loud enough to have tumbled Prince Gorsedrycough off his perch, av he was roosting on it on the north side of Sebastopol."

"Why, Mickey, she hasn't her match in this world, hasn't my Liz," exclaimed the Sergeant, clearing his throat. "Lord bless you, she says all that to cheer me up in spite of her own trembling fears.

'Her true kn'ght in battle
    Too well doth she know,
Will ever be foremost
    Where thickest's the foe.'

And I'll be sworn when she wrote that she was crying out of very fright for fear I should be doing the very thing that she advises me to do. Look here, Mickey; do you see that watery blot—and that, and that—tears all of 'em—hem—ahem! Bless her; she talks about boldly meeting the foe, and striking nobly for the honour of the country I left behind me. Why if she had only seen us, Mickey, my boy, march up to those batteries on the heights of Alma, she'd have dropped all that striking bold talk, and fainted at the very idea of my walking up to meet that peppering storm of iron hail, eh? Aha! Sergeant Grey," he suddenly cried, as he caught sight of Clifton, "you never were more welcome than at this moment, Here's a long letter from Lizzie to me. It has been a deuced time coming, but it has found me at last. Here, take it, and read it out to us. I have read some of it, but not all; there is no secret in it, I know; and it will cheer your heart as well as mine to hear something from old England."

Clifton clutched at the letter, eagerly. Haverel was right; it did cheer his heart to read a letter from England, although there might not be a word in it which directly or by implication referred to him. Still there was an indescribable charm about news from home, even to him, isolated and lonely as he was, without a connection he could claim as his own, that made a communication greatly interesting, and with avidity he accepted the invitation to read it out.

It was not the first letter by several that Lizzie had written to Haverel, and, as in those already received, she had always addressed a few lines to Clifton, dictated in a grateful spirit for the succour he had afforded her in a moment of need; and as well in a hopeful strain, for she knew enough of his history to sympathise with his friendless condition, he regarded the arrival of an epistle from her with almost as much interest as did Haverel. Then she would tell him such news as she thought he might be pleased to hear, and banter him upon the ladye love he was to meet in one of the distant lands war took him to, who was to be a foreign princess at least. Her reasoning was plain, simple, and, in her own mind, conclusive; for, she said, she knew that there were such ladies of title as foreign princesses—the Sultan's daughter, for instance—and as a lady of such high rank always, of course, had her own way in everything, so she had it in the choice of her lover. Now the English troops could not fail of being very attractive to such eyes, and when they appeared in the foreign capital, drawn up in martial array, the foreign princesses, as a matter of course, came out to look at them. Then the thing was done. One of the loveliest would cast her eye upon Clifton—insist upon having him for her husband—and the end would be that she would elevate him to be a Grand Turk, which she thought much better than being, as most men were, a great Turk. Thus cheerfully would she communicate with him; and while she thanked him for his kind and brotherly counsel to her, endeavour to raise in him a hope that the day could not be far distant which would clear up the horizon he now found enveloped in clouds and mist; and so, as we have said, a letter from Lizzie was an event to him as well as to Haverel.

He seated himself, and began at the very commencement, in which Lizzie acknowledged the safe arrival of Haverel's last letter, and he went on with all the news;—how she had advanced in her business—and how she had been subject to the annoying importu-

nities of the puppy Beverley Winslow, even after the knock-down blow he had received from Clifton, to avoid which she had obtained another situation, in which she was happier, had shorter hours of labor, was treated with tenderness, and had a much higher salary—an announcement she was sure would prove satisfactory to Haverel—for it enabled her to do many little things she had at heart, and to put by as well a trifle for the time to which she trusted they both looked forward hopefully.

And then she proceeded to tell him pleasant things about his mother—how well she looked—and all she said—and, saving the care his absence in active warfare gave her, how happy she was. And then she went on to say that the absence of that same very careless and reckless individual gave her a share of uneasiness because she knew that he did not take all the care of himself he ought to do; so she counselled him to be thoughtful and prudent, but at the same time to remember that the eyes of England were upon him and his companions, that the Queen wept and prayed for them as she Lizzie did, and though it might break her heart to hear that he had fallen, yet never to forget that he was a son of England, and through all difficulties, and opposed to all odds, to help to maintain its honour, to strike boldly and nobly to sustain it, and though it might fill England with weeping women and aching hearts, to fall where he stood rather than bring disgrace on the proud land of his birth by giving way before the hordes of the northern barbarian.

A general hurrah burst from the lips of the three men as the repetition of her words fell from Clifton's lips. Although Haverel had read the passage out, and Dunigan had heard it, the bright tear glistened in both their eyes when it again came before them, and Clifton in strong terms expressed his warm admiration of the spirit by which she was directed and in which she had written.

Now, as he expected, came a passage in the letter addressed to him. As soon as he saw his name in her hand-writing, he felt as if he could have pressed her epistle to his lips. There was something to him so inexpressibly delightful in having a line—if it were only just a line—from some one far away, if it were only to shew that he was not so alone in the world but that one—humble she might be, true hearted nevertheless—thought it worth her while to write earnestly and pleasantly to him.

As before, Lizzie wrote to him in a cheerful strain, first thanking him for his own kind words in Haverel's letter to her, and promising to strive and make herself worthy his good opinion; then launching out into hopeful speculations for the future, and bidding him prepare himself for some great and wonderful revelation in respect to himself which Providence, who never deserted the good and handsome, had in store for him.

CAPTAIN WINSLOW AND MYRA.

And now came a passage which not a little startled him :

"If you have not yet been captured by a Turkish princess, and made a viceroy at least," wrote Lizzie to Clifton, "I wish you would wait until you come back from the Crimea, for there is a young lady I know of who far excels the most beautiful Eastern princess of them all. Her name is Aston, and she comes from Arundel"—

Clifton uttered a cry of astonishment, and gasped for breath. Stifling, however, his emotion, he read, with a rapidity which Haverel and Mickey Dunigan were wholly unable to follow, "I think, by the bye, you have been at Arundel, and perhaps you have seen her; if you have, you could not have looked on her without falling in love with her, for she has the most lovely face I ever saw, and she is so quiet and so kind. My cousin Lucy is her maid ; she is very rich, and would make you the most darling little wife in the world. Shall I speak a good word for you, and ask her to wait for your coming back, eh ? If you have seen her, don't write and tell me you don't think much of her, for I'll never believe you if you do. So please set her down as your wife that is to be."

There was more in the letter addressed to him, but nothing more about Myra ; three or four times he read it over, and cared little, in the frame of mind into which this passage wholly unexpectedly threw him, for what followed.

But Haverel did ; and after several fruitless efforts, he succeeded in getting the whole of it read, greatly to his comfort and delight, for it wound up by intimating to him that she Lizzie had the greatest trust in his memory of her, that although there must, she knew of necessity, be plenty of her sex in the foreign places he visited, young, pretty, and weak as respected soldiers, yet she believed heartily that he would not resign her for the best of them ; it is true she might not be so handsome in form, so pretty in face, so high in rank, or so wealthy, but she defied any of them to have a truer heart to love him more dearly than she did."

"For the best of them," iterated Haverel, taking back the letter from Clifton, "for any hundred of the best of them. She, my Lizzie, is handsomer in figure and more beautiful in face than any other woman in the world—"

"Axceptin' Bridget Boyle of Ballynacraggy, County Limerick," suggested Mickey Dunigan, mildly.

"The whole world!" cried Haverel, with emphasis, raising his voice, and at the same time enlarging the orbits beneath his brows :

"In your eyes, Haverel," exclaimed Clifton Grey, as if there was more than a remote possibility that he or any other person might entertain an opinion that the merits of another individual of the fair sex entitled them to a claim to the enviable distinction:

"Av coorse!" ejaculated Micky, complacently, as

he shut his eyes, and in his mental vision gloated on the beauties of the warm-hearted Irish girl he had left in Limerick.

"Without exception, and in everybody's eyes!" persisted Haverel.

"Say no more!" interrupted Clifton, "she deserves all that you can say or think of her—when do you write to her—by the next mail, of course? You must let me say a few words in your letter in reply to her jokes?"

"To be sure, Sergeant, but I shall have a long letter to write, for this has been such a devil of a while getting to me, that I have got to tell her all about the Alma and Inkermann, and lots of things. It strikes me, Grey, if you want to write to her—"

"Want to write? What do you mean, Haverel? Would you have me leave unanswered—?"

"No, no, no! I am sure you would not do that, but you had, I think, better write on your own paper, I mean a regular letter from you to her—and I can enclose it in mine, you know."

This was precisely what Clifton wished, for he had a series of instructions to give Lizzie, as well as a number of questions to ask—upon a subject which he did not exactly like should be discussed in another person's letter. Many reasons presented themselves to him why it should form the staple of a special communication, and he caught, with avidity, at the sergeant's offer ; notified to him that he accepted it, and that he should have his letter ready to despatch by the next mail.

"I rather think I shall, too," said Haverel, "for I shall begin to-morrow. I am not quick with the pen, but I've plenty of perseverance, and something else to back it when writing to her. So, Grey, be sure the mail will not go without my being beforehand with my letter ; aye, early enough to prevent the commander-in-chief, in one of his freaks, starting it a day before its time without my letter."

"An' av I could send a line to Bridget Boyle," said Mickey thoughtfully, "she'd tell the ould people that I'd been made a corporal bekase of the villin I've been, but—."

"! but what, Mickey ?" asked Clifton, as he paused."

"But you see," replied he, with some embarrassment of manner, "I'm slow with the pen. An' I could use it as I can my rifle, I'd have written to Brighidia ban mo Store long since, the Lord's my judge ! but then—oh ! the murdtherin' spalpeen I was when I wint to school. I turned me back on me larning, an' now its sarved me the same, an' turned its onmannered back on me. Oh, wirrasthru ! an' av we knew when we're boys what raparceing loses us when we're min, what incredible dacent boys we'd all be. Ah, thin, its bad for me, it is, and Bridget, too ; but God's goodt sure he'll raise up in her heart something good an' holy as will stand her instead of hearing from the ignorant ragabone Mickey Dunigan, although it goes to my heart, sore, not to let her know she's the bright flower of my soul. An' its die like a thafe of a dog I would sooner than make her heartache by letting her think I'd not got her sweet face ever before me like the brightest star in the dark blue heaven."

Mickey, shall I write for you?" asked Clifton, in a kindly tone, so as scarcely to make it appear an obligation, while he deprived the offer of anything approaching a sneer upon his ignorance.

"Mickey Dunigan placed his thin worn hand upon Clifton's arm and said:

" Shall you ever do anything for a poor boy like me, that isn't kind an' good, an' like a livin' saint. The Lord's blessing on you, sergeant, an' you wouldn't think me the unconscionable vagabone I am—always throublin' you—I 'ud say to you, av' all the favours you've done me, and the Lord knows the're many and weighty, were put in a heap, they would'nt, in my eyes, in my heart, in my soul, half equal that favour, av you'd do it, av writin' to my—my— colleen dhas—my —my—musher, its a babby I am!"

The poor fellow covered his face with his two hands, and, for a minute, sobbed like a child. Clifton placed his hand kindly upon his shoulder and said :

"Mickey, my friend, you know that I have no relatives, no friends in the wide world but such as I can make by little attentions and services, which cost me neither exertion nor inconvenience, and which yield me satisfaction and pleasure. The obligation is therefore all mine. So think no more about it, but get together in your head all you want to say to your friends at home, and I'll come when off duty and write it for you, and mail it, so that it will reach its destination safely."

"God's blessing on you, Sergeant Grey," cried Mickey fervently; "its the load you've taken off my soul entirely. Oh, I'll be on duty again afore the week's out. Oh, its my heart's that light as a feather flake—whoop! Ha, ha! An' I see the dear an' shadowless face of my Bridget a readin' my letter, an' a laffing and a cryin', an' a sayin' 'the poor boy has'nt forgotten us. Ah, mother, darlin', an' the villin's a full corporal, he is—an' we'll get the good praste to write to him for us.' An' I shall get the letter from Bridget, an' you'll read it to me, sergeant, an' its oh I shall be burstin' wid joy; till the colonel 'ull say that's not Mickey Dunigan; sure an' its some roorin' turkey-cock dressed in his clothes a strutting about."

"Bravo, Mickey," cried Haverel, "I like the man who thinks of and is true to the girl he left behind him. Aha! Grey, you may rub your hands now and sing—

'Thus, thus, I'd play the enchanter's part,
And scatter bliss around ;
Till not a tear or aching heart
Should in the world be found'—

at least where you are."

Clifton turned the conversation, which was becoming embarrassing to him, by relating what had occurred at head quarters, and the honor he had received at the hands of Lord Raglan.

"Ah, I see," said Sergeant Haverel. "I'm a prophet, in spite of myself. Do you remember, Grey, when I enlisted you?"

"As well as if it were yesterday," he replied.

"And so do I. I told you, although I honestly confess that I thought myself then merely pitching palaver, that—"

"I should say it was a lucky moment when I met Sergeant Haverel ; he chose the path for me to win fortune, and a bright and honorable name," interrupted Clifton Grey. "You see, Haverel, I have not forgotten it. I had occasion to be struck by the words. They tallied with a resolution I then formed, and if I am not struck down by a Russian bullet I will win that bright and honorable name—"

"And be a general," cried Haverel, slapping his thigh.

"An' av the Lord spares me I'll follow you to the world's end, av you have to go there," cried Mickey Dunigan.

Clifton laughed, and then once more changed the subject. He exerted himself by an apparent flow of spirits to work them into a high degree of cheerfulness, and so far succeeded, that when the moment came for him to leave them for his dangerous and prostrating duty in the trenches, they were singing one against the other snatches of songs, sufficiently joyous and boisterous for an assistant surgeon to interfere, though in a pleasant spirit, and tell them if they continued their festivity in such lusty tones he should report them fit for duty, and bundle them out of the hospital tent.

Clifton hurried up to his tent; the hours for duty had arrived, and this night all the available men belonging to the guards were marched off to labor at the trenches—rather to repel a sortie expected that night in force. But it was something terrible to see, out of the strength which had landed in the Crimea, how few were left. It was absolutely horrifying to look upon the proportion of men yet styled effective. They were thin, gaunt, pale, fagged in their appearance, hollow-eyed, and pinched in the cheeks ; but they bore themselves bravely, and though many of them were ready to sink under the weight of their rifles, yet they breathed not a murmur—not one complaining murmur ; they knew what their country expected of them, and while a frail thread of life hung together there, they prepared to do it or die in the effort.

Noble fellows! Well may their queen display the interest she has throughout evinced ; they have deserved all the kindness, the womanly tenderness and sympathy which to her immortal honour she has so freely and so happily rendered to them!

The First Division, the very flower of the magnificent army, was at this time broken up. His Royal Highness the Duke of Cambridge, overcome by his anxieties and by his sense of the enormous responsibility imposed upon him, his naturally kind heart afflicted by the fearful losses his brigade had suffered by sickness as well as by the devastation of war, broke down; his mind gave way; his bodily health was prostrated, and he was borne on board the Retribution so ill as not to be expected to survive. The command of the Brigade devolved upon Colonel Upton, who exerted himself to the very utmost to stay the ravages, which, from the most reprehensible mismanagement, the soldiers were victims to. At the same time, conscious of what depended upon the bravery and endurance of the handful of men left, he felt compelled to call upon the energies of those able to perform their duties, and to tax them far more than would have been required if there had not been one half of the British army at that moment *hors de combat.*

Clifton Grey knew this, and sought to impress it on the men by a course of remarks which had the effect of inducing them to meet the extra demand upon their powers by cheerful and even eager efforts to make their individual exertions compensate for the miserable want of force for the magnitude of the task undertaken.

On this night rain, rain, rain; mud every where; cold, black, bleak, blowing, gusty—the most wretched dispiriting night men could have for any enterprise, the men set forth to their posts in the dykes, for such had the trenches become, with their usual undaunted courage—their unfailing chivalrous spirit, with a smile or a joke, though neither knew that himself or the man to whom he was speaking would return to quarters again. Up to the knees in mud, up to the waist in water, if a slip drew an oath, it was accompanied by a laugh. Want of warm or waterproof clothing—even a renewal of the garments destroyed by the war or the elements, or both, served to furnish food for mirth and pleasantry, though, at the same time, it helped to a grim spirit of determination to pay the piper on the Russians when they came in contact with them.

And on this night that opportunity was afforded to them—in truth it was seldom that it was not, for the Russian generals attached much to the harass they believed they inflicted by incessant sorties from their outworks upon the troops of the allies in the advanced parallels. They hoped to destroy faster than reinforcements arrived, and to call so constantly and so largely upon the energies of the foe, that they would be reduced to a state of comparative exhaustion, and become at a certain period an easy prey to an overwhelming force they would pour upon them. They under-estimated the energy and the resources of the two nations opposed to them, but they persevered in their tactics based upon them.

The men were marched down, in charge of Captain Astly, in front of the left attack, where there was an earthwork thrown up for infantry. This ran down towards the ravine, which here becomes a continuation of the military harbour of Sebastopol, dividing the civil from the military town, and this was marked as the boundary between the English and French positions.

The outlying pickets were posted so that the most advanced sentry of each nation was in communication with each other—that is, had been, when men were plenty and the boundary was first traced, but since battle and distemper had reduced both, a wide space of ground became unprotected, and the Russians, who appear to have been kept well informed by their spies, became acquainted with this piece of inattention, which, like so many other examples of a similar kind, was committed at the price of many valuable lives.

On this night, pitch dark, a heavy rain, rendered more violent by a gusty wind, a large body of Russians stole into this undefended space, and proceeding rapidly to the left, came upon the sentry nearest to the open spot before he was prepared for them; he was bayonetted, and they penetrated to the earthwork before it was discovered that the advancing troops were Russians. At first it was supposed that a French picket had overshot its mark, because exclamations in that language were uttered by the Muscovite leaders rather loudly. It was soon found that a terrible mistake had been made. The Russians commenced the work of slaughter before their adversaries were prepared to resist, and killed and wounded a number of men, captured three officers and a dozen men, ere an arm was raised to repel them or an alarm given. A party of the 34th were at hand, however, and drove them out of the earthwork, but, largely reinforced, they returned to the charge. It was at this moment that the men under Captain Astly came up, and a desperate struggle at once ensued, hand to hand, sword to sword, bayonet to bayonet, men fell on both sides, killed and wounded; some were captured and forced to the rear by both parties. Captain Astly, a man of large proportions, and of undaunted courage, fought like a lion, not only performing deeds equal to anything yet recorded in the annals of chivalry, but by his voice and gestures animating his men to emulate his own actions.

In his desperate efforts to repulse the enemy, his ardour carried him too far; he was surrounded and beaten to the earth; he would inevitably have been despatched or made prisoner, badly wounded, but that Clifton Grey, seeing his danger, rushed to his aid, shot one of his assailants, bayoneted another, and with the butt end of his musket felled a third; several of his comrades came rushing up at the same instant, for Captain Astly had won by his kindness and consideration for those under him the gratitude and attachment of his men, and, lifting him to his feet, they bore him away in safety until he recovered himself sufficiently to renew the charge. Waving his sword, and using his lusty lungs and his rapid feet, he led on a body of the men who had fallen back to reload. They swept the Russians before them, driving them down the ravine helter skelter, and halting only when it became a needless wooing of death to proceed nearer to the Russian batteries. Then they slowly returned to their earthwork to gather up their wounded and to bury their dead.

On marching back to camp the following morning, Captain Astly, after the men were dismissed, called Clifton Grey to his tent.

"Grey," said he, "but for your promptitude and courage, I should have been in that happy land where so many of our gallant fellows have gone before us. Although it seems a paradox to be thankful for being prevented journeying to those realms of felicity, it becomes more natural to be so, when I unhesitatingly assert that I am not so tired of my sublunary berth as to be anxious to change even the Crimea for Paradise. If you will, therefore accept this watch, the gift of a sister very dear to me, for remembrance of what has taken place last night, you will only add to the obligation. At the same time, if you at any future period can shew me how I may advance your interests, you have only to mention the affair of the ravine, and I will do my utmost to further your views."

Clifton refused the proffered present, but Captain Astly forced it upon him, and not needlessly to prolong a discussion embarrassing to him he accepted the gift — a very beautiful and valuable gold watch, at the same time he mentioned to the captain the flattering promise held out to him by Lord Raglan, and the hopes of advancement he entertained from it.

"His lordship will keep his word," exclaimed Captain Astly, "be assured of that. Be also assured, my dear Grey, that when you obtain your commission, one of the first to welcome and support you in your new sphere shall be Jack Astly, and let me see the man who in my presence offers you the cold shoulder."

Clifton much moved, thanked him with warmth, and retired to his tent.

There was a break in the clouds. He had heard of Myra, should probably hear from her; he had before him, almost within his grasp, the commission which would entitle him to the position to which he aspired. If it should please God only to spare him through the campaign, the bright side of the picture of life might yet be turned towards him, and he be a prominent object in it.

He drew his thin, worn, soiled blanket over him as he lay on the hard—hard ground, and with a peaceful, grateful heart, a smiling face, and happy visions, sunk into a sound slumber, while the heavy siege guns were booming, and the cracking rifles, the rolling muskets were dealing death near him, in front of and in Sebastopol.

CHAPTER XXII.

" Smack went the whip, round went the wheels,
    Were never folk so glad ;
The stones did rattle underneath,
    As if Cheapside were mad.
                                          *   *   *
That trot became a gallop soon.
                                          *   *   *
The dogs did bark, the children scream'd,
    Up flew the windows all ;
And every soul cried out—
                                          *   *   *
'Stop thief! stop thief!—a highwayman !'
    Not one of them was mute ;
And all and each that pass'd that way
    Did join in the pursuit."
                                          COWPER.

" Lara.—Be calm ; I will not harm you.
  Precious.—Because you dare not.
  Lara.—I dare anything !
Therefore beware ! you are deceived in me.
In this false world we do not always know
Who are our friends and who our enemies.
We all have enemies, and all need friends."
                                          LONGFELLOW.

THE steamer which bore Myra and Lizzie had not for its port of destination the comparatively near one Southampton, but the longer one London. That part of the journey, occupied by their throbbing anxious perusal of the fearful list of killed and wounded published in *The Times*, together with scraps and paragraphs of information relative to the battle and the war, passed over quick enough; but when their inspection was ended, and they were left only to communicate their speculations to each other, and to indulge in imaginings not of a very hopeful character, their passage began to grow long and wearisome to them. To add to its duration, they were encountered by a strong dead head wind, which not only rendered a seat upon deck extremely unpleasant, but almost impossible; and, therefore, they had to seek the close atmosphere of the cabin, where there was little to distract their attention from their foreboding thoughts, or to relieve the monotony of the voyage. Occasionally they heard remarks upon the battle which had recently occurred, and in which they were so deeply interested, and they listened with avidity to recitals of incidents happening in the engagement recorded in the various daily journals, but they heard not a word which coupled with the brilliant success or the many martial achivements the names of Clifton Grey or Sergeant Haverel. Neither had the heart to ask a question respecting them, but they could not help feeling considerable disappointment at not meeting with their names either in verbal statements or in the communications made by the special correspondents in the Crimea to their respective journals, or in consequence of entertaining despondent thoughts—sickening fears that some after publication would give, among the killed, those whose names they would shriek to meet in the list.

The fierceness of the contrary wind rendered their passage unusually severe and long, and it was not until ten o'clock the following morning that they reached the Custom House, London. What a welcome sight was the busy Pool; the Tower of London; the thronged London Bridge, with its swarm of foot passengers and vehicles passing to and fro. What a sense of security did the active life-thronging wharfs present. How sick at heart, how anxious Myra felt to be at home with her mother. What dread thoughts presented themselves of terrible results her absence might have produced. How glad she would be once more to fold her in her arms, and assure her of her own safety and immunity from harm; and also to satisfy herself that beyond mere fright and apprehension, her mother had sustained no harm. The captain of the steamer, who had behaved with great kindness and attention to them, now sent one of the crew with them to see them safely into a cab, and give the driver proper directions where to convey them. A cabstand close to the Monument was soon gained, and an active cabman ran up on suspicion of being required. He was at once hired; but before the seaman could give him the necessary directions, he suddenly delivered himself of a sharp whistle, and exclaimed:

"Well, I am blessed! Here's a go! You want to go to Baker-street?"

"Yes," said the sailor.

"A' course you do—I know'd both the young ladies the werry instant I clapped my precious eyes upon 'em."

Both Myra and Lizzie looked at the man with surprise on hearing his remarks.

"Look here?" said he, addressing them. "Didn't you a few nights ago hail me and ax me if I'd brought you from Baker-street, and took me for a kebbo who'd got the best on you to the tune of eight bob?"

"Are you the man who directed us to St. Paul's Church Yard?" responded Lizzie, by asking a question.

"The werry same, s'ep my golla; it's all right; there's been such a fillalloo after you—bobbies, detectives, and I can't tell you what. They're nabbed the cove who welled your tin; but he couldn't tell 'em nothink, but that he'd set you down, an' waited until he was tired, and so he druv off. But that bird wouldn't fight, so he's in quod, as I heerd; but there's a good reward hoffered for you both, for its bee'n feared you've been g'rotted and taken off to a 'orspittle for resurrection. But its all right now, I see. Jump in, ladies, an' I'll have you up to Baker-street in two two's. I've a nag as can step along when I puts him to it, and I strongly 'specks that this 'll be for me as good a day's work as hever I did do."

The whole of this speech, which was uttered with the greatest volubility, and with an amazing amount of excitement, was hardly completed before he almost pushed both girls into his cab—he would scarcely wait while Myra gave the seamen, who had escorted them to the cab, a gratuity, but sprung on to the box, and whipping up his horse—which did not belie the good character he had given it—dashed up Adelaide-street and along Cannon-street at a pace which induced a city constable to whip out his note book and make a memorandum, to the effect that the driver of the cab, No. 6009, would be required on a certain day to attend at the Mansion-House, to answer a charge preferred against him for furious driving. Before, however, this mem. was finished, the constable discovered that he had put down four O's, and for the life of him could not recollect whether the number was 6009, or 9006, or 9060, or 6000, after puzzling himself—for the cab was out of sight—he scratched his head and scratched out the mem., looking sharp out for another cab to make up for the error which had robbed him of a case.

On went 6009, bumping, swaying, now on two wheels, then on four, now grating the curb-stones, by-and-bye in the middle of the road, now full tear down Skinner-street, anon at full gallop up Holborn-hill. Here is Holborn bars, there Day and Martin's, whisk past Tottenham-court-road, in and out of the way of omnibuses now scraping a wheel with sufficient violence to make a 'bus driver look fierce and use bad language, anon crossing a wealthy merchant's horses as he drove in his mail-phaeton to business, so that he was obliged to pull them up on their haunches so short as nearly to strangle them, and to make him insist on John's jumping down and taking "that —— cab's number," which John obeys, but 6009 is too far off to see it, and he returns saying ing it is 1748, intending when the mistake is found out to declare he meant the badge instead of the plate, or vice versâ, as the case might require. Now Regent Circus is gained—slow round doth 6009, and gallops up until he reaches Mortimer-street, round which he swings and upsets a donkey and vehicle laden with market produce. In an instant the street is carpeted with potatoes, greens, scarlet beans, cauliflowers, winter spinnach, apples, nuts, &c., upon which a party of small boys go in for a scramble. One stout woman with a basket of linen is down in the mud, tripped up in her efforts to get out of the way of the cab, and the contents of the basket are fairly divided between the street, the pathway, an open area, and the air; and as a high wind is still blowing, some night-caps, having filled, are level with first-floor windows, accompanied by a pocket-handkerchief or two and some lace sleeves, the whole performing a reel, or whirling here and there in frantic gyrations.

But regardless of all, 6009 pursues his frenzied career, not, however, unattended, for a stout policeman, nine men—some with no business anywhere, and others with no business there—eight boys of varying respectability, five confirmed ragged blackguards, three women, a few children in the extreme rear, and some mongrel barking curs, who persisted in getting in the way of the pursuers, trotted after him, at first rapidly, but gradually settling down into a steady determined run, which no distance could knock up, keeping on, resolved never to stop until they had run the chase down.

This queue was, however, not in sight when 6000 arrived at the residence of Mr. Randolph. He dashed up to the door, and then pulling up his reeking and panting steed dead short, gave his jolted, tumbled, exhausted, and affrighted fare a momentary rest. In a moment he was off his box, and seized the knocker—rap, rap, rap, rap, r-r-r-r-r-ap resounded through the street, and might have been heard at St. John's Wood. The man-servant was trying a little pea-soup at the instant, scalding hot, and the suddenness of the summons caused him to leap off his feet and jerk about half-a-pint of the burning fluid down his throat, and empty the rest of the contents of the basin into his bosom, where the warmth of its presence was as immediately recognised as when taken inwardly. The knock had, however, alarmed the whole house, and despite his suffering and discoloured aspect, the man was compelled to rush to the door, raising, as he went, a steaming fragrance of pea-soup along the hall which threatened to scent the entire fabric. When he opened the door he found the cabman standing cap-in-hand, a cab at the curb, from the horse in which ascended wreaths of steam that obscured the opposite side of the way. He stared with surprise.

"I have brought 'ome the young ladies as was lost," said the cabman, in a tone in which excitement struggled with an effort to appear calm.

"What!" shouted the footman, extending his eye-balls, already somewhat stretched by the scalding soup, and catching a glimpse of Myra and Lizzie in the cab, he hallooed, "I'm blow'd if it aint, too!"

He darted to the foot of the stairs and yelled out: "Master! Sir! Missus! Ma'am! Young missuses! The young ladies 'ave come 'ome: they're come back, sir, and no mistake!"

Feet in the room above might have been heard rushing with speed. Pr-r-r-r-rew came a pair with swiftness down the stairs. It was Lucy. She flew along the passage and was at the door of the cab in an instant.

"Oh! miss!" she said, as she wrenched open the door; "Oh! cousin Lizzie!" and she burst into tears as she assisted them out of the cab.

In the hall, assembled, they met Mrs. Aston, who caught Myra in her arms and sobbed as though her heart would break, Mr. and Mrs. Randolph, Everett, and his two sisters, all making exclamations and uttering welcomes, electrifying and bewildering Lizzie with questions, who, pale as a sheet, was unable to utter a word.

At this moment a low hoarse murmur was heard,

as of an advancing tumult, and the cabman suddenly shot into the hall. He addressed himself to Mr. Randolph anxiously.

"Here, governor!" said he, "I vants a visper vith you."

"In a moment," said Mr. Randolph, who looked upon it as an intimation that he was about to claim the reward—one which he was only too willing to pay, as soon as he was convinced that the claimant was fairly entitled to it.

"Look sharp, good luck to you!" exclaimed the cabman, having just hurried from a position from which he could command a good view down the street, which Mr. Randolph had not.

"Don't be in a hurry, my good fellow," said Mr. Randolph, preparing to follow his family and the estrays into the drawing-room.

"Volker!" exclaimed the cabman urgently. "I shall vant your purtection, owin' to bringing them two young ladies 'ome."

"Protection! What do you mean, my man?"

Before the cabman could answer the approaching uproar became so great as to attract Mr. Randolph's attention, and to his great astonishment there paused before his door a huge mob.

How it had grown! There were three frightfully excited policemen, some forty or fifty men, some twenty or thirty boys, a troop of dirty women and girls, and a small army of children, clustering round the doorway. One active policeman instantly seized the quiet cab-horse, and the other two darted into the hall and pounced upon the cabman. In one moment such a clamour of voices arose in the hall, that Mr. Randolph was stunned and bewildered. The policemen commenced dragging the cabman away, but he clung to Mr. Randolph. They shouted to him to come on, and he hallooed to them to keep off; while Mr. Randolph, roaring at the top of his voice, asked what it all meant, and after becoming in a state of red heat with exertion, he began to obtain something like a lull, with the chance of an explanation, when the peripatetic greengrocer, absolutely frantic at the dispersion of his goods, appeared on the scene. Then the abating uproar increased again to a perfect hurricane of voices, these without adding to it by shouts and whistling, which gave the whole scene anything but a respectable aspect. The greengrocer had given himself up to an idea of fistic retaliation, and it was with great difficulty that one of the policemen could prevent him flinging himself upon the cabman, who, attended by Mr. Randolph, to whom he clung tightly, was dragged all over the hall by the policeman. The bankrupt greengrocer gave out incessant invitations to the cab-driver to come outside and be smashed, and Mr. Randolph was repeatedly requested to make one of the party. At length exhaustion prevailed, and Mr. Randolph succeeded in clearing his hall of all but the policemen, the cab driver, the greengrocer, and the washerwoman, who had just arrived, and was speedily the most clamorous of the lot. He took them into the parlour, gave the greengrocer more than twice the amount of the loss he had sustained; and, no easy task, satisfied the immoderate washerwoman, whose accident was the result of her own stupidity; took upon himself to produce the cabman, should any charge of furious driving be made against him, and so got rid of the policemen; gave the cabman the promised reward—a handsome sum, which he said would enable him to buy a cab and "Purwide for his missus and kids"—and at last succeeded in restoring his house to its wonted quiet.

He sought the drawing-room, and there, from Myra, obtained a brief narrative of the events which had occurred. He left her to seek repose after the fatigue she had endured, Lucy being instructed already to take care of Lizzie Hastings, of whom Myra had spoken in terms of the highest character, while he proceeded to Woolwich to see if the brig which had taken Saul Waters on board as a prisoner had reached there, and if so, to at once prefer the charge of abduction against him, in order, by conviction and transportation, to prevent him from ever repeating the offence again.

Myra soon recovered her health and strength again, perhaps because she had obtained a clue to Clifton Grey, and there was a prospect of communicating with him through Lizzie's letters to Sergeant Haverel. She had told, without disguise, her mother, the reason she had left Baker-street on the eventful night when she was captured by Saul Waters, and her mother, without comment, handed to her the letters which had occasioned for the time so much unhappiness. Mrs. Aston feared to enter into explanations with Myra; She would much rather have it appear she attached no particular importance to the impression Myra had displayed in Clifton's favour, hoping that a non-interference, absence, and other faces, might efface it; when, by a declared hostility, she should probably found an antagonism that would serve to strengthen the attachment rather than diminish it, and precipitate matters she wished to avoid. So Myra was left unmolested to hope and expect whatever she pleased. Her mother had but a faint notion how passionately and enduringly she loved Clifton, and how she nursed herself in the hope of being some day his—his only, in poverty or wealth, she cared not which, so that she was his, or she might have pursued a different course.

Lizzie Hastings expected daily a letter from Sergeant Haverel, and as in her last communication she had written to Clifton, she was quite sure she should have an answer from him in Haverel's letter to her. How anxiously Myra anticipated and prayed it coming, for the reply to it would let Clifton know where to communicate to her if he felt disposed, and she thought he was so inclined; she knew, she felt he must be. Lizzie had been received back by Mrs. Stewart upon an explanation tendered to her by Mr. Randolph of the circumstances attending her

compulsory absence, but Myra would not allow her to pass an evening without paying her a visit, or if too busy to come out, without sending Lucy to learn if a letter from the Crimea had reached her.

Beverley Winslow had been one of the first to welcome her back and express his "wage at the wascality of wuffians pwowling in wetiwed stweets to wob or wemove for outwageous pu'poses wespectable young ladies." He would have made himself very amiable to her, but she coolly repulsed him, and was so marked in her treatment of him, that both Isadore and Sophie Randolph questioned her whether Beverley Winslow had offended her; she replied in terms which led them to understand that she had a low estimate of his sense, and a lower one of his morals. They had thought him a mere fool, and as they believed that Myra had some deeper motive for her contempt than she had disclosed, they extended the cold shade to him too, so that he seldom came near the house after he detected that his presence was not hailed with signs of felicity.

And now arrived news of the battle of Inkermann. Again was the terrible list, published in the daily journals from the Gazette, carefully examined. Myra found not the name of Clifton Grey, after the most careful search, but she did that of Sergeant Haverel among the dangerously wounded. That night Lizzie sought her, and as soon as she was alone with her, gave way to a paroxysm of grief, which Myra tried to assuage by all the consoling speculations she could suggest.

"If I were only there," sobbed Lizzie, "to be by his side, to tend him night and day, to relieve him from pain, and supply the wants which in his helpless condition he will need, and which there will be no one to think of or provide him with! He will die in that horrible place, I know—I feel he will die, for he will get no help there."

Myra soothed her, and after talking earnestly with her, brought her into a calmer state of mind.

"He is not dead," she said, "and the name of Mr. Grey does not appear among the wounded; he will therefore, I am sure, act like a friend to him, and do all he can in his terrible state to help him."

"God bless him! I know he will—but if I were there, oh,—if I only were there, I could save him—I know I could."

And she sobbed, and drew pictures of his agony and suffering until she was almost choked with grief. Yet Myra's gentle soothings ultimately prevailed, and she went home to pray that he might recover from the injuries he had received from the Russians, whom she hated now more than ever.

Some time passed on, but there was no letter from the Crimea, and Lizzie grew very desponding—Myra very sad. One day Everett Randolph mentioned that Beverley Winslow had a brother who had just arrived from the Crimea, who had been invalided home.

LETTERS FROM THE CRIMEA.

"Oh!" cried Isadore, "how I should like to see him. Has he been wounded, and does he look pale and interesting?—if he does, bring him here to let us see him."

As every one of the family expressed a wish to see and converse with one who had been in the Crimea, Everett was easily prevailed upon to promise to bring Capt. Winslow home with him to a family tête-à-tête. Myra, who heard all that passed, resolved to be present to learn if something might transpire about Clifton; if it were improbable, still it was possible, so she resolved not to be away.

A few days subsequently, Everett mentioned that he had invited Captain Winslow and a brother officer, both invalided from the Crimea, to visit the family that evening; so Myra took care to be present about the time the guests were expected. At eight o'clock, Beverley Winslow, who felt himself immensely important since the return of his "bwother fwom the Cwimea," arrived, accompanied by Captain Winslow and Captain Mandeville, who had formed a close intimacy with him on their way home, and they were received with marked distinction. Captain Winslow's eye fell at once upon Myra. Notwithstanding Sophie and Isadore Randolph were both pretty girls, yet Myra's was a face which is rarely seen, and invariably eminently attractive wherever it appears. She was pale and delicate looking; her large resplendent eyes were thoughtful and sorrowful in their expression, and there was something so spiritual in her appearance that it was not possible to treat her like even one of the fairer members of her sex. Captain Winslow saw and was enslaved. He had fancied himself into a passion for Sylva at Malta, where he had stopped on his way home, but finding that she was in London, he had hastened thither. Her beauty paled before that of Myra—her reign ceased—she was deposed; he concluded Myra to have wealth, he resolved to have her and her portion. He soon became studiously attentive and obsequious to her, but she as immediately conceived a repugnance for him. She glanced at his sallow face—his furtive eye was enough for her; she read his character, and despised him.

Many questions were put to him about the war, which he answered, but with caution, for greatly to his annoyance his companion, Captain Mandeville, knew too much of the share he had not had in the battles and skirmishes already fought, for him to utter those lies which he would otherwise have unscrupulously indulged in. In Myra's mind all this time Clifton Grey was uppermost, upon her lip trembled his name, when suddenly her mother, as though she divined her secret thought, said to Captain Winslow—

"Permit me a question, Captain. I was much interested in a young—gentleman, I believe I may call him, who, under particular—nay, very peculiar circumstances, enlisted in the army. He promised to write to me, but has not; I should like, however, to learn something about him."

"What regiment did he enlist into?" enquired Captain Winslow, with a smile at the probable absurdity of her question.

"I cannot tell you," she replied.

It was on the tip of Myra's tongue to mention it, but she remained silent.

"His name," continued Mrs. Aston, "is Grey."

Captain Winslow started, as if bitten by a snake.

"Grey!" he exclaimed, turning red. "Grey!— there was a young fellow of that name, but he turned out a coward and a scamp. He has been either drummed out of his regiment or shot before this."

There was a malignant brutality in this reply which did not carry conviction to the listeners.

Myra felt as if nothing but a tremendous call upon her energies could keep her from fainting. It could not be true; but if it were, horror!

"Softly, Winslow," interposed Captain Mandeville. "I, too, know a young fellow named Grey, who is now in the Crimea. Do not let us confound persons."

"Really, I presume we have something more agreeable to say to the ladies than to talk of mere privates— common fellows, of whom, so far as my experience goes, the least said the better," interrupted Captain Winslow, hastily.

"Common fellows!" exclaimed Captain Mandeville, "who have won for England her proud name among nations. Let us have justice done them, if you please, Winslow; and with respect to Grey, Mrs. Aston asked you a question, which you have answered to the best of your knowledge. I, too, will answer it, for, as I have said, I, too, know a Grey, and my man may be the young fellow about whom she is questioning. My Grey is in the second battalion of the Scots Fusilier Guards."

"That is the regiment!" exclaimed Myra, with involuntary earnestness. The eyes of all were turned upon her—she had spoken with such emphasis. Captain Winslow felt cold blood about his heart. Was Grey to step in here, too, between him and his object? He became deeply interested in what followed.

"Then you will be gratified to hear of his progress, I expect," exclaimed Captain Mandeville, who had noticed her earnest manner. "His name is Clifton Grey."

"The same," exclaimed Mrs. Aston.

"Well then, ma'am, permit me to tell you he was looked upon as the smartest and most gentlemanly man in the ranks—indeed his comrades called him Gentlema . Grey—he bore a very high character for attention and sobriety with his officers, of kindness and general good offices with his comrades. He fought nobly and chivalrously at the battle of the Alma, for which he was promoted from the ranks to be sergeant, by his Royal Highness the Duke of

Cambridge; he saved the life of an officer—a dear friend of mine—who is enthusiastic in his praise. He fought with the most unflinching bravery throughout the dreadful day at Inkermann. He has never been absent from duty; and if it pleases the Almighty to spare a man who has been in the most dangerous and fearful engagements unscathed, he will receive a commission from Her Majesty, to which he will be well entitled."

"What a noble fellow!" cried all there but Myra—for her heart was full—and Captain Winslow, who hated Grey yet more than ever for this eulogium, which he could not disprove.

"He is a noble fellow!" ejaculated Captain Mandeville, "and Winslow can bear out my statement; for he is a captain of the very regiment to which young Grey belongs; he must know that I have rather underrated than over-estimated him."

"I should be sorry to lower Mrs. Aston's favorable opinion of him," said Captain Winslow, with a slight laugh, "but really, though there is some apparent truth in what you have said, I know the fellow to be so artful—to have such secret sins—that I cannot join in his praise if I would. He would deceive the very devil himself. The truth is, he is a blackguard, with a fair face and smooth tongue, and, mark my words, will meet with his deserts before long."

"I believe he will," said Captain Mandeville, drily. "I believe, too, that you have seen in this matter farther than you can justify: however, I may say, that hitherto this young man, in whom Mrs. Aston confesses herself interested, has won as yet only praise of a very high character. When the blame is clearly known, to be deserved, then we will condemn him; until then, let us give him the benefit of what he seems so well to deserve. You understand, Winslow," added Captain Mandeville after a moment's thought, "I can have no motive in defending the character of this young man in his absence, but that which induces any man possessed of honourable feelings to be commonly honest when called upon to speak of another of whom he has some knowledge."

"Possibly," remarked Captain Winslow, coolly.

"Personally, I know but little of him."

"Pray let us change the subject," cried Captain Winslow, "I am sick of the fellow's name. You, Mandeville, speak from hearsay, I—from absolute knowledge of his cunning and knavery. I am sure, too, we shall be able to furnish topics of conversation far more pleasing to the ear of Miss Aston than this."

Never was he so mistaken in his life.

A few days after this, Captain Winslow called in Baker-street. Mrs. Aston, on law business, was at Lincoln's Inn with Mr. Randolph; Mrs. Randolph and her daughters were at the Botanical Gardens, Regent's-Park. Myra was at home alone, she preferred it to accompanying either her mother or her

friends. A letter might come from the Crimea at any hour; Lizzie was certain to bring it to her immediately she received it. Myra had an inkling that her mother would in some way interpose between her and its perusal, and though she did not desire to act in opposition to any expressed wish of her parent, she saw nothing wrong in fulfilling her own wish in a particular direction, so long as her mother refrained expressing herself upon it; so it was pleasanter to her to be at home, with the chance of arrival of the letter, than to be stifled in heated law offices, or inhaling the fragrant perfumes of wonderful examples of modern floriculture at the Botanical Gardens. So she remained at home.

Captain Winslow, on hearing from the footman that Mr. Randolph and family were out, inquired whether Miss Aston was at home, and was answered that she was then in the drawing room. He expressed a desire to see her, and with a *nonchalance* which compelled the footman to succumb, he expressed his intention of having an interview with her, and of announcing himself. The man bowed, and the captain skipped up the stairs, tapped gently at the door, and then opening it, entered the room, and closed it behind him.

Myra was there. She was perusing a much creased and often handled letter. She started and uttered a faint exclamation on seeing Captain Winslow, at the same moment rapidly put the letter into the pocket of her dress. Said Captain Winslow to himself. "That epistle was being perused in secret, doubtless from a man. I must learn, if possible, more about that—some infernal agreeable young vagabond, of course." He was jealous already.

He bowed with an air of excessive politeness, almost of reverence, to Myra, and then, advancing, said, with studied amiability of manner:

"I have a thousand apologies, Miss Aston, to make for thus intruding upon you unannounced, but the truth is, I wished much to speak with you, and as I learned you were alone, I feared that if I deferred to the usual courtesy you might, out of mere formal etiquette, deprive me of the desired gratification. There are cases, you know, my dear Miss Aston, in which the cold forms of politeness may be dispensed with, and I trust this is one, nay, I may say it is one. We old soldiers understand these matters better than you fair demoiselles, so I am an authority, and really, if that were not the case, the generous British public have been so lavish of favour to us Crimean fellows, that we may be pardoned if we stretch a freedom into a privilege."

"Crimean heroes are entitled to privileges to which Crimean fellows can surely have no claim. I am afraid, Captain Winslow, you are dealing in misnomers, and wrong yourself."

Captain Winslow bit his lip almost until the blood came; a tinge of scarlet, not often seen there, appeared on his sallow countenance. Myra spoke with emphasis, and he felt the sarcasm; he knew himself to be no Crimean hero; he believed that she knew so too; and hence her remark. He could see she did not approve his intrusion; her countenance did not, decidedly, express satisfaction at his presence; but truly it was very beautiful, even in its present almost scornful aspect, and roused his worst, as well as his best passions.

He had never loved before. Woman hitherto had been his toy—his plaything for the baser amusement of his idle hours; he measured the members of the sex with whom he came in contact not for what was estimable or loveable in them, but for the beauty of face and form which lent a zest to his libertine appetite. He had frequently spent labour, time, and money in accomplishing the ruin of some handsome girl who had caught his fancy, and had exerted himself in order to effect his purpose, to persuade her that he loved her; this was but one of the lies employed; he cared for or loved no one but himself. He had played the profligate and heartless scoundrel many times, and hitherto had escaped its consequences; now, even, he only fancied his taste was slightly captivated, not his heart enslaved. He congratulated himself upon the ease with which he had banished Sylva from his mind. He deceived himself into the belief that he was smitten with her, and she was connected with large properties to which he was making claim. His original idea had been to marry her; now it assumed another form; he liked Myra best, and, unlike the first impressions raised by other women, that which struck him on seeing Myra was connected solely with a matrimonial alliance; and this grew upon him not only while in her society, but after he had quitted it. He was even now prepared to lay his fortune, with his hand, at her feet, should an *éclaircissement* occur.

This is a somewhat long digression, but necessary to show that the observation made by Myra cut Captain Winslow to the quick, because he naturally was most anxious to stand well in her eyes; but he interpreted her meaning to be, that not being a Crimean hero, he was, as he had himself expressed it, a Crimean fellow, and disentitled to the privilege he sought to avail himself of or claim. And he was right in his interpretation—that was precisely what she did mean.

As we have said, he bit his lip until the impression of his teeth was left upon it. And for the moment he hated her. Then again the feeling came upon him that he could snatch to his breast, and devour her with kisses. He had never before been thus affected; he trembled—he knew not wherefore. His chest was on fire, and to himself he could not explain it. He knew only that an exertion of self control was essential.

"I lay no claim to being a Crimean hero," he re-

plied, in a quiet tone,—"a debilitated frame kept me down when I would fain have done as my brother officers did, but in this I fancy I am somewhat the more entitled to your sympathy and to your consideration, for to the pain and depression occasioned by a distressing malady, there was superadded the bitter agony of being unable to take a share in the glorious encounters which took place, either as skirmishes, sorties, or general engagements. Chained down by illness in supine bondage, the chance of signalizing oneself was wholly removed. Miss Aston will at least do me the credit to believe, that had the opportunity been afforded me, I should have striven to earn the glory won by many a gallant comrade opposed to the Russian foe."

"It is not I who have questioned your readiness to face an English foe, Captain Winslow," exclaimed Myra, coldly.

"No one else would have dared," he exclaimed, with a sudden imperiousness of manner. Myra walked to the window and looked out.

The ground was rotten beneath him—he felt it. It flashed through his mind that some one had been speaking against him to Myra. The guilty mind is ever the readiest in suspicion. Who could it be? He could not for a moment conceive. Suddenly he remembered the letter Myra was perusing when he entered. Was that from the Crimea? It looked worn and tumbled. Who, there, would speak indifferently of him? In an instant Clifton Grey recurred to him: to be sure—who else? Mrs. Aston had spoken of him—the daughter had acknowledged that she knew his regiment—it must be so. He remembered, with an inward curse, his handsome, manly face, his well-knit, well-proportioned, and graceful form; he recollected how Sylva had been struck by his personal qualifications at Malta. It was not so wonderful that it should have made its due impression upon the romantic nature of a young girl, with warm impulses; but the bare thought that she could love him filled his heart with rage, the more violent in its effects because he was compelled to keep down all sign of it. He determined, however, to ascertain whether there was any foundation for his supposition by inquiries, which must be prosecuted with caution; and if he found that his surmises were correct, he would leave nothing undone or untried to consummate a most vindictive revenge upon Clifton; while, with respect to Myra, rather than she should give her hand to the man for whom he entertained such deadly hate, he felt that he could remorselessly slay her.

He quitted the seat he had, uninvited, taken upon entering, and followed Myra to the window.

"Miss Aston," he said, in his most gentle tone, "I have much need of your pardon:—illness has made me petulant, suspicious—unlike, in truth, what my real nature has ever been; and, if either by manner or by speech, I do or say aught to offend you, I sincerely hope you will extend your kind consideration to the infirmities occasioned by physical prostration, and smile at my folly and weakness, rather than look grave at my irritability."

Myra turned towards him.

"Captain Winslow," she said, "your apology is uncalled for. You seem to have forgotten that we are comparatively strangers."

"No, in truth," he said, in the same tone, "I have not forgotten that; it is because I would seek to alter that state of our relations that I beg you to bear with me. All intimacies must have a beginning—all friendships a commencement. I am most desirous that the acquaintance which, through the kind introduction of my friend Everett Randolph, has entered upon the first stage of its existence, should ripen into the closest friendship. It would be preposterous in me to feel other than that, while dependent upon you for a large share of generous courtesy, the onus of inducing the cementing that friendship will rest upon me. Having proved myself worthy of your good opinion, I trust not to be shut out of a place in your good graces."

Myra remained silent; she really had no answer to make to it. She certainly had no desire to cultivate the friendship of Captain Winslow, and however positively he might establish by proof his worthiness, it would not make any alteration in her indifference to his merits. In truth, if she did not feel indifferent, it was because she disliked him, entertained a repugnance to him, and would be much better pleased by never seeing him again, than forming that close intimacy to which he had alluded.

"I have offended you?" he exclaimed, as she remained silent.

"Offended me!" she reiterated. "Oh, no." He had annoyed her by his intrusion, she could have added, but she left it to him to infer.

"I will tell you why I think I have," he said; "and I may add that you are unconsciously so, and I have been guilty, unintentionally, of an act I am truly most desirous to avoid."

She looked upon him with surprise. Those lustrous eyes, how deep their beauty sunk in his heart! He cleared his voice and went on:

"It was my lack of consideration which induced me the other night, when I had first the happiness of meeting you, to speak of a young soldier in the Crimea, named Clifton Grey, in certain terms."

He paused. Myra felt that his small eyes were fixed upon her like those of a serpent regarding its prey. She felt her color heighten her cheeks, but by an effort she gave no other token that his words affected her.

"I know him, of course, by being under my command," he continued, "and spoke of him hastily, without considering that I might have pained the feelings of Mrs. Aston, whose *protégé* I presume he was."

"No," exclaimed Myra, coldly.

He repeated her negative with surprise.

"Am I equally in error in presuming, Miss Aston, that you were interested in him," he asked, eyeing her keenly.

Her lip curled.

"May I ask, Captain Winslow," she said, "whether I am expected to submit to a cross-examination, and duly answer every question you may put to me?"

"Not unless it may please you to do so. For God's sake! Miss Aston, do not misunderstand me! What in another might be provocative of offence, I beg—I entreat you not to consider such in me. I am so anxious that you should believe me incapable of this very intention, that I have introduced the subject of Grey to prove myself possibly inadvertent, but at the same time free from any design to give the shadow of an offence. Your mamma assured me that she was interested in the young fellow, and that led me to presume he was a *protégé* of hers, which I now learn he was not. I intended to say—that while under this impression—it was inconsiderate of me to speak as I did, and to fear, in telling an unwelcome truth, that I had offended her—and you—, of all the world, whose favour I would at any cost secure."

"Sir, the acquaintance between Mr. Grey, my mother, and myself, was brief; its duration, indeed, very short; but sufficiently long to assure both that he was a gentleman in appearance, in principle, and conduct; high couraged and noble in spirit, and of nature so generous as to sacrifice, as it seemed—as I am happy to hear from Captain Mandeville it has not—those prospects which one in his position had a right to consider ought properly to be his. Of his esoteric nature we have not to learn; of his exoteric character Captain Mandeville has been sufficiently explicit. What you have said—you will pardon my candour—has not had the weight to make it offensive. You may be labouring under some extraordinary misconception, or may mean some other person; but to believe that you are either mistaken or misled is the extent of my feeling upon the subject."

"You imagine this, Miss Aston. I see clearly my speech has offended you; and upon this very subject I trust to win your good will yet. I must, however, in justice to myself, say that I have not confounded persons; I have not been mistaken or misled in the fellow's character. I regret that you have been deceived in him, because— "

"Captain Winslow, you spoke just now of being desirous of not being misunderstood."

"Most assuredly."

"You say that you have not confounded persons?"

"Undoubtedly not."

"Are you prepared to deny what Captain Mandeville asserted?"

"He *is* mistaken, if you will."

"In saying that Clifton Grey was at the battle of the Alma, and was promoted for his bravery ?"

"Well,—no."

"In stating that he fought with unflinching bravery at Inkermann ?—"

"Well—no."

"That he bears a high character with his officers, and has been promised a commission ?"

"Well—a—a—no—but—"

"Captain Winslow, I am satisfied, and whether you are misled or deceive yourself, it is immaterial. You will see that it is unnecessary for me to be offended at what you have said."

"Miss Aston, really—you appear to place my word at a very low estimate. I—who had constantly the fellow under my eye—surely I must best know what he was."

"I desire, Captain Winslow, to hear no more upon what appears likely to become a painful subject between us."

"Miss Aston, it is plain that you take a great interest—a very great interest in this fellow."

"Sir!"

"It would be preposterous to call it love—madness, insanity. You may be romantic and fancy this, but it would be mere raging lunacy for you to throw yourself away upon a worthless vagabond. At least, I will step in here, and stop such a frantic sacrifice."

Captain Winslow's passion got the better of his prudence. Myra indignantly recoiled before him, and rang the bell violently. The footman appeared quickly.

"The door!" she exclaimed. "Captain Winslow will leave at once."

With burning cheeks she hurried past, him without taking any further notice of him, and rushed to her own room. Captain Winslow found himself in a false position, and cursed his own intemperate rashness, which had induced him to commit himself. The footman saw that something was amiss; having an impression that Captain Winslow might probably have insulted Miss Aston, because of the manner in which she quitted the apartment, he was divided between the propriety of showing him out or the duty of kicking him out. The captain settled the question by thrusting him on one side, and proceeding, with hasty strides, to the door, opened it for himself, and slammed it it after him with a very undisguised degree of ill-humour and excitement, which did not promise to prove advantageous to the interests of any inferior with whom he might come in contact. In this frame of mind he pursued his way to an appointment in the City. Pausing before a large warehouse and mansion, united, he glanced at the name upon a well worn brass plate on the counting-house doors, and after a moment's hesitation he knocked at the private-door with a long peal, influenced by the angry feelings

raised by Myra. A powdered lacquey in the service of high nobility might have envied such a rapid performance on the knocker. The door was speedily opened by a man servant, ready to prove obsequious to such a knocker; Captain Winslow, whose regimentals were a passport to flunky respect, enquired:

"Is Mr. Jayne within ?"

The man responded with a bow.

"He is, sir, but engaged."

"Unfortunate," exclaimed Captain Winslow, at the same time slipping out an oath. Then he drew out his card-case, and putting his card into the man's hand, he added:

"Give that to Mr. Jayne, and ask him to be good enough to write me to say when it will be convenient to see him."

"Perhaps he will see you now, sir," exclaimed the obsequious man. "There are occasions when I may inform him, even though he be engaged, that gentlemen are desirous of seeing him on matters of importance. Shall I do so now ?"

"By all means!" exclaimed Captain Winslow, and slipped a half crown into his hand. The man thanked him, skipped lightly up the stairs, returned, stating that Mr. Jayne would see him, and ushered him into a well furnished room, in which he perceived a tall, stern looking old gentleman and two ladies. The former bowed, the latter half rose at his entrance; he delivered himself of the usual formal bow, and then said:

"Mr. Jayne, I presume ?"

"Yes," replied the elderly gentleman, and added, "Captain Winslow?"

"The same," replied the captain, and added, "You have received my note, I have no doubt?"

"I have."

"Upon the subject it contained I am here."

"Of course, proceed."

Captain Winslow glanced at the ladies, and said:

"Is it not an affair to be discussed in private."

"Clearly, but these ladies are interested in it, and in fact, we were talking it over upon your arrival. It is a singular and complicated case, and will require to be carefully disentangled. Your note was, I suppose, necessarily brief, but at the same time, is not altogether clear. Will you have the goodness, Captain Winslow, to state as clearly and succinctly as possible, what you intended to convey in your note to me."

Captain Winslow caught, at this moment, sight of the face of one of the ladies, which previously had been averted from him, he uttered an exclamation of surprise, and hastily advanced to her.

"Signora Sylva," he exclaimed, "can it be possible! What happens to meet you in England."

He sought to take her hand, but she rose with sudden abruptness from her chair, and retreated from his touch; an expression of scornful disdain curling her upper lip.

"Pardon me, Captain Winslow," she exclaimed haughtily, "I cannot so easily forget the unmerited and unmanly insults forced upon me by you at Malta. Let me assure you most unequivocally the pleasure of meeting is not shared by me. I shall remain sir in your society, only to hear your pretensions to the claim you have made, and upon what they are founded. I confess to much incredulity respecting their justness, and am prepared to oppose them to the utmost."

Captain Winslow bowed with affected humility.

"It is my misfortune," he said, "to be constantly misjudged. Something in my manner, in the tone in which I deliver my observations, cruelly belies my real intention. I acknowledge, fair Signora, that on that evening at Sliema, to which you allude, I was in a provoking humour for banter, but if I remember rightly, I apologized to you, and expressed my sorrow at my indiscretion."

"Add not meanness to your impertinence, sir," interrupted Sylva, almost imperiously. "I too keenly remember all that occurred on that eventful evening to be deceived by any paltry attempt to gloze over your most contemptible proceedings."

"And I too well remember what took place on that night," he said, drawing himself up with sudden anger; then, remembering it would be better for him to control himself, he curbed his emotion of rage, and said, in a meaning tone, "but you need not fear; I will say nothing more to offend you."

"You dare not—dare not, sir! This is Saxon, is it not, and not difficult of comprehension? I say you dare say nothing more to offend me, because it would only be at the cost of truth; and for that you would have to render an account to those who would demand it, unmoved by bluster or unaffected by attempts at deception."

"I cannot fail, madam, to be surprised at this reception," exclaimed Captain Winslow, pretending to be hurt by her manner, "or at the tenor of your remarks. I dare do much, as even you might learn; but, as I have before said, you have misconceived me. I would not, for worlds, offend you; for I am anxious to be your friend—not your enemy. Few of us can afford to make enemies, fewer still have friends. When we may secure the latter we should not fling away the opportunity ——"

"I desire to hear no more on this head," again interrupted Sylva. "You have already said too much to alter the opinion conceived of you by me. You will, if you please, for the remainder of the interview, address yourself to Mr. Jayne, with whom your business lies. My province will be to listen—or to make a remark, when necessity alone compels my interference."

As she concluded she resumed her seat by the side of the young lady, her companion. Captain Winslow gazed at her savagely, but disguised his malignant feeling under an air of superciliousness, as though his dignity had been improperly wounded, and he had just discovered it in time to resent it.

'Really!' he exclaimed, "we are certainly playing at cross-purposes here. As Rip Van Winkle says, 'I am not myself—I am somebody else.' Upon my honor, signora, I am by no means flattered by the portrait you have painted of the humble individual before you; and being loth, as I have said before, to give you pain, or in any degree to offend you, I will retire and leave you to the greater enjoyment of old Jayne's company, solus, deferring my communication to a period when that person calls upon me to hear what I have to say to him."

Then, turning on his heel, he added, as if to himself, but yet audibly :—

"An Italian shrew—a thorough scold, by all that is virago-ish. What a lucky escapade!"

"Stay, sir," cried Mr. Jayne, in an elevated tone, as he was about to quit the room, and with a tone which had the effect of arresting the captain's departure, in spite of that individual's intention to quit without exchanging another word. "One moment, if you please? You have put in a claim to large property, in default of the heir coming forward. You state yourself to be in a position to prove that there was a rightful heir recently existing, but that he is dead, and that under the terms of the will you, as next of kin, claim the whole of the estates and personal effects which have been left."

"Exactly, old gentleman; and when you choose to extend your city movements to the west, and will call upon me, I will perform what I have promised in my note."

"Preposterous and impertinent, Captain Winslow."

"Impertinent, man? Bah! your age protects you from my horsewhip."

"And the law, Captain Winslow. Make no mistake respecting my mode of doing business. Were you to make any attempt to play the part of the mere vulgar ruffian, I should claim satisfaction, it is true, but it would be to place you in the felon's dock."

"The felon's?" hissed Captain Winslow through his teeth.

"And murderer's. The law appoints not different docks for various grades of delinquents. But this is the folly of senseless boyhood, captain. To put all this ridiculous and contemptible exhibition of temper aside, and to keep to the point, you will be pleased at once to assert the nature of your claim, upon what it is founded, and what your anticipations of the result may be; for, as I have said before, both these young ladies are interested in the issue, and may either accord your claim or see fit to oppose it."

"It will please me to do nothing of the sort. My claim can be affected by no such necessity as even a mere recital of its points to you or to the young ladies. If they are interested, they must wait until they or you, or whoever may be the trustees or executors of the will, hear from my solicitor. My communicativeness has been abruptly cut short by Signora Sylva, who can cool her anxiety by such process as she may think proper to employ. After the initiative to her temper with which I have been honoured, I can be at no loss to conceive what that process is likely to be. As a measure of precaution, I should recommend shower baths occasionally."

He made a very low bow, as he concluded, to the ladies, put on his hat, and sauntered out of the room with an air of insolent indifference he was far from enjoying. Once more he cursed his own want of self-command, for he knew his claim was wholly dependant on proving that which was not true, but to do which there would not be much difficulty if too close enquiries were not made into his proof. He had expected to carry Jayne by a *coup de main*, and get possession of the property long before the rightful heir could have the opportunity first of discovering he was the heir, and secondly coming forward to substantiate his claim. He was well aware of the value of possession, of the difficulty the heir would have in proving his identity, in providing the means of carrying on the trial, and surmounting all those minor obstacles—not much in themselves but of moment in the aggregate—which impede the prosecution of a suit for the recovery of property. He was quite conscious of all this, and flattered himself, that once quietly in possession, he would not easily or quickly be ousted. He correctly assumed that Jayne could be of important assistance to him in accomplishing this, and had come prepared to employ all the arts of fascination and cajolery he possessed; but he had first been ruffled by Myra, and then the unexpected appearance of Sylva had flung him off his guard; her behaviour completed the overthrow of his self-command, and he committed himself as we have seen. He was a rogue and a villain, but a shallow one withal, a mean, paltry scoundrel, without even the ability to be a clever knave.

As he departed, he felt that he had committed himself, and raged inwardly until he almost threw himself into a bilious fever, but he comforted himself in the hope that he might yet get hold of the city man, and cajole him by flattery and by bribes yet to further his views.

He was mistaken. Mr. Jayne was a man of a different composition. He was by no means insensible of the value of money—was always ready to take it and make it; but, to do him justice, it must be legitimately. He could do nothing without his commission, but he would not have accepted a bribe—as a bribe—if it equalled in amount the bullion in the Bank of England. He was a most proud man withal.

He had a peculiarly elevated notion of his position as a wealthy city man, and of the respect thereby due to him. Captain Winslow had treated him with the supercilious contempt he would himself have exhibited to a small trader—it was an insult he could neither forget nor forgive. His whole internal economy bubbled with fury, but he kept down every trace of it under the cold, calm, stern exterior he usually wore, and when he heard the slam of the door following Captain Winslow's departure, he turned to Sylva and said:

"That fellow's an insolent puppy, presuming upon his aristocratic connections; but he shall find that if he were Her Majesty's own brother, it would make no difference with me in the consideration of his claim. I will examine into it with a not easily-satisfied scrutiny, which will probably prove far from agreeable to him, and he may satisfy himself that he shall not take possession of the estates left so strangely by your father, Signora, without proving beyond the possibility of a doubt that he is the only surviving heir to them."

"I have not for one instant entertained a doubt that the young soldier I met at Malta, is the same youth you brought up, and the true heir," observed Sylva, with considerable emphasis.

Mr. Jayne shrugged his shoulders.

"I confess," he said, "your description of his face tallies with that young man, and the name is absolutely identical; indeed, I may acknowledge my belief that the young soldier you encountered at Malta, and Mr. Grey, reared under my surveillance, are identically the same person; but I am not so sure as to the other claim you put forward."

"But, sir, I repeat I am," exclaimed Sylva, with energy.

"We shall see. I will make every inquiry respecting him, and report progress. Captain Winslow speaks of his death—"

"Oh no, no, no!" exclaimed the other young lady, with exciting earnestness. "He is not dead—I am sure he is not dead. I should have seen his spirit, if God had called him hence. No, he is not dead! I have searched the blood-stained roll of names, but his is not among them. This man, who is just gone, is a falsider—a wretch unworthy of belief. You, too, have tried to lead me to such a belief, but there is no truth in it," she added with vehemence. "The same Almighty hand which guided him to the spot where my life must have been sacrificed but for his intrepid deed, will warn me when he quits this earth, if he is to be snatched away before I surrender up my soul."

"Calm yourself, Mistress Precious," said Mr. Jayne, with a cold tone and colder smile. "All that can be done to prove him the true heir shall be, but you will agree with me that it would be unwise to raise in him hopes which may never be realized."

RA-TAT!

THE VALLEY OF THE TCHERNAYA.—MEETING BETWEEN SISTER GERALDINE AND CLIFTON GREY

The postman's knock resounded through the house at that moment, and a pause took place. Almost immediately the serving man appeared with a letter on a silver salver; he handed it to Sylva.

"A letter for you, ma'am, from abroad," he said. She took it up hastily.

"From Malta—from the Crimea!" she exclaimed, and then ejaculated, as if she were about to faint, "Merciful heaven!"

She drew a long breath, and then, with a pale face and a voice trembling with emotion, she said—

"Come with me, Preciosa, darling, to my chamber. This is a visible interposition of Providence—this letter is from Clifton Grey!"

CHAPTER XXIII.

"What a wonderful man the postman is
  As he hastens from door to door;
What a medley of news his hands contain,
  For high, low, rich, and poor.
In many a face he joy doth trace,
  In many he grief can see;
As the door is opened to his loud rat-tat,
  And his quick delivery.
  Every morn as true as the clock,
  Somebody hears the postman's knock."
                                THORNTON.

          "Oh! child, child, child!
Thou hast betrayed thy secret, as a bird
Betrays her nest, by striving to conceal it.
I will not leave thee here"
                                LONGFELLOW.

LETTERS FROM THE CRIMEA. AN ECLAIRCISSEMENT.
CAPTAIN WINSLOW FLINGS A BOOMERANG.

RA-TAT knocked the postman with sudden violence at Mrs. Stewart's in Baker-street. The young ladies screamed in chorus, and three of them pricked their fingers with their needles. Mrs. Stewart looked round at the heap of work, and sighed.

"More work!" she ejaculated, "it can never be done, that is certain."

The waiting-maid entered the room with glittering eyes, and held out two letters. Mrs. Stewart put out her hand for them, but the girl drew back.

"No, mem," she exclaimed, pointing to a young girl who sat bending over a bonnet with a face as white as that of a ghost, and a heart beating violently, "for Miss Hastings, mem—two, mem, from the Crimee, mem."

"Give them to me!" gasped Lizzie.

The maid, with a knowing smile, handed them to the trembling girl, who saw nothing but the two square pieces of folded paper, which she clutched

convulsively, pressed passionately to her lips, and conveyed to her bosom.

Mrs. Stewart watched her for a few minutes, and the tears sprung into the good lady's eyes as she saw how the poor girl shook, and tried to use her thimble on an imaginary needle, the real one having, in her excitement, dropped upon the floor; but when she began to cut up valuable blonde lace into lengths for bonnet strings, Mrs. Stewart interfered.

"Miss Hastings," she said, with the considerate kindness of giving her an opportunity of recovering her calmness, "will you be good enough to put on your bonnet and run over to Miss Aston with a message from me. Say I shall esteem it a great favour if she will permit her last order to stand over to the end of the week."

Lizzie rose like lightning from her seat, and as she passed Mrs. Stewart she murmured, so that the good lady could just catch the sound:

"God bless you, dear madam, for this kindness!"

How many minutes elapsed before Lizzie was tapping at the door of the prettily-furnished apartment in which Myra studied, under the first masters, every branch of the accomplishments necessary to form and complete a first-class education?

"May I come in?" she exclaimed, holding up the two letters to Myra's view.

Myra uttered a cry, and ran up to her.

"From the Crimea?" she asked.

"From the Crimea!" replied Lizzie, "both from the Crimea!"

There was one at that moment passing the door of the apartment; his ear caught the words, and he stopped to listen, for the sound of the place named had a spell for him. It was Captain Winslow, who had paid another visit to Baker Street, in the hope of retrieving his false step, to be accomplished either by abject attention to Myra, or to her mother, or both. He gently inserted his head in the door way, and saw Myra extend her hand for the letters; he heard her ejaculate, as she gazed eagerly upon them, "Both from the Crimea!" and then, with considerable emotion, add: "Both, indeed. Oh, Lizzie, here is one from Clifton Grey!"

"Clifton Grey," he repeated, between his teeth, and muttered a fearful oath. "Is it so, my disdainful prude! It is proper that thy mother should be present at the perusal of this letter, and she shall."

He disappeared, still muttering, and hurried to find Mrs. Aston.

In the meanwhile the two maidens were absorbed in the letters. Lizzie, true to her love, thought not of the letter from Clifton, until she had perused every line of Haverel's long, long epistle to her, wherein he detailed the embarkation at Varna, the disembarkation at Old Fort, the battle of the Alma, with the celebrated incident of the battle of the standard of England, in which he had won distinction; the flank march, and the battle of Inkermann, where, but for Clifton Grey, he had received his death-wound. He made light of his hurt, but spoke heartily and earnestly of the attention our hero had paid to him; he eulogised him as a soldier, as a brave, daring, and skilful tactician, and as a sincere and tender friend. Words, he said, were too feeble to express his worth, thoughts too limited to conceive his true goodness: he had known him to have but one enemy, he said, and, thank God, that one had left the Crimea, which, bad as it was, was a sort of paradise without him. The whole of this letter was interlarded with lines from songs or scraps from poetry, with passionate exclamations of love, and an amazing variety of marks which were, as he explained, intended for kisses. Lizzie read out every word; she did not miss a letter, or fail to kiss one mark, but it is extremely doubtful if Myra had heard more than ten detached sentences; her eyes were fixed on the bold, yet elegant penmanship of the superscription upon a letter she held in her hand, addressed in Clifton's hand to "Miss Lizzie Hastings, Mrs. Stewart's, Baker Street, London, England." That she read and re-read, as if it were a lesson to con by heart, and she thought that Haverel's letter would never, never end, until at last Lizzie, devouring it with kisses, and pressing it to her heart, launched out into hyperbole, the subject being Sergeant Walter Haverel, his inexhaustible store of good qualities, and the high estimation in which she held both, and should continue to hold them as long as she breathed.

Before she had exhausted her commentary, Myra suggested to her that there was a letter yet unread, and thought it would be as well at once, while they were alone, to inspect its contents.

"To be sure," said Lizzie, hastily, "how selfish of me! But I am so happy to think Walter is not so dreadfully wounded as I feared he must be, that I seem to have forgotten everything else. Pray open and read it, miss?"

"But it is addressed to you," said Myra.

"No matter—there is no secret in it; and who knows, it may be as much for your eyes as for mine."

Myra would have refused to comply with her request—felt that it would be proper to do so, yet found it impossible to follow these intimations uttered by the small, still voice, and so she opened it, trembling as she did so.

The letter was of no great length. It commenced by telling Lizzie of the sensation the arrival of her letter had occasioned to those most interested in its receipt. It thanked her warmly for so much of her letter to Sergeant Haverel as had been devoted to himself. "You did not think—can perhaps never know, Lizzie," it proceeded to say, "what joy the sight of those lines brought to my heart—mine, so lonely, so friendless, so isolated—mine, that knew of no other in the wide world, most of all in dear, dear England, to respond with sympathy to its throbbings, to keep pulse for pulse with it in its hopings, to joy in the realization of its aspirations, to mourn over its blighted expectation, or its untimely destruction."

"Poor fellow!" exclaimed Lizzie, wiping her eyes.

"He is unjust!" thought Myra, with a swelling heart, but she said nothing: keeping, with difficulty, her emotion under, she went on with the perusal. "You will not, therefore, be surprised to learn that I kissed the only hand-writing I have received from England, or that I failed to register in my very warmest affections that kind-hearted girl, who, in the absorbing nature of her own long attachment to another, proved herself yet sufficiently unselfish to devote herself to the expressions of kindness and goodwill to one who needed both greatly—to him whom they reached, to contravene an opinion fast seizing possession of his soul, that the wise man had but too truly asserted "all is vanity and vexation of spirit,"—to whom they came like balm on a bleeding wound—came in time to prevent him falling into the cold errors of misanthrophy."

"Misanthrophy!—what's that?" asked Lizzie.

Myra explained. Lizzie pouted and pished.

"Poor fellow!" she exclaimed, "no doubt he was very dull and bad just then, but he has too kind a heart ever to be such a fusty, disagreeable old mopus as that."

Myra went on, and in one minute both became greatly excited, and totally unconscious of approaching footsteps.

"You must not smile at my morbid fancies," continued Clifton, "for, in truth, my strangely friendless position makes me at times very sad and sorrowful, and renders my efforts to win name and fame almost aimless. This was not always so, and—I do not mind letting you into the secret, Lizzie—is the reason why I have never looked after any Turkish or other princess since I have quitted England. I look not back upon my early days in comparison with my present position as a source of sorrow; but I do unceasingly regret that change of circumstances has, from some causes with which I am wholly unacquainted, deprived me of one whom, I fondly hoped, would have been my correspondent—my only one while in the army. I care for no other. In your communication to me you mention a young lady from Arundel, named Aston. Lizzie, indeed, you touched my soul when you spoke of her. I did meet with her at Arundel. It would be impossible for me to intimate what you suggest. I, who from the first moment I beheld her, so well appreciated her true worth. Although I feel most acutely, most keenly, most deeply—nay, Lizzie, without ceasing upon this subject, I will now say no more, than that in accordance with a promise made to Miss Aston, I, previous to my departure from England, sent to her a long letter—"

"I never—never received it!" ejaculated Myra, with the greatest agony of manner. She paused for an instant, but, by an effort, once more collected herself. Wiping the hot tears from her eyes—she went on:

"It was returned to me with an official notice that she had quitted Arundel without leaving her address —"

"Yet this was not so," interpolated Myra, and added, as if some new light had broken in upon her: "There is something wrong in this. Perhaps a clue is here to the unaccountable silence of Ellen Fairfax." Without further remark she, with avidity, continued reading the letter.

"Since then I have not communicated with her because I know not where to address my letter. And now, Lizzie, if ever you felt disposed to do me a favour, you will confer upon me an obligation which I can never repay, never sufficiently esteem, if you will —and I leave the management of this to your own dear woman's nature—ascertain whether the Miss Aston of whom you have spoken is the same being in whose dear society I passed the only really happy hours of my life, who is never absent from my memory, nor from that place in my heart to which she was elevated ere we parted. Should it be, and she has not forgotten me—if all interest in my present, my future, has not been effaced by other and perhaps worthier objects —"

"Not worthier," exclaimed Lizzie. "Never! never!"

"If," continued Myra, unheeding the interruption, and reading rapidly, "I have not become wholly indifferent to her, will you endeavour to discover whether a few lines from me would be received by her, even upon those terms I arranged with her at Arundel. If she assents, you will not, Lizzie, I am sure, waste an instant of time in communicating with me. You cannot half conceive the rapture such news would give me; how entirely it will reward me for all there has been to suffer, surmount, and endure here; nor can you imagine the value I shall place upon this, the crowning obligation of your kindness —"

Lizzie that instant dropped from the sofa, on which she had been sitting by the side of Myra, upon her knees, and clutching at Myra's hands, she said, with much excitement of manner:

"You will do what he asks, miss?—Oh, remember how alone he is in that place of blood and death! Not a friend, a relative in the whole world, to send to him one little line to cheer him—Oh, miss, say that you will receive his letter. He will never, never abuse your goodness; it will make him so happy, and God will bless you for the kind act!"

"Hush, hush, Lizzie!" cried Myra, equally excited. "Rise, there's a dear, good girl. Receive his letter!— aye, Heaven knows with what happiness. Lizzie, I

will myself answer this letter—I will write to him first—"

"Myra—Myra! do my ears deceive me? Can it be my child who utters this unmaidenly, immodest resolve?" exclaimed a female voice, suddenly and harshly.

Lizzie screamed and sprung to her feet. Myra uttered no sound, but she almost fell to the ground in a fainting fit. The words she heard were uttered by her mother, and in a tone she had never before known her to adopt—certainly when addressing her.

Behind Mrs. Aston appeared Captain Winslow, in the dress of a civilian. He stood in the attitude of one who was either much shocked or much pained by the éclaircissement which had just occurred; his eyes were turned upon the floor, and altogether his aspect was infinitely more humble than it had been shown beneath this roof previously. Myra's first impulse had been to fling herself at her mother's feet, and pour forth some passionate acknowledgments respecting Clifton Grey, and to make a fervent appeal to her heart; but at the instant she caught sight of Captain Winslow, and her impulse was thrust back, she felt to be suddenly transformed to stone, ice, or any material rigid and pulseless.

It flashed through her mind that he had to do with this sudden interruption. She knew her mother's habits so well; it was not her custom to watch her daughter's movements; to pry into her actions; to come upon her at any moment unexpectedly, by intention, or to look upon her, or to speak to her with harshness: yet she had done this, and by design, too. It was clear, therefore, that she had been moved to act thus by representations which had wrung her to the quick, and in which she had placed sufficient faith to act upon them. Myra easily concluded that Captain Winslow had made the representations, and she despised him accordingly. She was resolved, too, that he should not count the incident as a triumph. She turned to her mother and said, firmly and coldly—

"Mother, you wrong me. You are unjust. I deserve no such imputation as you have flung upon me. When have I so acted, that you should, unacquainted with facts, unhesitatingly challenge me with resolving upon an act at once immodest and unmaidenly."

"Oh, Myra!" cried her mother with anguish, "do not add to your folly by attempting to conceal your error, or by affecting to brave it out. I know all."

"May I beg, mother, to know what is comprised in that word 'all?'" asked Myra, as coldly as before.

Mrs. Aston, who idolised her daughter, looked upon her affrighted. She had never seen her under this aspect; ever to her she had been tender, gentle, submissive, and most affectionate, in word, look, and gesture; she was now cold, repelling, and, as it seemed, sullen. Upon every other occasion, did a shade of vexation cross the brow of Mrs. Aston, a word of remonstrance rise to her lips, Myra had always sought to remove it by flinging herself upon her mother's neck, by kisses and promises to implicitly obey her slightest wish—and she never failed to succeed in the effort; but now she drew herself up to her full height, appeared firmly determined to maintain a spirit of opposition, to throw off the trammels of girlish obedience, and assert a claim to think and act for herself.

"Myra, my dear child," exclaimed her mother, "it is not in this tone or in this spirit you have hitherto received admonition from me. I am most painfully hurt to see you thus changed. Have you forgotten the relation in which we stand to each other?"

"Indeed, mother, I have not," responded Myra, in clear, firm tones. "Not for an instant have I ceased to remember the link—the tie that binds us so closely together, that makes you to me, and should me to you, the first, the paramount consideration in our earthly career. For you, readily, unhesitatingly, without one poor sigh, would I resign the little share of happiness I may hope to have in this life. To you I have ever striven to act as becomes a dutiful, loving child; for the sake of my own self respect I have never, at any time or under any circumstances, intentionally or involuntarily been guilty of an act which should bring the blush of shame to my cheek, or that of indignation to yours. I challenge you to name one occasion upon which you can convict me of speaking an untruth."

"Myra, my darling, speak not to me in this strain. Come to my heart, from which not for a moment have you been displaced. I have every faith in your integrity, your modesty, your good sense; but you, the child of nature, the simple and the guileless, have suffered yourself to be deceived and misled."

Mrs. Aston had, on the commencement of her speech, folded Myra in her arms, and kissed her tenderly; but as she concluded, Myra disengaged herself.

"It is you, dear mother," said she, "who are deceived and misled. As you love me, speak out plainly any charge you have to make in reference to aught I may have done, or you may imagine I have in contemplation. Do not hesitate to prefer it openly. I will not hesitate truly to answer to it."

"The fact is, Miss Aston," exclaimed Captain Winslow, "you are too innocent, too unsuspecting. You are thus easily made the dupe of the designing and the artful."

Myra looked at him with a glance of undisguised contempt, but made no reply. He winced beneath that flash of scorn; but was determined neither to be abashed by it, nor to retreat. Mrs. Aston was, however, much troubled by the position her daughter had taken up, and was evidently bent upon adhering to. It was her conviction, hastily formed, it is true, that it would be better to come to an explanation at once

with her, while able to produce a witness, and shewing Myra how she was the victim of artifice, withdraw her, with her own consent, at once and effectually from the gulf into which she was about to leap. Mrs. Aston was well assured, if Myra were made to see her error, she would abandon it on the instant, and do her utmost afterwards to retrieve it; therefore, before Captain Winslow could add to his observation, she said to Myra:

"You have received a letter addressed to you from the Crimea?"

"No!" said Myra, firmly.

Mrs. Aston looked astounded. She was sure Myra would not, to screen herself from any amount of anger, deliberately utter a falsehood. She turned to Captain Winslow:

"Pray sir," said she, "how can you explain this?"

"Does it require explanation?" he asked, with a shrug of the shoulders.

"Indeed, sir," said Mrs. Aston, with stern gravity, "it requires very clear explanation. You informed me that you had seen my daughter, in a greatly excited state, perusing a letter addressed to her from an individual in the Crimea, of whom you gave me a most painful report."

"May I beg to ask you, madam, whether upon your entry into the room you did not hear Miss Aston say she would answer the letter she had received?" returned Captain Winslow. "You could surely also see in her hand the letter—since conveyed out of sight —but I must, after your promise to me, really deprecate being brought forward as an informer. You had, madam, the opportunity of judging for yourself. Positively, I cannot see what other explanation you can require."

"My daughter, sir, denies having received any letter from the Crimea," exclaimed Mrs. Aston, with an air of perplexity.

Captain Winslow again gave his shoulders what he intended should be an expressive shrug.

"If you can reconcile that declaration with what you have witnessed, I have nothing further, of course, to say in the matter," he remarked, and walked to the window, humming a tune from a favourite opera.

All this while, Lizzie Hastings had looked from one to the other with no little astonishment and fright; but the observations made by the Captain seemed, in some degree, to restore her to self-possession. She saw, the instant she became more calm, the true state of the case; it was plain to her that the captain had by some means or other, not very creditable to him, made himself acquainted with the arrival of the letters from the Crimea; that he had laboured under the error, however, that one had been especially forwarded to Miss Aston, and he had, believing that it had been received sub rosa, communicated the fact to Mrs. Aston. Lizzie perceived, too, that she had been pointed out as something worse than an accomplice, and she by no means felt her position to be agreeable or gratifying. She determined, however, not to suffer herself to be aspersed, and especially by this man. She, therefore, plucked up heart and advanced to the captain. The words "designing and artful" were ringing in her ears, which burnt as though some spiteful person had pinched them.

"If you please, sir," she commenced, "may I ask you a question?"

He turned and fastened a penetrating look upon her. "What have you got to say to me, my good wench?" he asked, superciliously and suspiciously.

"I beg your pardon, sir! I am not your wench—nor have you any right to use such words in speaking to me," returned Lizzie, indignantly. "I believe you are the brother of Mr. Beverley Winslow."

"Well! what then?"

"Merely—that as he is an unmanly scoundrel, who has several times infamously and grossly insulted me, I suppose that I ought not to be surprised at anything you, as his brother, say or do."

"What do you mean, woman!" he cried fiercely.

"That I wish to know, sir, when just now you told Miss Aston she was made the dupe of the designing and artful, whether you intended me as the person by whose arts and designs she was being misled."

"It is a question I beg to decline answering," he replied, with a sneer.

"Very likely!" she returned; "but that won't do for me. It is bad enough to play the spy and informer: it is worse to try and blacken the character of a defenceless girl who has only that to enable her to hold her head up in society; but it is far more contemptible to do this, and to refuse to give the person traduced an opportunity of clearing themselves."

Captain Winslow elevated his eyebrows, and turning to Mrs. Aston, said :—

"Really, madam, I must throw myself upon your protection. I trust you will release me, during my visit to you, from the attacks of a vulgar spitfire."

"How dare you use such an epithet to me!" exclaimed Lizzie, stamping her foot with passion; and then bursting into tears, she turned to Mrs. Aston. "Madam!" she exclaimed, excitedly, "I do not know what this contemptible fellow—he may be a captain, but he is no gentleman — may have said to you respecting me, but I beg and entreat you to repeat it to me, without keeping back a word. I will answer every question truly and honestly, madam, without the least disguise or falsification—as I hope God to be merciful to me. You will then learn if I have been artful and designing, as I have been represented."

"Absurd!—ridiculous!" cried Captain Winslow. "Pray, Mrs. Aston, do not trouble yourself to do anything of the kind. You must see it is not needful.

You must know, from what has already occurred, that this assumption of honesty is a mere blind."

"Really," said Mrs. Aston, stifly, as she addressed Lizzie, "I must say, young woman, appearances are not in your favour. Before you came to the house I had not one thought with which Miss Aston was concerned to vex me. I have suffered the most acute anguish, the greatest unhappiness, anxiety, and misery, out of the peculiarly strange connection formed—much against my wish—between you. It is unnecessary to allude to the past—"

"Mother!" exclaimed Myra, reproachfully.

"I say," persisted Mrs. Aston, "it is unnecessary to allude to the past, but I cannot forget that upon one occasion you took Miss Aston from this house, under circumstances—I may perhaps admit them to have originated in thoughtfulness, but they were not the less indiscreet and improper—and from which most disastrous consequences ensued. Notwithstanding the lesson which such a painful and distressing affair should have imparted, I find that Miss Aston is again on the verge of committing herself in a matter, the result of which she does not appear to me properly to comprehend. I find, also, that she is incited, induced, urged, to the step she was about to take, by you. I withhold the assertion, which seems to pain you, that you have an artful design in doing this, but I am quite convinced that the whole thing is indecorous, unbecoming, nay, highly improper. If Miss Aston is not alive to her own position, it becomes me to make her fully to understand, and see that she supports it. I must, therefore, request that from this moment the intimacy between you shall cease, and I must further insist that you do not attempt directly, nor by artifice, to see, speak, or communicate with Miss Aston again, unless by my especial permission, and under such conditions as I may think proper to impose."

Lizzie Hastings gasped for breath. She felt as if she should choke. She tried to articulate a mass of incoherent words that struggled for mastery, to exculpate herself from the odious imputation cast upon her. Before, however, she could get a single word out, Myra said earnestly to her:

"Lizzie, for my sake, be silent. Let me answer this. Upon me rests the responsibility of removing this unjust, this cruel attack upon you, so undeserved, so unworthy in those who make it."

"Myra!" ejaculated Mrs. Aston, her eyes sparkling with indignation.

"Mother," responded Myra, "I hear what you have said in sorrow and shame."

"It is time, Miss Aston, that you retired to your chamber," exclaimed Mrs. Aston, with much anger. "If I am to receive a homily from the lips of my own child, she should, I think, at least have the prudence—I avoid the harsher word—of refraining from doing so in the presence of those who cannot fail to be grieved and surprised at such an exhibition."

"My dear mother," exclaimed Myra, gazing upon her mournfully, while her eyes swam in tears, "would we had never left dear Arundel—would we had never changed the position we held there. If we were more humble, we at least never sought a false grandeur at the expense of truth and justice. I am ready to resign all dignity—all elevation—all that society in London seems to worship—if it is to be purchased at that price. I will never accept it at such a cost. Nor will you, my ever dear mother, when free from an influence at which a little while hence you will shudder to remember you were ever moved by. I love you, dearest mother, as tenderly and fondly as I have ever done. I would not, to ensure my own happiness, inflict on you one moment's pain. I never have been, never would be, to the most affectionate, devoted parent, undutiful; from you I have never had disguise; I would, from my soul, scorn, abhor to descend to employ it to deceive you. You, mother, must, in a calmer moment, feel that to charge me with intending you a homily, is to challenge me with an intention foreign to my nature. To suppose that any opinion Captain Winslow might form respecting me would, in the least, affect me, is equally to treat me with injustice. Whether he be grieved or pleased, surprised or gratified, is not, nor ever will be of any moment to me; but I cannot and will not permit any such person to make assertions respecting me, or any one whom I may respect—esteem, love—as I do Lizzie Hastings—" she held out her hand to Lizzie, which the poor girl seized, kissed, and sobbed over—"without at once denouncing them as false and malicious."

"You are severe, Miss Aston," exclaimed Captain Winslow.

"I am just, sir," she replied, coldly. "Briefly, dearest mother, and I pray you to believe me, who never yet concealed, directly or by evasion, the truth from you, when I declare by all that is sacred, whatever may have transpired between me and Lizzie Hastings in the direction to which you allude, has been not from her suggestions, but by my own solicitation. When we are alone, dear mother, I will, as I have ever been, be candid and open with you, but ask me for no further explanation now. I will prove to you that I have not received, to me addressed, any letter from the Crimea. The communication I have seen you shall read. You shall judge whether I erred in saying I would write to one far away—an act I should never have committed, but with your assent and under your counsel. I will prove to you, dear mother, that I am undeserving of the observations you have used to me—that Lizzie Hastings is equally so; but not here, not now, not in the presence of one, who, having played the part of eaves-dropper, consistently followed it up by the rôle of

tale-bearer—one, who, appearing in the character of an unbidden guest, seems desirous to glide by a natural transition into that of mischief-maker, striving to create division in you and I, dearest mother, between whom never before has any vexed question over arisen."

"Miss Aston," exclaimed Captain Winslow, with an assumption of dignity, "you make a strong claim to being actuated alone by truth and justice, withal you are unjust and to me. Older and more experienced in the world's ways than you, I am able to see things in their proper light, while you only receive them through the pure medium your own guileless nature enables you to adopt. I am sincerely desirous of saving you from being drawn into a scheme which, for a time, may lull you into an intoxicating and fascinating dream, but from which you must shortly awake to horror and despair, without the power of redeeming or retrieving the false step you have unconsciously, and out of your own unsuspecting generous nature, been led to take. I repudiate the unworthy character you would fasten upon me; I claim to appear in that of a true friend. I know that to prove myself such I must be content to rest for a time under the ban of being prompted by unworthy motives, but the time must come when I shall appear in my true colours—when you will have the opportunity of testing my sincerity—when you will know me for what I am—when you will earnestly thank me for taking the step you now condemn. I am content to abide the coming of that time. Fully conscious of the influences by which your vision is now distorted, I take no umbrage at the indignant contempt showered upon me by you. You will yourself, at a future time, amply reward me for the pain you have now inflicted, by an expression of sorrow that so unfortunate a delusion should have led you to have thus misjudged me. Farewell, Miss Aston; for the present I ask from you only the exercise of calm reflection and the exertion of your own natural sagacity: divest the present artful attempts to mislead you from its interested purpose, and the whole fabric of selfish deceit will fall to the ground shattered."

He bowed low, as he spoke, and left the room to Mrs. Aston, her daughter, and Lizzie, whom Myra would on no account permit to depart until a full explanation had taken place. Nothing was reserved or concealed, and Mrs. Aston was compelled to admit that the charge of duplicity and design against Lizzie was not sustained, although she did not at all approve of, nor feel disposed to countenance any of the proceedings in connection with Clifton Grey, nor could she be brought to acknowledge other than she was opposed to them, and that she set her face wholly against them. Under all circumstances she thought it advisable at present, at least, for Lizzie not to repeat her visits, and that high spirited girl needed no further intimation to keep her from making her appearance there, even though Myra was desirous she should form no such determination. But of this new arrangement anon.

Captain Winslow as he left the room slowly drew on his gloves and set his hat to his comfort, intently at the same time trying to divine what was to be his next step. He was aware that his last words would be taken for what they were worth, and that he should actually gain nothing by the position he had taken up. He did not like the aspect of affairs, and saw plain enough that he was neither prospering in his prospects of obtaining the wealth belonging to Clifton Grey, nor the hand of Myra. Further, that upon whatever he decided as a means to ensure that success, it was necessary to adopt it at once; but what the plan was to be was the difficulty, he puzzled his brains for an idea.

As he approached the hall, a hasty glance at the man's face, who was ready to open the door for him, suggested the outline of a scheme. He put his hand into his waistcoat pocket and drew forth a sovereign; he placed it in the footman's hand, who, when he saw it, and comprehended that it was largesse to himself, opened his eyes, if possible, wider than when he had been scalded by the pea-soup.

"What is your name?" asked Captain Winslow, after he had told the man to put the gold into his pocket.

"Perk, at your service, sir," replied the man, with a profound bow.

"I am desirous of having some conversation with you, Perk, upon a matter in which you can help me. I do not want everybody to know this, however, and presume you can be secret—if well paid?"

"As the grave," said Perk, with another bow.

"And will not object to afford me some little assistance quite in your power—if well paid?"

Perk placed his hand on the left side of his plush waistcoat, and made another bow.

"When, Perk, can I see you for this private talk, and where? Be quick man."

"This evening, sir, at the 'Last and Lapstone,' Stingo Lane."

"Stingo Lane. Where's that?"

Perk explained, and Captain Winslow, with an air of satisfaction, departed to take his brother Beverley out for an airing.

That night, at the "Last and Lapstone," the two worthies met and sat together in a retired corner of a smoky and not very aristocratic parlour. There they concocted certain arrangements, and when they separated, both went their way, smiling. Perk with five new sovereigns in his pocket, and Captain Winslow with a splendid scheme in his head which he hoped to realise.

CHAPTER XXIV.

"He started up, with more of fear
Than if an armed foe were near.
'God of my fathers! What is here?
Who art thou? and wherefore sent
So near a hostile armament?'
   *   *   *   *
The rose was yet upon her cheek,
But mellowed with a tenderer streak;
Where was the play of her soft lips fled?
Gone was the smile that enliven'd their red,
The ocean's calm within their view,
Beside her eye had less of blue;
But like that cold wave it stood still,
And its glance, though clear, was chill.
   *   *   *   *
Ere yet she made reply,
Once she raised her hand on high;
It was so wan and transparent of hue,
You might have seen the moon shine through."
                    THE SIEGE OF CORINTH.

THE VALLEY OF THE TCHERNAYA. SISTER GERAL-
DINE. CLIFTON GREY, THE UNFORGOTTEN.

CHRISTMAS day in the Crimea was passed by the British troops as cheerfully as circumstances would permit. The weather was still of the most wretched description, the mud was in many places up to the girths of the transport mules and horses. The cavalry horses, owing to want of foresight and the commonest precautions, had died off at the rate of 40 per cent., and were not available to do the work absolutely essential to provide the men with common necessaries. The Times fund, so nobly and liberally subscribed to by the people of England, not only began to afford comforts to those who had desperate need of them, but of very shame to cause the authorities to bestir themselves in order to effect some alteration in the state of things. The loss sustained by the British army, by sickness and privation alone, was something terrific—it is doubtful if it will ever be really known. Individual families know that they have lost relatives, but the tremendous aggregate of those who perished from sheer want of proper precaution, and that, too, in the face of every facility for providing any possible requirement, will never be permitted to be made known, even though so much has been openly and broadly stated—though such damning admissions have been unintentionally made at the Board of Enquiry into the Crimean commission at Chelsea, by the very men who would have the public think that the charge of imbecility and incapacity does not apply to them, although the facts need not the aid of an index finger to point out the guilty culprits.

It was a pleasure to Clifton to have once more beneath the roof of his tent his comrades, Sergeant Haverel and Mickey Dunigan. It is true they were not yet restored to health, not yet fit to do aught but the lightest duty, but as daily they saw how the room

CAPTAIN WINSLOW'S PLOT.—STRUGGLE BETWEEN HIM AND CHARLEY ROWE.

they occupied in the hospital was needed by many battered down by starvation and rags, they refused to longer keep the space allotted to them, and surrendered it to two fellows of their own regiment, in a far worse condition than themselves.

Clifton took upon himself the duty of supplying the place of the doctor to them, and made them promise not to attempt the performance of duties which would throw them back again into the hands from which they had just been emancipated. He tried to impress upon them that their country needed their best assistance, for the drafts arriving out, to supply the, stalwart, well-disciplined men who had been swept away by bullet or disease, were mere boys, raw recruits, who were undisciplined, inexperienced, and, save by careful management on the part of those who had their disposition, physically incapable of performing the service they were brought hither to perform.

Clifton had written for Mickey Dunigan the letter to Bridget Boyle, of Ballynacraggy, County Limerick, and the poor Irishman counted the days the letter would take to reach Ireland, to be handed all over Ballynacraggy and its vicinity, to be commented on, and to be answered by the priest. Sergeant Haverel also enumerated the probable number of days absorbed by the mail in the performance of its duty to and fro—the very brief interval Lizzie would permit to pass before she replied to it; and though the sum total was greater than he liked, he yet comforted himself by thinking that at all events he should have an answer from Lizzie just about a month before the priest, of whom Mickey spoke, had mended his pen and commenced the first line to him from Bridget Boyle. Clifton Grey, too, speculated, and counted, and surmised, and fidgetted respecting the period occupied in the transmission of the letters, and looked forward for the arrival of the return mail with an anxiety it is not possible to describe. Would Lizzie see Myra? Would she repeat his words to her?—would Myra respond to them? Even as he repeated these questions his heart beat violently, and he felt a sick longing, which almost unnerved him for a proper performance of his duty. Still he was never absent from it—always ready when required—now in the trenches, anon on picquet duty, frequently engaged to repel sorties, but, with the exception of some three or four slight wounds, which he attended to himself, he escaped the hazards of the tremendous warfare unscathed. The mortality in his brigade had been truly horrible; no more forcible example being needed than that a draught of 150 men to the Scots Fusiliers, which arrived out under Lieutenant-Colonel de Bathe, was reduced in an incredible brief period to twenty men. About this time the picquets in the Tchernaya Valley were furnished by the brigade of Guards, and they extended over a considerable space of ground. As they were subjected to constant harassing from the enemy, who frequently advanced upon them in force, the brigadier was instructed to strengthen his pickets, and when he had done so the force of his brigade was represented by thirty men. This is a painful proof of the enfeebled condition to which the effective strength of the army was reduced by the devastating sickness which seized the men, owing to the deficiencies of food, clothing, and shelter, to which they were subjected.

Clifton Grey, on picket duty down in the valley of the Tchernaya, one bitter cold night had been engaged in a skirmish in which, with his comrades, he had proved successful and driven off the Russians, but some sharp firing still continued where the French held the ground. The roll of musketry—the cries of the combatants—the groans of the wounded were brought down by the wind, which was sharp and frosty and was clearing the sky of rolling masses of heavy grey cloud, so as to bring out the broad blue light of the moon. Clifton's force being in greater strength than usual that night, after a brief consultation with the captain, he marched up a body of the men in the direction of the firing, in order, if necessary, to assist the French, should they require the aid; but, before he could reach the spot, the moon broke out brightly and lighted up all the gloomy spots and hollow places, and the Russians ceased their efforts, to make a rapid retreat into Sebastopol, or such of the batteries as they might have emerged from. Nevertheless, Clifton pushed on with his men, and only paused when he thought it advisable to reconnoitre alone, before he precipitated himself and comrades into a difficulty, from which escape would be no easy matter. A turn in the hill along which he wound brought before him a sight which made him pause, and his whole frame thrill with emotion. Upon the ground lay several dead men, slain in the recent skirmish; by the side of one, however, knelt a Sister of Mercy: she was rendering to a departing soldier the last consolations of her religion. In his dying eyes she elevated a crucifix, and some feeble moaning attempts at utterance made by the man, told that he recognized her purpose and was grateful for it.

Clifton leaned upon his rifle for a moment, and regarded the solemn scene in silence; and then, as he saw the man's head droop and fall on the shoulder of the *religieuse*, as if fainting, he moved forward and tendered his assistance. He gave a hurried glance round him—both French and Russians had retired—and in this lonely, terrible spot, while the missiles of death were flying about, a young and tender woman, risking hazard of the most fearful kind—unmindful of dangers from which even stout-hearted men would shrink, made her way to afford aid to the wounded and helpless—or the last offices of religion for those whose fleeting breath was fluttering in their bosom, and whose dying aspiration—whose last feeble sigh she received—having afforded them a satisfaction in quitting this world of care, which, without her presence, they would not have known.

Clifton, with a brief apology for his intrusion; offered his services, if he could be of assistance to her;—he saw that she was French, and he addressed her in that language. She turned her quiet, calm face to him, neither startled nor disturbed by being suddenly addressed, and thanked him, but feared it would be of no avail.

"I see," exclaimed Clifton, "a fatigue party is approaching;—let me relieve you of that wounded soldier. I will support him until they arrive."

She looked on the face that rested calmly upon her shoulder, and shook her head.

"*Il est mort!*" she said in a low tone—"he is at rest. The Holy Virgin be praised, he died a Christian —*Requiescat in pace!*"

She crossed herself, and her lips moved in prayer. Then, with the aid of Clifton, she slowly laid the poor fellow upon the damp grass a stiffened corse. She looked around her. Of all those who lay upon the ground none longer needed her aid. The stillness of death was on all. The light laugh of the party approaching to remove the wounded and dead was heard ringing in the sharp air. She shuddered, and turned to Clifton, saying at the same time—

"Ah, but this war is a frightful scourge! it is merciless and insatiable; the healthful and the ailing, the innocent and the sinful, are alike struck down, and many a death-dealing bullet has not alone destroyed the body, but has borne to destruction the soul with it. Ah, Mon Dieu! it is too terrible."

Clifton acquiesced, but suggested that as a dispensation of Providence, it was only left to mortals to bow to the decrees of the Almighty Power without questioning its wisdom or commenting upon its necessity. He then diverted the subject to an expression of surprise that she should be so far down in the valley of the Tchernaya, almost beyond the outposts of both armies, and expressed his fear that she might meet with harm in thus venturing so far beyond the limits of the allies.

"I fear not danger from man," she exclaimed, with a soft smile. "My mission is known and recognised, and, pass where I may, testimonies of respect, proffers of service, observations of gratefulness is the treatment I experience. Yet, I have strayed beyond intention—in fact, I have lost my way. I set out to pay a visit to some of my religion in the English camp, and have evidently wandered out of my route."

"What division?" asked Clifton Grey.

"The First."

"Indeed you have wandered far from your destination. My regiment forms part of that division, and if you will accompany me, I will contrive to forward you to the nearest path to it. One of our men, who is a catholic, shall accompany you."

The sister thanked him, and rather gladly accepted the offer. They waited until the French soldiers arrived and took charge of the dead, and then they moved slowly away. Clifton Grey soon got into conversation with her; he found her sensible, agreeable, and with far less of the affectation of sanctity than he expected. He hinted his surprise at the discovery. She smiled.

"Religion," she said, "ought, by its possession, to make us cheerful, lively, happy. Sensible that as far as our capacity enable us, we obey the precepts of our holy faith, why should we wear long faces? We cannot avert the fiat of the Creator—we must resign ourselves to His will—we reverence, love Him, with our whole hearts, and in trying to make ourselves worthy of His approbation, it is unnecessary and it is wrong to be miserable and doleful. It is a sin to laugh when it would be wrong to laugh; but it would be a sin to appear dolorous when the heart should leap with innocent mirth and joy. I believe that I have a mission, and I exert to the utmost of my frail powers every effort to fulfil the duties of that mission; but as it takes me to the bedside of the sick and the dying, so it takes me to the dwellings of the healthy and the happy. As I am borne by it to the hovels and huts of the wretchedly poor, so am I at times compelled by it, too, to enter the halls of the rich. My province is to be ever among the poor, the afflicted, the wretched, and the dying, yet I am called upon at times to mix in the innocent festivities of those in a happier condition. As I am, I truly hope never without an earnest devotion when it is needful, so I am not without cheerfulness when it may be harmlessly indulged."

Clifton walked on for a moment, in silence, and then he said:

"May I enquire of you, whom you wish to see belonging to the first division?"

She mentioned two or three names of men with whom she had been acquainted. They were all dead— they had fallen in the Battle of Inkermann. He conveyed to her the sad news, and she prayed audibly for the repose of their souls. Then she enquired for a Catholic priest, the Rev. Mr. Wheble. He was attached, Clifton said he thought, to the Fourth Division, but the man he should select for her guide would be enabled to afford her the necessary information. She then remembered that she had a letter for a soldier of the Scots Fusilier Guards.

"Ha!" cried Clifton, hastily, "what name?"

She could not remember, after repeated trials. It had, she said, been brought by an Irish sister who had come out to the Crimea. She had almost brought a mail with her. She had been a long time distributing them, for many were dead, and others were difficult to find.

At the mention of Ireland, Clifton thought of Corporal Mickey Dunigan, but he dismissed the thought as being improbable. Twice or thrice the suggestion intruded itself, and, more to get rid of it than with any hope that it would be answered affirmatively, he mentioned the name of Mickey Dunigan, and the sister clapped her hands. That was the name. The letter was from his friends in Ireland, and she hoped that he was living to have the pleasure of receiving it.

Poor Mickey! Clifton's heart glowed as he thought of the delight the simple-minded fellow would experience at receiving an epistle from Bridget, for he felt sure it was from her. He sighed. Epistles for all, for everyone—from the highest to the humblest—save him. There was none for him. He sighed again, and heavily. The Sister of Charity heard it. She knew the sound well; she looked in his face.

"You are *triste*," she exclaimed. "Have your friends at home failed to communicate with you?"

"Nay," said he, with a sad smile, "it is not that—for I have no friends."

"No, that cannot be true; you, young, in manner amiable—it is not possible."

"Yet it is true. Letter for me indeed! Ah! no," he sighed again, "I have neither friend, nor relative, but those by whom I am at any time surrounded; nor home, but wherever I may locate."

"This will not always be so."

He shook his head despondingly.

"I have had bright hopes—glorious visions—blessful anticipations. I am afraid they will end—like all such dreams—in an awakening to disappointment."

"Nay, despair not; the good God often chasteneth those whom he ultimately showers happiness upon."

He shrugged his shoulders.

"I am in that," said he, "resigned; yet I feel often most keenly that I am alone in this mighty world, and of a verity know not one who wastes one thought upon me—cares whether I live or perish."

"There is One," she exclaimed with emphasis.

"Who may that be," he asked bitterly.

She pointed her hand impressively to heaven. He bowed his head reverently.

"I acknowledge, with humility," said he, "that He knoweth when the sparrow falls. I spoke of earthly ties of human sympathies, I have none of these upon which I can rest a claim."

"And yet there may exist those who are more deeply interested in you than you imagine."

"I have no reason to think so."

"Listen," said she, "I have promised to seek out one in your army circumstanced like yourself. Before I reached Marseilles I sojourned at a convent of our order, at Havre. Two young English girls were there in consequence of a remarkable incident. To one of them I conversed upon my expected journey to this vast graveyard, and she told me that she knew a youth who had joined the army of England, who was without kindred, or, as he believed, a friend in his own land to sigh for his absence, to hope for

his advancement, his safety, his glory, and she expressed her fears that he would be sad and cheerless in his isolation. But she supposed that he would hail with gladness the kind word that in his loneliness told him there was one yet in England who had never forgotten him; who prayed earnestly for his safety; who, conscious of the bright visions he had formed of fame and glory, constantly put up fervent wishes for their realisation; who was fully aware that he might be bowed down by a sense of desolation, but would have him rise up out of it in the full belief that though thousands of miles and wide seas divided them, she had never, never forgotten him, and that while she breathed she never would, nor cease to pray that, escaping the horrors and the dangers of his dread profession, they might be re-united in peace and happiness. But were this not even permitted, yet she would not have him think his memory was not cherished; that though absent, he was no more remembered; that though deserted by all the world beside, there were not bright eyes turned to the same sky upon which he gazed, in the hope that his were gazing there too, that there was a heart beating for him truly and steadfastly, though it were the sole one left, still there was one, and he might not lie down in sorrow and despair, believing in the living world there was none to care for him, no, not one.

"See, monsieur, here is an example," remarked the sister, with vivacity, "even the loneliest being in your grand army may not with justice despair, for to him shall I come with tidings to lift his heart out of the dullest gloom into sunshine. And, monsieur, these admissions were made to me specially by the beautiful young English girl of whom I have spoken, in trustfulness that when they were made known to him he would become happier, and bear his hard lot with more cheerfulness and resignation."

Clifton listened with attention to these observations. He felt a strange sensation pass through his breast—an increase in the action of his pulses—as he heard them; it was impossible not to identify them with his own case, or not to feel a presentiment that he was the very youth to whom she alluded. Yet she had mentioned Havre, and a convent, as the scene where this communication had been made to her; and Lizzie Hastings had spoken of Miss Aston as dwelling in Baker Street, in London; he heaved a deep sigh again, for that reflection seemed to settle the question, so far as he was concerned.

"Are you still a sceptic?" enquired the sister, looking at him seriously.

"Not of the truth of your assertion, that you are the messenger of happy tidings to some one who may be in their circumstances as lonely and sad as myself," he returned, "but I do not see how my assent to this entitles me to be more cheerful."

"It might be your own case," she suggested.

"Alas, it is not," he observed, sadly, and added, "it is calculated even to add to my gloom, for it is but another instance that while all around me are obtaining some comfort, even from unexpected sources, I am still left isolated and alone."

There was a pause. The sister shrugged her shoulders, and told him he lacked faith. Suddenly he said:

"You have not forgotten the name of this soldier, to whom you are the gentle courier of such blissful tidings?"

"In very truth I have not," she replied, quickly; "for often in my visions, brought up by day reveries, or in my nightly dreams, I see again that young, pale, English face turned towards me so earnestly—those large, deep, thoughtful eyes bent on mine with such appealing anxiety. Ah, Mon Dieu! may that English boy be yet living, for the sake of her pure, young, innocent heart."

Clifton was interested by this description, and a little eagerly said—

"Tell me the name of this soldier!"

"I made from her lips a memorandum, and I have often referred to it. I remember it well: it runs thus," she said, repeating word for word what she had written down, "M. Clifton Grey, Soldat Anglais, 2ᵉ Bataillon Scots Fusilier Guards."

Clifton stood still, and removed his cap; the moon shone brightly on his clear, manly face.

"I am Clifton Grey!" he exclaimed, "of the Second Battalion of Scots Fusiliers, and the name of the lady who sent to me the words of comfort you have briefly communicated—was it Mademoiselle Aston?"

"Mademoiselle Myra was the only name confided to me," replied the sister. "Tell him, said the fair English girl, "that Myra has never forgotten him, and that she never will—never—never!"

Clifton fell upon one knee, and seizing her hand, kissed it with passionate fervor. A gush of tears came to his eyes. He uprose and turned away, his emotion was so great he could not speak—could not even attempt to affect a calmness he was far from feeling. He paced up and down to endeavour to bring his feelings under control, while the Sister rightly resolved to preserve silence until he became more placid, for she knew enough of human feelings and sympathies to be aware that kind words and soft consolations, in a moment like this, would be unheeded.

Oh, what joy was brought to Clifton's heart—what bliss—what, as he estimated it, ample reward for his long, long season of doubt and despair, for the struggles and trials of his vocation! What a new stimulus to win honor, fame, promotion—what an impulse to move buoyantly onward in his career, to render himself worthy of one so dear, so tender, so thoughtful! How he was lifted out of his sorrow into delight!

At length he was in some degree enabled to calm down his extravagant joy, and to return to speak with the Sister, who had brought him such happy, happy news.

"You were right in bidding me not to despair; I wrong in indulging it," he said. "I acknowledge with reverence and humility the kindness and goodness—as I may hereafter also have to confess—the wisdom of Heaven in all connected with my course; and I freely confess, that as my heart had sunk to the lowest depths of despondency, and is now on the very pinnacle of hopefulness, so it is not just to Heaven to believe, even in the toils of misery and wretchedness, that we are wholly abandoned, cast off, left to perish, without a tear or a sigh being wasted on our memory."

Now he questioned her closely, and made her repeat to him all that she knew of Myra, every word she had uttered, all she imagined that she even thought. He was greatly perplexed to account for the presence of Myra and Lizzie Hastings at Havre; and the Sister could afford him no other information than that it was owing to a remarkable incident, with the particulars of which she was unacquainted, not having had the curiosity to ask for them; and he was obliged to content himself in the hope that when Lizzie wrote she would not fail to give a history of this strange circumstance. Clifton drew from the Sister that her name was Geraldine, and that she was on her way from the camp of the first division to the hospital at Balaklava. He told her he should see her again, and should he have the good fortune to hear from England, which he now felt some title to expect, he would certainly endeavour to see her, and communicate to her that further pleasing intelligence of which she was now the harbinger.

By this time he had reached the spot where a dozen of the men were stationed, and with the permission of the officer, the man of whom he had spoken was despatched with Sister Geraldine to the camp, where Mickey Dunigan was lying dreaming of Bridget Boyle, but not that a letter from her was so close at hand.

Clifton returned again to the sentries stationed near the neutral ground, and found all still, save that one of them, a keen-eyed, good soldier, said he fancied he had observed something dark moving lower down in the valley, but he could not make it out. It was a suspicious object, because it bore no form by which to class it. He pointed out the place where he had observed it moving slowly and stealthily; but it was not to be seen at the moment he mentioned it to Clifton. Our hero, struck by his remark, determined to reconnoitre, and moved cautiously but quickly down to where the hill was in deep shadow; he sprung from knoll to mound, leaped over gullies and fissures, and sprung round a mound, about ten feet in height and some thirty feet in extent, which shut out the view for some distance further down the valley, to find himself the next instant struggling in the arms of a troop of Russians.

He contrived to discharge his rifle, although the bullet went careering in the air; he struggled with desperation, but he was thrown down, and a voice in French bade him remain quiet and save his life; resistance was wholly useless against the force by which he was surrounded, and his struggles would end only in compelling them to despatch him. He cast his eyes round—upwards of two hundred men were crouching under the mound ready to carry out some enterprise, and he saw, therefore, that he had nothing to do but resign himself to his fate. His rifle had been already secured, and the Russian officer tried to extort from him a promise not to attempt to escape, which he would not give; he was passed to the rear, and two Russian soldiers were placed to guard him, with their rifles pointed to his head, and strict orders to shoot him if he offered to move.

With satisfaction he soon learned, from exclamations passed from one to another, that the discharge of his rifle had alarmed the picket, and the enterprise, whatever it might be, was frustrated, but it was with gloomy anticipations he found himself seized, the whole party moving rapidly from their cover, and preparing to return to Sebastopol. He had longed for the hour that should bring with it the entry into Sebastopol, but not in this way—he had not contemplated that.

At a given order, the Russians made a dash, and were soon down the hill. A few shots were despatched after them by the picket to which Clifton Grey belonged, but not one of them took effect. The soldiers were soon in the road, and, as the day began to dawn, they were admitted within the gates of the town. Clifton, reflecting that if his heart had been greatly elated by the communication made to him by Sister Geraldine, its joys was considerably modified by the disheartening, unhappy fact, that he was a prisoner in the hands of the Russians.

CHAPTER XXV.

"E'vn daylight has its dangers; and the walk
Through pathless wastes and woods, unconscious once
Of other tenants than melodious birds,
Or harmless flocks, is hazardous and bold.
Lamented change! to which full many a cause
Invet'rate, hopeless of a cure, conspires.
The course of human things from good to ill,
From ill to worse is fatal, never fails."
                  COWPER.

" And then with glassy gaze she stood,
As ice were in her curdled blood;
  But every now and then a tear,
    So large and slowly gather'd, slid
     From the long dark fringe of that fair lid.
It was a thing to see, not hear!
And those who saw it did surprise
Such drops could fall from human eyes.
To speak she thought—the imperfect note
Was choked within her swelling throat;
Yet seemed in that low hollow groan,
Her whole heart gushing in the tone.
It ceased. Again she thought to speak,
Then burst her voice in one long shriek!"
                  PARASINA.

CAPTAIN WINSLOW PUTS INTO EXECUTION HIS PLOT.
WHAT FOLLOWED IN CONSEQUENCE.

LIZZIE HASTINGS, to use her own expression, when Myra begged her to come and see her still as she had hitherto done, was resolved to "die first." She assured Myra that to her she should always act, and of her always think, as she had up to the present moment; but she could not possibly darken her mother's doors again until she herself was convinced that the injurious and unjust suspicions of that lady had ceased. She was, for some time after the scene at Baker-street, of which Captain Winslow had been the occasion, hot and irritable; as Beverley Winslow experienced, on meeting her one afternoon alone in Portman-square, for that gentleman "wejoicing" in having presented to him another opportunity of speaking to her and urging his passion for her—for, if the truth must be told, he was really more smitten with Lizzie than Myra—resolved it should not be lost or thrown away. He had perceived her suddenly walking slowly, as if in deep thought, a few paces before him, and he drew nearly up to her before she was conscious of his approach. He stole up close behind her, and in a low voice murmured:

"What a widiculous demmed little shy maff it gwoes! And wuns away fwom its own intewest too. It knows how my heart and bwain is wacked with love for it, and what wolls of wiches I would spwead awound it—what wegwets I would shield it fwom, and yet shwinks fwom and wetweats fwom me as if I was a wegular wetch."

Lizzie knew the voice well. At another time she would have fled away; now she stopped short and turned round, so that Beverley restrained himself only with the very greatest difficulty from running over her.

She pushed him back, and said, fiercely:

"How dare you annoy and pester me in this way, after my repeatedly telling you that your conduct insults and offends me?"

"Thats where its so demmed widiculous. I would not insult it for the world—I love it too much, and would make it a lady."

"And I tell you once for all, I do not wish to be spoken to by you."

"Not when I love it so?"

"I despise and hate you, and those connected with you. I hate your brother, because I think him a scoundrel. I despise you as a fool; and I insist upon your not following me, or I will claim the protection of the police."

"Weally now—weally now, its vewy angwy, and it looks so wemarkably pwetty, too, when it is ewoss."

He laid hold of her chin, and pinched it, as he spoke, and she responded by a smack upon his face, given with such vigour that it might have been heard at some distance. Beverley Winslow's hat was knocked off by the shock, and was whisked away by the wind, at the rate of twenty miles an hour, across the square. A red impression of five small fingers was left upon his cheek, and there was created a ringing in his ears which shut out every other sound. The pain was very sharp, and his eyes were filled with water, and, to add to his mortification, Everett Randolph and his two sisters came up at the moment, having seen the whole transaction. Everett laughed boisterously, and would have spoken, but his sisters, angrily, dragged him on, disdaining to utter a word to the hero of such a scene in the street. He saw that they cut him, and that Lizzie was no longer visible. He had nothing left but to retreat, feeling wofully at a discount; but he saw the necessity of recovering his hat, which was rolling with extraordinary rapidity round the square, followed by three boys and a dog. The dog, however, exhibited the greatest speed, and overtook the hat, which he shook frequently, as though it were a rat, and it was proper to do this; he rolled over it twice or thrice, bent in the crown, and broke the brim, and declined to give it up when called upon to do so by the three boys, who, all anticipating reward, seized it and struggled with the dog for possession. The hat was not benefitted by the process, nor was Beverley Winslow's appearance improved when, dirtied, torn, and out of shape, he put it on, not noticing, in his agitation, its unfavourable aspect. He gave to one of the boys a half-sovereign in mistake for sixpence, and retired to find a cab in which to secrete himself until he reached home, vowing never to have anything more to say to such a "fewocious viwago" any more, and leaving the boys to have a desperate fight for "halves," until a policeman appeared to take a part in the performance.

Lizzie wrote a long letter to Haverel, and one to Clifton Grey, to whom she related everything that took place in respect to himself, fearing that Mrs. Aston would refuse Myra permission to write to him. She counselled him to write boldly to Miss Aston, and assured him, if she were a judge of a woman's heart, she was sure that Myra loved him with her whole soul. Night after night she sat up until she had got these letters written, and she went with them herself to the post office in Old Cavendish-street. At the mystic window she asked every possible question of the snappish official there, satisfied herself that she had complied with all the requisite forms, and that the letters would go safely to their destination.

She further satisfied her conscience by the reflection that she had given Myra to know that she was engaged in writing to Sergeants Haverel and Grey, and that she had also given to Myra the exact direction for a letter addressed to Grey, and by which it would find its way through the post office to him in the Crimea. But she could not put her little foot over the doorstep of Mr. Randolph's house. No; she could not do that. Myra was thus left to the companionship of her own thoughts. The Misses Randolph were extremely kind and sociable with her, but there was no real friendship between them; their intercourse did not take that shape. They did not seek her confidence from the mere delicacy of good breeding; she shrunk from bestowing it upon anybody. Even Lizzie guessed far more than she knew. With her mother she had been very explicit; had confessed that Clifton had, at least, won her esteem in a higher degree than any other person with whom she was acquainted; indeed there was no other person of his sex for whom she experienced similar sentiments. She thought it illiberal and harsh to treat him with coldness and distance because of his position, and frankly confessed she found it impossible to do so. She argued the question with great earnestness and force, and so far with success, that a compromise was entered into between her and her mother, in which Mrs. Aston withdrew her ban against all future correspondence with Clifton Grey, and Myra promised not to write until she received her mother's permission to do so. And then they glided once more into their former relations. Captain Winslow still came to the house; but though he met Mrs. Aston, Myra avoided him; she did it so openly and decidedly, that in the sitting-room, when he entered, she at once retired from it. His passion only became more and more inflamed by it; and a plan he was concocting to make her his own, was only hastened by her behaviour to him.

Perk, bribed by the promise of a large sum, was the principal agent in the plot, and on the night on which it was to be carried out, was an active participator in it, for without his aid it could not have been accomplished. The whole family of the Randolphs received an invite from a fashionable friend to a splendid re-union, and accepting it, went there. On this night Beverley Winslow called, and was ushered into the room, where Mrs. Aston and Myra were sitting, by Perk, without that individual having ascertained whether they would receive him. Mr. Beverley Winslow, instructed, but without knowing the purpose for which he had been tutored, observed Myra disappear, without attempting to detain her, but at once entered into a long history about some poor family in whose behalf he said he was "desirous of winning her generous assistance," which kept Mrs. Aston chained to her seat listening to a dreary tale, of which she could comprehend little or nothing.

In the meantime, Myra retired to her chamber, and seated herself by her dressing-table, to indulge in the luxury of free and untrammelled thought. Her maid Lucy, by a contrivance of Perk, had gone to the theatre with a fellow-servant, Myra having granted her permission; so that she was quite alone, and not, as she thought, likely to be interrupted.

She had scarcely been a minute seated, when she became conscious of a most powerful and beautiful scent, different to anything of the kind she had ever before smelled, and her attention at once was drawn to a very handsome pocket handkerchief upon her toilet-table. She took it up and examined it; it was bordered with the most extravagantly expensive lace. She put it to her nose; it was this which bore the fragrant scent, which had so immediately excited her notice. Again and again she drew its delicate odour within her nostrils, and while wondering to whom it belonged, became insensible.

It was dark within—without. In five minutes from that time, closely enveloped in a huge military cloak, she was carried to a travelling carriage, standing at the corner of Portman Square, and was supported in the arms of Captain Winslow. The horses were lashed into a gallop, and the vehicle rolled down to the Brighton Railway Station. There it was placed upon a truck and conveyed by the mail train to Brighton.

Captain Winslow had kept the carriage window down, and paid first class fare for himself and a lady, an invalid preferring to ride in his own carriage. He had a lamp with him, and having thoroughly acquainted himself with the means of keeping Myra in a state of insensibility for a certain period, without affecting injuriously her system, he, as soon as he observed signs of returning animation appearing, laid her head gently on his breast, and poured down her throat a potion, which once more restored her to her helpless unconscious condition.

She was very pale, and lay as though dead; he was extremely nervous and anxious, he feared detection—was afraid she might perhaps die from the effects of the drug, was altogether too much agitated and apprehensive to take, as he had intended, a most base and infamous advantage of her powerlessness.

At the Brighton terminus he was in a state of trepidation, until his horses were put to and he had fairly started on the road to Chichester, where he intended to change his route for a quiet and retired spot, with which he had been made acquainted. On reaching Worthing he was compelled to stop and refresh, and then it transpired the carriage had sustained an injury during its progress, and would be unable to proceed any further. He was in a fearful passion, but that availed him nothing; he then took the landlord aside, and told him he had his sister in the carriage, that she was afflicted with occasional attacks of raving insanity, and when travelling it was found essential to give her a sleeping draught; that as he was anxious to get her to their destination, he must provide him with a post chaise, as it would be impossible to sleep there. The only post chaise belonging to the establishment was out, and would not be back till four in the morning, and as there was no alternative, Captain Winslow was obliged to remain. The horses were put in the stable, Myra was left in the carriage; he remaining with her, drinking deeply of brandy, and smoking furiously of cigars.

At four the post-chaise returned. The jaded horses were taken out, and those belonging to Captain Winslow were put in. A fresh post-boy was placed on their backs, the captain's servant being left in charge of their carriage, and away they went, and continued journeying for some miles. Day dawned, and Captain Winslow dropped into a doze—a dream—he was at the battle of the Alma, and deafened by the rolling musketry and the shouts of contending foes; then he became conscious of a succession of shrieks, and opening his eyes, found that Myra had become alive to her situation, and finding him sleeping, had put down the window and was screaming for help.

Some one had answered her appeals, for he could hear the voice of a man shouting to the postilion to stop. This the man could not do, for the horses, startled by Myra's sudden screams, had taken fright, and were flying madly along the road. Now there was a frightful crash, the wheels of the swaying vehicle went into a ditch, and over went the chaise; the horses kicked and plunged, broke the splinter bar, and galloped away. The postilion, fortunately unhurt, assisted Captain Winslow and Myra out of the carriage, and without waiting to see whether they were hurt, darted off after the horses. Captain Winslow had not time to address Myra, ere a young man, who had been running after the carriage, arrived; he was out of breath, but he cried aloud—

"Dost thou need help, young lady! Good lord! Why Miss Myra—be it thee! I be Charley Rowe—dont'ee know I?"

Myra screamed with joy, and ran up to him, but Captain Winslow pulled her back. Charley Rowe, however, in an instant caught him by the collar, and held him firmly; there was a desperate struggle between them.

SAUL WATERS.—CAPTAIN WINSLOW IS AGAIN FOILED.

"Ruffian," shouted Captain Winslow, "release me, or I'll make you bitterly repent this. Dog! take your filthy hand from my neck!"

"Neither of those be my name," said Charley Rowe, still holding him with a strength which Winslow could not shake off. "And I shan't let go of you at your bidding. You've been playing the rogue to that young lady, I'll be sworn, and so I'll stick to you until justice be done; and so I will. Look'ee, Miss Myra, I swore to Mr. Clifton Grey that if I had ever the power, I'd watch over and serve you, and I'll shed my heart's best blood to do it, too."

Clifton Grey! how the name stung Captain Winslow. He struggled desperately with Rowe, but he was still a prisoner.

"What is it all about, Miss Myra?" asked Charley, when Winslow, finding them ineffectual, ceased his struggles, though he chafed with rage and intense vexation at thus finding himself a prisoner.

"I know not—oh, I know not!" she exclaimed, clasping her hands convulsively; "it seems to me all a horrid, fearful dream. It appears scarcely a few minutes back that I was with my mother—was in my own chamber in London. Yet am I here—far, far from my home."

"But not far from the old one," responded Charley, "we be only a few miles from Arundel, and I'll soon take you there."

"Heaven be praised," ejaculated Myra.

"Aye, Ellen have often wondered she never heard from you, she'll be glad to hear from you surely. As for this chap here, we'll take un to the police inspector and see what he's got to say to un."

"Never!" shouted Winslow, terrified at the considerations that it called up. He struggled desperately with Charley, and they swayed to and fro, Winslow trying to throw Charley, but in vain. While in the heat of their tussle—Myra, in deadly affright, unknowing whether to remain or fly—three low looking fellows made their appearance from the other side of the hedge. They were busy in a moment, and wanted to know "What was up?" Captain Winslow, at a venture, declared that the ruffian who held him had attacked him, as he believed, to rob him, and he offered them a handsome reward if they would seize Rowe, and take him where he could be consigned to the custody of the law.

The sight of the overturned chaise, and the gentlemanly attire of the captain, seemed to support his assertions, and the offer of a handsome sum was an inducement to believe them, whether he spoke the truth or not. So, after a moment's conference, they set upon Charley Rowe, who, compelled to release Captain Winslow, tried to keep the fellows at bay with his stick, but, Winslow being added to his assailants, his chance of even escaping, with the purpose of obtaining assistance, was destroyed, and he quickly was overpowered, and his arms bound tightly to his side.

Captain Winslow was unable to contain his exultation; he laughed joyously, and taunted Charley Rowe with the turning of the tables; but the young man, though deeply hurt and vexed at his position, only said:

"Never mind; my turn will come again bimeby. Don't be alarmed, Miss Myra; he daren't hurt you; there'll be help along presently, you'll see."

"Miss Aston," said Captain Winslow, "pay no heed to what this brutal lout says, and fear nothing; no harm is intended you. I only seek to rescue you and keep you from danger. I beg of you to calm yourself; to ask no questions; to wonder not at the novelty of your situation—at least not now to agitate yourself respecting it. All shall be cleared up and explained to your satisfaction. At present it will only be needful for you to be quiet and resigned, under the solemn assurance that no danger can come near you—no ill is designed you."

Myra turned from him in great distress. What to do she knew not, the place was so lonely; there was no one near who would help her, save Charley, who had been deprived of the power of doing so, and there seemed nothing left for her but to remain quiet until an opportunity was afforded her to obtain assistance. Her mind, too, was yet clogged by the effects of the drug; her brain was racked with pain; everything was still confusing, and she felt it useless to resist when Captain Winslow placed the military cloak round her, and prepared to lead her to a cottage in a bye lane, belonging to one of the three men, where they could rest and await the means of conveying them on to their destination.

Charley Rowe was forced to accompany them. Captain Winslow had no notion of his being permitted to depart; he was anxious, if the presence of the police became a necessity, to give Rowe into custody at once, and to make a strong case against him. He, a gentleman, a captain in the army, would be listened to with attention; his word would go infinitely farther than that of a country boor, and therefore it would, as a matter of personal safety, be necessary not to lose sight of him until his point was gained.

It was a wretched looking hovel by the way-side into which they were ushered, and they were roughly bid to make themselves as welcome as they could. A prompt demand was now made by the men upon Captain Winslow for the award, which he sought to defer, for he was not yet he felt in a secure position, but they all refused to wait; indeed they exhibited a remarkable anxiety, which contrasted strangely with the apparent want of occasion for it, and they told the captain in very unqualified terms that if he did not give them what he had promised, they would release Charley Rowe, and bind him in his place. Captain Winslow made a virtue of necessity, and not only gave them, as he had promised, five pounds for what they had done, but he promised them fire more if they could right the post-chaise and bring back the horses, which the postilion had pursued and probably recovered, so that he might be enabled to get away from this desert place. The men seemed readily to comply with his request, and left the cottage, as they said, for that purpose.

When they had disappeared, Captain Winslow spoke to Myra, and endeavoured, by the most specious language, to induce her to believe that he had not been the immediate occasion of her being brought from London, that he had but one object in life, and that was to be the slave of her will.

She answered him not—the very sound of his voice sickened her, and she estimated, at their true worth, the tenour of his asseverations. She began, too, to comprehend more clearly the situation in which she was placed, and, though agitated and alarmed, to feel that in these days of enlightenment, of an extensive police system, no serious danger would probably befal her. Although, in the hands of a bad and determined man, there was no telling to what villany she might not be subjected, still there was the hope, the possibility of escape—the probability that he would not dare proceed beyond a certain limit, and she must trust to her own energy and firmness to protect her so far, and this she resolved to do—even to death. She turned from him, as he spoke, and gazed from the open door, hoping—against hope—to see some persons come that way who could effectually afford her the aid she so much needed.

Captain Winslow, unable to extort a word from Myra, pandered to a miserable meanness in his composition, a low and contemptible weakness, which shone out whenever an opportunity for its indulgence occurred. He walked up to Charley Rowe, and exhausted his invention in taunting him and to try to sting him into a foaming passion, but without succeeding, for Charley Rowe by no means seemed so depressed as might have been anticipated. Whether he had a source upon which he relied for a satisfactory change in the circumstances he did not let drop, but he listened to the sneers and sarcasms—the jeers and low insults—with a smile of contempt; he replied to some in coin as good as that flung at him. A remark made about Clifton Grey by Captain Winslow, who had, by his previous observation, gathered that Rowe was his warm friend, gave him the most pain; but he consoled himself by telling the Captain that he was not to deceive himself into any notion that he would ever stand in Clifton's shoes—he might some day clean them, but that was all he would ever have to do with them.

Captain Winslow's hysteric cry of rage was interrupted by a short scream of horror from Myra. A shadow darkened the doorway. The next moment a man, in rough seafaring costume, entered the room. His face was pale, his beard unshaven, his counte-

nance haggard, and his eyes blood-shot. He cast his eyes quickly round, and running up to Myra, he pulled her face rudely round.

"By the living God!" he cried, "it is Myra."

"What!" shouted Charley Rowe. "Why—be that you, Saul Waters? Why I thought thou wert transported."

Saul Waters, for it was he, turned round and looked with surprise on the speaker.

"Charley Rowe," he exclaimed, "an' bound. What does 't all mean?"

"Who are you, you ill-mannered ruffian!" cried Captain Winslow, hectoring. "What do you mean by entering this cottage in this blackguard manner, and by daring to lay your filthy paws upon that young lady?"

"What do I mean!" echoed Saul Waters, fiercely; "you shall soon see what I mean. You be too glib of tongue, you be; calling names afore you know who's who. Lookee, soldier—for you be a swaddy, I suppose, by that dog's tail under your nose—my name's Saul Waters, and if truth be told, I dessay no more a ruffian and blackguard than you be, an' I've perhaps more right in this cottage than you have, as I'm likely to shew you by flinging your ugly carcase over into yon ditch."

Captain Winslow spluttered with passion, but Saul waved his hand contemptuously, and turned to Charley Rowe.

"Charley," he said, "what do this mean? How be it Myra's here, and you be bound? Tell me truth, or 'twull be worse for'ee, that 'twull."

"I don't care for your threats, nor for you, Saul," replied Charley; "you know that; but I don't mind telling you all I know, for I do hope you will ask forgiveness for the past, and not let any harm come to Myra."

"Harm to Myra!" repeated Saul Waters, his eyes glaring with unnatural brightness. "No, never!" He uttered a fearful oath, attesting his determination to prevent it, if an attempt was made to injure her, and then asked Rowe to tell him the quarter from which she was likely to meet with it?"

"There it stands," said Charley, nodding his head towards Captain Winslow. "He was carrying her off by force in a post-chaise, but it was overturned; I interfered to save her, but some fellows who came up took his money to help him, and brought Myra and me here."

Saul Waters looked fixedly and with a growling aspect at Captain Winslow; then he turned his glance on Myra, who sat with her face buried in her hands. He gave one look at Charley Rowe, then he stepped to the door and gave a hurried glance, right and left; he returned and confronted Captain Winslow—all the work of a minute. He fixed his gleaming eye upon the officer, and exclaimed, through his teeth—

"You have some design upon Myra, then. You perhaps love her, and would carry her off, so that she should be yours. You have found her scornful, and you have tried to bring her to a satisfactory way of thinking; but you have not been altogether successful, though not far off. Now mark me! Myra is my foster sister. I have a design upon her, for I love her to madness. I will carry off and she shall be mine."

"Insolent scoundrel!" cried Winslow, furiously. "How dare you——"

"I dare a great deal," cried Saul Waters. "I have that which makes me do as well as dare much, and I have sworn that Myra shall be mine, and she shall. You will not step in to hinder my making her so."

He produced a pistol from his pocket, as he uttered these words, and pointed it at Winslow's head. The captain staggered back at once, alarmed, and frenzied with passion. Myra screamed, and threw herself upon her knees.

"Captain Winslow," she cried in agony, "if you have one spark of honour—if you are not utterly lost to all that is just and honourable, you will forego your own misguided intentions, and save me from this man."

What Captain Winslow would have said is not necessary to record, for he was prevented speaking by a voice at the window, which exclaimed:

"That is he. Forward, lads, and take your prisoner."

Saul Waters turned round at the sound of the voice, and, with a shout of horror, saw, at the casement and in the doorway, a party of the coast-guard. With a terrible oath he dashed into a little out-house, and, breaking through the window, leaped out, and sprung into a plantation at the back, closely pursued by three or four of the coast-guard. The officer in command, accompanied by the remainder, entered the cottage. Charley Rowe uttered a loud "Hurrah!" as he recognized him.

"Thank God! You have found us out, Lieutenant Lawrance," said he, with a face brimful of joy. "You have not come a moment too soon. Lord help me, what a sweat I have been in! Here, just untie these cords, there's a good fellow!"

"Aha! Charley Rowe, and bound. What does this mean? Unbind him, Wilson."

"Hold!" cried Captain Winslow, assuming a proud demeanour, "I hope you will order nothing of the kind. Whom may I have the honour of addressing?"

"Lieutenant Lawrance, R.N." returned the officer.

"And you, sir?"

"I am Captain Winslow, of the Scots Fusilier Guards. It is by my orders that the young ruffian is bound; he attempted to commit a robbery upon me, but, fortunately, timely aid arriving, he was secured, and I have retained him until I could give him in custody of the police."

"What—Charley Rowe?—impossible—absurd!" exclaimed the lieutenant. "What have you to say to this, Charley?"

"He!" exclaimed Captain Winslow, with a contemptuous hiss, and added authoritatively, "You wear Her Majesty's uniform, Lieutenant Lawrance. I hope, sir, you will do your duty."

"I hope I shall, sir," he replied, haughtily; "at all events I shall not come to you for instructions, if I do not. What is the meaning of this charge, Charley? Unbind him, Wilson—did you hear my order?"

"Ay, ay!" sir, replied the sailor, "but—"

"No replies, sir; obey orders," exclaimed Oliver Lawrance, peremptorily.

Charles Rowe, as he was being unbound, answered the query put to him by saying:

"I can just tell you that it is a shocking, wicked lie. You ask that young lady there all about it, Mr. Lawrance. She will tell you the truth, I know."

Lieutenant Lawrance turned to where Myra sat upon a chair, half fainting. She had, however, heard Charley Rowe's observation, and she upraised her wan face so that he could see it. He did so, and at once recognised it. He started, removed his cap, and advanced hastily to her.

"Good heavens!" he exclaimed, "Miss Aston!"

She at once remembered him by the sound of his voice, and felt a sense of safety instantly. She tried to rise and speak to him, but she found herself too weak to accomplish it, and she sunk back again, and burst into tears.

"Pray compose yourself, Miss Aston," he said, respectfully and tenderly. "Be assured of your safety. When you feel more recovered, you can speak; but do not distress yourself to do so."

Myra looked at him gratefully; at the same time Captain Winslow came up to him and tapped him on the shoulder, and with a haughty, arrogant demeanour, said:

"Mark me, Lieutenant What's-your-name, I must protest strongly against all these proceedings."

"Indeed!" responded Lawrance, coolly.

Yes. Firstly, I object to your addressing that young lady in such familiar terms."

"Do you?"

"Yes; I object to your addressing her at all."

"Really!"

"Emphatically, sir. It forms no part of your duty, and I shall not permit it. I have given into your custody a fellow who sought to rob me, and for aught I know, to take my life, and you, in defiance of representations to that effect, have seen fit to release him, and for which highly improper conduct I shall report you to your superiors."

"Sir, if you are as you profess to be, an officer in Her Majesty's service, you must be well aware that it forms no part of my duty to take into custody persons guilty of the act with which you have charged this young man. You will have the opportunity of doing this to the proper authorities by-and-bye. You will, therefore, perceive that your observations are gratuitously impertinent, and as such I fling them back to your teeth; at the same time, if I may be permitted an expression of opinion, I think I may justly challenge your title to forbidding me addressing Miss Aston, to whom I most unequivocally deny having spoken in familiar terms. I further have the very strongest doubts that young Rowe ever thought of attempting the criminal act with which you have charged him, and were it my duty to detain him—which it is not—I should hesitate much ere I did so on your testimony."

"Insolent audacity! But I see how it is: you and the fellow are in collusion. I, however, do not intend that he shall escape, and shall therefore go at once and seek for a constable to take him in charge."

"Stay, sir," exclaimed Lieutenant Lawrance, standing in his path as he was about to leave. "You cannot be permitted to depart at present."

"What do you mean, fellow?" cried Captain Winslow, with pretended indignation—in reality filled with apprehension.

"Plainly, sir, that I have strong doubts respecting your conduct, and it is my intention to detain you until those doubts are cleared up."

"At your peril lay a finger upon me, villain,' cried Captain Winslow, excitedly.

"No one will lay hands upon you, unless you make an attempt to go hence, and then I suspect that in no gentle manner you will be restrained. Let me also suggest to you, to be less free in your use of misapplied terms when speaking to me, or you may have to rue the consequences.

"I insist on quitting this den," roared Captain Winslow, now fairly frightened at the possible and looming consequences of the act he had committed with such recklessness. "Who will dare to detain an officer in Her Majesty's Guards."

"I—Oliver Lawrance, most assuredly," exclaimed the young officer of the coast guard, "and that, until I am certain he is guiltless of the suspicion now attaching to him."

"If you don't, I shall," exclaimed Charley Rowe firmly. "He spoke about finding an officer to give me in charge, he shall have one sooner than he wishes for him, I'll warrant."

"Miss Aston, if you are now sufficiently recovered to speak," said Oliver Lawrance, "will you be so good as to inform me, if this individual who styles himself an officer in Her Majesty's Guards, has any claim to direct your actions.

"None whatever," exclaimed Myra earnestly, "he has—"

"Pardon me, Miss Aston," interrupted the captain, "let me entreat you, for your own sake, not to be

too hasty. Consider, reflect upon your position, before you make any statement."

"Reflect upon my position!" she repeated, with indignant emphasis. "I do not understand you—I do not desire to understand you. I request that you will not again address me. Lieutenant Lawrance," she continued, addressing that officer. "I claim your protection, I have been brought here under some strange and mysterious—"

"Miss Aston, for the sake of your fair name, let me urge upon you to maintain a reserve on what has happened," exclaimed Captain Winslow, striving to convey an imputation from which he thought—he hoped she might shrink. But she was really too innocent to divine his intention, and paid no heed to what he said, but in brief terms related her waking as from a dream, and discovering herself in a post chaise with Captain Winslow at her side, her shrieks for aid, the overturning of the carriage, the attempt at her rescue by Charley Rowe, and the incidents following it, so far as she was able to take cognisance of them, until the arrival of the lieutenant and his men.

"I had a misgiving that you would give me some such explanation of your presence here," said Oliver Lawrance to her. "However, you may rely upon me for protection. We will make the best of our way to Arundel, and there you can telegraph to your friends to tell them of your safety, where they may find you, and so relieve their minds. As for you, sir," he added, turning to Captain Winslow, "you, who have been so free in your application to me of the epithets fellow and villain, allow me to say that my impression of your being a consummate scoundrel does not appear to have been in the slightest degree erroneous, nor the determination to detain you for magisterial inquiry unjustly formed. You may consider your detention in what light you please, and take, after you are out of my hands, any steps in respect to it you may have in your power; but I shall enforce your attending me to the station at Arundel, where I shall place you in the hands of the civil authorities, and you will there learn that when an officer in Her Majesty's Guards commits an act which renders him amenable to the law, who the parties are, as well as myself, who will detain him?"

The lieutenant called up two of his men, both armed with pistols and cutlasses, and to their safe keeping he consigned the captain, who inveighed bitterly and passionately against this interference with the liberty of the subject, and vowed revenge, threatened actions, and raved like a madman, but to no purpose. Oliver Lawrance ordered his men to conduct him to Arundel, and promised to meet them there at the police station, so the captain was marched off with as little ceremony as if he had been a smuggler of the lowest caste.

Just at this time the three fellows who had made

prisoner of Charley Rowe, under the influence of Captain Winslow's bribery, returned to say the postillion had succeeded in recovering his horses, and with the aid of some ropes had managed to repair the damage sufficiently to the overturned chaise, which had been set on its wheels again, in order to reach, at a steady pace, the town of Arundel. But when they saw Rowe at liberty, the captain a prisoner, and a party of the coast guard within the cottage, they decamped at the top of their speed. Charley, calling to two of the seamen to follow him, darted off after them like a roebuck, soon doubled upon them, and run them into a close, where they were all captured. This, in some degree, compensated for the escape of Saul Waters; the men in search of him having returned to say he had eluded them, and got clear away. Captain Winslow was, therefore, marched on foot, in company with the low rascals he had employed, along the dusty road to Arundel, Charley Rowe accompanying him to see that he did not escape. Oliver Lawrance handed Myra into the post-chaise, and taking a seat by her side, bade the postillion drive to Arundel.

Upon reaching the town the chaise was stopped, at Myra's wish, at the residence of Mr. Fairfax, and Ellen was not a little astonished to see, on running out to the door to ascertain what visitor had thus early made a call, Myra Aston, handed out by Oliver Lawrance, her person loosely enveloped in a military cloak, her hair in disorder, no bonnet, her face white as ashes, and her whole manner distracted. She caught hold of her hands, and wrung them warmly and earnestly.

"Dear Myra," she exclaimed, with tears in her eyes, "I am very—very happy to see you; I thought you had forgotten me."

Myra could hardly articulate a word in reply, and Ellen hurried her into her own room.

Oliver Lawrance, taking a brief farewell, and promising to wait upon her shortly, ordered the postillion to drive the chaise to the nearest inn. Then he took the man's name down, and bade him follow him to the police station, as his evidence might be required. Before, however, he made his way there, he went to the railway station, and there, having received the particulars from Myra, transmitted a telegraphic message to her mother in London to say she was safe, and inform where she was staying; he then went on to the police office, and stated the heads of the charge against Captain Winslow. The inspector thought it advisable to go up to the magistrate at once and prefer his complaint, so as to secure an early decision, as he, the magistrate, might be called away to London, and detention possibly might prove inconvenient to Oliver Lawrance. The young lieutenant caught eagerly at the proposition, and walked with the inspector to the magistrate's residence, some two miles from the town; and when Captain Winslow, being dusty and weary,

reached the police station at Arundel, overcome with disgust at his situation, worried and anxious as to his future, vexed and annoyed by his blackguard associates, he was yet further distressed by the announcement that he had two miles further to proceed, a portion of which was through the town. He found, too, that he was none too soon in his arrival for the rabble to muster. Arundel can plead no exemption from the curiosity that prevails among the humbler classes, and on this occasion it furnished a strong complement of idlers— men, women, girls, boys, and dogs—who kept up a running commentary, as they followed the prisoners to the dwelling of the magistrate, not calculated to console or re-assure them, and especially irritating and offensive to Captain Winslow. He felt sick and woebegone; this degradation seemed but a foretaste of what was to come. He cursed his precipitancy, which had urged him to the act of the previous night, without providing for a contingency of this kind which had befallen him; in fact, he reflected with dismay, that he had made no provision against the consequences of detection, he had assured himself of success, because, by one atrocious portion of his plan, he had assured himself Myra would be compelled, in order to save herself from the most shameful disgrace, to become his wife, and thus secure to him immunity for the infamous means adopted by him to complete his purpose.

But then he had not executed this piece of infamy. As we have said before, he was not a bold and determined villain. He had all the elements to make a thorough paced scoundrel, excepting those essential qualities, courage and nerve—want of both had saved Myra from a dreadful fate, and had brought him into his present critical position—want of both now prevented him seeing a loophole of escape, and he was quite down; all the arrogance and haughtiness had disappeared, and, quite chapfallen, he prepared, with terrified apprehensions, to encounter the stern glance of the magistrate, and his yet sterner remarks when the facts were placed before him.

On reaching the magistrate's residence, he found there Oliver Lawrance and the inspector of police, who in his manner to him rather curiously mixed up brusqueness with a sort of half deference to the position he was understood to occupy in life, and put a few questions to him, administering, however, the usual caution. This caution was beneficial to Captain Winslow, for it operated on his fears and kept him silent. The magistrate was not yet visible, and the whole party were obliged to wait his coming, in the room devoted by him to the cases brought before him

While all were in this state of suspense, a little, active, bustling man in black entered the chamber, and looked sharply round him. The attire and military appearance of Captain Winslow at once caught his eye, and he approached him with a brisk air. He smiled, rubbed his hands, and bowed obsequiously.

"Beg pardon," said he, addressing him, "will you permit me a word with you?"

Captain Winslow looked at him with surprise;—he nodded assent.

"I understand," he continued, "that is, I perceive, you have been placed in a position both embarrassing and painful to you. Some charge, the result of a serious misconception, which no doubt you are able to meet and overcome, has been preferred against you. Now, the most innocent man in the world may become a victim to the law if he does not have proper aid to battle with it. And"—here he fixed his eye steadfastly on the Captain's—"even a guilty person, by skilful professional assistance, may, unscathed, escape its fangs. Do you comprehend?"

"Fully," replied Captain Winslow, quickly. "I am quite sensible of the great advantages to be derived, by persons entangled in the meshes of law, from able professional assistance. I do not think," he added, cunningly, "the value of such aid can be over-estimated."

The little man rubbed his hands and exclaimed:

"I see—I see! You are an educated man of the world. I am a professional man—excuse me—have you engaged the services of one?"

"No," replied Captain Winslow.

"Do you require such assistance?" pursued the little man.

Drowning men catch at straws. Captain Winslow caught at this straw. Strange to say, the services of a lawyer in his difficulty never occurred to him. Now he saw its great importance. He would not appear too eager, however; for he desired to enlist the best ability the man could display in his service; and by artifice he hoped to obtain it. He looked steadfastly at the little man, and replied—

"I do need such assistance, of course; but it was my intention to telegraph to town for my own man of business."

"I should be loth to interfere with the practice of any member of my profession," said the little man, quite as cunning as he was. He made a bow and turned away, as if about to leave the room.

"One moment, if you please!" cried Winslow, eagerly.

The little man stopped—and with an air which seemed to say—'I listen, but only be quick,' prepared to hear what the Captain was about to remark.

"Will you do me the honor to acquaint me with your name?" said Captain Winslow.

"Knipe—at your service, sir; John N. Knipe. There is a business card—on some other"—

"Stay! I presume you have had some experience in your profession?"

"Pretty well, sir; and some sharp work, too; in which I have no cause to be dissatisfied with my success," returned the lawyer.

"Then, Mr. Knipe," said Captain Winslow, "as my man of business is in town, and you are on the spot, I shall avail myself of your services. As an earnest, here are five guineas; and your success in clearing me from an odious and unjust charge shall meet with a proportionate reward."

"My dear sir!" exclaimed Mr. Knipe, promptly pocketing the money offered to him—"We will do our best. Now, if you please, let us know how matters stand. And, whatever you do, reserve nothing from me. Upon that our success will mainly depend. Be as quick as you can—because it would be as well to be prepared to meet the charge at first as well armed as we can be."

Winslow nodded,—and the two retired into a corner, where they conferred together in a very low tone; and as Winslow perceived the sort of character he had to deal with, he was very explicit. Knipe chuckled—for he now had him in his power—and he had also a shrewd notion of the line of defence to adopt.

Just as their conference was drawing to a close, Mr. Knipe called out to the Inspector of Police—

"Mr. Grabble, I shall be compelled to give you a little trouble."

"Me, sir?" responded the inspector.

"You, sir, as the proper person to apply to under the circumstances. That young person there, sir, Mr. Rowe. Will you be good enough to take him into custody upon a charge of attempted robbery with violence?"

He pointed to Charley Rowe, who was talking to Oliver Lawrance when he spoke. The inspector started:

"Charley Rowe!" he repeated, "surely there must be some mistake!"

Charley sprung forward, and said indignantly:

"Why, Mr. Knipe, you don't believe it—you don't mean to say you'll dare—"

Mr. Knipe waved his hand.

"Mr. Grabble," said he, "will you do your duty?"

"Certainly," replied the inspector, "but do you give the charge?"

"Only on the part of my client," responded Knipe. "Not on my own, certainly."

"Your client must give it himself, then," said the inspector bluntly.

"Oh, by all means," said Captain Winslow. I distinctly give him in charge for assaulting me with intent to rob me."

Grabble shrugged his shoulders, and turned to Charley Rowe.

"You hear," he said, "you must surrender yourself I must take the charge?"

"It's a lie! the scoundrel knows it to be one," cried Charley passionately. "Why I prevented—"

"Will you do your duty, if you please, Mr. Grabble," interposed Mr. Knipe. "Mr. Rowe will be able to convince the magistrate of his innocence, perhaps; it is clearly of no use talking to you about it."

"Stop!" said Oliver Lawrance, "I know something about this affair; the charge is monstrous."

"Pray, Lieutenant Lawrance, were you present when Captain Winslow was attacked?"

"No, but—"

"That is enough, Mr. Grabble: you must do your duty," urged Knipe.

"Then I'll bail him," observed Oliver Lawrance, quickly.

"Ridiculous!" exclaimed Mr. Knipe, shrugging his shoulders and laughing. "Felony is not a bailable offence."

"Mr. Rowe, you must consider yourself my prisoner," said Grabble; "it's unpleasant, but I must do my duty."

"Of course," said Knipe, rubbing his hands.

"But," said Charley, burning with rage, "I am not guilty, and I won't be taken into custody for a thing I never thought of. No; d—n me, you shall tear me piecemeal first."

He tore himself out of the grip of Mr. Grabble as he spoke, and would have given way to a very dangerous kind of excitement, but that Oliver Lawrance restrained him.

"Peace, my good fellow," he exclaimed; "be calm. I'll stand by you—"

"But to be taken into custody like a thief—no, that I 'ont."

"Hush—hush. Any man may for a time be made the victim of a base and lying charge," said Oliver Lawrance; "but only for a time. You have a witness, you know."

"Where?" asked Knipe, eagerly.

"You'll find out quite soon enough," responded Oliver Lawrance; "and let me tell you, Knipe, there is such a thing as being too sharp."

Knipe grinned.

"Can't be too sharp," he said.

"Not when it cuts both ways? I tell you what, Knipe, you may have thought it a deep trick to advise your client to this step; but he won't be likely to think it so clever when he has to pay for it."

Charley Rowe doubled his fist.

"Aye, and he shall pay for it, too," he said, grinding his teeth.

Oliver Lawrance, however, drew him on one side, and whispered to him to keep himself calm; he shewed him that Myra Aston would be clearly able to exonerate him, and that he should have a good action of damages, with swinging amount for false imprisonment; he counselled him, therefore, as a matter of policy, to submit with the best grace he could. Charley Rowe did not seem to accept the reasoning very willingly, but he remained quiet, save that he preferred his charge of assault against the men who,

for a bribe from Captain Winslow, had attacked and bound him with cords. And Lieutenant Lawrance caused the charge at the suit of Myra Aston against Captain Winslow to be properly entertained, so that he would not be able, under a plea that there was no charge against him, to leave the custody in which he had been placed.

All this having been done, the magistrate's appearance was awaited with impatience. After a short time longer had elapsed, the clerk made his appearance, and commenced arranging the books upon the table, and to place some papers ready for perusal by the awful functionary when he made his appearance; he cast his eyes furtively at those present, shuffled about the table, chatted with the inspector of police, nodded to two or three of the spectators present, who appeared to think his notice elevated them into a position of importance. Then he made some enquiries about the charge—looked steadfastly at Captain Winslow, doubtful whether to consider him a gentleman, and treat him accordingly, or a swindler, and frown at him. He sent an over inquisitive boy out of the office, and made some remarks to one or two women present, who bobbed and curtesied as if he were the justice himself—he examined some pens, looked over a book or two, scribbled, with rapidity, some hieroglyphics upon some foolscap paper, and, having gone through a series of other performances of like character, he stood, having carefully separated his coat tails, with his back to the fire, and altogether felt himself to be a fac simile edition of the magistrate, only that he was more condescending, and had not got the income.

Presently a loud hushing, and the exclamation "Here comes his worship," told that the magistrate was approaching, and every eye—many very anxiously—was bent upon the door of the apartment.

CLIFTON GREY IN SEBASTOPOL.—INTERVIEW WITH PRINCE MENSCHIKOFF.

CHAPTER XXVI.

"The tale is old, but love anew
May nerve young hearts to prove as true."
                                        BYRON.

"I loved and was beloved again ;
In sooth it is a happy doom,
  But yet where happiest ends in pain.
*   *   *   *
            I would have given
My life but to have call'd her mine
In the full view of earth and heaven."
                                        IBID.

"Away, away, my steed and I,
  Upon the pinions of the wind
All human dwellings left behind :
We sped like meteors through the sky,
When with its crackling sound the night
Is chequered with the northern light ;
Town, village, none were on our track,
But a wild plain of far extent,
And bounded by a forest black ;
  And save the scarce seen battlement
On distant heights of some strong hold."
                                        IBID.

SIMPHEROPOL. THE STORY OF THE PACKET. THE
ESCAPE. THE PURSUIT. THE DEATH STRUGGLE.

THE sombre gloom of that darkest hour before
the dawn, had given place to the dull grey
haze of a cold and misty morning, when
Clifton Grey entered Sebastopol a prisoner. A wind
had sprung up suddenly, and from seaward huge masses
of dark, damp vapour, swept over the city, giving a
cheerless, comfortless aspect, to that which needed
no such medium through which to observe its sad
condition. The air was bitter cold, and Clifton felt
it more acutely, perhaps, because he was much
fatigued, having been on duty from dawn the morning
before, and because he was depressed in spirits at
having been captured in such an unexpected manner,
and, as it seemed to him, with so little credit to his
sagacity, for, suspicious of the presence of the enemy
near to the spot on which he was advancing, he had
absolutely run into the arms of the foe, without
having left himself a possibility of getting away upon
discovering them. He cursed his precipitancy, which
had caused him to throw away his usual caution,
and regretted that the delightful news communicated
to him by Sister Geraldine should have operated so
as to drive him, in his zeal to excel all his former acts,
into an act of indiscretion, for which he would now
have to pay the penalty, perhaps with his life. Here was
a sudden stop to his elevation, a rude destruction
of all those dreams which had in his onset animated
him, and which, if they had been weakened under the
influence of a painful uncertainty, had been renewed
with greater vividness by the assurance from Myra,
that she had not forgotten him, and never would. No
wonder that he was depressed in spirits, that, with
the addition of fatigue of no ordinary kind, he felt

the bitter cold of the gloomy morning act distressingly
on his frame, and give a dismal character to every
thing he gazed upon.

Heaven knows, the sights he beheld on entering
Sebastopol required no such frame of mind to add
force to their horrors, and in fact, despite his
melancholy sadness, they were of a character to
excite his interest and attention.

The town, with its high and capacious houses
covering the hill sides, and in sunnier times smiling
with white and shining faces upon the harbour,
seemed now deserted ; here and there a mass of ruins,
an unshapeable heap, told where the heavy shot
and shell of the allies had produced fearful mischief.
Some buildings were merely marked and chipped,
others were excoriated and seamed with destructive
iron missiles hurled at them. The civilians, men,
women, and children, seemed to have vanished. In
every direction he saw soldiers, mostly on duty, and
actively engaged moving about the otherwise deserted
streets. In the harbour, between Forts Siever-
naia and Constantine, lay at anchor the Russian
vessels of war, which were afterwards scuttled and
sunk ; upon the waters of the harbour boats were
moving to and fro, engaged in bringing stores and
ammunition from the North to the South side, and
an active steam-tug travelling here and there, as
though nothing passing its vicinity could get along
without its aid.

As they passed on through the streets, Clifton saw
that he was eyed by the Russian soldiers employed
on various duties ; but they, with one or two exceptions only, made no remark upon his disaster ; in fact,
it struck him that they looked wearied and ill, and,
at least a large proportion of them unfitted for the
arduous labours they were compelled to perform. In
the open places, or barrack squares, masses of soldiers
were drawn up, and were being inspected. In other
places fatigue parties were being told off, and in
some spots he observed, where a guard was stationed,
the duties of relieving him were performed with the
same orderly precision as if no siege of the city had
been going on.

At length a guard-house was reached, and Clifton
was conveyed within and there searched for weapons ;
he was afterwards forwarded to a building appro-
priated to the purpose of confining those prisoners of
war, who were of a condition above the private. It was
evident that Clifton was considered to be a commissioned officer, for the Russians treated him with a
degree of courtesy for which he was hardly prepared,
and he was placed in a room where there were three
French officers, who had been taken prisoners during
one of the midnight engagements, and with whom he
soon became on friendly terms. Able to speak their
language fluently, and with an elegance of diction
which proved him to have received a higher order of
education than common, or to have mixed in the

upper circles of society, he was at once accorded a footing similar to their own; and when they learned, by a course of inquiry which they pursued, without being offensively inquisitive, that he had fought at the Alma, Balaklava, Inkermann, and in various skirmishes, sorties, and other struggles, their respect for him proportionably increased.

They lamented with pathetic earnestness the hard fate which consigned them to captivity; but they did not fail to endeavour to extract as much comfort out of it as their situation would afford. One source of consolation to them was the tremendous havoc among the Russian troops occasioned by the desperate bombardment of the Allies, and the fearful results of incessant sorties; but they were also moved to wonder and admiration by the ceaseless activity of the Russians, their restless perseverance, the bravery which rivalled martyrdom, the apparently inexhaustible resources, or the unflagging fertility of invention for creating or supplying them.

At the same time, it seemed marvellous to them that such wondrous long convoys, laden with provisions essential to their very existence, such strings of arabas piled up with materials for war, should swarm into the city. Two days after Clifton had been in the town, he counted two hundred and twenty waggons laden with stores which had come up from the interior without molestation or even attempt on the part of the Allies to intercept them. Some few days passed, and Clifton had recovered his strength by rest, but not his spirits; on the contrary, he became thoughtful and sad; for as he cast his eyes about him, he saw little or no prospect of escape, a hope in which he had indulged from the first moment he had been seized by the enemy. The works without the city walls were bewildering—within they were swarming with Russians, toiling with never-ending labour to repair the damages effected by the bombardment. Even if he contrived to get out of the cage in which he had been placed, there seemed no possible chance of getting away undetected; for, if he adopted the dress of a Russian soldier, he could not speak the Russian or the Polish language, and would be in constant danger of being discovered by the soldiers straggling everywhere, with whom it would be wholly impossible to avoid coming in contact. Still he would not give up the idea, nor lose any chance that might offer itself, although every day the prospect seemed more hopeless.

He had been a prisoner a fortnight when, one morning, a Russian officer made his appearance at his quarters, and addressing him in French, asked him if his name were Clifton Grey. He responded in the affirmative; and the officer immediately requested him to attend him, and further informed him that he was about to appear before a general officer. He suggested that he would find it to his advantage to answer all questions put to him

promptly and without hesitation; to adhere to the truth strictly, as the officer before whom he was to appear was well-informed, and would be able immediately to detect falsehoods; and, he added, the more ample his explanations were the greater would probably be the benefit which he would derive from them. Clifton answered him coolly, that he would follow him, because resistance to the command would be a piece of Quixotic folly; but that he should use his own judgment as to the replies he might give; he might, however, be convinced that whatever they were they would not be of a description to compromise his own or his nation's honor. The Russian smiled, as it appeared to him, with significance. He felt proportionately determined to be as reserved, as it appeared to be expected that he should be communicative. He followed the officer into the streets, where an escort awaited them, and he was marched to a large building in the city, guarded by Russian soldiers, in a manner which left him no opportunity for doubting that he was a prisoner, to whose safe custody some importance was attached—wherefore, he was somewhat at a loss to surmise; but though he was disposed to think it arose from a misconception, there was no doubt of the fact.

A large body of troops surrounded the handsome building to which he was conducted, and officers, brilliantly uniformed and almost profusely decorated with medals and orders, were in and about all the approaches to the apartments in the interior of the building. The guard which had escorted Clifton hither remained without, and he followed, attended only by two Cossacks and the officer who had summoned him to attend his general, and now conducted him to his presence. They ascended a flight of stairs, and passed along a corridor, which, like the hall and its avenues, abounded in the presence of military officers. The officer paused before a chamber door, at which stood sentry a formidable looking Russ. A communication was made to another fierce-looking Cossack within the chamber, who had the care of the door on the inner side; and he, after a short interval, announced that admission was granted. The chamber door was thrown open, and Clifton followed his conductor into a spacious chamber, the Cossack instantly closing the door behind him and his two Cossack attendants. The room had the air of an official chamber; the table was covered with papers and documents of all kinds, important, as being connected with the management of the Russian armies in the Crimea, and the defence of Sebastopol. Large maps hung round the room, where, upon chairs and on the floor, engineers' drawings and plans were plentifully strewed about. Orders and requisitions were scattered in all directions, and though, in some parts of the large table there was some order and method, yet the general aspect was one of confusion and disorder, consequent upon active and multifarious occupation in this department. Clifton saw from the window the harbour of Sebastopol, its waters alive with huge lighters, sailing to and fro, approaching laden with stores or returning empty to be re-freighted, Dockyard galleys with officers were dashing here and there, and at the mouth the forts Constantine and Sivernaia were frowning over the entrance and showing their teeth to the dark mass of sea. Beyond and far away on the gloomy Euxine, the vessels of England lay still silently and ceaselessly watching this entrance to the town, longing for permission to run in and belch fire and flame on all around. To the right, and above the town, were visible the batteries and trenches of the allies, known, however, only by the volume of white smoke, rainbow-tinged in the sunlight, which every now and then bounded from them suddenly into the air, breaking into irregular wreaths, followed by a heavy boom, then a hissing scream close at hand, an explosive crash, and a cloud of splinters from some building shell-struck. The dark green of the hills, too, were constantly enlivened by small puffs of smoke, arising in many parts, which the quick and practised eye of Clifton recognised as rifle discharges from the small pits in which the crack shots of both armies lay concealed, firing at every object in the shape of an enemy—rarely missing it. An instance of which precision was given by a young officer to a friend whom he had conducted into the trenches. Desirous to prove to him how vigilant the Russians were in the rifle-pits, he held up his hand above the surface of the trench, and was rewarded by an evidence of the truth of his assertion, in the immediate loss of two of his fingers, cut off by a Minié bullet, from the rifle of a watchful Russian in a pit.

Clifton here observed, too, more plainly, the results of the bombardment in the utterly destroyed suburbs of the town, which now were nothing more than huge heaps of stone, mortar, and beams. Above them, upon the heights, there were a series of low batteries, rising tier above tier, pierced with embrasures, and mounted with an ample supply of guns. In the direction of Inkermann and down to the Belbek, there were visible earthworks, trenches, and redoubts, on a scale that surprised him, and to an extent which was enormous and startling; in, upon, and about them were bustling some three or four thousand men, actively engaged in rendering them effective for the purposes of defence.

All that he here observed might be said to have been taken in at a glance, for his attention was at once called to a general officer seated at the table, who immediately he was introduced proceeded to interrogate him.

Clifton looked steadfastly upon him, and saw that he was a man somewhat advanced in years, with bronzed and hard features, but with a countenance stern and intelligent, and with an eye peculiarly bright and piercing. He looked at our hero as though he would penetrate his most secret thoughts, but Clifton met the gaze firmly and without shrinking, for he esteemed it his duty, as an Englishman, to preserve a bold and brave bearing in the face of every trial and danger, and to endure with unflinching coolness and hardihood whatever tests of his courage and his sense of honour the barbarism or the curiosity of his captors might impose.

The breast of the Russian general was covered with orders of a brilliant and distinguished kind; it was clear that he held a high and important post—nay, Clifton did not for a moment doubt in whose presence he stood. Nevertheless, so far from feeling abashed, he was, if possible, strengthened in his determination to permit no information of any value to be eliminated from his knowledge.

He was not permitted to remain long in suspense, the general at once addressed him:

"You are an officer in the British army," he said, in the French language; and immediately added, "you speak French, I presume?"

Clifton replied in the affirmative. It was at the tip of his tongue to state, that although an officer, he was but of non-commissioned rank; but the Russian general proceeded so rapidly in his interrogatories, that he was spared the confession. He inquired the name of his regiment, and whether he was on the staff.

Clifton, in answer to the first, said he belonged to the Guards, and to the second he replied in the negative.

"What is the number of the allied army at the present moment?" asked the Russian general.

"I do not know," replied Clifton.

"You will not, perhaps," said the Russian, sarcastically.

"If I were acquainted with the actual number of our forces, I should not reveal it," replied Clifton firmly; "but there have been so many losses and renewals, so much sickness and restoration to duty, that what is the effective force I am wholly unable to say."

"You can give a shrewd guess, I suppose?"

"Undoubtedly."

"Well, how many do you guess?"

"Enough to take Sebastopol, if they are permitted to try."

The Russian general did not appear offended at the remark; indeed he laughed.

"More than enough, after the battle of the Alma," he exclaimed; "less than half enough to take it now."

"Nevertheless the attempt will be made."

"Of course, and the Allied armies annihilated. Your generals have lost the happy moment, and they will never recover it. Heaven has declared for us, and we are now invulnerable. Every fresh attempt proves it. Say, what is Lord Raglan's state of health —is he not sick and depressed?"

"No; he is well and confident."

"I am differently, and I believe better informed. What are the relations between him and General Canrobert? The *entente cordiale* is scarcely preserved, Ha!"

"For aught I know to the contrary, they are in as perfect accord as ever."

"You are then ignorant of what is the fact—Bah! You must not attempt to deceive me. You Guards—where is your strength now, where your brigade? Will you tell me that it is as strong in health and calibre, as flush in numbers, as when it swept up the heights of Alma a host of fiery warriors, reckless of that blazing flame of death dealing red-hot shot poured upon them—a *feu d'infer*—or will you acknowledge the truth, and admit that it no longer exists?"

Clifton bit his lips, and remained silent, feeling the hot colour rise up in his cheeks as he heard this bitter allusion to that host of brave fellows that had melted away, not one-fifth from the bullets of the enemy, but two-thirds from the gross incompetency and mismanagement of those whose duty it was to provide them with the commonest necessaries and did not, and who have met every attempt at enquiry with shameless denials, bullying and blustering, endeavouring to make up with invective what they want in common honesty.

"You are silent," said the general, after a moment's pause. "You perceive that I am well informed as to the condition of your army."

"If so, where is the necessity for interrogating me?"

"Because I would have my intelligence confirmed by what I consider to be an authority."

"You will commit an error in estimating me as one."

"I think not. However, explain to me, why you should not constitute an authority. You are young, active, intelligent, have taken part in the numerous engagements which have already occurred between us, you have been constantly employed on active duty, have been in contact with the officers of brigade, the commanders of division, probably with the commander-in-chief himself—is it not so?"

Clifton bowed.

"You must have therefore been placed in a position to know the disposition of the forces, the numbers employed on active duty, the force maintained in reserve, the courses of the parallels, the position of the guns, the situation of masked batteries, and the day appointed upon which a general assault is to follow the opening of that tremendous cannonading with which we have been so long threatened, and which, in fact, we have partially experienced. It is impossible that you should be unacquainted with all, and more than I have here suggested. I therefore desire you to give me a brief sketch, embodying in its relation all the information I

have now shaped out, and which I desire to receive."

"Sir," responded Clifton, speaking with firmness, "whatever I have seen, whatever has come to my knowledge by revelation, has been ascertained through my privilege in being a member of the British army. It has been revealed to me as one taking part in the operations with which it is connected, and under that view it has become to me a sacred and secret trust. I decline, therefore, with proper respect to you, to communicate any information calculated to be of benefit to those in command of an enemy's troops, or disadvantageous to the soldiers of my nation, or to those of its ally."

"What! You refuse to comply with the request I have made to you?"

"If it pleases you to adopt that harsher definition."

The Russian officer frowned.

"I will compel you to furnish me with this information," he said; and added brusquely, "obey at once."

Clifton's lip curled in contempt.

"I cannot obey you," he said haughtily.

"You will not?"

"I will not!"

There was a pause for an instant. The Russian general bent his glittering eye sternly upon him, but Clifton met his gaze calmly, and neither blanched nor even seemed at all affected deferentially by it. The general drew forth a superb gold watch; he looked at it, and placed it upon the table.

"I will give you five minutes to reflect," he said, "upon the policy of obeying my command. I do not usually accord such indulgence, but in your case I shall depart from my customary practice. If, at the expiration of that time, you persist in your refusal, you will be handed over to a detachment, led hence, and shot."

As he concluded, he made a memorandum upon a piece of paper of the time, and then continued the writing in which he had been interrupted by Clifton's entrance.

The Russian officer who had conducted our hero hither made a sign to him to comply, but he waved his hand impatiently.

"I require not five minutes—nor one, for reflection," he said firmly to the Russian commander. "At the expiration of an hour, a day, a month, a year, I shall be as decided and fixed in that resolve as now."

The Russian chief looked up from his writing, while Clifton spoke, but when he ceased he went on again with his work.

Clifton folded his arms and gazed upon the general, who was now the arbiter of his fate; he regarded him attentively; saw that he was not the man to trifle with his word, or who had too much sympathy with human life to be particular in sparing it when thwarted in any purpose. But this reflection did not affect his decision; he was not moved by it to give way; in truth the possibility of saving his life by compliance was not for an instant entertained. He did not, therefore, expect to be spared. Death appeared to him to be now certain. A throng of thoughts rushed through his brain. Was this to be the termination of his career—this the goal at which he was to end his race? Well, he believed sincerely that the disposal of every man's life was in the hands of the Creator, and he resigned himself to His will. Perhaps there was a sigh trembling upon his lips, that he should end his life thus, but he suppressed it, for he felt that if his hour were come, he had to meet it as became a brave man and a true Englishman; to implore of Heaven that it would shower down its blessings on Myra, and grant her a happier lot than his chequered career had proved, and then, with a smile at fate, receive the messenger of death when it came to nestle in his bosom, as calmly as now he stood awaiting the expiration of the term fixed for his decision.

"The time has elapsed," exclaimed the general, emphatically, as he suddenly examined his watch, and returned it to his pocket. "What is your answer?"

"You have had it," quietly responded Clifton.

"You accept the alternative?"

"I do."

"The prospect of immediate death does not induce you to alter your determination?"

"No. I faced it too constantly at the Alma, at Inkermann, Balaklava, the Tchernaya, by day and by night, to fear it now," he responded, almost contemptuously.

The Russian gave a brief order, in his native tongue, to the officer who had brought Clifton hither, and once more referred to his watch.

"You can make your peace with Heaven!" he exclaimed. "You will be shot within five minutes from this time."

"I have no heavy account to render," said Clifton, a faint smile illumining his features, "I have some mercies to be thankful for, some short comings to acknowledge in humility, a short prayer for one I have left behind me, and my preparation is made."

The Russian chief waved his hand towards the door. The two Cossacks wheeled about: one touched Clifton upon the arm, and pointed to the now open doorway, and the Russian officer, who had been his guide, with a depressed and disturbed countenance, giving a military salute to the general, led the way from the apartment. Clifton gave his English military salute, and went out of the room, betraying no sign that his condemnation to death in any respect affected painfully his spirits. He was calm, collected, and resigned, prepared to face his Maker, if it were His will that he should do so, without exhibiting an unworthy fear, betraying a bitter regret.

He had reached half way down the corridor, when the little cavalcade was summoned to return to the apartment they had just quitted. The Russian chief, as Clifton entered, motioned him to advance close to him, and said—

"Have you not a word to advance why you should not be shot?"

"Only that I protest against it, as a barbarous use of power, and opposed to the custom of civilized nations, who do not slaughter their prisoners in cold blood."

"I am not troubled by such weak considerations, when my will is thwarted. Besides, the difficulty you suggest would be easily got over, by not acknowledging your capture."

"The false evasion would scarcely avail you, General, for I shall be missed by my comrades, who know me too well to believe that, if not killed, I should be other than prisoner, if away from my regiment without leave. I have left behind me warm friends, who will lament and strive to revenge my fate."

"The thoughts of them—the permission to rejoin them——"

"Will not move me to be a traitor to my country."

"Nor that one of whom you spoke but now—that fair one in England for whom your last sigh will be given?"

"Could I, General, prove the wretch you seek to make me, she would spurn and execrate my memory. My death, for honor's sake, may draw forth regretful tears from her gentle eyes; but they will not be those burning drops which would sear her lids did she know I had purchased existence at the base price at which you offer it."

The Russian looked steadfastly at him, and then said—

"You have decided not to preserve your life at the expense of affording me merely a confirmation of certain intelligence."

"I am decided," he replied, firmly.

"I am glad of it," said the Russian chief, a smile breaking over his features. "You have stood the test well, and worthily represent your nation. You are also deserving of the admiration and affection of your fair lady, who writes to you from England."

He took up a letter as he spoke, and handed it to him.

"Do you know in whose presence you stand?" he asked abruptly.

"I surmise that it is Prince Menschikoff whom I have the honour of addressing," returned Clifton.

"A shrewd surmise, too," returned the prince, for he it was. "Open that letter—there is a marked paragraph—read it aloud and at once."

Clifton opened hastily the letter; he recognised the hand, it was from Lizzie Hastings. He cast his eyes rapidly over the paragraph to which his attention had been directed. A broad ink line had been run round it, he started as he saw the following remarks, which, in a voice by no means so steady as that he had before employed, he read audibly as instructed. "I am delighted to hear so enthusiastic an account of your gallantry, my dear Mr. Grey. Walter tells me you did wonders at the Alma, but that at the dreadful battle of Inkermann you surpassed all that you had done before, and proved yourself a true Englishman. So bravely you fought, that the remembrance of it would have been a sustaining consolation if it had pleased Heaven on that occasion to have taken your life. Now, as it seems you have been, through all the frightful bloodshed and destruction, spared, you are doubtless reserved for some great purpose; and let me urge you to set to and take Sebastopol at once, and so put a stop to this frightful war. I am told for positive truth that this war arose all through the scandalous conduct of a horrid old Russian, who wore a very bad white hat, when he was at Constantinople, and he is carrying it on now—I mean the war, not the hat. So I think the very best thing that you can do is to take the detestable old Russian prisoner as soon as you can, and send me a button off his coat in proof of your success. I'll have it made into a brooch to wear for your sake; and when you come home, if Walter don't object, and somebody else don't pout, I'll give you a kiss for your bravery."

When he concluded the prince laughed heartily, and then said:

"A brave girl—but I fear misinformed on some points. I suspect you are likely to find the capture of Sebastopol a more difficult task than the young lady calculates; and, as circumstances at present are arranged, the probability of capturing me is somewhat distant; perhaps, however, as it is not possible to accede to the lady's wishes on two of the points, we may contrive to gratify her on the third."

He lifted his sword as he spoke, and separated from his coat one of the handsome buttons with which it was decorated, and handed it to Clifton, who received it with some embarrassment.

"Tell the lady," said the prince, "that the detestable old Russian regrets having in her eyes so bad a character, and that he cannot redeem it by surrendering Sebastopol or himself to you in order to stop the war; but that as she has expressed so strong a desire to possess one of his buttons, he begs, through you, to forward it to her, in the hope that in addition to some little satisfaction the article itself may afford, it may ensure her a brooch and you 'a kiss for your bravery.'"

Clifton bowed, and intimated that the observations which had occasioned this incident were mere badinage from a young, innocent, and lively girl, who had no idea that her remarks would meet any other eyes than those for whom they were intended.

Prince Menschikoff made an inclination, and said, in a complimentary tone:

"Your nation may well preserve her prestige, when her sons so sustain her honour, and her daughters entertain such sentiments. I hope that you will think better of me and my nation than to suppose that I really intended you to be slain, and I beg you to believe that, while in our possession, you will receive nothing but courteous consideration. You will to-day be forwarded to Simpheropol, and from thence to Russia, there to await for an exchange or a termination of the war. Farewell."

Clifton bowed, and left the room, this time with pleasanter feelings; while the countenance of the officer who accompanied him was lighted up with joyous animation.

"I had a horror," said he, to Clifton, "that he was in earnest when he ordered you out for death. He gave me the necessary instructions, and had he not have countermanded his order, you would by this time have been laying beneath five feet of earth. For the honour of Russia I am glad he altered his mind; it is seldom that he does change it, but I rejoice in your escape; in sooth, it was a narrow one."

Clifton thanked him for his expression of good will.

"You should have asked him for your parole," continued the Russian; "he was in good humour with you, and would have granted it. Shall we return and ask it?"

"Not for worlds," replied Clifton, eagerly.

"As you please," said the Russian. "But I do not suppose you will try to escape, for the effort would be useless, and only bring death upon you; therefore your parole would be of great advantage to you—especially in Russia."

"I will not ask it now, at least," returned Clifton. "I am quite prepared for the consequences of any step I take, and, therefore, fear of death on account of ill success would not deter me from making an attempt to regain my freedom. However we will leave the matter in abeyance, and, as we say in the Fusiliers, we will keep our powder dry, and trust in Providence."

That night Clifton, with a number of other prisoners, English and French, was with an escort of considerable strength forwarded on to Simpheropol. The sky was clouded and dark, the air dense and obscure, so that he was unable to observe the features of the country sufficiently to be of service to him in any attempted escape. He perceived that their way lay through deep ravines, over high ground and mountain fastness. Now they were winding through mountain gorges, anon passing over rugged and irregular mountain ridges. In many of the places along which they passed large bodies of troops were stationed, and parts of the road-way, rough as it was, had been under the hands of the military engineers, to render it at any given time inaccessible to an enemy. Vast and perpendicular walls of rock were succeeded by a winding descent to a country which, in the obscurity of the atmosphere, appeared to be hilly, wild, and but little under the cultivating hands of man.

He was not sorry when Simpheropol was reached, for his journey had not been of the most agreeable character, the horse upon which he had been mounted being of the short and shaggy kind bestrode by the Cossacks, sure-footed enough, but with a shambling gait, which, together with its want of two or three hands in height, made the long legs of Clifton difficult and awkward to dispose of with comfort, so that to alight was the pleasantest part of the progress.

Simpheropol disappointed him. It possessed a large body of troops, certainly, but his first impression was, that it not only was incapable of an enduring defence, but that much preparation in anticipation of the necessity of any such event had not been bestowed upon it. However, he had not much time permitted to him for notice, but was hurried into a large building and ushered into a tolerable sized apartment, along with his three French companions, who had shared his prison in Sebastopol. The door was locked upon them, and they perceived that the windows were barred; they had, therefore, only to make the best of their condition, which the Frenchman quickly did, and Clifton also.

The Frenchmen appealed to their pipes, and entered into a lively conversation, detailing with tragic emphasis the disasters of their journey, and lamenting that France had lost the services of three of her best sons, who were doomed to an inglorious inactivity through the beastly stupidity of circumstances daring to take upon themselves to act differently to what these individuals would have ordered them.

Clifton removed himself to a window, and withdrew from his pocket the letter of Lizzie Hastings, which he read with the greatest avidity, and with somewhat different feelings to those which had possession of him when he read an extract before Prince Menschikoff. Lizzie, having acknowledged the receipt of his letter, was as communicative as he could have wished; her long letter, crossed and re-crossed, testified this. She gave him a sort of diary of her acquaintance with Myra, in which she recounted the expedition to Little St. Thomas Apostle, the capture in Thames-street, the incidents which succeeded it, and which satisfactorily explained the mystery of the presence of the two young maidens at Havre. Then came the receipt of the letters from the Crimea, of her interview with Myra, and what took place on that occasion through the intervention of his old friend, Captain Winslow, whom he heartily cursed, and whom he made up his mind to call out and shoot if ever he got the chance. She added her belief that Myra loved him—there were three dashes ending in a scribble under that—and she bade him keep up his spirits, for if a letter from Myra did not accompany

hers, it would be through the machinations of Captain Winslow; but he might rest assured that a letter would be written to him by Myra, who had heard of his brave feats in battle, and of his promotion with an enthusiastic delight, which no words could express; and then she urged him to proceed on his career for Myra's sake, and went on until she delivered herself of that paragraph to which Prince Menschikoff had specially called his attention, and ended in a prayer that Heaven would protect and guide him, for she had made up her mind to dance with her Walter at the wedding of Clifton and Myra, and she should certainly not die happy unless she did so.

Clifton had hardly concluded the letter when the door flew open, and a Russian officer, attended by four of the eternal Cossacks, made his appearance, in order to inspect and examine the prisoners who were now placed under his charge. He was young, fair, and his features were strikingly handsome; their contour was of no common order, and attracted Clifton's attention, the more, perhaps, because they appeared familiar to him. They had a decidedly English character, but it was not that which excited his notice; it was that the face had been somewhere seen before by him under circumstances to fix it upon his memory. He could not at the moment recollect, however, where he had seen it, although he had not a doubt upon the fact; so strong, indeed, was the impression, that he would have at once spoken in free terms to the officer, invoking him to recall to his memory where they had previously met, but that the Russian, who looked fixedly at him as he had at the other officers, betrayed no sign of recollecting him; and so clearly was this exhibited, that Clifton felt immediately the recognition was all on his side. He was, nevertheless, induced to commend himself to the Russian's attention, and experienced a strange prompting to cultivate a good understanding with him; this did not promise to be difficult, for as both conversed fluently in French, and the Russian seemed disposed to be courteous, the chief obstacles were at once smoothed away.

It was the duty of this officer, whose name was Captain Eimanoff, to visit the prisoners frequently, to see their requirements attended to, and to be responsible for their safe custody. He was agreeable in manner, was kind and considerate, and sought to enliven the captivity of his prisoners by affording them various means of passing their time pleasantly. Clifton and he soon became very good friends—so far, at least, as frequent conversations and the utterance of mutual good wishes went. This was in some measure brought about by Clifton himself, who, as we have said, was moved to improve their acquaintance by an inward prompting for which he could not altogether account. Captain Eimanoff responded to his advances readily, and sometimes, when relieved

CLIFTON GREY PURSUED BY THE COSSACKS.

from duty, would come and pass a spare hour or two with him. He had visited France and England, and he seemed pleased at the opportunity, not only of recounting the impression he had received during his tour, but of affording himself the gratification of recalling the scenes he beheld and the hospitalities he experienced.

Clifton noticed, that although frank and brisk in his manner, appearing cheerful generally, at times very chatty and lively, there was, withal, an under-current of sadness and gloom, as though some heavy grief were tugging at his heartstrings unceasingly, and was too deep-seated to be rooted out. Often would he, in the midst of a conversation, become silent and abstracted, and when roused for a reply, betray that for a few minutes he had been utterly unconscious of all that had been uttered. Clifton guessed that home remembrances were the cause of these occasional fits of absence, and too much sympathised and respected them to rally him upon them.

One night, however, Captain Eimanoff appeared so pale and melancholy, that Clifton Grey could not help making a remark respecting it, and trusted that while he was excused referring to it, the occasion was one that admitted of alleviation or ultimate relief.

"No!" replied the Russian, smiting his breast. "No, it is not possible. My unhappiness lies too deep for any hand on earth to aid it. Cure is hopeless. I strive to master the sadness which at times almost crushes me, but in vain. I pray you to pardon and excuse me."

He walked to the window to conceal his emotion. After he had regained his composure he returned to Clifton, with an assumption of gaiety, which he very ill supported, and, unable to continue the effort, he declared his intention of retiring.

"I confess," he said, with a sad smile, "that I am acting unkindly, for it is my duty to cheer and enliven you under the calamity of your imprisonment as much as lies in my power; but there are memories too sad for control, and I, unfortunately, am afflicted with them; at times they obtain the mastery, and then I find that my wisest course is to bury myself in solitude until the fit is exhausted, and I am once more resigned to my hopeless fate."

"Not hopeless."

"Hopeless!"

Clifton laid his hand upon his shoulder.

"In the Latin philosophy it is writ '*Nil desperandum*,'" said he, earnestly, "I have experienced its truth. No condition is so utterly past redemption that all hope is denied to us. We may see no break in the gloom which overhangs us; but when it seems most dense, a light will break upon the horizon."

Clifton, in support of his argument, briefly related his position previous to his meeting with the Sister

Geraldine—how blank his prospect—how dull and dark his future seemed, yet, in his moment of deepest despair, the voice of promise and of joy breathed its delicious music in his ear.

"I had lost all hope," he exclaimed. "All the romantic aspirations for fame and elevation were, as it seemed, trampled out of my heart. There was but one in the wide, wide world for whom I would have even wrenched fame's wreath of laurel from the grisly skull of death, and from her I had not received one word—one line—one brief communication to even give me a hope that she remembered me. She was my lode-star at the Alma——"

He paused and uttered a low cry, for at the moment he uttered the last word—while yet gazing upon the wan, sad countenance of Captain Eimanoff, an association of ideas with the name of that now historical river, at once solved the mystery of his acquaintance with the features of the Russian officer.

"Merciful heaven!" he exclaimed, suddenly, "were you at the Alma?"

"No," replied Captain Eimanoff, "I was on my way to the Crimea when that battle was fought. My first action was at Inkermann. I accompanied the Grand Duke Michael thither."

"It is a singular coincidence," exclaimed Clifton. "Upon the battle-field I saw an officer lying dead, whose features most closely resembled yours."

"Ha!" ejaculated the Russian, a hectic colour rushing to his cheeks and forehead. "Repeat those words?"

Clifton did so, and added:

"So remarkable is the resemblance, that if you had replied in the affirmative to my question respecting your presence at the Alma, I should at once have considered that my opinion respecting the death of the officer I saw lying there was premature."

"Gracious heaven! Should this have been him?" muttered the Russian. Then fixing his eye anxiously on Clifton, he said: "You cannot divine how deeply your communication interests me. I had a relative, a son of my father's only brother, whose resemblance to me was most remarkable. Should it be him you saw stretched dead upon that bloody field, you will at once bring me, in a breath, joy and sorrow. Sorrow, because I loved him; yet joy, for he stood between me and happiness. I almost wish you had not mentioned this, for, destitute of proof, it will upheave a sea of doubt, of hope mingled with sadness, of joy allied to despair."

Clifton remembered the packet, the watch, the ring, and the purse. The packet was in the lining of the coat he had on; the ring was upon his finger; the watch was in his pocket; the purse, with other valuables, stowed away in his knapsack, which was in his tent.

He drew off the ring from his finger:

"Do you know that ring?" he asked, as he presented it to the Russian to examine. He looked closely at it, and after scrutinising it carefully, said:

"I do not recognise it."

"Or this?" said Clifton, drawing forth the watch. After inspecting it, the Russian shook his head:

"I do not know it," he replied, returning it.

Clifton now opened his coat, and with a penknife, ripped open a part of the lining, and drew forth a packet tied with ribbon. It was directed, and his eye caught at once the name upon it, which was the same as that of the Russian captain; he handed it to him.

"That," said he, "may give you the desired proof."

The captain took with trembling hand the packet, and looked at the superscription. His face became of ashen whiteness; he passed his hand over his brow, as cold drops of sweat stood upon it. Clifton, for the moment, thought he would have fallen down in a fit, but he rallied again, and, by a tremendous exertion, preserved a calmness of demeanor scarcely to have been anticipated from the severe inward struggle which the sight of the hand-writing on the packet occasioned.

"The ways of Heaven are inscrutable!" he at length exclaimed, "this packet is addressed to and is for me—with your permission I will open it."

Clifton, of course, immediately assented; and, with quivering fingers, the young Russian removed the ribbon and tore open the packet. He took out a daguerreotype portrait, and having gazed upon it, pressed it to his lips, and then hastily put it away within his coat and nearest to his heart.

"The portrait of a pretty girl, I would stake my existence," thought Clifton, but made no remark. The Russian then perused the written contents of the packet; and when he had finished, he turned his eyes on Clifton—they were glittering with tears.

"This epistle is from my poor cousin," he said—"written in the event of his falling in battle. It was to have been forwarded to me, if discovered after his death, by any of the soldiers of his own nation. Such, however, it seems, were not the means Heaven saw fit to employ for its own wise purposes. Yet it has reached me; and though I grieve for his fall, still it has lifted me out of my despair—and what is of far deeper interest, has saved from hopeless misery one whose happiness he, as well as myself, would have died to secure. My heart at present is too powerfully affected for me to enter into explanations; but, to-morrow, I will spend an hour, and clear up what must seem now to you a strange and childish mystery."

Clifton then gave to him the ring and watch which he had taken from the lifeless person of Captain Eimanoff's cousin, and they were gratefully accepted as relics, which the family of the deceased would so much desire to possess. Captain Eimanoff fervently thanked Clifton for the restoration of the ring and watch, and especially for the packet, the value of which to him, he said, it was not possible to measure. He wrung Clifton's hand, and rushed out of the apartment. Three days elapsed, and he did not appear, much to Clifton's surprise. His place was supplied by an older officer, brusque when he did speak, but whose characteristic was taciturnity. He seemed to think he ought to be very stern, in reply to any remark by monosyllables, in order to impress the prisoners with a wholesome fear and a proper sense of their position and his authority. The effect upon them was to make them laugh, and him the subject of endless jokes. It was towards the close of the evening of the sixth day that Captain Eimanoff made his appearance, and then the change in his manner was such as to surprise Clifton exceedingly. His eye was bright—a smile lighted up his features—his cheeks bore a healthier hue—in truth, he seemed to be another being. After shaking hands warmly with Clifton, he said:

"I have been to Sebastopol. I have had an interview with Prince Menschikoff, and have obtained from him a release from military duty, and return at once to Moscow."

"Your heart is not then in this war," said Clifton.

"My heart, my hand, my life, are my country's, does she actually need them; he replied with animation, and so soon as she shall absolutely require all, so soon shall they be rendered up for her. But I can be spared, and grave interests are involved in my return. I acknowledge they are my own private affairs, but I much feared that I should have been unable to obtain my wish; the simple truth however touched the prince's heart, and he granted me the leave I asked. Of the importance I attach to this, and the communication you have placed in my hands, be you now the judge. I am the son of a noble, my mother was an English lady; you will therefore judge that I have some sympathy with the natives of that favoured land, though now opposed by the will of the Czar to them. My father had a brother who married my mother's sister, and my cousin Ivan, whom you saw dead at the Alma, and I, were the results of these marriages. Our parents were married at the same time, beneath the roof of the same church; we were born on the same day, and at nearly the same hour, and were christened by the same name. As you have observed, a remarkable resemblance existed between us, which, perhaps, is not very extraordinary; our tastes, dispositions, and habits were similar, and as we were brought up together, we became much attached to each other. Out of this similarity of tastes, however, sprung a circumstance that occasioned to me the keenest anguish, and, as I erringly believed, a misery which should embitter my existence unto its close. My uncle, Ivan's father, at some time previous to his marriage had rescued from death a wealthy noble, who vowed eternal gratitude, and to prove his sincerity, when he heard of my uncle's marriage, which had taken place shortly before his own, he came to him and begged him to enter into an arrangement with him, under which their children should be married if they happened each to have one of an opposite sex. The Count vowed that had he a son, and my uncle a daughter, his son should marry my uncle's daughter; or did Heaven grant to him a daughter, and my uncle a son, that he would bestow his daughter's hand upon his son. The latter event was that of which there was every prospect would be fulfilled, for the baron had a daughter—lovely as an angel in Paradise—my uncle a son—my cousin Ivan. We three were brought up together, and I passionately loved the daughter of the count. My cousin did so too, but it was not until their solemn betrothal took place that the eyes of at least two of the parties were opened. My love for Alexina was returned. Much as my cousin Ivan resembled me, there were still points of difference in our character, which so far influenced her gentle heart, that, although attached to my cousin Ivan, she loved me. When the betrothal was announced, and I saw that we were about to be sundered—that our union would be rendered impossible—that our innocent, though passionate, soul-absorbing love for each other would become guilt, I became frantic. I rushed into the presence of the count—I fell at his feet—I wept—I entreated, prayed that he would rescind his resolution, and not render both his child and myself wretched for life. In vain! He was deaf to my entreaties;—nay, swore that she should be the wife of Ivan Eimanoff, or he would immure her in a convent. I became frenzied—mad—and for months I was laid upon a bed of sickness. On my recovery I was despatched to join the regiment to which I had been appointed, stationed in Poland. I parted with my beloved mother, my noble father, in despair—they mingled their tears with mine, but they gave me no hope. Ivan loved Alexina as passionately as did I, and he refused to forego his claim. He said without Alexina life would be valueless to him, and if, in violation of the expectations he had borne from childhood, and the solemn promise by which her hand had been promised to him, that hand was awarded to me, he would not live one hour after he knew such a decision had been arrived at. So Alexina and I were separated;—both were consigned to a despair it is hopeless to describe;—her fate far worse than mine, for she was doomed, not alone to be parted from me for ever, but to submit to caresses which would be abhorrent to her. This tangled web Heaven has unravelled. The war between Russia and the Allies ensued. My cousin has perished. That packet you so providentially recovered and delivered to me, contained his will, in which he expresses, in the strongest language, his dying request, that the hand of Alexina be given to me, to whom he leaves

all his possessions, such as were his own at the time of his death, and calls upon his father to make me his heir. I doubt not that his wish will be complied with, as though 'twere a voice from above. The count's oath will not be violated; for in wedding me Alexina will become the wife of Ivan Eimanoff, and save the grief that will severely afflict his parents on receiving the tidings of his death, happiness will be spread in all the families affected by this occurrence. You see, therefore, why your gift so affected me, and can understand why I am anxious to return to my home—why I quit the field of honor at a moment when it would be presumed that I had every inducement to remain—aye, and remain I would, under all these circumstances, but that I fear the heart of the gentle Alexina may give way under the load of sorrow which even at this moment burdens it."

Clifton congratulated him upon the promises of happiness which now smiled upon him, and laughingly reminded him that he had bidden him not to despair even though fate seemed to have relentlessly consigned him to hopelessness. He had experienced—even as himself—that the blackest frown of fortune did not preclude a following smile.

"True," said the now happy Russian; "and though you are plunged into the misfortune of captivity, you must not despair." Then, in a lower tone, he said rapidly—" You are not in my custody now—indeed I am no longer in the service. You are not on your parole of honor. You have served me—I would serve you. Beneath your bed you will find a bundle —it contains a note—I dare say no more;" then changing his voice into a louder key, he said—" I do not ask you—but I insist upon your accepting this ring and this watch in remembrance of me, in place of those you so handsomely and so kindly surrendered to me. Keep them and wear them for my sake. I bid you a hearty and sincere farewell. May we meet again in happiness and more peaceful times."

Clifton felt it would be absurd to raise a difficulty in accepting the trinkets, and took them in the spirit in which they were offered; he also warmly bade him farewell, expressing an earnest hope that all his fondest anticipations would be realised. And thus they parted. He was not a little anxious to retire to his sleeping room, which was a small one, with barred windows. His room door was locked and barred on the outer side at the ordinary time, and as soon as he had retired for the night, he looked beneath his bed for the bundle of which Captain Eimanoff had spoken. He found it, and opening it, saw that it contained a Cossack cloak and cap, a brace of revolvers, a dragoon's sabre, and, as he had stated, a note, which ran thus:

"Two of your centre window bars are loose, and can be easily removed. The height to the ground beneath is not greater than will enable you to drop without injury. Leaning against the wall, beneath your window, you will find a lance. Make for the bottom of the town. On the inner side of the gate you will see a man standing with a Cossack pony, fleet and enduring. You may safely trust to it for your long journey. Utter the word 'Sebastopol' only, and it will be resigned to you. The same word will enable you to pass the gate. Pursue then your track over the plain; consult frequently the plan which is here enclosed, and which will direct you to the British lines in the Valley of the Tchernaya. May we meet again. God be with you!"

There was no signature; and when Clifton had finished its perusal, he consigned it to the flame of his lamp, and burned it. He attired himself in the cloak and cap provided for him, stuck the pistols in his belt, attached the sabre to his side, and then blew out the light. He advanced to his window, and looked out: the night was dark, for the moon had not yet risen; but the sky was clear, and the dark blue vault of heaven was studded with innumerable stars. He gazed anxiously beneath him, but all was still and silent; occasionally he heard the martial tread of soldiers, passing to and fro; but after a time even this ceased, and he believed the hour had come to attempt to effect an escape, and to succeed, or to perish in making it.

He tried the window bars, as directed, and they came out from their places almost at a touch. They had been previously removed and replaced. He was now enabled to look right and left—not a soul was in sight; in an instant he forced his body rapidly through the opening, and dropped to the ground. He remained motionless for a minute, then groped about for the lance. It was on the appointed spot, and he took possession of it. With an increased action of the heart, he made at once for the principal street.

Simpheropol is a large sized town, with rather wide streets, and excellent boulevards. Along the latter he proceeded, until he reached the lower part of the town. Perhaps his pace was quicker than caution would have dictated, but the few military and civilians he met appeared to take but little notice of him: a hurrying Cossack was an object too familiar to attract their attention. After he had proceeded some distance, he began to fear, as he saw no sign of a person in charge of a steed, that he had missed his way, and he paused for a moment to assure himself; but no, the works for the defence of the town were before him, and he pushed on again. As he neared the bottom of the town he beheld, in an angle of the street, where the houses were in deep shadow, a Tartar standing motionless, holding by the head one of the unmistakeable shaggy Cossack ponies. Clifton advanced swiftly, and, seizing the rein, said in a low tone:

"Sebastopol!"

The man in charge nodded, and Clifton vaulted into the saddle: the Tartar instantly glided away like a spirit, and Clifton clapped spurs to the pony. He soon reached the outlet, which was guarded by a formidable body of Russian troops. As he approached he was challenged, and in a loud voice he replied:

"Sebastopol!"

The clanking chains fell from the gates, and an opening in them, large enough for a horseman, was made, and he passed through. Some words were addressed to him in the Russian language, which he could not understand, but he shook his lance, hissed through his teeth the word "Sebastopol," and pushed along the road which lay before him.

Between Simpheropol and the plateau to which Clifton was directing his steed, the country is a succession of huge plains, or rather long sweeping downs, which do not however, save in some instances, possess the height or steepness of those which are to be met with in various parts of England, but are more extensive. Clifton dashed along in sight of the military works of Simpheropol, and commanded by those upon them, expecting every moment to hear the *ping* of a Minié bullet close to his ear, followed by shouts commanding him to stop. But all was silent, save that it seemed he could hear a dull sound every now and then in the direction of Sebastopol, as if the siege was proceeding, even though it was close upon midnight. Perhaps it was a sortie upon the lines, a renewal of the Inkermann struggle, and he was away from it, losing in this interval of capture and attempted escape the opportunity of distinguishing himself—of doing aught to aid in the realisation of his country's noble intention. He kicked the sides of his steed, who responded by increasing his speed, and proving himself to be deserving the good character which had been given to him.

It was not until Clifton had ridden some miles, and that not in the direct track, that he paused to look behind him. He was in a valley, and the ridge which rose against the sky shut out from his sight the town of Simpheropol; to the right and left, in front and in rear, no living thing save himself and steed were visible, and this he thought an admirable opportunity for consulting his map, which the Russian had enclosed with his disguise, in order that he might be the better able to proceed direct, and with less chance of interception than if he attempted to find his way without any such help.

He produced it, but, after a careful inspection and straining his eyes to no purpose, he arrived at the conclusion that he should be compelled to wait until the moon was up before he could employ it to advantage; he could scarcely distinguish enough to get the general bearings of his route, but the information he acquired was insufficient to follow it correctly, or to understand wherefore he should pursue certain deviations from the regular beaten track. He had just determined to proceed along to the right of the road and select a spot where he could conceal himself until the moon obtained sufficient altitude to enable him minutely to inspect the plan, which he now regretted he had not examined previous to his departure from Simpheropol, when he observed his horse prick up its ears; presently it gave a low whinny, and showed symptoms of a desire to proceed. Clifton swept the horizon with his eyes, and, at a point in the direction from whence he had himself just come, he perceived above the ridge the tips of several lances, which he knew to be borne by Cossacks. Suspicion alone made him charge himself as the object of their advance; he believed his escape had been discovered, and they had been sent in pursuit. He had no notion of being re-captured easily. He felt to see that his revolvers were safe, he knew them to be loaded, and every nipple was provided with a cap. He made up his mind to fight for his liberty, for, if the worst came to the worst, and he was completely overpowered, he could but become a prisoner again.

He clapped his heels to his horse's sides, and gave his head the rein. The animal replied with a snort, and set forward at its best pace, as though it was conscious his safety depended upon its speed. It breasted the hill gallantly, and, as it mounted the crest, Clifton's anxious eyes perceived on the brow of the hill, behind him, a small band of about a dozen Cossacks, who were urging their horses forward at their top pace, and who, when he caught sight of them, were shaking their lances in the air and pointing, in seeming excitement, to him.

He heard a faint shout rise on the air—it came from those following him, it was distant—he could hardly have imagined it so distant as it appeared to be, and it was evidently intended for him. He made no response, only patted the neck of his horse, and spoke a few cheering words to him, which the beast seemed to feel an encouragement, and responded to by, at least, maintaining the speed at which he had now for some little time been going.

The top of the hill they had surmounted, continued a small plateau until it descended by a gradual slope into a valley, the other side of which seemed bounded by broken and uneven ridges. There was not a bush, a tree, to afford a cover; it was plain he should have to continue his flight, in sight of his pursuers, for some time yet, and have no chance of plunging into any hollow space or thicket to conceal himself from observation. He gazed with anxiety on his pursuers, and saw that they gained upon him; at least, so it seemed, for they were now palpably in sight, and were pushing rapidly down the slope he had descended. He had, it was true, a straight and level surface before him, for, at least, a mile, and, after that, a descent along a course so favourable for speed, he should be galloping while they were slowly mounting the hill, and he calculated he should be descending into the valley when they had reached the spot over

which he had just passed. In the valley, perhaps, he might find a cover, and there secrete himself until the succeeding day passed away, taking, again, the advantage of the night to pass over the country between him and the Tchernaya, and once more rejoin the British army; but, to accomplish this, there was no time to be lost, neither need his steed fail him. Being a good horseman, he sat his steed so as least to impede its progress, and he made it understand that now, if ever, he needed its best speed. He looked steadily at the way before him—that was clear; and, again, he looked behind at those who were pressing on after him, and who, he was quite sure, knew that he was an escaping prisoner; they were certainly nearer to him. The moon broke out suddenly through a haze which had obscured its beams, and proved itself to be higher in the heavens than he had presumed it to be. As its light swept over the hill, he discovered that one Cossack was far in advance of his fellows; that he was better mounted than they, and that he, at every stride, gained upon him—would, at the difference in their rate of speed, soon be up with him.

It was not difficult to calculate, that a struggle only with one would afford the others an opportunity to come up, and end the affair much to his, Clifton's, discomfiture. So he saw there was a necessity for getting rid of his Cossack attendant, whose proximity, each moment, becoming palpably and disagreeably nearer, proved that he was admirably mounted, probably upon one of the steeds captured in the fatal Balaklava charge. That thought settled the matter, so far as Clifton's intentions were concerned, and he drew from his belt one of the revolvers, and examined it: it was ready; and turning round, he calculated his elevation, and discharged it, watching, with no little solicitude, its result. To his surprise, he saw no sign that it had reached the persevering pursuer in advance of the others, but he saw one of that party fall to the ground, and confusion immediately observable among them. His follower, immediately in his rear, kept on, however, as steadily and as rapidly as before; if any alteration was observable, it was that he drew nearer still, and that his horse appeared to increase his speed. Clifton aimed once more the small but terrible weapon at his pertinacious pursuer, and when he had got as he believed his range, and the proper elevation, he pulled the trigger. The smart report awoke up a hundred echoes in that wide plain, where it seemed no echo could have answered. The white veil of smoke wreathed up into the air, but there was the Cossack, shaking his lance—it is true, a little excitedly, for the bullet had deprived him of one whisker, and it seemed to him that a thousand bells were ringing a frantic peal in his ears.

Clifton saw that he had missed him again, but he saw also unmistakeable signs that he had been dangerously close to his mark. On came the Cossack.

There were six charges in each revolver, and Clifton resolved this man should, unless fortune gave him a true aim in his next discharge, have expended the whole six upon him. By the gestures in which his Cossack pursuer indulged, it was apparent that he regarded him as a foe, and meant him evil; therefore, before he "came to grief," he determined, if possible, to send the Cossack there.

He put his steed along at a steady pace—the willing thing, with its ears pricked up, seemed to comprehend that much depended upon its efforts, for it kept on without faltering or making a false step, while its gallop was as uniform and even as though its propulsion was an effect of mechanism, free from any erratic movement consequent upon failing strength or renewed vigor.

Having satisfied himself that so far as this was an advantage he could avail himself of it, he turned again and levelled his deadly weapon, glancing along its polished barrel with a keen eye, and as he brought it once more to bear upon his intended victim, at the moment he had got his aim he pulled the trigger. The report was sharp and loud, and ere the wreathing smoke was whistling away in concentric rings above his head, he saw the heels of the Cossack fly up in the air, and his horse keep on, at a frantic pace, riderless.

Now he pushed on his own little steed, and as he found himself on the descent he pressed it, for he hoped to reach the valley, where he could obtain a cover, before the party—to whom the Cossack he had first brought down belonged—again came in sight, and where he could hide in safety until night. He knew that it would not do for him to prosecute his journey in the daylight, his disguise was not sufficient for that. It would pass muster at night, or at a distance, but in the daylight, and in face of the enemy's picket or any of their troops, wherever stationed on his route, it would not stand an instant's inspection. Besides, beyond a few words, he knew nothing of the Russian language, and a simple remark addressed to him demanding a reply would prove fatal to his incognito. It was of vital importance, therefore, to obtain some place in which he could hide until he could leave his shelter with some better prospect of escape than he should possess in the daylight.

Upon gaining the bottom of the hill and passing into the valley, he saw that there would be the opportunity desired, in pursuing the course of a stream which ran through it, for in some places dense brushwood came down to the water's edge, in others there were rugged cavernous embankments; of the most eligible of these he determined to avail himself. He guided his steed to the stream, and was no sooner in it than he, in order to avoid being further tracked on the morrow, directed the animal along its course to a part where the land rose abruptly, and was covered with a coarse, scrubby brushwood. At this moment he heard the clatter of horses' feet in the valley, and he started almost nervously, for he at once attributed it to a new enemy appearing from an unexpected source; but, to his unspeakable relief, he found that it was the riderless horse of the Cossack he had shot, and the animal, with a sagacity pertaining to its species, galloped up to keep company with the one which Clifton bestrode.

A glance told him that it was a powerful English bred animal—its appointments that it had belonged to an English dragoon regiment. At first he puzzled his brain how to get rid of it, for it whinnied, and joined him in the stream, seeming delighted to have company once again. He spoke to it a few words in his own tongue, of the character usually employed by cavalry soldiers to their steeds, and the beast pricked up its ears, gave a low whinny, snorted, and betrayed its satisfaction at being in the vicinity of one of the race by which it had been formerly commanded. It is hardly necessary to say this is no fiction, having actually occurred, and those who have much to do with horses, can vouch how readily they not only recognise a voice, but language.

Clifton, however, thought this accession of company no gain, but how to get rid of the animal he could not devise; indeed, he had no time to spare, and he pushed on, determined to leave the result to Providence. At length he reached a kind of bluff, crowned with trees and underwood, some of which came straggling down into the water. He tore the branches hastily on one side, and saw that there was plenty of room for him to crawl between the intertwining stems and branches of trees to a depth beyond his sight, and here he immediately decided upon establishing his lurking place; he, however, passed on, and soon found a passage beneath over-arching trees, springing from a kind of natural terrace, beyond which was a series of rocky ridges, some of them crested with scrubby brushwood, others with long rank grass shooting up in wild luxuriance from their uneven surfaces. He guided his steed up a somewhat steep ascent, and the other horse followed him with the docility of a dog. Dismounting when progress became difficult, he led the animals through some intricacies into a natural cleft in the earth, where there was room for them not only to stand but to lay down, if they felt so disposed. He quickly collected some fodder, of which there was an ample supply, and arranging it in a heap before each horse, left them to enjoy a day's rest, while he returned to seek out his own covert, and secrete himself in it.

Having marked his way so that he should be able again to recognise it on the following night, he retraced his steps, and wading through the stream, soon discovered the bluff again, whose shelter he was about to claim. He was not altogether satisfied that contiguous to it was a slope, even smooth and velvet-like, which might have given it a claim to a home at Windsor. It stretched down to the water, and if the course of the stream was pursued in search for him, it was just of that nature to draw attention to him. Nevertheless, it appeared to afford the only means of cover in the vicinity of absolute extent, and yet close in its nature, and he resolved to trust to it.

He pressed the bushes on one side and entered. It was very dark—he groped his way along—now stopped by thick tree stems—anon by straggling bushes; but his progress was not entirely checked: and where the opening for advance was very small he forced his way on. The smell of dank earth—the slimy damp of decaying vegetation—the feeling that creeping things and crawling horrors were in profusion—deterred him not; he went on as long as he could force a way. At last he found himself in empty space; the darkness was impenetrable. He stretched forward his hands, but they touched nothing —he put out his foot, but, save the damp earth, nothing encountered it. He groped for a short distance, right and left, and above his head; nothing whatever met his touch. He drew his sword, and stretched out his arm as far as he could reach— nothing but empty space met the point above— around him.

He paused—for an indefinable dread took possession of him. The intense darkness prevented him distinguishing an object of any kind, or whether he was advancing to destruction. He had read of such places as these;—natural caverns, under hills, in which were noiseless pools, bottomless, so far as attempts to fathom them had proved. He knew not but that he might be on the edge of one, and another step forward precipitate him in. He could swim well; but a struggle with such a lake for life would not be altogether agreeable, even if not fatal.

Then, again, a yawning gulf might be beneath his feet—some fearful depth, that would make a fall into it annihilation. He shuddered, and stepped back. Then he laughed at his surmises, which he declared to be very like ridiculous fears; and feeling round for a space, to ascertain that nothing was in the proximity likely to be disagreeable or dangerous, he seated himself, and prepared to count the time; for it was doubtful whether he should see daylight in that place.

He found his Cossack cloak invaluable to him, and he proceeded to draw it round him tightly, in order to stretch himself upon the earth, and rest—not to sleep for in his position that would be dangerous. In doing this, his hand came in contact with something within a portion of the cloak, and examining it, he found a capacious pocket. It instantly struck him that the thoughtfulness of Captain Eimanoff had provided him with some food, and he dived into the pocket and brought out a bottle; a further search produced a paper parcel, which smelt fragrant in his

nostrils, for he was hungry, and there was no doubt about meat being within the packet; he dived his hand in again, and brought forth a small pipe and a little box, which to his great joy had an unmistakeable scent, for it contained lucifers. A light, in his present position, was worth all the rest put together. He returned everything to his pocket but the lucifers, and with one he quickly obtained a light, but it was feeble and revealed nothing. He had in his pocket a considerable portion of an English newspaper, over which he had beguiled some of the hours of his captivity, and he determined to grope his way back to where the foliage was abundant, and breaking a quantity of twigs, endeavour to kindle a fire, if only to enable him to see what sort of a place he had got into. The project was quickly executed: he was pleased to find that at some distance from the ground, the leaves and their small twig-like branches were dry, and snapped easily. He collected at his feet a large heap, and gathering it up in his arms, returned as near as he could possibly guess to the spot upon which he had stood when he found the treasure in his cloak. He arranged it lightly, and beneath, near the bottom, he inserted the paper, and then set fire to the mass. At first there was a dense volume of smoke, then it burst into a flame, and he found that he was in a cavern, of tolerable width, extending farther than his eye could penetrate. It was a natural excavation, arched and dry, and, as well as he could perceive, somewhat sinuous. Where it led to was a question, it struck him, he was not likely to satisfactorily elucidate—indeed, he was well content to find that the firm earth beneath extended in every direction, and that, without danger of falling a thousand feet below, he could either promenade up and down, or lay himself at length to obtain the rest necessary to fit him for the further exertions he should have to make ere he could reach the British camp.

He drank from his bottle, and eat from his paper of provisions. Some of the wood he had fed his fire with was resinous, and burned brightly and well; other portions were damp, and evolved smoke, but his fire still burned steadily. When he had completed his repast the warmth was agreeable, and the light cheerful, and he stretched himself, with his cloak folded around him, at his fire side, with the intention of passing at least twenty hours in that dark place, as best he could.

He thought, by way of amusement, he went back from the present moment to his earliest recollections. Strange scenes—stranger events—passed before his eyes. Now he was mixed up with pleasures and delights, anon struggling with difficulties, which appeared insurmountable; there was a strange agglomeration of incidents, and at last he seemed to become conscious he heard voices and loud laughter, and he started up and rubbed his eyes.

The darkness was intense.

CLIFTON GREY RESCUING A ZOUAVE AND VIVANDIERE FROM THE RUSSIANS.

He had been asleep; slept soundly for hours—many hours—the fire was out, there was only a smell of charred wood, and not a glimpse of light anywhere.

But the voices—he surely had heard voices;—their sound had disturbed him. He started; for a loud laugh struck his ear. It sounded from no great distance off—was that of a man—a rough, stalwart man. Hark! there was a woman's voice, speaking in sorrowful tones, followed by a rapid remark from another voice, and again a loud laugh.

Clifton sat breathless—the sounds were not far from him; but the darkness was so profound he could see nothing. He listened intently, and again the voices spoke; but he could not catch a word. He drew a pistol from his belt, and crept in the direction from whence the sounds had proceeded. He soon came to the entangled labyrinth of stems and branches between which he had crept on entering, and he forced his way between them until he perceived a glimmering light, and quickly reached where things became quite visible and palpable to him. It was broad daylight—there was no doubt of that. He could hardly realise that he had slept the long night away; but the strength and wakefulness he now felt, assured him that such good fortune had been his.

He moved with great caution, and now heard the voices with great distinctness; even heard the gurgling of the stream as it raced by the valley to the place in which he was concealed. He got nearer and nearer to the persons who were speaking, hoping to be able to see them, without being seen. Nor was he disappointed in this; for, after a serpentine motion, with cat-like care, he was enabled to look on to that slope he had noticed the night before, as rendering less secure the covert he had selected for safety.

What were his emotions on seeing a party of at least thirty Cossacks dismounted from their horses, seated on the grass, partaking of a hasty meal. They were not a dozen yards from him. In the centre of a ring which they formed was seated bound, and a prisoner, a Zouave; by his side, but also a prisoner, a vivandière, a young French girl, whose remarkably pretty face commended itself greatly to the Muscovite taste.

Fortunately the impression she made was felt by nearly all the rough troopers there; and each desiring to be the object of her favour, prevented any or either of his companions forcing upon her his loving attentions. The Zouave was in despair. The girl was half frightened, but tried to carry it off with an air of cool defiance, and did her best to comfort her comrade and countryman, although her position was by far the most dangerous of the two. The Zouave was, however, greatly concerned about her. He repeatedly assured her he cared not for himself, but he was in despair about her fate. He hissed and

sputtered, and rolled the r's about with wonderful emphasis, and it was his passionate exclamations which drew from the Muscovites those loud laughs which had disturbed Clifton. The latter speedily discovered in the French prisoner, his friend, M. le Zouave, whose life he had saved at Varna, and who had returned the compliment for him near the Inkermann heights. The vivandière he did not recognise; but he was struck by her handsome face, and the dissimilarity she exhibited to others of the same profession he had seen in attendance upon the French army. He felt a wonderful disposition to rescue them, but how? Any attempt he could make single handed, would not only be futile, but ensure his own captivity. However, he resolved to lie *perdu*, and watch events.

He lay upon his breast on the watch for, at least, half-an-hour, when, of a sudden, a trumpet was heard in the distance. The Cossacks sprung to their feet, and one, who appeared to hold the rank of sergeant, addressed a few words to the fiercest looking of the troop, the effect of which was to make him resume his seat by the side of the Zouave, while the others all mounted their shaggy ponies, and rode off, leaving the Zouave and the vivandière in the care of this one Cossack.

Clifton's heart beat violently. Surely he could now accomplish the liberation of his little French friend and his pretty countrywoman from this one Russian's custody at least; and, what was more, he resolved to try it. The thing was to get out and fasten on to the Russian before he was discovered, and as they were at the moment placed, this was next to an impossibility, because of the positions in which the three sat; but this was soon altered, for the Cossack, being now beyond the control of his companions, resolved upon regaling himself with a kiss on the sweet lips of the pretty French woman. That was a language common to all nations. He could not speak French, nor the lady Russian, and he concluded that there would be no difficulty in conversing thus, but he was mistaken; for on attempting it, he received a most violent smack on the face from the small, but vigorous hand of the French girl, which almost sent him reeling, while the Zouave uttered anathemas, wonderfully interlarded with *sacr-r-r-r-r-r-ies* and *mille tonner-r-r-r-r-r-es*, together with voluble promises to have a sanguinary revenge for the insult offered to his countrywoman. The Muscovite re-seated himself upon the grass, and rubbed his cheek, regarding, as he did so, the pair with a gloomy look. A murderous expression, which promised them a shorter career than might otherwise be theirs, twinkled in his eyes. The blow had roused the devil within him, and he drew from his belt a formidable knife, determining to revenge the blow he had received by cutting the girl's throat. As he rose to execute his sanguinary project, a human figure burst from the network of shrubs and leaves behind him, seized him by the long hair which descended to his shoulders, and dealt him with the butt-end of a pistol a blow of such tremendous force, that the fellow was in an instant stretched senseless upon the ground.

The vivandière uttered a smothered shriek, and the Frenchman an exclamation, but Clifton quickly made himself known to him, and dragged him and the vivandière into his covert, leaving the Muscovite still senseless upon the earth, the blood slowly trickling from a wound in the temple.

It was not without difficulty that Clifton conveyed them into that part of the cavern which was free from vegetation; but when there, he explained his own position, and how he had discovered them. They were not a little delighted. In return they told him briefly that the night previously they had met to talk about their friends in La belle France, near the Belbek, when a sudden sortie, made by the Russians, overwhelmed them, and they were borne away prisoners. They were on their way to Simpheropol when Clifton rescued them.

The Zouave, whose arms were now at liberty, had no notion of leaving the body of the Cossack where it laid, as he said, "to tell tales and point to their lair," so he volunteered to remove it, and requested the pretty Fanchette, for that was the name of the young vivandière, and Clifton to remain where they were until he had accomplished the feat, which they consented to do. But he had no sooner gone, than Clifton proceeded to gather an armful of twigs and kindle a blazing fire. When the cave was lighted up, he produced his flask and the provisions left from the previous night's repast, and Fanchette did not hesitate to avail herself of them, thanking him warmly for his services, and intimating, that if he attempted after such kindness to imitate the act of the Cossack, for which she had struck him in the face, it was highly improbable that she would so resent the copy he made of the example set him. Whether Clifton accepted the invitation and kissed her pretty lips, and whether if he did so she displayed no anger whatever, is not to the purpose of the story, let it suffice, that the Zouave, on his return, detected in them no such close proximity as to lead to the belief that a passage of the kind had occurred, and he was a close observer of her movements at least.

The Zouave had accomplished his errand effectually, for he had run his knife across the Cossack's throat, and then stripped the body; after which, as there appeared no sign of any Cossack or other enemy near or far, he carried the body to the stream and threw it in it, and, as he said, "it sunk like a stone." He brought with him the clothes of the dead man, and proposed to attire himself in them, and having secured his horse, start, when night came on, for the French lines with Fanchette, where he hoped to get back in safety.

Clifton now told him of the two horses he had stowed away, and the Zouave resolved to fetch the shaggy pony belonging to the slain Cossack, lead it to where the others were stationed, because, he said, should any of the party who had recently left them return and find no trace of the prisoners or the Cossack, they would conclude that he had gone on with them to Simpheropol; whereas, if the shaggy pony was discovered, a search would probably be made in their vicinity, and they perhaps unkenneled.

No sooner said than done. The Frenchman, attired in the Cossack's uniform, a world too big for him, obtained possession of the little steed, and, following closely the directions he had received from Clifton, soon found the cleft where the other two horses were; having secured his addition to the stock of horseflesh, he returned to the cave, where he found Clifton and the pretty vivandière engaged in pleasant and harmless conversation.

M. le Zouave was in ecstacies at his deliverance so far; he vowed eternal friendship, and promised personal aid to the death should our hero ever require it at his hands, and he be able to render it. He made Clifton repeat the particulars of his escape, and was especially comforted by the account of the death of the Cossack who pursued Clifton over the plateau on his way hither. He examined with satisfaction the revolvers, and, finding that three of the barrels were empty, unlaced one of his greaves; he exhibited a leg infinitely thinner without the leathern gaiter than with it. From the part which undulated over the calf, he, with a burst of almost childish mirth, exhibited to the astonished gaze of Clifton a couple of small pockets, and these were closely filled with cartridges wedged in. No wonder his leg seemed stalwart for such a little fellow: the secret was explained. The empty barrels of the pistols were now charged, and this important act was scarcely finished, when, to the dismay of all, the crackling of leaves and branches as of some one approaching the cave in which they were seated by the leafy entry was heard. A heap of leaves collected by the energetic Zouave to feed the fire had been compulsorily put aside as being too damp for the purpose—they gave out smoke instead of flame. In a moment the Frenchman whipped up the heap and deposited it on the fire, which was burning brightly, and completely smothered it; then whispering to Clifton to remain still, he threw himself upon his face, and commenced a serpent-like movement, to meet the new comer, be it friend or foe.

The cave was once more in utter darkness; the vivandière stretched out her arms and caught hold of Clifton; she clung to him tightly—he could feel her heart beat against his breast—he bent over her and whispered some words to reassure her—her face nestled upon his shoulder.

"Mon Dieu!" she murmured, "I am fainting; we

shall be killed. O, my brave friend, protect and save me. I shall die with fright."

He placed his hand over her mouth gently, and for at least two or three minutes they stood thus. They could hear the crackling of leaves, slowly and with little noise, proceeding as though there was yet some one cautiously moving among the interlaced branches and stems at the mouth of this natural cave. Once Fanchette shuddered, and clung even yet closer to Clifton, for a hollow groan distinctly sounded in their ears. Still the displacement of the boughs went on, and Clifton began to grow excited at the impossibility of forming a guess as to the real cause—or rather as to who occasioned this much dreaded sound. At length it ceased entirely and all was still; he could hear it no longer. The suspense was tremendous, and he was just on the point of begging Fanchette to remain where she was, while he sought to discover the meaning of this strange interruption, when he felt a strange hand seize his arm; in an instant he shook it off, and, throwing the young French girl on one side, stood prepared for a death struggle with some mortal foe, when he heard the voice of the Zouave addressing him. Clifton eagerly asked him if he had discovered the cause of the disturbance.

"Oui, mon ami," he replied, "Les Cosaques, there's half a hundred of them looking for their friend, whom I have sent into the other world to keep company with others whose term has been shortened by the brave soldiers of my nation. The mouth of this place is surrounded; they are hunting and nosing about like a swarm of ferrets, and when their patience becomes exhausted by the absence of their comrade, they will follow in search; then for a short shrift and an introduction to purgatory, without troubling us to give our consent."

"We must not remain here," said Clifton.

"C'est vrai," responded the Zouave, "but how to get away? The Cossacks will not permit us to pass, and we cannot walk through the solid bank of earth."

"There is a passage unexplored at the end. We will have a light at all hazards, and see where it leads to."

"Vive la bagatelle," said the Zouave, and kicked the smouldering embers.

Clifton, however, knew that there was a resinous pine springing out of the earth, surrounded by an undergrowth of younger plants, and he procured, not without difficulty, embarrassed too by the necessity for the utmost haste, enough to twist into a kind of torch, and kindled it. It threw a red glare around, and the keen eyes of the Zouave instantly detected the sinuous passage at the further end of the cave; he uttered an expression of joy, and made it a low bow.

"Ouvrez la bouche," he said, and added a promise, if it obliged him by doing as he requested, to remember it in his prayers. "En avant, mes enfans," he cried, "we shall get further into trouble or get out of it by this door."

Neither Clifton nor Fanchette needed urging to follow him closely up, as he hurried along the winding passages of the murky den, waving in one hand the torch, and bearing in the other the sword with which Clifton had been provided by Captain Eimanoff; our hero having lent it to him, as he had the brace of pistols, and the Zouave had been deprived by the Russians, who had captured him, of his arms.

The passage, which continued for some distance uninterruptedly, suddenly divided into three, leading in totally different directions, and it became a perplexing question which to select. There was nothing to assist the judgment—not an indication by which they could form a notion as to which of the passages had an outlet, or whether any of the three had one at all. It was necessary to choose one, and as hitting on the best would be a mere matter of chance, they agreed to leave it to the decision of Fanchette, who promptly decided upon taking that on the right hand, because — she thought it was the right. She could furnish no other than her woman's reason for the adoption, but she was very decided on the point, and they accepted it.

The path soon grew narrow and very tortuous, but they persevered, and ultimately it entered on an ascent which became abruptly steep, and required some agility and strength to clamber up it, but, nothing daunted by the difficulties, they proceeded, hurrying along as much as was possible, for their torch had burned down to an unpleasant closeness to the Zouave's hand, and afforded but small light. Clifton, however, observed what seemed to be a star in the darkness, and pointed it out to his companions.

"There is daylight," he exclaimed, "shining at the mouth of this passage. Fanchette was right; she has chosen the correct route."

"Fanchette is an angel!" cried the Zouave; "she is always right."

"But you do not always think so, Henri," the young vivandière responded, almost sharply.

"Eternally!" he ejaculated, with a vehement gesture.

"I am afraid, my friend," she replied, with a laugh, "that you occasionally indulge in falsehoods. I have a very clear remembrance of being many times challenged by you with being very decidedly in the wrong."

"Nay!" he exclaimed. "Ma belle Fanchette, you are seeking to effect a surprise upon me. If I have ever suggested to you that you have been in the wrong, it is only when you have felt disposed towards love, and in some moment of affectionate tendencies you have for the time made a mistake in the Henri on whom you desired to lavish your fondness. You should not thus charge me, when my act has been the simple one of reminding you of your error."

"Bah! Ha! ha!" returned Fanchette, "Your ridiculous jealousy; besides your language, M. Henri, ma foi, that was not so simple—"

Clifton suggested that as they were not out of the lion's den, it would be as well to be cautious in the use of the tongue, to which advice his two companions assented, and they proceeded in silence until, after traversing a longer distance than they had calculated, they reached the mouth of the excavation, or rather, a natural tunnel.

Both Clifton and the Zouave stole warily into the open space; the former, to his surprise, within a few paces of the entrance, discovered that they were contiguous to the cleft where the steeds had been stabled, and that they were there standing quietly, yet feeding on the herbage which had been provided for them. This was an advantage, if the Cossacks, in search of their now two missing comrades, did not reach the cavern which had sheltered the trio; if they did—and this was an event highly probable—they would explore every part of it, and coming out at the outlet which they had just quitted, and at which Fanchette yet remained, nothing could prevent them discovering the steeds, and eventually the fugitives. This was, at least, the chain of reasoning Clifton followed out; he therefore deemed it advisable to devise some plan by which they could quit this locality, or if they remained, arrange a mode of concealment likely to prove secure.

He summoned the Zouave to his side; after a consultation, the Frenchman decided on selecting the cleft in which the horses stood for the spot in which to remain for the night, and explained to Clifton that he would speedily construct a screen of the thick brushwood, if Clifton would aid him by lopping with his sword material for the purpose, of which there was plenty in the immediate vicinity. Clifton doubted if there would be time to accomplish it, but the Zouave, with the agility of a cat, sprung up the ridge above them, and tore down several saplings, while Clifton applied himself to the task of rooting up, where he could, the brushwood and long fern-like grass, working with such good will that he soon had as much as he considered would be enough for the object required, and he proceeded with as much as he could carry to his little agile friend, who was already engaged in scooping out earth with the aid of a knife, in which to plant his young trees. With Clifton's help this was soon done, and the activity and skill of both combined soon effected the leafy screen which the Zouave had designed. His aptitude at arrangement, the taste with which he interlaced and planted shrubs and the tall grass, struck Clifton forcibly. No practised floral decorator would have surpassed him in skill and quickness, and in a space

of time almost incredibly short the task was done. Fanchette was summoned from her lurking place, and when all were within the clift the Zouave placed up the last trees which completed the covert. With what he had left—not a vestige or leaf had he suffered to remain without, so as to draw attention—he stuck up a second screen in front of the horses; then he made Fanchette lie down, and covered her with grass and brush, and pointed out a place for Clifton and himself to lie, spreading over them loose leaves and grass, so that any of the Cossacks on the search who might pause in front of their lurking place, and peep into it, should be unable to see them. Well it was that he had taken this precaution; well, too, that they had completed their task with the speed they had done, for they had hardly disposed themselves in the order mentioned, when the quick ear of Clifton caught the sound of an approaching footstep.

He caught the arm of the Zouave and pressed it; the little fellow nodded, and lay quite flat, but watching with the eye of a lynx for the coming stranger.

The heavy tread of footsteps was almost immediately heard, and the tramp of many feet broke on their ear with startling rapidity, telling them the crisis of their fate was at hand. To add to their excitement, they heard the voices of Russians calling to each other in their native tongue, and a party of ten or twelve of these stalwart and ruthless fellows, stopped actually in front of the artificial screen of leaves. Clifton gripped his pistols, and set his teeth: he was not very sanguine that the eyes of these men, accustomed to the natural arrangement of the scrubby brushwood and tangled coverts, would be deceived by the artificial; he concluded they would detect it at once, and dash in upon them as soon as they discovered it, so he prepared to spring to his feet, and sell his life dearly, for he had not a single expectation of being spared. Fanchette, who heard the coming of the Russians, lay quite still in a state of perspiration, saying her prayers, but the Zouave had a better opinion of his skill. He did not for a moment anticipate that his labour would be easily recognised, and himself unkenneled, so he lay curiously watching the movements of his foes, and breathing profanely a number of sacres, because the Cossacks conversed in the Russian language, a language of which he even knew less than Hindostanee, and he wanted to know what they were talking about, but he was not destined to be gratified, for the men passed on and were soon out of hearing.

Others, however, followed, but without pausing to inspect their lurking place, although it was evident they were searching right and left. Once, indeed, a hand pushed aside the leaves directly above Clifton, and he saw the glittering eye of a Russian rolling round, but the hand was withdrawn, the eye shut out from his gaze; a trumpet, at a distance, sounded, and the Cossacks disappeared.

All became silent and still—the rustle of the wind in the leaves was the only sound heard—but none of them offered to move; even Fanchette laid close—it is a question whether she did not like the stillness less than the noise made by the Russians—but in a little time the Zouave whispered to Clifton:

"It is permitted to us to doubt, and I don't believe there is a Cossack in the vicinity. I'll creep out and survey."

He did so—employing the wriggling mode which he had adopted when he left the cave to meet the Cossack whom he slew.

Some time elapsed, but the Zouave did not return. Clifton had not breathed a word to Fanchette, and she had lain perfectly silent, until silence became unbearable to her, and she rose up and looked about her. Clifton heard the rustle, and looked up too.

"Ah!" exclaimed Fanchette, "I shall suffocate if I remain here. What with heat, and what with fright, I have not a dry garment upon me. Then Henri is so adventurous. A soldier may be brave, but he has no occasion to be a fool with it. He has been gone hours from here, and you may be sure he has put his head into the lion's mouth, and had it bitten off for his pains."

Clifton laughed, and bade her rest herself contented. He believed Henri to be safe, but, to ease her mind, he told her that he would depart in search of him. He counselled her not to grow alarmed at a lengthened absence, for he assured her he should be cautious in his movements, and would, unless any unforeseen circumstances occurred, return to her.

"You are kind, my friend," she exclaimed, "as complaisant as you are handsome. Ah! mon Dieu! it is better for you to go in search for Henri, it is dangerous to one's heart to be much alone with you." She breathed a sigh as she spoke, and looked with tenderness beaming in her pretty soft dark eyes, too, and Clifton, who noted the look, albeit he smiled, thought as she did, so, without a word, he impelled himself to the other side of the screen.

Upon doing so he encountered the Zouave stepping back with the lightness of a cat: he started on seeing our hero, who smiled, and divined the object with which Henri was returning with a step so stealthy. He made no remark, but questioned the Zouave upon the result of his investigation, and he replied, "That there was not a Cossack anywhere within view." Further, he had cautiously crept to the top of the ridge, from which he could see the country stretching away for miles, and he was much deceived, he said, if he had not heard the booming sound of the cannonading which was proceeding against Sebastopol; he, therefore, looked well at the road it would be necessary for them to take, and he observed several land marks which would be useful to them as guides; but Clifton remembered his own map, furnished by Captain Eimanoff, and together they consulted it.

It was plain, distinct, and easily understood. Clifton found that the path over the ridge would somewhat anticipate the route marked down in the plan, but he saw he should be able to get into the course to be followed without difficulty, and he determined to take it, proceeding to make the necessary preparations for departure.

The night was fast approaching, and, by the time the sun had sunk, a haze spread over the surrounding country, and shut out of sight everything beyond a hundred yards. This, while it was of service to keep them out of sight of their foes, possessed also the disadvantage of probably bringing them into the company of the enemy before they had an opportunity for avoiding them.

But all risks must be incurred, for remain there they could not; they had fasted some hours and had nothing left from Clifton's supply—even the little barrel attached to the vivandière's side had been emptied by the Cossacks—so, as soon as the moment came for departure, they brought out their horses, having well searched the immediate neighbourhood first, and mounted. Henri and Fanchette each upon a Cossack pony, and Clifton on the English charger, set forward, Clifton taking the lead. The horses were fresh and cantered on at a smart pace, and as soon as our hero discovered that he had got on to the route marked down on the little chart, he followed it closely, and increased his pace, because he believed that the Captain had marked out for him a track but little likely to be infested by the mounted soldiers of his own nation, and, as time was everything, he should be adopting a wise policy to use as much rapidity as possible. The haze continued—even grew thicker—but he did not slacken his speed, though he was several times in doubt whether he had not missed the route—he believed he had not, and so pushed on.

Once he heard the clattering of a troop of Cossack cavalry, by far too near to be pleasant, but he pushed on without stopping, passing over hill and dale until the Zouave declared it his belief the Crimea was made of an expansive material, which some spiteful Number Nip stretched out when any one like themselves, for example, desired very anxiously to get to the sea coast. They knew, however, they were nearing the desired haven, and that they were not far from it, for a rattling fire of musketry, continued for some time, told the story of a sortie in the trenches. Their hearts beat tumultuously, and their steeds were urged forward, although they had before exhibited signs of being tired. Down hill, now up-hill, anon again to descend, and then they found themselves in a stream somewhat wide: they were soon up to their saddle girths. The vivandière uttered a cry of alarm.

"Sit firm, my dear child," cried the Zouave, "your pony will swim like a duck; as for me, if I get wet, it will be the clothes of the Czar that will suffer—"

His pony slipped as he spoke, and the little Zouave was shot into the stream instanter, but his agility was unconquerable; he scrambled on to the beast's back almost as soon as he was off, sputtering and spitting, and anathematizing all animals that stumbled. Both Clifton and the vivandière were convulsed with laughter, and the Zouave heard their merriment as they all landed on the other bank of the stream. He shrugged his shoulders.

"*Marchand qui perd ne peut rien!*" he cried, merrily; "I shall peel in a few minutes, and be once more in the costume of des 3*mes* Zouaves, and will cry *Vive l'Empereur* with—"

"Stand—who goes there?—give the word, or I'll fire!" exclaimed a voice from a man who sprung up immediately in front of them, and presented a minié rifle at them.

"English!—Scots Fusilier Guards!" cried Clifton, loudly and rapidly, he did not, of course, know the word, but he found, to his great joy, that he was once more safe on the soil possessed by his countrymen. It was not, however, until Clifton exhibited to him his attire beneath his cloak, and the Zouave had declared himself a faithful subject of the Emperor of France, that the sentry permitted them to pass. The soldier, forming part of a picket, told them they had better look sharp, and pass along up the hill at their best speed, for an attack by the Russians in force was expected to take place very shortly, and they would find themselves awkwardly situated if they remained.

Clifton shortly afterwards, in following his advice, came upon the officer in command of the picket, who listened to Clifton's narration, briefly told, with interest, and directed him where to find the ground held by the Guards, our hero soon availed himself of the information. It was dawn when he reached his colonel's quarters and reported himself, and then he proceeded to his own tent; he met Sergeant Haverel just stretching his arms, yawning, and coming out to obtain a mouthful of fresh air. He uttered a shout of delight when he saw Clifton, and he wrung him by both hands with a force which pretty plainly told that he was fast recovering his strength again.

"Aha! Hurrah! God save the Queen, and d—n the beadle!" he cried. "Escaped from the hands of the Philistines! Bravo! I told Mickey that you'd get out of their clutches before they shed their eye-lashes, I said to Mickey said I—"

"Never mind that now, sergeant," interrupted Clifton with a smile, "I'll hear all this by-and-bye; I'll tell you how I was fool enough to suffer myself to be taken prisoner, and how I got away; but I want to sleep my friends here, and snatch a few hours myself. Where's Mickey?"

"Snoring, like the Malakoff bellowing at the French. He is such a fellow is Mickey, he takes half of his life out in sleep, and likes it, but I'll disturb his slumbers for him."

And so he did; Mickey jumped up as soon as he heard of Clifton's return, and after expressing his delight he bestirred himself to place something to eat before Clifton and his late companions, for they felt like starving, and as soon as the repast was ready they fell to it without much pressing.

The sun was shining brightly—the bombardment was going on heavily—musketry rolling incessantly—shot and shell from battery and earth-work; from trench and from rifle-pit. The sky above bright and blue and calm—the earth beneath red with flashing fire, or white with the smoke of gunpowder, and during this work of devastation the young guardsman, the pretty vivandière, and the bold Zouave were fast asleep in Clifton's tent, and dreaming soft and pleasant dreams of home and loving faces.

CHAPTER XXVII.

Gra. O, upright judge! Mark, Jew! O, learned judge!
Shy. Is that the law?
Por. Thyself shall see the act:
　For as thou urgest justice, be assur'd
　Thou shalt have justice—more than thou desir'st.
Gra. O, learned judge! Mark, Jew! A learned judge!
　　　　　　　　　　　　　　　　SHAKSPERE.

" His boat appears—not five oars' length—
　His comrades strain with desperate strength—
　Oh! are they yet in time to save?
　　*　　*　　*　　*　　*
　Fast from his breast the blood is bubbling,
　The whiteness of the sea-foam troubling—
　If aught his lips essay'd to groan,
　The rushing billows choked the tone!"

THE MAGISTRATE—THE EXAMINATION—THE REMAND
　　—THE FATE OF SAUL WATERS.

THE appearance of 'his worship' in the chamber, converted into an office, was followed by the sound of a general rising up of those who were seated, and a sharp cry from the clerk for silence, while he looked round frowningly to observe if there were any delinquent regardless of the injunction, and, if any, who he was.

The magistrate was a short, stout, elderly gentleman, dressed in black, and wore round his neck a white cravat of rather ample proportions. He looked much as if he belonged to the church, yet his countenance was of that apoplectic tint which so very plainly pronounced 'port wine,' that one would pause ere such profession were actually assigned to him. His eye was small and a very light blue, and surmounted by a bushy eyebrow, which gave it generally a severe character. His hair was short, and stood up brush-like and decided, as though it were of strong growth, but was kept cut down close to the roots; whether this process of cropping made it prolific, and the young shoots starting above the surface titillated, we do not profess to say, but the worthy magistrate appeared to be constantly occupied in scratching his scalp with one finger nail, while the other fingers were spread out, fan-like, during the operation.

He rubbed his hands and glanced round at the mob assembled, and as his eye fell upon Captain Winslow, he elevated his eyebrows and bowed—he mistook him for a prosecutor, because of his style and gentlemanly appearance. The captain returned it with studied politeness, and then the magistrate was seated.

"Silence!" cried the clerk, as soon as all was hushed, "will you be silent, pray," and he looked fiercely round; but as nobody was making a noise but himself, he turned and whispered to the magistrate, who nodded repeatedly, as he listened without comprehending, even if he attended to a word that was uttered. The clerk having finished his statement, the magistrate leaned forward and poured out a glass of pure spring water; he took up the tumbler with a tremulous hand, and it might have been heard to chink against his teeth as he swallowed or rather gulped down its contents. When he had drained it he replaced the tumbler, and gazing sharply about him, said:

"Hah! Now—a—now, what is the first charge?" Mr. Knipe pressed himself forward.

"With your worship's permission, we have a charge of felony to prefer against a person now in custody before you."

"For whom do you appear, Mr. Knipe?" asked the magistrate.

Mr. Knipe pointed to Captain Winslow, and said: "This gentleman, your honour; an officer in Her Majesty's Scots Fusilier Guards, who has just returned from the Crimea, wounded, having nobly bled in his country's service."

"Oh,—in-deed!" exclaimed the magistrate, bowing and extending his hand to shake hands with the captain. "Captain Winslow," he added, "it gives me considerable pleasure to make your acquaintance—very glad indeed. England is deeply indebted to her brave defenders, and, as a nation, very proud to acknowledge it. Your regiment, I believe, is an especial favourite with Her Majesty?"

Captain Winslow brightened up, and bowing: "It has that distinguished honour," he said.

"I beg your pardon, Mr. Tickelpenny," interposed Oliver Lawrence, abruptly, and speaking to the magistrate with bluntness. "I am also an officer in Her Majesty's service, and entitled to be heard with some respect for my word. Permit me to suggest, that as I have a very serious charge to bring against that individual to whom you have just spoken, he is now in custody respecting it. You are premature in fraternizing with him, as justice requires from you the

strictest impartiality, and not the display, either of sympathy or good-will, for prisoner or prosecutor."

Mr. Knipe extended his head, and turned his face full upon the magistrate, but he addressed the lieutenant.

"His worship, I presume," he said, "is quite acquainted with his duties, without requiring to be instructed in them by a lieutenant in the Coast Guard Service,"

"Or the impertinent interference of a lawyer of sharp practice," responded Oliver Lawrence, and added rapidly: "I was desirous of guarding his worship from being entrapped into an error by a remark which fell from you, and which you had no right to make."

"No right, Lieutenant Lawrance?" snapped Knipe.

"No right!" repeated the lieutenant. "You are not the clerk of the court, yet the magistrate addressed himself to that gentleman, but you officiously prevented him replying, by making a statement which must come from the inspector who has taken the charge, and through the clerk, who will submit it to his honour."

"I contend, Mr. Coast-guard-officer," cried Knipe, in an insulting tone, "that I ——"

"Silence! Mr. Knipe," cried the clerk, sharply, having suddenly been reminded, by Oliver Lawrance, that his dignity had been put down by the lawyer's forward conduct, and being now resolved to claim and maintain it, "his worship will come to your case in its proper turn."

"But I beg to inform you—"

"And I you, sir, that you can speak when you are called upon to defend your client; but you must not interfere with the proper course of business. Your honour, the first charge is a case of turnip stealing, if you will be pleased to take it."

"Oh, certainly; by all means—certainly," cried Mr. Tickelpenny, rapidly, being at that moment in a state of bewilderment and mystification, astonishment and vexation. The remark of Mr. Knipe, and the gentlemanly appearance of Captain Winslow, had led him to believe that he was present solely in the character of a prosecutor; but the observation of Oliver Lawrance had caused him to alter this opinion, and to make him believe that he had committed himself. As he was a stickler for what he termed the blind impartiality of justice, being at the same time grossly partial, he was annoyed at being even suspected in public of having made a mistake in this direction, and he determined to be cautious during the remainder of the proceedings, but to give Lieutenant Lawrance, if opportunity were afforded him, a rubber for the bowl he had received at his hands. At the same time he determined to prove the majesty of the law in his administration was not weakened by sympathy. The turnip-stealing case proved to be that of a poor boy, ragged, wan, and half starved in appearance, who was charged by a portly farmer with having stolen and eaten more turnips at one feast

THE FATE OF SAUL WATERS.

than an ox would have been able to have consumed. The farmer swore to the boy's having stolen them and eaten them. The boy was not asked a question about the matter, but his face and half-starved condition were evidences against his having partaken largely of anything for a long period. However he was declared guilty, and the magistrate sentenced him to be imprisoned for three months and thrice privately whipped.

A shudder ran through those present at this wholesome example; but as Mr. Tickelpenny, on a former occasion, had given a starving vagrant six months at the tread-mill for stealing and eating a carrot, they ought not to have been surprised. However there was one there whose face was crimsoned as if with sudden passion; he was a remarkably half-starved gentlemanly looking elderly man, attired in black. He rose up, and in a clear voice, said:

"Mr. Tickelpenny, I shall give notice of appeal against that sentence."

What! charged with being wrong again? Mr. Tickelpenny grew angry.

"Who are you, sir?" he cried, sharply; "by what right do you talk about appealing?"

"My name is Herbert," he was answered. "I am a solicitor, resident in Arundel, and, if I mistake not, your worship has occasion to remember me. My right to talk about appealing is that right which every Englishman has to appeal against an unjust sentence, against which the law allows appeal."

"Unjust, sir! How dare you say it is unjust?" roared the magistrate; "I will commit you for contempt of court, if you talk in that fashion."

"Oh, sir, I say it with all respect for the court," replied Mr. Herbert, bowing; "but I contend the prisoner has not been asked whether he is guilty or not, whether he would be defended or not—in short, he has not been heard."

"Aha! what are you here to pick up a client, Herbert," said Knipe, with a chuckle, hoping, at the same time, by the sneer, to purchase the good will of Tickelpenny. Mr. Herbert turned, and looking steadfastly at the sharp lawyer, said—

"Mr. Knipe, you must be aware that I am not in the habit of imitating you in your mode of obtaining practice, or if I were guilty of such pettifogging, I should not poach on your manor, which I believe this is." Then turning to the magistrate, without waiting for a reply, he said, "I should have added, that in the event of a committal, I shall take the several points I have mentioned, as well as that the sentence is enormously disproportioned to the offence."

Now this was not the first time that Mr. Herbert had appealed against the decisions of Mr. Tickelpenny. On several occasions he had been instructed to do so, and had been uniformly successful; indeed, on the last occasion it had been intimated to Mr. Tickelpenny to be more careful in his judgments, or

he would be removed from the commission. He hated Herbert—more, he feared him.

"Perhaps, Mr. Herbert, you would like a rehearing, if you feel disposed to take up the boy's case," said the magistrate, coldly. "I have no objection to give the prisoner the benefit of such an arrangement, especially as a doubt has been thrown on his having had a fair hearing."

"I accept the offer," replied Mr. Herbert, "but I reserve—I must tell your worship, in order that there may be no misunderstanding—my right of appeal."

Mr. Tickelpenny hemmed, but made no other reply. He ordered the boy once more to be put on his trial, and Mr. Herbert, with great ability and firmness, cross-examined the farmer; he sternly reminded him that he was upon his oath, and that if he made a false statement he threatened to indict him for perjury. He elicited from the farmer that the boy was not near the turnip field in question, that when caught he had no turnips upon him, nor was there any trace of guilt about him; he denied the theft, and beyond that, the farmer could not swear his turnip field had been robbed at all—he only suspected it; the prisoner being the first person likely to be guilty that he met, he had taxed him with the theft, and had given him into custody.

Knipe, whose game it was to be popular, clapped his hands, and cried:

"Really, brother Herbert, a most triumphant refutation."

For which interruption the clerk informed him that, if again guilty, he would be ordered out of court.

The magistrate confessed, with manifest ill will, that after the result of that cross-examination, that the evidence against the prisoner was insufficient, and he should discharge him on that charge, but that he should commit him for fourteen days as a rogue and vagabond. But here one of the rusties got up and said his father lived in the parish and paid rates, but that he had been out of work for some time, which caused the boy to be poorly fed and badly clothed. Mr. Herbert now contended that the boy was not begging, and that he was on the public highway when seized by the farmer; and Mr. Tickelpenny being informed by the clerk that he could not altogether safely to himself inflict that sentence, the boy was discharged entirely; but the magistrate, determined to have a fling at some one, ordered an indictment to be made out against the farmer, who had distinctly sworn the boy was guilty of theft, which he afterwards acknowledged he was in no condition to prove; and the farmer, to the scandal of every one in court, snapped his fingers at the magistrate, slapped his pocket, and informed Mr. Tickelpenny that he might do his best and worst, for he had more there than would buy two such old scarecrows as he any day.

Abused thus on all sides, the magistrate was purple with passion, as well as port wine; he ordered the farmer into custody for contempt of court; and when the man was incarcerated, his braggadocio deserted him. Brought to grief and penitence at the same time, he sent up a snivelling petition for pardon.

The next case called on was that of Captain Winslow; Oliver Lawrance at once retained Mr. Herbert for Myra Aston, and Charley Rowe. The charge was about to be entered into, when Mr. Herbert, with great politeness of manner, which contrasted strongly with the stern abruptness he had previously used, addressed the magistrate, and said:

"Mr. Tickelpenny, I have been retained in two cases to come on before you. As one is of a minor character, and the other, extremely grave, I should esteem it as an especial favour if your worship would oblige me by taking the first of the two cases now, and let the other follow it. Your worship's urbanity in these matters is known to me, and I confidently rely upon its being extended to me in this instance."

"Oh! certainly—certainly," exclaimed Mr. Tickelpenny, "what is the charge you wish to be called first? because, if the prisoner and the prosecutor are here, we will take it."

"It is a case, in which a Captain Winslow, of the Scots Fusilier Guards, charges Charles Rowe with attempting to commit a robbery, accompanied by violence."

"I object to its being taken out of its proper order," exclaimed Mr. Knipe, who thought Mr. Herbert had some motive for the arrangement. He was correct in the surmise he had made. Mr. Knipe's objection, however, was overruled; he was sharply reminded by the clerk, that the arrangement was one he had wished for, and that he had no ground for objecting to it; to do so would be to prove himself captious. The case was therefore called on, the captain standing at the witness bar, and Charley Rowe in the place allotted to prisoners. Mr. Tickelpenny had the night before taken, as his share of a revel, four bottles of port, and he was thirsty and feverish; water made him feel qualmish, and he made an excuse of sudden faintness to retire for a while, to refresh himself with a pint bottle of the same fluid, in order to give him strength to administer justice on the number of cases to be heard.

As soon as he had retired, Mr. Herbert despatched a note dictated by himself, but written by Oliver Lawrance, by a messenger who drove his gig rapidly away into Arundel, and then he rapidly proceeded to cross question Charley Rowe, and Oliver Lawrance, and quickly obtained an insight into both cases. When Mr. Tickelpenny re-appeared with a brighter eye, and a more smiling countenance, for the pint of port had done its work, he was ready for him.

The case was now called on, and Captain Winslow made his statement, which was to the effect that while proceeding from Worthing to Arundel, at an early hour that morning, in a carriage, the prisoner had

knocked the postilion off the horse he was riding; that the pair took fright, and overturned the carriage, and upon his getting out, Rowe made a demand for his watch and money; that a struggle ensued between them, and at the moment two men coming up, they assisted him to secure the prisoner; but subsequently he was released by the coast-guard men, under the direction of their officer, whom it was his intention to report for his disgraceful interference for the purpose of frustrating the ends of justice.

"Be assured the ends of justice shall not be frustrated," cried Oliver Lawrance emphatically.

"Silence!" exclaimed the clerk.

"Pray, Captain Winslow, at what hour did this alleged attempt at robbery take place?" asked Mr. Herbert.

"I cannot exactly answer, for I was awakened from my sleep suddenly."

"By what?"

"A scream."

"Who screamed? Remember, sir, you are upon your oath."

"We decline to answer that question," cried Mr. Knipe sharply.

"But I insist upon having it answered," returned Mr. Herbert; "my client's interests demand it.

"He must answer it," said the clerk.

"But," persisted Mr. Knipe, "your worship will please to remember that there is another case in some degree connected with this, and my client cannot be compelled to make admissions in this case, to be used injuriously to himself in the other."

"Well," said Mr. Herbert, "the scream came from some person within the carriage, did it not."

Captain Winslow remained silent; he bit his lip, for he perceived that he had made a slip.

"You must answer my question, Captain Winslow," continued Mr. Herbert.

"It is irrelevant, and we decline," said Knipe.

"I am the best judge of that," responded Mr. Herbert, "and I insist on the question being answered."

The magistrate was appealed to, and decided that the question must be answered. Mr. Herbert repeated it, and Captain Winslow, in a low tone, answered in the affirmative.

"That scream woke you?" observed Mr. Herbert. "It did."

"Pray what was the cause of that scream?"

"The—the horses had taken fright, and were in full gallop."

"Oh! then you did not see the prisoner knock the postilion off his horse?"

Captain Winslow hesitated.

"Be careful to what you swear, Captain Winslow," said Mr. Herbert, impressively; "let me remind you that your words are taken down, and will have to be sworn to again, and signed in the form of a deposition. I ask you, did you see the prisoner attack the postillion?"

"No."

"I thought so. The chaise was overturned before Charles Rowe came up?"

"Ye—yes. The horses, taking fright left him behind; he came up running, and attacked me at once."

"Have you any witnesses to prove this?"

"No—no."

Captain Winslow uttered this negative hesitatingly.

"Not of the commencement of the struggle," suggested Mr. Knipe; "but subsequently you had two witnesses, I think, had you not?"

"Oh, yes, decidedly," cried Captain Winslow, eagerly, knowing he might make this admission, by the question being put by his advocate.

"Are they here?" asked the magistrate.

"They are," replied Mr. Knipe.

"Then they have no business to be while the examination is proceeding," said Mr. Herbert; "they are instructed in their story; let them be removed."

This was done, and then he continued his cross-examination, and in spite of the shrewd sharpness of Mr. Knipe, he succeeded in making the captain prevaricate and hesitate so much, remember so little, and so often contradict himself, that the magistrate, under the counsel of the clerk, confessed that his opinion in the value and truth of his testimony was greatly shaken. The two witnesses were examined, but they so entirely contradicted themselves on the important points, and made such irreconcileable statements, that Mr. Tickelpenny told them plumply he did not believe one word they had stated. Mr. Herbert, when Mr. Knipe confessed he had no further evidence to offer on behalf of the prosecutor, spoke for some little time in favour of the character of Charles Rowe, whom he had known as an inhabitant of Arundel from childhood, and during the time was unacquainted with a single act of dishonesty or impropriety on his part; he was doing well as a workman at his trade, and there was no need for the commission of the crime with which he was charged, and of which he was as convinced, as he stood there, he was innocent; and more, that he should, before the examination was ended, prove that he was so, and that Captain Winslow had deliberately sworn to that which was false. He then called Oliver Lawrance, who related all he knew of this matter. The magistrate pricked up his ears. The young lieutenant's story materially altered the position of the case.

"Where is the young lady?" asked the magistrate; "she will be a most important witness—nay, the fate of the prisoner depends upon her statement."

"I am willing to stake it upon that," said Mr. Herbert.

"And I," said Oliver Lawrance.

"And I," cried Charley Rowe; "she can and she will clear me, I know."

"The young lady is an interested witness," exclaimed Mr. Knipe, "and I object—"

"Not to her evidence being received, surely," exclaimed Mr. Herbert.

"Absurd!" the magistrate observed. "Object to her evidence? Ridiculous, Mr. Knipe! why it is the very thing we want."

It was the very thing Mr. Knipe did not want.

"I was going to observe," said he, "if I had not been interrupted in the most unprofessional manner I ever remember in my life, that the witness, being interested in my client's not being able to establish his point, I should request your worship only to admit it under strong suspicion. Also, that as the young lady is not here, I should object to an adjournment for the purpose of her production."

"Upon what ground?" asked Mr. Herbert.

"The offence with which my client is charged not being a bailable offence, he would be made to suffer the inconvenience of imprisonment until the further hearing of the case."

At this moment a murmur arose near the door, and Myra Aston, accompanied by Ellen Fairfax and her father, entered the apartment.

"Miss Aston is here," exclaimed Mr. Herbert, triumphantly. "We will put her in the witness-box, if you please."

Myra was duly installed in the box, and trembled excessively at her unusual position. There was scarce a person present who did not recognise her, and a buzz of friendly acknowledgment passed round the room. Mr. Herbert, in order to reassure her, addressed a few words to her in a friendly tone, and conducted her examination in such a manner that, before it had concluded, she had quite recovered her self-possession. Her statement perfectly exonerated Charley from the base charge. She related all the circumstances, as they had occurred to her, and her artless, simple manner carried with it a full conviction of its truthfulness. The magistrate, who was much struck with her appearance, made some enquiries, and was answered by the clerk in such terms of enthusiasm, for that young gentleman was struck by her appearance also, and was anxious to make himself estimable in her eyes, that Mr. Tickelpenny declared his entire belief in her testimony. He therefore discharged the prisoner from custody, and said he would leave that court without a stain upon his character. He expressed his regret that an individual wearing her Majesty's uniform, and professing to be one of the heroes of the Crimea, should have disgraced his most honourable profession and himself by a charge as base as it was proved to be false.

This speech elicited considerable applause from the spectators, which was speedily suppressed by the clerk. Mr. Herbert said that the case would not be permitted to rest there, as he should prefer an indictment for perjury against the captain; but he now had to enter upon the grave charge of abduction. And Captain Winslow, as a prisoner, was at once escorted to the dock which Charley Rowe had left; his appearance there gave the greatest satisfaction,—a murmur of applause again filled the magistrate's room, but the clerk, as before, suppressed it.

Once more Myra gave her testimony, and related all that had transpired, so far as she knew, during which she was frequently interrupted by Mr. Knipe, who put questions to her in a brusque tone, with the intention of rendering her nervous and embarrassed, but Mr. Herbert was on the alert, and, by his manner and words, rendered her efficient support. When she had concluded, Mr. Knipe commenced the cross-examination.

"Was Captain Winslow in the house when you retired to your room, Miss Aston?" he asked.

"I know not."

"Did you not expect him?"

"Most certainly not.

"Did you not address a note to him that day, stating you desired earnestly to see him?"

Myra returned an astonished and indignant negative—her manner carried conviction with it.

"You did not see Captain Winslow enter your chamber?"

"No."

"Nor when, as you state, he carried you off?"

"No."

"You were not conscious of *anything whatever* that transpired during your insensibility?" he asked, with peculiar emphasis.

"I remember nothing from the time I placed to my nose a handkerchief I found upon my table, which had been placed there by some one, but did not belong to me, until I awoke in a travelling chaise this morning, at dawn, and, to my horror, discovered myself in it, alone, with Captain Winslow."

"Really, your worship," said Mr. Knipe, addressing the magistrate, "I don't see how this case can be carried further. There is not a tittle of evidence to connect my client with a forcible abduction at all. I do not see upon what ground he can be a moment detained, for it comes to a mere question of credibility of testimony. For the young lady's sake I would forbear asking my client any questions, or I could prove that she was in that post-chaise with Captain Winslow by ——"

He paused for a moment, and looked at the captain.

"Her own consent?" asked Mr. Herbert, abruptly, and added, "I would caution Captain Winslow against further asserting that which he is unable to sustain."

Mr. Herbert then called upon the magistrate to grant a remand, maintaining that sufficient evidence had been given to shew that, by some scandalous complicity, an article had been conveyed to Myra's dressing-table, charged with chloroform, and placed where she was likely to take it up and inhale it; that she had been carried from thence, while insensible, by the captain or his agents, had been brought down there, certainly, by him, had been rescued from him by Rowe, therefore, there was enough evidence to connect him with a plot and abduction, and to justify a remand, in order that further evidence might be procured to bring it clearly home to him.

Mr. Knipe argued against the remand, and made the most infamous insinuations, for which Mr. Herbert attacked him fiercely, but he sheltered himself by saying—"He was so instructed." He boldly asserted that Myra was with Captain Winslow by her own consent, and if he were in London he should be in a position to prove it.

"Ergo, a remand is of as much importance to your client, in order to clear his character, as it is to mine to sustain the purity of hers, and punish the flagrant wrong inflicted upon her," cried Mr. Herbert, with emphasis.

The clerk, against Knipe all through the piece, strongly counselled the magistrate that the circumstances against the captain were so highly suspicious a remand ought to be granted, and Mr. Tickelpenny, who was very sick of the case and wanted some port, granted it, refusing the most earnest exhortations of Mr. Knipe to take bail. Captain Winslow was removed in custody, that day week being named for the fresh hearing. The two men who had taken the bribe to make Charley Rowe prisoner, were sentenced to three months' imprisonment for the assault, and being recognised as a brace of poachers, for whose apprehension a reward had been offered, they were informed that at the expiration of their present sentence they would be tried upon the other charge.

Myra returned to the residence of Mr. Fairfax, accompanied by her friend Ellen and her other friends. Arrangements were entered into with Mr. Herbert to carry on the case, and the opportunity was given for the arrival of Mr. Randolph, who, upon receiving the telegraphic message, had taken the first train down to Arundel, having left Mrs. Aston in a state of considerable excitement.

It seems that the absence of Myra had not been discovered until the following morning, when her maid, entering her chamber to help to dress her, had discovered her bed without its tenant, and that it had never been lain in. She communicated with Mrs. Aston, who was, of course, greatly alarmed, and roused the family. The former abduction led them all to entertain painful forebodings respecting her present absence, and when it was subsequently discovered that Perk was missing too, it was at once suggested that an elopement had taken place—but, with whom! Mrs. Aston scouted the idea connecting Myra with it as a consenting party, but thought that her refusal to permit her to communicate with Clifton Grey, might have induced her to withdraw herself from her mother's protection. She said she was a strange girl and a little self-willed, therefore this might be the case. Lizzie Hastings was at once visited and questioned, but she could communicate nothing but her terror and her fears. She, however, suggested her belief that Captain Winslow had something to do with it, and advised that his residence should be immediately visited. In the interim, however, the telegraphic message was received, and Mr. Randolph volunteered to go down to Arundel to see her. The message had merely stated that she was well—was safe at Mr. Fairfax's residence—and would be glad to see her mother; but Mrs. Aston, believing that this message but confirmed her suspicion, accepted Mr. Randolph's kind offer, and bade him inform her daughter that if the suspicions she entertained were correct, and she had been induced by them to quit her care, that she would withdraw her interdict against her writing to a certain individual in the Crimea, and when she reached home they would together discuss the matter, with a view to effect an arrangement which would prove satisfactory to her.

But Myra was unable to return, owing to the adjournment of her case against Captain Winslow; at least it was thought to be the best plan for her to remain in Arundel until after the case had been heard, and the captain committed for trial, for neither lawyer had any doubt about that result. Indeed, Mr. Randolph expressed his conviction that the rascal Perk had been an agent in the incident, and hoped to find him in custody on his return to London. He thought there would be no difficulty in obtaining from him, under the promise of pardoning his complicity, sufficient proof of the guilt of the captain to convict and remove him for a time from the chance of doing mischief. Mr. Randolph determined to leave no stone unturned to capture him, and produce him on the following hearing, or at least, sufficient evidence in respect to him to warrant a committal.

Before he returned to London, he had a private interview with Myra, and acquainted her with the message her mother had entrusted to him, without mentioning names; but he saw by the kindling eye and roseate blush with which her cheek was mantled, that it alluded to some attachment she had formed, to which her mother was indisposed. He, however, delivered the whole of the message he had received to her, and then said:

"It becomes my duty to inform you Miss Aston, that on leaving town this morning, a document was placed in my hands, informing me of the satisfactory completion of your legal business, which I have so long had in hand. It is my province, briefly to inform you, that a rapid mortality having taken place in your father's family, which would never acknowledge your mamma as the lawful wife of one of its younger sons, you became next of kin, and entitled to vast real and personal property. I asserted your claim in time to prevent occupation by the other branches of the family, and in spite of determined opposition, I have succeeded in proving you to be the legal claimant of the property, and heiress to not less than fifteen thousand per annum. There is a handsome sum accruing in arrears, and therefore, as having the power, and the title of moving in an elevated circle, I am anxious you should accept and adorn it. It is not because I have been the instrument in obtaining this handsome income for you, that I found any claim to offer my counsel to you, but, rather because I was an early friend of your estimable father. I have delivered to you a message which makes allusion to a person in the Crimea—"

"Mr. Randolph," interposed Myra, rising and speaking with earnestness, and yet with dignity, "you are about to allude to a circumstance the details of which you are wholly unacquainted with, and you would found your remarks—your advice, upon a surmise which could not fail to be erroneous. Pray spare me. I am most grateful for your services, quite irrespective of their success, and should listen with respectful attention to any counsel you might tender me, being convinced that it had its origin only in a desire for my welfare; but, in the present instance it could only be painful, and, pardon me, offensive, because it would be directed to an intangibility."

Mr. Randolph bowed and smiled.

"Upon my word," he said, "I believe you may be trusted to think for yourself. I take my farewell of you for the present, but I shall return in a few days, and I fully expect to be able to complete then the case of the scoundrel who so infamously abused my hospitality in respect to yourself. Until then, adieu. I leave you in safe hands now, and shall entertain no apprehension about you during our separation."

But Myra was not permitted to be free from danger, and though in these later times the events we record may be deemed improbable, they occurred nevertheless; aye, as have stranger circumstances than ever were the offsprings of fiction. Myra found herself happy enough with Ellen Fairfax—happy, perhaps, because Ellen never omitted an opportunity to speak of Clifton Grey, nor Charley Rowe either. It was a theme she was not by any amount of repetition tired of listening to, or they of descanting upon, and so it formed the chief topic of their conversation. We may as well admit, too, that having received the permission of her mother to write to the Crimea, she availed herself of it that very day, and wrote to Clifton. What a delightful task she found it! what an amazing long letter she wrote to him! how much she had to say! Often she paused, and her cheek burned, for she could find that her inclining was running away with what strict propriety would not have parted with—that is, she sat down determined to write in the spirit of a sister writing to a brother, to whom she was tenderly attached, but she found herself writing several times as if to one to whom she was tenderly attached, but who was *not* a brother. At length her letter was finished, but not until every spare inch was absorbed; she grudged the blank space claimed by the envelope, but contented herself with writing the superscription fully and clearly, and with sealing it firmly with the very prettiest seal she had got, and the very bluest wax she could purchase. She posted the letter herself, and paid the registration fee, because that gave an additional chance for its safe delivery. In two days from that time, Lieutenant Lawrance paid her a visit, bringing her a pressing invitation from her foster-sister, who in a letter entreated her to come and see her. The letter stated that Nelly's father was very ill, and confined to his bed; she was therefore unable to leave the house. She expressed her regret for her brother Saul's conduct, but she assured her that he dared not present himself in the locality. She was aware of his recent visit, but she said, being conscious that the coast-guard were in hot pursuit after him, he would be afraid to venture near home, especially as he knew that Lieutenant Lawrance, who was strictly enjoined to take him, if possible, was a constant visitor there. She wound up her epistle by again urging her, in remembrance of their former loving association, to come and exchange a few words with her, who was now so sorrowful and so lonely. Myra had loved Nelly Waters as a child, as dearly and fondly as if she had been truly her sister, and she was not proof against this appeal—she therefore promised to go. Ellen readily offered to accompany her; Charley Rowe, too, if he could spare the time; the Lieutenant said he should be there also, and if the weather was calm, he promised a sea excursion in one of the coast-guard galleys.

Myra assented, and on the day appointed they all went. Myra was received by Nelly with grateful delight, and by old Waters, who was in bed to whom she paid a visit, with a grim aspect on his ghastly face which might mean satisfaction, or something very different. He was fond of his son Saul, and he thought that his "misfortunes" were in a large degree owing to Myra, so that he felt that he had no forgiveness to ask for—rather that Myra had some forgiveness to ask; he, however, said nothing, but, as we have said, grinned with an expression to be variously construed. Nelly, however, understood better how wickedly her brother Saul had acted, and, while she attempted to extenuate nothing, attributed his conduct to the pangs of disappointed love rather than to innate brutishness or desire to harm her. Upon no point is a woman's sympathy so soon roused as upon that of disappointed love. She makes more ready and greater allowances for short-comings and criminal conduct arising out

of this cause than for any other, particularly where she is the occasion. Myra, therefore, in reply to Nelly, tried to console her by assuring her that she freely forgave Saul for all that had transpired, but she hoped he would never again induce her to retract the forgiveness by in any way again molesting her. Nelly appeared much more at ease by this acknowledgment, for she supposed that the hot pursuit after Saul would now cease, erroneously presuming that it was persevered in by Myra's instructions, and she hoped fallaciously that her brother, restored to society, would become an honest and good man. She acknowledged to Myra that Lieutenant Lawrance had offered her his hand, and that she had found him open-hearted, single-minded, generous, and brave. She had accepted it. There might be some love in the matter; she thought there was—a little. She certainly preferred him to any other man she had ever seen, and she seemed to feel that she would be more likely to be happy with him than any one else. Her father had said "Yes" to the match. The only painful thing was his being set to catch Saul; but she trusted, now, that difficulty would be got over, and that they should be able to get married without any unpleasant drawbacks.

Myra hoped they would, and told Nelly that it might be in her power to serve her, and begged of her to communicate with her when she could be of any help or aid.

The day was extremely beautiful, sunny, and cloudless; the sky was blue and clear, and the sea, no less blue, had not a ripple upon it. The proposition of Lieutenant Lawrance for an excursion upon it was agreed to be carried out. Before he went to the station to have a galley launched, he pointed out a sheltered spot where embarkation was easy, and requested Myra and Ellen to meet him and Rowe at that spot, and the boat should be brought round there. To this they assented, and they proceeded towards it, across a field, through a small plantation, and so down to the beach. At the water's edge lay a small boat ready for launching. As Myra and Ellen, observing it, made some remarks respecting it, the former heard a sudden exclamation in her ear, which horrified her. She felt herself seized and lifted up from the ground, and borne to the boat, in which, in spite of screams and struggles, she was almost thrown. The boat was launched, and shot far out into the sea. Another minute, she found herself alone upon the sea with Saul Waters.

With all his strength and skill he pulled from the shore, and under his practised hands the boat skimmed over the tranquil surface with remarkable speed, until a mile, at least, was gained from the beach. Even then he paused not, but while he spoke he pulled with his utmost strength. It was his hope to be able to cross the channel in that frail boat, for the sea was calm, and there was no sign that it would change, while his expectations of getting away undetected or checked rested upon his putting as great a distance between him and the land in as short a space of time as possible. Myra appealed to him to cease his persecution of her. She assured him that it was useless, and, at best, could but result in her death.

"I know't!" said the ruffian; "I mean't. If you still refuse to have me, if I dosnt hav'ee, none else shall, by God!"

In vain Myra told him of her recent interview with his sister, and how she had begged her to forgive him; that she had done so under the promise that she should be no more molested or persecuted by him.

"What right had she to make any promise?" cried Saul. "Nobody asked her—not I! And as to forgiveness, why I've suffered enough for'ee—and I've sworn you shall be mine, or I'll kill'ee, if I swing for it! When I know'd thou'd gone to Ar'ndel I guessed you'd come to see our Nell, so I laid watch for'ee. Ha! ha! you fell into 'trap—I ha' gotten thee, have I?"

Myra told him that death had no terrors for her, and that he should slay her rather than she would consent to be his.

"We shall see," he exclaimed laconically, and still pulled with his best strength, knowing that if he exhausted himself, he should have the long night to recover himself in.

He had no notion of the arrangement which had been made for Oliver Lawrance to bring a galley round to the spot where he seized Myra, or it is doubtful whether he would have adopted, at once, the step on which he had decided, for those galleys were manned by four men, whose long oars and strong arms made them skim like a gull over the sea, and if chase were given would render all his exertions to get away from them utterly hopeless.

As it often happens in cases of crime, his very cunningly devised plan for escaping unnoticed was precisely that which excited attention. The look-out at the station observed the boat suddenly shoot out from the beach, that the rower was exerting his utmost strength, while the female who sat in it had a crouching look, as if frightened, and an intimation to this effect was conveyed to Oliver Lawrance. Just as they were launching the galley he directed his powerful glass at the object, and, with a sigh, handed it to Charley Rowe, who exclaimed :

"Good God! that's Myra in there. Why, I be hanged if that' isn't Saul Waters—the scoundrel! Tumble in there, and give chase," he cried lustily to the men, and himself sprung into the stern-sheets, followed by Oliver Lawrance, who said no more to the men than the brief order :

"Give chase!" adding, "Give way, men, give way—pull together."

"Put out your strength, boys," cried Charley Rowe, excitedly, "there's a prize in that boat for you."

The men gave a cheer, and away they went.

"Lend me your pistols," said Charley to the lieutenant ; "let us see if they are ready for use." Oliver handed them to him without remark. He was full of thought : it seemed that fate had designed for him that painful task of making prisoner the brother of the girl he loved best in the world, and whom he was about to marry. It was natural that he regarded the enterprise with no satisfaction, though he would do much to save Myra, and had not the smallest tenderness towards Saul. He had as lief he were hanged as high as Haman as not, but for the grief it might occasion Nelly ; and nothing now would have pleased him better than to have gone in pursuit of them, had Saul been any one but the brother of his bride elect. Still the duty, however unpleasant, must be performed, and he determined to execute it. He did not observe that Charley Rowe did not return his pistols, but that young gentleman, having a shrewd guess how the land lay, had a fear that Saul might be dealt with too gingerly, and he remembered his promise to Clifton. He was determined to carry that out at every cost, and so he saw the pistols were in fit condition for use. He resolved to use them, too, if he did get a chance.

The two boats kept on their course, but the galley, when she had full way on her, went two feet to one of the other. Strange that Saul looked not in the direction of the coast guard station. He had kept his eye upon Ellen, who had run about the shore, shrieking, but she had disappeared, and he expected every moment to see a dozen people on the beach where he had obtained his prize, but he was startled from gazing in that quarter by an ejaculation from Myra's lips.

"Thank heaven!" she exclaimed with fervour, "there is aid at hand." He cast his eyes round, and, perceiving the galley, uttered a fearful oath, and redoubled, if possible, his exertions ; but in vain, the galley gained on him every instant ; but he abandoned not his exertions until he saw that they were hopeless. What was to be done now passed rapidly through his mind. Escape was hopeless. He had a brace of pistols in his belt. Murder was in his thoughts : one bullet for Lawrance, another for Myra, and a grave in the deep sea for himself. He bent his gloomy, frowning eyes on Myra, and drew his pistols.

"Say your prayers," he said through his clenched teeth ; "for before you shall get away from me again to be another's, I'll shoot you."

"Have mercy!" she exclaimed, clasping her hands appealingly to him.

"You had none for me," he answered, "and I'll have none for thee. Say your prayers, girl, and ask me not to spare you, for I will not, so help me God."

She compressed her hands tightly in agony, and said no more. Saul, with knitted brows and clenched teeth, spoke not either ; he awaited the approach of

THE ATTACK ON THE GREAT REDAN.

Lawrance, with his finger upon the trigger of his pistol. He knew well that his sister loved the young coast-guard officer with all the genuine intensity of a first and passionate love; he was conscious that his death, especially by a brother's hand, would break her heart, but he cared not for that; he believed it to be the intention of Lawrance to capture him, if he could, and, therefore, he resolved to forestal him by what he deemed the consummation of a fierce but just retaliation and revenge.

He remained motionless until the galley was close up, then he suddenly sprung up to execute his terrible purpose; he levelled his pistol to take a deliberate and deadly aim; but ere he could discharge it a hasty shot from the galley was fired, the bullet passed through his heart; he leaped up with a shriek, and fell back into the sea, in which he found that deep, deep grave he had intended for himself, though not by such means.

As his body slowly rose to the surface, crimsoned with his blood, his eyes fixed on Myra's; with horrified gaze, she observed his reappearance, and his death glare was terrific. She pressed her hands over her own; when she again removed them, the waters had surged over the lifeless body, and all that was mortal of the unhappy wretch sunk to the depths of the insatiable sea.

Charley Rowe leaped into the boat in which she was seated, and his cheering voice bade her fear no more, for henceforward he would remain near her, whether she would or no, to protect her until the return of Clifton Grey; or, if he met with a soldier's death in the Crimea, so long as he, Charles Rowe, lived; for, in that case, with his death only did he consider that he should be released from the promise he had given to Clifton at parting. Myra replied only to his promise of protection by becoming senseless. The boats were now directed to the shore. Myra was tenderly lifted into the galley, and borne to land to the nearest point to the "Bonny Bark," where Oliver Lawrance knew she would have the best attention paid to her, and where it would be his painful duty to break to Nelly Waters her brother's fearful death.

The passage over the sea was performed in silence. The keel grated on the pebbly beach, as Myra, heaving a sigh, recovered from her swoon, and, being put on shore, was led by Charley Rowe and Oliver Lawrance to "the Bonny Bark," which they gained, to find Ellen Fairfax fast recovering from a fit of screaming hysterics, into which she was nearly relapsing at the sight of Myra restored unharmed. While she was expressing her joy, in tones feeble from exhaustion, Oliver drew Nelly aside, and said to her:

"My own dear Nelly, I have sad news for you, but I know that you have a strong sense of right to direct you, and more than ordinary nerve to bear such tidings as I bring. I may rely upon you lis-

tening with calmness, and bearing with resignation the trial it has pleased God to impose upon you; but if at this moment you do not feel equal to receive my communication, I will reserve what I have to say to another time.

"It is about Saul," she said, sadly; "tell me the worst; I am prepared to hear it."

"He is dead," he replied.

She gasped for breath.

"I did not expect that," she murmured, hoarsely. Clutching him by the arm, she fixed her staring eyes upon his, and asked, "Did he fall by your hand—yours, Oliver?"

"As God is my judge, no, Nelly," he answered, solemnly.

She wrung his hands, and, bursting into tears, fell on his breast, saying:

"This will be a sad blow for my poor father."

A hollow groan and crash was heard above the stairs at the foot of which they stood. They both ran up, and, to their horror, beheld old Waters stretched on the floor—dead.

He had overheard their discourse; and the intelligence of the desperate fate of a son who, notwithstanding his faults, he loved tenderly, coming thus abruptly, was more than his weakened frame could bear. The shock killed him.

CHAPTER XXVIII.

"He that outlives this day, and comes safe home,
Will stand a-tip-toe when this day is named."
                                        SHAKSPERE.

"The bursting shell, the gateway wrenched asunder,
    The rattling musketry, the clashing blade;
And ever and anon, in tones of thunder,
    The diapason of the cannonade."
                                        LONGFELLOW.

"Glory is like a circle in the water;
Which never ceaseth to enlarge itself."
                                        SHAKSPERE.

            "The din of war 'gan pierce
His ready sense, when strait his doubled spirit
Requickened what in flesh was fatigate,
And to the battle came he; where he did
Run reeking on the lives of men as if
'Twere a perpetual spoil; and till we call'd
Both field and city ours, he never stood
To ease his breast with panting."
                                        IBID.

THE ATTACK ON THE QUARRIES. A LETTER FROM
HOME. ATTACK ON THE GREAT REDAN.

IT is impossible to follow in detail all the movements of Clifton Grey for the few succeeding months, and therefore we may say that he was welcomed back by his superior officers with pleasure, by his comrades with delight.

As heretofore, he was unsparing of himself in the performance of his duties, and his attention to the wants and comforts of his men drew down upon him blessings from them, and praises from his colonel. Ever ready to volunteer for sortie, trench, or picket duty, he was one of the first selected in any undertaking of importance. He could handle the men as he pleased; they would obey a gesture of his more readily than a loudly uttered order from any other officer, albeit, where he was, there was no absence of discipline. The sick, the faint, the wan, and the wasted, he nursed as tenderly as if he were a woman, and they were children. In the assault, the storm, the repulse, his actions were those of a hero; on all sides he was praised; he won the goodwill of every one with whom he came in contact, making no direct attempt to obtain it, and he deserved all the commendations he received, for his deeds were such as to entitle him to them.

Since his escape from Simpheropol he had been in many desperate skirmishes and night attacks, but had yet escaped unwounded, although Sergeant Haverel and Mickey were both again wounded, one twice, and the other thrice after Inkermann, and they swore that he bore a charmed life—that Providence was making a pet of him, and preserving him in order that he might be set down quite whole and perfect before the very person who would prefer to receive him in that condition; not that an arm or an eye less would turn her heart from him. Still she was mortal, and she had no more desire than any other young lady of her age would have, that one she so much esteemed, and whom she looked upon as her own private property, should be shorn of his fair proportions.

The registered letter he received safely. When it came, he looked at the superscription, and wondered what fair hand had traced his name in such beautifully shaped characters. At first he thought it was from Sylva, but the writing was not hers; then he thought of Preciosa, but yet doubted she was the writer. It was not Lizzie Hastings, certainly. He opened it, and the first words greeting his eye was the signature Myra Aston! He kissed the letter with an emotion it is impossible to describe, and put it away safely in the breast of his coat, nearest his heart, that he might read it alone, unobserved by any other eye save that of Heaven's. Alone! it was easy to decide upon that, not so easy to accomplish it, for soldiers were at his shoulders, before him, around him, whenever he was awake and moving, so he obtained leave from his colonel, on being relieved from the trenches that night, to occupy a rifle pit, on pretence of having some ball practice. His colonel endeavoured to dissuade him, but in vain, and so he reluctantly assented to his request.

Clifton had selected his pit; it was one which had been unoccupied for some time, because it was

covered by one or two in possession of the Russians. He supplied himself with a pick and spade, and some stout pieces of wood, and when in the darkness, occasionally lighted up by the blazing fire of shot and shell from the English and French attacks, or from the Russian lines, he stole to his coveted spot. As he neared it stealthily, to his surprise he heard sounds proceeding from it; he crept up and saw a stout Cossack within, busily occupied in rendering it comfortable for his own occupation. Clifton laid down his rifle and implements, and threw himself suddenly upon him. A fierce struggle ensued, but the Russian contrived to tear himself from Clifton's grasp, and bounded away from the pit like a deer towards his own lines; but, ere he had reached a hundred paces, he fell pierced by a dozen bullets. His form had been seen against the sky, and his feet heard as he ran, by unerring marksmen, and they brought him down as they would a fleeing wolf.

Clifton, recovering his rifle and implements, took possession of his pit, which he soon turned, throwing up earth embankments, and making a small embrasure, yet having a good sweep, which enabled him to command a large portion of the Russian earthworks. Dawn was breaking when his task was completed; it certainly could not be called daylight when he found his work had been already detected, and was the target for the bullets of all the Russians who could get a shot at it. He was well supplied with cartridges, and he replied to the shots directed at him, through his long, narrow slit of a loop-hole, with fatal accuracy. After he had for upwards of two hours fired at every foe who shewed even the tip of his feather, he was left in comparative repose, and now he took out his letter.

He read with avidity every word of it. In vain, the booming sound of guns from Sebastopol, from the Inkermann heights, and from the English parallels, crash and thunder in his ears; in vain, so far as distracting his attention, did small puffs of white smoke rise up, and bullets bury themselves in the earthwork with which he had surrounded his rifle pit. He had eyes, ears, observation, for nothing but the words before him, every one of which might be said to be photographed upon his heart; the tenderness of some passages, the general sweetness of all, rendered him, when he had brought himself to the close, one of the most happy, delighted young heroes in the world. Somehow, he could see that she loved him—the style, the tone of the letter said so; yet there was not one word there which her mother in reading would have condemned—yet, perhaps, she might have hesitated to have accorded her free consent to the closing words, "Yours, ever affectionately, Myra Aston."

"'Yours, ever affectionately,'!" he repeated, as he kissed the words again and again. "Aye, Myra, ever, for ever, ever yours affectionately, while life beats within this frame. At last the ice is broken, and fate smiles upon me. My destiny is united with hers, that I feel; I love her truly and devotedly, that I know; I will win her and wear her, God willing, that I swear. Oh, that I may be able to perform some deed in her honor, as did the knights of old. Well, I can try, though the warfare is of a different character to that employed in the fourteenth century. Still, an act of gallantry tells the same, and—what's this?"

From the ground he picked up a narrow-folded piece of silver paper; it had evidently fallen out of the letter; it contained a lock of hair. He knew it; it was Myra's hair. Perhaps Mrs. Aston might not have approved of *that* being inserted in the letter; nevertheless, there it was. The paper ran a risk of being spoiled; it was kissed so much, and then that went close to his heart in the safest place he could find for it.

"Your cavaliers *sans peur et sans reproche* wear the colours of their ladies on their breasts or shoulders; I have mine near my throbbing heart, and I will do honour to it or perish," he exclaimed, placing it carefully, and then taking up his rifle, and peering cautiously through his small embrasure. He did this in time. He had not noticed that rather a heavy shower of bullets had whistled over, about, and into his pit, a short time previously; for "Yours, ever affectionately," was floating about in his eyes; but now he observed, to his startled surprise, three Russian sharpshooters making a dead rush at his pit. Several shots were fired at them, but missed. Crack! went his rifle, and one fell; he snatched up the rifle which the Russian whom he had found there had left; fortunately it was loaded; there was no time for thought, less for aim. Bang! he discharged it, and the second fell from its aim. The third Cossack was now at the pit, but Clifton met him with the muzzle of his rifle, and forced him back. He then sprung up on to the outer edge, clubbed his musket, and swinging it round his head like lightning, it descended with a terrific crash, and the Russian fell brained. He stood up, waved his hand, and gave a lusty cheer. A hail of bullets poured, and one hit him, passing through the fleshy part of his left arm. He waved his rifle, gave another cheer, and dived into his pit again, the feat eliciting cheers right and left from friend and foe.

It was night, dark and stormy, before he quitted his lair, and then it was only when one of the gallant Rifles, who had been eagerly watching his opportunity, had made for the hazardous post, and filled it, that Clifton quitted it with credit to his country and honour to himself.

Thus passed the successive days, with our hero always occupied by military duties, rarely missing posts of danger, because they were posts of honour. Time wore on; the loud wailing cry of famine, sick-

ness, devastation, and death, arising from blind and blundering incapacity, had been responded to by an indignant and sympathising nation; the evils complained of had been partially remedied by the benevolent offerings of the public, and increased activity in the various Departments which had been before inactive and inoperative. Ministers were put on their trial, and sought to redeem their short-comings. Those ministering angels, the Sisters of Mercy, and the nurses banded under the angelic Miss Nightingale, had brought consolation, comfort, and relief to the fevered, dying soldiers. Clothing, huts, tents, were sent in profusion, and military stores, fabulous in quantity, were supplied. The shorn battalions were restored to their proper number, and once more the British army mustered in pride and strength, and health, yet greater in number than when it had landed in the Crimea.

Clifton had passed through every phase with credit —through many with distinction—through all with honour. Several times his name had been brought before the General Commanding-in-chief, Lord Raglan, as the hero of some dashing exploit, and the heart of that gallant soldier warmed as he heard the narration; he privately sent to the war-office a hope that the merits of so brave and valuable member of the subordinate in command would not pass unrewarded.

Clifton, during this after period of which we speak, had written at length to Myra; he had not forgotten that though he might love, and the maiden to whom he addressed his letter might love too, no acknowledgment on either side had taken place, nor a sentence or intimation actually expressive of it had passed between them. He remembered upon what terms he had asked Myra to write to him. He had not forgotten in what character he had assured her he should communicate his progress to her, and in the composition of his letter he did not once lose sight of this throughout—it was respectful, if tenderly so. Still he lost not sight of their respective positions, nor trenched upon one which, though he hoped for and thought would be, had not yet been granted to him. There was an air of manly sincerity in his observations and expressions of good-will towards her and her mother, nothing adulatory or fulsome; his history of himself was modest, but the mere mention of the different struggles in which he had been engaged, itself told a tale flattering to his bravery. When he had completed his epistle, he, too, registered it, and directed it to the old place, Arundel, as she had desired, but to the residence of Mr. Fairfax. It need hardly be added he sent kind remembrances to the pretty Ellen and to Charley Rowe, both of whom were in ecstacies on receiving them, and at hearing how free he had passed through fire and bloodshed— how well he had advanced—how nobly he deserved the promotion he had received.

Clifton received, too, a packet from Sylva, in which

the history, intercepted by Captain Winslow, was repeated. Its contents told of a lost child, heir to great wealth, and established a chain of evidence respecting him to prove his title and claim to the property up to his third year. From that time he had been missing, and attempts to find him had hitherto failed; but Sylva reiterated her belief that from the extraordinary resemblance he bore to the father of the missing child, he must be him whom they sought, and brother to her, Sylva, and Preciosa, the link wanting to prove their relationship having been discovered. In Clifton's letter to Myra, he gave her the heads of Sylva's communication, but confessed he was at a loss how to supply the connecting link, for his earliest memory was confined to the nursery of Mr. Jayne, and he knew nothing whatever of his origin but what Mr. Jayne had told him. The accidental mention of this matter had an important result, but we must not anticipate. He replied to Sylva, thanking her for the warm interest she had displayed, urged by mere suppositions, and informed her with regret that he could supply her with less information concerning himself than Mr. Jayne, with whom she was residing; but he saw that there was still a missing link, which he might be able to supply, that he had written a letter to Captain Eimanoff, a Russian officer resident at Moscow, to obtain it for him, and as soon as he received it he would forward it to her, but some time must elapse, as he was obliged to adopt round-about means to get his letter to its destination.

June commenced; the siege was dragging its slow length along, but an enormous gathering of guns into position foreshadowed another opening of the ball, as the commencement of the successive bombardments were called; and on the 6th of June, 157 guns and mortars on the English side, and 300 on the French, opened upon Sebastopol, or rather, its outworks, filling the neighbourhood, and miles round, with its deafening clamour. The Redan, the Malakhoff, the Garden Battery, all were subjected to a terrific fire throughout the day, hotter, indeed, than the Russians could bear, for they replied to it only ineffectually, the iron hail ploughing up the earth, and tumbling into crashing ruins the suburbs and various points of the objects attacked. Men were told off, and at last it was expected that a "go in" at Sebastopol was to be allowed, but the night passed away, and no such order was issued; the men were eager, anxious, and disappointed, comforting themselves alone under the idea that the Commanders-in-Chief knew best. The firing was kept up, however, and on the following day Clifton observed, with anxiety, the progress of the bombardment. The perpetual hiss and crack of shells, the booming of heavy guns, the deafening roar of heaven-knows-how-many pounders only served to animate and excite him. He now had hope of reward—he thought of Myra—he longed for

some opportunity of performing a daring act for her sake, that she might be proud of him, and he saw that it was coming. All day a stream of men and officers crowding into the trenches announced that some important undertaking was in progress, and at length it transpired that the French were to take the Mamelon, and ours the quarries. Clifton pressed forward, and volunteered, as his own regiment was not ordered out, and he received permission, to his joy, to join. His tall figure soon made him conspicuous, as did his Guard's uniform; and when the rocket soared into the air as a signal for the men to dart into the quarries, Clifton Grey, with spirit-stirring shout, gripped his rifle, and rushed out like a deer, out-pacing his comrades, and leading them ten yards in advance.

"Who is that?" cried Lord Raglan to one of his staff near him, as he pointed to our hero. The officer looked through his glass.

"Sergeant Grey, of the Guards, my lord," shouted the officer, excitedly.

"One Clifton Grey," exclaimed his lordship.

"The same, my lord," returned the officer.

"Brave fellow! he will be killed," exclaimed his lordship, watching the result of what appeared little less than an act of madness; but he was not killed, and, entering the quarries, bayonetted the first foe, and made good his position. A wild yell behind him told him that Micky Dunigan had also volunteered, and was after him at a pace almost equal to his own. He came in with a dash, and firing his deadly rifle at close quarters, supported Clifton. The noble and brave men whose duty it was to take the quarries, animated by the example of the two guardsmen, raced after them at the top of their speed, and came into the quarries with a cheer and at a bound. And now ensued a sharp bayonet fight, accompanied by flashing shots in all directions, fired with rapidity, and continued with desperate determination; flame darted here and there, leaping and springing, carrying death in its path, and lighting up the darkness like running lightning in a heat haze. A tremendous effort to retain the quarries on the part of the Russians was of no avail against the resistless bravery of the British, and they were swept out of their stronghold at the point of the bayonet. Reinforced, they poured back again in masses to meet a withering fire from the British, and Clifton Grey's voice might have been heard far above the din, animating the men, and leading them on to drive back the foe. Corporal Mickey, with lusty voice, ably seconded him, and the brave 88th, and gallant 62nd, answered with ringing cheers the exhortations to press forward and make the place their own. Throughout the night, these tremendous onslaughts were made by the Russians; six desperate efforts to retake the won position failed. One most murderous sortie was made at about three in the morning. A blaze of shot and shell poured in from the Strand Battery, and lighted up this ravine of death, but did not succeed in driving out the gallant men who had taken it. Now was the opportunity for taking the Redan. Clifton urged, entreated, implored the officer in command to lead them into the Redan; he had been up close to it, and had seen that it was scarcely defended.

"The men, flushed by victory, have heart for it now," he cried, with excitement: "let us make the attempt; my life against it we win it gloriously."

"We have no reserve—no orders to go beyond the quarries," answered the officer. "My orders are to take, if possible, this ravine, and maintain it, and I'll not yield it now I have got it. I would be glad to do as you wish; I have no doubt of its success; but I dare not comply; the risk with this handful of men would be tremendous; and if it failed, what excuse should I have for exceeding my orders?"

"The opportunity of winning an important position," returned Grey. "He is your true general who seizes his opportunity when it offers, and depends not alone on more systematic arrangements."

The captain shook his head, and turned on his heel, and Clifton, blackened and grimed with powder, turned away with a sigh of disappointment.

"Stand to your arms, boys!" he cried, "here come the Russians again in force;" and they did come, but it was their last assault. It was in this rush that lance Corporal Quin distinguished himself so greatly. That night the Russians were driven back right into the Redan, and when morning dawned, the British held unmolested possession of the quarries. That night the French gallantly assaulted the Mamelon, and, after a bloody fight, took possession of it.

The English lost, in killed and wounded, one third of their force in action. The French loss was yet greater; and as Clifton returned to his quarters, and proceeded along the road which led down to the attack on the right, he met the pretty Fanchette, who had, in spite of the shot which came angrily from the Malakhoff about the spot where she had crossed, come hither to find her Henri, who was either in the Mamelon, or among the wounded. Fanchette's little barrel was soon in requisition by the wounded, who came thronging by in the ambulances; and, while serving out the liquor, she made enquiries of some Zouaves for Henri. He was safe, she was told, and in the Mamelon; he had greatly signalised himself, and would be mentioned in a despatch, and thus brought to the notice of the Emperor.

"Vive l'Empereur!" she shouted. She kissed Clifton on both cheeks, and, waving her hand to him, said they should meet again. He, accompanied by Mickey Dunigan, went on to his quarters.

Nearly a fortnight passed away when, once more, the siege, which had, after the capture of the quarries and Mamelon, languished, was renewed with vigour. On the 17th a tremendous fire was kept up inces-

santly, and on the 18th the several regiments were told off for the attack on the Redan. The French were to make a simultaneous assault on the Malakhoff; and once more Clifton and Mickey Dunigan obtained permission to volunteer; and this time Sergeant Haverel joined them. He had no notion of their having all the fighting to themselves. They volunteered, at Mickey's earnest wish, with the 18th Royal Irish; General Eyre addressed them, when ready to push to their destination, the Cemetery.

"I hope, boys," said he, "that you will this morning do something which will make every cabin in old Ireland ring again."

A loud cheer followed this speech.

"Sure, general darling," cried Mickey, "I know a cabin whose roof I'll lift off wid the glory I'll win this morning."

"And return home a captain," exclaimed the brigadier, smiling.

"Long life to your honour, I'd go back to Bridget a giniral, av the queen, God bless her! would make me one," he replied.

A loud laugh followed this speech, and then the order was given for the skirmishers to advance, and a dash make at the Cemetery. With a wild stirring whoop the men darted at their prey, and their ardour proved resistless; the Russians in defence fled, save a few who were made prisoners. The gallant 18th absolutely got into Sebastopol. Clifton Grey, with a mere handful of men, stormed the Wasp battery, and carried it. And here he maintained himself for a short time; but though he shouted for support, none came. The Russians, seeing him unassisted, came out in hundreds, and he was reluctantly compelled to relinquish his prize, but he made for some houses in the suburb of Sebastopol; and there he, Mickey, Haverel, and about a dozen of the bold 18th, got into a house, and from the windows fired at the Russian embrasures, drawing down upon themselves shot and shell, and grape, but without making them retire. They held their place until nine o'clock at night, when hungry, worn out with exertion, black as soot with the smoke of the powder, they made their way back to their lines, sad enough, for they knew the attack on the Redan and on the Malakhoff had failed. The English troops seem to have been moving without concert, or without a definite object—they attempted to accomplish too many things, and gained nothing but honour for the determined bravery with which they fought. The French attack also failed, and once more there was a lull in the siege—a kind of solemn gloomy silence—a mourning for the loss of many a brave officer, many a gallant soldier, sacrificed to an unaccountable mismanagement which will never be explained.

In ten days after this failure, the Field-Marshal succumbed—Lord Raglan was dead. He was much grieved and perturbed at the unhappy result of the

18th, and was thrown into a nervous, morbid gloominess, which prevented his being able to resist the attack of diarrhœa, which seized and carried him off in a few hours. A grand procession attended the remains to the ship that was to bear them to England, and after that melancholy duty was performed the siege went on under Lieutenant-General Simpson, but with little more satisfactory progress—nay, perhaps a little less. Sorties and struggles took place for the next six weeks; when Prince Gortschakoff, now in command of the Russian armies in the Crimea, conceived the idea of attacking the allies on the Tchernaya heights, and relieving the Malakhoff and Redan by driving them back from these positions. Upwards of 50,000 Russians were assembled with this object, and they crossed the river at several points, but they were met by the Sardinians, French, and English, with firm steadiness, and a devastating fire—the attack failed in its purpose, and the Russians retreated in disorder, with a loss of six thousand killed and wounded. This event took place on the 16th of August, 1855, and but little happened after it until the 5th of September following, when for the last time the bombardment opened under General Simpson and Marshal Pelissier, the Sardinians and Turks taking no part in the engagement. At daylight on Wednesday, the 5th, the signal rocket sprung hissing into the air, and, instantaneously, the whole of the lines occupied by the English and French, facing the Russian works, belched forth one terrific flame of shell and shot, and continued a *feu d'enfer* without intermission for three days, at the expiration of which it had been previously decided at a council of artillery and engineer officers, held before the Commanders-in-Chief of the Allied armies, to give the assault. Accordingly the morning of the eighth was determined on; and, on the part of the English, General Simpson decided on entrusting the arduous and glorious task to the Second and Light Division, under Sir William Codrington, since Commander-in-Chief, and Lieutenant-General Markham, the first named holding the command. The operations were to be the grand attack on the Malakhoff Tower by the French, and, simultaneously, an assault on the Central Bastion and Quarantine Forts. The English were to storm the Great Redan. Clifton Grey was on the previous night in the trenches, and at his earnest exhortation he was permitted, when his company was relieved, to remain behind, and volunteer into the storming party. When, in the morning, at the appointed hour, as the roar of musketry and cannon, the iron hail destroying everything in its path, told that the French were already pouring up under the gallant Bosquet to carry the Malakhoff, the signal was given for the English assaulting column of 1000 men, composed equally of the two divisions, to advance; as it marched out of the fifth

parallel Clifton joined it, and was received with a loud cheer, accompanied by cries of "Here comes the fighting Guardsman!" and he, with gratification, took his place with the sergeant of the nearest company. Fifty yards further out sprung Micky Dunigan, who also volunteered, along with a bold fellow, one Sam Goodram, of No. 6 company of Coldstreams. Both had secreted themselves in the trenches, and were absent without leave. Sergeant Haverel, eating his knuckles with rage, had been ordered out on outpost duty, and could not get a chance of going to glory.

The distance between the trenches and the salient angle of the Redan was unfortunately great, and, although the troops sprung forward with rapidity, the hail of shot, shell, and grape, poured upon them, committed fearful havoc, many perishing before they had being able to strike a blow, but the brave fellows advancing, never faltered. They were up at the crest of the ditch in a remarkably short space of time. A ladder-party of 350 were preceded by a covering party of 200, and as soon as they reached the walls the ladders were planted. The first to spring up, before even it was firmly planted, was Clifton Grey. Gripping his rifle, with its bayonet fixed, close to the lock, he sprung up the rounds, and was over the wall into the salient angle in an instant. In accomplishing this feat, he received a graze in the side from a bayonet, and a bullet through the fleshy part of the arm, close to the yet unhealed wound; but heeding them not, he fought with desperation, clearing a space for those who came leaping after him.

"On boys!" he shouted, "the eyes of England are on us! Let us redeem our last failure—give 'em the cold steel, boys."

"Three for you, Grey darling," roared Micky, "an the lasses in ould Ireland are waiting to dance a jig at the bating we'll give the Rooshians this blessed day."

The soldiers, pouring over the walls, fought hand to hand desperately with thrice their own numbers, and soon cleared the salient angle of their foe, but beyond, there was another work which commanded this angle, from which a perfect hurricane of shot from bristling cannon and Russian riflemen poured upon them, slaying heaps of gallant fellows, who were now in desperate need of ladders and supports, but they came not. The officers within the Redan, in exciting anxiety, looked for them, asked for them, but they were not at hand. The men were falling fast—they were like rats in a trap—and Clifton Grey, who saw the imperious necessity of the immediate arrival of the supports, volunteered to run back to the parallels and hasten them,

"If I am shot on my way, Colonel Wyndham," he said, "you will do me the justice in your report to say why I did not fall here."

Colonel Wyndham wrung his hand, and he bounded

over the wall into the ditch, and entered the shower of shot, but he reached the parallels in safety, and implored the generals in command of the storming party to despatch instanter the reserves. He was coolly informed the wishes of Colonel Wyndham should not pass over unnoticed. Hurt, and sick at heart, he returned to the scene of blood and slaughter—again in safety—and reported the message he had been entrusted with.

"I must have supports," cried Colonel Wyndham, passionately, "all will be lost without them ; I will go back myself." Then, turning to the next in command, he said to him, "If I fall, you will state why I left my post." And away he went, hoping, vainly, that he should return with a body of men sufficient to execute the proud wish of his heart.

In the meanwhile, the Russians, finding that the same blind mismanagement which had marred so many glorious opportunities previously, was in operation here ; that, as on the 18th of June, a mass of the British soldiers were devoted to a hopeless sacrifice, without the assistance which was necessary to enable them either to win a victory or retire with the least possible damage, they poured a large force of Russian infantry into the salient angle, and a bloody contest with the bayonet ensued. Here Clifton Grey exerted himself in such a distinguished manner as to excite the spirits of his fellow soldiers, and animate them to deeds of desperation. He was lustily cheered in reply to his shouts to them to maintain their character of English "Die-hards," and frequently exclamations of approbation burst from the lips of officers as he rallied the men, when, overwhelmed with numbers, they were compelled to give back, and with a rush led them up, so as to drive the Russians again into their second work. For one whole hour was this most unequal contest maintained ; fierce and sanguinary, conferring immortal honor on those engaged in it, but yet a murderous sacrifice. No supports were sent ; the men, exposed to a withering fire, which thinned them frightfully, fought on against hope, and budged not an inch. At length an enormous mass of Russian infantry were forced into the salient angle, and their mere numbers enabled them to oust the British troops, forcing them to retire over the wall into the ditch. Here the gallant Ensign Massey exhibited his noble bravery, fighting like a hero until shot down, being hit in both thighs. Clifton was one of the last to leave the angle. Sore at heart, mad with despair at the failure, he stood his ground like a lion at bay, and refused to move. He clubbed his musket and dealt blows right and left. Bayonets were thrust at him, shots fired, but he moved not. Now he hurled a fellow to the ground with the butt-end of his rifle, and recovering it, ploughed others with his bayonet in a frenzy of excitement. In vain Mickey Dunigan, and even fighting Sam Goodram, who loved this dangerous occupation be ter than any other,

halloed to him to retire ; he moved no foot of ground until Goodram came behind him, whipped him up in his arms, and flung him over the parapet, himself and Mickey following. Partially stunned by his fall, he uprose, and at the same moment a party of brave and excited Russians leaped into the ditch after them ; here Ensign Massey would have been ruthlessly bayonetted, had not our hero, who had filled his pockets, breasts, and cap, with cartridge, in addition to his ordinary service of fifty rounds, covered him. He loaded and fired as fast as he could, using his bayonet when closer quarters were occasioned by the rushes of the Muscovites.

The ditch was at last cleared of foes, and only heaps of wounded, or men who sought opportunities to dash across the open, to get into the trenches, were left within it. Clifton, however, would not do the latter, but, getting into the broken glacis outside the ditch, he there constructed for himself a rifle pit, and he kept up his fire upon the walls of the Redan, in spite of the hail of bullets directed at him. He could see poor Mickey, once more badly wounded, lying in the ditch ; and he saw a Russian rifleman, who probably was the man who hit him, trying to cover him with his rifle, to give him the finishing touch. Clifton marked him, brought his rifle to bear upon him, and, before the man could execute his cold-blooded murder, he fired at him, and despatched him into eternity. Loading again, he looked sharply out for any other who designed deeds so ruthless, or who attempted to shoot the soldiers passing from the ditch over the open space on their return to the trenches.

He saw the tri-colour triumphantly waving from the Malakhoff, and he gnashed his teeth at the sight ; for the British flag was not to be seen over the Redan, though beneath it, wounded and slain, lay some of her best and bravest sons. This repulse, he was sure, would never be allowed to pass without a struggle to redeem the disgrace ; and he calculated that another storming party would that night be formed ; he resolved to make one in it, for he felt sure the second—or, rather, the third assault—must be crowned with success. Fortunately, he had a supply of food with him, which he now brought out, and ate with a hearty appetite ; and he took a draught of water from his canteen, which tasted like nectar to him, though a fastidious lady would have choked at the flavor. He sought for some repose, but the bullets fired at his pit kept up such a spitting and spattering, that he found sleep impossible.

Night came on, but he clung to his post ; for he resolved to try and get into the Redan, to see what vigilance was being exercised by the Russians in its care, and to report progress to those who purposed having another dash at it. He waited until he thought that the men might be retiring to rest, after their fatigues, and the guard fewer and less observant

THE PRIZE ACHIEVED.—THE COMMANDER-IN-CHIEF PRESENTING CLIFTON GREY WITH A COMMISSION

No. 35.

than usual, and then he stole cautiously out, and moved into the ditch. Making direct for where he saw Mickey Dunigan laying, he came up to him, and whispered his name to him. He put his canteen to his parched mouth, and the poor fellow sucked in the water as if it were the very breath of life.

"Ah, thin, God's blessings on you for that, sergeant dear!" he murmured, "I'll do now. Faith, I'd been kilt widout it, tho'."

"Are you much hurt, Mickey?" asked Grey.

"I've a hit or two in the legs," was the reply, "but nothing bad—sure I'll do well enough when the dochter sees me." Cheerful, patient, and resigned, he submitted quietly to his condition, where others would have wailed and mourned and quarrelled with their fate.

Promising to return to him, Clifton clambered stealthily up the wall, and then slid over into the salient angle. To his astonishment, not a Russian was there. He passed in, and clambering again over the second works, got into the Great Redan. Not a soldier was visible; he went further, and peered cautiously round; the place was in darkness and in silence; he listened intensely, but without hearing a foot-fall; he examined it now more boldly, and ascertained that it was deserted. He now took an opportunity of gazing towards the city, and he could see dark masses moving with rapidity along the harbour; he saw the bridge of boats over the waters, thick and black with moving troops.

"Great Heaven!" he ejaculated, "the Russians are abandoning Sebastopol."

The instant the idea crossed him, he retraced his steps—sprung over the works into the salient angle—over the wall into the ditch, quicker than over the Russians had forced him to move; and approaching Mickey he knelt down by his side, and said, hurriedly:—

"Hurrah! Mickey, my boy, the Russians are flying from Sebastopol."

"Wishha! is that thrue?" cried Mickey, huskily.

"I have seen them moving away—the Redan is abandoned," replied Clifton.

"Oh, thin, blessings on the good God, Sebastopol is ours. Hurrah!" exclaimed Mickey, with more vigour than might be expected. "Sure its mind the bit wounds I don't a morsel; an now' I'll back to ould Ireland, and see Bridget a cuishla machree."

"Aye, and when she holds you in her arms Mickey, she'll have a sergeant there," cried Clifton.

"Plase God," responded the brave fellow.

Bidding him lie quiet, Clifton now made at the top of his speed for the trenches. On his way he was startled by a sudden blaze of light, followed by a tremendous explosion, then a burst of flame from a large building on fire.

"It is true," he cried, as he gazed upon the dull red glare of the conflagration, "they are evacuating the city."

He increased his speed, and quickly entered the advanced parallel; here he found, as he anticipated, a whole division, the Third, under Sir Colin Campbell and Brigadier General Eyre, swarming in the trenches, making ready for a renewal of the attack, which this time it was intended should redeem all past failures. He was speedily recognised as the "Fighting Fusilier,"—"the Fire-eating Sergeant,"—"the Pet of the Guards," and other names equally familiar, but not a jot less flattering. He asked to be conducted to Sir Colin Campbell, when he learned he had the command, and he was readily obeyed. Upon being brought before the brusque chief, he briefly related his discovery.

"The Redan deserted!" cried Sir Colin, surprised, "impossible!"

"And yet true," replied Clifton.

"How did you discover it?—begin at the beginning. Were you in the attack of this morning?"

Clifton related to him, as concisely as possible, all he had done that day up to the entry into the Redan.

"You are a gallant fellow, and deserve your commission," exclaimed the brave general, glowing at the narration, "and you shall have it too, if a word at Court from me can do. Now tak' a company and reconnoitre; you will be better able to examine it, and then bring me the report."

With joy Clifton retraced his steps at the head of a small company, and they reached the ditch unmolested, entered the angle, and from thence into the great Redan. They found it unoccupied. They searched for infernal machines and found one or two, the connections of which they destroyed. They gazed down upon Sebastopol: it was a sheet of flame; explosion, too, succeeded explosion. Magazines blew up, and hurled whole buildings into the air; the flames leaped, and licked everything within reach, enveloping it, in its destructive embrace, and leaving to the Allies, as Prince Gortschakoff said to his imperial master, only a heap of blood-stained ruins.

Having completely searched the building, and assured themselves that the Russians had deserted it, they returned, and reported the result of their examination to Sir Colin Campbell, who, when he heard it, no longer doubted it, but deemed it prudent to remain until the morning before he attempted to occupy it. He, however, granted to Clifton a fatigue party to bring off his friend Mickey Dunigan and some others who were lying wounded in the ditch. Clifton had his Irish comrade conveyed to their own quarters, where, before he considered himself, albeit he felt weak and faint, he caused Mickey's wounds to be examined and dressed, learning with pleasure that though severe, they were not at all dangerous. It was while bidding Mickey cheer up, that he felt a tightness round the upper part of his skull, as though a cord were suddenly compressed there, attended by a violent thrill and a sensation of giddiness. His eyes became sightless, his lips vibrated, his teeth grated, he was conscious of no more.

Sergeant Haverel stood by his side, watching him. He had noticed his haggard countenance, blackened and begrimed with powder; his lips white, parched, and crusted, as if salt was exuding from them. He noticed that there was stiffened blood all down his coat sleeve, his breast, and his trousers. He saw that he was trembling, as he believed, from over exhaustion. Then he observed him swaying to and fro, like a drunken man, froth bubble from his lips, his eye-balls turn into his skull. Haverel stretched out his arms and caught him as he fell lifeless. The sergeant lifted him, as if he were a child, and placed him upon his bed. He commenced to undress him, but was compelled to abandon it in despair: the cloth, matted with congealed blood, adhered to the coat and arm, and Haverel was afraid to remove it with violence, for fear of injury to his comrade, to whom he was more attached than if he were his own brother; so, bathing his temples and mouth with some cold brandy and water for a few minutes, he then darted down to the hospital, and brought back with him Mr. Surgeon Wilson, of the 7th Hussars, who quickly accomplished the disrobing, and dressed the wounds which he found, in a masterly manner.

"He has entirely prostrated himself with exhaustion;" he said, "and he is sharply wounded. He is a plucky fellow. There's ninety men out of a hundred would have sought the rear if they had had such slaps as these. Nothing serious, my man," he added, as Haverel excitedly put the question. "No, no, his wounds are angry and inflamed, but there is nothing that can not and *shall* not succumb to knowledge and skill."

"You will try your best to cure him, sir, won't you?" asked Haverel, appealingly.

Mr. Wilson laid his hand upon his shoulder and said, very emphatically:

"If you had seen him fight as I did at Inkermann, you would put yourself out of the way to cure him, and serve him too."

"*If* I saw him fight at Inkermann," almost shouted Serjeant Haverel, astounded, "Well I am dauged! I should think I did—I wish the Queen had."

"Wisha!" murmured Mickey, "av he'd a seen him fight about that redoubt as we did, Sergeant dear, sure he'd know more about fighting than he does av cutting a poor fellow's leg off. Musha! av the Queen, God bless her, *had* seen him, its sorry I'd be for Prince Albert's cocked hat."

Mr. Wilson laughed, and bade them be quiet, and he hoped in a short time to bring him round again.

Clifton was now reported severely wounded, and orders were given to remove him to the hospital.

Mickey was also carried there, and it was not a little to the satisfaction of the latter that he found their beds were side by side, for if he got well first he foreshadowed the numberless little kindnesses he should have it in his power to display to Clifton, and he yearned for the opportunity that he might shew how deep and heartfelt was his gratitude, and how glad he was of any chance which enabled him to evince it in any shape, however humble.

CHAPTER XXIX.

"Come home!
Come to the hearts that love thee, to the eyes
That beam in brightness hot to gladden thine:
Come where fond thoughts like holiest incense rise,
Where cherish'd memory rears her altar's shrine.

"Come home!
Would I could send my spirit o'er the deep—
Would I could wing it like a bird to thee,
To commune with thy thoughts, to fill thy sleep,
With these unwearying words of melody—
Come home!"
                                    ADM.

"Till now the stars and garters
Were for birth's or fortune's son,
And as oft in snug home quarters,
As in fields of fight were won.
But at length a star arises,
Which as glorious will shine,
On Smith's red serge vest, as upon the breast,
Of Smythe's scarlet superfine.

"Too long mere food for powder,
We've doomed our rank and file,
Now higher hopes and prouder,
Upon the soldier smile.
And if no Marshal's baton
Private Smith in his knapsack bears,
At least in the war, the chance of the star,
With his general he shares."
                                    PUNCH.

COME HOME! THE REWARD OF VALOUR. THE COMMISSION. THE RETURN HOME. ENGLAND.

CLIFTON GREY, while stretched upon the bed of pain and sickness, had a convincing proof that the bread he had cast upon the waters was returned to him tenfold. Kindness begets kindness: he had been kind to men with word, with active deed, with money, with counsel; and now he was helpless and struck down, battling with death—for fever and dysentery attacked him—it was as if every regiment in the army had sent a company to the hospital daily, to enquire after his health.

Officers sent little luxuries and nourishing things in the very kindest spirit; the men also procured them from such sources as they were able, and were far happier in the knowledge of his acceptance, and partaking of them, than if they had thrice the quantity for their self-enjoyment. Why, there was Mrs. Seacole, "from Jamaica," who so approved of his handsome face, and yet handsomer conduct, looked up all the delicacies she could, and took especial care that they were placed within his reach. Then, as it happened that Sister Geraldine gave her womanly tender ministering to Mickey Dunigan, so he entreated her by the love for that God whom she served entirely to exhaust all her watchful care, her thoughtful tenderness, upon Clifton, and he, Mickey, would make a vow, which she should dictate, and he would solemnly keep. She needed no such adjuration : it was her heavenly duty to succour the distressed or helpless, without regard to favour or preference ; but she recognised Clifton, having met him on the plateau, and she remembered his kindness of manner, and his respectful treatment : it was only natural that this should have its influence on her woman's heart, and so Clifton was well nursed.

Again, he was not at a loss for society : there was his watchful friend Mickey ready to talk to him when he saw that he was disposed for conversation ; there was Sergeant Haverel, who, whenever off duty, or he could get away from service, would come and sit and talk, and read or sing to him. In addition, there were as many soldiers of the Guards or regiments of the line that knew him, came to sit a few minutes with him, as were permitted by the regulations of the hospital ; and to crown all, many of the best surgeons in the whole army, when they knew the "Star of the Guards Brigade" had been struck down, came to give the benefit of their skill, and their good-natured observations to cheer him up.

One morning Sergeant Haverel came in elated; there was a letter for Clifton from Myra. He tore it open with avidity, and found that she commenced by regretting that she had only a few moments at her command to send him a few lines in reply to his letter, of which she acknowledged the receipt with expressions of warmth that made his heart glow with pride and pleasure. But he also found that she had so well employed those few minutes as to completely fill four sides of a sheet of bank post, and to cross them. Without referring to her position, more than she had been placed in critical situations, and that she was still in complicated circumstances, she begged him to come home, to purchase his discharge even, if necessary, and for which funds would be found him ; but to come home as soon after the receipt of that letter as possible. The news of the fall of Sebastopol had reached England, and she told him the impression was, that with it the war had ended. She begged him, for his own sake, far less than hers, to come home. She said there were some strange circumstances connected with him afloat, which his presence would alone set at rest ; and she begged him, if not

for his own, for her sake to come home. A few more remarks, and again the same entreaty ; from the commencement to the close of the epistle it had only the refrain "Come home."

"Come home !" he thought, with bitterness, "what home ? I have no home."

Yet, for all this despondency, when he thought of his isolation, he determined to go back to England as soon as he could ; for where Myra's home was, there was his home.

While he was reading his letter, serjeant Haverel was spelling out one from his darling Liz, occasionally breaking forth into snatches of ballads, in the intensity of his delight. When he had finished, and had kissed his letter a thousand times, he comforted Mickey by telling him, that according to a close computation he had made, the next mail in would bring letters from Ireland.

"And then, Mickey, my boy," said he, "you will receive one from your Anna :

　　'Pride of every shady grove,
　　　　Upon the banks of Banna.'"

Mickey smiled with pleasure at the suggestion, and answered—

"Bridget it is, you mane. Sure it's the happy boy I'll be when I get the paper scored by her purty five fingers. An' I ought to be patient, for God's good, sure, an' He's sint me a prisint from another swatcheart in England."

Haverel whistled.

"Mickey," said he, "I did not take you for a libertine.

　　I left my love in England,
　　　'In sorrow and in pain,'

but I be screwed if I left one anywhere else. Is she pretty, you villain, this number 2 ?"

"Why dy'e ax me ; sure shouldn't I say yes," returned Mickey, with a feeble laugh.

"What's her name ?" asked Haverel.

"Sure, the swatest name in the calendar. Mary, it is."

"Mary," repeated Haverel. "Molly asthore :"

　　'Mary, I believed thee true,
　　　And I was blest in thus believing.'

I have a passion for the name of Mary. Ah, Mickey, you are a sad dog. What's that you are twiddling in your fingers ?"

"Sure, isn't it a lock of her purty hair," he replied.

Haverel took the paper handed to him, and opened it. It contained a lock of light-brown hair, plaited in three, and tied with blue and yellow silk threads. While Haverel was examining it, Clifton turned his large sunken eyes upon Mickey Dunigan, and said—

"Mickey, I wrote a long letter for you to a poor girl in Ireland, who, judging from the letter she has sent you, has her whole existence bound up in you. I have always believed you truthful, tried you, trusted you; but I hope that you are faithful, that you will be able to explain that lock of hair by some better history than the one you have given, or, as Heaven hears me, I will have no more to do with one who acts to a poor, trusting, loving girl, like an accomplished scoundrel."

" Wisht—wirrastru! musha to the bad likes av my tongue; sure, Sargeant Grey dear, its joking I am. May my tongue be blistered, an' my soul black, if I do not tell you the truth now. When the packages came from the noble people of England for the poor shivering soldiers widout a shoe to their back or a coat to their foot—no, I mane—"

" Go on, Mickey; never mind, we know what you mean," interrupted Haverel.

"Well, as God's me judge, I had a flannin shirt sarved out to me, an' it was a new one, and a very good one, and warm and comfortable to a poor fellow who needed it as I did. Well, sargeant dear, inside it was pinned a paper—a letter—here it is," he handed it to Clifton as he spoke. In this was the lock of hair. The superscription, written in a humble style of writing, was as follows :

"This is for you, And I
Hope it is A young
Man ;
If not, Give it to one."

Within, in the same handwriting, were the accompanying words : "My dear Friend, I write these few lines to you hoping that they will Cheer you A little. I think you are dull, but God will help you. I am A young woman, and I hope that you are A young man. This is my Hair Keep it for My sake, from MARY. You are now laughing: it is bad writing."

"God bless her !" said Clifton, earnestly.

"Amen !" exclaimed Mickey Dunigan, reverently.

"God bless her !" cried Sergeant Haverel, fervently. Not one of them laughed, but tears stood in the eyes of all.

The gift of the generous hearted girl was warmly appreciated, and if she could feel that her kindness had been rewarded by the strong estimation in which the sentiment that had dictated the gift was held, herself being included in the favourable opinion, she was well repaid.

"Whatever her station, that girl has a kind heart, and everybody about her likes her, I'll be sworn," cried Haverel.

" 'All nature seems pleased as she trips it along,
Her smiles make the lark swell his rapturous song;
The shepherds their cares and their labors forget,
To gaze on the charms of my sweet Robinette.' "

"Sure, she was my swate heart, an' yours, an' every one's, any way," cried Mickey, triumphantly, believing that he was offering a justification for the slight and harmless deception he had practised.

Clifton Grey, when he had admired the lock of hair, beautiful both in softness and color, returned it with the note to Mickey, and said—

"Keep them both, Mickey, and give them to Bridget to treasure when you get home. Be assured, that when she knows the contents of that note, she will keep the writer affectionately in her memory."

"Its hug her, she would," said Mickey, "av she could get sight av her purty figure, as I should, too, an' no harm done."

"And I," cried Haverel, "to the delight of my Liz, if she knew it.

"And I," said Clifton, "in proof that the exquisite emotions of sweet charity and tender benevolence so universally exhibited by the gentle women, and the kindhearted maidens of England have not been met with indifference by those it was intended to help and serve—nay, that their open-handed charity has been received by the suffering army of their nation with an enthusiasm it would gladden their generous souls to witness."

"And a mighty pretty way of shewing one's gratitude," laughed Haverel :

" 'Her rosy lips you'd love to kiss, but then
You'd pause awhile ;
Because a kiss would interrupt the sweetness
Of her smile.' "

In this way did the weary hours of illness glide away, and months elapsed before Clifton or Mickey were able to leave the hospital convalescent. Yet this desirable condition at length arrived, and our hero was once more a tenant of his tent. He was compelled to wear his arm in a sling, and his appearance was that of one who had but recently stood on the threshold of the grave; but he felt all the symptoms of returning vigour and strength—he had lightness of spirits and cheerfulness, and the surgeons confidently predicted a speedy return to health. Mr. Surgeon Wilson, however, having received a private intimation—not from Clifton, certainly—that a return to England, now that active warfare was at an end, would be very desirable, declared that he needed a change of scene, and that the air of England was necessary to restore him to perfect health. This statement was conveyed to head-quarters, and his name and that of Mickey Dunigan appeared on the list of those invalided home to England.

Clifton made his preparations—they were not many —for his return, and now longed for the hour that should bear him away from the spot on which he had done and endured so much, and where he had won so much honour.

One morning he was summoned to the head-quarters of the general-commanding-in-chief, now Sir William Codrington, for another change in the command had taken place. Upon attending, he was at once ushered into the presence of his commander. The interview was brief, but most flattering and gratifying to him. After a short colloquy, he received a communication and took his leave.

Three days after, the First Division, under Lord

Rokeby, were paraded on the plateau, and were, after some evolutions, formed into square. Almost immediately after this General Codrington arrived on the ground, accompanied by his staff, and having inspected the Guards, complimented the general and brigadiers on the efficiency and healthiness of his men. After a few more complimentary remarks, to which the brave fellows were well entitled, and which were as handsomely bestowed, Clifton Grey was called from the front, where he was at the head of his company, and by the side of that glorious flag which proudly exhibited so many marks of desperate conflict, to the immediate presence of the commander-in-chief. When he stood before General Codrington, the latter having alighted from his steed, he was thus addressed by him :—

"Sergeant Grey, a recruit in the army of England, you volunteered into the Guards, and accompanied your regiment to the Crimea. From your admission up to the present moment you have been distinguished by those qualities which are eminently valuable in the soldier. I do not allude to bravery and disregard of death, for that is to some extent the inheritance of every man, but to cheerful obedience, strict attention to discipline, great regard for cleanliness, scrupulous subordination and performance of duties, —the first to be ready to occupy a post and share its dangers, the last to be willing to leave it. I have examined your case, the successive reports of the colonels, brigadiers, generals, and others superior in command. In every instance in which it has been thought proper to make a reference to you, its purport has been to extol your conduct for the extremely creditable discharge of your duties, and the highly efficient state of the men of your company. With these statements, in every respect so honourable to you, are coupled warm eulogiums on the chivalric gallantry with which you have led your men into action, and the determined bravery with which you have maintained when there the honour of your corps and of your country. In all the important actions in which your regiment has been engaged you have eminently distinguished yourself. Your officers have, in proudly forwarding details of them to head quarters, with great pleasure submitted your name for promotion to a commission. The late lamented Commander-in-Chief, Lord Raglan, forwarded the recommendation to the War Office— Lieut.-General Simpson, my honoured predecessor, supported it—and it was my agreeable duty, after the attack upon the Great Redan, to add to that recommendation. An ensigncy in the Guards is no mean gift, and the Government thought it advisable to institute very searching inquiries into the propriety of its bestowal in your case. The result has been favourable to you, in every point of view. It becomes, therefore, my gratifying office to present you with this commission in the Guards, forwarded to me by the Minister of War, with a request that I should inform you that on the circumstances connected with this promotion having been submitted to the Queen, her Majesty, upon learning your honourable claims to it, commanded it immediately to be despatched to you, accompanied by her earnest thanks for the brave manner in which you had helped to maintain the honour of your country, and with it the promise of the first vacant lieutenancy in your regiment, without purchase. Accept it, therefore, as a tribute of honour from a grateful country, proud of you as one of her noblest and most devoted children ; and I trust that every comrade who has witnessed your performance of the first duties of a soldier, your bravery in the trying moment of fierce encounter, and every soldier who now witnesses its fitting recompence, will take it as an example how to win that high reward which will never be withheld from the man who so justly merits it."

He presented Clifton Grey with his commission as an ensign in the Scots Fusilier Guards, as he spoke, and shook him heartily by the hand, at sight of which a tremendous rattling cheer burst from the men who, presenting arms, saw the bestowal of this honourably-earned distinction. Three times did the gallant fellows cheer the well-deserved reward of their late comrade, and the band struck up "God save the Queen."

The proud moment had come. Clifton's face was as white as marble, his heart throbbed violently, and his bosom heaved and swelled as the various passages in the Commander-in-Chief's address affected him. As he received his commission the bright water welled up from his heart into his eyes, his lip quivered, and, though he would have spoken, not a word came to his aid ; but the cheer of the men gave him the wished-for opportunity, and then, removing his shako, he said to the Commander-in-Chief :

"General, it is with the profoundest emotions of pride and gratitude I receive this promotion, and the communication from her Majesty. When I entered the army, a simple recruit, it was this honour to which I aspired ; it shone like a star before me, and guided me along the path I have pursued, to the door which has been thus thrown open to me and to others in my condition. I have esteemed the profession of arms as the most noble man can follow. I have endeavoured to support the name of soldier unsullied ; the result will, I am sure, induce others to emulate my efforts. I shall pursue my career with, I trust, the same scrupulous regard for the honour of the army as a soldier—of myself as a man and a gentleman. I am at a loss for words to express myself with the enthusiasm I feel ; but I am sure that, having won the prize I have received by a course of conduct thus guerdoned, I shall do nothing to disgrace the promotion."

General Codrington expressed his conviction that he would not, and offered his congratulations, in which many officers present followed him: among them none more enthusiastically than Major Linder, whose promotion, consequent upon heavy losses, had been very rapid.

Sergeant Haverel was next called to the front. He was commended and made staff sergeant; and our friend, Mickey Dunigan, was elevated to the rank of sergeant. The troops were then marched to quarters, the hearts of our friends being not a little gladdened by the events of the morning parade.

There was further honour yet in store for our hero; for our friend the Zouave, in accounting for his compulsory absence from duty, had given the details of his rescue, in which, with the true characteristic of his nation, he made the performance of Clifton little short of a marvel. Marshal Pelissier detailed the incident in one of his communications to Marshal Vaillant, Minister of War for France, as an instance of the *entente cordiale* existing between the men of both nations, and the minister submitted it to the emperor, who, ever alive to military merit, sent him the order of the Legion of Honour. Marshal Pelissier sent it by a French general officer, accompanied by high compliments, and M. le Zouave and the pretty Fanchette were permitted to be present at the presentation. General Codrington, in whose tent the investiture of the order took place, informed Clifton that he had no doubt her Majesty would grant him permission to wear it, as also the decoration of the Medjedjie, which the sultan had conferred upon all who had distinguished themselves in the Crimea, and to which he was therefore fully entitled.

With Henri and Fanchette Clifton passed the remainder of the day in his tent. Henri had been, for his very distinguished bravery in the capture of the Malakhoff, elevated to the rank of a sous-lieutenant. He, too, was going home, and when he reached La Belle France the pretty Fanchette was to become his wife. Having arranged where he could communicate with them in their own land, Clifton bade them farewell. Fanchette kissed him, when parting, on both eyes, to which he replied by kissing her lips; and then she promised that their first boy should be named after him, Clifton Grey, and so they separated.

The Himalaya was in the offing with her signal for sailing flying. Major Linder, invalided home in her, had got with all his effects on board. Sergeant Haverel was there, also, in charge of a company of invalids. Sergeant Dunigan was leaning over the side, gazing on the steep cliffs of Balaklava, and thinking of the first gem of the ocean, and his dark-eyed girl, who was then looking at the winking stars and thinking of him. The steam was hissing with a continuous drony hum from the safety-valves; the sailors were walking round with the capstan, with even tramp and cheerful song; and Clifton Grey was waving his cap in reply to the cheers of a vast body of troops, men of his own regiment and others, who were lining the cliff, assembled there to pay him the last tribute of respect they might have in their power so long as the armies of the Allies held possession of the Crimea.

Now the anchor's weighed, the huge paddles are put in motion, and the leviathan ship steams rapidly across the waters of the Black Sea. Constantinople is left behind, and Malta is soon gained. What associations did not this place raise! The brief time permitted for going on shore he availed himself of; but to his enquiries, the answer was returned that his mysterious friend Sylva was yet in England. Her last communication to him was dated from the residence of Mr. Jayne, and there he determined to seek her. He cared little for that gentleman's black looks or insolent remarks. He felt perfectly independent of him. He knew that he had been paid in full for any expense or trouble he might have been to him. Nay, he had yet money of his in his possession, which more than paid his expense of coming to Arundel to sunder the connexion with Clifton, if, indeed, he had not charged it to his account. As he was a man who did not make to anyone a present of his time, if he could avoid it, it was most probable he had done so; and Clifton, knowing that since that period he had asked nothing from him, no favour, indeed, of any kind, he felt that seeking an interview merely with one residing beneath his roof, there was no necessity for caring or heeding the likes or dislikes to his presence he might think proper to evince.

The run from Malta home was performed with remarkable rapidity, and when the coast of England rose up out of the ocean, Clifton felt a powerful emotion as he gazed upon it, for he remembered how acutely he had considered himself lonely and abandoned when it had sunk down into the bosom of the deep; yet now, when again he saw it, his prospects of position were far superior to any he had imagined, although he hoped would be so soon his, his chances of happiness infinitely greater, and he could not help anticipating, not far from realization. It was natural, therefore, that he should view it with emotion, that his bosom should throb with a nervous anxiety to be again treading its shores—to be where he could see and confer with Myra.

From Portsmouth he had departed, to Portsmouth he returned. Major Linder had placed him upon an equal footing with himself, and warmly cultivated his friendship. Upon landing, they were received with every token of respect and honour, and many and pressing invitations to become the guests of the most influential in the town were tendered them; but Major Linder was anxious to get to London, as well as Clifton Grey, and so, after one night's rest, they set off for the metropolis, at which place they arrived at mid-day, putting up at one of the first hotels. How strange London appeared to Clifton again, after an absence of two years! What an incessant roll, bustle, and turmoil! the camp was nothing to it; besides, it had been situated on an elevation, broad, expansive, open; here, everything seemed shut in, "cribb'd, cabin'd, and confin'd," while the thousands of persons moving to and fro were, to his seeming, rushing about like mad persons, all looking eager, and pushing along as if on a mission of life or death.

When Major Linder understood that Clifton purposed visiting Gresham-street, with the object of an interview with the young and lovely Signora they met at Sliema, he felt an inexpressible desire to accompany him. Ah! how well he remembered those magnificent eyes of hers; how they languished in softness while they were turned upon Clifton; how they had flashed and glittered when bent upon Captain Winslow; how dignified their expression when they fell upon him. He pleaded so urgently to be permitted to accompany our hero thither, that Clifton did not decline or deny him.

The family of Major Linder, to whom Clifton had been introduced, and most kindly received by, placed to his use a brougham, until he made his own arrangements during his leave of absence; and in this—a handsome vehicle of the kind—they dashed up to Mr. Jayne's residence. Mr. Jayne was standing at the window of his drawing-room, talking to both Sylva and Preciosa, when he observed the carriage stop. His exclamation of wonder at the possible business two officers of the army, "bearded like the pard," could have with him, drew the attention of the young ladies, who, of course, hurried to the window. No sooner did their eyes fall upon one of them, than both uttered a scream of surprise. At the same moment the footman entered the room, bearing on a salver the two cards entrusted to him by the officers below. Before Mr. Jayne could adjust his gold glasses over the bridge of his nose to ascertain the names of the owners of these cards, both ladies cried in concert.

"At home, William."

Whereupon William ducked his head, and leaving Mr. Jayne in possession of the cards, darted down the stairs, and returned, followed by both officers. Mr. Jayne, having had just time to mutter 'Major the Honourable Cuthbert Linder, Scots Fusilier Guards; Ensign Clifton Grey, Scots Fusilier Guards.' When those gentlemen were announced, Sylva ran up to Clifton, and shook both his hands with enthusiastic warmth. Preciosa was, however, not content with such salute, but murmuring:

"Heaven has blessed my prayers with your safe return! Preserver of my life, how I have prayed for your safety." She threw herself in his arms, and embraced him.

Mr. Jayne looked on in wonder. He was in a most ridiculously embarrassing predicament. At first he made up his mind to be cold and stern,

because of the past; and then it suddenly struck him that he was rich enough to be independent of those who had employed him in Clifton's affair, so if they were offended on learning that he had met the youth he had had so many years beneath his roof in a friendly spirit, they might be so, for what he cared; besides, there was a prospect that he would be proved heir to a large fortune, and that was a material consideration weighing with him; so he extended his hand, and said:

"Welcome, Mr. Grey, to England."

Clifton was not proof against this; so he seized the proffered hand, and wrung it warmly.

"I am proud to meet you, Mr. Jayne," he said, earnestly; "you will find, sir, that I have done no dishonour to the name I bear, nor to the education you superintended."

"I am quite prepared to hear that," replied Mr. Jayne, rubbing his hands. "I expected no less of you."

Major Linder was now introduced. Sylva at once remembered him, and a strong flush passed over her features; as she did so she extended her hand, and, with much sweetness of manner, welcomed him back to England in safety, after having honourably shared the dangers of the campaign, as their medals—one with four clasps, the other with three—testified. Linder raised her hand to his lips, and observed that his greatest happiness since he landed was his having the felicity of meeting her in England.

They sat together for some hours in converse, but it was not at this interview that they entered into the subject upon which they had already communicated: this was reserved for a second meeting, which, however, was named for the morrow; for Clifton was burning to see Myra; he was restless, unsettled, wished to see nothing, could think of nothing, but Myra, of whose whereabouts he knew from the letter he received from her, but about whom he should learn more from Lizzie Hastings. He was that night to see her. He had wisely determined to let the interview between her and Sergeant Haverel pass over before he visited her; indeed, he would, but for Major Linder, have gone direct to Arundel, but was dissuaded; but it was not possible to have prevented him seeing Lizzie that night, to hear her account of all those incidents which had but briefly been described in the letters he had received, and then determine upon his course of action in respect to them.

CHAPTER XXX.

"O my soul's joy!
If after every tempest comes such calms,
May the winds blow till they have waken'd death,
And let the labouring bark climb hills of seas
Olympus high; and duck again as low
As hell's from heaven! If I were now to die,
'Twere now to be most happy; for I fear
My soul hath her content so absolute,
That not another comfort like to this
Succeeds in unknown fate."

SHAKSPERE.

"Why, hark you!
The trumpets, sackbuts, psalteries and fifes,
Tabors and cymbals, and the shouting Romans,
Make the sun dance."

IBID.

"He shall flourish,
And like a mountain cedar, reach his branches
To all the plains about him; children's children
Shall see this, and bless heav'n."

IBID.

HOME. HAVEREL AND LIZZIE. CLIFTON AND MYRA. THE MYSTERY CLEARED UP. RETURN OF THE GUARDS TO LONDON. THE CONCLUSION.

SERGEANT HAVEREL having seen his men safely to Brompton barracks, where Mickey Dunigan was compelled to remain for some little time, owing to prostration occasioned by his voyage, and no little excitement consequent upon his return to England. The surgeon promised him, if he would remain quiet, that he would soon restore him to health and strength, so that he should be able to go back to Ould Ireland, and to those who loved him, as good a man as ever he had been; a communication he received with pleasure, and with promises to conform to the directions given to him.

When Sergeant Haverel had fulfilled all the duties he was required to discharge, he made the best of his way to London, by express train; even that seemed to go at a slow pace, but he was soon whisked up to London Bridge, when, obtaining a "Hansom," he went to Baker-street, by his own instructions, at about twenty miles an hour, if the horse could do it. The driver of course said it could, and certainly he went along at a rattling pace, and landed the Sergeant at Mrs. Stewart's residence, with a celerity which he himself considered quite creditable, and Haverel was well disposed to reward. A tremendous knock at the door, loud enough to have been achieved by the tall footman of the Marchioness of Londonderry, woke up the echoes of the street, for the cab-driver knew that he bore in his vehicle one of the Crimean heroes, whose return home would be welcomed with the greatest excitement and delight, and therefore a long and vigorous cadenza upon the knocker was precisely the proper proceeding to be observed. Mrs.

Stewart believed it to be the advent of a lady of tifle, and learned that it was a tall, moustachioed, and bearded officer, who wanted to see Miss Hastings. Mrs. Stewart guessed who the officer was, and hastened to have a look at him. A fine manly person she found him. She warmly and kindly welcomed him to England, paid him some graceful and well merited compliments upon his bravery; expressed her regret that Miss Hastings was not at home, and would not return that evening; but she immediately calmed some uneasy reflection which rose in the gallant sergeant's mind, by telling him that she had gone to pay a visit to Mrs. Haverel, his own mother. Haverel at once bade her good day, but she would not permit him to leave until he had partaken of a glass of wine. While she left the room to give the necessary directions to lay before him a lunch, Haverel became conscious of pretty faces suddenly popping in at the door-way, and as suddenly popping out again. There was a succession of them, and, at last, when the face of a pretty dark-eyed girl presented itself, he laughed and nodded, and then, like a naughty girl as she was, she nodded and laughed in return, and ran away, for she heard Mrs. Stewart's step upon the stairs. Those faces were belonging to Mrs. Stewart's "young ladies," who, learning from the servant-maid that Miss Hastings's "beau" had come home from the wars, immediately felt dying to see him; and as young ladies rarely feel to be dying for anything but they gratify their wish somehow, so Mrs. Stewart's young ladies, one and all, had a peep at the beau, and instantly considered Miss Hastings as one of the most fortunate "young ladies" in the universe. "But there," observed the shortest apprentice, who was busily engaged plaiting up blonde for a bonnet cap, "some girls have the luck of it. I have often looked at one of those handsome officers of the Guards riding down St. James's Park of a morning, but he never takes any notice of me a bit, any more than if there was no such person." The girls laughed merrily; but they all agreed that Miss Hastings certainly had considerable luck.

All this while Miss Hastings was comfortably situated alone with old dame Haverel, to whom she had brought home, as a present, a new dress, which she had bought, and, with the help of Myra's maid Lucy, had made for her at night, after she had done her own long day's close work. It was so smart, being a lustre, with a handsome pattern upon it, and it shone so, and fitted her so well, that it did one's heart good to look upon it. And then she also brought her a new cap, quilled up so "full" and with such lots of the "best" flowers in it, and certain adornments of ribbon, red, white, and blue, that the beadle of her parish, if he had at that moment seen her, would have removed his cocked hat, and made her a low bow.

Lizzie had dressed her up in the new dress, had

pinched her in at the waist, and patted, smoothed out its wrinkles, and pulled down the skirt, arranging its folds, so that it seemed full and handsome; and she had put on the bran-new cap, smoothed her grey hair tenderly, setting its plaits, and giving a flower a pinch here, and a pull there; and when she had done all, she turned her round once or twice, and clapped her hands, laughing with delight; then she placed both hands on the cheeks of Mrs. Haverel, and, with swimming eyes, said:

"There, there, dear Mrs. Haverel, you can't think how well and how nice you look. I declare you seem quite worthy of so brave, noble, dear, good son, as you have got."

She kissed her affectionately, as she spoke; and Mrs. Haverel returned her salute with warmth, declaring that she loved her quite as dearly as that dear son; for in his absence she had been to her as thoughtful, affectionate, generous, and good, as the most loving child possibly could have been. Then there was a silence; for the hearts of both were full. At this moment a voice through the key-hole of the door sung:

"'There's one down by the green Savanna,
    One that I love;
Ah! how that dear form haunts me,
    No matter where I rove.'"

An affrighted shout from Mrs. Haverel—a shriek from Lizzie—and the door flew open. There stood Haverel, trying with his dim eyes to make out which was his mother, and which his Lizzie; and there they stood, gasping at him as if he were his own ghost, and then he, with husky voice, cried out:

"Liz—Liz!—mother!—all right, eh! Here I am, safe home."

Lizzie darted up to him, crying hysterically:

"Walter—Walter! O thank God—thank God!"

He pressed her to his breast, he kissed her with passionate enthusiasm, and then hugged his mother, leaving her arms to have another ardent embrace of Lizzie. He blubbered like a child, and Lizzie sobbed as if she was bent upon breaking her heart. Mrs. Haverel followed suit, by crying as if she had been distrained upon for rent. But it was all joy,—all pure, right down, sheer joy, although its aspect was one of grief. And then they all consoled each other, insisting that the other should leave off crying, which they did, to begin again presently at a word. Then, to see how Walter Haverel had to stand out, and how his mother and Lizzie admired him in his bran-new regimentals, with the tunic coat and gold lace, all bright and glittering, and then his great bushy beard and moustache, which his mother said were horrid, and made him look like one of the bears at the 'Locogiosi' Gardens, and Lizzie didn't know whether she did like them or did not—not that just now she could dislike anything belonging

to him. And how he handed his mother out, how he laughed, and how delighted he was to see her in such splendour, and how he hugged Lizzie when he learned 'twas all her doing, her gift, her making, her management, though, he added, that was a matter of course, for his mother, of herself, never cared to look smart, or give her clothes a fashionable touch in the shape.

Yet all this time how his eyes, his thoughts, his sense were filled with Lizzie, for she had grown, and her figure had filled out more during his absence. She was ever neatly dressed; now she happened to be prettily dressed in a light muslin frock, and a pretty riband bow upon her neck, which somehow directed attention to her face, the prettiest ever sun shone on, and gave back sunlight beam for beam. It is certain that Haverel was not so considerate about preserving the beautiful smoothness of this garment, as he ought to have been, for new muslin dresses are not every day purchases, or to be had for asking; but then he loved her, so it was impossible to keep his hands from her. Then they sat down to tea. Now Lizzie had brought a nice new loaf and a bunch of water-cresses, and Haverel, on his way, had purchased a bag of tea-cakes, enough for six, together with a large crab, and a quart of shrimps, so there was plenty to form an excellent meal if they had only appetite to bring to it. It was all set out by Lizzie, who laughed, and talked, and cried in a breath, and received every now and then a kiss to help her on. They were all falling to, when there came a loud knocking at the door, which Lizzie ran to and opened. Now Walter opened his ears at the same moment, for he certainly heard the new comer kiss Lizzie—his Lizzie, that, too, not once, but a dozen times, a sort of rapid fire of kisses, like the chirruping of a large bird. He jumped to his feet, determined to stand no nonsense of that sort, upon any pretence whatever, when the door opened, and in came Lizzie with a blushing face and delighted aspect, followed by Clifton Grey.

Well, to be sure, Haverel gave a shout of joy, and after a minute's explanation, which served to tell that Clifton, too, had seen Mrs. Stewart, and been seen by the 'young ladies,' who thought him, although he neither knew it nor said it, 'such a duck of a fellow.' He had, on learning whither Haverel had gone, followed him, and here he was with some remarkably fine hautboys, together with a bottle of Spanish wine, which he bought at Hedges and Butler's, in Regent-street, and which once tasted is not lightly remembered, nor easily forgotten. So there was quite a feast, and they all laughed and talked with such vehemence and volubility, that the neighbours believed Mrs. Haverel to have suddenly grown reckless, and had commenced riotously to squander her hoardings.

When tea was cleared, Clifton learned from Lizzie

a history of the events which had occurred since the arrest of Captain Winslow, who, not liking to trust to the issue of a trial, contrived to escape from the custody of the country officer on his way to Horsham jail, for which, no doubt, he paid a handsome sum. He remained at large until he learned that Perk had hanged himself, and then he surrendered to take his trial. Evidence was wanting to connect him with the actual forcible abduction, and though there was no moral doubt of his guilt, the legal proof was needing, and therefore he was acquitted. Clifton had learned, just before leaving the Crimea, that Captain Winslow had sold out, on being peremptorily ordered to return to his regiment. The permission to sell was accorded to him in a manner and with a readiness which was far from being flattering to him. What had become of him since he had appeared at the trial Lizzie could not tell; she had not heard of him, and she had had one last, and she believed final, interview with Beverley Winslow. It seemed that her cousin Lucy—that 'bit of a girl,' had got a sweetheart—seventeen, and with a full-grown sweetheart! What a strange thing it is a girl, with difficulty, can manage to do without a new bonnet, or a new dress, or a new mantle, though always wishing for, and thinking of one or the other; but she cannot contrive to do without a sweetheart, if there is a chance of getting one. No, no; she cannay, she will not do without one, if he is to be had. And so, quiet, prim, innocent Lucy had got a sweetheart, a master's-mate on board a man-of-war, who dressed and looked like a half-blown lieutenant in the navy. His ship having come home from the Baltic with despatches from Admiral Seymour, he had a few days' liberty, and he took Lucy—who would take Lizzie with her—to the theatre, and on their way the latter posted a letter to Haverel, leaving for a moment her friends while she did so. Beverley Winslow happened to be posting a letter also, and at sight of her sweet face he could not resist the temptation of laying hold of her, and begging of her to "wefwain fwom tweating him so wigowously." He swore that "he loved her little toes better than the whole body of many a lady of wank, and if she would give up her demmed bonnet building, and come and live with him, he would instal her in a little pawadise—a wegular little pawadise." He placed his arm tightly round her waist, vowing he would have his answer—and he did. Lizzie, knowing that the young sailor was rather fiery, she was fearful of making an outcry, because she was not desirous of a scene; but Lucy had suddenly cried out: "Why, I declare if there is'nt a rude fellow insulting my cousin Lizzie." The remark was enough for the young sailor; he let go of Lucy's arm, and, in more expressive terms than we think it proper to give, bade him "cast off," and, at the same time, he delivered some very severe hits, which seemed to bear

Beverley away to the very heart of Japan. The sailor knocked him down, and set him up again; and then knocked him down once more, where he laid and kicked; but our sailor lifted him up and shook him, boxed his ears, slapped his face, and when he was out of breath, gave him his toe. Being released, and thus helped on his way, Beverley ran away, affrighted, sick, sore, and disgusted, fully resolved to take no more notice of Lizzie, not even if she went down on her "mawwow bones and entweated him to pawdon and fo'give her." Haverel and Clifton laughed heartily at the poetical fate of Beverley Winslow, and the sergeant vowed to be a sworn friend for life with Lucy's young man.

Clifton, having heard from Lizzie all he could expect to hear respecting Myra, now announced his intention of at once proceeding to Arundel, where Myra, Mrs. Aston, and the Randolph family were. They were living, he ascertained, in the house formerly in possession of Mr. Gibbon, who was dead, and whose family had departed from Arundel; thither he resolved to bend his steps, greatly to the satisfaction of Lizzie, who thought it was quite what he ought to do; nay, she hardly liked his having stopped so long in London, and she hinted as much. He explained, that he possessed not the claim to rush into Myra's presence that Haverel had to hasten to hers; but Lizzie cried "Fiddlestick!" and said he had. And off by mail train he went. Remembering, on his way, that he had promised to meet Sylva and Preciosa on the morrow, he stopped his cab, wrote a note to his friend Linder, begging him to go in his place, and excuse him, making a promise to call upon them in three days, as a pressing engagement, which he had strangely overlooked, had called him away. Lizzie's face and Haverel's happiness had done it all. He felt that he could not rest until he had seen Myra; he was quite convinced he could attend to no business or affairs of any kind until he had had an interview with her.

He reached Arundel at midnight, and went direct to the inn kept by Mr. Chesney, who had, under the instructions of Mr. Gibbon, behaved with such kindness to him before he left England; and here, after knocking up the inmates, he obtained a bed and retired to rest. He slept but a few hours, however, and arose with the dawn, making, immediately afterwards, his toilet with strange and scrupulous care, and then he departed out for a stroll.

It may be surmised that he directed his footsteps to the banks of the gentle Arun, where it went meandering clear and pellucid through most charming scenery, murmuring a song "beyond the reach of art." He desired to refresh his memory with a sight of the spot where he had seen Myra, almost for the last time —where he had taken his farewell of her; and he felt that it would afford him a remarkable satisfaction to find out the tree against which he had, on that morning, seen her lean; the spot on which she had sunk to the ground in anguish too deep for words, and where he had pressed a burning kiss upon her hand, and left her sobbing.

Soon he saw the wide spreading elm beneath which, on that memorable visit, he had first behold Myra standing. Strange that now there should be a female there at the moment he came to renew his acquaintance with it, but who seemed to be lost in contemplation, instead of the perusal of a book. As he drew near slowly, the female changed her posture, turning partly from him, and gazing in the direction the stream was flowing. He would rather there had been no one there; however, he paused not, and, as he approached the figure, his heart began strangely to pulsate. Surely he recognised the proportions of that form; there was but one being in the world who, in his eyes, could possess that graceful outline—and that one was Myra. Yet, the Myra he had parted with was neatly but plainly dressed, this young lady was most elegantly attired.

A few paces more, and he was almost at her elbow; the sound of his feet upon the waving grass attracted her attention, and she turned her head towards him. Heavens! what a face of exquisite loveliness was presented to him; how clear and alabaster-like the skin; how large, deep, and gazelle-like, the eyes; how small the mouth; and how transparent and red the lips. There was no doubt in his mind respecting a face, every lineament of which was deeply impressed upon his memory—it was Myra—of that he had not one wavering uncertainty. She looked upon him with eager and enquiring eyes; he had left her with a face almost boy-like; he now had dark-brown mustachioes, and a beard. Yet she could not be mistaken in the eye, the elevated white forehead, for he had removed his undress cap as soon as her sweet face was turned towards him, his finely formed figure, displayed to such advantage in his uniform. As his heart beat with emotion, so here palpitated violently. She heard his low, soft, musical voice exclaim—

"Myra!"

Then the place seemed to move round with her.

"Clifton—Clifton!" she exclaimed, with quivering lips, and stretched her hands out towards him.

"Even him, Myra," he replied with fervour, and, opening his arms, she fell into them. He twined them round her fair form, and her arms were folded fondly round his neck; he kissed her sweet lips with an ardour which only such love as his could display; and she had no thought to shrink from it—no perception but that the happiness of that moment was worth a life-purchase.

The prospect of a meeting had been a constant presence to both. How they should deport themselves the source of constant reflection. Neither had said to the other, "I love you;" and though each loved, and passionately, too, yet that they were beloved by the object of their affection was a question rather of hope than certainty. Clifton had resolved to meet her with a respectful manner, which would expand or contract according as he was received. He did not much fancy her being rich, it seemed to place a fatal bar to his hopes, and he was too proud to seem to court her favour if there was displayed the smallest symptom of a sense of difference of position. So he intended to be polite and gentlemanly, and as well behaved as Mrs. Aston could wish. It was Myra's prayer that she might meet him on his arrival in England, alone. She felt that it would be a painful trial if she were called upon to receive him in the presence of her mother and the Randolphs, for it was probable that he might mistake her intense efforts to keep down her emotions from being gazed upon by unwished for eyes, for pride and coldness she did not, could not, feel. They did meet alone, and how they acted we have described.

Before they separated a long explanation took place between them, and when they parted there was no doubt remaining as to the state of their affection for each other. After breakfast, Clifton paid a ceremonious visit to Mrs. Aston, and was received by that lady with a frank and friendly air. He had come home an officer in the Guards, if he had gone away a recruit in the ranks, and it was astonishing, even with the sensible Mrs. Aston, how that circumstance altered the case. Mr. Randolph and Everett welcomed him with manly friendliness, and the Miss Randolphs with marked destinction. Mr. Randolph elicited from Clifton—and oh, how his modest recital made Myra's heart glow!—the part he had taken at the Alma, at Balaklava, Inkermann, the Great Redan, &c. His medal, with its clasps, hung honourably from his breast, and it is amazing how he commended himself to the hearts of the young ladies and the gentlemen present, when they knew how gallantly he had served his country, especially when he rose and said;

"Mrs. Aston, on parting with you I assured you that if I could not renew my intimacy with you ennobled by honours, I never would in disgrace. I have come to renew my intimacy, and I trust, in doing so, you will consider that I have not violated my promise."

Mrs. Aston pressed his hand warmly.

"Mr. Grey," she said, earnestly, "I am very proud to receive you. There has been an interval in which I have not done you justice, and I have been punished for it as I merited; henceforth I will strive to do better by you."

She placed, as she spoke, his hand in Myra's, and hastily quitted the room to conceal a violent flood of tears. Clifton raised Myra's hand to his lips and pressed it. She, with a smile but a blushing face, gently disengaged it, and hastened after her mother to console and embrace her, to tell her that she thought her the dearest, kindest, best mother upon earth.

Mr. Randolph proposed a stroll, while the ladies prepared for a ride, knowing that by such an arrangement all emotion would have been got over; and Clifton, anxious to see Charley Rowe and Ellen Fairfax, readily consented. They had barely got into the High-street when, most unexpectedly to all parties, Clifton suddenly encountered ex-Captain Winslow, who had that morning arrived in Arundel to put into operation a devilish plot against the happiness and virtue of Myra, and was not a little astounded to see him in the garb of a commissioned officer of his late regiment. He was about to slide past, but Clifton stopped him:

"Mr. Winslow," he said, "at length we meet on equal terms. I am now in a position to demand satisfaction for the insults you have heaped upon me—the calumnies you have unsparingly uttered in respect to me—and the unmanly and infamous treatment I have received at your hands, so long as you had the power to inflict it, and I was debarred from resenting it. You will, therefore, name your friend, who will act with Major the Honourable Cuthbert Linder, and arrange the time and place."

"Bah!" cried Winslow, trying to affect contempt. "Go out with you! No! I only go out with men of my own position."

He knew Clifton was a first-rate shot—to go out with him was death.

"You shall not shelter your craven spirit under a plea so contemptible," said Clifton. "I am an officer in your late regiment, and I trust—what you have never been—a gentleman. I insist, therefore, that you accept my challenge."

"Never! I tell you, you are beneath me, and I will not fight with you."

"You are a liar and a coward!" said Clifton, calmly, "and, with both, a poltroon. You are also no better than a common burglar, which, hereafter, I believe I shall be able to prove. I have given you a chance of which you were wholly unworthy. You were a bully in power—you are a coward now. The hour of reparation has arrived; but I do not intend to let you escape, revelling in the acts of a scoundrel with impunity. As you can descend to the acts of a petty, paltry villain, you shall have some part of his punishment as an act of retribution."

He seized Winslow's riding-whip—an elastic, but, for its purpose, a formidable weapon—and he collared the ex-captain at the same moment with a firm grip; then he lashed him until his arm ached—until the contemptible wretch roared for mercy, and lay down on the ground shrieking. He struggled up again, and, breaking away, ran off as hard as he could towards the railway station, covered with stripes and weals, suffering the most excruciating torture, and

knowing that he dare not appeal to the law for redress —knowing that his game was up, that he had lost all chance of the property, which he knew to be rightfully Clifton's, and all prospect of gaining the hand or possession of the person of Myra, whom he loved with a frantic passion amounting to frenzy— knowing that he had been lashed as a rank hound— knowing that now he must sneak into a circle that knew him not, and in which it was unlikely he could come again within contact of the toe of Clifton's boot.

It flew round the town that an officer from the Crimea had horse-whipped most soundly some fellow in the garb of a gentleman, and it came to the ears of Charley Rowe; so he called on Ellen, who was soon to become his wife, to tell her what he had heard, and to inform her that it was his intention to seek out this Crimean hero, and make some inquiries of him about Clifton Grey. At that moment Mr. Fairfax came into the parlor, from the shop, somewhat flurried, and said—

"Charley and Ellen, my dears, here's an officer from the Crimea making inquiries in the shop about you both; and, 'pon my soul, I believe its the same young man that took your place as a recruit."

There was a rush of two into the shop instanter. Mr. Fairfax was nearly upset in the struggle, and Clifton suddenly found a pretty pair of arms round his neck, and a pair of soft lips glued to his own, while, at the same instant, his hand was nearly wrung off, and his arm wrenched out of its socket by the enthusiasm of our friend Charley, who capered and sung as if he were mad. Mr. Randolph's respect for Clifton proportionally increased, upon hearing the incident narrated by Mr. Fairfax, which had led to this grateful attachment of the couple, who knew not how to express their delight at seeing him back well and unhurt. Charley said that though so long as he had life he could never forget the service rendered to him, yet he felt now to be able to breathe freely for the first time since Clifton had gone away. Now he could get married without a pressure on his mind, and Ellen Fairfax iterated all he said, and we think would have kissed Clifton again, but for the strangers present.

Lucky dog, that Clifton Grey! to be thus saluted by so many pretty girls, and to be looked at by so many more, who would have been glad to have had similar titles to do the same thing.

To be sure, Charley Rowe rushed home to tell his mother the good news. To be sure, Ellen Fairfax understood now why Myra had sent a special messenger, inviting her and Charley to dine with her, to which invite no refusal would be valid; and to be sure, a very pleasant—nay, delightful evening, was spent among them. Both Sophie and Isadore Randolph were delighted with Clifton—he was such a contrast to Captain Winslow, and they quite envied Myra her good fortune in obtaining such a prize.

Ah! but ere long there were two of Clifton's friends came home from the Crimea—all in good time—and when they had got over the first interview with these girls, could get no rest until they married and made sure of them. How they joked Everett Randolph about his near sight compelling bachelordom; and to think it should turn after all that he had got a pretty, very pretty girl for a sweetheart, poor, but respectable, a governess in a friend's family. As soon as he gained her consent, he came forward like a man, acknowledged his love for her—and though it was unneeded at his home—said where he was received she must be even as himself, and so she was. Near-sighted, indeed! You should have seen the wife he chose. Many a longer-sighted and wealthier man might have sighed in vain, for one far less beautiful.

Events crowded upon Clifton now. As he walked the next morning with Mr. Randolph towards the railway station, he was astounded to meet Major Linder, with Sylva and Preciosa hanging on each arm, and Mr. Jayne following in the rear. Mr. Randolph, after the greetings were over, invited them to the house at which his family and Mrs. Aston were staying, and they hastily consented. They were compelled to settle the question of their relationship with Clifton, and had been forced to do it in a very unexpected manner. Captain Winslow had, through his lawyer, served notices of ejectment upon all the tenants renting the property, and had given notice to the trustees that he should enter on possession on a certain day, the heir male having failed, and he being next of kin. The whole party made for the house, and after dinner, in the evening, they all assembled in the drawing room, to compare notes and see how matters stood. Briefly, this was the state of the case:

Lord Howard Mortimer, a noble of great wealth, and greater pride, had two sons, the eldest a fine, handsome, manly fellow, the counterpart in mind and person of his mother, an elegant and accomplished woman. The second son needed the personal qualifications of his brother, and he had all the craft and pride of his father. The very common circumstance of an unequal attachment between Herbert Mortimer and Adela Gower, created a division between father and son; and the latter, as secretary of legation, was sent to Madrid, in order to sever the connection. But Herbert and Adela were already married, and a son was the result of their connection. When Herbert, who was yet under age, went to Madrid, he made arrangements for his wife and infant son to follow him. Adela and two younger sisters—they were orphans—with the child, therefore, joined him, and two more children were born—both girls. Herbert Mortimer was now of age, and inherited a handsome property, in right of his mother; he considered himself, therefore, independent and able to brave his father's displeasure; he wrote to him to announce his marriage at the precise time that his father had contracted a matrimonial alliance for him with the eldest daughter of a noble and wealthy house. Lord Howard had deemed it quite unnecessary to consult him in the matter, but had made the whole of the preliminary arrangements. The lady had seen Herbert, and, liking him, readily assented to the match; in Lord Mortimer's eyes there was nothing wanting to complete the union but the ceremony, and his despatch to this effect crossed in its passage the one from Herbert to his father, which rendered the whole scheme impossible. The passionate rage of Lord Mortimer knew no bounds; placed in a false position with the Earl, whose daughter's hand he had asked for his son, thwarted in his ambitious projects, he grew all but frenzied by his disappointment. Suddenly, Herbert Mortimer disappeared. He had been out for a ride, and returned no more. It was afterwards discovered that he had been shot—it was supposed by brigands —for the purposes of plunder, but there was subsequently reason to presume that a hired assassin had committed the murder. Adela's reason fled at the shock occasioned by his mysterious absence, for she feared he had left her. She was dead when her husband's murdered body was brought to Madrid. An agent now made his appearance with powers granted to him by Lord Howard Mortimer, and conveyed away the children in spite of all entreaties and remonstrances. Adela's two sisters were left friendless in Madrid. But the Russian minister there had seen and fallen in love with the eldest sister, solicited her hand; being accepted, he married, and conveyed her and her sister with him to Russia. Sylva and Preciosa were the two daughters of Herbert Mortimer; Sylva had been carried to Malta, where she was brought up in charge of a young couple who had just embarked in trade, but who, strangely enough, had, through Adela's nurse, previously known the child, and recognised her at once, although they said nothing about it at the time; and it was through the exertions of the person whom Sylva thus considered her guardian that she became enabled to trace their history thus far. A Spaniard, named Huerta, had had the charge of Preciosa, and they had traced him—but he was dead. But what had become of the boy? Presumption pointed to Clifton, for his features were remarkably like those of Herbert Mortimer, and Huerta it was who desired Mr. Jayne to prevent a meeting between Clifton and Preciosa. But, alas! proof was wanting, and this was what it was needful to discover.

"Have you discovered the nurse?" asked Clifton.

"No," replied Sylva, "we have searched in vain for her. Her name was Margey—a peculiar name—but we have failed to trace her."

"My mother's name was Margey, before she was

married," cried Charley Rowe, suddenly starting up, and she was abroad just before I was born, I know. I'll fetch her."

Before a word could be uttered he was out of the room, on with his hat, up to the cottage, and without telling his mother more than that Clifton Grey, who she knew had come home from the war, wanted to see her, he brought her down full trot, and landed her, quite out of breath, into the centre of the party in the drawing room. After her greeting of Clifton and welcome home had passed over, she was asked whether she knew the name of Herbert Mortimer. To the great delight of all, she answered, "Yes." She had been nurse to the Honorable Mrs. Mortimer before her death. She was then asked, Did she remember the infant son, and if there was any token by which she could recognise him in after years. With what intense anxiety her answer was awaited! She replied in the affirmative. She said the son of Herbert Mortimer had upon his throat a ruby mark, which they had called, when he was an infant, 'a cherry.' Instantly every voice clamoured for Clifton to take off his stock, and display his throat; they would hardly wait for it to be unbuckled, it was almost wrenched off. His throat—so white—was laid bare.

"There it is. I'll swear to it," cried Mrs. Rowe, and clapped her finger upon a small, clear ruby spot just above Clifton's collar bone. There was a general hurrah! Everybody was about to embrace him—particularly the young ladies—when Mrs. Rowe stopped them.

"One moment," she said: "I can identify Mr. Grey, if he be the son of the Honorable Herbert Mortimer, beyond the possibility of a doubt. While his nurse, knowing his history, I feared he would be subject to foul play. I mentioned my fears to my late husband, then servant to the English ambassador at Madrid, and he prevailed upon me to let him prick a coronet, and the letters 'H. M.,' on the back of the child's left arm, just below the shoulder. It was done, and a document was drawn up, which we both signed and swore to before a magistrate in Madrid. A catholic priest witnessed it, and kept a copy. That priest is in London now, at Spanish Place, and I have a copy at home."

A general demand was now made upon Clifton to off with his coat, and up with his shirt sleeve. It was useless to object, and there—the first thing seen were two deep holes—wounds received in the war, from which he had just returned. A pin might have been heard to drop in the sudden involuntary respect these honorable scars received; and when Myra bent her head over to hide her tears, and kissed them, there was not a dry eye present, or one there who did not desire to pay them a similar homage.

Clifton, in a red heat, and with a face as scarlet as his own coat, at his novel position—thrilled to the very marrow by that kiss from Myra's dear lips—now turned, almost shamefaced, his arm round for inspection, to Mrs. Rowe. He had never seen the mark in question, and the place was a little difficult to get at; but when she succeeded, she pointed out the mark. There it was—a coronet, plain enough, and the letters 'H. M.'

"God has heard my prayers!" ejaculated Mrs. Rowe. "I prayed that I might be of service to you, and I trust I have. You are the son of the Honorable Herbert Mortimer—of that I will stake my existence; and I will prove it."

"He is then Lord Herbert Mortimer, for the old lord is dead," exclaimed Mr. Jayne and Mr. Randolph in a breath.

"And our brother!" exclaimed Sylva and Precious, in a breath, as both hugged him in their arms, a proceeding which Major Linder would fain have shared in so long as Sylva might have liked; but he contented himself with proposing three cheers, which were given lustily by every one, Myra elevating herself on her toes in her excitement, and Charley Rowe almost ready to leap out of the window, and run round the town, by way of letting off a little of his superfluous joy.

That evening was a happy one, in truth.

* * * * *

The scene now changes to London. The priest named by Mrs. Rowe was visited, remembered the circumstance of attesting the document mentioned, saw the marks on Clifton's person, and declared them to be the same. Captain Winslow proved to be Clifton's father's brother's son; and it turned out that Linder's friend, Captain Mandeville, had followed out the suggestion given to him by the major. He had discovered that Captain Winslow had a deep project on foot to obtain possession of a title and great wealth, and he succeeded, without appearing to have any desire to do so, in obtaining from Winslow a document in the handwriting of Huerta, which stated that the son of Herbert Mortimer had been in his charge until his third year, when he had consigned him, with the fictitious name of Clifton Grey, to a commercial man in the city of London, named Jayne; that on his reaching his twenty-first year he had been cast adrift to do as best he could, and, unknowing his origin, it was not possible for him to discover it, as the guardian to whom he had been consigned knew nothing connected with his birth. A similar proceeding had been adopted with the daughter placed under Mr. Jayne, who, also, at an appointed time, would have been subjected to the same process. This document was most important; and Mr. Randolph, undertaking the business, employed the most able means to aid in the establishment of Clifton's claims, which were, upon a chain of evidence without one link wanting, fully established, and he was duly installed in his title and vast possessions, under the title of Lord Herbert Clifton Grey Mortimer, as he would not abandon that name under which Myra had known and loved him.

It was just at this time that Myra, the history of whose descent was not unlike his own, was put into possession of her property, and Clifton arranged with her to be married as soon as the peace negotiations, then pending, were settled, so that he might at least, if obeying Myra's wish, he retired from the army, take his leave of it when there was no war in which his country claimed his services; then they would take public possession of their estates, that their respective tenantry might have an opportunity of receiving them with the rejoicings that they very unequivocally expressed their desire to do in the very heartiest manner.

Now came the presentations at court. Lord Mortimer, on the accession to his title, and upon his promotion, was presented to Her Majesty at a levee. It was a proud day for him. He wore, by permission of Her Majesty, the decoration of the order of Medjedjie, sent to him by the Sultan of Turkey, the cross of the Legion of Honor, sent to him by the Emperor of France, and by his right, his medal, with its clasps. His reception by the queen was most gracious. She had been informed of his bravery in the field, and of his conduct, which afforded such an admirable example to every soldier in the army. She thanked him for the services he had rendered to his country and to her, and she further informed him that so soon as the order of valour, preparing now for the adornment of the gallant men who had signalized themselves by deeds of martial daring, were ready to be presented, she should feel it her pride, as well as her pleasure, to append with her own hands one to his breast. He kissed hands, and passed on with a proud gratification, rivalling that which he experienced when he received his commission at the hands of Sir William Codrington, commander-in-chief of Her Majesty's forces.

Peace prevailed in the councils of the Emperor of Russia : the propositions of Austria were accepted. A congress was held in Paris, and all the demands of the allies were acceded to. Peace was signed, and the joyous illuminations and fireworks indicating the public rejoicings at the happy event followed in due course. The order for the British regiments to return home were issued, and to Clifton's gratification the government decided upon the public entry of the Guards into London. The Scots Fusiliers, in the war-steamer Princess Royal, reached England safely, and the soldiers being landed at Portsmouth, were borne to the camp at Aldershott. Here were assembled the Grenadier Guards and the Coldstream, and here Clifton joined them, and Sergeant Haverel, and our friend Mickey Dunigan, who vowed he'd march into London "wid the bould Fusiliers as' he died for it," and so he did. The

morning came, and the men were borne by the railway carriages to the Nine Elms station, and here they formed in three lines, the Grenadiers in the centre, the Scots Fusiliers and the Coldstreams right and left, marching on to St. James's Park, where they saluted the queen, and from thence into Hyde Park, where they were inspected by Her Majesty. An immense concourse of people assembled to greet and welcome them on the footways, in the windows, on house-tops, in vehicles, carriages of all kinds—wherever a view was to be obtained, there were squeezed persons of both sexes —young and old, gentle and simple, rich and poor —cheering with lusty throats the arrival of those who had done so well in their country's cause. The muskets of the soldiers were adorned with bouquets, their breasts with flowers, and never were men in such heavy marching order. There were curiosities ancient and modern, birds, goats, dogs; one shaggy old rascal, of the latter breed, who had been wounded at Inkermann. Clifton Grey proudly bore the flag 'neath which he had fought, and which had been so nobly maintained by those in charge of it at the dreadful days at the Alma and Inkermann. As he neared the balcony on which stood the Queen, the royal family, and royal guests, she, much affected, pointed out its tattered condition to the King of the Belgians. It was noted that he looked up at one especial house on his route, and that as he went by there was an increased waving of handkerchiefs and stentorian shouts proceeding from it; that at this very house Sergeant Haverel looked up and smiled, and shouted to Sergeant Dunigan—"There's my Liz, Mickey!" And Mickey did'nt know which of a dozen pretty faces was the one to which his attention was directed, so he kissed his hand to all; and how he wished in his heart, poor fellow, that Bridget Boyle, of Ballynacraggy, in the county of Limerick, had been among them, so that when he was released from duty he would have nothing to do but pour his full heart at her feet.

This ovation being over, and the whole of Clifton's affairs being arranged, he nominated Sergeant Haverel steward upon his own estate, and Sergeant Dunigan steward of Myra's property. The latter was despatched to Ballynacraggy to fetch over Bridget, and having married her first, return to England, in order to take possession of their new home. To be sure Biddy screeched awful when the sergeant came upon her at a most unexpected moment, and to be sure she hugged her boy to her heart, and he squeezed his *colleen dhas* to his breast ; and to be sure that night all Ballynacraggy was uproarious at his return home, and the whole village turned out to see the wedding of the bould soldier boy with the prettiest and best lass in Ballynacraggy, and danced on the green all the day, and got very jovial in the evening, in honour of the event. It was certain that there was great festivity, and that all Ballynacroggy turned out again when the happy couple left and came to England. It is no less certain that when they reached it, and Myra and Clifton welcomed the new bride to a new country, they confessed, that in the dazzling fair skin, the deep blue eyes, the long, very long eyelashes, silken and slightly curled, the rich dark brown tresses, that the county of Limerick could produce some of the most beautiful girls in the world. When Haverel saw Bridget Dunigan, he whistled and poked Mickey in the ribs, and said, with a rich laugh—

"'Axceptin' Bridget Boyle.' Why, Mickey, you were right, boy; you have got the exception, too."

Sergeant Haverel kissed the exception, and told her she might consider herself the happiest woman in the world—excepting his Lizzie—for she had got the best fellow for a husband in the universe.

"Axceptin' Sergeant Haverel," said Mickey.

"Av coorse," replied the sergeant.

Now the sight of Mickey's felicity was more than Haverel's nature could endure without emulating it; so, as he found that some little time would yet elapse before Clifton and Myra were united, he got Lizzie alone one morning; he suddenly seized her in his arms, and burst forth :

   " 'Oh, name the day, the happy day,
      And I will buy the ring ;
     The lads and maids in favors white,
      And the village bells, the village bells shall ring.' "

Lizzie was so coaxed and teazed, and pleased, she did not quit his arms without naming the day, and Haverel immediately communicated it to Clifton, who, in turn, informed Myra, for they had promised to be present. As there was another marriage shortly to come off, it was arranged that Charley Rowe and Ellen Fairfax should be married at the same time, and, with this purpose, they came up to London. Such a wedding as it was, too. Why, there was, of course, Old Fairfax and Mrs. Rowe, with a number of friends, including Clifton and his sisters, Myra, her mother, and all the Randolphs; then there were the Haverels, and all their relations, Mrs. Stewart and all the young ladies from Baker Street, every girl of them, all dying for a soldier, to be taken in the same way that Lizzie was then accomplishing the feat— the short apprentice was almost dead over it—and our Lucy, and goodness knows who. And after the flurry and flowers, and rustling of white silk, and sobbing, which constitute a wedding, was over, there was such a banquet provided at Clifton's new large mansion in Park Lane for them; such happiness at it, such speechifying after it, and such dancing when the happy couples had started off to Brighton to spend their honeymoon! Really Clifton himself began to grow very impatient for his own marriage to take place; but lawyers will not be hurried. Yet there is an end to all things, and so, at last, there was to the delay which kept him from calling Myra his own

dear little wife. The settlements were all completed, the deeds were all signed, and everything wanting finished, excepting the marriage, and that **now only** depended upon Myra. And when he **told her this** alone one morning, she placed her hands in **his, and,** with a look of unspeakable happiness, said :

"When you will, dearest Clifton. My happiness can scarcely be greater than it is now; yet to be assured that I am yours—yours only for life—for ever—will consummate the greatest possible felicity I can know on earth."

He pressed her to his heart.

"It will mine," he said, with passionate emphasis.

So the day was fixed, and it was made known. Astonishing! how infectious it was! There was Major the Honourable Cuthbert Linder, madly in love with Sylva Mortimer; and Lord Montmorency with Preciosa; there was also the Miss Randolphs and their brother; and all of them seemed to think it would be the proper thing to be wedded on the same day, at the same church, at the same moment, and go down to the same piece. Clifton thought so too, and as Sergeant Haverel was already on his estate in the West of England, so it was agreed that the weddings should take place at one time, and that Clifton should proceed to take possession of his mansion **and** park—one of palatial proportions and splendour— accompanied by all his married friends, immediately afterwards.

At St. George's, Hanover-square, they were wedded, and after a splendid breakfast they proceeded in carriages and fours to their destination. Although relays of horses were on the road, it occupied quite two days to reach his noble home. On the morning of the third they entered upon the confines of the estate, and here they were met by the tenantry, whom Sergeant Haverel and Sergeant Dunigan had set to work and drilled into certain evolutions to be performed in honour of the coming guests. How Haverel had sweated and swore over them, but how well they repaid his exertions! Clifton was quite electrified to see them fall into line, wheel to left or right, form a square, deploy, fire a volley of cheers, now in rounds, now in platoon, and he laughed until he was so convulsed that Myra became quite frightened, for he knew what exertion it must have cost Haverel to have accomplished it.

It was quite delightful to see how active and busy he was, and how admirably the tenants obeyed his directions. The horses were taken out of the young lord's carriage, and garlands of flowers (with thick ropes inside) attached to the splinter-bar, which twenty young fellows seized and ran away with the carriage full trot. And there were the rich farmers on horseback, and their wives and daughters in chaises of various kinds, and there were the humbler tenants on foot, and a marvellous quantity of little girls strewing flowers and singing, lifting up their little legs under the impression that they were dancing. And, such a band! It had been got up under the direction of Mickey, who was something of a musician, and was composed chiefly of wind instruments and drums. He had borrowed two fifers and two drummers from the band of a neighbouring regiment, and he had clarinets and French horns, trumpets and bugles, one fiddle—which was rather out of place—and an Irishman with the union pipes, which had already flung two pigs into convulsions, and the player was therefore privately advised not to use his pipes until the dancing took place at night. When the carriage was set in motion, the band struck up "See the conquering hero comes," and though the novel sounds terrified every crow out of the neighbourhood, yet the tenantry thought it splendid. They cheered all the way through the park, in which flags were flying and cannon firing, and ceased not until the house was reached.

It was a fine old mansion, of an earlier period even than Elizabeth, capacious and strong. It had stood the storms of time bravely, and now, embowered in trees, it looked as though it could yet withstand the assault of centuries. It was gaily decorated with flowers and flags, while from some of the windows depended rich draperies, as in the manner of the olden time. From the turreted roof in the centre of the building waved in the air the banner of his house; from the western wing, the flag of England floated; and from the southern, the flag of the Scots Fusilier Guards, which, under Haverel's direction, had been exactly reproduced. On the steps were arranged the household, and at their head Sergeant Haverel, with a face glowing with heat and perspiration. Greatly to the marvel of all the civilians present, to the amusement of Clifton, and to the intense delight of Major Linder, every servant, male and female, up with their hands to their forehead, and gave the military salute. Then Sergeant Haverel stepped forward, and in a speech of hearty and even eloquent language, welcomed him to his ancestral halls. Major Linder took the opportunity to congratulate him, and all his friends, tenants, and neighbours, set up a burst of cheers, which might almost have been heard for miles. The band, under the sudden inspiration of the Scotch gardener, struck up "The laird shall hae his ain again."

As soon as Clifton could get an opportunity to speak, he thanked them for their welcome to his home; he assured them, that he trusted, when they knew him better, they would not believe him altogether undeserving of their good wishes. As he considered their interests identical, he begged them, in all their perplexities, their trials, and their afflictions, to seek him. It would be his most constant endea-

vour to remove their cares and anxieties, to improve their position, and to ensure their happiness; for he was well convinced that when a lord found all his tenants happy and thriving, he was never so wealthy; but that when they were poor, discontented, and unhappy, he was himself a sufferer, and should look to himself as the occasion of the distress and the misery, and upon himself as the only physician that could cure it. He was interrupted by loud cheers. Sentiments like these appealed to the hearts of those who keenly felt their import. He bade them be happy that day, everything that could be thought of he hoped had been prepared for their enjoyment, and he begged them to fling away all restraint, do just as they pleased, so that they were all animated by the one object of making each other as happy as they could.

Sergeant Haverel and Lizzie (oh, her delight!) had the task to keep everybody in a state of felicity. Mickey Dunigan and Bridget aided them. The latter was followed by swarms of children as sheep follow a bell-wether, for she distributed to them cake and sweet drink, and fruit and bonbons, and everything that was of heaven in a child's imagination, seeming, like a fairy, to find them in places where they were not expected to exist. And Sergeant Dunigan looked up drink for the thirsty, and Haverel looked after the girls, while Lizzie put in a state of frenzy half the young gentlemen farmers present.

As the day wore on, Clifton and his wife, and Linder and his wife, and Randolph and his wife—in fact, almost all the world and his wife, joined those in the slopes and the glades beneath the over-arching trees, mixing in the festivity, and in the dancing Clifton led off Sir Roger de Coverley with old dame Ransom, and Myra followed with Gaffer Plumtree. Major Linder dashed down the dance boldly with old Mrs. Thumbtwig, and Sylva danced Farmer Spurn, entirely out of breath; while Ellen Rowe darted off with neighbour Primrose, Charley following with Gammer Wittle, until the country pair were quite bewildered, suffering themselves to be pushed in here, dragged out there, taken anywhere, in the confident belief that in the end they should turn up somewhere.

For a long summer's day, even up to midnight, for, indeed, one whole week, these festivities were kept up, and then Clifton Grey, happy in the possession of a young, beautiful, and loving wife, in the society of friends to whom he was much attached by the ties of esteem and friendship, sat himself down to realise that happiness which he had gone through such a probation to obtain, and to prove himself a hero both in LOVE AND WAR.

www.ingramcontent.com/pod-product-compliance
Lightning Source LLC
Chambersburg PA
CBHW020848020726
47497CB00005B/1311